The Brotherhood of
DISTRICT 23

The Complete Series

BESTSELLING AUTHOR
AMY BRIGGS

TABLE OF CONTENTS

BOOK 1 – FIRED UP

BOOK 2 – FULLY INVOLVED

BOOK 3 – CONTROLLED BURN

BONUS CHAPTERS

INTERVIEWS WITH THE CHARACTERS

FIRED *up*

BESTSELLING AUTHOR
AMY BRIGGS

DEDICATION

For my parents

I couldn't find anything suitable to wear to my own dad's funeral. Everyone was going to be there, wearing their Class A Dress Uniforms, which was completely acceptable, since he was a Fire District Chief, but I won't be wearing mine. I haven't worked at that department in almost a year, and it just doesn't seem appropriate at all. My aunt also informed me that my father's only daughter shouldn't be dressed like a boy the day he's laid to rest; her words of reprimand have been ringing in my head all morning.

At least my best friend, Matt will be there, along with his brother Brian and the rest of the department of course. Brian was actually appointed into my father's position when he died last week. We have a bit of a history. We had a moment really; a hot, steamy moment that I'd never be able to get out of my head apparently. I felt a moistness pool between my legs thinking about his beautiful green eyes, his well-defined muscles and the tattoos that couldn't be more perfectly placed on his chest and arms. *Jesus Christ, it's your dad's funeral, get your shit together, Josephine Meadows.* That was a one-time thing, just kiss, a really great kiss. No matter how great it was, or how much deep down I actually wanted him, having those thoughts at this time and place was inappropriate. I shook my head to clear it; reminding myself that

Brian was a cocky asshole anyway.

Matt was picking my aunt and I up, she was my only biological family left now and my dad's older sister. My mom died when I was three, leaving me and my dad to fend for ourselves for the most part. After she died, he never dated, or married again; he was more or less married to the fire service. He worked the job until his last breath; when he passed away from a heart attack while out on a call. It was no secret that the stress of firefighting made heart attacks the number one killer of firefighters, but their shitty diets certainly didn't help either, no matter how hard I tried to get him to be healthier.

"Josephine! Matt's here, let's go!" Aunt Molly yelled from downstairs. I finished putting on my favorite red lipstick that I never wore except to go out or for events, grabbed some black heels that were probably a bit too high for walking around all day, and took a deep breath as I went downstairs. It was going to be a long day, but everyone that I'd be greeting loved us, they were all our family.

BRIAN

It's the day of Jack's funeral, a day I've been dreading as I felt like I lost my own father. He was my fire chief for as long as I can remember as I moved up the ranks. Technically, he was the only father figure I had. My dad left my mom with me and my little brother when I was five and he was three. Our mom, and Jo's mom had been friends, and Matt and Jo have been best friends since they were born. The two were born in the same hospital in the same week; making them almost inseparable for as long as I can remember.

When our dad left, Jack Meadows stepped in to help out; teaching us how to be boys, and then how to be good men. He and our mom stayed friends and I always thought there might have been something going on there, but who knows. Jack was an honorable man, and when his wife died, around the same time our dad left, he made it a point to check on my mom, and that was good enough for us. From what I know, he never really involved himself with a woman again. They ended up being really close. When we were old enough, we couldn't wait to join the fire department, and we've both made a career out of it. That fire department was our calling and definitely our family.

It was time to lay to rest the only father I've ever known, and to make sure his family had everything they needed from the fire department; that was my responsibility now and we looked out for our own. I adjusted my uniform, making sure it was all in place and thought about Jack's family. His only family besides the department was his sister, Molly who lives out of town, and Jo.

Josephine Meadows. I started to get a little twitch in my dick; she was always so fucking sexy and had absolutely no clue how hot she was. She was a firefighter too, it was in her blood. We used to all ride together, and my God, her ass in a uniform. It would stop you in your tracks if she walked by. She was off limits though, her dad had been my boss, and my brother was her best friend--that's like two bro code fails in one. I haven't seen her all that much since we drank too much, and got a little handsy with each other at one of the fire academy graduation parties last year. We said some stuff to each other that probably should never have been said.

Jo

We'd decided to do only one service, viewing, whatever you wanted to call it. My dad knew it would be a production, he was a Fire Chief, and as humble as he was, he was a fucking good one, and well respected across our state as well as several others. We'd casually discussed what he wanted over the years. It's something you got comfortable talking about in emergency services; you knew how short life could be. We were going to the funeral home, then straight to my dad's house for a reception that the fire department stepped in and took care of for me.

In traditional fashion, I was up at the front of the room by the memorial, thankfully with my aunt, and I had asked Matt to be with me too. Normally, he would have come with the rest of the fire department, but as a show of support, he arrived with me instead. Dressed in his Class A uniform, he stood by my side, ready to be my crutch if I needed it. It was a lot of people, he knew everyone, and could help me say and do the right thing. I honestly think I was still in shock, I had yet to shed one single tear. Matt was a little worried about it, but I knew it would happen after all the "business" of the funeral was over. Matt's mom, Catherine, was also sitting in the front row, she'd been really close to my dad, and

I could see she was grieving as well, dabbing at her eyes with a beautiful little white lace handkerchief that appeared to have tiny blue flowers embroidered on it.

My dad was cremated, as per his wishes. He was a firefighter, and as sick or crazy as it sounds, he thought it was amusing to be cremated. Whatever, it was what he wanted, and at the end of the day, what did it matter? It was the only thing my aunt and I disagreed on about this whole situation, she felt that he should be traditionally laid to rest. We compromised, and I let her buy a plot and a headstone, and I'd promised that we'd have a private non-burial sometime after the service, but not that day.

My feet were killing me from my heels already, and the service had barely started. The fire department had wanted to do an honor guard and I asked them not to, but they were all there, showing their support. There was a sea of navy blue uniforms, and I truly appreciated their presence even though it was a little overwhelming. My heart thumped against my chest thinking of how supportive these people all were. I've shown up to a lot of these in the support role myself, always knowing this day would come, but was still in awe at the amount of people in attendance.

Matt leaned over to whisper to me. "How are you holding up?"

"I'm alright. I probably should've worn more sensible shoes though," I giggled, and my aunt threw me a glare. I leaned over to her. "You know my dad had a sense of humor, lighten up a little bit." She took my hand and squeezed. She knew I was right and that even if we didn't know all of the firefighters, EMTs and police officers coming through to pay their respects, they had all been touched by my father in some way. It was important for us to not make their hurt any worse either. We were a family, a big crazy family that most folks didn't understand, but family nonetheless. He had even indicated, should he pass, that we should play upbeat music at his "funeral." We did just that, turning the service into an almost cheerful gathering.

Matt checked his phone and smiled. "Looks like our department is here, just got a text from Brian." They could all be so annoying and crude, but would do absolutely anything for you. I basically had one hundred brothers, which was the coolest thing since biologically, I was an only child.

"Ok, so here we go. No crying."

"You can do whatever you want you know. I'm here for you." He put his arm around me and gave me a squeeze. He looked down at me with a soft smile, eliciting a small smile from me in return. Matt always knew how to keep me calm and I was so grateful he was there for me.

"I really appreciate it, Matt, thank you. I just want to be strong, he was so loved by everyone, I really want today to be a celebration and I know that's what he would want too." I sighed.

Matt smiled and leaned into me. "I think that's exactly what he would want."

The funeral director came over and let us know people were arriving and that he'd direct them where to go. I thought it was pretty obvious where to go, and we already knew, but I kept my mouth shut for a change. I was planning to really make the effort to not offend anyone or give too many of my opinions which would be a change of pace for me. The first to walk in the door was Brian, and the rest of the guys filed in one after another. I noticed those goddamn sexy eyes right away, and felt myself getting warm and flushed in his presence. Brian looked me straight in the eyes and nodded, before holding the door for his men to come in and pay their respects. They were so professional looking. I mean they were professionals, it's just that I grew up with so many of them, sometimes I'd forgotten how handsome and well put together they could all look when they needed to, especially right now.

Each of the emergency services well wishers that came through the line, said something wonderful about my dad, gave me and my aunt a hug, shook Matt's hand, and then took residence in the back of the funeral home. That's how it worked, the "family department" basically stood watch at these events to see if anyone needed help. Brian didn't come through the line with the rest of the guys, which seemed odd. I spent the greater part of the afternoon shaking hands and hugging my friends, my dad's friends and several people I didn't actually know. That felt like it went on for an eternity and I was growing uncomfortable from all of the talking and hugging. My uncomfortable shoes weren't helping me either.

As the guys from my old department, which was my dad's department came through I thought about all the things I loved about each of them, and what I know my dad loved about them too. Scotty was always the driver, and ran the pumps. He was kind of young for a full time driver with that much responsibility at twenty-three, but he took it in stride. He was also our engineer, he could get water to flow out of anything, and was often called upon to teach rural departments how to get water when they had hydrant problems or couldn't get water at all. He was so smart, and had such an instinct for reading a scene and knowing where equipment needed to be efficiently and effectively.

Our engine officer, Kevin Taylor, was quiet and cool all the time. Never lost his head, always had a good answer to a question, and could read a fire like nobody else. He was almost forty, and had never settled down himself. He was actually older than Brian who was thirty-five and now our chief. Taylor had ladies throwing themselves at him, but he never took the bait, at least not in front of any of us. He could be a bit of a loner, but I had the best late night conversations with him in the kitchen at the firehouse, I could have sworn he was the most interesting man in the world like in those silly beer commercials.

Jax was, well he was Jax. Seth Jackson was actually his real name, but he reminded us all of a tall, Australian guy on a soap opera we saw one time, named Jax. It just stuck once we started calling him that as a joke years ago. He was tall, blonde, blue eyed and handsome like a model. An ex-marine, he was so fit and good looking, he was always beating the girls off with a stick. Matt lived with Jax. He bought a house when he got out of the marines, and figured he'd offset costs by having a roommate. I think all those years in the marines, he didn't really like being alone that much, even though he was kind of quiet. We always got along well, and he was a great firefighter. Always training, and reading about the latest thing in fire suppression. He was a walking encyclopedia of new technologies.

Matt was usually on the same shift as me when I was riding regularly. He's also an engine guy. Back in the academy, I had to coax him off of a fire escape that we were training on when he got paralyzed up at the top. It's no joke, and if I wasn't helping him myself, we were partners on that training exercise, I probably would have frozen too. That's the thing I love about firefighting, you always, and I do mean *always* have a partner; it was actually a very common rule. No going off on your own and freelancing at a fire, everyone has a partner. Since we're so close personally, we work together really well and were usually side by side until I left the department to work several part time and per diem jobs at different departments and for the county, which seemed like a great way to branch out at the time. . He dates the worst girls ever, I hate them all, and that's not because I have a secret crush on him, I saved that for Brian. Matt just has horrible taste and dates the dumbest girls I've ever met in my life, but they sure do love firefighters. Most girls love a sexy firefighter, we've all seen the movies. As a female firefighter, it was both nauseating and hilarious to watch the dating rituals of the guys around me.

I tried to smile as much as I could and worked to not think about what I was going to do with myself at thirty-two years old with no parents left. When you're little, your thirties seem so old, but here I am, and I'm not ready to have no parents. I'm not ready to let go. Sure, I had the fire department, and I had my aunt, and Matt of course, but I was basically out of family and it was starting to hit me hard, causing a pain in my chest that felt like a hole being drilled right through my heart. As I felt that hole get bigger, my eyes started to well up. *Well shit, here it comes, now I'm going to cry.*

Last to come through the line was Brian. He gave my aunt a kiss on the cheek, and stopped in front of me. He was obviously sexy, but he looked so well put together and handsome in his uniform. He reminded me of my dad a little, looking very serious and very much in charge. I'd tried to avoid eye contact, I *was not* liking how he was consuming my thoughts throughout the day today and at this point, I was definitely going to cry at any moment and I didn't want to do that in front of him or anyone else for that matter.

BRIAN

Fuck she's beautiful. Seeing those steely blue eyes filled with tears, I just wanted to grab her and take her someplace away from all this madness. These things can get really crowded, and with someone as awesome as her dad, I knew this would happen. I watched her from the back of the room for two hours, just smiling at people, sharing stories, thanking them for coming, I don't know how she can look so calm. She's a fucking warrior. The thing is, when this many firefighters, cops and EMTs get together, it becomes overwhelming, even for some of us that know to expect it, and that includes her. She's a firefighter, one of ours, and always will be, even if she isn't riding with us right now. There's stories to tell, guys you haven't seen in forever, and then the responsibility of looking after the family. It can be a lot to deal with, when they're grieving themselves. Everyone would want to share their "Jack story" with her. Jo knew all of that, but something inside me wanted to protect her anyway. I sure as fuck wasn't going to let anyone know that. I didn't go through the receiving line with my department when we arrived, I hung back and kept an eye on things, not quite ready to face her.

Once it was time for me to go up there, I had to say something. "Jo, are you okay? I know we haven't spoken in a while, but I'm so sorry about your dad. I'm sure you know how I felt about him."

"I'm fine, Brian. Congratulations on your promotion. I'll be by sometime next week to get both his and my stuff from the station." she said calmly.

"That's not even a little bit important right now. Please let me know if there's anything that I, or the guys can do to help you out. You know we're all family." And I meant that.

"I'm okay, thank you." She gave me a quick, friendly hug. I felt an electric charge, and I could smell the orange blossom or whatever it was in her hair. I had to walk away, immediately. It was not okay to have those thoughts about her, and definitely not at that moment.

I was Jack's Deputy Chief, and was recently appointed to take his position temporarily, possibly full time later. As far as I was concerned, that meant looking out for everything he cared about, which included Jo, whether she liked it or not. The last time we had a real conversation just between the two of us, she told me what a fucking asshole I was. She also mentioned how I needed to grow up, and how she felt that I wasn't the person she thought I was. I've been thinking about that conversation a lot this week, but at the time, I was only concerned about my career and getting laid. Messing around with her wasn't going to make either of those things work. So, maybe she was right. Today, I'd sent the Ladies Auxilliary to Jack's house to handle the reception, so Jo could stay here as long as she wanted before going back to the house and continuing to entertain people. It was the one small thing I could do, and since she *did* speak to my brother a billion times a day, he helped me arrange her okay with it.

I went back to my post at the back of the room and watched

the last of the people trickle through. The crowd had dwindled as people were leaving to go to the reception, and I saw Jo's demeanor change suddenly. She went from a wistful sadness to what appeared to be pissed off in an instant. Some guy that I sort of recognized, but wasn't sure from where, was standing next to her and as I watched, he grabbed her arm. What the fuck was that about? I watched my brother grab the guy's arm, and motion for him to leave. I saw red. I rushed to the front of the room, grabbed the clown by his jacket lapels and got in his face.

"Is there a problem here?" I snarled at him.

"You need to get the fuck off me, bro. I'm talking to my girlfriend right now, you can back the fuck up." I looked over at Jo to confirm what this jackass was saying.

"I'm not your goddamn girlfriend, you fucking asshole, and you have absolutely no business being here. This isn't the time or the place, and regardless, we have nothing to discuss. Please leave." she literally hissed at him. She turned toward me and my brother. "Brian, Matt, it's fine. Danny, please leave, you don't belong here." She pointed to the door.

"Fine, I'll leave because you're causing a scene at your own father's funeral, but we aren't done talking, Josephine. Not by a long shot." The douche stormed out of the funeral home.

"Well that was fucking perfect. Sorry, Dad." Jo said to the sky. "Thank you both for being here, I really do appreciate it." She huffed. "I think it's time to get back to dad's house so I can hug some more strangers and hear fish stories about my dad. At least I can have a drink there, cause damn, I sure need one."

"Well, I'll take you there now and we'll do some drinking for your old man," Matt said. She smiled and walked toward the door with her aunt who didn't respond to the scene at all, and Matt hung back to talk to me.

"What the fuck was that all about, man? That guy is a douche. Are they seriously together?"

"That was Danny, Jo's *ex* boyfriend, the lying, manipulative Fire Inspector from Station 19. He went to the academy with me and Jo and was a prick then too. Well he never got any better, and somehow, they dated for the last year, and big shocker, he cheated on her the entire time. Anyway, she has some stuff at their old apartment together she wants to get back. He wants to get back together and he thought today, at the funeral, would be the perfect time to approach her about this." His eyes got big, letting me know he thought it was a dumbshit idea just like I did. I'm actually kind of surprised Jo didn't punch him right in the throat.

"That guy is a dick. What the fuck did she date him for? We need to go get whatever shit she left there for her." I'd be damned if I let her go anywhere with that guy. I couldn't believe he'd grabbed her, I'd like to rip him apart for that alone.

"I honestly don't know why she dated him. I was actually going to ask for your help, I wasn't sure you would though."

"Why wouldn't I?" I was offended.

"Listen, Jo and I never discussed whatever it was that happened between you two last year before she started dating, Danny the Douchebag, but it's no secret that something went down. I know you haven't spoken more than two words at a time since then, and it's fucking awkward, man. I don't really want to know but I know you well enough to know you can't keep your dick in your pants with the ladies, so how about you not do that to my best friend who not only lost her dad, your boss, but is basically family to us."

Now I was mad. "I'm not going to talk about that with you now, but I will tell you that I would do anything to help her out. That's it. Just call me later and let me know what you need. I'm going to meet the guys at her dad's, I'll see you there."

I was fucking pissed. I know what I did, and at the time, it seemed smart, but now I felt like a fucking asshole. It gave me a pain in my gut thinking that I might have hurt her and drove her into the arms of that prick; although I didn't think I did at the time. I glanced over in her direction, and she nodded back at me, but it was icy and expressionless. Her black dress hugged her body in all the right places, and those fucking heels. Goddamn, I wanted to bend her over a chair and fuck her until she saw stars. And there it was, she still made my dick hard as a rock and I needed to go before that became noticed.

tugged at my heart strings, bringing those old feelings right back to the surface in an instant. I wanted to comfort him the way I needed to be comforted. I wanted to make him feel better, not so alone in his grief. I know that my father was the only father Brian had ever really known, and their bond was special and unique, as was his loss.

"You know you were very important to him, right? Not just at work. He loved you and Matt as much as he loved me really." He gave me a much bigger smile then, looking like he might even laugh.

"How do you always know how to make people smile?" Leaning in close to me again, he rested his chin on top of my head for a moment, hugging me again. He smelled so good, I inhaled his manly scent and forgot about the day for just a moment, lost with him. He let me go, and moved to lean back on the railing of the deck and put his sunglasses back on. Mine were still on top of my head, so I slid them down and took up the spot next to him, letting out an audible sigh.

"Anytime. That's one of the many things that our little family is for." I gave him a little elbow to his rock hard abs and mused to myself a bit. It was kind of nice just hanging out with Brian, not uncomfortable at all. The last time we were alone ended in an argument about a kiss we shared, which seemed unlikely to happen at this moment thankfully. I thought about it quietly, hoping that maybe we were past the point of avoiding each other, and potentially leaving room for us to be friends again. I'd always want more, but I'd certainly have taken friendship over nothing at all.

I wasn't sure how much time had passed, but I realized I had been gone for a bit, and needed to get back to the reception. "I've got to go back in and say goodbye to some people, but anytime you want to talk, you know where to find me," I gave him a tiny peck on the cheek, leaving me with a little electrical charge.

"Thanks, Jo, and obviously the same here. We'll talk later okay?" he said as I walked back inside.

Finally, the reception was over. My aunt had decided to head back to her place, which was about two hours away. I was staying at my dad's, like I have been since I moved out of Danny's apartment. I never saw Brian leave, but I was now alone, like I felt I needed to be. Truthfully, I'd had enough men and firefighters, and questions about my life to last me a lifetime. I felt like I might be able to be friends with Brian again and that was nice too even if deep down I'd always want more. I wanted to drink, and I wanted to forget about being sad. Or maybe I wanted to think. Either way, I definitely wanted some quiet. I sent Matt home with the rest of the guys, they were all going out to the local watering hole.

It had been a couple hours since everyone left, and I wandered around my dad's house, touching pictures, talking to myself as if talking to him. *What am I supposed to do now without you here?* I heard a knock on the screen door and jumped. It was Florida, and a typical 80 degrees in October, but no humidity so I had the door open for some fresh air.

"I'm sorry I scared you, may I come in?" Those green eyes penetrated right through me. Brian was dressed in a black t-shirt, jeans that hung low on his hips and showed just a bit of that V leading to...oh you know. His beautifully sculpted arms were covered in tattoos that I couldn't admire earlier today, and I think I forgot to reply while assessing him as he repeated his question. "Jo, can I come in and talk to you?"

"Oh, yeah sure, come on in, Brian. Did you need something?" *Besides fucking me on this recliner? I obviously need to stop drinking, there's something wrong with me.*

"No, I don't need anything at all. I wanted to come and see you, check on you really. After the drama with your ex, and well, just everything, I wanted to make sure you're alright." He looked like he meant it, but I was in no mood at that point in my day. I was feeling kind of angry about life and losing my dad and I didn't want to be bothered. I'd been nice and understanding all day and while I did love admiring him physically, and daydreaming about those arms around me, he definitely wanted to come and play Chief of the Department with me right now and I wasn't up for it.

"Look, Brian, it's me, not some random civilian that doesn't get how this all works. You don't have to come over here out of obligation from the department and take care of anything. I'm perfectly capable of handling my shit. I appreciate you having words with Danny earlier today, but I can certainly take care of that situation myself," I was being mean, and I felt bad, but didn't stop myself. I felt like lashing out at someone, and he was an easy target.

"Listen here, Jo. I've known you your entire life, you can be pissed off at me, the fire service, the world, or whatever you want, sweetheart, but it *is* my responsibility to look after you whether you like it or not and not just because I'm the Chief. And while we're at it, we're eventually going to talk about what happened last year, because we can't keep ignoring each other forever. Today was the first time we've spoken more than two words to each other since last year. You need to let me be here for you now!" he raised his voice, making me angry and turned on at the same time.

I got in his face and put my hand on his broad chest in a gesture to push him away, but he didn't move an inch. "I don't need anyone's help, definitely not yours. Thanks for stopping by." He stood in front of me without moving just like a statue, and it was as if there was a magnet between us. I didn't move my hand either, it was glued to him giving me a warm static charge I couldn't let go of. I stared into his eyes, full of fire and wasn't sure whether this was a standoff or we were going to just argue about it, then he did it. He kissed me. For the second time in my life, he kissed me, drawing me into him like a tornado, consuming all of me.

BRIAN

I didn't know why I did it, but I grabbed her face and planted my lips on hers in a kiss like no other, and she let me. She didn't push me away, she let me devour her; it was so fucking hot, my cock was hard in an instant. Holy shit, she tasted like strawberries and wine, I wanted to ravage her. I ran one hand through her beautiful short hair, and the other I used to pull her close into me; she had to feel how fucking hard I was. She gave in, and even let out a sexy little moan as I shoved her up against the wall by the door where I walked in, and started to kiss her neck, inhaling her intoxicating scent.

After a moment, I stopped and looked into her dark gray eyes. "Look at me, Jo." I ordered her as she tried to look away. She obeyed and I swear to God, something inside me melted. Literally, I felt like my insides were turning to fucking jello. *What is going on here?*

"Brian, you should go. I don't know what that was about, but we're obviously both grieving in our own ways, and I don't want us to do something we'll certainly regret." I didn't want to let go of her. She was wrong—this was something else entirely, it wasn't my grief or my desire to console her. It was something different.

"I came to talk, I'm not going to apologize for what just

happened though, it was fucking hot, and I know you can feel what you do to me." Yes, I meant my rock hard cock. It was fucking aching, pressing up against my jeans, begging to be freed.

"I can feel it alright, and I'm not interested anymore, we've been down this road. You need to go. I have things to do here at the house, we can just forget about what happened here tonight, and any other night for that matter. I'll be by the station next week to pick up my old stuff I know my dad kept as well as his things." She pushed me away.

"You really want me to go?" I couldn't believe she was kicking me out. We were both flushed, and she was fighting it hard.

"Yes, I do. Please go, now is really not the time for this discussion or anything else," she looked down at the floor and wouldn't make eye contact with me.

"I'll do as you ask today, but we're not done talking, and after that," I waved my hands in between us. "We have more than talking to do." I wanted to press my body up against her again, and own her right there in the living room.

As soon as she'd stopped kissing me, I was missing it, feeling a pull to her. I've never felt that way. Ever. I loved it, and I was going to get to the bottom of it, but not today, I honestly don't want to upset her today, she doesn't deserve that. I probably shouldn't have pushed her today, I'm kind of a dick. We'd just spent the whole day at her dad's funeral and I even leaned on her for support. I definitely shouldn't have done that; I looked down at my cock, who clearly had a mind of his own.

"I'm sorry, Jo," I walked out the door, got in my truck and headed to the bar. I was off the following day, and I needed to drink off and shake the feeling that had come over me. I texted my brother and some guys from my shift and told them I'd meet up with them at Haligan's, the usual firefighter hangout.

Oh, shit. What just happened? I touched my lips and my breath hitched; I cannot believe he just did that. I didn't even fight back, I melted like butter right into him and it was so good. I was tingling all over, and even though it was so *so* wrong, I wanted it to happen again. Immediately. Ugh, how did I find myself in these situations? Well, it can't happen again, I won't let it. He's just upset about my dad, and we got carried away. It would crush me if he rejected me again like last time and there's no way he'd changed since then.

Brian was a notorious skirt chaser, and I already made the mistake of catching feelings for him a long time ago when we were growing up. Last year, when I told him how I felt and after the best kiss of my life, we parted ways with him saying, "we can never be together," I was crushed. I was drunk as hell and shouldn't have said anything to begin with, it was just a childhood crush anyway, but he was so cold about it that night. I can't even believe he brought it up again. I'm certain that my dad knew how I felt about him, and that he secretly hoped I'd end up with Brian someday, but that clearly wasn't going to happen. From what I knew, he couldn't keep his dick in his pants, and he was definitely not a one woman guy, which I always knew, and I was more of a serial monogamist.

I went back to rummaging through my dad's things, and fussing with things nervously around the house. I tried doing the last few dishes that were left out, and put away anything leftover from the reception, all in an attempt to not think any more about Brian. I should have been thinking about my dad, not about getting shoved up against the wall in a way that left me getting moist between my legs and shuddering with excitement.

I decided I didn't really want to be alone quite as much as I thought I did. Isn't that always the way. Most of my friends and a few people that were my dad's friends were all gathered at Haligan's, which wasn't really a surprise, that's where everyone in emergency services hung out. Since some of my dad's friends were going to be there, I felt like I needed to spend some more time hearing about how awesome he was, and also getting hammered. Drinking more would definitely take my mind off of that glorious kiss, and touching Brian's perfect body. I rolled my eyes at myself, remembering that I didn't think it could ever work out seriously, so it was a waste of time to keep fantasizing. But I still got butterflies thinking of his hands on me. I hoped he wouldn't be there tonight, but I think deep down I knew he would be.

BRIAN

I went straight to the bar from Jo's house, completely afflicted by her touch. Her lips on mine were all consuming to me and after waving my friends down, I headed straight to the bar to order a beer and a shot. I needed to get this damn woman off my mind. She's right, she isn't really just my responsibility, certainly not in the way I was making it, but I was feeling like I wanted her to be. That had to be my closeness to her father. She was practically my little sister if you think about it. Somehow my cock doesn't know that though. Just thinking of her gave me a stiff dick and I had to adjust myself under the bar.

Matt and a bunch of the guys from the department were all there, the place was packed. "Hey, bro, what's going on?" he asked me.

"Not much, stopped by to see Jo before coming here. She wasn't in the mood for company though." *Except when she kissed me back,* I thought.

"Yeah, she sent me on my way too, but I guess she changed her mind, she's on her way here now too."

I tried to hide my anxiety, or was it excitement? "Oh that's cool. I'm gonna go play some pool with the guys." I ordered another beer, and headed over to the pool tables, which had a perfect view of the front door. I'd be able to see when she came in. There were way too many people here for me to look like something was up, and I didn't think I'd be able to talk to her about what happened between us yet after she pushed me out. Hell, I'm not even sure I would know what to say. All I really knew was that I wanted to get my mouth on hers again, as soon as possible. About fifteen minutes later, she walked in and headed straight to Matt and a couple of the guys at the bar. I couldn't hear what they were talking about, but they both looked in my direction, and I caught her eye. I held up my bottle of beer in greeting and smirked at her. She froze like a deer in headlights and darted her gaze away. I wasn't letting her off that easy. I wouldn't confront her in front of everyone, but there was something going on between us, and I was determined to find out what it was.

I played a couple games of pool absent-mindedly; I couldn't stop looking over at her talking and laughing with a crowd of guys around her. It was pissing me off. I knew they were her friends, and friends of her dad's, but something's different, and I didn't like all that cock hovering around her. I couldn't take watching all those guys around her, and before I could even think through what I was doing, I was storming over in her direction.

"Jo, I need to speak with you," I growled in her ear.

"I'm busy, Brian." She wouldn't look me in the eye.

"Look at me. We need to talk, right now." She met my eyes, and my heart started racing.

"Ok." she said quietly. "Hey, I'll be right back, need to go talk to Brian about something real quick." She walked past me, toward the back door and disappeared outside. I followed closely behind. I was pissed.

"What is your problem, Brian? I was talking to the guys and having a good time," I could see she was getting drunk, her words were slurred and she was smirking at me, almost taunting me.

"Yeah, I can see that. You had a crowd of sharks swarming around you. You need to stay away from that." I couldn't believe how mad I was; I was jealous. I was the only shark that should be circling. She leaned up against the building, and I caged her in with my hands on either side of her face.

"Seriously, what are you doing? Why are you giving me a hard time? I told you I'm not your responsibility once already today." She looked me dead in the eyes and I felt it in my chest. I leaned in close enough to feel her breathing.

"You *are*," and I crushed her lips with mine. God, she still tasted so good. I grabbed her behind the neck with one hand, and pulled her close at the small of her back with my other hand, pulling her into me. She opened her mouth, and I explored her with my tongue. I swear to God, I was seeing stars and angels and I don't know what the fuck else. She had one hand on my chest, and the other reached around to my back. It was like a raging inferno where she touched me. I felt like I was getting a fever from the heat between us.

She came up for air and looked down, I grabbed her chin and lifted her eyes to mine. "Don't look away, Jo," I said softly, still pulling her close to me with my other hand.

"What are we doing? I mean really, what is this?" she asked me sounding exasperated.

"You know I care about you. I don't know what this is, but I don't want you being available to those other guys." That probably wasn't exactly what I should have said, but my dick was rock hard

"Where are we going?" I asked quietly, forgetting he'd already told me. I was starting to sober up, and wondering if this was a good idea, even if I really did want him to do bad things to me.

He grabbed my hand while he drove with the other and looked over at me. "*We*, are going to my house, where *we*, are going to talk and explore each other and see what's going on between us. Just us. I'm going to kiss every inch of you, Jo. That's where *we*, are going." He brought my hand up to his lips and kissed it gingerly.

Holy shit, I think I just came hearing him say that. That's the hottest thing I've ever heard in my life. Danny and I'd had sex obviously, we were together for a year, but never was I turned on just from the words he spoke. We had a pretty vanilla relationship. Not that I was into kink per se, but a little feistiness in the bedroom was a turn on, but that was not his thing, at all. With just Brian's words I was going to melt right into the seat. I forgot to respond I think because then he asked, "is that ok with you, Jo?"

I looked up at his face and smiled before whispering my reply. "Yes."

We pulled into his driveway, he had a beautiful home. Really nice for a single guy. It was a typical Florida bungalow style house with a perfectly landscaped yard in the front, and the back. I'd been there before for events and parties; he had the perfect backyard for entertaining. We hopped out of the truck and he came over to my side. "When you're with me, you need to let me open the door for you." He kind of growled under his breath at me.

"Okay," When our eyes met, it was like he could see through me. He leaned down and kissed me softly on the lips, then taking my hand and leading me inside. This was happening.

BRIAN

I'm actually a little nervous, and I'm never fucking nervous. I also never bring women here. I have had my fair share of action, but I preferred going to their place, or anywhere that isn't mine, so I could get out of dodge when the party was over. This was different, she needed to be with me, in my space. We walked inside, me still holding her hand, almost dragging her behind me. I was acting like a caveman, but I wanted to claim her as mine.

She was standing in front of me, staring at me looking confused and nervous too. "Can I get you something to drink?" I asked. I was forgetting my manners, and practically my own name right now. I walked to the fridge and got us both a beer.

"Thank you." She took the beer from me and never broke eye contact. We stood in the poorly lit kitchen in silence for what seemed like a really long time. I needed to do something. She broke the silence first.

"We don't have to do this, Brian, I think we got carried away in the heat of the moment and—" I stopped her right there, slammed my beer down and lunged at her, ramming my tongue into her mouth, and wrapping her up in my arms. She was still trying to hold her beer, while kissing me back, letting me explore her mouth with mine. I grabbed the beer bottle from her, without breaking our kiss, and put it on the counter, and she grabbed me roughly. She was so fucking hot. I lifted her up, she wrapped her tiny legs around my waist as I shifted us over to the island in the kitchen and set her on top of it. She had her hands under my shirt at my back, and I was groping every inch of her. I yanked her tank top over her head.

"Fuck you are so gorgeous, Jo," I grabbed some of that sexy short hair and pulled her head to the side giving myself access to her neck. She moaned softly at my touch. "We need to take this to my room," I scooped her up and carried her, legs wrapped around my waist.

I put her down gently on the edge of the king size bed, and took my shirt off. Her breath hitched, and I smiled. "You like what you see?" I workout a lot, and my job demands I be in shape; it certainly looked like she was pleased.

She stood up, and started to lightly touch my abs, and kiss my chest. I was going insane. "You need to lose the pants," I said as I unbuttoned her jeans. She started to lower her hands to the hardness pressing up against my jeans and I thought I'd explode right there. I had her pants off, and she was standing there in nothing but a lacy black bra, and matching panties. Fuck me, she was hot. She had a cardinal tattoo and some flowers that went around her shoulder and back, they were so colorful, on her pale, beautiful skin; I couldn't take my eyes off of them.

She finally spoke. "Fair is fair, time to lose your pants," she unbuttoned my jeans and reached in freeing my aching cock from the constraints of my boxers. She was still kissing me softly and her touch set my skin on fire all over again. She was starting to kiss me lower, and I stopped her. If she put her mouth anywhere near my cock I was going to come apart, I wasn't going to let that happen so fast.

I pushed her back down on the bed and climbed up next to her. I kissed her softly and reached around to undo her bra, taking it off with one hand. Her nipples were stiff little peaks, and I began to suck and knead one, and then the other. I reached down between her legs and groaned. "You're soaked, Jo," I ran my finger along her slit under her panties and felt her juices. She was so wet for me. I brought my fingers to my lips and licked them. "You taste so sweet."

"Brian, are you sure you want this?"

"Woman, I'm about to taste you, all of you. I've never wanted anything more in my entire life." I had no idea how true that was.

Jo

I was coming undone. He sucked on my nipples and started to kiss me lower, I just leaned back on his bed and let him. He was like an animal, sniffing and licking me and I loved it. He took charge, and was going to have his way with me, and I wanted to relish in it. My entire body was flushed and when he got to my panties, he growled, and ripped them off. I let out a little startled sound and leaned up on my elbows.

"This is mine, Jo, once this happens, it's mine," he looked me in the eyes, and I was mesmerized and speechless. "Say it. Josephine," he demanded, and used my full name. I fucking loved it when he called me Josephine.

"Yours," I barely get the word out. I could feel his hot breath between my legs, a little bit of five o'clock shadow grazing my thighs and I wanted him to touch me so badly I could hardly think. I would be his any which way he wanted at that moment.

"That's right." He began to lick me softly between my thighs, massaging my clit with his tongue, and I swear to all that is holy, I saw heaven in that moment. He slid one, and then two fingers inside me, massaging me from the inside while licking my clit soft and slow. I've never had anyone make me feel this way, I was literally coming apart from the inside out. I was going to explode at any moment. I didn't want this feeling to end, I was shaking all over and ready to lose it.

Once he began fucking me with his fingers, I lost control and he was coaxing it out of me. "Yes, Jo, come for me. Come on me now!!" He demanded while pumping in and out of my hot, wet pussy. I obeyed, and lost complete control, screaming his name while he continued to lap at my clit like he couldn't get enough. It felt like he was feeding on me, and he was starving.

"Oh, Jesus, Brian! It's too much, oh, my God," I screamed. When the raging orgasm subsided and I leaned back panting, he crawled up over me and kissed me hard. I could taste a little bit of myself on him as he devoured my lips with his. That tongue of his was soft and rolled around in my mouth like it was finding it's home, it was so sexy and I was still recovering from the orgasm I had just had, getting turned on again just from him exploring my mouth with his.

"I'm not done with you yet. I need to be inside you, Josephine," he was hovering above me now, my hands on his broad shoulders. "I don't think I can be gentle, baby, you have me too hot, I need to fuck you. I need to fuck you hard." He growled and leaned in to lightly suck my neck, sending shivers through me. He reached over to the nightstand and grabbed a condom then looked at me intently, awaiting a response to what he said.

"Please, Brian, yes, I want you so bad," I uttered, wanting him more than anything I could fathom. He rolled the condom on, and grabbed my ass underneath me pulling me to him. He lined his cock up to my slit, I honestly couldn't imagine it fitting inside me it was so big and hard. With one thrust, he was filling me and I was seeing stars.

He groaned on top of me. "Jesus Christ, you're so tight and so wet, fuck!" He pulled almost all the way out, and began pumping into me hard. I felt another orgasm welling up inside me almost immediately, forcing me to call out. "Fuck yes, Brian, oh, my God!" He was ramming his length inside me, so hard, but he was connected to me. He never took his eyes off me. I was ready to come, and I knew he was too as he moved faster, and harder and we both began to lose control. I felt him come with me, even through the condom and he yelled out my full name. "Josephine, my God!" When we finished, I was shaking all over and he grabbed my face and planted soft sweet kisses on my lips and all over my face. He was still pumping lightly into me, as I felt the aftershocks of the greatest orgasm I've ever had in my life.

"You're so beautiful," he was staring into my soul, and I was letting it happen. I was so fucked.

BRIAN

I was so fucked. That was the most intense sex I've ever had in my life. "You're so beautiful," I whispered to her while staring into her eyes. I pulled out of her with a groan, and went to the bathroom to get rid of the condom and to grab a towel to clean us both up.

"Thank you," she said quietly as I cleaned her up. The room smelled like sex, and she was glistening from a little bit of sweat. I was starting to get hard again already. I laid down and pulled her to me, she rested her head on my chest and sighed. It was the most comfortable I've been in my entire life except that she was so quiet, which was definitely not like her in general. One of the things I loved about her is that she says whatever she's thinking. Except in this case; she was quiet, staring off a little.

"What are you thinking about, Jo?" I was almost afraid to ask, but I needed to know what was going on in that pretty little head of hers.

She giggled before answering. "Well, it's been a hell of a day." Thinking back to the events of the day, her dad's funeral, our argument at his house, the bar, and now me holding her, yeah, it had definitely been a hell of a day. I relaxed and laughed too, "Yes, babe, it sure has. Are you okay?" I kissed the top of her head. She hesitated, and took a deep breath.

"Uh, yeah, I'm okay," she propped herself up on her elbows and looked at me. "I just want you to know, that uh...This doesn't have to mean anything, okay? It's been a kind of fucked up day, and we both know this isn't what you do really, so—" What just happened? Now I was pissed off.

"Whoa, wait a minute there, Josephine. We just had mind-blowing sex, and now you're here, with me, at my house and I'm trying to talk to you. Please give me the benefit of the doubt for like five fucking minutes, woman. What I *want*, since you failed to ask me, is *exactly* what's happening *right* now. Without all the angry yapping though. Jesus Christ." I huffed, and she started to giggle. "What's so funny?"

"You are. I'm so sorry, I didn't mean to upset you. I just don't want either one of us to feel like we have to turn this into something it's not. We're both grieving right now, we've been drinking, and these things happen, and I just didn't want you to think I had some kind of expectations," she laid her head back down on the pillows and sighed.

"What kind of expectations?" I genuinely didn't know exactly what she meant, and I wanted her to clarify before I argued with her. I leaned up on one arm staring at her intently.

"I don't know, Brian, can we just change the subject?" she sighed again and I wasn't going to let her off that easy. I didn't really want to push my luck, but pushing my luck was kind of my thing, and after today, I wasn't going to be taking no for an answer.

"Let me be clear. I do have expectations. I told you that you were mine, and I meant it. I don't want you messing around with other guys from the station, any other station or anywhere else. While we're doing whatever this is, and we'll definitely be doing it again, you're mine." There, I said it. I meant it. I've never given a shit before now, but fuck that, I would kill another dude if he went near her. And this was absolutely not a one-time thing. I was feeling pissed off just thinking about it. And I'm pretty sure I sounded like a fucking caveman or something and I didn't care at all.

She sat up, looked me in the eye and smiled. I pulled her to me and kissed her, I was marking her as mine, again. She climbed up on top of me and I was instantly hard again. The things this woman did to me, where the hell did this come from? She whispered in my ear, "I want you. Again. Now. And, I'm on the pill." Knowing we're both clean from our normal FD physicals every six months, she slid herself on top of my length. I sat up with her tits right in my face and started sucking on her stiff little nipples while she slowly bounced up and down on my cock. We had clearly come to an understanding. I massaged her breasts and continued licking and sucking on them until she picked up the pace, and I felt my balls start to swell again. She felt so fucking amazing. She grabbed the headboard behind me, and started fucking me hard. "Brian, I'm so close!" I could feel her body tensing up, and I let myself go too, coming inside her and thrusting as hard as I could; holding her hips to mine. I didn't think I'd ever stop coming, and I could have died a happy man in that exact moment. Oh, I was definitely fucked.

Wow, well that was an interesting turn of events. What the fuck was going on with me? Not only had I just fucked Brian, the hottest man on the planet—*twice*—he called me his. At first, I thought about saying I don't belong to anyone, but him demanding and saying those words, *you're mine*, entranced me. It was hot. He did things to me, and I knew it would not end well. I slept next to him for a while, I was downright exhausted from the best sex of my life and an emotional day in general.

When I woke up, he wasn't there, but I heard noises in the kitchen. I grabbed one of his fire department t-shirts, I had the exact same one, but his smelled like him, and was so big to fit that ridiculously ripped body of his, that it hung down to mid-thigh on me. I looked for my panties, then remembered he ripped them off of me last night. Damn, they were cute too, *oh well it was worth it*, I giggled to myself. I opened a few of his drawers until I found a pair of his boxers, and put them on. I went to the bathroom, and tried to make myself presentable, which was damn near impossible. I settled on washing off the prior day's makeup at least.

I tiptoed to the kitchen and what I saw made my jaw drop. A perfect specimen of a man, shirtless, wearing basketball shorts was humming, and cooking. I just stared at him, he was so fucking hot.

He turned around and caught me; giving me the biggest smile with the whitest straightest teeth I've ever seen.

He came over to me. "Leannán," he said, kissing me softly.

"What does that mean?" I asked, kissing him back.

"It means lover in Gaelic. You are my 'leannán. Mianach. Mine." He said it again, and I felt myself get flushed all over. How did I not know he used Gaelic phrases. Who cares, he should do it all the time. I kind of wanted him to fuck me on that kitchen island we started on last night.

I settled for a very soft, "Yes." This was intense.

"I made breakfast, and there's coffee over there," he pointed to the counter and just like that, the intensity was gone, like it never even happened. The whole thing was so crazy. When I turned around to walk to the coffee maker he smacked me on the butt. "Nice outfit. You're lucky I'm hungry and I know you need to eat or I'd take you right here again." He gave me a devilish grin. I really am a sucker for a great smile, okay, I'm a sucker for *his* smile.

"Thank you very much. I forgot to eat yesterday, I'm actually starving. And you know, coffee makes me very happy too." I made myself a cup, and he brought breakfast over to the table for us to eat. He set the two plates down and got himself a cup of coffee too.

"I have off today, which you already knew. I was thinking we could get out of town for the day and go to the beach. Get away from everything for a while, what do you think?" he asked.

"You want to spend the day with me?" I was kind of surprised we were even having breakfast together, let alone discussing spending the day together.

"Of course I do. Plus, I thought maybe a day of not being busy would be a nice change of pace for you. And it's a great day for the beach, I mean it's too cold to swim, but the sun is shining, it should be nice."

God his smile was amazing. He should seriously do toothpaste commercials or something. His eyes were sparkling as he tilted his head like he was waiting for an answer.

"Um, sure. That would actually be really nice. I need to get my car from the bar, and I would like to shower and get a few things from the house first. Is that okay?"

"Of course. I showered earlier so after we eat, we'll go get your car and drop it off at your house. Now eat..." he looked so serious. I'm not withering away, that's just not genetically possible. I have come from a long line of people with a pretty round ass and some curves.

"Yeah yeah, I'm on it," I laughed. This was kind of surreal. I wasn't really sure what' was going on, but I didn't hate it. We couldn't let anyone know about this at all though. I mean good lord, in this town? But a day away, on the beach, sounded absolutely glorious and he's right. I totally deserved a day to just kind of be free. I figured that I would take what I could get for a day and deal with real life another day.

BRIAN

After we got her car back home and she took a shower, we headed out. It was all I could do to keep myself from getting in the shower with her. I could hardly be in the same room as her without getting turned on at that point. I really wasn't sure what the hell was going on, but I liked it. I liked *her*. A lot. I wondered if I always felt this way. I mean I've always been attracted to her. She's beautiful. I was such a dick to her last year, but things were different. Her dad warned me very clearly that my intentions had better be on the up and up and I was not willing to get involved in anything that would jeopardize my relationship with him. I was pretty sure she didn't know her dad talked to me, and it was probably better that way.

It's about an hour drive to the coast and it was a really warm day for October. But that's Florida for you, it was basically second summer here. We could hang out on the beach and get some sun. It's good for the soul, and I thought it would make her happy. Making her happy made me feel happy. Yep, I was fucked.

She was staring out the window, and we were jamming to some early 90's alternative rock so we didn't talk much on the ride; it was making me a little nervous. I wanted to know what was going through her head, she looked deep in thought. I put my hand on her tan thigh just below where her skirt ended and she jumped and looked over at me startled. "Are you okay?" I asked her. I could feel myself scrunching my face at her.

She relaxed and smiled. "Yeah, I'm good. Just thinking about things is all. It's a beautiful day," she took a really deep breath in and sighed out with a smile. I took her hand and brought it to my lips, kissing it softly.

"What are you thinking about? Your dad?" I didn't want her to be sad, I was hoping to give her a distraction from all of that.

"No actually. I was thinking about last night," she laughed and was definitely blushing. I started laughing too, and took her hand in mine again, weaving our fingers together.

"Pretty great night. There's more where that came from. I could barely stay out of your shower this morning." There went my dick again, with a mind of it's own, getting excited. "We're going to have a fun day today, Jo," and I meant it. She smiled back at me and rested her head on the seat. She looked so relaxed, I couldn't wait to get to the beach and just put my arms around her.

We got to the beach in record time, and I specifically chose one we could drive the truck out onto. It was a perfect sunny day, the sun was warm and there was lots of people there enjoying the surf. That's Florida living man, it's like no other. There were surfers out there, people fishing, kids playing. I pulled out a huge blanket I had in my truck, and a picnic basket, yeah I have a picnic basket that my mother gave me years ago, and set up a spot for us just beyond where I parked us. Jo had already hopped out and walked to the water. I watched her kick off her flip flops halfway there, and lift her skirt up a little bit, even though the water didn't stand a chance of getting her clothes wet. She never really showed her body off in a provocative way at all, and that made her that much sexier. She was never on display.

I watched her get her toes wet, and jump a little. I had told her that water was too cold. It was adorable watching her keep sticking her little feet in. I finished setting up a spot for us, kicked my shoes off and quietly snuck up on her. She was staring off into the water; her hair was blowing a little in the gentle breeze. I watched her for a minute, thinking about how perfect she looked, so relaxed and beautiful.

I put my arms around her from behind, and inhaled her scent. She smelled like flowers and that, mixed with the smell of the ocean, was my idea of heaven. I buried my face in her neck and just breathed it all in. "You look happy. It's nice."

She held me a little tighter. "I am. I love the water. Even with all the activity here, it's so peaceful. Thank you for bringing me here today. It's definitely what I needed."

"I want to make you happy, Jo." I turned her around and brought her closer to me; kissing the top of her head. She was intoxicating. She felt like home. She relaxed into me and we both sighed. She's it for me, I didn't know when it happened, but in a moment somewhere in the last twenty-four hours, she had my soul. I couldn't possibly imagine not holding her and having her in every day of my life. She was meant for me.

"I am happy," she pulled away and smiled up at me with her perfect little mouth. She leaned up on her tippy toes and gave me the sweetest kiss I've ever felt in my life. Her lips were like little pillows, so soft. It wasn't even an erotic thing, even though I was basically at half mast in her presence at all times, it was like sweet sugar on my lips. She took my hand and walked us back to the blanket. "Come on, let's have a drink, and enjoy the view!" She cheerfully pulled me along and plopped down on the blanket, her flowing skirt falling around her.

I grabbed the mimosas we made back at her house out of the cooler, and poured two cups, handing her one. They were really delicious, not nearly as delicious as her lips, but it would do for the moment. I sat down next to her and we both faced the ocean. "Do you remember when we used to come out here fishing with your dad?" I was hoping that wouldn't upset her, I really was having some fond memories sitting here with her.

"I do. They're some of my favorite memories. Not at the firehouse, just sitting out here waiting for fish to show up," she laughed. "My dad loved it here. I think he wanted to retire on the water and just fish, or pretend to fish, all day," she smiled. "We had a lot of fun as kids before you grew up first and became a big jerk." She poked me and laughed.

"Aww, come on now. I'm trying to make up for it now. That's gotta count for something." She was right, I was kind of an asshole as a teenager to her and my brother, and then again as an adult. I took myself way too seriously.

"Well, maybe you should keep trying, buddy," she said and gave me that look. The kiss me right this fucking minute look. And I did. I grabbed the back of her neck and brought her to me. She started exploring my mouth with her tongue and I felt myself wanting to climb on top of her right there in front of everyone.

Until a little kid yelled, *eww* at us. We both started cracking up and immediately stopped our public show. She rolled over on her stomach and couldn't stop laughing. "What is up with us, Brian?" She was still laughing.

"I don't know, but I like it." I smiled down at her.

"I do too." She rolled over on her back and I settled in next to her on my side, just looking at how sweet and beautiful she looked.

She didn't look at me as she spoke. "Did you talk to my dad a lot lately?" I wasn't sure what she meant exactly.

I rolled over on my back next to her, and nudged my arm around her and she laid her head on my shoulder. I Inhaled the salt air before answering. "I'm not sure what you mean. I talked to your dad every day when we were working together, and then when you taught him to text, we communicated daily more or less." I kind of chuckled about that. God, Jack learning to text on the smartphone Jo bought him was hilarious. He used to get so pissed off at it like it was the phone's fault he couldn't get it to understand the words he wanted to send. He was the king of autocorrect fails and it never disappointed on making me laugh.

She giggled. "No, I meant about anything besides work. He had seemed kind of distracted the last couple weeks, and I was wondering if he ever talked to you about it. Like was he extra stressed out or anything?"

I thought about it, and Jack was always kind of a chill guy unless he was pissed off at his phone, or one of us for doing something careless. He seemed like maybe he didn't feel well the last couple weeks, but I didn't realize it at the time. I decided to keep that to myself for now though.

"I don't think so, babe, he was mostly his usual self from what I could tell. I'm not sure that he would have told me if something was troubling him, or if he wasn't feeling well." Which was true. We have a 'man up' philosophy in the fire department. Basically, if you don't feel well, suck it up pussy. So, if he didn't feel well, he wouldn't have told me unless he thought it was serious. I didn't think she meant his health though.

"Hmmm, I was just wondering," she said, seemingly in thought about it.

"Do you think something was going on with his health?" I asked. He wasn't as fit as the rest of us, but he was also a lot older. He certainly could have worked out a bit more, and maybe staved off the heart attack longer, but our job was stressful, and it could happen to fit guys too.

"Well, he wasn't the poster boy for health and fitness, but no. I don't think that's it. Maybe it was nothing, I'm just doing a lot of thinking about the last year, and how much time we spent together. That's all. It's nothing really. Just thinking," she said.

I squeezed her closer and kissed her forehead. "Babe, you know you were everything to him right?"

She squeezed me back tight. "I do know that. I just miss him, and I wish that I'd talked to him about a lot of things before he was gone."

"I know, baby, I know." I didn't know exactly what to say, but I knew she needed me to hold her. She sighed deeply, and snuggled into me. She was the perfect little fit in my arms. I was holding her hand on my chest, and had my other arm wrapped around her. It was the most comfortable I've ever been with a woman.

We spent the rest of the day sharing stories about her dad, drinking mimosas, and just enjoying each other's company. I can honestly say that I kind of always thought I'd be solo, playing the field. Sure it would be nice to have someone to come home to after a long shift, someone to worry about me being in danger, but that's the job. I found plenty of people to keep the sheets warm, but if this is what a relationship is like, I've been missing out. It was awesome; I'd never felt so relaxed and content in my life.

Jo

It had been the best day I've had in as long as I could remember. Brian was so kind, sweet and gentle all day. Not at all like the last couple years. Talking about my dad, talking about the fun we had as kids, it's just been so fun and relaxing, and it's not the mimosas talking. I didn't want the day to end, but I knew it would have to. Then it's back to real life. I was going to push that off for as long as I could. We watched the sunset, and Brian asked if I wanted to head back to town.

"If we must," I said wistfully. It was kind of like a vacation fairy tale.

"We can stay here all night if that makes you happy, Jo. You happy is all I want today." He sounded like he really meant it, but the escape had to come to an end at some point.

"We should head back I guess. It's been nice being away from reality all day. Thank you so much," I rested my forehead on his chest and sighed. He put his arms around me.

"What's wrong? You seem upset." He asked and I tensed. Having this conversation was really the last thing that I wanted to do, but I realized we probably should.

"I'm not upset; I'm just not thrilled about going back to reality is all. I mean it's been a wonderful day, but we have to get back to our lives," I didn't want to say separate lives, but it was what I meant knowing deep down that the other shoe was bound to drop, I was sure of it.

"Back to our lives isn't so bad. You've got a lot of support back at home, Matt, the station...me," he looked at me questioningly. He knew where I was going.

"You're not suggesting this become a public 'thing' are you? We can't be together in public, Brian if that's what you're implying," Okay, there I said it. I stiffened up, and he pulled away from me, looking angry. It needed to be said by me, before he did.

"What do you mean we can't be together? I thought we established this last night. And this morning." He was furious.

"I don't want to go public. We don't even know what this is. Especially after last year, and my dad, everything that's happened. I don't need people thinking that I fell into the arms of the guy that got my dad's job at my old firehouse. And to be perfectly honest, this has been an amazing day and I don't want it to end, but I don't think either one of us is ready for what showing up 'together' really means, do you?"

I was feeling exasperated but it had to be said. I was anxious and paranoid just thinking about it. The last thing I needed is the public humiliation of this falling apart after a weekend fling the day after we said our goodbyes to my dad. Seriously, I didn't need the gossip at the station or the county for that matter and I didn't need the heartbreak that he was going to lay down on me, I mean let's face it, I was hooked. I'd been hooked my whole life on him. But he's a heartbreaker plain and simple. I felt tears welling up in my eyes, and now I'm going to cry too? If only a bolt of lightening would've stricken me down right at that minute. He was staring at me, and he looked hurt and angry, like really pissed off. I felt like a caged animal and I wanted to flee. But I meant what I said.

He took a deep breath, shutting his eyes for a moment. I was waiting for him to raise his voice at me, and I was holding my breath anxiously. "Look, Jo, I honestly don't know what this is between us, but I can tell you that it's been one of the best days of my life sitting out here with you all day, touching you, kissing you, and watching you smile. I know what I said to you last year was shitty, and we can talk about it at some point. I promise I will explain, but not now. Right now, it's me and you, baby, and nothing else really matters. I need to be with you, inside of you, around you, and I know you feel it too. If you want to keep this a secret, I can agree to that for now, but I refuse to never kiss those delicious lips again." He leaned in for a kiss, and I met him halfway. It was soft and deep and felt as if it were meant to prove something. It did, I was getting hot and wet, and I almost forgot everything I had just said. I lost myself when he touched me. I always lost myself with him.

"So, you're suggesting that we sneak around?" I whispered when we stopped kissing. I was resting one hand on his chest and holding myself up in the sand with the other.

"No, *you're* saying we have to sneak around. I'm willing to go along with that for now because I crave you, Jo. I'm not nearly done with this, and I know you're not either, if I have to sneak around behind people's backs to get to you—I will. It's not like we have to climb out the bedroom window and sneak away from our parents, people know we're friends. I've known you your whole life." He grabbed me and rolled on top of me in the sand, holding himself up and caging me in between his huge arms. "But make no mistake, you're mine, Jo. There's no one else in the picture while this is going on. Understood?" He looked me right in the eyes.

"Does that go both ways?" I had to ask, and he let his lips spread wide in a handsome grin; trying to disguise his urge to laugh.

"Yes, it goes both ways. I mean it, both of us. Only you. Only me. I know that you don't believe me, but you'll see." With that, he leaned in for another kiss. It wasn't the animalistic crazy devouring kiss we had so often, it was deep and loving, and I forgot my name when it happened. He literally took my breath away. This couldn't possibly be real, could it?

BRIAN

Honestly, I wanted to flip the fuck out when she said we couldn't 'go public' whateverthefuck that even means. I'm actually totally impressed with myself that I didn't, and I somehow came up with a game plan on the fly. I usually do what I want and generally, especially when it comes to women, I get what I want. That being said, I didn't want to scare her off and I sure as hell didn't want to stop fucking her. I didn't really love the idea of having a secret from my brothers at the firehouse, or my actual brother for that matter, but if it kept this thing going longer then I was all for it. I couldn't get the woman off my mind and if it meant sneaking around to see her naked and otherwise, then so be it. For the time being.

I'd never actually had a girlfriend that I brought out with me anywhere anyway, so this was fine until I figured out what is really going on between us. I was going to ride this out because I'd get to see her, and she wouldn't be seeing anyone else. Apparently, I'm more fucked than I thought. When did I start becoming such a pussy? God, I needed to get to the gym and workout or something. *Do something manly.*

We pulled into her driveway, and she reached to open the door. "Hey!" I snapped at her.

"What?" I startled her and hopped out of my side.

"What did I tell you about letting me get the door for you?" I smiled across the bench seat at her.

She immediately blushed and smiled, so my mission was accomplished, as she took her hand off the door. I came around and opened her door for her, taking her hand and helping her out of the truck.

"You've become quite the gentlemen, Cavanaugh," she took my hand and we walked to the front door of her dad's old place.

"You like it?" I caressed her face with the back of my hand.

"I do, very much," she whispered.

"Are you going to invite me in, Jo?" I kissed her softly.

"Would you like to come in, Brian?" she smiled up at me, her gray eyes sparkling.

"Why yes, I would like to come in and get you out of that dress. Immediately please," I started reaching up under her dress, finding her wet, just how I liked her.

She opened the door, and pulled me in behind her. I shut and locked it, turning to pin her with my stare. Her back was to me; I stopped her and pulled her into my chest. Kissing her neck, I slid one of the straps of her dress off her shoulder and she leaned into me more, making my cock hard as hell. I was wearing basketball shorts, so there was no hiding what she did to me.

"Let's go to my room," she whispered and took my hand, pulling me behind her. We got to her room and she turned to face me, grabbed the hem of her dress and pulled it up over her head in one motion. Standing in front of me, braless, wearing nothing but a pair of white lacy panties, she smiled and then looked down.

"Álainn...beautiful...you're so beautiful. Look at me,

Josephine," I took her chin in my hand and lifted her face to meet my eyes. "Don't look away, baby," I told her as I yanked my shirt up over my head. Looking into my eyes, she didn't say anything and it made me question if she was okay. I took her face in my hands again, bringing her close. "Talk to me, Jo," I stroked her face gently.

"Now is not for talking," she smiled and leaned in to kiss me. My heart was racing, as I pulled her in tight to take her mouth to mine, all the blood in my body rushed right to my cock again, igniting my need to be inside her. Playing with the waistband of my shorts, she reached in and freed my cock and sunk to her knees, dragging my shorts down with her. Taking me in her mouth, she licked the tip of my cock which was just starting to drip, and then took my entire length.

"Oh fuck, Josephine, that feels so fucking good," I was holding the back of her head as gently as I could while she used one hand to stroke my shaft, and the other was massaging my balls. She used just the right amount of pressure with her tongue as she bobbed her head up and down on my aching cock. My balls were getting heavy and I was going to cum any minute. "I'm going to cum baby, you gotta stop," I tried to gently push her away.

My girl grabbed onto my ass and began sucking even more vigilantly, I couldn't take it anymore, I let every bit of cum I had hit the back of her throat and she swallowed every drop. I yelled out with my release, grabbing the back of her head as gently as I possibly could at that moment, which wasn't very gentle.

Holy shit, was that fucking hot. When I was done, she let my cock out of her beautiful mouth with a pop and she looked up at me, still on her knees with a satisfied smile on her face. Goddamn she's so hot and so beautiful, and she's mine was all I could think looking down at her like that. "Oh, my God, that was amazing. Now get up and turn around," I demanded. I was going to fuck her so hard she'd feel me all day tomorrow, but not before I taste her sweet pussy again.

She got up slowly, touching me softly all the way up, kissing my torso, my abs and my chest on her way up, rubbing those full perky breasts up my body. She turned around, her back to me, rubbing so closely and softly against me, I was instantly hard again. "Bend over," I demanded gruffly and she obeyed immediately, leaning her hands onto the bed with her ass in the air toward me, still wearing those white lace panties.

I softly rubbed the small of her back, and gently rolled her panties down to her ankles and helped her step out of them, widening her stance, and running my hand back up her leg between her thighs. She took a breath in, and I caressed that perfect round ass with my other hand and gave it a squeeze. I fucking loved her ass, I was going to get it eventually, but not yet. I got down on my knees, and bent her further over on the mattress, her legs spread wide in my face, and began licking her sweet juices.

She started moaning softly, and I stuck a finger deep inside her, lapping at her wet pussy. "Oh, Brian," she called out, sticking her ass even further into the air, and pumping her sweet little clit on my finger. Just as she started to cry out, ready to cum, I pulled my finger out, stood up, and thrust all of my cock inside her. She cried out. "Oh, my God, Brian, fuck fuck fuck!!!" She met me, pushing back into every thrust, calling out my name. I fucking loved it when she screamed my name.

I could tell she was almost ready, she was panting and clawing at the sheets on the bed. "Come with me, Jo, come with me, baby!" and I fucked her even harder, with everything I had, while she screamed my name out into the mattress, arching her back and pulling the sheets toward her. I pumped her pussy full and when we were both done, I practically collapsed on top of her, my heart beating out of my chest. We were both shaking and panting, relishing in the aftershocks. I scooped her up onto the bed, planted a kiss on her lips, and went to the bathroom to get something to clean us both up.

When I came back, she was laying on the bed, totally naked, smiling at the ceiling. I stopped for a minute and she looked over in my direction. "Hey you," she grinned.

"Hey, beautiful, whatcha thinking over here," I climbed on the bed next to her, and cleaned us both up with a warm washcloth. "That was pretty amazing, Jo."

"Yes, yes it was. I think I'll be feeling that tomorrow," she laughed.

Feeling some pride, I replied. "That was the plan. Gotta have me on your mind tomorrow," I dropped the towel on the ground, and scooted in next to her, pulling her close. She sighed into me, and I squeezed her a little tighter and planted several kisses on the top of her head. Inhaling her scent, that freshness that reminded me of spring mornings when the orange blossoms were blooming, I felt more at ease than I ever remembered feeling and the more time I spent with her like that, the more comfortable I became.

"Oh, I'm sure I'll be thinking of you tomorrow, Brian." She gave me a squeeze, then started to get up.

"Where are you going?" I reached out to keep her in place next to me. She dodged me, and went over to her closet and grabbed some little shorts and a fire department t-shirt to put on.

"I'm not going anywhere, but the shower, however you gotta get home," she laughed. I frowned back at her, I didn't want to go. I wanted to wake up next to her. I was about to throw a temper tantrum.

"I think I'd rather just stay here in bed with you."

"Yea, as nice as that would be, and it would be nice," she came over to the bed and kissed me. "We both have early shifts tomorrow, babe, and my house is pretty much on everyone's way to work, so your truck needs to not be sitting in my driveway in the morning," she got back up off the bed.

"How about this? How about if I join you in the shower, and then I'll go home to my lonely bed without you tonight if I absolutely must?" I tried to negotiate.

"That sounds like a fair deal, Cavanaugh, I like how you do business." Her smile was so bright it gave me butterflies. She came back over to the bed, leaned over me and planted a sweet kiss on my lips, taking my hand, and dragging me with her to the bathroom.

After stripping down again, she leaned over and turned the water on, and I stood watching her in awe for a moment. It was like watching art that you couldn't understand, but you loved anyway. As my eyes roamed her beautiful body, taking in her colorful tattoos, I was hard again. She turned around to look at me and a smile formed at the corners of her mouth "Come on, let's get in, babe." she whispered. Okay, yeah I loved it when she calls me babe. I loved it when she calls me anything actually, but that, I really loved, it sent a warm sensation straight to my chest.

I followed her into the huge walk-in shower, unable to keep

my hands off her. She was standing under the water, and pulled me in to kiss her. "This is really nice, Brian," she whispered with her lips just barely touching mine.

I wrapped my arms around her and agreed. "Yes it is, baby, we'll have to make this a habit." I seriously couldn't stop smiling around her. She's sexy, smart, she's everything, and my carnal need was beginning to take over. I grabbed the body wash and some poofy sponge thing and started to wash her. She had a perfect body. She wasn't tiny, she was fit and strong, curvy, with that nice round ass that I couldn't get enough of.

She started to make quiet moaning sounds as I rubbed her body down gently, the hot water rolling over both of us, wrapping us in warmth. She in turn, was rubbing soap around my shoulders and neck, massaging me with just enough pressure to send tingles through my whole body. I was so relaxed, and so turned on that I dropped to my knees in the shower, and pushed her against the shower wall. I grabbed her leg and threw it over my shoulder, I was going to taste her delicious pussy again right now.

I looked up at her, and she was watching me, smiling and breathing heavily while the water continued to roll over both of us. "Baby, I need to taste you again," I started to circle her clit with my thumb, watching her react to me by touching herself, massaging her own breasts, and pinching her hard pink nipples. Fuck, that's hot. My dick was aching to be inside her, but I was hungry for that pussy.

I went in with one finger, and started to lick that hard little nub causing her to suck in air and cry out softly. "That feels so good!" She was trying to steady herself on one leg, leaning into the shower wall and reaching out on the tile, but I was holding onto her so tight, she wouldn't fall. I kept licking and sucking at her folds, pumping two fingers inside her slowly, coaxing out her release.

As she got closer, she gently grabbed onto my head with her other hand and started to moan and cried out, "Brian, I'm going to cum! Oh, my God, baby!" Her whole body shook and I could taste her juices as I continued licking gently, making it last as long as I could. When she was done, I stood up and kissed her hard, wanting her to taste herself on me.

"Do you taste how delicious you are?" I growled at her, pressing my hard cock against her. "I need to be inside you, baby," I said, not waiting for her answer. She looked satiated and I wasn't done with her by a long shot.

"Yes please," she whispered to me, and gently bit my bottom lip, then ran her tongue across it.

I grabbed her by the ass, lifted her and pressed her into the shower wall as she wrapped her legs around me. I slowly guided her down on my cock which was aching for her now. She grabbed onto me, yelling out as I thrust into her. Fuck her pussy was so tight, I could feel it adjusting to my size inside of her, squeezing my dick just enough to send chills all over me while I was slowly pumping into her and holding her against the wall. Sex has never been this amazing, it's like bees buzzing all around me.

"You like that, baby? You like my cock inside you?" I whispered in her ear. She was holding on to me tight while I fucked her against the wall.

"I can't get enough, baby," she panted.

I could feel my release coming, and I was trying to hold off until she was there. I started to try moving faster, and she moaned;

giving me the go ahead. I started pumping into her hard, causing her to cry out with each thrust, driving me even crazier than I already was.

"Oh yes! Brian! Fuck me, baby, that's so good!" She started to shake, and I could feel her pussy tighten around my dick, bringing me to my climax, I pulled her down on my cock as hard as I could and let myself go inside of her, crying out myself.

"Jo, oh, God!" I yelled out as every bit of cum I had was released inside her. I fucking loved coming inside her, there's no greater feeling. As we both finished, I gently let her down to her feet again, and just pressed my body against her, under the steaming hot water, relishing in the moment.

"Damn, that was amazing. You have no idea how fucking sexy you are, do you?" I looked down at her beautiful, gray eyes looking back up at me.

She smiled. "That *was* fantastic, baby," she said. "I've never had shower sex, we'll have to keep this on the regular list of things to do in secret," she laughed.

After we got out and dried off, we dressed in her room. She put on leggings that had me staring at her ass and forgetting everything else. I laid down on her bed and sighed.

"Tired, babe?" she climbed on top of me straddling her legs around me and looking down at me smiling that beautiful smile of hers. I grabbed her hips and rubbed the sides of her legs.

"Not really, just super content actually," I smiled from the inside out. "I'm really happy, Jo, I really like being with you." Her presence was so warm and inviting, even when it wasn't sexual, which it was for me almost all the time, but it was something different. I just wanted to be near her.

"I'm happy too, Brian," she replied, but she looked like she had something else to say.

"But? It sounds like there's a but," I pushed myself up, causing her to put her arms around me to stay upright.

She held on tight to me, bringing me in for a hug, and playing with the hair at the back of my neck, sending tingles through my head. "There's no 'but', this is actually really wonderful," she kissed my temple sweetly, and rested her head on my shoulder. I brought her in tight, rubbing her back softly while she sighed into me. I'm in, one hundred percent. This chick is all that's right in the world. How did I even consider saying no to this in the past? I have seen the error of my ways, everyone should feel this content with someone.

"I promise you, it will always be wonderful," I pulled her away just enough to get lost in her eyes. "I'm serious. You need to understand I don't consider this a fling, something is happening here." God, I almost wanted to tell her I love her right now, but I've never said that to anyone, ever.

"I don't consider this a fling, Brian, honestly I don't," she smiled sweetly, leaning in for a kiss. I wrapped my arms completely around her, kissing her as softly as I could. She stirred up an animal need in me, but the passion in just that sweet kiss overwhelmed me. I held onto her in a hug that felt almost desperate, like I was afraid to break it and let her go. She sat up and released me first, to my dismay. I could have held her all night.

"As much as I'd love you to stay, babe, you've gotta go," she crawled off me and walked across the room, grabbing a sweatshirt and pulling it on over her head. She looked kind of like she just woke up, she was fucking adorable.

"Alright, alright. You win this time, but I prefer waking up next to you, in my bed. So that needs to get on the schedule asap," I was going to insist on this in the very near future.

She slinked her sexy ass over to me, and put her arms around my midsection and looked up. "I think that can be arranged," I leaned down and kissed her. God, I'd never get tired of kissing her, I needed my lips on her constantly. "Now next time you swing by, park out back. That big truck of yours is a pretty huge eyesore in my driveway for all to see," she gave me a sideways glance, meaning business.

"Ugh, Jo, I hate hiding. Do we have to hide? Seriously?" I was still holding onto her and rolled my eyes.

"Yes, we do if you want to keep doing this. It's not anyone's business anyway. And before you ask, no, I'm not telling Matt either, so don't think it's easy for me. This is just the best for now, trust me," she laid her head on my chest.

Kissing the top of her head, I agreed. "Okay, for now. But let me be clear, this isn't just about sex. Do you understand me?" Honestly, I'd do anything to keep her, to keep this feeling. She was like a drug and now that I'd had her, I couldn't get enough.

"Yes, I understand," she reached around me and scratched my back softly, sending chills up my spine. "Now get your ass out of here," she laughed.

"Booo. Fine. I'll text you later, baby," I cupped her face in my hands and kissed her.

I left her house a few minutes later, after we made out like teenagers in the doorway. Even though it was getting a bit late, I went to the gym at the firehouse. I called my brother and he said he'd meet me there. While I had a twenty-four hour shift the next day at seven a.m., a shitload of paperwork due to the new Chief appointment, I seriously needed to hit the gym a little tonight. Jo gets me so fired up, and I just couldn't fathom how Jack dealt with all the bureaucracy and red tape bullshit that comes with being Chief.

Matt was already there when I pulled up. "Where have you been all day, bro?" he asked me.

"I went fishing at the beach," I lied, like she wanted me to.

"You don't have any poles in your truck, man," *Christ, I suck at this lying business already apparently.*

"Well, I went to the beach intending to fish. Since I didn't have my poles, I basically just hung out. It's been kind of a long couple days dealing with everything here at the station since Jack..." I trailed off.

"Yeah, it has. I sure do miss the old man. Closest thing to a dad we ever really had. It's not the same without him giving us shit." Matt chuckled. He was right. "It was probably nice out there just relaxing. We should actually go fishing like we used to out on the beach soon."

"Yea, let's definitely do that soon. Come on, let's pick up some heavy shit and put it down," I laughed. Okay, so I covered myself that time. I was gonna have to get better at that though. I grabbed my cell out of my pocket and sent her a text.

    My lips need to be all over you. When can
    I see you?

She replied immediately

    You just left!

76

I'm already hard thinking about you. When?

I couldn't help myself.

Oh please lol. I can come by the station tomorrow after my shift at 19 to say hi, but we can't do anything there. Day after maybe when you're not working.

You're working at 19 tomorrow? We need to discuss that. And maybe nothing. You're mine. Tomorrow.

Now I was pushing my luck but fuck it. I was already getting half hard just thinking about it. And as for her working at 19 with that dickbag? No. That needed to stop immediately.

I have to work, there's nothing to discuss. And we'll see about tomorrow. Goodnight, Cavanaugh.

Goodnight my beautiful, Josephine.

She has no idea who she's messing with. I get what I want. We were absolutely going to discuss her not working at all these different places though. And definitely not with that Danny asshole, something about him really bothers me. He's shady as fuck and I don't trust him. I put my phone away and killed my upper body at the gym.

Jo

I loved that he called me by my full name sometimes. No one did really, even my dad rarely did. Actually he and Brian are the only two people to call me Josephine, ever. It was my mom's middle name. Everyone else called me Jo. After he left, I laid down on the couch and thought about how excited he makes me. I wondered if he really meant what he said, that it wasn't about sex, that it was something more. Lord knows it was something more to me, but I just wasn't sure with him.

I was disappointed that I told him to leave, and I was almost disappointed in myself that I was letting this happen, but it felt so good. Couldn't really be bad, could it? Something that felt so right? Okay maybe, but maybe it was time for me to start living a little instead of being so wound up all the time. I had a reputation for being pretty high strung and fussy. Not in a girly kind of way, just particular about things. Around the firehouse, even as a young girl, I was like the "mom" of the group always making sure nobody got hurt if I could avoid it, always knowing all the "rules". That probably had a bit to do with my dad too, but it was my nature to look after people. It was in my genes to take care of people.

I really needed to make some decisions about work too; I had too many part-time jobs. I had been working per diem at another fire department —Danny's fire department actually, and as a fire inspector I picked up some work, in addition to co-teaching a class at the community college in fire science of course, and a part time gig as a per diem paramedic sometimes, but I had not picked up any shifts at Station 23 in quite a while. I wasn't sure why I had been avoiding working there, it was actually my favorite place to work. I didn't have to prove myself anymore, and I liked just about everyone there. My teaching semester was over, and Matt had suggested I talk to Brian about picking up some shifts at the station and stopping work at Station 19, since it was the same department Danny belonged to. I needed to be there for work tomorrow though, I had been on the schedule a while. I'd need to think that over. Brian certainly didn't like it. I didn't like personal issues becoming work business, but Danny showing up at dad's funeral was too much. I didn't need him making work unsafe. Something about his behavior really gave me the chills.

After my shower, I made myself a sandwich for dinner, and sat down at my dad's desk. I wanted to go through some of his papers, and start getting things in order. Since I was living at Danny's until a couple months ago, I didn't have another place except here, and I was planning to stay here until some other plan came to mind. I needed to start sorting through my dad's stuff and getting rid of some of the junk he'd been collecting. And the papers, that man had notebooks and papers everywhere. He kept regular and meticulous notes on calls he was on, in case he ever needed to refer to them in court, or for his reports. I turned the scanner on; I liked the background noise, and hearing what emergencies were going on across the county actually made me feel safe, and sometimes people said some really hilarious, and dumb, stuff over the air.

There was a small car accident on the other side of town, an MVA, with no injuries, and some fluids on the ground. A boring gig for a firefighter, you're basically spreading cat litter all over the road to soak up the oil and grease, and sweeping it up. There was a respiratory emergency at the nursing home, which didn't require the FD, just an ambulance. That was a pretty common call unfortunately. That, and slip and falls. In Florida, you're required to be both a paramedic and a firefighter to work, and I admitted, with the exception of helping the elderly, and people that have been in car accidents, fire was really my favorite. The camaraderie of the brotherhood as we call it, is a lot like police or guys in the military. They become your family, and really you're only as good as the sum of your parts on the team. Everyone has a specialty of some kind, something that they love about the job, and a role they have on a truck. There were no calls for our department, which made me feel good. As fun as it is to be a firefighter, when the tones drop, you don't always know what you're walking into, and I did always fear for the safety of my friends.

My favorite was engine work; I just wasn't a ladder girl. I hated ladders at the academy, and I'd climbed on top of buildings to do work when needed, but I really hated it. I hated carrying heavy shit up a ladder even more. That vertigo-like sick feeling that you're going to fall. I'd read someplace that there are only two fears we're born with, the fear of falling, and a fear of loud noises. You didn't grow up in a firehouse maintaining a fear of loud noises, in fact, I loved the sounds of the trucks, the saws, the sirens. The fear of falling, that never went away.

I was smaller than most of the guys, so rescue in tight spaces was usually my job. I was on the tactical rescue team, which was ideal since I could squeeze into cars that are all smashed up to help stabilize patients, crawl in a storm drain to save baby geese easier, things like that. I could haul hose wherever it needs to go, and carry all the same stuff the guys could, we just all have our specialty and our preference. On a fire, I was usually on the hose, or doing some searches, that kind of thing. The engine was for fire suppression and water supply and the ladder was for ventilation, search and rescue. This was all relative, and depended on what you saw when you showed up at a scene and what other stations or equipment were available.

My dad insisted that if I was really going to make a career out of it, that I get certified in basically everything there was and made myself as good as possible at every activity in the service I could. He knew that even with him at the helm, I'd face some challenges as a female firefighter, and he knew I didn't want special treatment. Even though he felt the real learning was on the streets, there was something to be said for attending all of the classes, for exposure to other departments, and for credibility later on. It's actually helped me a lot, I'd kind of become a jack of all trades and literally, I had a laundry list of certifications that while interesting, aren't especially common.

Brian was a ladder guy, so we didn't ride the same truck usually, although he didn't ride a truck that much anyway now since becoming deputy chief, and now chief of course. He had his own duty truck to take to scenes. Ladder guys, or truck guys, love climbing on roofs, going up ladders, hell as a kid he loved climbing trees and stuff like that so I guessed it made sense. Matt and Brian are actually on the same schedule and typically work together most of the time. I used to be on the same shift pretty often as well, just a different truck than Brian. We used to have a lot of fun at the station. I was the only woman, but our department is progressive, so it was never an issue really, plus I guess looking back, my dad being the chief meant that people would respect me, or at the very least be nice to me. In fact, I think that people expected a lot more out of me than others sometimes because my dad was so good at what he did.

Matt and Brian have been in my life literally since Matt and I were babies, and Brian was three. We grew up together. I didn't want this fling with Brian to ruin what little family I really have left, but I also couldn't stop thinking of getting him back in bed. As long as it remained a secret, that was okay. I wished it didn't have to be a fling, but I knew that we could never go public, and to be totally honest with myself, there's no way that he could be serious about me for long. It's just not who he is.

BRIAN

Thinking about her working at Station 19 was making it a long day. It made my blood boil, I knew that douchebag Danny was going to do something, I just didn't know what. He rubbed me the wrong way for more than one reason, there's something just off about him, I didn't want him anywhere near Jo. He's up to no good, and I made a mental note to do some digging on the guy. She needed to just come back to this department already. I was sitting at my desk with a mountain of paperwork in front of me and a huge cup of coffee, but I couldn't concentrate, I tapped my fingers, just being pissed off about her working there, and also half turned on because I was thinking about her.

I pulled out my phone to text her,

Morning, beautiful. When are you coming by?

I sat and waited for her to reply. I know she doesn't have a call, because I've been listening to the scanner, and I would know if there was a fire or an EMS call in her district. After what seemed like forever, but probably was a few minutes, she replied.

Hey, there. After my shift I can swing by.

Everything okay?

I ask.

Yeah, why wouldn't it be? I'm just working. Like you.

You're working where we both know you shouldn't be.

I was going to be honest. She definitely shouldn't be there.

Look, I'm just working. Please don't give me a hard time.

I'm protecting what's mine.

I don't need protection, I'm just working. I'll be by after my shift around 4. Now settle yourself ;)

Okay, I got the wink, so she wasn't pissed.

Just be careful. I miss you. ;) I don't care if I sound like a pussy, I do miss her.

Be careful too.

And then she sent a second text, *I miss you too.* I grinned like an idiot and stared at my phone. She missed me and I loved it.

The tones dropped, and I hopped up and shoved my phone in my pocket. I was listening for the dispatcher to announce where the call was and what we had in store for us today.

"Engine 23, Ladder 23, Visible Smoke in the area of North Orange and Virginia Ave," I heard over the intercom. I was wearing my duty radio, so I replied on my way to my new Chief's truck. "Central, 2300 responding." The rest of the guys were racing to their trucks, and they also responded accordingly.

Normally we'd have an actual address, but since it was the middle of the day, someone must had spotted smoke, and called it in. That meant we'd either have to find which house it is, or it would be really obvious which house it is. Because it's a home on the end of town, the neighboring town's trucks were called as well. We all went lights and sirens to the scene, something I'll always love. The rush of excitement that comes with getting to the scene is something you just can't describe unless you've done it. I arrived first, and immediately saw which house it was and called it into dispatch. I threw my jacket and helmet on, and walked around the house doing my 360, sizing up the scene.

The other trucks arrived shortly after I did, and I instructed them where to set up. It looked like there was a fire somewhere in the back corner of the house, probably the kitchen. The smoke alarms were audible now, and I could see a lot of smoke in the kitchen window. It appeared that no residents were home, but we still needed to do a search. My guys ran like a well-oiled machine. I went back to my vehicle to set up command, and instructed the ladder to set up and conduct a search to make sure there was no victims in the house. Then instructed the engine to attach to the nearest hydrant and prepare to go in the back side of the house. The interior crew reported that there was no visible fire, however there was smoke coming from the wall near the oven.

I sighed. That meant that if they didn't find the hot spot with the TIC (thermal imaging camera), they'd have to start ripping the wall apart looking for the fire. That could go a lot of different ways for us, and get complicated. In a concrete block house, you couldn't exactly just rip the walls apart obviously, and it could be a little trickier to find the source of the fire. Also, our job was not just to find the fire and put "the wet stuff on the red stuff", but we had a moral responsibility to try not to do a bunch of damage to personal property as well. The house had an addition to it, so it wasn't traditional cement block like most homes in Florida. It definitely had a truss roof construction on the addition of the second floor, and I was pretty concerned there was fire in the addition walls making its way to the roof. In central Florida, most of the homes start as one story cement block, and they're on relatively small plots of land. The only way to have a bigger house is to move outside the city, or build up. This house had done that, and it wasn't looking good for the likely pricey addition. I called for additional personnel to the scene, it was definitely a fire and we'd need reinforcements. It was going to be a long job.

Jo

I heard Station 23 get tapped out for what sounds like might become a real fire. That made me a bit tense. The thing is, firefighting isn't really what you see on television. There aren't that many fires in real life. Yes, in a city, there's more than our fair share, however it's not racing from one fire to the next, so when you do have a legitimate fire, it's a big deal. Brian knew what he was doing and those guys are really the best around, so I was sure it would be fine. It's unlikely for me to get called there, it's all the way on the other side of town. I decided to listen to the call on the radio to stay up-to-date.

I'd been avoiding Danny all morning, who wasn't supposed to be on the schedule, and yet somehow miraculously was on shift. He's up to no good, and while I probably should talk to him to make arrangements to get a few things I left at his place, I'd almost rather buy new shit. He approached me this morning when I got in, and I told him I needed to go check my duty rig. I was not riding a fire truck today, I was medic du jour today, and my partner was another girl who's also a per diem. I didn't know her that well. Her name was June, and she was a tiny thing, about three inches shorter than me, and I'm only five foot four, and she means business. I'd partnered with her before, and she was a nice chick and not competitive, which was a wonderful change of pace in a medic partner. I prefer when everyone just shows up ready to do their job and that was definitely June.

We hadn't had a call all day, and so we were sitting in the engine bay listening to Brian's call. They called for additional staff, so there was definitely a fire. I loved hearing him on the radio, he sounded gruff and sexy. I felt myself grinning hearing his voice give orders and provide updates.

"Central, place all companies in service, and request back-up EMS. Active fire in progress." I heard him demand over the air. This perked me up, that's pretty serious around here. Suddenly, our tones dropped too.

"Rescue 19, EMS Fire Response to North Orange & Virginia for active fire." My partner and I hopped up and headed to our duty rig. I replied immediately over the air. "Central, Rescue 19 en route."

The fire was actually about fifteen minutes in traffic away, it's a congested area, and even with lights and sirens it's difficult to get through it. It was "my treat", which basically meant, my partner drove, and I got the first patient. In those situations, you took turns unless a call was something that was the one thing that you "just can't" and you made a deal. In this case, it was just my treat, so I rode shotgun, and laid on the sirens, a lot. I was a little anxious knowing that Brian was there. It would be the first time I'd see him since everything that was going on, and we were both working. It was never an issue when I had a mad crush on him from afar, but I felt invested differently. I was there to do a job, so that's what I'd do. I was actually relieved that he wasn't interior fighting the fire himself, although all of my other friends were.

My partner knew that Station 23 had command, and that it was my old station. "Hey, do you know if it's your old shift on today?" June asked.

"Actually, yeah they are on today. It's Matt, his brother, and our friends inside right now." I laid on the queue hard, people drive like assholes here and they needed to get the hell out of our way for Christ's sake.

"Must be a fucking mess for us to get called all the way out here. I didn't think the county was that busy today, although I was napping this morning, so what do I know?" June laughed.

"It's actually busy as hell today, I think all the other rigs were out and that's why we got called all the way over here. You'd think it was a full moon or something. I'm actually more than happy to get out of the station today. At least we can sit outside and watch the firefighters." June knew about Danny, and commented this morning over coffee why he was on the schedule when he wasn't supposed to be. She never cared for him. The more time that passed it seems nobody really liked him. We were rolling up to the scene, and I saw my dad's old truck, now Brian's truck.

June pulled up next to Brian and yelled out the window. "Hey, Chief, where do you want us?" He had a serious look on his face, and when he looked up, he looked right at me and smiled.

"Pull back out in front of my truck. Thanks for coming," He went back to what he was doing; he had several guys around him providing reports and waiting for orders. It was such a turn on watching him. He had on his Class B uniform, but he had his turnout coat and helmet on and was pointing at the rear of the house where you could see brown smoke puffing out of the roof seam steadily. He looked so commanding, and honestly, it was making me wet. I was definitely staring at him.

He looked up and waved us over once we'd parked, and had our equipment in hand. We were really on standby, there were no active injuries at this time. "Meadows, Cruise, thanks for coming. Looks like a busy day in EMS, and fire too it seems. You can hang out here for now, we already have a rehab unit set up in the neighbors yard over by the B side of the house. I'm hoping not to need you...for EMS." His gazed locked with mine. Damn that was smooth. I felt myself get hot, and not from the fire.

"Sounds good, Chief," June replied, and we wandered a few yards away to watch the scene and stay out of the way. We stood off to the side of Command, where Brian was and watched the crews go in and out of the house, listening to the ops channel on the radios we were wearing. The ops channel is the channel you switch to once your scene is active, so you're not clogging up the dispatch channel. Everyone on the scene switches to that channel so you can talk to each other about what's going on with your job, what you need, all of that kind of thing.

The interior crew was able to find active fire in the attic, which was part of what looked like an addition to me. The fire probably started in the electric in the kitchen, it was an old house, but had two stories, which is not at all traditional for Florida homes. I knew Brian knew all of that, so I just minded my own business, I was there as EMS support, and with a different station. He's the boss and it was his show. He was kind of always the boss, since he was ahead of most of us at the academy and all, but I have to say it was strange to be at a mutual aid call like this and not see my dad running Command. It made me a little sad.

June seemed pretty bored, and to be honest, if it weren't for lusting after Brian, leaned up against my ambulance, I'd be pretty bored too. She wanted to see if we could leave after we'd been there about an hour. "I'm gonna go ask Command if we can get out of here; it's been over an hour and our shift is almost over. They can get a crew that's closer by now, you cool with that?" she asked me.

"Yeah, that's fine," I actually wanted to stay and more or less stare but she was right. We could leave then, sit in traffic, and probably get to our station just in time for our shift to end. That would mean I could totally avoid Danny today. She walked over to Brian, and although I couldn't hear the conversation, he glanced at me, and he looked annoyed. I didn't know what he wanted me to do, they didn't really need us here since by now the scene was secured, the fire appeared to be out, and they had another crew that was doing rehab that could be assigned. He was going to be there for awhile, but that wasn't my job today.

"He seemed grumpy about it, but he released us from the scene. The fire is out anyway; they don't need us loitering." She hopped into the driver seat, and as I was climbing into the passenger seat, I caught Brian's eye. I gave a little wave and got in my rig. He didn't wave back, and that made me sad, even though we were at a scene. Well, I'll just have to deal with it later, I'd text him or something when I got home. He wouldn't be done here, and back at the station when I got done, so there was no point in planning to stop by. Based on his scrunched up face, I'd be hearing from him sooner rather than later anyway, and that was alright with me. Watching him in action today, made me feel proud, like he was *my* hero.

BRIAN

Even though I didn't need Jo and her tiny partner on scene anymore, I was still annoyed when they left. I looked at my watch when Cruise came over, and immediately realized that I wouldn't be done here by the time Jo was originally planning to stop by and see me. Both myself and my cock were very disappointed. I grabbed my cell off the tailgate of my truck, and sent her a quick text and then put my phone in my pocket.

`I'm still getting my hands on you tonight.`

I didn't wait for a reply, I really wanted to wrap it up here, and I needed to go take a look inside the residence so I could write my reports up. Jack was very serious about maintaining records, and that is something he taught me very early on. He said that it could save your ass if a resident came back and thought we did something wrong, or needed to use our report in court to back up their claims against a shitty contractor, or a million other reasons. He made it very clear that complete concise reports, even for fires, not just EMS, were critical.

I felt my phone vibrate in my pocket, and knowing it was her gave me a stiff dick. I couldn't wait to get the hell out of there and see her. But I still had some work to do.

We finished up about two hours later, and it was hot. I was sweating from the Florida heat, my guys were exhausted, and it was finally time to head back to the station. I checked my phone to see what Jo's reply was, and I grinned at the screen.

> Hope you're thinking of a creative way to make that happen, Chief.

Oh I most certainly was. I couldn't stop smiling, and Matt came over to me as we walked back to the trucks to leave. "What are you all smiley about? You look like an idiot," he laughed at me.

I quickly shoved my phone back in my pocket. "Ah nothing, just a girl." Well, it wasn't a lie, it was a girl. It was my girl.

"Oh, you've got a new one do you? What's she look like? Got a picture of this one?" he asked and leaned in to nudge me to take my phone back out, which obviously I wasn't going to do.

"No, but you know she's hot." I laughed and walked off to my truck. Fortunately for me, this was pretty typical banter between us when it came to the opposite sex. Matt and I really don't discuss these things outside of your typical chiding. None of us has been in a real relationship for as long as I could remember, so our conversations were always pretty superficial. I didn't even think anyone in our little circle even tried seriously dating anyone. That made me think of Jo and I, and how this would all play out. I was already completely unwilling to let her go. That was pretty much the long and short of it, she needed to be with me always, and I needed to figure out how to make that happen. In any event, she would be stopping by to see me later, and the nice thing about working twenty-four hour shifts at a giant firehouse is that there are plenty of places to disappear to when you needed some "alone time." I'd be making sure we had some of that one way or another.

In the meantime, I also had another little surprise for Jo. I wasn't sure she'd love it, but I thought she'd be open to it.

Jo

I was just getting out of the shower when I got a text from Brian letting me know they were back at the station finally. It really did take forever to clean up a scene sometimes. I was already home, and fussing with myself over how I was going to play this tonight. Was I going there as a casual friend stopping by? What was my real excuse for coming there? I didn't really want to come off suspicious. This whole sneaking around thing in public was a little harder than I anticipated.

I texted back that I'd be there in a half hour or so. I kept fussing with my hair, which was short and black, and had kind of a messy pixie thing happening which I actually loved in my general line of work, it was never in my way. I stared at myself in the mirror, swiped on some red lip gloss, and called it a day. I was going to the firehouse, not out to dinner. I had on ripped up jeans that even I thought made my ass look pretty good, a white t-shirt that was probably a little more snug than it had to be and a black bra, since I was feeling a little feisty. Fuck it. Time to go.

The anticipation of seeing him was making me nervous and excited at the same time. It seemed every time I thought of him, I got tingles and butterflies, and I could already feel myself getting wet in anticipation. I didn't know if I'd be able to touch him at the firehouse. I mean it's definitely not something they encouraged, fraternization. Whatever, Brian is the Chief now, and I'm just stopping by to "talk". I actually giggled to myself like a teenager. I was literally giddy with anticipation.

I pulled up to the station and parked in the visitor parking in the back of the building. The bay doors were open, so I walked around and entered that way; where I ran into Matt.

"Hey, what are you doing here?" he asked genuinely surprised. Usually I tell him what I'm up to. Since the thing with Brian started I actually haven't talked to him that much. I'll have to catch up with him later, it's only been a couple days.

"Oh, I'm just here to talk to Brian about my dad's stuff. I saw him at the fire today, and he said he'd be doing paperwork and stuff tonight if I wanted to stop by since it would be convenient," I lied innocently.

"Ah, that's cool. Well, I'm going to the day room to watch a movie and hopefully fall asleep in a recliner. Text me later and we'll catch up," he laughed.

I laughed too, that was pretty typical by the last third of a twenty-four hour shift. Sleeping in a recliner and hoping for no calls. "Alright, sounds good. He in his office?" I was already walking in that direction.

"Yep, sure is," he pointed in the direction of Brian's office, which obviously I knew where it was. I walked toward the back corner of the building where the offices and conference room were. It was getting kind of late, so most of the lights were off, but there was a glow coming from below the closed office door. *Why did I feel like I was sixteen-years-old all of a sudden and too nervous to knock on the door?* I sighed to myself.

Just as I raised my hand to knock, the door swung open and Brian literally ran right into me like a brick wall. I didn't even see it coming, and as I was falling to the ground, he grabbed me and pulled me into him.

"Oh, my God, Jo, I didn't know you were standing there, are you okay?!" he grabbed my face with both his hands and was inspecting me. I started laughing immediately.

"Yeah, I just got hit by a super hot truck, but other than that, yes, I'm fine," I really thought it was hilarious. He looked at me like I was crazy for a moment, then pulled me into his office and shut the door behind me. Before I knew what was happening, he had his mouth on mine, and he was exploring me with his tongue so passionately, I melted right into him again. He had me pushed up against his office door. I started to wrap a leg around him, pulling him in closer. I simply couldn't get enough of his taste and I was drinking him in.

"I've been waiting to do that all day," he said in a raspy, low voice.

"Me too, Brian," I managed to breathe out. He had his hand at the small of my back, drawing me closer to him, something I could never get enough of, and his other was caressing my face while he planted soft kisses on my lips. I swear, our lips were molded for each other, every time he kissed me, I just wanted more. I didn't want to undo his uniform, so I had my hands on his back pulling him into me, and I could feel his hardness pressing up against me. He reached next to me and locked the door.

"What are you doing?" I was surprised.

"I'm going to have you right here in this office. I can't wait another second, or couldn't you tell?" Oh I could tell. I was going to pretend to be coy and shy about it, but we both know why I'm here, so I took a step back, and grabbed at his utility belt, undoing it, and freeing his huge cock from the restraints of his thick uniform pants. He yanked my t-shirt over my head, and admired my lacy black bra.

"So fucking sexy, Josephine," he growled into my neck, and began to suck and kiss my shoulder near my cardinal tattoo. "Pants, off. Now," he whispered in my ear, undid my jeans and they fell to the ground revealing the matching black lacy panties. "You have me so hard, baby. Jesus Christ," he grabbed my face and kissed me with so much tenderness, I was putty in his hands. His kisses were so deep, I felt them to my core.

As I undid his uniform shirt, he continued kissing my neck and nibbling at that spot between my shoulder and my neck, and I was losing my mind. He dropped his pants, took off his uniform shirt hastily, and moved me over to the couch with him. He was completely naked now, and I was still in my bra and panties. As I was getting ready to take them off, he stopped me. "No, leave them on. It's so sexy," he whispered and pulled me onto his lap, straddling him. I was so wet with anticipation; I could hardly stand it anymore. Moving my panties to the side just a bit, he started circling my clit with his finger, causing me to moan involuntarily. I was going to come already. With his other hand, he pulled my bra down and latched on with his mouth sucking and lightly biting, flicking my hard nipple with his tongue.

"Brian, I'm going to come, oh, my God," I was panting as quietly as I could manage. He stuck two fingers inside of me, and began pumping them into me, while sucking on my nipple. I felt the waves coming, and I couldn't stop it.

"Come for me, Jo. Come on my hand right now, baby," he moved to the other nipple, and I began riding his hand to get my release. It came almost immediately, and I gasped for air as my orgasm washed over me and I grinded myself into his hand. He kept pumping me with his fingers until the waves had subsided, and then repositioned me so he had access to enter me fully. "Baby, that was so fucking hot, but I'm not nearly done with you." He positioned his rock hard cock at my entrance, and I pushed myself onto it letting out a gasp as he entered me. I was slowly riding up and down him, feeling the wave come again when he moved us quickly so I was on my back. Lifting one of my legs up on his shoulder he was so much deeper, I couldn't think straight all I could do was feel his length filling me up causing a buzz over my whole body. Thrusting harder and harder, I couldn't control my release and I felt him getting close too.

"Baby, come with me, I can't wait. It's so fucking good, come inside me now!" I willed him to fuck me harder, and grabbed him, pulling him as tight as I could. As I fell over the edge into ecstasy, he cried out my name, and pumped me harder, filling me up and getting his release with me. We laid there for a few minutes, catching our breath in silence. We started to get up, and when I grabbed for my clothes, he pulled me back to him for a kiss.

"Baby, that was fucking amazing," he smiled, making me smile back like a teenager again. He was right, that was amazing.

"It was alright," I jokingly smiled and winked at him, hopping up to get dressed, I mean we're in a public place. Looking shocked, he smacked my ass and laughed too.

"Alright, my ass. You know that was the best sex you've ever had." He gave me a sideways look.

"It was pretty good. We'll have to do it again for me to be totally sure I think," I kidded with him some more. I was having some fun with him, and he looked a little perturbed, making it that much more fun to mess with him.

"Well I'm all for more, lets get to it, Jo," he started to try undressing me again.

"No, no, no...not here. We're pushing our luck as it is, we shouldn't be doing this in here and you know it. It was amazing, Brian, I promise." I got up on my tiptoes to give him a tender kiss. "You know I like messing with you." We both laughed and we finished getting dressed quickly. This sneaking around was hot, and we were having fun, and being playful, I was truly enjoying it.

BRIAN

We got ourselves dressed and were joking around in my office. It's never been like this for me, so hot and then so comfortable and fun. I loved being around her, she was intoxicating, and when she smiled, it just lit me up inside and made me feel warm, like home. We opened the door to my office in case anyone had any notion of swinging by, although unlikely, it was still work and I knew we shouldn't do things like that, but honestly, I wasn't officially the Chief yet, and who could help themselves in my position really?

I actually did want to talk to her about some things and she probably wasn't going to love it but too bad. I cared about her, and it was important. I went around my desk and sat on the other side, and she settled into one of the visitor chairs and put her feet up on my desk. I smirked at her because that was kind of ballsy, but I was guessing she used to put her feet up there from that side her whole life when she was in here talking to her dad. All of his plaques and awards were still on the wall, I wasn't ready to take them down, and I thought that was something she should be here doing with me. That wasn't what I wanted to talk to her about though.

"So, how was your shift over at 19 today? Did you have any problems?" She knew exactly what I meant by the scrunched up face she made at me.

"If you're referring to Danny, he tried to talk to me this morning but I was busy, and then in the afternoon, we got called to your fire, so my day was uneventful from a professional standpoint," she was fairly terse with me about it and started looking around the room when her eyes landed on the pile of gear next to my desk. "Is that my gear?" she asked me looking surprised.

"Actually, yes, it is. I wanted to talk to you about that today..." I had practiced this in my head a few times, and now I felt like a teenager all over again for some reason. Before I could continue, she interrupted my thoughts.

"I can clean it out and decommission it if you want. It's been here for quite a while, I'm sure you'd like to be able to reissue it. I'm sorry I've left it here for so long..." she trailed off, seeming to be unsure of what to say, and then she sighed.

"Jo, I actually had your gear brought out, because I'd like you to start riding here again. I don't have a full time spot open yet, however we've been rotating per diems regularly, and honestly, no one that's passed through here knows the guys, the station or the town like you do, and you're working like ten different shift jobs all over the county, and that seems like a pain in the ass, and—"

"Wait, you want me to quit taking shifts at other places and come here essentially *full-time*?" her eyes got huge and I honestly couldn't tell if she was mad, happy or in shock at the suggestion.

"Yes, that's what I want. Actually, it's what your dad wanted, and its certainly what Matt wants. And yes, it's definitely what I want." I repeated myself because it was worth repeating.

"My dad?" She tilted her head quizzically at me and softened her expression.

"Okay, I'm gonna be straight with you, Jo. Your dad and I were tight, we ran this station together, and we discussed staffing regularly. He was planning to ask you to come back to 23 and quit working all these different jobs, he was just waiting for the right moment to approach you. He didn't want you to feel like he was pressuring you into coming back to work for him, he was hoping you would have approached him yourself." I sat back and waited for her response. She was completely still and just looking at me with those steely gray eyes.

She sighed again. "Why did he want me to come back?" Her eyes dropped to the floor and she seemed hopeful for an answer that she must have been looking for.

"We don't have any other women at this station, there aren't that many in the department that do both fire and EMS to begin with. He trusted you, we all trust you, and he called it 'getting the band back together'," I laughed a little thinking about that conversation with him. "He and I agreed for the record, that you're good for the department, and you bring a lot to the table. And on a personal note, we like having you around, and being honest here, nobody wants to juggle shifts like you have been, we thought it would be perfect." I was being honest. Jack and I had agreed not to approach her about this, but to maybe plant some seeds so she would think of it herself, we even got Matt in on the plan, but then Jack died. And now, with things going on between us, I wanted her near me, where I knew she was safe, where her family could look after her, where I could look after her. She can take care of herself on the job, I didn't worry about that, but we are her people. It's like her dad said, we're like a band, and it was time to get the band back together, he was totally right.

She wasn't saying anything, she took her feet off the desk, and put her head in her hands, looking down at the floor. I wanted to come around the desk and comfort her, do something, but I was frozen. I didn't want to do the wrong thing and I honestly couldn't tell if she was mad, sad, confused, or what. Uncertain, I asked her what she was thinking.

She moved to look up at me, and rested her chin on her hands, and took a deep breath. "I don't know. It's something I've been thinking about actually, but don't you think that what's been going on between us complicates that? I don't want to keep doing all this shift work all over the county either, but coming back here? I just don't know," she leaned back in the chair and looked up at the ceiling.

"Look at me, Jo. It's me. At the end of the day, we both know that we can work together, so that can't be the issue. We're your family, and you belong here with us. It's a good team, and as far as you and me..." I paused, looking for the right words and leaned forward putting my hands on my desk. I needed to say the right thing here and I wasn't sure what that was, I didn't know how she felt yet. *Fuck it, I have to be honest, I've dicked around for way too long,* "As for you and me, I only see this getting more serious between us regardless of where you work. I told you that first night that you were mine, and I meant it, and I don't intend for that to change in the foreseeable future." There. I said it.

"Are you serious? We couldn't keep seeing each other if I work here. You'd be my boss!" That was not the reaction I was hoping for. Shit shit shit.

"For now, nothing has to change. Work is work, and personal is personal, and we can keep them separate. Do you want to work here, Jo? Do you want to keep seeing me? I think you do, and I damn sure know I want to keep seeing you outside of work," I was starting to get freaked out that this was about not wanting to continue what we have before it gets a chance to go where I want it to.

"I do. I do, both. I need to think about it though. I don't know if we'll be able to keep us a secret if I'm working here, and I don't want to get a reputation, or for people to think there's some kind of favoritism going on," she seemed really conflicted. This was kind of a lot of information all at once.

"First of all, there is favoritism. You're definitely the only firefighter, or person for that matter, that I'm sharing my bed with. That being said, we're professionals. You and I know how to behave, we've fought fire and been on tons of calls together in our lifetime. So, how about this, how about you take a day or two and think it over, and maybe pick up a couple shifts here so you can see exactly how it would work?" Man, I pulled that out of my ass. Hopefully that worked.

"Okay, I'll think about it. I'm just not sure that we should keep—"

And then the tones dropped. We had a goddamn call.

Jo

"Rescue 23, Engine 23, two car MVA at the intersection of I4 and Colonial Drive. Number of injuries unknown."

I've actually never been so relieved to be interrupted by the tones dropping. Brian hopped up of course, he's on duty.

"Jo, grab your shit. You're coming." He commanded.

"What the fuck are you talking about?" I snapped at him.

"Grab your gear. It's late, it's a rescue, more hands are better and it sounds like it could be bad at that intersection. Just grab your shit, you can ride with me, and we'll see what we have on scene." He was walking out the door as he demanded my presence at the scene.

Fuck it. I grabbed the pile of gear and followed him to his Chief's vehicle. The other guys were already hopping in the trucks and Matt looked over and grinned at me as I trailed after Brian. I made the shoulder shrug, I don't know what I'm doing face, and just kept on moving. I hopped in the passenger side of the truck, and started donning my gear over my jeans, and checking my pockets to see if my tools were still there.

"Central, 2300 en route," he got on his radio.

"2300," they acknowledged.

"Central, is there an update on victims?"

"No, Chief, no update. Two cars, head on collision, one car into the guardwall. That's all we've got."

"Thanks, Central." He put his radio down and looked over at me rifling through my pockets. "Everything should be there, I checked it earlier today. I don't know everything you keep in it, but you sure are prepared with all your pink duct taped tools," he chuckled.

Yeah, the handles of all my shit was wrapped in pink duct tape. That's thanks to the fact that people "accidently" take your shit all the time, and none of those motherfuckers would dare keep my wire cutters, knife, or anything else if it was wrapped in pink duct tape. I've been doing it for years.

"Shut up. You know why I do that." I glared at him. "My safety glasses are missing. I need safety glasses for a wreck."

He leaned over me while driving lights and sirens to a call, opened the glove box and pointed. "Take mine, I shouldn't need them." Then he smiled and I couldn't help it, I smiled back. I didn't really know what I was feeling, but the rush of going to a call and helping people was getting me fired up. Car accidents and rescue, that was my wheelhouse, and I guess I was going to hop right back in it with my guys.

He switched channels on his radio so he could talk to the rescue truck. "Rescue 23, it's 2300."

"2300 go ahead," I recognized Scotty's reply. He was driving.

"I brought Meadows as extra personnel for this one. You've got an extra crew member tonight," he looked over at me and smiled again.

"No shit, Chief. You brought JoJo?? Sweet. We'll see you there." Brian started laughing and I just glared at him.

"JoJo? Nobody calls me JoJo. Good Lord," I rolled my eyes even though it was kind of funny. We arrived on scene first, and I grabbed a radio and hopped out and ran over to the SUV that had flipped upside down. I could hear the rescue and the engine in the distance coming up soon.

"Chief! I've got one victim here, still buckled in, and fluids leaking!" I yelled across the intersection to him where he was evaluating the second vehicle which appeared to be pinned up against the guardrail wall. "Fuck, this is a mess," I muttered under my breath, and got down on the ground to check on the victim in the SUV who was seatbelted in, upside down and basically dangling.

"Jo! My guy is stuck, his leg is under the dash, and he's got a serious head wound!"

"Are there any other victims?"

"It doesn't look like it!" he yelled back. The rescue and the engine both pulled up and staged so that we could get tools off the trucks, and get to work. I squished myself as flat as I could and shouted into the vehicle to the patient. "Ma'am! Ma'am! I'm with the Fire Department, can you hear me?"

She opened her eyes and turned her head to look at me. "Yes," she whispered and tears started to roll down her face. She was scared, hell if I were strapped upside down in my car I'd be scared too. She didn't look too banged up which was a good sign.

"Ma'am, my name is Jo. I'm here to help you. I need to you to look straight ahead, I don't want you to move your neck, I don't want you to move at all in case you've hurt your spine, okay?"

She looked straight ahead. "I don't know what happened. He came out of nowhere," she replied. She was definitely in shock. A paramedic rig rolled up, and two medics that I actually knew came running over, Mark tossed himself to the ground next to me.

"Ma'am, we can worry about that later, we need to ask you some questions, and then we're gonna get you out of here." I told her. Now that the medics were here, I could go get some tools to free her from the vehicle. She was going to need to be cut out of that seatbelt and it was going to take a few people to make sure she didn't just come crashing down. "Mark, I'm gonna go get some tools, I'll be right back," and I jogged back to the rescue, leaving him to assess and treat the patient.

"Jo! Chief needs you over at the other vehicle. The space is too small for anyone to secure the patient, and you're the smallest. I'll take over for you at the SUV," Scotty had come running to meet me.

"Okay, no problem, the lady seems alright, but she's gonna need to be cut out of her seatbelt, so take another guy with you so she doesn't come falling down, she's suspended upside down." I took off toward the other car, about fifty yards away. When I got to the other car, more or less all of the heavy rescue tools were out and Brian and Matt were discussing next steps with one of the medics from the second rig that had arrived. "What's the situation?" I asked as I assessed it for myself.

The victim appeared to be a young man, unconscious but breathing, who was trapped in the driver's seat, up against the guardrail wall. The dashboard had been crushed enough to trap one of his legs under it, and his spine wasn't stabilized due to the passenger seat getting shoved in the way. This made him out of reach without crawling into the vehicle, which they were all too large to do without jostling the patient too much. If I wasn't here, they would have had to, but I was there, and I knew what to do.

"We can't get in to stabilize the patient before we cut out this dash to free him, I need you to get in there," Brian said.

"Absolutely. Give me that blanket to cover the patient up, so when you pull the tools out, I can cover him up." I made my way into the passenger side of the vehicle, over the damaged passenger seat, and then over the console into the back seat. It was a sedan of some kind, but only had two doors, so it was definitely a tight squeeze. I took the blanket and covered up the chest and torso of the victim, so any more broken glass or debris wouldn't fall on him. As I looked him over, I could see an extremely deep head wound, as well as a better view of his left leg, which looked like a broken femur, thankfully not through the skin, but still nasty. "Anybody know this kid's name?" I yelled out as I positioned myself behind the driver's seat so that I could stabilize the kid's spine as best as possible without moving him too much.

"Kid's name is Marshall, it's on the insurance card from the glove box. Be careful in there, Jo," Brian leaned in. "What can you see over there?" he asked me.

"Okay, the only way to get this kid out is gonna be through the passenger side, but you're gonna need to cut that whole passenger seat out for us to get him out on a board properly. Get me a collar, I'm gonna stabilize his neck while you get set up." I demanded, and Matt took off to get it for me.

Brian leaned into the vehicle and lowered his voice. "Be careful in there. Glad you're here to help, we'll try to get you both out as fast as possible." We locked eyes, and I nodded. This is what we did, we put ourselves in precarious situations like climbing into crushed cars to help others get out. Matt came back with the collar, and I carefully manipulated it around the patient's neck, trying to not move him at all, you simply had no idea what kind of internal damage was done after a wreck like this.

The heavy rescue work was beginning. Most people think the Jaws of Life and the other large hydraulic tools they see on TV or hear about just come in and rip machinery apart like a hot knife through butter. It really doesn't work that way. In order for this to go smoothly, it had to be done in steps.

First, they had to pop the door off the passenger side. It was open, but the hinge was damaged, and the whole thing was just in the way and was going to make getting the patient out smoothly tricky. The whole point of this operation was to get the patient out to safety without any further injury. Matt got to work on that with the spreaders, which are actually commonly known as the Jaws of Life, because it looked like a huge set of jaws that open and close. What he needed to do, was position the points of the jaws into the door hinge and then open the jaws up, making the hinge pop. We called it a door pop. Once you heard that pop on both hinges, it meant that it was broken off from the main part of the car, and you could remove the door by just a quick yank. Some were easier than others, generally newer cars have a lot of plastic bullshit and wires that control window and locks that you can easily snip, or just pull away. Matt was able to remove the door in just a few moments, and it didn't even jostle the car a bit. I was crouched in the backseat, sweating my ass off, holding the patients head still and monitoring his vitals. I kept asking if he could hear me, and he would audibly grunt from time to time, which was a good sign.

The next step was to remove the passenger seat. It would probably be a real pain in the ass. It would require using the cutters, which look just like handheld cutters, but they're huge, and they're powered by hydraulics and attached to the truck from a hose, just like the Jaws. Because it was a bucket seat, it really was the best option for getting the patient out smoothly, and I knew it sucked, but this kid was in bad shape, the less he was moved around the better off he'd be. Matt stuck his head in the car before he started cutting the seat out. "You alright in there?" he asked with a smile. We'd always made great partners.

"Yep, all good. Hurry up though, it's uncomfortable and I'm sweating my ass off," I smiled at him.

"Your wish is my command. Let me know if anything changes," and with that he pulled his safety glasses back down, and crouched down to start cutting the seat out. It was going to require at least four cuts to get it loose enough to actually remove it. Car seats were definitely not designed to come back out. I looked around, and it appeared there were a lot of people on scene now, and traffic, while light at this time of night, needed to be diverted. I didn't see Brian anywhere, I'm sure he was bossing people around, I mused to myself.

I could see Scotty was back at the truck operating the other end of the tools where the power was, and there were other people helping that lady out of her SUV. I sighed with relief that she appeared to have minimal injuries. Seriously, a seatbelt will absolutely save your damn life. She had her window down, and without her seatbelt, she could have been ejected right out of that SUV.

After about ten minutes, Matt had two of the posts cut and then stopped to check on me and the patient again. "We're halfway there. When I get to the final one, if you could push it with your foot, I'll have Joe back here pulling while I cut, and we should be able to yank it out pretty smoothly, okay?" He was dripping sweat now too. It was stifling hot in the gear, shoved in the backseat, however I was just holding onto the victim, Matt was maneuvering a giant tool, and it was heavy.

"You got it, chop chop," I said. I saw the third little post snap, and connected eyes with Matt signifying I was ready. The medics were waiting right behind him with a board, ready to help get the patient out. As Matt started to cut the final post holding the seat in place, the metal twisted, and the seat snapped backwards, knocking right into my ribs.

"Aww fuck!" I winced, and fell backwards, letting go of the patient for just a moment. "Dude, get someone to hold the fucking seat man!" I yelled at Matt. Joe rushed forward, he had been standing right there, and grabbed the seat, pulling it toward them, instead of me and the patient, and within a few moments, the seat was out.

"Sorry, Jo, didn't see that coming. I thought you were gonna kick it back in my direction," Matt said and put the tool back on the ground where they were all set up.

"It's alright. I just wasn't ready. Hey, I have an idea, I think we can get away without rolling the dash, if I can reach the seat adjustment, and lean this driver's seat back, we should be able to slide him out onto a board without fucking around with this dash." It was going to require me to crawl down and seriously reach, but it could save a lot of time if it worked.

"Works for me, what do you need me to do?" Matt asked.

"Get in here and hold the patient's head still. I need to crawl down on the floor and see if I can reach between the door and grab the lever without smooshing myself with the seat."

Matt immediately got in, and took over securing the patient, and a little crowd formed around the vehicle while we tried to make this happen. I was never going to reach it with my turnout coat on, so I took it off, and took off my helmet so I could get my head low, and sprawled my lower body across the back seat. I immediately felt cooler, I was completely soaked with sweat. I scrunched way down below the driver's seat, and managed to stretch my fingers out just enough to reach the lever. When I pulled it, nothing happened. Fuck. It needed more weight to actually push the seat back.

"Okay, I need you to push *gently* back on the seat, he's not enough weight to move it. But I might get stuck down here, so get someone over here to pull me out too." I sighed. Maybe this wasn't the greatest idea, but it was still faster for the patient than getting out any more tools and cutting the car apart more. "Okay, on three," I yelled.

"One, two, THREE!" I grabbed the lever, the seat came back on me, and I was definitely now stuck. Fucking hell.

"Jo, the patient is almost flat on top of you and his leg is free, are you okay?" Matt yelled down at me.

I was pinned down underneath the seat now, not in pain, but extremely uncomfortable. "Get the patient out on a board now, then I can get out!" I couldn't see a damn thing except for the floor of the car, and I could hear scrambling above me.

Then I could hear Brian yelling, *oh fuck*.

BRIAN

"What the fuck is going on? Is she stuck under there?" I yelled. I knew the answer to my own question, and I was pissed off.

"Uh, sort of, she'll be out in one sec," Matt yelled at me while he was helping the medics get the patient onto the board. "Jo, one more minute alright?" he called down to her. All I could see was her lower half kicked out onto the back seat of the car, and her entire torso and head were covered by the flattened out driver's seat.

"Yea, hurry the fuck up," she said from underneath the goddamn driver's seat, sounding muffled. Seriously? I bet this was her idea. It was definitely faster for the patient, but now my girlfriend is stuck under the seat. *Crew member. She's a member of my crew.* At least I didn't say that out loud. I rubbed my temple and shook my head.

The medics had the patient out, and rushed him to their rig and took off. Matt jumped back in the car to get the seat off Jo. She lifted her head up and laughed at him then lightly punched him in the chest. Her face was bright red, probably from being mostly upside down for however long this was going down.

"Ow! What was that for, I just freed you!" he grabbed at his chest where she hit him.

"That was for hitting me with the passenger seat. What the fuck, man?" she laughed and rubbed her ribs. Was she hurt?

"If you two are done, both patients are now on their way to the hospital, we can clean up and get home. You okay, Jo?" I asked in all seriousness.

"Yeah, Chief, I'm great now. Let me know how that kid makes out." She smiled, grabbed her coat and helmet from the backseat and climbed out of the car. I got a good look at her. Her shirt was completely soaked, and you could see right through it, that sexy black bra that was for my eyes only, was now visible for everyone to see. Matt noticed right away too.

"Oh, hey now, putting on a show for us out here?" He laughed, and the guys around the truck started whistling. I was pissed. Nobody needed to be looking at her like that; nobody but me.

"Oh, shit! Well I wasn't exactly planning to be out here tonight," she turned bright red, and put her coat back on right away, but didn't buckle it up, left it hanging open. I was going to lose my shit.

Matt walked off to grab a water, and Jo followed him until I stepped in her way, stopping her. "Buckle your goddamn coat up. You don't need to be showing everyone out here what's mine," I growled quietly.

She stopped, stunned, and gave me a fierce look, "Listen, *Chief*, it's hot as fuck. I'm not wearing a uniform, because I hadn't planned to be out here, so how about you just back off," I think she actually hissed at me.

"You could have gotten hurt today, *Meadows*. Next time you're going to try a stunt like that get me over here." Okay, she really didn't need me to make that call, I was being a dick now

Jo

That motherfucker. Check with him? Before making a call that gives a critical patient extra time? *Oh, fuck you, pal. Fuuuuuuuuck you.* That vehicle was perfectly safe, and Matt would never in a million years let me put myself in a precarious situation on a scene. So fuck him, fuck his micromanagement, and sure as fuck, fuck his attitude about my outfit. I was wearing jeans and a t-shirt, because that's what I wore to come and fuck him in his office. I knew this fling was a bad idea. I couldn't work here, and keep this up with him.

It was time to go, and I decided I'd ride back in the duty truck with the rest of the guys, not in the Chief's vehicle. I wasn't going to ask permission to do it either. I was expected to be part of the crew today, and I was going to ride back to the station with them. And I didn't want to talk to Brian even though I knew I'd have to back at the station.

"Hey, I'm riding back with you guys," I said to Scotty and Matt who were standing with me next to the rescue truck.

"So, are you gonna join us permanently, or what, Jojo?" Scotty asked.

"Uhhhhh when did you decide calling me Jojo was cool," I gave him the fish eye and raised an eyebrow in his direction. I didn't even hate it, it was just so ridiculous.

"Today," he laughed and went around the truck to get in the driver's seat. I actually started laughing too. Of course he decided today, probably at the moment he said it on the radio.

I looked over in Brian's direction, and we connected eyes. I wasn't going to ask him if I could ride the truck back, I was just doing it. And to be truthful, that's the right thing to do anyway. He acknowledged me with a nod, and actually didn't even look mad that I was riding back with them, so that's good.

Matt opened the door to the back for me. "Your chariot awaits, madam," he chuckled. I hopped in, I was just short enough, that I always have to kind of launch myself into a fire truck by grabbing the 'oh shit' handle and propelling myself up the first stair.

"Thank you, kind sir," I laughed back. Jax and Taylor were already in the back as well as a young guy I wasn't acquainted with, and after I hopped in, Matt got in the front right seat, the officers seat. We all put our headphones on so we could talk to each other; fire trucks are just loud in general, and we were lucky enough to have each seat wired with a set of headphones and a microphone so we could communicate with each other, or with Central dispatch if we needed to.

Matt asked from the front seat. "So, Jo, what was that little chat with the Chief about back there? He mad about something?" He was laughing.

"Oh, he was just giving me his thoughts on me squishing myself under that seat. He was somewhere between thrilled and ecstatic about it," I laughed.

Scotty chimed in from the driver's seat. "Eh, whatever. He needs to get his panties out of a bunch. So seriously, Jojo, you going to come back full-time or what? It feels like we got the band back together tonight."

I wasn't sure how I felt about it after getting yelled at. "I'm not sure. There's a tentative offer on the table, but I've got some other commitments I need to work out. Why, you guys need a den mother?" I teased.

"We need some better eye candy around here than these clowns, that's for sure," Jax spoke up, sitting across from me, he winked.

"Watch yourself, Jax, she'll kick your ass and not even feel bad about it," Matt joked.

I smiled. That is what it was like. I fell right back into a groove with them. It was nice. The kid I didn't know giggled but didn't say anything.

"Hey, what's your name, kid?" I covered my mic up and leaned over to him.

"Jason. Jason Barrett," he reached over and shook my hand.

"Nice to meet ya. You old enough to ride a firetruck?" I had to give him a hard time, he looked twelve.

"Yes ma'am. I'm twenty-one. Been riding on this crew for a few months now. I came from Seminole county."

"Uh, yea. Don't ever call me ma'am again, or I'll have to kick your ass too. It's Jo. Jo Meadows." I gave him a dirty look. Ma'am? I'm thirty-two. Sheesh. He looked scared now that I threatened him, and Jax was laughing hysterically because he could see and hear the entire exchange.

"Yes ma'—uh, Jo. Sorry," he said quietly. I smiled at him, he meant well I could tell, and he smiled back. Maybe they do need a den mother, I thought.

We were just a few minutes away from the station and Matt turned the stereo on and started playing Kenny Loggins "Danger Zone." We all settled in, rocked out and not talking. We were lucky with this truck, it was pretty much equipped with everything you needed for an accident, and it had a CD player and stereo which was just a nice treat.

I leaned back and thought about what I wanted to do. I wanted to come back. I loved this job, I loved this station; it was my dad's legacy. Getting involved with Brian was a bad idea. I needed to put an end to it when I got back and if the job offer was still available, I could get myself off of the District 19 rotation within about a week and come back full-time. Yeah, that's what I would do. Thinking about what we were doing in Brian's office before the call, made my body betray me as I started to feel myself get warm between my legs. Apparently, my pussy didn't understand what's best. I needed to shut that down immediately.

We pulled into the station, and everyone was getting out of their gear and putting it away in their gear bins. I didn't have a gear bin anymore so I was going to have to go ask Brian what to do with my stuff which I was absolutely dreading. I'm in no mood for his Neanderthal attitude right now. It's now been a long day, I'm dirty, I'm angry at him, and I need to go home and shower this day away. My shoes and my keys were in Brian's Chief truck though, because that's where I got dressed in my gear, so I was without other options.

"Meadows, a moment of your time?" Brian poked his head into the engine bay and summoned me. Nobody thought anything of it, and just kept doing what they were doing. I think after all the adrenaline of the call wore off, they were getting tired. I knew I sure was.

"Sure, Chief," I carried my coat and helmet with me, still dressed in bunker pants and

not really sure what was going to happen.

BRIAN

She came back in my office, the office we had sex in a few hours prior, sat her coat and helmet down on my office couch and took a seat in my visitor chair. I needed to do the reports on the call, so my desk had fresh paperwork all over, and after she sat down, I shut the door and sat down at my chair on the other side of the desk.

"Your shoes and stuff are in my truck, you can grab them after we talk," I said. I felt like I had a million things to say to her, but I honestly wasn't quite sure where to start. We were officially in that gray area where I wanted to have a Chief to firefighter talk, but I also wanted to ask how she felt about being back with us, and I wanted to know why she was rubbing her ribs earlier, and kiss whatever it was that was making them sore.

"Okay," she replied.

The sweat from earlier had mostly dried, but I could still faintly see her black bra under her white t-shirt and it was distracting me and my cock. I stared at her, forgetting what I wanted to say altogether until she spoke up.

"What do you want me to do with my gear, Brian? I do want to come back, but I have other commitments as you're well aware, and I'll need to see them through. After that, I would like to get back on the schedule. And while I'm at it, let's just face it, we need to quit seeing each other, or sleeping together or whatever this is. This is work, and I need the job as you're well aware, and I don't think after our argument today that we should keep doing—" I cut her off right there.

"Whoa, wait a minute, you want to what? It was a disagreement and wasn't a big deal. Why would we stop seeing each other? You can't be serious," I was stunned, and certainly didn't expect that response. I understood that we'd had a small argument at the scene, but she shouldn't be letting everyone get a look, and no, just no, we can't stop now. She can't be serious. My face had to be bright red, I felt my entire body temperature rise like I had a fever.

"I'm serious. I can admit that this was just some fun, and maybe an escape for a bit, but if I'm going to come back here to work, I don't think either one of us needs the bullshit that happened today to happen every time we work together. When I'm here, I'm more or less one of the guys, and I've always been that way. You can't treat me differently because I've sucked your dick, Brian," she said matter -of-factly; as I balled my fists up at my sides.

"I don't consider this a fling at all, which I've said several times. Do you really think that's all that's going on here?" She had to feel something; I knew she did. An unfamiliar wave of desperation came over me, giving me a horrible sick feeling.

She looked me squarely in the eyes. "I do. I would like the rest of my firefighting career to be at the station my dad ran my whole life, but it's your station now, Brian, so you tell me if that's going to be a problem." She was cold and as my heart started racing, she just kept staring blankly at me waiting for a reply.

I took a deep breath, and thought of what to say. I needed her to be here, with us, with me. "Jo, if that's what you want, then I'm not going to beg you to keep things going. I think it's a huge mistake, but I want you as part of the crew here. That's what your dad wanted." I didn't know what else to say, I was feeling my heart sink that she was slipping away, but I didn't know what to do to stop it. I couldn't bring myself to say how I really felt; it was bubbling to the surface, but I just couldn't say the words to her. I wasn't ready. "There's an empty gear bin next to Matt's that we cleared out a while ago, and it's yours if you want it. It was all I could get out.

"Okay. I'll put my gear out there, and I'll work my schedule out at 19 tomorrow; then I can be on the schedule here. Should take a week to work it out, two tops. Will that work?" She was like a stone; I don't understand how everything changed so fast. I honestly didn't know what to do and I just couldn't be totally honest with her, even though I felt the stabbing pain in my chest of her leaving. I was losing her and it was the last thing I wanted.

"Yea, that's fine." That's all I could say. She stood up to leave, and I sat in my chair, frozen.

She grabbed her stuff, and got up to leave, stopping in the doorway. "I'm sorry, Brian, I'm not the girl for you, and it's better if we just try to be actual friends, or whatever. Last time we had a moment it was a huge mistake and we barely spoke for a year. We can't do that, you're my boss now. Thanks for the job offer. I'll let you know when my schedule is worked out; I'll try to have it handled tomorrow," and she walked out, shutting the door behind her.

"FUCK!" I stood up and yelled when I was pretty sure she was out of earshot. I threw my dirty coffee cup from this morning across the room, shattering it into a million pieces, and sat back down putting my face in my hands.

Jo

I stopped outside the door after I left, and rested my hand there trying not to cry, and keeping myself from going back in and running into his arms. I loved him, and I couldn't let this keep going, knowing full well it was headed for a crash and burn. Working at the station, and remembering my dad was way too important; I needed to honor my dad, not fulfill a childhood crush. It hurt so badly; my heart actually ached. I heard him yell and throw something in his office after I left, and it ripped my heart in two. He'd get over it though, I knew he would, but I honestly wasn't sure I would. In my view, for him, it was pride. For me though, I had a taste of what I always wanted, and Brian didn't end up with anyone, especially not me. He'd never been the guy that was going to love me, be by my side for better or for worse. He's the guy that's a good time, with a brilliant smile, the charming guy that gets your panties wet, but you can't ever keep. It's better to just end it now, on my terms, before I got in any deeper, as if that were possible, and cut my losses before he did the inevitable himself.

I took a deep breath, went out to his truck; grabbing my shoes and keys from where I left them on the seat. I came back in to the engine bay where the gear racks were to find Matt standing there waiting for me.

"Hey girl, he super pissed at us or what?" he smiled. He had the same charming smile his brother had, no wonder he was a hit with the ladies too. He was leaned up against his gear bin, next to an empty one, which was apparently mine.

"Nah, he didn't even bring it up. He wanted to tell me there was a gear bin already here for me. How long have ya'll been planning this, and why were you so sure I'd say yes?" I tried to pretend nothing was wrong of course. Matt and I shared almost everything, but I obviously couldn't tell him how I was feeling or what was going on with Brian.

"We honestly weren't sure you'd say yes. I was pretty sure when your dad was here you might, but after he died, I wasn't sure. So you said yes?" he smiled at me, clearly realizing that I was going to be joining him back at the station.

"Of course I said yes," I gave him a smile. It really did feel so good to be there. "This is my home; you know that better than anyone. I just have to finish out my schedule at 19, and then I can be more or less full time here in about a week or so." It just occurred to me that the change would require a conversation with Danny. That was unfortunate. Whatever, this was what I really wanted in my heart, even if my heart was hurting over Brian. Nobody needed to know that part.

"Sweet! Well, here's your rack, next to mine. I kicked Travis, the C shift guy out of this spot because—well because I can," he laughed, and I joined in. He does his best to look out for me. I hung my coat up in the wire rack, and put my helmet on top and stared at my name already on it. J. Meadows FF/EMT. That was me; it was also my dad I thought. I reached up and traced the letters with my fingers softly.

"He'd be so happy right now, Jo," Matt put his hand on my shoulder and pulled me in for a hug. I grabbed onto him really tightly, more than I normally would and rested my head on his shoulder. "You okay? Is something else going on?" he asked, giving me a squeeze, then pushing me out so he could look at my face.

"No, no. Everything is great. I'm actually exhausted. I'm really happy," I lied. "I'm gonna head home and shower and call it a day. I picked up a short afternoon shift at 19 tomorrow; just covering for another guy, and it's been a long day. I'm so happy to be back though." I took a step back from him, and took off my bunker pants, situating them just right in my bin, the way I like them and put my regular shoes back on. We all have our own way of pushing the pants down around our boots, so we can step into them in a hurry.

"Alright, sounds good. Text me when you get home." People always thought we were dating over the way we looked out for each other, but it was never like that with us. Thankfully, neither of us ever felt anything more than friendship. We were just tight is all.

"Will do," I smiled and waved as I made my way out to my jeep. Meanwhile, I felt my heart beating out of my chest over the end of Brian and I. I loved him. There's just no denying it. That love is a drug, and my body was in withdrawal.

BRIAN

I don't know how long I was sitting there staring at the ceiling when my brother came to my office.

"Yo, what the fuck happened here?" He waved at the shattered ceramic that had spread across the floor.

"Nothing. It's nothing," I was completely aware that we both knew it wasn't nothing at all, but I wasn't sure telling Matt anything was a good idea.

"Uh, yeah, it's something. Spill it," he sat down in the chair Jo had just vacated. Fuck it, I'll just tell him a little bit, maybe he won't want to kill me.

"Had a small disagreement with Jo over some things, but it's fine now. No big deal," I knew he didn't believe me. He looked at me like I had two heads, and I knew I was going to have to tell him. "Okay, it was more than a small disagreement, but it's personal, so I don't want to talk about it," I said.

"This explains why she looked like someone kicked her fucking puppy on her way out of here tonight. What did you do man? Seriously, didn't we talk about this? Did you fuck her?" he yelled at me.

Technically, the answer was yes, but now I'm feeling protective and don't want to say that. What we had is more than that. It's more than sex, way more...it is..,it's just more than sex. I didn't say anything, I just looked at him in silence, choking inside trying to find the words I was too afraid to say.

"What the fuck is wrong with you, Brian!? She isn't one of those dumb whores you mess around with!" He was getting red, and really angry, and I was getting angrier by the minute too. "Seriously? You fucked her. Her dad—basically the only dad WE ever had just died—and you fucked her. I can't even fucking believe you would sink so low as to take advantage of her like that," he threw his hands in the air waiting for an explanation from me. I honestly wasn't sure that I had an explanation to give him, maybe he was right. Maybe this was all my fault for starting something and not coming clean as soon as I realized how I felt about her. Maybe she wouldn't have ended it if I told her the truth. How my heart ached right now, how making her smile was all I cared about now.

"It wasn't like that, Matt," was all I said.

"Oh? It wasn't like that? So tell me, what exactly was it like, man? You don't use up friends. You don't love 'em and leave 'em to family, dickhead. I can't believe she said she'd work here for you. What the fuck happened? I want the truth," he was pointing at me to drive his point home, and I blurted it out without even thinking.

"I love her, dude! I fucking love her. But she doesn't want anything to do with me other than working here, so that's how it's going to be. Now back the fuck off!" I screamed back. I said it out loud, and it felt so good. But it should have been her I was saying it to. With my lips on hers, touching her and confessing my feelings to her. But no, I just screamed it at my fucking brother.

"You what?" He leaned back in his chair and ran his hands

through his hair, clearly stunned by my confession. "Oh, Jesus, dude. What the fuck," was all he muttered.

Yeah, what the fuck indeed.

"When did all of this happen? You need to come clean, because eventually I'm going to hear about it when she's ready to talk to me, and I'm your brother, and her best friend, and fucking dude— ugh. What a goddamn mess." He shook his head at me, and I leaned back in my chair, putting my hands behind my head and letting out a big sigh myself.

"I'm not sure when it happened exactly, but we've been sneaking around together for a little bit since the funeral, she didn't want anyone to know," I confessed, and actually felt hurt that she still didn't want anyone to know now, after the fact.

"Yeah, because she's smarter than you. You can't tell anyone else that you two had something going on. You think you're in love or whatever, and all you're going to do is make things hard for her. And I'm not letting you do that. She deserves better than to deal with your bullshit or firehouse gossip, especially now," he was lecturing me like a little kid now, and I'm not appreciating it.

"Hold on one minute. It takes two people to make a decision like this. I wasn't exactly in it on my own." I tried to defend myself.

"Yeah, I'm sure. While we're at it, why don't you tell me what happened last year that made you two stop speaking more than two words to each other. Is that how long this has actually been going on? Oh, God, it hasn't has it?" he looked sick, likely because he knew I had been with other women in the last year, that wasn't a secret. Thinking about Jo, and other women at the same time made me feel ashamed that I wasn't ready for something when she approached me last year. I just didn't know how I felt, and now I wished so badly that I had thought more of it. I thought back to my discussion with her dad.

"You wanna come in here, son?" Jack motioned for me to come to his office. I had been staring at Jo, and I'm pretty sure I just got caught.

"Yes, sir, of course," I felt my face get hot and followed him into his office where he shut us both in.

"You know I love you and your brother like my own sons, right, Cavanaugh?" he sat down at his desk his stern expression letting me know he was about to give me shit. His lips curled up and the lines above his eyes furrowed.

"Yes, sir, we feel the same. You're the only father I've ever known, and I hope we make you proud," I meant that deeply.

"That there is my only daughter, Cavanaugh," he pointed out his door. "She's the single most important thing to me in the world."

"Yes sir, I understand," I nodded my head. I was deathly afraid of where this was going.

"I'd love nothing more than to see two of my favorite people end up happily ever after, Brian. But if you're not—ready shall we say—for more than what it takes to be serious, I'd like to warn you to keep it in your pants, son," he looked almost as uncomfortable as I felt. "Josephine is my life, Brian, and I'm not going to allow a broken heart to keep her from her dreams in the fire service, here at this station. I expect you to be Chief after me and when I'm gone, I expect you to look after her."

"Sir, I'd never do anything to hurt her. Jo is family. I'm sorry if I gave you the wrong impressi—" he interrupted me.

"I think I know exactly what's going on, Cavanaugh, and

when you're really ready, you have my blessing. You better be ready though and not one minute beforehand, are we clear?"

"Yes, sir, we're clear," I was going to try to explain myself more, but wasn't really sure what to say, and opted to just shut up, sitting there looking at him.

"That'll be all," he pointed at the door, signifying it was time for me to get the fuck out and think about things.

"Yes, sir," I got up and made a hasty exit, with my tail between my legs wondering what he thought he saw. And giving me his blessing? What was that about? What did he think was going on, because nothing was going on except I got caught staring at the hottest firefighter I've ever seen in my life.

It was about two weeks after that talk with Jack that we were all partying at Jax's house, celebrating something, I can't even remember what, when I went outside to get some fresh air and found Jo sitting on the front porch drinking her beer. She was pretty drunk and so was I, but I sat down next to her, admiring her beautiful tanned legs she had stretched out on the railing.

"What are you doing out here," I asked her. I looked around, expecting to see someone else, that she wasn't just sitting out here alone.

"Just enjoying the fresh air, I love it out here. It's such a beautiful night. Too nice to stay cooped up inside," she looked at me and smiled, those soft lips revealing her perfect smile. "What brings you out here, Cavanaugh? Lose something?" she laughed at me.

"Lose something? No. I just wanted to get some fresh air. What do you mean lose something?" I didn't get it.

"Oh, I saw you show up with some girl, I figured you were

looking for her is all," she said.

I rolled my eyes. "Oh her, yeah no. I didn't lose her. She actually belongs to someone else as it turns out, and I don't play that game, so I sent her on her way awhile ago," I kicked my feet up on the railing too. This is a nice night, she's right.

"Ahh, I see, well better luck next time," she looked away and took a long sip of her beer. I don't know what about it was so hot, but I very suddenly wanted to be that beer bottle, with her lips around my cock like that.

"Eh, whatever. It wasn't going to go anywhere anyway," I wanted to change the subject desperately. She was still looking away, and I could feel myself staring at her profile, admiring her features. Her short hair, which I just loved on a chick, her pouty lips which always looked pink, and those legs. They're worth mentioning twice. She was wearing a fire department hoodie, cut offs, and Chuck Taylor's. She was so effortless, and so fucking pretty.

She turned and gave me a skeptical face, her eyes were all squinted at me. "Oh, you're looking for something to go somewhere?"

I froze a little, "Uh, well...I don't know. I'm not not looking for something to go somewhere?"

She took her legs off the railing and swung herself in my direction. She looked me dead in the eyes and asked me. "So you're telling me, Mr. Single Player Cavanaugh, is no longer just looking for his next lay? Enlighten me sir, I'm shocked and intrigued," she was totally mocking me.

"I didn't say that. I just said that I'm not opposed to it necessarily is all."

"And describe this woman you're not opposed to, will you? I'm fascinated," she leaned in, and I felt myself being pulled toward her.

I was whispering now. "I don't know, she understands what we do for a living and appreciates it. Not in a badge whore kind of way, but genuinely appreciates what it means to us. That's all." What I was describing didn't really exist. Women say they understand, and that they're supportive, but deep down, they don't feel important enough if they've never been a firefighter, and to be honest, most female firefighters aren't like Jo. They're not smoking hot, they are masculine and act like they have something to prove. Whether or not Jo felt like that, she never acted that way.

"There's a handful of us out there, I guess you'll just have to keep looking," she whispered back.

"None like you," I said, and as I leaned in closer to whisper it to her, she leaned in to meet me halfway and our lips just barely touched.

"Like me, huh?" she smiled, still millimeters away when I reached up to touch caress her cheek and bring her in closer for a proper kiss that I now couldn't do without.

"No." I brought her in gently and kissed her more softly than I've ever kissed anyone in my life. It was full of passion; the kind of kiss everyone thinks their first kiss will be like but it isn't of course because you're a sloppy mess. It was the perfect kiss. She parted her mouth, and let me explore it with my tongue gently and I brought my other hand up around the back of her neck, playing with the short hair back there. She brought her hand up to my chest, sending tingles all over my body. It was a kiss that

made you forget you ever kissed anyone. I had butterflies; I was buzzing.

"Let's leave," she whispered, and I came to my senses, back to reality and what it would mean if we did leave, no matter how badly I wanted to. My back stiffened up and I pulled away, stopping the most amazing moment with a woman I've ever had in my life.

All I could think of was Jack. Her father. My Chief. 'I'm not going to allow a broken heart to keep her from her dreams in the fire service, here at this station. I expect you to be Chief after me and when I'm gone, I expect you to look after her'.

"We shouldn't be doing this, Jo, I'm sorry I did that," I stood up to leave. Really, I wanted to run away at top speed. She stood up too.

"Why not, Brian? This works," she gently waved at the air between us.

"No, no it doesn't. We've been drinking, and this just isn't going to happen. I'm sorry I let this happen Jo. I didn't mean—I don't—" I couldn't even think of the words to say. I wanted it to happen, but all I could think of was her dad, and I wasn't ready for that discussion. With her, with him, with myself.

She changed her demeanor; straightened her posture, rolling her eyes at me again, "Oh I get it, Brian. All of Orange County is good enough, but not me. It was a big mistake. Let me guess, 'you're drunk', 'we work together', 'you're like a sister'...I'll save you the trouble Cavanaugh," and she started to walk away when I grabbed her arm.

"Don't act like a baby, Jo, it was just a kiss. You're not my girlfriend and you're not going to be, nobody is," I immediately

regretted saying that, it was mean and I knew it as the words escaped my lips.

She turned to stone. "Let me go. Now." I let go of her arm, and honestly thought she was going to punch me but she didn't. She inhaled. "Don't act like a baby? Are you serious? I was wrong about you, Brian. I've always thought you were someone you aren't, and you never will be. Enjoy the revolving door of women while the rest of us move the fuck on. You're right, it was just a kiss, it was a huge mistake." She walked off the porch out to her Jeep and I just stood there wishing that I'd said something, anything except what I said.

That day, I felt like something had changed, like I had lost something, but I didn't own it. She stopped speaking to me for anything other than business at the firehouse or cordial hellos after that, so I definitely lost something, I lost her once already back then. I felt incomplete, not whole every time I saw her after that and I felt like an asshole. I told my brother a much shorter version of all of this while he listened, completely speechless just looking at me like a wide-eyed cat shaking his head every once in a while. I didn't get into the details of the last week with Jo, Matt knew what he needed to, that we'd been sleeping together, and that I loved her and that was a lot. Anything more than that wasn't any of his fucking business; even if she wasn't speaking to me, again

When I was done being as honest as I could allow myself to be, we sat there in silence for a minute that felt like an hour until finally he spoke. "You're a dick." He got up and walked out of my office.

He was right, I was a dick.

Jo

Once I got home, I immediately got in the shower. Along with all the dirt and grime, I tried washing my heartbreak away, even if I sort of caused it myself. I had what I always wanted for a little bit and honestly now I don't know if having a real taste was better than nothing or not. I wept on the shower floor, letting everything I'd been holding in for who knows how long just swirl down the drain with my tears. Deep down, I thought maybe it could work with Brian, I mean we've been friends forever, and my dad absolutely loved the guy, but he didn't fight me on it, so my instinct to break it off must have been right.

I guess it didn't really matter anyway, my dad's not here, and Brian was going to be my boss. I spared myself the pain of more heartache by ending it,, and cutting my losses before things got any more serious. Being alone is probably what I needed anyway, right? Something about growing and whatever. I knew I was going to have to tell Matt what happened at some point, but for the moment I had planned to just focus on getting myself out of Station 19, and back to my home. Then I'd worry about my next move.

The next day I slept in late. Really late. I missed four text messages from Matt, two from Danny, but none from Brian. Even though I expected I wouldn't hear from him, it was still disappointing. Matt was just texting me because that's what he does; none of his were important, but Danny hasn't texted me in ages.

> Can you come in early to cover a couple more hours?

> Hello? Can you help me out or not, Jo? I'd appreciate a reply either way.

I rolled my eyes. The text messages were from about twenty minutes ago and they were about a minute apart. God he's so impatient—what did I ever see in him? Danny wasn't really my type, he never was. He was good looking, don't get me wrong, but he was Mr. Clean Cut, ass kissing, work his way to the top guy in a schmoozy kind of way. Not in the put in hard work and make it happen kind of way. I decided to go ahead and take the extra couple hours, it never hurts, and I was going in anyway, so I texted him back.

> Just got your messages. Long day yesterday. Yes, I'll take the hours, I can be there at noon. Good?

Then I sent a second message,

> I need to talk to you about my schedule as well.

He replied immediately,

> Long day? I see. I'm not in the station today, I have fire marshal inspections around the district. What's wrong with your schedule?

I guessed he had inspections to do, he was always so vague

with how he spent his time when he was out doing "fire marshal stuff". Generally, a fire marshal does inspections and investigations, as well as handling fire prevention week and activities like that, but it wasn't close to fire prevention week. He could never just be specific with me about what he was doing though, a major reason our relationship failed miserably.

We can talk about it later. I need to change my schedule.

I'll come by this afternoon.

Great, of course he's going to make a special trip. I didn't even bother replying. I'd been so nice to him, because I cared so much about him having a good reputation especially with my dad. When I found out that he was cheating on me, I didn't get upset. I talked shit to Matt about it, and let that be my outburst. Besides the fact that it was embarrassing to be cheated on, part of me was kind of relieved because our relationship was more out of a convenience than anything else. I also just didn't believe in creating a scene. I wouldn't get anything out of pitching a fit or getting over emotional; I definitely learned that trait from my dad who would be mad as hell at someone and talk calmly as if he were whispering to a baby.

I rolled my ass out of bed and put a uniform together. I honestly didn't like doing laundry or chores of any kind. I had plenty of uniforms to choose from so I didn't have to be washing them every day unless something really gross happened. I was riding the firetruck today, not the ambulance, but it was the same uniform either way. Since I showered the previous night, I just washed my face, brushed my teeth and fixed up my short hair. If I had to do any work today, I'd have a helmet on anyway, so it wasn't really worth getting too fussy, and I honestly didn't want to seem attractive to Danny. The last couple times I saw him, he gave me this awful dirty feeling when he looked at me, and he wasn't ever even that into me so I don't get it.

I had no energy, my limbs felt heavy, and I dragged myself around the house getting some coffee going, and changing my clothes. I couldn't stop thinking about Brian, and how I ended things last night. Part of me had really hoped there would be a message from him this morning, because I know I'd have gotten another taste if he had tried at all. He was so convincing even when he wasn't trying. One look at those eyes, and I forgot just about everything. Convictions? Out the window. Inhibitions? Please, they don't exist. But this was different. My feelings were so deep for Brian Cavanaugh; I just couldn't let it be a fling. He says it's not, but I couldn't sacrifice what my dad always wanted for a few rolls in the hay. Fucking glorious rolls in the hay. I was getting turned on and wet just thinking about him growling in my ear, and fucking me; just the thought of his touch made me shudder. *Okay, Jo, get ready for work, fuckkkkk.* I rolled my eyes at myself, poured some coffee in a thermal mug and got on my way.

I worked at Station 19 a lot over the last year or so out of convenience. It's not a particularly busy station, but we were back up mutual aid on a lot of calls and that's more or less how Danny and I ended up dating. After Brian and I kissed last year, and it ended abruptly, and I was super pissed and hurt, Danny started flirting with me at work. He's a good looking guy, and had a lot of women that wanted him, and I decided that if he was into it, why shouldn't I go for it. I mean, I wasn't going to wait for Brian, and I had already put myself out there and got the proverbial smackdown on my heart anyway, so why not date someone new.

Danny and I started dating, and within months, it quickly escalated into me moving in with him. I think I did it so that I wasn't scraping by, and honestly, at the age of thirty-one, which I was at the time, who doesn't want to feel like they should be with someone? I figured that this was the guy I was supposed to be with mostly because we had the fire department in common and he was good looking, and that even though we didn't have the passion I had longed for in my life, maybe that was just a fantasy. My dad did not like me living with Danny at all. It was something we didn't see eye to eye on at all, and I pretty much knew he was right deep down.

After a few months, we were not working the same shift, which is where it turned out he was cheating on me. While I was at work. Funny how when we were dating we never ended up on the same shift, but now that we're apart, he kept showing up on my shift all of a sudden.

Now I was feeling the anger toward Danny, the loss of my dad and the loss of Brian; it hit deep. How I ended up in the situation was more than depressing, I felt an ache down to my bones. My body was hijacked by loss and there was no ransom that could fix it.

BRIAN

Matt wouldn't speak to me the rest of the night at the station, and I slept like shit. I couldn't get her out of my mind. I tried to rationalize what happened in my head, to make myself angry with her, to think of reasons why being with her was a bad idea, and all I could come up with was that I fucking missed her, and I had a huge pain in my chest. In my heart. She is mo chroí. My heart. Mo chuisle, My pulse, as my mom would say. I felt weak thinking about her leaving me. I knew that her happiness had to be first, not mine.

Our mom was born in Ireland and taught us the Gaelic. It was all bits and pieces, and sometimes when we were growing up and getting into trouble, she would yell at us in Gaelic phrases I still don't understand. She moved here when she was a young girl, maybe 10 I think, and so she didn't have much of an accent unless she was really fired up about something, then she would start talking fast, and you could hear it a little bit. It's funny, how when you feel like shit, you want your mom. I want my mom right now. She'd know what to do. I'm gonna have to tell her what I've done though. Fuck it. Jo's worth it; she belongs with me, and my mom will help me figure out how to get her back.

I basically moped around my house most of the morning, feeling like a big dick and an outsider since the people I give a shit about weren't really talking to me. My brother wasn't speaking to me, I obviously couldn't talk to Jo right now, this was a good idea, I'm gonna go see my mom. I'm way overdue for a visit; I hadn't seen her since Jack's funeral anyway.

I'd been sitting around sipping my coffee all morning which was just leaving an awful bitter taste in my mouth like everything around me. Literally, everything was making me sad or annoyed. Mom lives about 20 minutes away, so I showered and shaved and got my shit together, tail between my legs, knowing that my Irish ass reaming would be a big part of my begging for her help.

"Mamai," I said when she opened the door. She looked surprised to see me. I guess I needed to come by more often. We used to do regular dinners, but the fire department schedule didn't make that super easy, and once we were getting called away all the time, she just kind of gave up on us boys showing up on a regular schedule.

"How are you, my love? Get in here, come come!" she exclaimed when she opened the door, clutching me into her arms in the best hug ever. Seriously, there's nothing like a mom hug. It just warms you all over.

"I'm alright, Ma. I'm sorry I haven't seen you since the funeral," I knew my mama had a fondness for Jack and I left it at that. If it were any other man on earth, I may have—no I would have—had an issue.

"So sad, my love. I know how busy you are helping people. Get in here and give mama some love and let me put some coffee or tea on. Which are we having today love?" she was always so welcoming.

"Let's have coffee, Mama, unless you've decided it's whiskey time?" I loved teasing her. She only drank when things were really bad, or really good.

"It's one in the afternoon, Brian Patrick. We Cavanaugh's don't do that unless times are tough. Are times tough?" she gave me a furrowed brow and a concerned look as she led me to her sitting room which was super traditional old school old lady. I loved my mama, however this room was the room you weren't allowed in until you were an adult, the furniture looked so comfortable when I was younger, and then when you finally were allowed in as an adult, you wanted to go back to the kids' room where you could actually get comfortable on the furniture. She had flowered chairs, and *the* most uncomfortable couch on earth in this room, but you were an adult in this room. She led me to the sitting room, and then rushed herself off to the kitchen to make coffee.

"Mama, you don't have to do that, I'm a grown man, I can get coffee. I came to visit with you." She was getting older, and with Jack's passing, it made me think of my lineage, and how my mama was no spring chicken. I don't want her fussing over me of all people. I did however, know better, so I sat my ass on the old fashioned flowered couch where I knew she wanted to sit across from me and I waited for her to come back with coffee.

A few minutes later, she returned, probably because Matt and I bought her a fancy automatic coffee machine with pods so she wouldn't get out the ancient multi person brew pot she used to. She handed me a cup and I took a sip and pursed my lips from the fire that the whiskey sent chasing down my throat.

"Holy cow, Mama, what he hel—heck?" I tried not to curse in front of her unless it was the holidays and we were all drunk. She laughed at me.

"I know you need it, my love. Something must be happening in your life for you to come by unannounced. If it makes you feel better, I have a splash in my tea, in case it's too much for me to handle," she winked at me and sat down on the same couch as me, turning herself to me.

"Mama, I can't just come to see you and check in?" I asked. She was onto me. I didn't swing by as often as I should.

"Don't play a game you did not invent, my child. I know you are here searching for something, so let's get to it. I have plenty to keep me busy in my grief over my dear friend," she was referring to Jack, and I felt like I knew something had happened there. "How is my dear dear, Josephine?" she asked me. My heart sank even further, which I didn't think was possible.

"Uh, she's okay?" I made it a question. "I've talked to her a lot the last week or so. I got her to come back to our station sort of full-time," I again, said it like a question I was asking for approval.

"Your feelings are no secret, my love. What happened that made you come here for comfort? I know you, love, and I know your ways...Has something happened? Talk to your mama..." she patted the couch between us. My mom's voice was so soft and soothing, with that faint Irish accent. The sweetness in her voice always made everyone want to spill their guts to her. She was everyone's mama.

"Mama, everything is fuc—messed up, and I don't know what to do about it. Jo is going to come back to Station 23, so me and Jack's plan worked, but..." I just didn't really know how to say it.

"But you're in love with her," she finished my sentence for me and smiled. I let out a huge sigh that I'd been holding in since the day before when I talked to Jo last. I didn't say anything at all and she continued. "Why does this leave you exasperated, Brian? Does she know how you feel?"

I looked up at her, how did she know? "Not really, no, I don't think she knows how I feel, but I do know she doesn't want anything to do with me except for working together I guess. I don't know what to do and I thought I could just let it go, but Mama, I'm sick over it. I've never felt this way about a woman before, and it's like my brain doesn't even work right now." It's true. I couldn't see straight without knowing she was mine. "She is *grá mo chroí*". I admitted to my mom.

"Ah, she is your eternal love." Now mama was smiling so big she looked like she would laugh.

"Why do you look like you're going to laugh? This isn't funny. This is terrible." I poured the rest of my coffee down, feeling the burn of the whiskey all the way down to my stomach.

She grinned and got up and went to the liquor cabinet. She pulled out two tumblers and poured us both a healthy amount of Jamison's. "Well my dear," she said as she passed one to me, then clinked my glass with hers, "Jack and I always knew this would happen eventually," she giggled and took a sip of her whiskey.

"What are you talking about? Jack told me to stay away from her," I recalled that conversation in my head again.

"I know exactly what Jack said to you. He didn't tell you to stay away from her. He told you not to lust after her like a conquest. I also know that he told you that you would have his blessing when you were really ready for what that sweet girl deserves," she said matter-of-factly, and sat back down on the couch looking pretty satisfied with herself. "It seems you are now ready, so tell me, why doesn't she want to be with you?"

"How do you know all of this, Mama?" I was now very sure she had a relationship with Jack and I was kind of mad about it.

"Jack and I had a very special friendship, Brian. You and Matt were like sons to him, and he was a wonderful person to us especially in our time of need. Jack and I were very close and he often came by to check in on us, and we talked. You don't get an opinion on this, your mama is a grown woman you know." She looked away and I could see the hurt and sadness of his passing in her teary eyes.

"I'm sorry." I really was sorry. If she loved Jack half as much as I loved Jo, her sadness breaks my heart too.

"It's fine, we all go eventually. Jack and I often talked of the dangers of the job for him, and for you boys, and for Jo of course. Now, tell me why you think she doesn't want to be with you, and why you are so sure this cannot be fixed." My mama thought everything could be fixed. With whiskey and hugs mostly, which was actually mostly true if you really think about it.

"Well, we started seeing each other...secretly," I waited for a reply or judgment, but she just motioned for me to continue. "After a little bit, I told her about how Jack and I wanted her to come back to our station and work with us, and the old crew, and she seemed to like the idea. Then we got a call, and we went out to handle it, basically like old times, great teamwork, everyone got saved, the whole thing. But..." I really didn't want to tell my mom what a dickhead caveman I was at the scene, but I had to come clean.

"Go on, Brian, you may as well tell me, because you know if you don't I will just call Matty and ask him later," she winked at me. I gave a little sarcastic laugh. When she wanted answers, she got them, so I drank the rest of the whiskey in my glass and told her.

"Honestly, I didn't treat her like one of the guys on my crew. I was overprotective, and unprofessional about it and gave her a hard time because I wanted to protect her. And she was mad. Mama, really really mad. I was a jerk. I thought it was just a little argument, and that we'd talk about it later, and she didn't want any part of it. She said that she wanted to come back to the station full-time, but we couldn't see each other anymore. I had to decide if it was going to work for me or not. I wanted her to be happy, and I knew that being at Jack's station is what she wants in her heart, so I let her go. I didn't fight for her," I hung my head. Getting the full story off my chest was a relief, but didn't take away the pain in my chest that her absence had left.

"Oh my dear, I'm quite certain this can be fixed. But I'm going to give you the hard truth, as you do to your boys down at the firehouse," she lowered her eyes at me, and looked at me over her glasses. Oh shit.

"Okay, Mama, shoot," I said and took in a big breath.

"Man up," she said. She took her whiskey down, and put her glass on the coffee table and looked at me.

"What?" I almost choked. That was her advice?

"You heard me, son. Man up. You love this girl? Go fight for her. Go get her. Don't sulk and whine like a little baby. You go tell her the truth, and you tell her how you feel. She'll see you're serious. A serious man fights for his woman. This I know." And with that, she folded her arms; was clearly done with her advice.

I thought about it for a moment, and realized she was right. I was a total pussy not to stop her in my office. We were tired, she was mad and I just let her go. What the fuck kind of way is that to show a woman you love her? I needed to get a plan together for getting her back, for good.

"Mama, you're right. I'm gonna get her back. Thank you," I scooped her into a big hug and wouldn't let go.

"You're welcome, sweetheart, sometimes we need someone to point out the obvious to us because we cannot see what's right in front of us."

I got up to leave, and then decided I better tell her that Matt and I weren't speaking before she heard about it.

"I forgot to tell you that Matty knows about this, at least some of it, and he's pretty pissed off at me right now too," I started to put my hand over my mouth for saying pissed.

She waved her hand at me and laughed a bit, "Oh I know. He called me this morning and told me everything." She already knew everything I had come to tell her. She's a wily woman; I couldn't even be mad. I needed the kick in the pants, we all do sometimes.

"I'm not even mad," I laughed.

"You have no reason to be. You need to set things right with your brother though. He loves Josephine too in his own way. Those two have always been very close, and he feels like you betrayed a trust, a sacred bond. He doesn't understand true love yet, but he will someday, and you can teach him once you get your affairs in order. But until then, he wants to protect her from getting hurt too, just in a different way. Go see him, he will talk to you, I made sure of it," she instructed me.

"Okay, Mama I will. I'll go talk to him later tonight," I gave her another hug and a kiss on the cheek. "Thank you, Mama. I'm gonna make her my wife, you'll see."

"I have no doubt that you will, my love. I have something for you, hold on a moment," She walked back to her bedroom and came back with a small box, and put it in my hand.

"What's this?" It looked like a ring box.

"This is a gift that Jack gave to me a long time ago, and I think that it's the perfect thing for you to give Josephine when you set things right. Now go," she shooed me out of the house. I didn't open the box, I needed to go home and formulate my plan and talk to Matt. Time to make Jo mine. For good. Operation MJM, "Make Jo Mine". Yeah, it was game on.

Jo

I had about four days to get my shit together, and be okay seeing Brian at work on a regular basis. I had managed to get a couple other guys to take some of my shifts at 19. Towards the end of the time frame, I was looking to leave, so I should only have to put in another two, maybe three shifts here before getting on the schedule over at Station 23 more or less full time.

It had been a slow afternoon at the station, and I was only here for a quick six-hour shift. I was covering for another guy that had kids, and there was some kind of event at his kid's school. Matt and I had been texting since I woke up, and he wanted me to come out for beers tonight, which I really didn't want to do, but I had no reasonable excuse not to. It would be better than sitting at home feeling sorry for myself, but I wasn't convinced it was the best idea. I did want to talk to him about how uncomfortable Danny had been making me with his comments and looks lately. I'd been avoiding him like the plague and I just felt like something was up with that. Hopefully tonight wasn't a "gathering" and it won't be all the guys, and Brian of course. I'd love a night to chill out and talk to Matt. I just didn't want to see Brian, until I figured out how to cope with the situation. I was going to have to pretend that I'm perfectly okay with the things that I said, which honestly I wasn't. I regretted it.

In my panties I regretted it, and in my heart I regretted it, but my brain came out on top this time.

Matt filled me in about some new girl he met that sounded about as interesting as watching cement dry, when our tones dropped for a car accident. I was actually covering for the first officer that afternoon, so I shoved my phone in my shirt pocket, and headed for the truck. Stepping into my gear, I got that same rush I always do from emergency response.

As we were pulling out of the station, Danny was pulling in and gave me what I'd call a death stare. He glared at me in such a way that pierced me with his glassy eyes. Hey, it's not my fault we got a call, and I never told him to come here to talk to me in the first place. Station 19 does not have a heavy rescue truck like Station 23 does, and so often we called for them to join us on a car accident because they have some of the tools for a bigger job. This was a tractor trailer accident, sounds like it flipped on it's side and no one was hurt, but we called for them to join us anyway, just in case. It wasn't my shift that would be working, they all got off at 7am this morning, so at least I wouldn't see Brian there. And it was 19's scene anyway, even if he were there, he wouldn't be in charge of this one.

We got to the scene, and it was more of a big mess than anything else. The driver of the vehicle had "lost control", hit the guard wall, and flipped his semi on its side. He was standing around yelling about some mystery car that cut him off and caused the accident. The semi was filled with citrus. Lemons, oranges, limes and grapefruits were everywhere. Literally all over the road, and a whole bunch of them had gotten smooshed into the road already from passers by, and it smelled delightful. We were all chuckling about it, and working on cleaning up the mess so the truck could be hauled away and become someone else's problem when I saw Brian's Chief truck pull up.

Come on, seriously? What's he doing here? It's not even his day to work. I tried not to stare, and to just do my job, but I wanted to see what he was doing there. My heart started racing as he got out of his truck and walked over to the on scene commander for a minute, then went over to see his crew. It wasn't station 23's mess to clear up and they would probably be released from the scene as soon as enough of the mess was cleaned up to open the roadway back up. I looked away, but I swear I could feel him looking at me. I was wearing my bunker pants, t-shirt and helmet, but no coat because there was really no danger, and as usual it was pretty hot out. I thought about our argument the last time we were on scene together and chuckled to myself; today I'm wearing a uniform shirt which is navy blue with the fire department insignia on the chest. There would be no public sweaty show today, *so there, Chief.*

I couldn't help myself, I looked over his way and he was staring in my direction, wearing jeans and a t-shirt that accentuated those beautiful muscles of his. His visible tattoos on his arms were so sexy, and he was standing with the officer of the 23 truck, with his arms folded in front of him, and his sunglasses on. He must have been on his way somewhere, or on his way back from somewhere because he lives on my side of town. It was none of my business what he was doing, but I couldn't help myself. I felt desire rising within me just from seeing him, and I think I was staring, because he smiled right at me. *Oh shit, I got caught staring. Fuck me.*

I shook myself from my Brian trance, and helped my crew

finish up what we were doing. I tried not to look in his direction again. I saw him leave out of the corner of my eye, as we were winding up, and his guys got sent home. It took a little longer than expected to wrap up; citrus can be a little unruly—who knew? I had about an hour left in my shift by the time we got back to the station, and Danny was in the day room, presumably, waiting to talk to me.

After I put my gear back, I went over to talk to him. "Did you want to talk about my schedule?"

He looked up from the paperwork he was reviewing. "Yeah, that's why I'm sitting here waiting for you." He was curt with me.

"I can't help when there's a call, Danny, so lose the attitude," I didn't know what his problem was, but I didn't need his shit today.

"Yea, I get it. What's the deal with your schedule?"

"I'm going to take myself out of the per diem rotation for awhile. Well indefinitely actually. I've been offered a more steady gig, and I've decided that it would suit me better to have a more normal schedule, so I'm going to take it. I have two more shifts here this week; I got the rest covered." That pretty much summed it up. I waited for a response and got a smirk.

"Going back to daddy's old station I assume?" he asked smugly.

I was pissed. "Yes, I am. It's closer to my house, I grew up there, and they're offering me a full-time spot, so yes." *Fuck you, Danny, fuck you, fuck you, fuck you.*

"Fucking the Chief over there now?" he demanded, his anger beginning to show.

I didn't even know I was going to do it until it happened, but I slapped him right across the face. I could've gotten in a lot of trouble for that, and honestly I didn't care, even if I didn't plan it, he deserved it.

"Wow," he said as he rubbed his cheek where I hit him. "Sensitive subject, eh?" he laughed at me. He *laughed* at me.

"No, Danny it's not," I lied. "It's actually none of your fucking business, this was about a job opportunity. And you don't get to talk to me like that. What the fuck is your problem?"

"No problem, Jo. No problem at all." That smug look of his was infuriating me. "I'm sorry if I offended you. How's going through your dad's stuff? Have you gone through all of those notebooks of his yet?"

Now he wanted to make nice? The guy was a dick; I honestly have no idea what I ever saw in him. I did just hit him though, so I figured I would make a little bit nice. "No, I haven't gone through them yet, probably this weekend. I need to make sure there's nothing in the notebooks that needs to be sorted." Who knows what's in all of those notebooks, my dad journaled in addition to keeping meticulous call notes. I definitely wanted to read his journals, but I didn't even know if they're all in the same place. I hadn't really gone in his room yet to poke around.

"Ah, I see. Well good luck. If there's nothing else, then I guess that's it. Your shift is about over, I can cover the last half hour if you want to leave now," he offered.

"Uh, alright, cool. Thanks." I was a little confused, but getting away from him sooner rather than later sounded ideal to me at this point. I started to walk away.

"Oh, Jo?" he called after me.

"Yeah?" I turned around to see what he wanted.

"Looking sexy today," he laughed. "Really sexy." He narrowed his eyes at me.

A chill setttled all over me. That was completely out of the blue, and totally creepy. *Looking sexy? What the hell is that about?* I didn't reply.

I got out of there as quick as possible. There was something seriously wrong with him, and the way he'd been glaring at me the last few times I've seen him disturbs me. And why would he care about my dad's notebooks? I made a note to schedule time to go through them this weekend, I felt like something in those notebooks intrigued Danny, and if that was true, I needed to find out why.

BRIAN

I showed up on that scene to see her. I knew she'd be there. I was on my way to go see my brother straight from my mom's when the call went out. I had hoped to have beers with Matt tonight, but he told me he was meeting up with Jo, and frankly, I needed to make things right with Matt before he saw her so he would help me get her back. The plan would start as soon as possible.

I thanked the Lord above when I saw her she was wearing a dark blue uniform shirt, her uniform looking like everyone else's. Except that no one else on that scene makes my cock hard. No one anywhere, actually. I'd been getting a few texts here and there this week from girls I had gone out with recently, and I told every single one of them that I was off the market and wished them well. Even if Jo didn't know yet, there's no other woman for me and she will find out soon enough. I honestly couldn't stand the thought of touching anyone but her and I cringed at the thought.

As I headed over to my brother's house, I thought about how different life felt since I tasted her. Like I was carrying a weight around before I realized how I felt about her. I was so excited about my future with Jo, I wanted to call her and talk to her about it like she was my best friend. She wasn't really speaking to me, but that would change soon enough. I was absolutely going to man up, and be the man she deserved in her life. I'd protect her and love her forever. The sappy shit made me so happy I could burst, I didn't even care, I could shout it from the rooftops.

I pulled into my brother's driveway, he lived with Jax in a house that belonged to Jax. It was their bachelor pad more or less. I preferred my house being my sanctuary, and I kept most of my partying outside of my place. Jax was probably down at the station tinkering with things or researching stuff, I didn't see his truck there and you could find him there most of the time, even on his time off.

It was a nice afternoon, and I was pretty sure my brother was out back in his back yard, so I walked around instead of coming to the front door. Sure enough, there he was, lounging in a chair beer in one hand, phone in the other.

"Hey, Matt." I approached the beast carefully. I really did need his help, and since we've both already talked to our mom, I wasn't quite sure where to start and I was hoping he would actually.

"Oh, hey dickhead. How was your visit with mom?" he laughed sarcastically in my direction, not really making eye contact with me. Obviously he wasn't going to make this easy for me.

"It was...you know, enlightening. Apparently she already knew everything. Nice mouth," I got a beer for myself out of the cooler next to him and grabbed myself a seat.

We sat in silence drinking our beers for a couple minutes, when Matt did finally speak up first. Thank God.

"Look. I have to just ask you, because I don't even get it right now, but mom told me to listen to you. So, are you serious? Like really serious about this? Because this changes everything, man, you can't be kinda sure, or whatever. You have to be honest with me, do you really love her?" He looked over at me and waited for my response.

I turned myself to face him and took in a deep breath. "Matty, I've never been so sure of anything in my life. She's my heart. Like Mama used to talk about love. My life is empty without her in it. I'm in physical pain without her right now and I don't know what to do to get her back, but I have to. I was put on this earth to take care of her and to love her. I need you to help me." I meant every word, and I hoped it was enough for Matt to understand the depth of my feelings for her. I didn't really know what else to say.

Matt was looking at me intently, and then he finally spoke up., "Okay, I get it. If she's the one for you, then I'll talk to her tonight when I see her. I'm not making any promises because she doesn't even know I know anything yet, but I had already planned to bring it up tonight. She is meeting me out for drinks later. Okay?"

"Yeah, absolutely. Seriously, man, I owe you one. I'm telling you I've never felt like this before and I swear to you it's the real deal."

"Do you think she feels the same way about you?" He asked me.

"I think she does. I think she's afraid of what people will say, but I don't care. I'd give up being Chief to be with her," I'd have given up whatever it took to make that empty feeling go away.

"Okay, settle down. Let's not go resigning from our jobs. I'm pretty sure you can make this work one way or another if she really feels the same way. She's squirrely though, and you know that about her. She starts on Sunday with us, so don't do anything before then. I'll talk to her tonight, but that's so she can tell me what's going on from her perspective. The only way to win this game is patience. You're gonna have to take it slow or you're gonna piss her off, and you know what that means," he laughed.

I laughed too, when Jo was pissed off, she'd go to the end of the earth to make sure you knew she was right and you were wrong out of principle alone. And she would win. Every time. "Yeah, I definitely do. I'll try to keep myself in check, but you gotta tell me how she is after you talk to her. I haven't seen or heard from her, and I can't stand her working at 19 this week with that Danny Russell wrapping up her shifts."

"Yeah, something about that guy really gives me the creeps lately. I used to just think he was a dick, but I feel like something else is up and he's actually been showing up on Jo's shifts this week when he's not scheduled," Matt confessed.

I stood up and clenched my fists, "What? Is he giving her a hard time? What's going on?" I was consumed with rage, if he was harassing her or even sneezing in her direction, I'd fucking kill him.

"Relax for right now, she says it's under control, and in less than a week, she'll be full-time with us. Let her play this out her way so she feels like she did the right thing. I don't like it any more than you do, I feel like that guy needs a swift punch in the dick myself."

"Alright, it's only a couple days, but you need to check in with her about it. A lot. I don't like it one bit. We're her family regardless of anything else, we have to take care of her." I don't like feeling helpless, but Matt was right. I needed to let Jo have her space to work this out her way. I couldn't control everything in her life, but one thing was for damn sure, after she was done at 19, I wasn't letting her out of my sight, and if I had any say in the matter her beautiful face would be the first thing I saw in the mornings, and the last thing I saw every night.

Jo

I really needed to start going through my dad's stuff, and organizing his notebooks and stuff. I wonder if maybe I can just give the notebooks to Brian to hold onto in case he needed them for anything. I made a note to ask Matt to talk to Brian about it. I was trying to avoid initiating a conversation with Brian until we were working together, because it hurts. I've got a pit in my stomach, and every time I've thought about him, I felt my face getting warm, and my eyes becoming full of tears. I knew the feeling would pass, it had to eventually.

I was meeting Matt tonight, just the two of us, to catch up and hang out and have a couple drinks. We hadn't really spent any time together since I left the bar with Brian that night. That night, that sealed my feelings, and makes me weak in the knees. I started to get a tingle just thinking about how hot it was. *Stop it, stop it, stop it*. Oh, but it was so good. It could never be that good with anyone else, ever. I actually rolled my eyes at myself and finished getting ready.

Matt and I had decided to meet up at a place across town for some food and drinks, and we didn't really feel like running into everyone we know, so it was worth the extra fifteen minutes on the road to get there. It was actually a little Irish place kind of close to

Station 19 that I had discovered one night after a shift there with some of the guys that lived on that side of town.

I wasn't an especially high maintenance girl, I was definitely a t-shirt and jeans chick, but I still liked to feel pretty when I wasn't riding a firetruck. I had messy short hair that I thought looks pretty cute when I put some makeup on, so since I was feeling so shitty, I decided that I would definitely do my face tonight. It wasn't a date, but I was leaving the house and trying to put on a brave face, so it was a bit like painting on confidence.

I absolutely needed to tell Matt what happened. I couldn't keep this secret from him, and I was so afraid he was going to be angry with me about it. Scotty and I had been texting, and he said something was going on with Matt and Brian at work and they were barely speaking the other day. I was really hoping that it had nothing to do with me. I was sure it didn't, but I couldn't help the thought. I felt so fucking guilty for being dishonest in the first place. Really, this was probably never a good idea, since we couldn't be together publicly, I couldn't help but think that I set us up for failure by trying to keep him in secret. Well in true Jo fashion, it is what it is. Now it's time to clear the air, confess to Matt, and talk about what's next.

I pulled in to the parking lot of Erin's Pub, parking next to Matt. He obviously beat me here. I checked myself in the mirror real quick, freshened up my lipstick, and got my ass in gear. When I walked in, he was sitting at the bar with his back to the door, wearing his usual beat up fire department baseball hat, t-shirt and jeans. I could have spotted him a mile away.

"Excuse me, is this seat taken," I whispered in his ear trying to sound as sexy as possible. Hey, why not have a little fun with him.

He turned around quickly, and then looked shocked to see me, and I couldn't help laughing hysterically. He definitely thought I was a strange new possibility. Mission accomplished.

"What the fuck, Jo?! You can't do that to a guy! I'm in a dry spell! That's so not fair!" he pretended to be mad at me and it was making me laugh that much harder.

"Aww come on, Matty, that was funny. *Is this seat taken?*" I mocked him further.

"Yeah, yeah, hilarious. Come on, let's get a table," he stood up, still pretending to be mad, leaving a few bucks on the bar for his beer.

I followed him over to a booth where he sat facing the door, and I sat across from him, my back to the door. Something a lot of emergency personnel do is evaluate a room—anywhere they go—for the different exits. It's called a means of egress. We're always calculating how we would get out, if there was an emergency. Normally, we all like having our eyes on the door for some reason, it was just instinctive, but in this situation, I was fine letting Matt have eyes on the door, as long as one of us did. If I were here with someone who wasn't a partner, or in emergency services, I would have insisted sitting on the other side, just to have eyes on the exit. It's just an instinctive thing we all do and you don't even realize you do it until you are out and about with people who don't do it.

"Are you hungry?" he asked, and grabbed a menu from the little metal tray holding them, handing it to me.

"I can always eat," I grinned. "But I'm definitely thirsty more than anything," I poked my head up and around like it was on a swivel, looking for a waitress. Before I even sat myself right, an adorable little blonde girl popped up in front of us to take our order.

"Hi, I'm Summer, what can I getcha, hunny?" she asked me with the sweetest little southern accent.

"Hi, Summer, I'll take a Jameson's and ginger please," I smiled. She seemed really young, but she sure was perky. Matt was definitely enjoying the view himself.

"I'll have another one of these," he showed her his beer bottle and she smiled.

"Do you two need a few minutes with the menu?"

"I do actually, thanks," I said, and she smiled again and took off like a little fairy. "She's pretty cute, you should talk to her," I said to Matt.

"She's cute, but she's not my type. Looks a little young. Anyway, I'm here to hang out with you. How's it going? I feel like it's been the longest week ever, and we haven't really had time to catch up much. How are you doing?" He asked me a bunch of questions.

"I'm alright, it's still weird being in that house without him if we're being honest. And now, I really just can't wait to be done with 19," I didn't really want to tell Matt exactly how creeped out I was becoming by Danny, but I think he could tell.

"Is that motherfucker giving you a hard time?" he asked.

"I wouldn't call it a hard time exactly," I scrunched my face up trying to figure out how to describe it. Matt was waiting for me to clarify. "He just keeps showing up, and he's made a few kind of inappropriate comments, but I don't think it's a big deal. He knows I'm moving on and taking up residence at 23, so it is what it is. It's only a few more days, then I won't really ever have to see him."

Matt looked at me sternly before he replied. "It's important that you tell me if he's doing anything that you know is over the line." He awaited my response.

I sighed, knowing he was totally right. "I promise I will. I think he's pushing his luck with me for some reason, I don't know why now, but whatever. I don't think it's that bad. I promise I'll tell you if it's otherwise."

"Okay. I'm serious though. There's something about him that's really been bothering me lately and the sooner you get out of there the better."

"Yeah, I agree. I have a shift on Sunday overnight before I start with 23 on Monday morning that I'm trying to get someone to just cover for me. If that works out, I'll only have to see him one more time maybe, if he shows up on Saturday when I'm working in the morning." I had actually decided that the money this week wasn't worth seeing him, and instead of switching shifts with other guys, I offered mine up to people that just wanted to work a little extra this week.

"Uh huh," he prompted me to continue. He knew something was up. "So, how about you 'fess up and tell me what's clearly going on in that head of yours, because it's totally obvious you have something to tell me. What's really going on with Danny at work?" he fucking knew me and although that wasn't bothering me like the Brian situation weighed me down, he knew something was up, and he knew me better than I could ever pretend to hide.

"Eh, he's just hanging around all the time now like I said, and he made some 'you're looking sexy' comment that was fairly awkward and definitely uncalled for. Other than that, I'm just riding out the rest of the week, and trying to find someone to take my shift there Sunday so I can just be done with it already." The

Danny thing nagged at me a little bit, but I really don't think he's up to anything weird or nefarious, I think he's just a dick and is using his last bit of time to make me uncomfortable.

"Did you report him to 19's Chief?" Matt asked.

"Of course not. It's not that big of a deal, and let's be honest, I've heard way worse at 23, than 'you're looking sexy' and you know it," I gave him a sideways glance. Firefighters can be raunchy at times, and while there's obviously a sexual harassment policy, more often than not, the intent was not to harass, it was just messing around.

"I don't like that guy, Jo, and I especially don't like that he's left you alone all these months since you broke up, and now he's showing up all the time, making comments. Something isn't right about it." He looked genuinely concerned.

"So far, it was one comment, and he's just 'around' all the time," I waved my hands around, "I don't think it's anything to be worried about, however I promise you that I will report in immediately if anything changes, okay?" I put my hand over my heart, and promised sarcastically. I honestly deep down was a little creeped out by Danny, but I'm sure that it's nothing. I decided not to tell Matt that I'd slapped Danny earlier.

"Alright, you better," he ordered me, then changed the subject. "So what else is on your mind, we've barely talked, and that's unusual to begin with, but you seem really distracted about something. If it's not Danny, then what is it?"

I guessed it was the time for me to confess my sins to my best friend. Just then, Summer walked up with our drinks, and took our order. We were more snackers than anything else, so we got a bunch of appetizers to share which was pretty much our standard.

"Uh, everything is alright I guess," I was definitely stalling and he looked down at me indicating that he knew there was more.

I took a deep breath, I mean I did want to 'fess up, "Okay, okay, you're right. I need to tell you something, and I really don't know where to begin, because I really don't want you to be pissed off at me, and I need your advice, but I'm one hundred percent putting you in the middle of what I would consider a situation." My eyes got big and I waited for the go ahead.

He leaned in over the table. "I know. And you're my best friend, Jo, so let's get to it, and solve whatever the problem is now. There's literally nothing you could say that would make me not love you, you're my family. So just spill it and let's fix it," he reached over, giving my hand a squeeze, signaling the go ahead.

"Alright, fuck it. Here's the deal, I slept with your brother. Okay? More than once. I did it, I'm sorry, please don't fucking hate me, it was a thing, and now it's not a thing, and I'm sorry, and I probably wasn't thinking, but now it's kind of fucked up, and I'm sorry—" I was rambling when he cut me off.

"Okay! Okay! You're sorry, I get it. Relax, Jo. *Relax*." He laughed a little. Okay, that was a good sign right? Wait, was this funny?

"This isn't funny," I scrunched my face at him. My face was hot, and I wasn't sure if I wanted to cry, or run away.

"You're right, it's not. Obviously you've been thinking about all of this a *lot*, so tell me what's going on before I even consider giving you my opinion on the matter. And before you even ask, I'm not mad exactly," now he looked stern.

I needed to just spill it, all of it. "Look, I've had a crush on your brother since I started liking boys. He was so mean to us, but I didn't care. I always had a thing for him," I started. "We kissed and had kind of a moment, and he blew me off bad last year. I'm sure that's what you're wondering about, right?" I asked. Matt never ever pressured me about what made me stop talking to Brian regularly last year. He knew something happened, but we never talked about it.

"Okay, so something happened last year, that's not a shocker since you barely spoke for a year, but what the fuck happened now?" I was borderline mortified; I couldn't even believe I was saying it out loud. I felt like Matt deserved to know, and I want his advice, but I also feel like I cheapen my 'moments' with Brian by bringing them up for discussion to his brother.

"Well what do you want to know exactly?" I was dodging for sure, but I also didn't really want to discuss the exploits in detail. I felt like he knew something and was coaxing confirmation out of me or something. "Do you know something? Did you talk to Brian about this, Matt?" I know I was sounding defensive. They were brothers, they very well may talk about this stuff, I actually have no idea. Oh, God, I hope they didn't talk about me in bed. Oh, God.

"Alright, in the interest of full disclosure, Brian told me a *little* bit of what happened. Not really any details though. And don't *you* tell me any details either, dear God, that's all I need is a visual I can't get out of my head," he rolled his eyes dramatically. "I'm more interested in where your head is at, and what is going on with you," he said.

I sighed and rolled my eyes too. So, he already knew. Ugh. "Ugh, okay great. Wonderful in fact," I put my head down, let out a huge sigh, looked back up and let it roll out, "Ok, so Brian and I had ourselves a fling if you will over the last week or so. I thought it might be something more, but it's not. And now, I'm coming back to work full-time at the station, and so that's it more or less."

"So, is it more, or is it less exactly?" he questioned me.

"Uh, it is what it was? I mean look, we can't be together. I haven't talked to him, and I'm gonna pretend that it's back to normal except for you know, that he's gonna be my boss for real now," I took a huge gulp of my drink. Maybe this going back to the station was a bad idea. I didn't know if I could look at either of them that often after this.

"So, explain to me...why can't you be together? Do you *want* to be together?"

I hesitated. The answer was yes. But it felt more complicated than that. We couldn't have a fling, and then go back to working together like nothing happened, and if he started seeing someone after me, I might die of the heartbreak.

"What did he tell you, Matt?" I was dodging the question.

"Honestly, he told me he didn't want to stop seeing you, that you ended it, not him."

"That's true. I thought it was for the best. You know that I want to stay at 23 for the foreseeable future, maybe the rest of my career, and I don't think that having a relationship with the Chief is a very professional way to do that, do you?" I asked.

"I don't really think you answered my question, Jo. I think you're dodging me," he tilted his head at me like a puppy.

"Did I want to break it off?"

"Yea, that is the question on the table."

"No. No I didn't. I've loved Brian my whole life Matt. Not like me and you, that's weird," I nervously laughed. "You and I both know how he is, and I care about working at 23 more than anything," I paused. "Look, honestly, I've been in love with Brian from the beginning; since as long as I can remember. But I know I did the right thing," I got serious, and sad. It felt so sad and so wrong to tell Matt, and not tell Brian what my real feelings were.

"So, you're in love with a man, who wanted to be with you, possibly loved you back, but since you have no idea how he felt, you think you did the right thing because of *work*? That's where we are, correct me if I've missed anything," He summed it up about right.

"Yeah, pretty much. Sounds about right," I just stared at him blankly. I didn't know what to say. I felt empty after telling him everything. He sat there in silence, making me super uncomfortable and I shifted in my seat. "What?" I finally said, frustrated. "What do you want to say? It's obvious you have something to say about all of this."

"You're both so fucking stupid." He put his face in his hands and groaned.

BRIAN

Basically, I spent that whole evening trying not to text Matt and ask him how she really felt about me, or if she said anything about me. Like a damn teenager, I paced around. I went to the gym for a little while, but I felt like shit. I spent the whole night fretting, sick to my stomach, nervous and anxious, hoping and wishing that Matt could help me fix what I should have never let get broken.

I had to work in the morning, so I thought I'd go to my office and do a little paperwork, to maybe take my mind off things for awhile. If I texted Matt, he'd be pissed at me, and while patience isn't really my thing, I thought better of irritating him, since he was technically trying to help me. I had some reports to write, and I was still going through a lot of things that Jack was working on that he hadn't finished. I needed to work on grant proposals soon, and thank God, Jack had started to teach me how to do a lot of these things over the last year or so or I'd be totally fucking lost.

It's really a lot of bullshit sometimes, and often I miss actually fighting fire. I'm not that old, and the idea of spending the rest of my career not actually getting to go in and 'do work' was frustrating. I cared very much about being a leader, but this whole thing with Jo has me thinking a lot more about what I really want in my life. If this job is the real reason she won't be with me, I'll go back to being a black hat firefighter right now, I don't need to be in charge of shit at the station if that's what it takes.

I didn't have the attention span right now to do any of this paperwork, I was just shuffling things around on my desk. I decided to just save it for tomorrow, so I wandered around the station shooting the breeze with a couple of the guys on shift before making my way out. Finally, I got a text from Matt, he was on his way home.

Yo, I just left.

And?

I replied.

You're both so fucking stupid.

Fuck you.
Are you going to tell me what happened or not?

Yea, what are you doing now?

I was just heading home

I'll meet you at your place so we can talk

Is it bad

`    I don't know, I'll meet you at your place`
`  and tell you what's up`

Ugh, I didn't know what that meant, but it didn't seem that great. We weren't really phone talkers, and Matt only lived about five blocks away, so it was usually just as easy for us to meet up in person to talk, but I didn't like the sound of this. I got in my truck and headed home. Contemplating my future without her in it just wasn't feasible. Regardless of what Matt had to tell me, I knew she had feelings for me and I was going to do whatever it took to bring us together.

It was only a ten-minute drive to my house from the station, and I had to pass Jo's house to get there. I stared at her jeep in the driveway as I rolled by, she was home now too and the light in her bedroom was on as well as the one in the living room. I wondered what she was doing, what her and Matt talked about. My mind wandered to what she might be wearing too. She was so fucking sexy, especially when she wasn't trying. She was probably wearing little shorts and a fire department t-shirt like she usually did. *Fuck, I've gotta make this right.* I flipped open the glove box to make sure the box from my mom was still in there. Safe and sound, right where I left it.

Matt was parked on the street in front of my house, he knew it irritated the shit out of me when he parked in my driveway. It was only big enough for my giant truck. I thought about how I'd either make the driveway bigger or let Jo park her Jeep there if she wanted. My God, I was so fucked for her. He hopped out of his truck as soon as I pulled in.

"So, what did she say?" I cut right to the chase. The suspense was killing me, literally.

Matt laughed. "Geez, bro, calm down."

"Honestly, dude? I can't." And really, I couldn't. I was obsessed. We walked to my front porch and sat on the steps, both of us staring out to the street. "Okay, let me have it. What's the deal?"

"Well, first of all, we need to look into this Danny more. He's making comments to her, and I think something is up."

"What do you mean, comments?" I was furious in an instant. I'll kill the motherfucker.

"She didn't really get into it and kind of blew it off, but I think something else is going on. He honestly didn't give a shit about her for months, now he's showing up on her shifts, making inappropriate remarks and shit. Something doesn't add up. She has a thick skin and all, but I think something is just off about the whole thing," he said. He looked like he was trying to figure out what it could be, and so was I. Whatever it was, I'd put a fucking end to it. An end to him. Nobody will mess with my Jo, even if she won't have me back.

"Okay, we'll pay this dickhead a visit ASAP," I said. "So, let's get to it, did she talk to you about me?"

"Yeah, Romeo, she did. Settle yourself. She fucking loves you, so calm the fuck down." The heavens opened up and released some of my pain immediately. *She loves me!* I could do a fucking Irish jig in my own front yard. I tried to restrain myself from the dancing and attempted to be cool like a cucumber, but inside, seriously, I was bursting with fucking hearts and flowers.

"Oh yeah?" Was literally all I could say. I didn't want to sound like a fucking pussy, I'd already poured my heart out twice today, once to mama and once to Matt. That's more than enough to revoke

want to be together, you should. I'm not a total heartless douchebag you know," he rolled his eyes at me. "Jo is like a sister to me, and I don't want her getting her heart fucking broken by anybody, including you. I want to protect her too, you know? And it hasn't exactly been her year."

"Alright, man, I just wanted to make sure there wasn't something else there, like maybe you had hoped things between you..." he cut me off.

"Ahhhh no. I don't feel that way about her. At all. I never did. She's basically always been one of the guys to me, and just as tough as any of them too. So you should probably watch your ass too or she'll punch you just like ol' horsey face back in third grade," he laughed at me.

I couldn't help but to laugh. When we were little, Matt was kind of scrawny, and Jo was a tomboy. Some kid was giving Matt a hard time, and little pigtailed Jo punched him right in the lip. The kid ran home to his mom, who went straight to Jack's house to confront them, it was hilarious. When Jack asked Jo why she did it, because of course she didn't deny it, she told her dad right in front of the kid and his mom that the kid was a horse-faced bully, and so she punched him in his big horse teeth to teach him a lesson. I was a little older, so I wasn't around for it, but all the other kids talked about it for years, and nobody ever messed with either one of them after that. Jack told me the whole story one day when we were shooting the breeze down at the station during a random shift. I couldn't catch my breath I was laughing so hard. Jack told me that it took everything he had in him not to laugh when it happened too. That was Jo, tough as nails, a protector, and a fighter.

Matt grew up to be tall and athletic like me, and had his own good luck with the ladies. Since he and Jo really were like two peas in a pod; it never occurred to me that he might have a thing for her until this moment. I was fucking glad he doesn't.

"Alright, as long as you know she's mine," I laughed.

"Yeah, yeah, Tarzan, I get it. Just don't fuck it up. Give her a tiny bit of space to get her bearings, and I think you might actually end up the white knight on the horse and all that shit," he started laughing at the horse reference, and then we both couldn't stop laughing like little kids again rolling around on my porch.

Jo

So, after Matt told me how stupid both Brian and I are, he proceeded to tell me that he thought that I was being a real asshole for not giving Brian a chance when it seemed like it was more than a fling to begin with. He said that I put Brian in a losing situation by making our relationship about his becoming Chief of the department instead of owning up to my own feelings. While that may be somewhat true, I sure didn't appreciate hearing it.

I admitted that I may have reacted too quickly, but that for now it was for the best because I didn't want to mix work and my personal life anymore. He didn't buy it, but said he'd leave me be about it for now, whatever that means. In any event, we basically agreed to disagree, and agreed to get together the day after tomorrow to go shooting. Another hobby we have in common is target practice. It's fun, and the local range lets all firefighters, EMTs and police officers shoot for free.

He was right. I didn't give Brian a chance, I basically made an excuse for him, his promotion, and bailed out after that. He didn't try to fight me though, and if he really loved me, he would have argued or fought back or something. He just let me go, and that's all the proof I need that his feelings aren't the same as mine. Matt didn't really know what he was talking about, he wasn't there, and frankly, he had no room to talk about feelings anyway. He was a bit of a playboy himself, running around with every blonde in town that has a thing for *hoses*. He didn't have any response for the other women comments that I made about Brian other than that I didn't give Brian a fair shake, and that was all he had to say about it.

Matt made it really clear that he didn't want to be in the middle of it, that he would not tell me exactly what Brian said, and that if I wanted to know, I had to ask him myself. That's just not happening.

When I left the bar, I told Matt I'd think about it and I apologized for putting him in the middle. I didn't want to do that, it was not my intent, but he was glad that I shared with him what was going on; at least the PG rated stuff. Now, I have two days off if Jonah, the guy that always wants extra hours takes my last shift at 19. Then, we'll see what happens. After all of this, maybe it's just better to stay friends with Brian anyway. Who was I kidding? I couldn't be friends with a man who fulfills every fantasy I've ever had in my life. *Fuck. This sucks.*

I sat at my dad's desk for a while going through his stuff when I got home. These notebooks are everywhere. My dad had some journals in his bedroom as well, but I wasn't ready to go through those, and he kept them hidden, I knew they were personal. I was tired. I was tired of thinking about Brian, tired of being angry at Danny, tired of being sad in general.

I happened upon a shoebox in my dad's bottom desk drawer and pulled it out. It looked like he was in and out of it a lot because it had worn corners, but I don't ever remember seeing it. I pulled it out and sat it on the desk, taking the lid off carefully. Inside, was a stack of envelopes, mostly a soft pink color. As I looked through them gingerly, they all had my dad's name written on them, "Jack" in lovely cursive, definitely a woman's handwriting.

Suddenly, I felt like I was snooping, and I even looked around to make sure nobody was watching. I took the box over to the couch, and opened the letter on top that was dated two weeks ago.

My Dearest Jack,

I so love that after all these years, we continue to write these beautiful letters to each other. Even though I see your sweet face grace my home often, it still tickles me each time I receive one of your letters. I look forward to seeing you on Wednesday, I've been thinking about what you said regarding telling the kids about our relationship, and you've worn me down. We'll tell them next week, and then you must get Jo to come back to the firehouse. Then the family will all be together. See you soon, sweetheart.

Love Always,
Your Catherine

I looked around again. Is this real life? It *is* real life. Brian and Matt's mom, and my dad were in a relationship? I'm not even mad, but man, am I shocked. I think we all kind of suspected it, but this was actual proof. My heart was racing, and I wanted to tell someone about this, but I didn't even know where to begin. I couldn't call Matt, this is just too crazy and it's been a rough night of talking to him. I immediately picked up my phone to call my dad, then realized I couldn't. I slumped over and felt tears forming.

My dad and I were so close; I still wasn't sure what I was going to do without him. He used to let me tag along with him no matter what he was doing my whole life. I never felt like I was in his way, and I could talk to him about anything. When I found out what was going on with Danny behind my back, I was so embarrassed, and so angry. I went to talk to my dad at his office about it and he never made me feel bad or stupid about it ever.

Jo, some people will never deserve the love that's in your heart. Don't let it stop you from loving again, he said to me.

I feel so stupid, Dad. I know it moved too quickly, and I just think I wanted to find someone. I was ready, ya know?

I had been crying and he just handed me some tissues from across his desk and kept going. *The man that deserves your heart is out there, hell you might already know him. You just keep being you. The strong, stubborn, hard worker that you are. You're just like your mother, Jo, and she'd be just as proud of you as I am. Don't let the actions of one fool change who you are.*

We lived together, Dad. What do I do now?

That seems like a silly question. You come back home.

Dad, I'm too old to come back home. I rolled my eyes at him.

You're not too old to take care of your old father. We both know I eat like shit, so you can help keep me on track while you regroup. You work too many different places, and could use some stability Jo. Maybe this is the man upstairs' way of telling you to take a breather and rethink your strategy. It's no different than on a fire sweetheart. Sometimes if something isn't working, we need to back out and figure out a new plan. So, come home and figure out a new plan.

He was kind of right. Who was I kidding, he was totally right. *Okay, Dad, thank you. It's just temporary though, while I regroup.*

Of course, just temporary. He winked at me.

No, seriously. I rolled my eyes at him again.

Oh settle down, he laughed. *Stay as long as you want. It'll be nice having you around, I absolutely hate texting you, now I can actually just talk to you.*

Seriously, Dad, you have got to get with the technology.

Yeah yeah, that's what you say. I like pen and paper best of all and I always will.

He sure did like pen and paper best of all. Between his notebooks, the journals I found in his room that I hadn't read yet, and these letters, he was a true old fashioned guy. It was actually one of the things I always loved about him, was his sense of tradition, coupled with his progressive attitude about me pursuing my goals. He was one of a kind.

I brushed my fingers over the date on the soft pink paper. This letter was sent two weeks ago. They were going to discuss telling the kids, who must be me, Brian and Matt, on Wednesday. That means that...my dad died the day before they were going to talk about all of this. Tears started rolling down my face. Over the next several hours, I sat on the floor in the living room, reading all of the letters, dated as far back as fifteen years ago, when they started writing.

There were letters that detailed their feelings, apologies for misunderstandings. These were genuine, old fashioned love letters. They were brief reminders of occasions and moments that they shared. It seemed that they had dinner together once a week, and they sometimes did other things. They enjoyed walking together out by the lake. I felt even closer to my dad after reading them.

After reading for hours, I gathered that they had been in love for years. They'd been intimate in every way. There were no details thankfully, but it was implied that they shared several overnights together over the years, and it was also clear that my dad had initiated this old fashioned tradition between them several years after my mom died, which was the sweetest thing I'd ever heard in my life.

I cried for them. I cried for their secret love that they didn't share with the world. I cried over the guilt I felt that they kept their love a secret from us kids. We'd been adults for so long, I felt ashamed that they were afraid of our reaction to it.

Then, I realized the loss that Catherine must have been feeling. I felt so terrible that she had to keep this secret that I was almost ashamed of myself. I assumed that I must have done or said something somewhere that made them feel like they had to keep a secret from me, and this brought the weight of guilt upon me. I truly would have loved for my father to find love, no matter who it was with. I've always been in love with love. The daydream of being in love always brought a smile to my face. Even just the fantasy of it as a teenager used to make me feel so enthusiastic about finding the boy I was going to marry. I didn't really remember my mom. My dad talked about her a lot, it was important to him that I knew who she was, so I knew where I came from, but I didn't miss her like I missed my dad. It was just different.

I needed to take these letters to Catherine; they belonged to her. I decided that I'd go see her the next day, I hadn't seen her since my dad's funeral, and she was the closest thing to a mom I'd ever had. She was always making us snacks, and letting us climb the trees in her yard. She used to yell at us for getting into trouble, and said we'd give her a heart attack one day with our shenanigans. Oh, man, if only she knew the shenanigans of the last week or so. I'd skip the confessions this trip, and give her the letters, she deserved to have them.

I went to bed that night feeling like I knew a part of my dad now that I didn't know even existed. But, I was also so empty inside. Sad that I didn't have someone I could talk to. Sad they felt they had to keep a secret from us. Brian would have loved to see these letters, maybe his mom will show him and Matt. That would be up to her, I feel like I've spied on something very private, and it's not my secret to reveal. And it's not like we're speaking anyway. I'd give her the letters and apologize for reading them all. Until then, I was praying for just one decent night's sleep where I didn't have the same nightmare I'd been having for days. I didn't understand it, but I'd been dreaming of Brian rescuing me from a fire. It's the same dream over and over again, and I wake up sweating and crying in the middle of the night every time.

BRIAN

Today I'm just aggravated. I'm spending my entire day trying not to think about Jo, and she's the only thing on my mind. I feel sick and weak, I kind of want to cry, and it's all because of her. How the fuck did I get here? To the place where I'm now just a pussy that couldn't have the girl. I knew she was worth it, but the waiting to take action was literally killing me.

I was driving around doing bullshit errands on my day off. I reminded myself of the plan; reaching down to my glovebox and taking out the box my mom gave me. I held it in my hands, and thought about my future. How I didn't want one without her, how every image I have of myself in the future includes her now. I also thought about how this ring, was given to my mother from Jack. It was a silver Claddagh ring, very simple, no stones. The Claddagh is a traditional Irish ring which represents love, loyalty, and friendship. It is two hands representing friendship, holding a heart for love, topped by a crown symbolizing loyalty.

I didn't ask her for details, I knew it was none of my business, but for my mom to encourage me to give it to Jo, says so much about how close she and Jack were. They were in love. I wondered why they didn't just tell us; we were all adults so it's not like we were going to be angry little kids. I'd have to ask my mom about it eventually; it really makes me sad that she felt she had to keep it from us. Jack too, he was a good man, he deserved to be happy. He was the kind of guy you would be okay with dating your mom.

As I drove around thinking about not thinking, I decided to go to the firehouse. I had an absolute shitload of paperwork to do. Normally when someone becomes Chief, there's a transition, a period of time where you work together on things and kind of do a handoff of responsibilities. That obviously didn't happen here, and it didn't seem like the district was in any big hurry to make things official one way or the other. It was frustrating to me that there had been no talk of any official announcement yet, even though they had appointed me to the position immediately two weeks ago.

Being the Chief was a lot of work, and I wasn't even sure that I really wanted the job right now. I always knew that I would eventually become Chief, it was my goal to be Chief *someday*, but it's a little early in my career to not fight fire anymore. I wasn't totally in love with being the Deputy Chief before any of this happened. The higher your rank in a mid to large sized department, the less actual fire you got to fight. The fewer accidents you worked on. You became the white hat dick at the top of the chain, and it wasn't as glamorous as many would think. People become firefighters because they want to fight fire, they want to save lives and make a difference. Nobody ever said, I can't wait to be a Fire Chief and sit behind a desk listening to other people's shit and doing budgets and schedules all day.

That didn't stop the need to submit the budget which would be due soon, and was extremely critical in terms of getting the gear and tools we needed replaced, as well as funding for some advanced training we were hoping to attend this year.

Jack had his own system, he had been the Chief for so long, I knew some of it, but certainly didn't comprehend his personal filing system, and I'm not sure what he kept electronically or not. Jack wasn't a lover of his smartphone or his computer for that matter, however he did believe that a progressive department technologically, as well as training wise was a sustainable model for a fire department, and he was committed to transitioning us to things like electronic maps in the trucks on tablets, and other 21st century treats for a department. The only way to have those things though was to include them in your budget requests, nothing is free, and budgets were consistently getting cut year over year, even though it was getting more and more expensive to maintain equipment and keep up with the ever evolving technologies.

When I pulled into the station, I saw that Jax was there. It was his day off too, so I went looking for him to see what he was up to. Jax was kind of a quiet guy, he went to high school with us, he was actually in my graduating class, but he didn't join the department until he got back from two tours with the marines. He was infantry, so he probably saw some shit, but he really never talked about it with any of us. Always cool, he never got mad at the dumb petty shit that can happen when you spend twenty-four hour clips together.

I found him in the computer room reading some stuff on the internet, not unusual for him. "Hey, man, what's happening?" I asked.

He looked up from the screen at me. "I was just reading about these new flat airpacks that allow you 'theoretically' to get in and out of a confined space more easily. I'm not convinced they're any better than what we have, and you know how I love new shit." He smiled. He really did love to ask for the newest and hottest thing in fire suppression, and it was usually really expensive too.

I laughed. "Why theoretically?"

"Well, in order to have the same amount of air that a firefighter is used to, while making the pack flat, it seems that they have elongated the whole setup. This means that anyone that isn't five foot ten or taller is going to have mobility issues with it. So, it's crap if you ask me. It looks cool though," he pointed to the screen. It did look pretty cool, but his point was valid.

"So don't ask me for it in your next wild request then, eh?" I laughed.

"No worries. I was thinking we should get a boat though," he grinned at me.

"Oh I'm sure you were. None of us even knows how to operate a boat," I rolled my eyes.

"Scotty knows how to work on anything. Just sayin', a sweet boat would be nice," he laughed at me. Thank God, he was only half serious.

"Yeah, he sure does, however the only thing we'd do with a boat is tow it in parades, so we're gonna pass on that for this year. Besides, I need to see where we stand with our current requests, and the budget for next year. That's what I'm doing here today. What brings you in on your day off besides free internet?" I questioned.

"Basically free internet. Matt and I are going to hit the gym in a little bit, then maybe go out for some drinks and look for some ladies. You should join us. You've been kind of crabby lately, man. Maybe you should get some ass," he chuckled.

The thought of any ass except Jo's turned my stomach. The

---

last thing I wanted to do was go to the local bar and pick up hose whores. All I wanted to do was to come home to her, kiss her, talk about our days, and make love—yes, make love—to her every night.

"I'm gonna pass, you two have your fun, may the odds be in your favor. I'm actually going to try to get through some of Jack's stuff and figure out what we can afford for next year before they decide to bring in some new asshole as Chief and tell all of us what they're going to give us from behind a desk," I replied.

The real fact of the matter is that the district could be taking their time because they're screening other potential Chiefs. They could decide to move someone from another station to be our Chief leaving all of us with a new boss. That would suck, mostly because we have such a great team, and a great camaraderie, a stranger would really put a kink in that. Even if I wasn't sure what I wanted to do in terms of my own career advancement, it was better for my guys, and our team if I did the work now without ruffling feathers, and then figured out what I wanted to do myself along the way.

"Your loss. It's ladies' night at the Yard." He went back to reading.

"Have a good time. I'll catch you later," I left and went back to my office.

I sat down at Jack's desk, my desk I guess, and turned the computer on. I hadn't really had much of a chance to get into the meat and potatoes of the job with everything that had been going on the last two weeks. I started looking through the budget requests for the upcoming year, as well as the expenditures from last year. I already wanted a drink.

Jax needed new gear, his was old and worn, so that was a must in the budget. We already purchased the tablets last year, so we were going to have to get the software that goes on them. It basically told you all of the hydrants and other pertinent information in a location when a call comes in. It's synced to the paging system, so it already knows the address of the call you're going to, and this enables the officer in the truck to assist the driver in proper truck placement by hydrants or whatever they may need for a particular call. In the old days, you either had to know already, or you had to look for it when you got there, which takes time. Maybe a few minutes, but a few minutes could save lives. That was definitely going to go in for the upcoming year.

I mulled over some call reports that needed a signature on them. It was our policy to have a senior officer or the Chief review all call reports to ensure they were accurate. After about an hour of that, I was done reviewing the ones that still needed a signature. I closed them up, and decided to poke around on the computer to see what kind of electronic filing system Jack had, if any.

An icon in the lower left corner lit up awhile ago, it was a message that looked like it was synced from someplace else. I opened it, and it was Jack's text messages, they started popping up from the last two weeks. As I watched it load, I saw messages from myself, from Jo and from several others all pop up. Most of them were over two weeks old of course, but there were several from one number that wasn't programmed in as a contact, and it seemed like they didn't know that Jack had died.

I read through the messages from the unknown number.

```
Jack—I think you're right, there is
definitely racketeering going on, we need to
get a file on this with the evidence you have
and then build a case
```

`Where are you? We need to get together.`

`Are you getting my messages?`

`Shit,    why    aren't    you    replying,    is`
`everything okay?`

Then they stopped. They were all from about a week ago, one week after Jack died.

Jack found out there was some type of racketeering? He had evidence to support this too? Who was he talking to about this? I stared at the screen for awhile before deciding that I had to get in touch with the person on the other end.

Nobody ever thinks of their parents as anything other than parents until they're confronted with it. I knew for me, my dad was my dad, and he was the fire Chief. He was my friend and my confidant and advisor too, but I didn't really remember him as a husband to my mother. He was a friend to a lot of people, but since they were all mostly fire and emergency services people, it almost didn't even count, because it was still kind of work related.

Realizing that my dad had a relationship with Mrs. Cavanaugh, Catherine, was a real revelation for me. I decided not to call before making my way over to her place, I didn't really know what to say I thought that swinging by would be better. I grabbed the box of letters, looked at them one more time quickly, and packed them and myself up for the short trip over to her place.

She still lived in the same house the boys grew up in, and I'd always loved it there. They had a huge climbing tree in their front yard just like my dad's, and Matt and I used to basically just sit in the tree planning out our lives. We didn't need a tree house, just a good solid branch. Brian would join us once in a while when we were really young, but when we became teenagers, he was off doing his own thing. God, I missed him. I missed his touch. I missed the way he took control. He made me feel like I didn't have to worry about anything; he was so strong and assured. He felt like home.

I needed to get a move on, it was already noon. I had spent most of my morning lazily re-reading the letters I was about to give over, and thinking about what I'd say to Mrs. Cavanaugh. It was time to get to it. She deserved these letters.

I pulled up in her driveway, and her front door was opened, leaving the screen door to the porch open. My Jeep isn't exactly super quiet, so she probably heard me coming, since she came out to the porch when I pulled into the driveway. She started waving immediately, and looked happy to see me. She was so pretty, she had her red hair, which had started to gray over the years, up in a cute loose bun, and she always wore a dress. Always. She was no nonsense, but she was also very feminine.

"Well, Josephine! How lovely to see you!" she called out.

"Hi, Mrs. Cavanaugh, I hope this is an alright time to just show up?"

"I've told you one hundred times, love, it's Catherine," she scolded me.

"I'm sorry, Catherine. I hope it's okay I just showed up without calling?" I asked.

"Of course it is, love. Come on in, let me put on some tea for us and you can tell me what brings you by, sweetheart." She was so warm and inviting all the time. I really loved her as much as I would my own mom.

"Thank you," I made my way into her sitting room, which was just for adults and looked around, waiting to see where she wanted me to go.

She looked at me standing there, holding the box and laughed. "Sit, sit, my dear. You're a grown up now, you can sit in here," she chuckled on her way to the kitchen to make us tea. I wasn't a huge fan of tea unless it's iced tea, but whatever she wants. The visit was feeling pretty awkward. I sat on the flowered sofa and looked around at the pictures of Matt and Brian, and a few of all of us doing a variety of things through our adolescence. We were some real goofballs back in the day. There was one picture of all of us making smiles with orange peels in our mouths that made me laugh out loud. That was definitely taken when we were playing soccer together on the Police Athletic League team. Since Brian was three years older than us, it was one of the rare times that our age difference put us all on the same team which was so much fun. Matt and Brian were always close, they never fought as brothers at all, and actually played really well together, much like they did at work as well. My dad and Catherine would come to our games and yell from the sidelines. I don't know if it's the Irish in her, but Catherine got yellow carded for screaming from the sidelines more than once. You'd never know that about her because she's so soft spoken usually, but man did she love some soccer, and she loved calling out the referees on what she felt were bad calls. I would have been so embarrassed, but the boys loved it, they always thought it was the funniest thing, and she'd have to go wait in the car for the rest of those games

"Oh, that picture makes me smile every single day, Josephine," she smiled at me and handed me an iced tea. She knew me.

"Thank you so much," I took the tea. "We were so silly back then," I said, drifting off into memories of what felt like one hundred years ago.

"It wasn't all that long ago you three were getting into trouble all the time," she laughed. "So what brings you by, dear? What's in the box?" She gestured to the shoebox I had placed on the coffee table in front of me.

I took a deep breath. "Well, I was going through some of my dad's things last night, and I found something that I think belongs to you." She was watching me, small lines forming around her lips and eyes as she smiled. I suspected she knew exactly what was in the box.

"I knew you'd come eventually, I just didn't think it would be so soon." She took my hand in hers. "I loved your father very much, Josephine, he was a very good man." She smiled sweetly, tears filling her bright green eyes. She and Brian had the same beautiful green eyes, I couldn't take my eyes off of them. "I'm sure you knew that already though, love." She paused. "Before you begin, let me tell you a little bit about your parents, and the side of your father that I came to know, and then you can share with me, okay?"

"Okay, yes please," I started to sniffle a little bit. I had a tendency normally to simply just not be soft, I'm not sure why. Maybe it was spending so much time with boys my whole life, but I didn't talk about my feelings much, and I didn't like acknowledging them, but being here with Catherine, about to hear about a side of my dad I didn't really know, gave me butterflies.

"I know you didn't know your mother very well, you were so young when she got sick, and you stayed with us quite a bit when your father was trying to take care of her, do you remember that?" she asked me.

"I remember that a little bit. I mostly just remember hanging out here with you and the boys a lot more than anything. I don't remember very much about my mom to be totally honest. My dad told me about her sometimes. He said he wanted me to know who she was, and said that I reminded him of her sometimes."

"Well, he was right, dear. You certainly look just like your mom, she was beautiful and you two have the same smile. You know that she was my friend, and she was a very loving person. She and I became good friends after we met in the hospital when we had you and Matt. She became sick soon after you were born though, and spent several years trying to get well again before the doctors realized what was wrong, and by then it was just too late to help her. Your father's job became to make her comfortable more than anything else. At the same time, my husband left me and the boys, and I developed a friendship with your father as we joined forces to take care of your mom and you little ones.

Your mother asked me to look after you and your father when she knew that her time on this earth was coming to an end. It was heartbreaking for all of us, but she knew that you would be raised in that firehouse, and she wanted you to have a woman in your life that you could come to when you needed, and I gladly offered to do whatever I could before she ever asked. It was shortly after your mom passed away that your father and I became closer. First, we shared our grief together, and then the challenges of raising you kids." She smiled as she was thinking about some memory. I'm sure the three of us were a handful back then, hell we were kind of a handful as adults too. I stayed quiet and hung on every word as she recalled the past I knew nothing about.

"One day, when you and Matt were about four years old, and Brian was seven, your father stopped by to see me, and he didn't have you with him, but he had flowers that he had clearly picked somewhere. When I asked him where you were, he said that you were at your Aunt Molly's house for the weekend, and that he had come just to see me. It was at that moment, that I fell in love with your father. He had come just to visit with me, and brought me those beautiful flowers. The boys were out back playing, and we sat on my front porch talking about where our lives had ended up and what we wanted for you kids, and for ourselves.

After that day, we began to have a romantic relationship. Don't worry, I won't go into details with you, but I want you to know that I never felt a love for anyone in my life like I did for Jack. He was my soulmate. He gave me a scanner so that I could listen to calls because I worried about all of you, and he taught me about what you do. Your father was a gentleman, Josephine, he was everything I hoped for my boys to become; kind and gentle, but tough when he needed to be. He showed me a love I never thought truly existed, and we shared our lives together quietly, because that's what felt right for us. When your father died, I too lost a piece of my heart, sweetheart." Those beautiful green eyes of hers started to fill with tears, tearing me up inside.

I felt my chest tighten, and tears started to fall from my eyes. "I'm sorry, I read all of them, Mrs. Cavanaugh. I feel like there's a whole part of my dad I didn't even know and I feel so awful you had this wonderful love between you and that you felt like you had to keep it a secret..." I trailed off and started really crying.

She leaned over and scooped me into a huge hug. "First of all, you call me, Catherine. And second of all, don't you dare feel bad. It was a choice that we made as adults, and we were quite comfortable with it over the years. Our relationship was unique, and we liked it that way, so don't for one minute feel like you kept us from anything." She comforted me like only a mother could, stroking my back and squeezing me in that hug. Some people give weak hugs like they can't wait for it to be over, not Catherine, she was all about a good hug, and I loved every moment of it.

I pulled away to wipe the tears from my face, and she smiled at me. "Shall we have a real drink and talk, Miss Josephine? I want to answer any questions that you have," she stood up and walked across the room to grab some tissues for me.

I laughed a little through my tears. "Okay, that sounds good." I took the tissues from her, and she turned back to go to the liquor cabinet, and poured us both some whiskey. She handed me one, and then walked over to a curio cabinet in the sitting room, and opened a drawer. She pulled out a beautiful round hat box with flowers all over it, and brought it, and her drink over to the couch.

Setting the large hatbox down next to the shoe box I brought, she said, "These are the letters your father wrote to me over the years, Jo. You are more than welcome to read them if you'd like. It may give you an understanding of who your father was besides the Chief, and your dad of course. He was a deep and loving man, who loved you more than anything in the world, and was always so worried whether or not he was doing what was best for you."

I dabbed at my eyes and my runny nose and looked up at her. "Are you sure? These are private, you don't have to let me read them," I felt like I was ten years old suddenly, and I didn't want to hurt her feelings or intrude any further than I already had.

"I'm quite sure. Now you sit and read, and I'm going to make us some lunch and then we can talk about anything you would like, okay?" She stood up.

"Okay, thank you so much." She smiled at me and reached over to squeeze my shoulder gently, and then made her way into the kitchen.

I opened the box and looked at the stack of letters, and took the one off of the top, touching the corners of it. You could tell it wasn't that old, the paper was bright white, and I recognized the handwriting on it as my dad's. I'd seen him write a million reports, and he was always writing in his notebooks or journals, so I'd know it anywhere. On the outside of the envelope, it simply said "Catherine" in his unmistakable penmanship.

I opened the envelope and pulled out the small piece of folded paper. It was dated about two and a half weeks ago.

Dearest Catherine,

I'm so excited to tell the children, I hope they won't be angry we've kept this secret for so long. At the time it seemed like the right thing to do, and then it was our special thing that was just for us, like a vacation from the craziness of everyday life. I love those boys of yours as if they were my own, and Josephine already looks to you as a mother figure, and for that I cannot ever express my gratitude.

You've meant so much to me all of these years, and shouting it from the rooftops doesn't begin to be a big enough celebration of our future together.

Love you always,

Jack

I smiled and put the letter back in the envelope and sighed. It was really sweet that he had someone, and in all honesty, I loved Catherine. You had to love her, she was the sweetest lady on earth, and she was also a good mother. She was always laughing with us, but also didn't take our shit either.

I pulled another letter out and opened it. They all looked pretty much the same, plain white envelopes, with Catherine's name on the outside, and the notes were written on plain white, unruled paper.

Dearest Catherine,

I know we talked about it, but I still wanted to send a note apologizing for canceling our dinner plans the other night. I look forward to seeing you always, and I don't like it when work interferes with seeing you. Soon, I'll be able to retire, and we can sit on the porch together and not worry about these things. You are my heart, my mo chroi (I Googled it to make sure I got the spelling right, are you impressed?) I love that you teach me so much, my heart is full.

I'll see you soon.
Love you always,
Jack

I giggled at that one. My dad really had a love hate relationship with technology. I considered it a big deal for him to Google something for a love letter. I read the rest of the letters, which were mostly summaries of how he felt about different things they did together, and about future plans. He talked about going to the beach with Catherine, she went with him fishing one time which shocks me, but apparently they had a lovely time not catching anything at all.

Another one detailed how much my dad loved going to a flower show with her. My dad at a flower show, now that's a sight I would liked to have seen. Apparently, they had a fantastic time smelling the roses, and they picked up a bunch of things that he planted for her here at her house. I saw Catherine peek out at me from the kitchen a couple of times to see how I was. When I was finished reading all of them, I relaxed and smiled. I felt happy, and relieved that my father had love in his life.

I got up and walked into the kitchen and without saying a word just hugged her from behind. She had been at the kitchen counter doing something, and I just couldn't hold back. She turned around and hugged me back.

"Are you okay, dear?" she asked me while we stayed in each other's embrace.

"I'm better than okay, Catherine. It makes me so happy to know how happy my dad was," I released her and stepped back. "I used to worry so much about him, and thought he spent way too much time worrying about what I was doing, or making his whole life about the fire department. I'm honestly bursting with joy that he had all of these wonderful experiences with you over the years. I just wish that we could have shared it together, that part makes me sad."

"Don't be sad, Josephine, to be honest, we talked about that a lot over the years, as I'm sure you gathered from the letters. At first, we just didn't want to complicate your lives, and then later on we kind of enjoyed our little secret. It was an escape for us. I'm sorry that you had to find out the way that you did, you know your father was going to tell you but then..." she trailed off.

She turned around to finish making us sandwiches, and continued talking while I sat down at the kitchen table to listen. "We can't change the past, but we can certainly make the most of the days that we have here with our loved ones. Your father knew that, and he knew that you would eventually find your way as well."

"Did he talk to you about me?"

"Of course he did! He would have been so happy that you are returning to the station, even though he's not here to see it." She said as she put a plate down in front of me. She set one down for herself as well, and sat across from me.

I smiled. "Did Matt tell you I was coming back?"

"Actually, no," she smirked at me. "Brian was here the other day, and he told me all about it."

"Oh he did?" I tried not to look as guilty or annoyed as I felt.

"Yes, he did. I understand you two had a bit of a falling out the other day. He was quite upset about it," she was definitely egging me on now. I didn't want to take the bait, but I was dying to know what he said. *So, he was upset?*

"Hmm, well you could say that. He asked me to come back to the station, but then he was kind of a jerk to me when we went out on a call together the same day. I'm still going to come back though, I belong there. I wish my dad was here to see it." I didn't want to say anything bad about her son to her, and honestly, I wished things were different anyway. If I could be with him, I would.

"Yes, he said that you two had become close and that his behavior pushed you away. Does that sound about right?" She leaned back in her seat looking at me over her glasses now, and I was getting anxious. Did he tell her what we were doing? Oh, my God, this is getting embarrassing.

"Uh, yeah sort of," I hesitated. I really didn't want to talk about this with her or anyone else.

She could sense I was in flight mode. "Jo, those boys of mine both love you like their own family. Sometimes they don't know how to tell us women how they really feel, but what they lack in communication, they make up for in their loyalty. I'm sure you two will sort it out just fine," she smiled at me again. She totally knew.

"Well Matt and I have always been tight. It's always been a different situation with Brian. It'll be fine though, we're all working together day after tomorrow. I don't know what he told you, but I'm not mad or anything. We just clash a lot, we kind of always have, we don't see eye to eye on a lot of things," I sighed a little bit. That was the best way that I could think of to summarize the situation without being blunt. I was still mad at him, and missed him at the same damn time.

"Well my dear, Irish boys are very strong willed, often to a fault. My boys, all of them," she smiled, she was including my dad in that statement, "have always wanted to protect you, whether you needed it or not. And us strong Irish lassies, just kind of have to remind them who they're dealing with," she smirked at me and had a fire in her eyes reminding me of how tough she could be if she wanted to, she just rarely needed to. Catherine had many layers, and it was so easy to see why my father fell for her.

"I'm so glad I came to see you today, Catherine. I hope this doesn't sound out of place, but you know I'm always one of the guys, and generally, I totally like it that way, but lately, I've really felt like I needed a mom, and you've always been the next best thing and I don't think I ever really expressed how much it has meant to me. I can't thank you enough," I reached across the table to take her hand in mine.

She squeezed my hand. "I'm always here for you," she rose and picked up our dishes, taking them over to the sink. I stood up, as it was time for me to go. I needed to take care of a few things and truthfully, this was an emotional afternoon.

"Thank you for lunch today. And thank you for letting me see your letters, I know how personal they are."

"You are most welcome, dear. You deserve to know the whole man that your father was, and I loved him very much, just as I love you. Those boys of mine both love you too you know. We're all family in our own special way." She hugged me tight again. I would definitely be coming back here for hug fixes when I needed them.

"I know they do. Hopefully, after we've been working together again for awhile, Brian and I will be able to get along better," I said as I moved toward the door.

"Josephine," she stopped me as I was walking out. "I'm not one to interfere..."

I laughed. "Why do I feel a but is coming?"

"Because you're a smart girl. I promise you that I don't know everything, but I know that Brian feels awful about how things transpired this week with you. I think he cares for you far more than you know, perhaps you'll give him a chance to explain himself when you're ready," she gave me a pleading smile with that sweet face of hers.

"I will, I promise," and I hugged her again and made my way out.

I thought about what she said; give him a chance to explain. He had a chance, it's not like I denied him the opportunity; he never took it. He still hasn't taken it. There's a shelf life on everything, and I'm not going to pine away for him, even though just the thought of him near me gives me chills, in a very naughty way.

BRIAN

I decided to text the phone number back from Jack's computer so that I'd get a reply.

I wasn't sure what to say, so I started with:

Jack passed away, I'm a friend that can help.

And I waited for a reply.

Almost immediately a reply came through.

I know about Jack. Who is this?

A friend of Jack's. I think I can help you.

Can you meet in person? I'll decide if you can help.

Yes, where?

Meet me at the Brewhouse downtown in one hour. Ask for Izzy. Someone will let me know.

Okay, one hour.

This was extremely strange. But I felt like if Jack was helping with some kind of an investigation, it was my duty to help see it through if I could. I wrapped up a few things, and made my way out to my truck. I was familiar with the Brewhouse downtown; it was someplace I've been to several times. A lot of cops hang out there, which in this moment, I was very grateful for since I didn't know what I was getting into exactly.

I drove past the Brewhouse, it didn't have it's own parking lot, so I had to park about three blocks away in a garage. There just wasn't any parking closer that would accommodate my truck. I didn't take the Chief's truck, in fact, I tried not to drive it on my days off anyway, it was just so conspicuous. I really didn't want anyone thinking I was out and about doing personal business in a department vehicle. Sometimes it was a pain in the ass to switch out, but integrity still mattered, and I really didn't know what I was getting myself into.

I walked into the place, it was actually pretty crowded, it was a Friday night, so I'm not really that surprised. I walked over to the bar and waited for a bartender to come my way.

A young guy, probably in his twenties came over. "What can I get you, man?"

"I'm actually looking for Izzy," I gave him a questioning look. He took a step back, looked me up and down and laughed. I don't know what that was about, but I don't like this.

"She's over there in that booth drinking a martini, watch yourself," he said.

"I'll take a Guinness with me," I said. He nodded and walked away to get it for me. I couldn't see this Izzy from where I was standing, the booth was in the back corner of the joint. The bartender brought me my beer, I paid, and made my way to the back of the bar.

"You Izzy?" I asked upon arrival.

A little tan-skinned girl with light eyes pointed to the seat across from her. "Yes, have a seat."

I sat down across from her, with my back to the door, which I absolutely hate. It made me feel trapped to not be able to see an exit wherever I'm at, so I was immediately uncomfortable.

"So, you knew Jack?" I wanted to disrupt the silence hanging over us.

"I did. And I suspect you did as well, since you texted me from his phone?" she asked.

"I actually texted you from his computer, he must have had it synced to his phone."

"Interesting. I wasn't aware that was possible, I'll have to keep that in mind. So you are?" she asked.

"I'm Deputy—eh Chief Brian Cavanaugh, of Fire District 23. I've known Jack most of my life, he was like a father to me. I was appointed to his position after his passing, which is how I happened upon your number," I was going to just be straight here. I didn't have anything to lose.

"Well, I'm Detective Isabel Cruise. You may know my sister, June, she's a paramedic," she held her hand out for me to shake.

Taking her hand, I took note of how petite she was. She was awfully pretty and tiny to be a detective. Not my type, because I'm still heartsick over Jo, however she's really pretty for a cop. "Nice to meet you," I said. "I do know your sister, she's a good medic, and often partners with a good friend of mine," I added.

"Yes, Josephine Meadows. I know who she is." That made me uncomfortable, and I started to feel defensive.

"So, let's cut to the chase here. You were working with Jack on something, and he was gathering evidence for you to build a case against someone who was clearly bribing or doing something dirty, correct?" I wanted to get to the point.

"Okay, sure, let's get to it. You seem like you have the best interests of the department in mind. Jack figured out that someone freelancing was essentially strong arming businesses into paying a little extra for a passing fire inspections when they didn't have passing standards."

I stared at her. So, basically someone was giving passing inspections to people who didn't deserve them. That puts lives at risk, and I felt my blood boiling about it. If someone was extorting money from businesses, they were unlikely to stop there.

"Okay, so how can I help?" I asked and took a sip of my beer.

She ran her fingers through her long dark hair and looked me in the eye. "Jack had evidence somewhere, but he died before he could get it to me. Someone has been extorting money from businesses all across town for at least two years. I need access to Jack's files, or I need you to look through his files and find the evidence so I can build a case against this guy."

"Do you know who it is?" I asked.

"Yes. You familiar with a Danny Russell?"

I immediately rolled my eyes and clenched my fists. That motherfucker was probably using Jo all along. I was gonna kill that fucking guy.

"So that's a yes," she glared at me.

"Yeah, I know him. He's a piece of shit. I'm not even a little bit surprised he had something to do with anything unsavory." I was furious at the revelation he might have been playing Jo.

"Jack said the same thing," she replied, and took a small sip of her clear martini. She was awfully small and good-looking for a detective. If I wasn't so into Jo, I'd definitely have some inappropriate thoughts about her, but right now all I could think about was pounding this motherfucker's face in. Anything I could do to ruin him, and I'm in.

"Yeah, that doesn't surprise me. Apparently, he was dating Jack's daughter for awhile. I've been watching her to see if she's involved," she said.

"Yea, she's not," I said curtly.

"Are you here for the greater good, or do you have some kind of thing for this girl?"

"That's none of your business, *detective*," Who does she think she is?

"If she was involved it is my business," she gave me a nasty challenging glare.

"If you were working with Jack, you already know she has nothing to do with this. Do you want my help to bring this dickhead down, or are we just going to banter all night, because I have plenty of other shit to do besides sit in this dive wasting my time with a cop," I wasn't going to take this chick's shit.

"Settle down, Romeo, you're right. I already know she has nothing to do with it, but I wanted to test you a little bit," she waved her hands for me to chill out.

"Okay, so where did you stand when Jack died? I have access to most of his folders, and shit. The rest of his information he kept in notebooks, he was always writing stuff down in them, but they're at Jo's house and I don't have easy access to them without saying something to her about it if she hasn't already read it for herself," which worried me. Jo could be a loose cannon, and was definitely not the first person who would reach out for help if she knew some kind of shit like this was going on. God, I hoped she hadn't figured this out for herself.

"I'm not sure where he kept his files to be honest, he said that he had gathered some witnesses that would testify that Russell had coerced them into paying him to sign bullshit documents giving them shortcuts. I gave him permission to promise immunity for their testimony, per my DA, however now I don't know who they are because he hadn't turned the evidence over to me yet, he kept saying he could get more, and he wanted to see if he could get Russell to confess first."

I ran my hands through my hair, sighing, and taking it all in. I can't believe that Jack kept all of this from me, but I also totally understand it too. He would never put any of us in a situation like this if he could avoid it, and clearly he thought he had this under control.

"Okay, well I can tell you that dickhead won't confess to me, even if he might have to Jack. He might tell Jo something, but I doubt it, and if Jack didn't want her involved, I want her involved even less. I don't get along with him at all and I want him as far away from her as possible," I was just going to put it out there before it ever became a question.

"Yeah, I know all about you. I heard about you grabbing him at Jack's funeral," she smirked at me. The sassy little detective had some balls.

"He fucking grabbed her at her own father's funeral, so yeah, I manhandled him, and I'd do it again," I was getting pissed off just thinking about it, and I waved for the waitress to bring us two more drinks. "What else is it that you *know*?"

"I know that Jack assumed you were going to look after his daughter," she said.

"He told you that?" I was shocked, but filled with pride and also feeling a little defensive and vulnerable. Jack told her all of this?

"Yes, he did actually. He said that you and your brother would look after Jo no matter what happened, and he was not going to let Danny continue to get away with the extortion." She was very matter-of-fact, and almost expressionless. She was a hard one to read, maybe it came with the job. She seemed awfully young to be a detective.

"Interesting. Well, that's true. Jack knew us, and he was like a father to us our whole lives basically," I wanted to change the subject. It was all still too raw, and I just wanted to be with Jo now that we were discussing her dad like this. "So, you need me to go through Jack's shit basically?"

"Yea, more or less, he was certain he had the evidence, so I need you to find whatever that is. I didn't know that he passed away until a few days after it happened and I'd been trying to reach him. Do you think by any chance that his death was anything other than an unfortunate situation?" she asked me seriously.

I felt like the wind got knocked out of me. "Are you asking me if I think Russell killed Jack?"

"I'm asking you if you think it's possible," her brown eyes were like lasers right now.

"It never occurred to me, but I don't think so, I just don't know. He wasn't a young guy, and he'd been on the job a long time. I think the stress may have gotten to him, but he died on scene, I tried giving him CPR myself. There didn't seem to be any foul play, it was more like thirty years of being a firefighter and dealing with that than anything else," I thought back over the last several months and wondered if I was right. Honestly, I think that it was natural causes, but really, what do I know. It would kill Jo if something more sinister had happened to her dad, especially if that douchebag was behind it. I silently prayed I was right, and that it was natural causes and years of working a stressful job that took him from us.

"I didn't really think so either, but it's something to keep in the back of your mind while you look for whatever he had found. I don't know how he kept it, we had talked about files, but I don't know if they were electronic, or paper, or what. So what I need is for you to find that out. And you cannot tell *anyone* until this gets blown open." She was very serious now.

"Are you sure nobody was helping Jack get the evidence?" I asked.

"I'm very sure. In fact, he's the one that reached out to me when he figured out what was going on. I'm not even sure that this Russell character is on to it yet. Which is good, because then I have the element of surprise when it's time to take him down," her eyes were even more serious now.

"I'll get on his computer tomorrow and see what I can find. He was getting better and better at technology, even though he hated it, so maybe something is stored there. If it's paper, I'm going to have to talk to Jo, because all of his notebooks are at home, he didn't keep them at work," I told her. I really didn't like the idea of involving Jo in this. She was going to be so upset no matter what, and if I asked for the notebooks without telling her what's going on, and before I get the chance to implement Operation MJM, I'd never be able to explain it.

Isabel and I were leaned in across from each other in the booth when I saw Jax and my brother walk into the bar out of the corner of my eye. Fuck. I don't want them seeing me with her, and I can't explain what I'm doing here yet. Hopefully they didn't see me.

Awww fuck. Matt walked up with Jax by his side. "Well hello, big brother, whatcha doing over here in the corner of a bar with this lovely young lady," he motioned to Cruise. "I thought you had some other things you were *sorting out.*" he said nastily.

"I'm actually here discussing business if you must know," I tried to explain without saying too much. Detective Cruise just watched the exchange and smirked.

"Oh business, that's what they're calling it now?" Matt gave a sarcastic chuckle. "Well this isn't going to get you what you say you're looking for." I sighed and dropped my head, when Cruise stepped in.

"Hi boys, I'm Detective Cruise, with the 23rd precinct. I was just discussing an ongoing investigation that I need some help from the fire department with," she smiled kindly at them both, and Matt wasn't buying it.

"Oh, a detective eh? What do they have a junior program now?" He was being an asshole, and I couldn't stop it.

"I'm older than I look, sunshine, and I don't have to explain anything to you," she stood up to leave, and looked over at me. "You know what I need, I'll wait to hear from you." She walked out of the bar, leaving me with an angry Matt and a completely clueless Jax standing there staring at me.

"Well she was fucking hot, dude," Jax chimed in. I buried my face in my hands, this was the last thing I needed right now.

"Yeah, she sure was. Not at all what I'd expect you to go after these days," Matt glared at me.

"It's not what it looked like Matt, you know how I feel," was all I could say.

"Oh really, do I? Because it looked like you were out in secret with some hot little Latina chick when you told me you had eyes for someone else," he said right in front of Jax.

"Are we talking about Jojo? We're talking about Jojo, aren't we...?" Jax asked the question with a childish grin. *Fuck, of course he asked.*

"I'm not explaining myself to either one of you right now," I got up to leave. "Matt, I need you to trust me, I cannot tell you what's going on, but I promise in a couple days I will. Nothing has changed from our previous discussion. You have to trust me." I repeated. I couldn't get him and Jax involved in this, there's just no way. Until I found out more information, I didn't want anyone else involved.

"I feel really out of the loop, but that chick was fucking hot. So, if you're not doing her, is she up for grabs?" Jax asked. I rolled my eyes.

"Dude, whatever you want. I gotta go," I was still standing there trying to leave, but I really needed Matt to acknowledge that he trusts me. "Matt, can you just trust me here?" I was pleading to him.

"Yeah whatever. You know where I stand, and if you're fucking around, I'm not going to stand for it and I'm definitely not going to help you," he said. Jax had to know what he was talking about but he didn't say anything else, and thankfully we just ignored his Jo comment earlier and he didn't press on it.

"I get it, bro. Look, I need to leave, I have to take care of some things tonight. You two have fun, and please for the love of God, stay out of trouble," I wasn't even kidding. The two of them often found themselves in some precarious situations when they went out. "And both of you," I motioned to Jax who was pretending not to be there by looking everywhere except Matt and I. "Need to keep this exchange to yourselves. It's important, and I can't tell you why, so don't fucking ask."

"Fine, whatever, settle yourself, Chief," Jax put his hands up in defense.

"Yea, fine. I'll call you tomorrow," Matt said.

"Ok cool. Are you still hanging out with Jo tomorrow?" I asked.

"Yea, we're going shooting. So, you should stay away," he laughed.

I rolled my eyes. "Just don't tell her about seeing me here tonight." I leaned in so Jax wouldn't hear. "It's important, I'm serious." I gripped his shoulder and looked him in the eyes. "This is really serious, Matt."

He stopped the smirk and laughing, and acknowledged my seriousness. "Are you sure everything is okay?" I sighed.

"It will be. I promise I'll fill you in as soon as I can. A couple days, tops."

"Okay." He looked concerned, but I honestly couldn't tell him what was going on.

"Alright, I'll catch you guys later, I really gotta roll," I tossed some money on the table and made my way out of the bar.

I couldn't believe that motherfucker, Danny Russell was taking bribes to pass inspections, and God knows what else. I wondered how Jack figured it out; how long he knew? Was Jo still dating that piece of shit when he uncovered this? She was going to be so fucking pissed off when she found all of this out.

It was too late to go back to the station tonight. I'd go through his computer the next day with a fine-toothed comb. I felt like if he was texting Detective Cruise, he was more comfortable with technology than he let on to us. There had so be something in his files that would bring this guy down, and I was going to find it.

Jo

I woke up the next morning with mixed emotions. I was happy I'd spent the day with Catherine, and that we'd talked, but I was still missing Brian so much. She obviously knew something was up, I wondered what he told her. Clearly he told her enough that she wanted me to give him a chance to explain himself. Honestly, there wasn't much to explain. He didn't fight for me, and that's probably because he doesn't want to be exclusive, like he said a year ago. And of course the working together thing, and him being my boss can't be explained away either. It happened, and we can't go back now, so the only thing to do is just put my mind on the job and hope that the longing for him subsides someday.

I had plans with Matt for the day, but I honestly didn't feel like doing anything at all. All this talk of love was just making me cranky. I wanted to avoid seeing any of them until work, but that's not how big girls deal with real life I guess. I decided that I'd try to get myself motivated by going for a run. I grabbed my phone and some ear buds, and made my way out of the house.

As I rocked out to some of my favorite music, I let the thoughts of my suffering heart float away for awhile. I was going to need to let go of all of this at some point, before I turned into some kind of a spinster. Once I'm on a normal schedule at 23 I can start thinking about how to move on and what my next moves are. While ending up at my dad's station again is important to me, it can't be my whole life either. I need to figure out what I'm doing.

I ran through town, and decided to stop at the station to get a drink of water before running back home. It was only a couple miles, and it made for a great halfway point so I didn't have to carry a water with me. As I approached, I saw that Brian's truck was there. *It's his day off. Maybe he won't see me.* Maybe I'd say hi and just show that we can be friends and that it's no big deal. Yeah, who was I kidding? I'm standing here in front of the firehouse getting turned on at the thought of saying hello to him. My body betrays me at just the thought of him.

I wanted to be close to him and I couldn't stop myself from walking toward his office, after I grabbed myself a water from the fridge in the kitchen. I held the cool bottle to the side of my face in an attempt to lower my body temperature from the run, and from the anxiety of seeing him. His office door was open, and he was intently staring at the computer screen. As I scanned him quickly, I couldn't help but get distracted by his delicious biceps and broad shoulders. I quietly knocked on the open door and his beautiful green eyes met mine instantly.

I forgot to speak, I was lost in his gaze.

"Jo, is everything okay?" he asked.

"Oh yeah. Yeah. I saw your truck was here, so I thought I would stop in and say hello. I'm sorry, I didn't mean to interrupt you," I started to retreat and he stood up immediately.

"You're not interrupting me, stop. Come in and sit down for a minute," he motioned to the couch and came out from behind his desk. The couch he'd ravaged me on just a few days ago. He was wearing jeans and a white t-shirt that was tight in all the right places, showcasing his muscles, and highlighting the colorful tattoos on his arms. My heart was beating out of my chest, I was certain he could see it.

"I, uh, I can't stay long, I'm on a run and was just stopping for a drink," my words say one thing, but my body still walked over to the couch, where he met me and we both sat down. I felt a magnetic pull to him that I simply couldn't control or explain anymore.

"You look amazing, Jo," he said softly.

I felt myself blushing and looked down to break our locked stare. "Thank you," I whispered. I was sweaty, dirty, and in the middle of a workout, he's crazy and I loved it. I can feel myself getting pulled into him, fighting it is impossible, it's magnetic. I was literally quivering, and the feelings I was having were so carnal. I wanted to crawl all over him right now.

He reached over and raised my face up to meet his. "Look at me." His touch was still like lightening rushing through my veins, nothing had changed. I met his eyes with mine, I still couldn't speak, I was in a trance. His eyes were scanning my face, he was looking for something and I gave him a shy smile.

I felt myself leaning in closer, as he moved his hand to my face, brushing my cheek with his thumb. He pulled me to him, with both hands and his lips were now barely touching mine.

"I'm going to kiss you, Jo," he whispered just before pressing his soft lips to mine. I melted into him, raising a hand and placing it on his rock hard chest. I could feel his heart beating, the same rhythm as mine. I let him part my lips gently with his tongue, causing me to forget all sense of right and wrong. This was against everything I said I wanted but it didn't matter in that moment. I slid my hand down his chest, feeling his abs tighten as I ran my fingers across them. He pulled me in closer, deepening the kiss and I didn't stop it, I relish in his touch. He brings me to life.

Suddenly, he grabbed me, pulling me up with him and moving us across the room by the office door. His hands ran all over my body as he kicked his door shut slamming me against it. He lifted both my arms above me with just one hand, pinning me to the door, kissing me savagely, desperately. I gave in to him, softly moaning at his touch. My brain told me to stop, but my body wasn't listening.

"Brian...we can't do this..." I caught myself saying as I lowered my hands, pulling him into me by the waistband of his jeans.

He grabbed the hem of my tank top, yanking it over my head. "I need you. Now," he growled into my neck, biting me gently and sending my brain into overdrive.

"This doesn't change anything," I breathed out, barely able to speak as I kicked my shoes off.

Grabbing both of my hands, pinning them out to my sides, he leaned back and looked at me hungrily. "Shut the fuck up, Jo."

BRIAN

I yearned for her. I was hungry for her. She tried to say something and I told her to shut the fuck up. I didn't want to talk. I didn't want anything but her sweet pussy wrapped around my cock. I was going to fuck her in my office again, and she'd feel me for days. I didn't give a fuck who was around either. The minute she touched me, my dick was straining against my jeans, aching for her.

I had her pinned to my office door panting, wearing just her sports bra and tiny little shorts she was out running in. Her tight little body was hot to the touch, and I couldn't keep my mouth off of it. As I kissed her roughly and moved my hands down the front of her, I grabbed her heaving breasts, pinching her stiff little nipples causing her to cry out in need. I roughly grabbed the bottom of the bra, yanking it over her head and taking a mouthful of her delicious tit in my mouth, rolling my tongue over her nipple and gently biting down on it. I moved over to the other one, sucking and kneading it, while she pressed her hips into mine.

She wanted me as bad as I wanted her, she unzipped my jeans and freed my cock from it's restraints; meeting my eyes. Those gray stormy eyes looked at with me the need I felt as well, and I was consumed by her. I was angry and frustrated with her for pushing me away, but I desperate to have her. I yanked my shirt off over my head, and she immediately started licking and kissing my chest, leaving my skin burning wherever she touched it. I fisted her hair in my hand roughly, yanking her head back, exposing her neck to me.

Her chest was heaving and I ravaged her neck roughly before I dropped to my knees, taking her tight little shorts and panties down with me. I rolled my shoulder between her legs and tossed her leg over me, opening her sex to me, inhaling her scent. I knew I was gripping her hips hard, but I didn't care. I almost wanted to leave marks on her, she was mine, she just didn't see it yet. I took a lick of that sweet pussy of hers, and she grabbed my hair roughly, pulling me into her folds. As I sucked and flicked at her hard little nub, she cried out, thrashing around and knocking a picture off the wall. She's moaned loudly, and I knew she was going to cum soon so I stuck two fingers deep inside her, pumping them to meet her unbridled desire. She couldn't stop this now, she didn't want to stop, and I loved every second of it.

"Yes," I growled into her pussy.

"Fuck me, Brian," she tried to breathe out quietly.

"You'll come for me first, then I'm going to fuck you so hard you'll never be the same," I told her with a mouthful of that sweet pussy. She was writhing with me, grabbing at the wall around her. It was exactly how I wanted her. Begging for it.

"Please! Oh God!" She started convulsing and I could immediately taste her juices. I slowed the pace while she climaxed. Looking up at her, I could see her eyes closed while she was lost in the moment. As she came down from her high, I stood up and kissed her roughly. I wanted her to taste herself on me.

"You taste so fucking good," I said as I dropped my pants and boxer briefs to my ankles, not even taking them off. "I'm not done with you yet," I pushed her back up against the wall.

"Brian, I..." she began.

"I said no fucking talking today, Jo," I didn't want to talk. I wanted to fuck her into next week. The corners of her mouth turned up into a devilish little smirk, she knew what was coming. I picked her up by her naked ass, she wrapped her legs around me, and I lowered her onto my throbbing cock.

She moaned again loudly, and I fucking loved it. I didn't care who could hear us. Once I was balls deep in her, I started pounding at her pussy, holding her up against the wall. She held onto my neck, panting and biting at my shoulder while I took all of my frustrations out on that delicious, wet pussy I just had in my mouth. She was bouncing up and down on my cock and I wasn't ready for it to end. I set her down and turned her around.

"Turn around," I growled at her.

"I can't... take..." she panted out, still obeying my command to turn around, and even spreading her little legs apart, knowing what was coming.

"Oh yes you can," I pumped my cock in my hand a couple times, and smoothed my other hand over that juicy ass of hers, right before I smacked it. She jumped, startled.

"Brian!" she cried out. She didn't move though; she actually backed her ass up closer to me, showing me she wanted more. So fucking hot. I lined my dick up to her slit and thrust it in all at once and smacked her ass again lightly. I knew I filled her up, and I could get so much deeper this way. I pumped into her hard, pushing her up against the wall, knocking more pictures and crap onto the floor. It made me even harder that she was moaning in pleasure, trying to quiet her own yells of ecstasy while pictures literally fell off the walls from our fucking. I reached around, and pulled her as tight to me as I could. I was so close, and I knew she was too, she was practically breathless, and I could feel her heart pounding against her chest.

My lips rested against her neck, while I continued to thrust into her, on a mission to ruin her. She's mine. "Brian, I'm going to come, I can't..." she whispered.

I felt her channel start to squeeze my cock with her release, and I pumped harder, wanting to come with her. She cried out, and I groaned as I emptied myself into her. She felt so good, and although I may have punished her pussy, she's covered in a slick sheen of perspiration, looking sated as well. I slowly pulled out with a groan, and released her from my grip, her skin was glowing pink where I smacked her ass and grabbed at her. Nipping at her shoulder before reaching down to pull my pants back up, I noticed she was quivering. I wanted to stroke her hair, hold her, but that's not what that moment was about. It was a reminder of what animal passion we have.

Walking to my desk to grab tissues for her to clean up with, I watched her gather her clothes up and start to get dressed. She was still out of breath.

"Brian, that was...I..." she looked for the words, but couldn't seem to figure out what to say. *Good.*

"Today isn't for talking, Jo." I reminded her in a gruff whisper as I reached down to gently clean up the mess dripping down her leg. She stared at me, mouth slightly open, clearly in shock.

I grabbed my shirt off the floor, putting it back on and then leaned up against my desk, arms folded, just watching her finish dressing. She put those tiny little shorts back on, and my dick started to twitch again. She had the sweetest ass I've ever seen. She opened her mouth to say something, and I held up a hand making the stopping motion.

"Don't, Jo. Just go home. We aren't talking about this today. I just can't." I went back around the other side of my desk and sat in my chair, pretending like I was going to get back to work, which was total bullshit. Her mouth was still open, and she was flushed all over, so fucking sexy. I wanted to kiss her so badly. I was so frustrated, but I couldn't talk to her, I just couldn't. With a stunned look on her face, she turned around and walked out. I watched that ass as she left. I laid my head on my desk letting out all the air I had sucked in while I was holding my breath to stop myself from saying more.

Jo

My legs were shaking from the fucking I had just taken, and my brain was in an overloaded electrical storm trying to process what had just happened. I attempted to jog back home, but basically trotted along or walked most of the way in a state of complete and utter shock. My legs were really not working anymore. Certainly not from running. Did I want that to happen? I certainly acted like I wanted it to happen. Holy shit. He devoured me, like he *needed* me. It was so fucking hot and he wouldn't even let me speak. It's a good thing too, because I would've done something stupid like stop it from happening.

I knew he was angry with me for pushing him away, but he was so turned on, so hard. It wasn't like before. He was even more demanding and controlling, and now I'm insanely turned on again just thinking about it. What he did to me is unreal, I was consumed and couldn't shake him loose. *Do I even really want to?*

Once I finally got home, I got in the shower and stood under the hot water for what seemed like an eternity. I was sore and my muscles were quivering. Definitely not from the run. He was right, I was feeling him. I felt him everywhere. Clearly, things are unfinished with us. *Today isn't for talking.* I kept repeating those words to myself.

After the water ran cold, I got out, got dressed, and gathered myself together. I was supposed to meet Matt at the range in about an hour, and needed to get my two guns and other stuff together. Similarly, to my pink wrapped tools, I have a handful of gun accessories that are pink as well, like my ear protection, and my eye protection for the range. It was hot out today, but I wore jeans and a fire department t-shirt anyway, I don't like to underdress for the range.

Matt was already there when I pulled up, setting up his guns. He had quite a collection including a couple rifles, three standard handguns, but then he also had a couple cool ones that he always let me shoot too. Jax was also there, setting up some of his guns. None of us had as many as Matt, he had become a bit of a collector over the last few years. Jax was a Marine, so he had a couple of pretty standard handguns as well as an AR-15, which was so goddamn fun to shoot. It made me giggle and laugh every time for some reason, it was so powerful.

"Hey, hope you don't mind I tagged along, Jojo," Jax quipped.

"Nah, I don't mind, as long as I get to shoot the AR," I laughed. "And why does everyone keep calling me Jojo all of a sudden?"

Matt and Jax both laughed. "I have no idea actually, but I'm pretty sure it's gonna stick, so better get used to it," Jax proclaimed.

"So what were you up to this morning?" Matt asked casually while we were all loading our magazines and getting our targets organized.

"Nothing, why?" I asked defensively.

"Uh, it's a pretty standard question actually," he gave me a confused look.

"Oh, yeah. I went for a run this morning, stopped at the station real quick to get a drink like usual. Well you know, when I run," I chuckled a little. I was a totally inconsistent runner. I usually only did it when I was feeling fat, or I was stressed out. But when I did do it, I generally always took the same route through town, stopped at the station for a drink and to pee, and then ran back home. I did this off and on through the years, which of course Matt already knew.

"Ah, stressing out? Or feeling fat?" he teased me.

"Go fuck yourself, Matty," I actually did laugh, he was a jerk, but he was my jerk and obvioulsy knew me well.

"Run into the Chief while you were there?" Jax asked.

"Yeah...I uh, saw him for a few minutes. He was working on something in his office and I stopped by to say hello." I tried not to sound like I was hiding something. I felt like I sounded suspicious, and that's probably because my sex was tingling at the flashback to my morning.

"He's trying to get caught up on paperwork and stuff I guess. He's got some side project going on too apparently," Matt said.

Jax laughed. "Yeah, side project." Matt gave him a nasty look.

"What's funny, Jax?" I looked at Jax, then at Matt and they both looked guilty as hell.

"Oh nothing, sorry, nothing." He was trying to cover something up.

"Oh something is funny, what's going on? What's this side project?" I was getting angry, surely it had something to do with me if they're both acting this way.

"I honestly don't know what it is, Jo. We ran into him the other night having a meeting with a detective at the bar. I don't know anything elsc, and we weren't supposed to say anything about it, *were we, Jax?*" He gave Jax a hard stare.

"You weren't supposed to say anything? To me? Or in general?"

"In general, I don't think it has anything to do with you if that's what you're wondering," Matt replied.

"Why would I think it has to do with me? You guys are the ones that brought up the big secret meeting with some detective, not me," I was actually curious. Why would he be meeting with a detective, at a bar in secret?

"Yea, she was some detective alright," Jax cooed. I felt my face get hot and I met Matt's stare with my own.

"Oh, she was hot?" I asked coyly.

"Oh, she was smoking hot," Jax daydreamed about it while we watched.

"Enough, Jax," Matt snipped. "Jo, it was a meeting, that's all we know. We went on about our business after we saw them," he explained.

"Why would I care?" I lied. Matt knew I was lying. He knew how I felt. My heart sank all over again.

"I don't know, why would you?" He asked me sarcastically.

"I don't, so anyway...let's shoot, I'm ready," and I walked off to install my targets.

I pretended that I didn't care, but I cared. I cared a lot. I was fucked six ways to Sunday raw by him this morning, and he was out at the bar with some hot cop the other night? This is exactly why I ended things with him. *Motherfucker.* What happened this morning will never happen again. Ever.

Jonah texted me to let me know he'd take the half shift I was supposed to have tonight, so I spent the rest of the afternoon shooting paper with the boys, pretending my heart wasn't completely broken again, and that I didn't feel completely used up by him. *Fucker.*

BRIAN

That, was the hottest thing I've ever experienced in my life. *Fuck me*. After she left, speechless, and I regained composure myself, I picked up the mess we made in my office. Four pictures, two trophies, and a flag all fell or got ripped off the wall while we went at it this morning. Nice work if I do say so myself.

I was so frustrated by the whole situation with her, it was tearing me apart inside. She obviously felt the pull we have. When she was near me, I could actually sense it. My brain didn't even know what to do with this except be grateful for her touch today. I know I probably seemed cold to her, but I couldn't tell her how I feel, it would just complicate things even more. She wanted me physically, and I knew she had feelings for me, I just needed to keep myself close to her and if amazing sex is how to do it, that's how it had to be.

I didn't expect for that to happen, but fuck if I'm not happy it did. I knew her. She'd be reeling right now, wondering what the fuck was going on because I wouldn't talk. She may have tried ending this, but after that mind-blowing sex, I'm going to be on her mind. And I really didn't want to talk right now, I knew that stunned her. I was frustrated and it's not the right time to talk. But I couldn't keep my hands off of her. If she thought about me half as much as I think about her, it would be a fucking lot. That was the plan all along, whether that particular delightful moment was planned or not. I'd see her tomorrow at work and we could keep this little game going until I win her back. I'd give her some space for to think about what we did.

I needed to get my head back in the game here with this investigation. I told Detective Cruise I would rummage through Jack's electronic files to see what I could find and that's actually what I was doing when Jo showed up. I had been going through folders on Jack's desktop, and had come up empty-handed so far. Where would he keep evidence? I'm not even sure what I'm looking for, and part of me thinks the cops should be sitting around doing this which is also frustrating.

Leave it to the cops to have me do their legwork. Fuckers. I clicked for hours, coming up with nothing. I tried accessing his Cloud, but frankly I don't understand the fucking Cloud, and it had a password on it that was probably synced to his home computer or something. I tried Jo's name, her birthday, her mom's name, I even tried *my* mom's name, and couldn't get in. Hell, it could be anything.

I got up to go get a cup of coffee, then it occurred to me, that if Jack had his text messages synced from his phone to his computer, maybe what I was looking for was actually on his phone. He had to be using that damn thing way more than we thought he was. I needed to get my hands on Jack's phone. Jo had to have it at the house, *fuck*. I'm going to have to tell her what's going on or find another way to get that phone to Detective Cruise.

I decided to give Cruise an update, and sent her a text.

Hey, it's Cavanaugh. I'm coming up empty

handed, but I have a thought.

Okay what's that?

She replied right away.

I think what you're looking for might be
on Jack's phone.

Why do you say that?

He's got synced files I can't get into,
but he was texting you through his computer,
so I think maybe he was using his phone more
than we knew

The more I thought about it; the more sure I was.

He not a phone guy?

Wasn't a technology guy, but the more I
dig, the more I think he was and just didn't
tell anyone

Ok, so where's his phone

At his daughter's house I think

Can you get it from her?

I hesitated. I wasn't sure how to answer that one after the

events of today.

    `I'll figure it out.`

I finally replied.

    `I   don't   have   enough   evidence,`
`circumstantial or otherwise, and no witnesses`
`are coming forward, so without it, we have no`
`case. Make it happen so we can bring this guy`
`down.`

    `Will do. I'll be in touch tomorrow.`

This was going to be a little more complicated than I thought. I'd have to think about the best way to get my hands on that phone without involving Jo in what's going on. I didn't want that motherfucker anywhere near her, and I'd like her to stay away from the investigation for that reason alone.

It was getting late so I decided to go home, and come up with a plan when I see her tomorrow. We have a twenty-four hour shift together starting at seven a.m. and I was sure I could find some way to make it seem like I needed to poke through the phone for work or something. It could wait though, I was exhausted physically, and emotionally, and needed to get some sleep. Maybe I would have one night where I didn't wake up wishing she was there. Probably not, but hopefully soon she will be.

I was so aggravated the remainder of the afternoon, and so relieved I didn't have to go in to work. After we were done shooting, we went out for a few beers and I was tired. The topic of the hot detective did not come up again while we were out, but it was definitely lingering in the air. Matt kept watching me, he knew I was mad because he knows how I feel. I wished I hadn't said anything to him in the first place.

I went home tired and cranky. Brian didn't actually owe me anything, but I had started to think that our romp in the office was his way of reconnecting with me. He didn't want me to end it after all. I guess that was all bullshit and out of convenience anyway. None of it really added up to me but at this point, I needed to get some sleep before working a twenty-four hour shift with him the next day. It was my first day back at 23 full-time, and I did smile to myself about that. My dad would have been really happy.

I walked into my house, and immediately dropped my keys in shock. I looked across the room, and Danny was in my living room at my dad's desk going through his notebooks. As I scanned the room, I realized there was a gun on the desk next to him. *What the fuck is going on here? Shit, my guns are still in my car and I just went shooting!*

"What are you doing in my house?!" I screamed at him. He rushed over to me, grabbed me by the neck, and shoved me against the wall by the front door, I had trouble breathing immediately. *Oh shit, what's happening right now?* I was terrified, and my heart started to thump against my chest.

"Shut the fuck up, bitch," his eyes were empty as he stared into mine. "You were supposed to be on crew tonight at 19," he looked around the room while still holding me against the wall.

"Someone is covering my shift," I whispered, grabbing at his hand around my neck. He had the gun in his other hand up against the wall, and I really didn't want to struggle with him until I could get my bearings. He was a lot bigger than me.

"Well, this wasn't part of my plan, but I can improvise. Sit down on the couch and do not move." He moved me slowly over to the couch where I sat, and he shoved the gun in the back of his jeans. He skulked over to an end table and grabbed a lamp, then pulled his multi tool out of his front pocket and cut the cord off of it. Putting the knife back in his pocket he walked back over to me with the cord, demanding I stand up and turn around. *Seriously, he was tying me up? What the fuck is happening?*

I did what he said, but pleaded with him. "Danny, what are you *doing* here? What are you looking for? I'm sure I could have helped you find what you need. What is this about?" He tied my hands up behind my back roughly and swung me back around and shoved me back down on the couch. Then he raised his right arm and backhanded me across the face, knocking me down hard. It hurt so badly that I cried out.

"I told you to shut the fuck up. And that, was for slapping me at the station. Someone should have beat the fucking sass out of you a long time ago," he menacingly stood over me. "I'll deal with you when I find what I'm looking for. Your father had information in his notebooks that I need, and I'm going to find it. Until then you will sit there and be quiet, or I'll fucking gag you next." I was reeling from being hit, he didn't hold back at all, he intended to hurt me. I was so confused, and scared. No one would stop by, no one would stop this. I needed a plan; the anxiety of the situation was making me nauseous. I kept scanning the room, looking for something that would help me formulate a plan to get out of this.

I continued to check the clock on the wall. For the next several hours, I silently watched him read my dad's notebooks with frustration, tossing each of them across the room when he didn't find whatever he was looking for. My face was throbbing from where he hit me; it had to have left a mark.

I couldn't figure out what would be in those notebooks that Danny would even care about. They were mostly notes from calls and things like that. They didn't have any personal information in them, because he wanted to be able to use them as testimony if he ever needed to be reminded of an incident. It was just his quirky thing. I was starting to get the feeling that what Danny was looking for was in my dad's personal journals, that were in his room, in the closet.

Whatever he was looking for, he wasn't finding and he looked angrier by the second. The sun was going to be up soon. He'd been at this all night long, and my body was stiff and fighting the fatigue of being awake for so long and left in such an uncomfortable position. I was dying to pee but didn't want to risk asking him; he wasn't in a stable frame of mind from the way he had reacted to me.

As the sun came up, I looked over at the clock and realized that I was supposed to be at my first day at work in about thirty minutes. My phone, which was in my back pocket, dinged with an incoming text message, snapping Danny out of his reading.

"What the fuck was that?" he demanded.

"It was my phone. It's in my pocket," I replied.

He stormed over to me, grabbing me roughly by the arm and pulling me up. "What pocket?" he growled in my face.

"My back pocket," I was trying to sound strong and angry, but I was fucking scared. This is not the guy I thought I knew, hell if I really knew him at all I wouldn't have stayed with him. He reached into my back pocket taking the phone. He looked at it and said, "Oh of course, its Matt. You fucking him yet?"

I didn't reply and the phone dinged two more times. "Jesus Christ, what a little bitch. He has to check in with you nonstop?" he retorted. "Are there any more notebooks, Jo? I need to know right now." He grabbed me by my hair and got in my face, making me wince. He was getting anxious. Beads of sweat were forming at his temples, and the veins in his neck were visibly bulging.

"Only what's there! What are you looking for?" I cried out. The fucking guy was off the rails and I wasn't sure what he was going to do to me, but I wasn't going to give up my dad's journals. He could go fuck himself.

He tossed me back to the couch and sat down on the coffee table in front of it looking at me intently, just a foot away from me. "Jo, your dad had evidence of some things I need to destroy."

"What are you talking about, Danny? What evidence?" Now I was getting really scared. Hopefully Matt would realize that me not answering would not make any sense since I was supposed to be at

would pass out.

"I see. Just your boss. So who are you fucking, Jo?" He whispered in my ear, still holding me in place by my hair. I could feel his breath on my neck, and it felt like bugs crawling all over me, I was disgusted.

"That's none of your business," I whispered and tried to jerk away.

"How about one more fuck for old time's sake? I did enjoy that tight little pussy of yours," he looked me in the eyes. He was actually serious? I thought I'd throw up, and before I could, he shoved his tongue in my mouth and tried to kiss me. With my hands still tied behind my back, I pulled away and squirmed out of his grip for a moment, ending the disgusting attempt at whatever he had in mind.

"NO! Get away from me!" I screamed. I felt tears start to fall. I didn't want to cry, but I was so scared, and so angry I just couldn't control it.

"Oh, I see how it is," and he hit me again, hard, in the same spot as before. I saw stars this time, and fell backwards onto the couch, reeling from the pain. "I'm not done with you yet," he said, yanking me back to him, and hitting me again on the other side of my face. "Not so pretty and feisty now, are you?"

This time, I stayed down, and he didn't pull me back up. He left me on the couch, where I could see blood dripping from my nose onto the couch cushions. I could also taste the metallic tinge of blood in my mouth. This was bad, and I didn't know what to do at that point to get out of this, but I didn't want him to hit me again. He had me overpowered, and the only chance I had was for someone to show up and help me.

He'd gone back to my dad's desk unsatisfied with what he was finding. "It looks like your dad was lying to me. There's nothing here that implicates me in anything. Such a shame I'm going to have to kill you over nothing. But now you know the truth, and that can't get out and ruin my career."

"You don't have to do this," I said. That's what you say when you know someone is going to kill you right? What the fuck else do you say?

"Yeah, I never considered myself a killer, hun, but I can't let this ruin my career. I've worked way too hard to let a little thing like skimming off the top of the county send me to jail. Besides, I'm way too pretty for jail," he laughed. "I'll be back, you stay right there," he got up and walked to the door. "Don't try anything, Jo. I'm serious."

I just stared at him as he walked out of the house. I looked around for my phone but couldn't see it. He must have had it. Shit. It was time to pray.

BRIAN

"Did you try calling her?" I snapped.

"Of course I did. She isn't answering, and that's not like her. Something's up," Matt said.

"Yeah, she changed her mind, and isn't going to show up. That's what happened," I didn't really believe that she would just ditch work. Even if she didn't want to see me, she wouldn't do that to Matt or the other guys. But what do I know? Here I am, giving her space, all the space she needs but maybe what had happened in my office sent her running.

"That's not it and you know that. Something must be wrong. Maybe it's that shitty Jeep of hers or something," Matt was clearly grasping at straws, although her Jeep could use some work.

"I'll try calling her from here. Maybe she's ignoring you," I tried to make a joke, even though I was having a slight pain in my gut telling me something was wrong. I tried calling her from my desk, and it just rang and rang, then went to voicemail. "Well it's ringing, so maybe she's on her way or something." If this is bullshit, I was going to have to lecture her on her first day about being on time, which I really didn't want to do.

"Let's give her a little bit. I'm sure she'll show up," Matt looked nervous, and I was definitely getting the feeling it was something else. We both got up and went to the kitchen to get some coffee, and avoid the elephant in the room which was the fact that we both know Jo is not only always on time, but to her, on time is early. She was already forty-five minutes late, and that was way out of character.

"Chief, did you find my gear request that I gave to, uh, Jack?" Jax came into the kitchen to get some coffee too.

"I actually did just find it this morning. I signed the approval, but it's got to go to the commissioners, so I sent it over electronically and requested they expedite it. Sorry, it's taken so long, the paperwork is a real bitch," I complained. I didn't think being a Chief was pretty much all paperwork. I didn't want to complain too much about my job to the guys, it was an honor, but I was really second guessing that this was for me so early in my career. Yes, I've been a firefighter since I was eighteen, and that's nineteen years, but I'm nowhere near ready to give up fighting fire and going on scenes to basically doing paperwork full time. I had those goddamn budgets to look forward to later in the week.

"No problem, Chief. I'm sure that coming into all of that suddenly wasn't exactly an easy task," Jax replied. He's a good guy. He always had his shit together, he's safe, and he's smart. He also follows orders, and rarely, if ever, questions anything. He's always keeping himself busy at the station training, watching videos of other stations fires on the internet, and keeping informed on the latest in safety technology. He's a class act too.

We all stood around the kitchen chatting, having our coffee, but all the while I was really getting worried about Jo. Even though I didn't think she'd reply, I pulled my phone out to text her. Something is wrong, I know it is. I can feel it.

Are you okay?

I didn't get a reply, which didn't surprise me really, but it did still concern me. I started to think of all the realistic explanations for why she wouldn't be here by now. I honestly couldn't think of a single one other than that something was wrong, something happened to her. If she was in an accident, we would've gotten a call, so it wasn't that, but something was definitely wrong, and it was nagging at me, bad.

"Hey isn't Jo supposed to be here today?" Jax asked.

Matt replied, "Yeah, I'm not sure why she isn't here yet. If she's not here by ten, we should just take the truck over there and see what's up. It's just too weird, and I've called like ten times. I'm a crazy stalker now," he laughed. His laugh had a hint of nervousness too.

Then the tones dropped. "Engine 23, Rescue 23, Ladder 23, Active fire reported at 243 Old Seminole Road. Victims unknown."

FUCK.

I dropped my coffee cup and made eye contact with Matt. It smashed to the ground spilling coffee and shards of ceramic everywhere.

"GO!" he yelled. "We're right behind you!" I ran to my truck without saying a word. It was Jo's address. Her house was on fire. *FUCK.*

Something *was* terribly wrong, and I needed to get to her immediately. I hit the lights and sirens, which escalated my adrenaline even more. I've always been a stickler about safe driving, but I didn't give a shit about any of that. I've never driven a department vehicle faster in my life, and I thanked God and Jack in that moment for insisting that we get a pickup with a huge engine as I hauled ass to her house. She was about seven minutes away on a good day, and today there was a lot of traffic. Every sound that my truck could make from the sirens was employed, I was beeping like it was a third world traffic jam, and hitting the airhorn as often as humanly possible. Traffic parted around me like the red sea, and while it felt like a hundred years, I'm sure it was just moments before I turned the corner to her street where I could see smoke billowing in the sky.

Oh, God no. This is bad. This is a real fire, please don't be home, baby, please don't be home, I prayed. The moral dilemma of being a firefighter is that we truly do love fire. We love when something is really burning because it gives us a chance to finally put our training to use. The downside is this. There are lives at stake. As I got closer to her house I could see her Jeep in the front where she always parked. *No no no. She's home. She's here somewhere.*

There was fire coming through the front windows, which had blown out already somehow. I could hear the sirens of the other trucks coming in the distance. I grabbed my helmet and my coat, but didn't bother putting my bunker pants on; I wasn't wasting one second getting into the house. I knew she was in there, and I knew she needed me. I grabbed an axe and ran through the smoke to the front door and tried the doorknob. It was locked, but with one blow of the axe to the door it crashed open, and a huge billow of smoke hit me immediately.

I started coughing, and put my face in the collar of my coat as I ran in. "Jo! Jo! Where are you?" I ran into the front room, where the fire had clearly started, it was extremely hot. Jack's desk was completely engulfed in flames, and it had spread to the walls, and curtains, which must have caught fire causing the windows to blow out. I ducked low and continued calling her name, coughing. "Jo! Baby, where are you?"

Then, I heard it. "Brian?" My heart lifted immediately at the sound of her voice and I started scanning the room.

"Baby, where are you? I can't see anything! Help me find you!" The smoke was getting very thick, and I didn't have anything with me but an axe.

I could hear her coughing, and then hoarsely, she called out. "On the floor, by the couch! Help!" I ran to her, she was only fifteen feet from me and she was on the floor, tied up. *What the fuck happened here?*

"Baby, I'm gonna get you out of here, hang tight," I grabbed my knife from my belt and cut off the restraints on her wrists and pulled her to me. She grabbed me and held on.

"Oh, my God, Brian, thank you," she was coughing, and her face was black and blue. Someone had done this to her, and I was going to kill them.

I touched her face gently and looked in her eyes, she looked so scared. I had to get us out of there now. "We gotta get out of here, baby. I want you to hold on to me as tight as you can, and put your face in my coat," the fire was getting hot and the front room was now almost fully consumed with fire. We needed to go out the back.

"We can't go out the back, it's on fire too," she said quietly, while coughing a bit. She started to sit up. "I can walk," she said, but as she started to get up, her knees buckled, and she couldn't stand up. Probably a concussion judging by the marks on her face.

"We're going to run for it, the guys are on their way." I could hear the sirens loudly now, and knew they were only moments away. "Hold on to me." I scooped her up in my arms, and she buried her face into my chest. I was starting to cough more too, so it was time to get the fuck out. I wrapped my arms around her head and face the best I could while carrying her, and I ran for it.

Through the front door, we ran into what was a bit of fire, but God had given us a little pocket where there was a safe enough opening to get out of there. I carried her out to the front yard and dropped to my knees in the grass as the trucks showed up. I laid her down gently, tossed my helmet to the side, took my coat off and balled it up to put under her head.

Her face was covered in bruises, and dried blood was crusted around her nose and the corner of her mouth. I felt a rage inside me like I've never felt in my life, I was going to murder whoever did this to her. The guys ran by me, setting up and getting water on the fire, doing what they do. Matt made eye contact with me as he took over the scene, and I nodded to him, signaling that I was staying with Jo, and the fire could be someone else's responsibility today.

I was inspecting her, checking her for other injuries and being as gentle as I could while I kneeled holding her to me. She looked up at me and I saw her eyes start to well up with tears, "Brian, I'm so sorry," she whispered to me.

I can't imagine what she could be sorry for, "Baby, who did this to you? I'm going to kill them, who did this?" I touched her face gently, looking into her eyes.

"Danny," she whispered. "He didn't think I'd be home. He was looking for something in my dad's stuff but he didn't find it," tears started to fall from her beautiful gray eyes. "I'm so sorry."

"Baby, what are you sorry for?" I leaned down and kissed her gently all over her face right there in the front yard for all to see. I couldn't keep it a secret anymore, "I love you, Jo, I love you so much, and I'm so sorry I didn't get here sooner. I'm sorry I didn't tell you what you mean to me. I can't believe I almost lost you today..." I pulled her to my chest and felt the sting of tears welling up in my own eyes. It was just then that the paramedics came rushing over to check us both out.

"Chief, we can take over now." They tried to push me out of the way.

"I'm not going anywhere, I'm staying with her," I clutched her even more tightly. I was never letting go.

"Chief, we need to check her out, and you for that matter, please let us do our job, you know we need to," that little medic, June, the sister of Detective Cruise pleaded with me, putting her hand on my shoulder.

"Okay, okay, but I'm staying with her," I relaxed my grip on Jo, and set her back down propping her up a bit on my coat.

June kneeled down and assessed Jo's injuries, her face was swollen and she was coughing from the smoke. June put an oxygen mask on her, and her partner came around to me.

"Sir, I'd like to put an oxygen mask on you as well," he said.

"No, I'm good. I wasn't in there very long," I shooed him away and looked at June. "How bad are her injuries?"

"Doesn't look like anything's broken, but we need to take her to the hospital for x-rays just in case," she looked down at Jo. "Jo, we need to take you to the hospital, do you want me to call anyone for you?"

Jo looked over at me and I shook my head side to side. "I'll ride with you to the hospital and I'll make any calls we need to." Jo smiled under the oxygen mask and I squeezed her hand.

While June and her partner loaded Jo up on a stretcher, I stood up and looked around at the scene, the fire was mostly under control now. Matt came running over to me as they were starting to wheel Jo away to the ambulance.

"What the fuck happened here, man?" he burst out.

"Danny Russell did this. He beat the shit out of her too, Matt. I'm going to fucking kill him," I was so filled with rage. "I need you to look for Jack's iPhone inside, and then call the police station and ask for Detective Isabel Cruise, the girl you met the other night, and tell her to meet me at the hospital. Bring the phone, it's important. I'm going with Jo; I'm not leaving her alone." I was praying it didn't get burned up in the fire.

"Holy shit. Yeah, man stay with her. I'll handle it, and I'll meet you there as soon as we're done here."

"Yea, thanks. I gotta go," I grabbed my coat off the ground, and started to hustle my ass to the ambulance they were loading her into.

"Yo, Brian," he called after me.

"Yea?" I turned around quickly.

"The cat's out of the bag now, so just take care of our girl," he flashed a smile at me.

I felt the corners of my mouth curl into a smile as I ran to the ambulance, "Will do. Thanks for handling this," I waved at the scene and took off. He's right, the cat's definitely out of the bag now. I'd told her I loved her, and kissed her in front of everyone. I'd do it again in a heartbeat, and planned on doing it every day from now on.

Jo

I felt weak all over, and my face was throbbing. I closed my eyes while June and her partner loaded me into the rig, I was so exhausted and everything felt like a dream, like it was in slow motion. Did Brian save me? Was that real, or another dream? I wanted to sleep now.

"Jo! I need you to stay awake!" Was that June Cruise yelling at me? It felt like a really strange dream. Then I opened my eyes and realized it wasn't a dream at all and I tried to get up. I needed to get the fuck out of here, and I'm strapped down to this stretcher. *What the fuck?*

"Whoa, whoa, baby, where do you think you're going?" I looked over and saw Brian, he was grabbing my hand. He was covered in soot and sweat, and then I remembered everything that happened and I started panicking. My chest tightened, and I started hyperventilating. I had never been a passenger in an ambulance before. I knew this one, I started looking around and I knew I'd ridden in it on a duty crew before.

"Jo, you gotta calm down. Lay back. Take a few deep breaths," June said, as she adjusted the height on the stretcher, raising me up a bit, then looking over at her EKG machine. I knew she was checking my blood pressure, which had to be through the roof right. I did not like being a patient.

I looked up at her and nodded, then looked over at Brian. His eyes met mine, but he looked different, he looked calm but scared. He leaned close to me, still holding my hand on top of me and whispered, "Baby, I'm here. You're going to be okay. I won't leave your side, okay? Just try to stay calm, and look at me."

I tried to talk, but my throat hurt so bad, and the stupid oxygen mask was annoying me. "I…" was all I could get out without coughing uncontrollably.

"Shhhh, don't talk right now. You ate a lot of smoke, babe, your throat is going to be hurting. Just relax and breathe," his voice was so calming that I forgot I was pissed at him. I squeezed his hand and nodded, and took a deep breath trying not to cough uncontrollably again. I just kept looking at him, and trying to take deep breaths which was calming me down, even if I was pissed at him.

I think we got to the hospital pretty fast, it felt pretty fast. The doors opened and the heat hit me right away, making me feel sick and I started to gag. I yanked the oxygen mask off, and kept coughing. God my face hurt, I wondered how bad it looked. The coughing was making everything hurt and I was getting angrier.

"Get this thing off me, it's suffocating me!" I yelled through coughs.

Brian was still right by my side, and chuckled. "You're going to be a pain in the ass about this aren't you, Jo?"

"You shut up!" I said through more coughs.

"Ah, feisty. You're gonna make out just fine, baby," he smiled at me. I was mad now. I was in pain, and what the fuck is he even doing here with me? Why didn't Matty come? He's my best friend.

Why is Brian here?

"I'm not your baby," I coughed and shot him a nasty look, scrunching my face in his direction, which hurt quite a bit.

"You are. We can discuss it later," he squeezed my hand and I tried to yank it back but he had a tight hold on it.

"Chief, wait here with her a minute while I give a report to the nurse," June said to Brian, and she and her partner left me with Brian at the ER entrance. This was bullshit, I need to get off this fucking stretcher. I started to undo the straps and sit up, and Brian realized what I was doing before I could get up completely.

"Jo! Enough! You need to sit still; you have to get checked out. That's an order!" He was serious, yelling at me in front of the entire ER.

"Why are you here? Why isn't Matty here with me?" I pouted and of course, coughed some more.

"Matt is running the scene and gathering some evidence. He will be here in a little bit. And I'm here, because you're mine, Jo."

"I'm not yours," I snapped.

"You are. You just don't realize it yet. You will."

"Oh really? Well what about the hot cop you're going to bars with?" He gave me a stunned look, his eyes opening wide. Yeah, I caught you, asshole. Everyone can't be yours. I started coughing uncontrollably, and he helped me sit up more.

"Detective Cruise?" he asked.

"I don't know what her name is. Whatever it is, obviously you're fucking other people, so I'm most certainly not yours." Fuck my throat hurt. I wanted to scream at him, and I could barely get my words out at all, everything was coming out as a raspy whisper.

He leaned in close and whispered in my ear. "Josephine

Meadows, you are *mo chroi*. There's no one else but you. There will never be anyone but you." He stood back up looking down at me. I felt paralyzed, not able to move or speak.

"But..." was all I could muster. And a stifled cough.

"Baby, I will explain everything soon. Detective Cruise is going to be by to talk to you about the fire, and about what that motherfucker Russell did to you. I've been helping her gather evidence against him, which your dad had actually started, we just couldn't figure out where it was right away. Now please, lay back, and let the staff here take care of you. I'll be right here, I promise," he said softly.

I was so confused. June and her partner came back over with a nurse who resembled a linebacker, as well as a pretty tiny little nurse trailing behind her. They wheeled me into a giant exam room, and moved me adeptly from the stretcher to the hospital bed.

"Jo, we gotta run, but I'll call you tomorrow to check on you, okay, girl?" June called out as she gathered her stuff to leave. She was on duty, she had to get her rig back in service and I totally understood that. It's always tough when you transport someone you know.

"Thank you, June," I hoarsely called back. I looked around, and the big nurse, the tiny nurse, and Brian were all staring at me.

"What?" I said.

"You need to put the oxygen mask back on, miss," the big nurse said. The little nurse was checking Brian out. *Seriously, bitch?*

"Fine, but let's get this moving, you need this bed for sick people, and I'm fine." I snipped at her and allowed the little slutty nurse to put a new oxygen mask on me while I tried to stifle my cough.

"I need to ask you some questions about what happened, and then we're gonna take you straight to x-ray and get some pictures of your face. Were you traumatized anywhere else?" She asked.

"No." I replied. I watched Brian as I answered the nurse's questions one after another. He stared at me intently the entire time.

"Were you sexually assaulted?" she asked me. I looked over and saw Brian's hands clenched into fists and he took a step closer to me.

"No." I replied.

"Are you sure?" she asked.

"Yes, I'm sure," I snapped at her, then looked back over at Brian. "Brian, he didn't do anything else to me, he just hit me," I didn't want him to have a stroke right there even if I don't understand what's going on with him right now.

"I think we have everything we need. Let's get you down to x-ray now. Sir, you're going to have to stay here," she motioned to a chair for him to sit in.

"That's not happening. I'm staying with her." He didn't move.

"Sir, it's not negotiable, don't make me call security. You're already overstepping here," she meant business.

"Brian, it's okay. I'll be fine, and I'm sure we won't be gone long," I looked at the nurse for confirmation.

"No, you won't be gone long. Audrey here is going to take you," she pointed to the little nurse who couldn't keep her eyes off my man.

"Audrey, I'm Brian Cavanaugh, the Fire Chief," she blushed

and smiled as Brian spoke to her. "This woman is a firefighter, and my girlfriend, and I love her more than anything in this world. Please take care of her and bring her right back to me." Audrey the slutty nurse immediately changed her demeanor to professional and nodded at him.

My mouth dropped wide open. I felt it happen and I couldn't stop it. He just said he loved me, in public. Out loud. The slutty nurse heard it too. I could tell it wasn't my imagination by the look on her face.

Well, holy shit. Brian leaned down and pressed his lips to mine softly. "I'll be waiting right here, baby. I love you." The slutty nurse wheeled me away to get x-rays of my face, which was apparently freaking some people out, so it must have been bad.

BRIAN

I waited for Jo to get back from x-ray in the ER room they'd assigned to her and pulled my phone out. I had a text from Matt saying he had found the phone upstairs in Jack's bedroom, which was unaffected by the fire. He was on his way to the hospital, he turned the fire scene over to the neighboring chief so that he could get there. I can't say I blame him. While this is a special situation because it's Jo, if any one of our guys was injured we'd all want to be here.

I couldn't sit, so I was pacing around the empty room looking at the chaos around me. I'm going to fucking strangle Danny Russell with my bare hands for touching my Jo. Who the fuck beats up a girl in the first place, let alone a girl you were intimate with. The thought made me even more angry. And she was tied up, that sick fuck. My blood pressure was through the roof, when Detective Cruise came rushing in.

"Jesus Christ, Cavanaugh, what the fuck happened?" she questioned me.

"It looks like Russell beat the shit out of Jo for starters," I hissed through my clenched jaw.

"Your brother called me and says he has the phone," she said calmly.

"Yeah, he has it. He's on his way here. I'm going to fucking kill Russell." That needed to be really clear, and she wasn't listening.

"Listen, you gotta let me handle this, I'm serious," she reached out and touched my arm just as the little flirty nurse Audrey I think her name was, wheeled Jo back in.

Jo looked immediately to where Cruise had her hand on my arm and then looked up to my face and scrunched her nose up. I quickly moved to her side.

"Jo, baby, this is Detective Isabel Cruise, she's actually June's sister," I explained. She looked at me quizzically, but I figured it would be best if she talked directly to Cruise.

"Hi, Detective," Jo's raspy voice whispered. She gave Cruise the once over and I took her hand, leaning over the railing of her hospital bed. She weaved her fingers through mine, and I expelled a sigh. I think I've been holding my breath since she was away from me getting her x-rays.

"Hi, Josephine. I'm sorry we have to meet under these circumstances. I was working with your father on bringing Danny Russell down for racketeering, and it seems now we can add assault and attempted murder to the list of charges. Can you tell me what happened?" She pulled out a little notebook, just like they do on TV and grabbed a pen from her shirt pocket.

"Sure, I can tell you what I remember." Jo whispered. I let go of her hand and got her some water from the sink nearby, her voice was so hoarse and I know she was trying to stifle her coughing.

She smiled up at me as I handed her the water. "Thank you," she whispered and took my hand again as Matt walked in, still dressed in his bunker pants.

"Hey, Jojo! You look like shit! You gave us a fucking scare. You alright?" he was trying to lighten the mood and ease his own anxieties, I could tell.

"Hey, took you long enough to come," she whispered at him.

"Had to take care of the scene for this asshole," he pointed to me and smirked. She giggled and started coughing a little.

"Alright, now that we're all here, Jo can you tell me what happened?" Detective Cruise brought us all back.

Meanwhile, Matt looked at my hand in Jo's and gave me a wink, which I replied to with a smirk of my own.

Jo took a deep breath, trying to find her voice. "Danny was in my house when I got home. He said he thought I'd be working, but I had found someone to cover my last shift at 19," she whispered, then took a sip of water with her free hand. "He had a gun, and he was going through my dad's desk looking for something," she stopped to cough. I helped her lean forward in an attempt to make it easier, she needed to get that shit out of her lungs.

"Thank you," she whispered to me and then continued. "He couldn't find what he was looking for but told me that he'd been stealing money and that my dad knew about it. He said that my dad was going to out him if he didn't confess himself," then my heart sank. *God, did he have anything to do with Jack's death?* I squeezed her hand so she knew I was here to support her.

She continued, "He hit me a couple times and then said that since I knew what was going on, even though he didn't find any evidence, he was gonna have to burn my house down with me in it," a tear fell from her eyes. I leaned over and rubbed her back softly with my other hand, it killed me that anyone would make her feel this way.

"Keep going, honey," Cruise said softly.

"He went out to his truck and got some gasoline and dumped it on my dad's desk, and then went to the kitchen where the back door is and lit the can on fire. I guess so I couldn't crawl out that way."

"Then what happened?" Cruise asked, taking notes.

"He yelled at me, saying that this was happening because I came home and it was all my fault, and he hit me again, and I guess I passed out. The next thing I remember is hearing Brian's voice calling out my name," she looked up at me, teary eyed and squeezed my hand which was still intertwined with hers. God, I can't believe this happened to her. I should have been there to protect her and I was sick over the thought I could have lost her. Detective Cruise spoke up again, tearing me from my thoughts.

"You did good, Jo. Your dad would have been proud of you."

"Thank you," she sniffled a bit and sat up a bit. "So what's next? I don't have the evidence anyone is looking for, and now my house is halfway burned to the ground, and he beat the shit out of me, so can you go find him and arrest him anyway?"

"Yes, we can, and my guys are out looking for him now. I was hoping that your dad's phone was recovered at the fire actually. Brian believes what we're looking for is on it," she looked over at me.

Matt walked up and handed Cruise the phone. "I believe this is what you're looking for then. It was actually in a different part of the house, not affected by the fire at all."

She took the phone and unlocked it immediately, scrolling through it and then smiling, "This is it, this is what we've been looking for!" She practically cheered, while the rest of us just stared at each other. Cruise pulled up a video, and turned the phone around to us, and then adjusted the sound so we could all hear it.

What we watched, was a video that was actually aimed at the floor, and you could see uniform pants of the person holding the phone, Jack, and the other person was Danny. What was undeniable though was the audio. It was a complete and fully recorded conversation of Jack confronting Russell, and Russell admitting to everything. All of the bribes he was taking, the inspections he was passing that shouldn't have, all of it. Jack told him that he had twenty-four hours to go to the police himself, or he'd be turning him in. It was everything they needed to put Russell away for the racketeering. What he had done to Jo would make it even worse, he'd go away for attempted murder.

"Holy shit, that's fucking amazing. How did you know the code to unlock the phone?" I asked.

Cruise just smiled, "I didn't know it, I just tried 2323 and it worked. I actually thought I'd have to take it back to the tech guys at the station."

Jo started giggling, and then so did Matt and I. That's Jack. He managed to record evidence with his phone, but his password was so easy anyone could've gotten into that phone. Just then, the big nurse walked in with a doctor and Jo's x-rays.

They both appeared startled by the number of people in the room. "Uh, well hello, everyone?" The doctor asked it like a question then looked over at Jo. "I've looked at your x-rays Josephine, and it looks like there's no fractures or breaks, so that's good news. But you definitely have a concussion from the assault, and I'd like to make sure that if I let you go home, that you'll have someone that can watch you for at least twenty-four hours and make sure you're alright."

"That would be me. I'll take care of her," I spoke up immediately. She was coming home with me and that's all there was to it. I wasn't not letting her out of my sight and wasn't asking her permission either.

"Are you sure?" she whispered up at me.

I leaned down closer to her. "Baby, I'm not letting you out of my sight. You're coming home with me, where I can take care of you and that's an order." As I leaned back upright, still not letting go of her hand, she looked up and smiled at me shyly.

The doctor nodded, "Ok, I'll prepare your release papers. You're going to be in some pain, so I've written a prescription for something to help with that, but you'll be right as rain in no time. The smoke should clear out of your lungs in a day or so, but you're going to have a sore throat, and you definitely need to take it easy for a few days."

"Thank you, doctor," Jo whispered. The doctor left the three of us there again and Cruise shifted her weight back and forth. She was an antsy one.

"Okay, guys, I'm going to take this back to the station, and see where we're at in terms of catching this guy. Hopefully he's not on the run and thinks he won," Cruise put the phone in her pocket and continued. "Jo, we'll probably need to be in touch in the next couple days to get your formal statement, but this is just about over, and you're safe with Brian," then she turned to Matt. "And, Matt was it? Thanks for bringing me the phone." She turned around and left the three of us standing there.

"So, is it safe to assume you two now have things out in the open?" Matt was never afraid to point out the obvious, even if it was uncomfortable.

THE BROTHERHOOD OF DISTRICT 23

"Uhmmm," was all Jo could mutter, but she did smile at Matt.

"We are working on that, thanks so much for making it awkward though," I replied and gave him a go fuck yourself look with raised eyebrows and an eyeroll.

"Yes, fuck you as well," he replied with a grin. "If you're going to take Jo home, I'm going to have Jax take me back to the station so I can cover for you. I drove your truck here so you'd have it, and took care of the other things you asked me to. He's out in the waiting room, they wouldn't let any more of us back here. The guys want to see Jo, so we'll probably bring the crew by around dinner time to visit you once you're settled, is that cool?"

She looked up at me for a reply, "Yea, that would be great. Is that okay with you, Jo?"

"Yes, that would be great, thank you." She whispered and coughed a little.

Matt tossed me my keys, and headed out, leaving Jo and I alone for the first time since the front yard. I was suddenly very nervous, she hadn't really said much, but she agreed to go with me, so that was something. I sat down next to her, rubbing her hand that I was holding with my thumb, not quite sure what to say next.

269

Jo

After Matt left, it was just Brian and I there alone in my hospital room. His fingers were still intertwined with mine, and he was running his thumb across my hand softly. I rolled over onto my side and examined him. He looked so worried, and tired.

"Are you okay, Brian?" I whispered. *Seriously, I hate whispering. I hope my voice comes back soon.*

He leaned in closer, placing both elbows on my hospital bed and bringing my hand up to his lips, kissing it softly. "I am now," he sighed out. "I thought I'd lost you, Jo. I don't know what I would have done without you. I'm so sorry for everything, baby. I'm going to spend my lifetime showing you how much you mean to me." He kissed my hand again, and rested his head in his hands, still holding mine.

Those eyes of his, I just lost myself in his beautiful green eyes again. I could see a tinge of hazel in them as I inspected his features while he was talking. "Brian, I'm going to be okay," I breathed out. I remembered everything he said to me in the front yard now, and I was afraid he had said it in fear, not really meaning it. He told the nurse he loved me too.

"Brian?" He looked back up at me.

"Yes, baby?"

"Did you mean all those things you said today?" I had to ask. It was just us now.

"What things, baby?" He smiled.

"You know, that uh..." He was going to make me say it? *Come on!*

"Come on and say it, baby. That I love you?" Now he was grinning and he moved himself to be seated on the edge of the bed next to me.

"Uh, yeah. That. Did you mean all of that? I mean I'm going to be okay now, so I mean if..." he cut me off.

"Josephine Meadows, I am truly, madly, deeply in love with you. It just took me longer than it should have to figure it out. I'm going to spend the rest of my life proving to you how much you mean to me. You're my heart, my mo chroi, and I can't live without my heart."

Swoon! He gave me that toothpaste commercial smile I can't resist, and leaned down to kiss me. That fire, that magnetic pull, it was there and it was intensified by a million. He softly opened my mouth with his tongue, sweeping it across my lips, sending shivers through my spine and waking up my sex. The way this man makes me feel is incredible. He growled a little bit and pulled away, making me pout.

"Come back here," I whispered with my new raspy voice, then started coughing.

"As much as I would like to take you right here in this hospital bed, the doctor said he was going to release you soon, so let's get you dressed, and get the fuck out of here. I want to get you home where I can take care of you better," he took my hand and started to pull me up.

"Kiss me again, and I'll get up," I was going to negotiate more kissing at all times.

He laughed and accommodated my request, taking my swollen face gently with both hands and pressing his lips gently to mine. "Oh, Jo, the things you do to me, even here." He pulled away and adjusted himself in his uniform. He was so fucking sexy. He had soot on his face from the fire, his hair was a mess, and he was beautiful.

He helped me get up, and just as I was finished getting dressed, the nurse came in with my discharge papers. "Now you know all the things the doc wants you to do, right? Few days taking it easy, not a lot of talking until your throat feels better," then Brian started laughing.

"Not talking? That's a good one," he laughed at me and I flashed him a look. When the nurse wasn't looking at me I flipped him the bird, and he winked at me in return.

"Thank you, ma'am. I will do my best," I whispered to her.

"Good girl. Now let this handsome man take good care of you," she patted me on the back and sent us on our way.

We walked out to Brian's truck, it was his regular truck, not his Chief's truck, which I thought was curious. He opened the passenger side door for me and helped me get in, noticing my confusion. "I asked Matt to bring my truck. I'm taking a few days off, so I didn't want the Chief's truck." He explained as he closed the door and walked around to his side, getting in.

"Are you going somewhere?" I asked. He never takes time off really.

"You're still not getting it yet, are you, baby?" He put one hand on the steering wheel, the other up on the back of my seat, staring at me, clearly awaiting a response.

"Uhh, no, I guess not?" I said.

"Jo, you're going to stay with me. Your house was on fire today and you were almost killed. We have catching up to do after the last few days. I'm staying with you and I'm going to take care of you. I've mentioned that I love you, and I intend to spend some time proving that to you," he awaited my response.

I felt my mouth curl up into a smile, he loves me. I think he actually meant it. "I'm going to take your smile as understanding, because you're not supposed to be talking anyway," he let out a little chuckle and started up the truck to take us home. My heart was full. I hadn't replied yet, I didn't get a chance, but I wanted to tell him how much I love him so badly.

The hospital was about ten minutes away at a normal speed which we were doing. We had to drive by my house on the way to his house, and when I saw the scene, I pressed my hand against the glass of the window in shock.

Brian reached over and took my other hand in his, weaving his fingers through mine. "Baby, it's not as bad as it looks. The guys got the fire out really quickly. You can't stay there for awhile, but the damage was only to the front room and the kitchen. The bedrooms are totally fine, just smoky, and that can be fixed. Matt already called the company that takes care of all of that, and they're coming over today to board up the windows and clean some of the damage up."

I looked up at him, tears in my eyes, "It's my home," I whispered.

"Baby, it's just a little damage, and we're gonna get it fixed up good as new. It's going to be okay," he brought my hand up to his lips, kissing it softly. "You're going to stay with me for now and then tomorrow if you're feeling better, we'll go get some of your things and look around okay?"

All I could do was nod. I was in shock. I was so tired, so sore, and I couldn't believe my house was on fire today. Brian was taking me to his home, to stay with him. He loved me. I couldn't find the words. For the first time in my entire life, I was speechless.

BRIAN

She looked so tired, and her sweet, beautiful face was swollen and bruised. It pained me so much to see what he did to her. When she saw her house, she became almost silent, and my heart ached for her even more. I should have taken a different route home, I wasn't thinking. I could really be stupid sometimes.

When we pulled in front of my house, her Jeep was in my driveway where I asked Matt to put it, so I parked on the street. She looked over and smiled knowingly at me, she knows my don't park in my driveway rule. *Good, we got a smile out of her.* I needed to shower, she needed to shower, and she needed to get some rest. The guys were probably going to stop by in a couple hours for their dinner break, and to visit with her, so I wanted to get her comfortable as soon as possible.

I parked out front and got out, while she waited patiently in the passenger seat for me to come around and help her out. God, that made me so happy. I helped her hop out, and grabbed the ring box from my glove box, shoving it in my pocket. I put my arm around her as we walked up to the front door. Just inside the door was a duffle bag with a couple things that I asked Matt to grab at her house. Some clean clothes mostly, so she had something to change into. I would never ask anyone but Matt to do something as intimate as that for my girl and I would have preferred to do it myself, but I just couldn't leave her side.

She followed me to the kitchen silently and looked around. We were both filthy, we needed to get cleaned up. "Baby, can I get you something to drink?" I asked her and opened the fridge to get myself a beer.

She mouthed the word water and smiled, then mouthing the words thank you silently as she took the bottle from me. I pulled her into me, and she melted against my chest as we stood there taking in what had happened. She held onto me, resting her head on my chest for a few minutes and then finally she sighed a big, relaxing sigh, as if she'd been holding her breath for awhile.

"Let's go take a shower and get cleaned up, then you can rest okay?" I said still holding her and kissing the top of her head. She silently nodded her agreement. She seemed downright exhausted at this point, and I couldn't say I blamed her. The adrenaline was wearing off both of us. I scooped her up in my arms and carried her to my bedroom, not forgetting the pink duffle bag of her stuff. She rested her head on my shoulder while I carried her. *God, I love this woman.*

I set her down in my bedroom near the bathroom door. "Go on in and get started, baby, I'll meet you in there."

She reached up, grabbing my face gently with both of her little hands, pulling my face to hers. "Thank you," she whispered, and planted a beautiful soft kiss on my lips before turning around to go into the bathroom. She had yet to tell me she loved me back, but I knew she needed me as much as I needed her.

Frozen for a moment, speechless from her sweet gesture, I was awakened from my daze when I heard her turn the water on. I grabbed her duffle and rifled through it to see what Matt grabbed for her to wear, I wanted to set it out for her. I found two pairs of leggings, a pair of jeans, three tank tops, and basically all of her lingerie. What a dickhead. I appreciate it, but what a prick. He was a funny guy going through her intimates drawer. Ah, whatever, he's my brother, fuck it. I laid out some leggings and a tank top for her, and a sexy as fuck pair of teal panties, and a matching bra.

I grabbed the ring out of my pocket, and opened the box, looking at the ring. I pulled it out of the box and put it on my pinky finger, it only went on about halfway, but that's fine, it won't be on long. I stripped off my filthy clothes and made my way into the bathroom to get in the shower with my woman.

I stepped into the shower to see her examining her bruises. Fuck, she had bruises all over her body. My rage took over, and I pulled her to me under the steaming water. "Baby, you're safe here with me, okay?" She looked like she had been crying. "Are you okay, Jo? Say something. I need to know you're alright," I pleaded.

She looked up at me, her gray eyes penetrating me. "I always loved you. I've loved you my whole life, Brian," she whispered, both of her hands resting on my chest.

She does things to me, things that make my heart soar, and my dick hard, all at the same time. Those words melted my heart, and I pulled her in tight, letting the hot water run over both of us and kissed her gently. After a few minutes, I grabbed the soap and started to wash her, and then myself. She stood perfectly still, letting me take care of both of us. When I was almost done, I took her right hand and looked in her eyes.

I took the ring off my pinky, and placed it on her right ring finger, with the crown and heart facing inward, a symbol that your heart belongs to someone. "Jo, my heart belongs to you. I'm sorry it took me so long to figure it out, but I'll spend the rest of my life showing you the rare and beautiful gift that you are to me." She looked down at the ring, and then looked up at me smiling. "My mom gave me that ring, it was given to her by your dad," I waited for her reply. That might have been awkward to say right then, but maybe she'd understand the symbolism to me.

She looked at it again, then looking up to meet my eyes, she smiled a huge beautiful smile. "I love you, Cavanaugh," she said.

I met her grin with my own. "You're mine, Meadows. Forever."

The End

ACKNOWLEDGEMENTS

My tribe is amazing, and I would never have considered writing a book without their support. Since it's my debut novel, I've got a handful of folks that deserve some public recognition.

First and foremost, even though I know he won't read this dirty little book, I have to thank my brother Jesse Briggs. Without his unconditional support of me pursuing my dreams, I'd still be wandering around looking for my passion. Thank you for always saying, "If you look at the worst possible outcome, its usually not that bad. Just do it." You're my guru man, thank you, I love you.

Carina Adams, who made this whole thing real by offering me the opportunity to do my first signing, setting the schedule for reality. Your book Forever Red, was my first romance read, and we became friends the moment we met. If you hadn't given me this gift I may still be mulling over the idea of finishing this book at all.

Janelle Picard, who reminded me that this book has actually been in progress for 20 years, the length of our friendship. I often reminisce of our days at the Jersey diners, writing, talking, and growing up together. Thank you for telling me to go *write*, not to go right to another bar for more drinks after brunch. We've been friends for so long, you're my family, and I love you. Jaisha Burr, thank you for always somehow knowing what my word count meant and encouraging my happy hour writing habits. The bars of Orlando surely want to thank you as well for my patronage. I love you, your family, and the craft beer tastings at TJ's. Donna Caruso, we were destined to be friends, and I'm so grateful for your friendship, and the ability to curse freely with you. Karen Bryda, you're the Meredith Gray to my Christina Yang, and I love our Skype sessions and ridiculous text chats. I'm so lucky we became close before I moved 1000 miles away. My NJ street team, Hillary Perryman, Stephanie Snock and Abbey Flick; drinks on me next time you're in FL. Thank you for your support through the last several years and thank God for FaceTime and autocorrect.

Aaron Heller, thank you for keeping my scene descriptions honest, and for allowing me to use your network for this book. You encouraged me to become a firefighter from the very beginning, and even with the pushback from some, it was one of the greatest personal achievements of my life. I'm grateful for your support and your tutelage during my firefighting days as well as now. Gene Pullen, Walt Lewis, Dave Hernandez all deserve thanks for their assistance in securing photos, equipment, and other fun stuff for me to help promote this book. I was recently reminded that once a firefighter, always a firefighter, and for that I thank all of my brothers and sisters. Delran Fire Department, Delran Emergency Squad, New Egypt Fire Company, New Egypt Rescue Squad, thank you for the privilege of serving with you and creating the inspiration for my stories.

The newest additions of my family, my writing family, deserves special thanks as well. Kristina Rienzi, thank you for your friendship, and thank you for taking me to a book signing with you. You stirred up my passions and you're an inspiration to me. To the authors that inspired and encouraged me to go from reader to author, MJ Fields, Stevie J. Cole, Carina Adams, Leddy Harper and LB Dunbar; thank you for welcoming me into the writing world with you, and for inspiring me with your smoking hot stories.

Judi Perkins, you're my yoda. I'm your kid now, and you're stuck with me, and I'm the luckiest chick around for it. Thank you for the beautiful cover, and for your no nonsense guidance on how to get this book done. Your introductions to my book family have been invaluable. And thank you for my new sisters, Sasha Brummer & Jess Epps; it's as if we've known each other forever.

My beta readers Kelly Williams (who gives fabulous story feedback and brainstorms with me), Mary Baird (who gave me my first author takeover on her blog and has encouraged me without ever meeting me), Chantal Zodarecky (the gif queen who loves my characters), Steph Gostin (we need some champs girl), and Martin Murphy (thank you for adding testosterone to the mix), your feedback was helpful and hilarious. Tiffany Holcomb, thank you for agreeing to being my PA and for sending me the most hilarious "you should be writing" memes. A special thanks to Jillian Crouson-Toth (who shares a brain with me and is truly my spirit animal), you got to know me and my characters and have shown me such love and support from the day we met online, I don't know what I'd do without you, and you're my friend for life. I'd be drowning without all of you! I'd also like to give a shout out to the bloggers I've met and been supported by; you make the romance world go round, and I've become an addict thanks to your reviews, shares and comments. I thank you from the bottom of my heart.

LJ & CB Creative Images and Services (Cassia Brightmore & Lance Jones), thank you for handling basically everything. I ask a million questions a day, and Cassia is always sweet to me even though I'm annoying as hell and a total control freak.

Thank you to my TR family from all over the world. Seth Miller, Laz Jefferson, Matt Salandra and so many more, your support and encouragement to take massive action and to go for it in every way means more than I could ever express. Ho'oponopono. I love you, thank you.

Lastly, and most importantly, thank you to my readers. I started as a reader, and your support, shares, love and kindness makes all of this worthwhile. I look forward to creating more book boyfriends for all of us!

BESTSELLING AUTHOR
AMY BRIGGS

DEDICATION

For all those who protect and serve

MATT

Everyone really needed a celebration or some kind of get together after everything that's happened in the last few months. After all the drama of my friend Jo's attempted murderer's arraignment and her house almost being burned to the ground, we were all ready to unwind and let loose. I was exhausted from all the fire calls last night, and while I'm normally not a party pooper, I had to force myself to go out, but not before taking a quick nap. I was definitely sound asleep and dreaming of a beautiful blonde when I heard Jax yelling for me.

"Yo, dickhead, are you coming with me or driving yourself?" My roommate, Jax, whom I also work with, awakened me. I was living in his house, renting from him. When he got home from his tours in the Marines, he bought a sweet house, perfect for entertaining. To offset costs for him and to avoid apartment living for me, I jumped at the chance to move in as his roommate. It was the best of both worlds. We had people over pretty often, and there was more than enough space for the two of us.

Rubbing the sleep from my eyes, I asked, "Where are we going again?"

"We're meeting the lovebirds at the Brewhouse in an hour. Most of the crew is coming, and a couple other people. It happens to be ladies night again, so get your shit together man. I'm hoping that hot detective will be there to celebrate with us."

The lovebirds in question were my brother, who was also our acting fire chief, Brian Cavanaugh, and my best friend, Josie Meadows, who also works with us. We all grew up together and used to work for Josie's dad, the old fire chief, before he died earlier this year. Jo and Brian have now fallen in love it seems, and are basically inseparable, except at work; you'd never know they were together there, because they go out of their way to avoid each other. They had one argument on a scene, and now they keep things quiet at work, although everyone is well aware of their coupleness. Them being together didn't bother me, but it was still weird and took some getting used to. Since her ex tried to burn her house down with her in it a few months ago, she's been living with Brian while her house was being restored, so they'd pretty much been inseparable.

The "hot detective" was Detective Isabel Cruise, who helped put away the guy who tried to kill Jo. She was working on a racketeering case against Danny Russell when things escalated and he tried to kill Jo to cover up everything he had done. It was kind of extreme, since he was basically just taking bribes, but he was fucking crazy. Detective Cruise was smoking hot, with long, dark hair, dark eyes, a tan complexion, and an absolutely perfect ass. Jax thought he had a chance. She was kind of a bitch if you asked me, definitely not friendly the handful of times I've met her, so I wasn't going to fight him for dibs of any kind. She seemed like a lot of work with all that attitude.

Jo and I have been best friends since we were babies; we were born the same week in the same hospital. I hadn't actually seen her all week, but we texted pretty much nonstop when we weren't working together. I was actually looking forward to spending some time drinking and hanging out with her. She has always loved giving me shit for my choice in the ladies, and I was sure tonight would be no different. She's never been known for keeping her opinions to herself, and I loved her for it.

I hauled myself out of bed and went to my bathroom to get ready. "Give me fifteen minutes and I'll be ready to go," I yelled to Jax. I washed my face, brushed my teeth, and fussed with my hair, which was all over the place from my spectacular nap. I probably could have slept all night, but I couldn't dodge celebrating the conviction of the maniac who'd tried to murder my best friend after beating the shit out of her. I'd left that part out; he seriously beat the crap out of her. Jo's face was finally healing up; she'd had a black eye for almost a month. Seeing that killed all of us, but she insisted on working all of her shifts, and none of us would argue with her. There was no point.

I changed quickly into some jeans and a t-shirt. It was a nice night here in central Florida; it was January and really not that cold at all. I mean, it's never that cold here, but it was kind of warm, particularly for this time of year. It was Jax's turn to drive, since I drove us out last time a few days prior. He was not patiently waiting for me to get my shit together and having a beer in the kitchen when I walked out.

"You ready, princess?" He gave me a sideways glance and a smirk and tugged on his bottle.

"Go fuck yourself. Yea, I'm ready. Let's go say hello to your bitchy little detective." I walked outside, creating the illusion I was now waiting for him to finish his beer to leave, which was of course total bullshit.

He laughed, "God, I hope so. So. Hot. And she has guns and likes to shoot things. All cops like to shoot things. Ugh, I love her." He made a curvy body silhouette motion with his hands. I just rolled my eyes.

"Let's go, Romeo. I got twenty bucks that says she doesn't show, and if she does, she doesn't give you the time of day." I laughed at him and walked to his truck, leaving him standing in the doorway to chug his beer.

Isabel

After a long day, I always needed a drink. It's just how you unwound in my family; with a nice stiff cocktail. I couldn't be bothered with making my go-to martini after the long day I'd had, so a glass of Pinot Noir would do just fine. My parents were both very successful; my dad was a lawyer, my mom a physician, and while they were on their A-game all of the time, once the workday was over, it was time for a scotch and a martini respectively, and I had picked up that habit easily.

I hadn't even taken my gun off yet when I was reaching up into the cabinet to get a wine glass. I wasn't sure why I kept them up so high; I had to stretch to put them away and grab them, which was counterintuitive. I made a note to move things around in the cabinets to make the wine glasses easier to reach. Then I realized I would never get around to rearranging anything. Who was I kidding?

I was supposed to meet some of the people involved with my most recent closed case, mostly all firefighters, to celebrate an attempted murderer's conviction we'd nabbed. I didn't really care for celebrations like this very much, but I wanted to show some support and solidarity with the fire department. Cops and firefighters sometimes got along, while we competed other times, and this investigation wouldn't have happened without their help. I was only sorry Jack wasn't here to enjoy the celebration himself. Although, since his daughter was almost murdered, it was probably for the best he passed away before the investigation was even completed. I wasn't completely sure we would have been able to convict with the evidence Jack had collected, but once that Russell douchebag tried to kill Jo Meadows and she lived to tell about it, we had him nailed.

I admired her courage, getting on the stand and telling the jury what he did, especially after they had dated. Thankfully, he hadn't sexually assaulted her, but it couldn't have been easy getting up on the stand with the shadow of the black eye he gave her showing, and telling everyone he'd tied her, beat her up, and left her to burn to death in her own house.

I couldn't believe he hadn't even been on the run. He thought he'd gotten away with it, so we'd found him at his house, watching porn and jerking off. Literally, with his dick in hand was how we'd found him. What a sick bastard. Her house was on fire, where he'd left her tied up, and he was at home stroking his tiny dick. Some people are just fucked up. With the help of the new chief and a couple of other guys, we had all the evidence we needed to put that guy away for the foreseeable future. Thank God.

I put the wine glass on the counter and decided if I was going to go out to see all these people, wine wasn't going to cut it. I poured myself vodka on the rocks and took it with me to the bathroom while I got ready. I realized I really did want to socialize a little bit. I hadn't really gotten out much lately. I didn't have that many friends; it was hard to be a detective and have friends who do anything other than the same work you do, and I've gotten a little tired of only talking about crime. It was depressing and not as exciting as one would think from watching television. Investigating is mostly a lot of paperwork and research. But I wouldn't trade it for anything.

My partner, Kevin Connor, was definitely my friend, although he was still pretty irritated with me for running an investigation without him. I hadn't had a lot of choice in the matter. My captain had known what was going on, I'd had to tell him, but until we'd had a real case, I was told to keep it to myself. Kevin would have to get over it eventually. It had been a big case for me, with no real evidence until the last minute.

I pulled my long, dark hair out of the standard ponytail I wore to make myself look serious and examined my reflection in the mirror. I was only twenty-nine, but I felt thirty-nine and couldn't decide if I looked as old as I felt. Even though I had always wanted to be a detective, it was exhausting work. The long nights and early mornings were never really something you got used to. Not to mention the awful sons of bitches you encountered on a regular basis.

I never really found being a detective harder as a woman, so I was luckier than many, but my parents never approved. They had always hoped I would become a doctor or a lawyer like them, and they had always given my sister June an even harder time for stopping her schooling at paramedic and not finishing med school. She'd actually always had a harder time than me, since she'd been so close to becoming a doctor when she'd started working as a paramedic. Our parents just had a different view of what success meant. As stereotypical as it sounded, putting bad guys away was the life for me. Becoming a detective was the icing on the cake.

I put some makeup on, which was also pretty rare for me, fluffed my hair, and poured the rest of my vodka down my throat. The liquid courage burn felt good, warming me from my lips to my core. I changed into some jeans and a low cut V-neck black t-shirt. I didn't really have a lot of cute, girly clothes; I was working most of the time. Technically, this was kind of work related, but it didn't feel that way. I wanted to celebrate with Jo and Brian, and truth be told, their friends were easy on the eyes. June had told me that, but I hadn't realized it until I met them. Firefighters are hot; they just are, and everyone knows it. I felt a little tingle I hadn't felt in a while and rolled my eyes at myself.

I decided not to wear my off-duty weapon, so I could have a few more drinks freely. Why not loosen up a little? It wasn't that having the gun with you wasn't allowed, but it was a great way to get jammed up if there was a situation and you'd been drinking. I would put it in the glove box of my car though, because not having it at all made me uncomfortable. I slipped on some purple pumps, because why not? I was only 5'4" and had a small frame. I just loved wearing sexy shoes, and if this was going to be a night out, then I wanted to create the feeling it was a night out from the start. I had the next day off, so I could actually enjoy myself a little.

I smiled in the mirror by my doorway, thinking it could be fun to let loose and celebrate a little. It was my celebration too; I'd put another douchebag behind bars.

MATT

We got to the bar, and it was already packed. I had to admit, I loved the excitement of a crowded bar. Most people didn't, but I was always kind of looking for a girl who would entertain me, and a packed bar was certainly better odds than a quiet one with all the same people all of the time. I immediately saw our little group of friends at the bar, and there in the middle was Jo, sitting on a stool, with my brother standing behind her. He had really become very protective of her. I did actually like seeing that, even if it was still kind of weird for me. She softened him up a little, and she was more relaxed when he was around her, like she felt safe.

She caught my eye, gave me a huge smile, and hopped off her stool. When I walked over, she threw her arms around my neck, giving me a huge hug. "I'm so happy to see you, Matty!"

I laughed and squeezed her back, lifting her up off the ground, returning the hug. "I'm happy to see you too. It's been like three days. What the fuck? Doesn't my brother let you out anymore?" I gave my brother a handshake and laughed.

"He does, he does," she blushed. It was actually kind of cute to see her act that way over a guy, even if it was my brother. Her happiness did mean a lot to me, even if now she was trying to get me to take dating more seriously, which wasn't happening in the foreseeable future as far as I was concerned.

"Jo can do anything she wants, man. I can't help if it she'd rather stay in with me than hang out with you losers after work," Brian joked. While he was possessive over her, which I didn't really understand, I knew he'd give up everything for her. They were without a doubt my favorite two people on earth besides my mother.

"Gross. I don't want to hear about it." I covered up my ears and laughed again. This was my tribe; these were my people. I honestly couldn't think of a group of people I'd rather be around, be it at work or outside of it. I trusted them with my life, and they were safe. I wasn't much into branching out, even if we really did know each other's business most of the time, which could get uncomfortable for most, but not usually for us.

Jo smiled and poked me in the ribs. "I'm not telling you anything you don't already know. Now we need to find you someone you can lock yourself away with!" She smiled at me and gave me that look. The look women who are in love give you when they want you to be in love too. I could not imagine feeling that way about someone. I'd never met a chick I could even remotely envision any kind of a relationship with. Most of the girls I have found myself spending an evening with just wanted to be with a firefighter because they thought it was hot, and not because they had anything interesting to say.

Oddly enough, I felt a kind of relief Jo had ended up with Brian. Not because he was my brother; men don't feel that way about other men, even their brothers most of the time. But I've always been so protective of her myself that it actually gave me a sense of peace to see her being taken care of. Okay, yes, by my brother, but whatever, taken care of nonetheless by someone who didn't suck. I thought I might enjoy taking care of someone, but it just didn't seem realistic for me with the type of girls I typically met.

We were all drinking and carrying on when Jax elbowed me in the kidney while pointing to the door. That damn detective did show up. I couldn't believe it. Jo went to greet her. She looked totally different than the handful of times I had seen her before. She had her long, dark hair down and was wearing a tight t-shirt and jeans with some sexy-ass heels. When I had seen her before, she was dressed like a TV detective with her hair pulled back into a stuffy, tight-ass ponytail. She had definitely not been the hot piece of ass I saw walk in now. I felt a twitch in my dick seeing her in those high heels and tight-ass jeans. That wasn't what detectives wore in my little bit of experience, and now I was into detectives.

"Oh my God, I'm so glad you came, Detective!!!" Jo squealed and hugged her. They embraced in a hug that looked a little uncomfortable for the detective, which made me grin.

"I wouldn't miss it. You look so good, Josie," she said and touched Jo's face, clearly noticing how much she had healed since they'd last seen each other. It was a sweet moment to watch. I looked over at my brother and saw him watching as well.

"Thank you so much, Detective," Jo smiled.

"Call me Isabel," she laughed.

"Ok, you can call me Jo then. What would you like to drink? It's a celebration!" Jo yelled out.

"Hmmm, I'll have a Ketel and Club with lime, please." Jo turned around to get the bartender's attention, and the detective looked at the group of us watching them. "Ok, none of us is working, so please call me Isabel, or Izzy if you're feeling really friendly," she laughed and smiled.

She seemed different, like she had softened up. Jax stepped right up to reintroduce himself, of course. "Izzy, so glad you could make it out. I'm Seth Jackson, but everyone calls me Jax." He stuck his hand out for a shake, which she took.

"I remember seeing you at the hospital briefly. Nice to see you again." She turned to me. "Matt, right? I know we met quickly as well. It's nice to see you again." She gave me a big smile, and it caught me off guard for some reason.

I stuck my hand out to meet hers, and when we touched, it felt like an electrical charge hit me. "Yes, Matt. Matt Cavanaugh, Brian's brother. It's nice to see you. I know Jo is super happy you came out tonight, so thank you." She looked me right in the eye while I was talking, and it made me feel like I was stuttering or something. Having me her full attention focused on me like that took me off my game somehow.

She smiled at me, giving me a warm feeling all over. "I wouldn't have missed it." She let go of my hand, and I immediately missed it for a moment. Jo handed Isabel her drink, and they walked off to girl talk, I guessed.

"Earth to Matt!" Jax snapped his fingers in front of me.

Shaken from my momentary trance, I looked up at him. "Huh? What?"

"Umm, I already called dibs, pal, so back off." He jokingly punched my shoulder.

"Yea, yea, good luck, buddy," I laughed at him. I actually didn't want him to go anywhere near her all of a sudden. I didn't necessarily want her for myself, but any girl Jax got his hands on was generally all about him, and I didn't want that to happen. There was something interesting about her I couldn't put my finger on. But bro code was bro code, and I had already said I wasn't interested. That didn't stop me from being annoyed as I watched him walk over to the girls to talk.

I saddled up into the seat Jo had vacated next to my brother and got myself another beer. "So how's the love nest, brother?" I teased Brian.

That motherfucker actually blushed. "Dude, it's amazing. Waking up to her every day is like holding warm sunshine, man."

I had to roll my eyes and groan dramatically. "Oh my god, did you actually just say that? I am going to have to revoke your man card. I'm speechless."

"Go fuck yourself, bro. You'll see. Some chick is going to come along, and you're not gonna know what happened to you in the head. I'm telling you, it's better than I could have ever imagined. Which leads me to something I need help with," he said.

"I don't see that happening to me, but anyway, what do you need?" I honestly couldn't imagine wanting to wake up to the same person every day of my life.

"I want to ask Jo to marry me, and I want your help," he whispered.

I almost spit my beer out, choking on it. "You want to do what?" I did not whisper at all.

"Shut the fuck up, man. It's a surprise." He got close and gave me the shut up hand gesture. I couldn't even believe we were having this conversation.

"I don't understand. You want to ask her to marry you? You've been together as a couple for like five minutes. Why now?" I just couldn't even comprehend why they'd want to get married so quickly.

"When you know, you know. I want to make it official, and I don't see any reason to wait. We want to have a family of our own, and we have plans for a future together. Do you have a problem with this?" He gave me a concerned look. I guess my shock and surprise gave him the impression I didn't approve. It wasn't that at all. I didn't know why I was even questioning him; they'd clearly been meant for each other. I guess I just didn't understand the rush; they'd just moved so fast.

"No, no. I'm sorry, bro. I didn't mean for it to sound that way. I'm just surprised you're moving so fast. It's like lightening fast for an outsider looking in. I believe you though. I know you love each other, and I'll help you do whatever you need. Seriously." I felt bad for making him think I didn't approve.

"Thanks, I appreciate it. Basically, I want to find a way to surprise her in the next couple of weeks, so I was hoping you might be able to help me come up with some ideas or help me get her where I need her to be," he said.

"Yea, of course, man. Whatever you need." I looked around and saw Jo and Isabel still leaning up against the wall, talking and smiling. They were both so pretty. As I looked around the bar, I noticed a lot of guys staring in their direction. "Did you get a ring?"

"Yea, mama went with me to pick it out. I wanted to be traditional and kind of do it the right way, and since her dad isn't here, I went and talked to mama about it last week, and we went shopping. I think she'll love it." He was glowing. When he talked about Jo, he was either pissed and defensive because someone was hitting on her, or he was being protective about something, or he was lit up like a Christmas tree. She definitely did something to him no one else ever did.

"That's awesome. Alright, well, let me know what you have in mind, and I'll make sure she's where you need her to be." I absolutely wanted to help in any way I could.

"Thanks, man. Ok, keep quiet. The girls are coming back. That detective is hot, dude. You should *investigate* that. It looks like Jax has moved on," he laughed and made air quotes when he said investigate. I rolled my eyes at him again and then looked back as the girls were walking up. Jax had taken up with a blonde across the room. He really did have the attention span of a fly when it came to talking to women.

"What's going on over here, gentlemen?" Isabel asked. She smiled at us, and her beautiful, full lips revealed the most perfect white, straight teeth. I was thinking about what I'd like to do with that mouth of hers. She was really sexy.

"Nothing at all, Isabel. We were just having brother talk, is all. Can I get you another drink?" I nodded toward her empty glass.

"Why, yes, you can, thank you very much." She stepped closer to me, so I scooted over to give her a spot next to me at the bar, and we leaned up together. I caught a hint of her perfume as she leaned in closer. I wasn't sure what it was, but it was light and sweet smelling, sending a signal right to my cock again. I almost groaned out loud. She was turning me on, and I didn't understand it, since frankly, I hadn't liked her all that much before I got here.

"So, Isabel, how does a pretty girl like you become a detective? Does it run in your family?" I flirted a little while we waited for our drinks.

She laughed. "No! Not at all, actually. My mom is a doctor, and

301

my dad is a lawyer. They never really loved the idea of me being a cop at all. I think they're used to it now, but they definitely would have preferred I did something else."

"Interesting. So you must really love it then?" I was fascinated that someone as pretty as her would want to chase after douchebags for a living. It was sexy, mostly because it was badass.

She looked off for a moment and smiled before meeting my eyes again, so I focused. "I really do love it. I can't imagine doing anything else. Every single day, even when I'm doing bullshit paperwork and dealing with red tape, I'm helping people. It was a calling for me, running investigations, chasing the bad guys, the whole thing. I was meant for it..." She started to trail off. "I must sound silly," she said and rolled her eyes at herself.

I leaned in closer, so she could hear me. The bar was noisy, and I simply wanted to get closer to her while we were talking. "It's not silly at all. It's how I feel about being a firefighter. I think it's comforting to know I'm doing exactly what I was meant for. So no, I don't think it's silly at all. I completely understand what you mean." Her intent stare into my eyes was throwing me off again. Then the corners of her mouth turned upward into a smile, making me smile too. She listened so intently when I spoke, like she was truly listening and interested in what I had to say. So few people did that, really. Maybe it was because she was a detective and was looking for answers or something. Whatever it was, it was attractive to have her focus, and it drew me to her in a way I didn't expect.

Isabel

I was listening to Matt tell me how he was drawn to firefighting the way I was drawn to police work, and I felt like he truly understood that pull to do something the same way I did. He was an attentive listener, and I kept getting lost looking into his green eyes. He and his brother had the same beautiful green eye color, but Matt's were softer in a way. He never looked away when I talked to him, and he was hot. I had to admit it. He was six foot three inches of rock solid, beautiful manliness. He didn't have tattoos all over his arms, but I could faintly see he had one on his chest and shoulder, and I found myself wanting to see more of them, without the obstruction of his shirt. His dark blond hair was perfectly trimmed, and he didn't have one bit of facial hair either; he was clean cut. I wondered how old he was. He had a bit of a baby face, but he was also seemingly mature in a way as well. He absolutely oozed sex appeal, and even though I didn't really need to be quite as close as I was, he smelled amazing, so I kept leaning in as his scent wafted around me.

As the moistness in my panties became apparent to me, I tried to shake off the attraction I was feeling. This was supposed to be professional, right? Or was it social? I could never tell, really, but I was certain I shouldn't have been so extremely turned on as I was at that moment. All we were doing was talking about our careers. I was lost in thought on that for a moment when he spoke again.

"Want to do a shot?" He raised his eyebrows at me and gave me a million-dollar smile, causing me to giggle a little bit.

"Sure, why not? I am off tomorrow. Let's have some fun." I was hoping I wouldn't regret saying that later. I did want to go to the range tomorrow afternoon for some target practice, and with a hangover, that would be damned near impossible. The bar was so crowded, we were standing really close to each other, and even closer when we both leaned in to address the bartender.

He ordered us two shots and got me another vodka soda and himself another beer. Handing me the shot of dark liquid, clearly whiskey, he flashed me that smile and raised his glass to toast. "To catching the bad guys." I clinked my glass to his and poured the warm liquor down my throat. I felt the burn all the way down but never broke eye contact with him. I couldn't stop looking at those eyes.

"Well, that was gross. What was that?" I asked as I put the shot glass down and took a sip of my vodka.

"Aw, come on now. That was Irish whiskey! It's good for you. Warms you from the inside out," he laughed at me, and I pursed my lips.

"Well, we live in Florida, so I don't generally need to be warmed up," I replied sarcastically.

"Oh, everyone needs to be warmed up every now and again, don't you think, Detective?" He leaned in close to whisper the last part, essentially melting my panties into nothing. Goddammit, he was so hot, and smooth too. He was definitely flirting with me, and I was loving it.

I didn't want to get into a situation I would surely regret later, like going home with this player, so I leaned back a bit, away from him, and said, "I suppose you're probably right. And I suspect you'd know far more about that than I do, wouldn't you?" A hot single guy like him, there was no way he wasn't a total womanizer, regardless of how nice his family was. He was just way too smooth for this to be his first rodeo.

"I don't know, Detective. I suspect you can hold your own just fine, maybe even teach me a thing or two." He stared down at me, challenging me with his eyes. We were facing each other, and I really had nowhere to go in the small space we had squeezed ourselves into. I could feel my heart racing. I enjoyed this cat and mouse game a little too much, and the alcohol was definitely getting to me. I watched his lips move as he spoke and couldn't help but think of what they'd feel like pressed softly against mine.

"You never know, Cavanaugh. Anything's possible." I smiled. I didn't know what to say. I didn't want to push him away, but I knew that anything happening tonight would be so wrong and only end in some kind of disaster. The intensity between us had grown. I had almost forgotten we were at a completely packed bar while we were talking. I wanted that to come out sounding like a joke, but it wasn't. In actuality, I'd have loved to leave right that moment to let him fuck me rough and dirty against the wall in the alley.

"I see you like to be vague, but I can tell you like me, Detective. Just a little bit, but you definitely want more, don't you? I can see it in your eyes." I couldn't believe he was just asking me that outright. He had some balls. Clearly, his ego was talking, and the alcohol, of course. He wasn't wrong though.

"I don't even know you, Cavanaugh. But you're awfully sure of

AMY BRIGGS

yourself, aren't you? You think your moves always work on the ladies, don't you?" His boldness was starting to irritate me a bit, and his obvious player tendencies were ringing in my head as they came to the forefront of my imagination. I could envision some little blonde bouncing up and down on his dick, and it actually aggravated the shit out of me. I couldn't begin to fathom why I cared, but it was making me mad nonetheless.

"I have my fair share of luck, if that's what you're asking me. Right now, I'm talking to you though." He leaned in to whisper something in my ear when Brian walked up with Jo. Matt took a step back, looking taken off guard.

"We interrupting something here?" Brian looked from one to the other of us in quick succession, searching for an answer to his question.

I spoke up first. "Not at all, Chief. Matt here was just telling me about how much he loves firefighting. And how he has plenty of luck with the ladies." I had stepped away from the bar, closer to Brian and Jo, and was looking directly at Matt with a smirk planted across my face. *Take that, pal.*

"Is that so?" Jo laughed. She looked at me and rolled her eyes in Matt's direction. "Well, his taste in those women he speaks of actually sucks, so don't let him tell you otherwise." She gave him an eye roll and a dramatic fake smile.

"Hey, wait a minute. We were just talking, weren't we, Detective?" He gave me a bit of a glare mixed with a look of desperation to be saved from the conversation. I was fairly pleased with myself; feeling like I'd knocked his ego down a peg. I didn't like cocky out of the gate, and I surely didn't care for his presumptuous attitude with me. Even if he was ridiculously good

306

looking.

In any event, I didn't want him to be completely angry with me. "I'm just having some fun with you, Cavanaugh. Lighten up." I took a sip of my drink while smiling across the glass at him.

"Uh huh, I see how it is." He took a sip of his beer and turned to his brother. "So, how are you two doing?"

"Well, we were actually just coming over to say goodbye. It's been a long day, and we're...tired," Brian said and wrapped his arm around Jo.

"Oh, tired, I see." Matt rolled his eyes at them. "Well, Jo, congratulations, or whatever we're supposed to say when these things happen. I'll wait a half hour to text you until you're done," he joked.

Jo laughed back at him, and Brian playfully punched his arm. "Ahhh, go fuck yourself, little brother. Text her tomorrow. We'll be busy in half an hour, and half an hour after that as well. For the remainder of the evening, in fact."

Jo turned to me and leaned in for a hug. "Thank you so much for coming tonight, Isabel. I'd love to go have a girls' night or something soon if you'd be up for it. I'm with these clowns twenty-four hours a day, so it would be wonderful to have some lady time."

"I'd absolutely love that. You have my number, Jo. And seriously, great job, and I'm proud of you." She smiled at me, and they left the bar arm in arm. They really were in love. I didn't quite understand that kind of love. I'd certainly never had it, but I admired it. I actually would love to spend some girl time with Jo. She was tough but also feminine and pretty, and we had a lot in common, working in a man's world. I thought about asking her to meet up for coffee later in the week when Matt caught my attention again.

"So, Detective, where were we?" His cocky smile drew me in and irritated me at the same time.

"Cavanaugh, we weren't. We were just about to part ways. It's time for me to go as well." I leaned in close to him to set my drink down on the bar, catching one last sniff of his intoxicating, manly smell.

"I feel like we were just getting started." He looked down at me, and I almost got lost in those pools of green again.

"No, you're mistaken. It's time for me to go. I'm sure I'll see you around somewhere, Cavanaugh. Have a good night." I turned around and walked out the back door to the rear parking lot where my car was without awaiting a reply from him or looking back. It probably looked like I was making an escape, and truthfully, I was. He had a charm about him you knew was probably not good, but it was goddamn irresistible.

MATT

I couldn't believe she'd turned around and left like that. I decided to follow her out. I didn't know why, but I was enjoying our little game. I thought she was kind of into me, at least a little. She wasn't normally my type, but then again, a guy like me didn't really have a type. But she was challenging. I liked a challenge. A moment after she left, I walked out the back door too, looking for her.

I saw her walking down the short alley to her car and ran to catch up to her when she quickly turned around, gave me an elbow to the ribs, and shoved me into the wall of the building.

"Jesus Christ, Isabel, it's me!!" I grabbed my side and crouched over in pain as I leaned against the wall.

"What the fuck, Cavanaugh? You don't run up behind a girl in the alley at a bar! What the fuck is wrong with you?" I couldn't believe she was mad at me! I was hoping she didn't crack a fucking rib. She was fucking strong and got me good.

"Well, Detective, I wanted to see you out to your car like a gentleman, but instead, you assaulted me." I decided to try to make her feel at least a little bit bad about nearly kicking my ass in the alley.

She softened her stance against me after the shock had worn

off, and I guess she realized I wasn't a threat. "I was already gone. Jesus. Well, shit, I'm sorry. Are you ok?" She came closer and put her hand on my ribs softly, attempting to lift my shirt to take a look at where she got me with her elbow, immediately making my dick hard.

Her touch sent chills through me, and I felt my breath hitch as she lifted my shirt up to see where she'd hit me. She rubbed her hand along my rib softly, and I flinched a little when she came to the tender spot, all the while turning me on at the same time. I watched her inspect my body for a moment and then grabbed her hand. I thought I'd explode if I let her soft little fingers roam across my abs any further.

She stopped, looking up at me while I had a hold of her hand at her wrist. "Am I hurting you?" she whispered.

"Not anymore," I whispered back, looking into her beautiful, brown eyes. My desire had taken over my entire body, and I wanted to taste her so badly. She gave me a small smile, and I pulled her into me with my other arm, letting my lips just barely touch hers, testing the waters of what I felt was our pull to one another.

She leaned into my kiss, letting me explore her mouth with my tongue and taste the citrus from her drinks on her lips. I released the hand I had grabbed to run my hands through her long, dark hair, while she ran her hands under my shirt to my back, gripping me just enough to send me into a spiral of want for her, feeling her pressed up against me, grabbing me like that. For a moment, we kissed passionately and softly, then, as her grip on me tightened, my animal need for her took control. I pulled away to look at her, inspecting her face for a reaction to what I was about to do.

Her hands were on my chest, and she looked at me hungrily,

biting her lip just a little and giving me doe eyes. I charged in, crushing my lips to hers this time. Her sexiness was more than I could stand, and I'd completely forgotten she'd nearly knocked the wind out of me just a few moments earlier. As she reached up around my neck, giving me her mouth roughly, I scooped her up in my arms, completely picking her up and swinging us around so I could press myself into her against the wall of the building. My cock was straining. I was practically fucking her through my jeans. I couldn't get enough of her. I wanted to fuck her hard right there in the alley, and she wasn't fighting it; in fact, she was clawing at me, while I held her tiny frame up against the wall.

"Isabel, come home with me," I whispered in her ear. I wanted to carry her to my car right then and there and have my way with her. As it turned out, she had other plans.

She hopped down and rested her forehead against my chest for a split second before she pushed me away. "I gotta go, Cavanaugh. That was fun." *That was fun?* She gave me a smile, patted my ribs gently, and said, "You're lucky I didn't shoot you. I'll see you around." She laughed a little bit, ducked under my arm, and started to walk away.

I spun in her direction, shocked. "Are you kidding me, Isabel? You're leaving?" My cock was throbbing, and my head was spinning.

"Yea, I gotta run. Lots to do tomorrow. But I'll see you, don't worry," she winked at me, then walked to her car, a fully restored 1969 Chevy Camaro that was black with racing stripes. She had a muscle car. Fuck me, she was hot.

Isabel

My heart was racing, but I knew I had to go. I couldn't get that close and let him know what I really wanted. That was just a momentary lapse in judgment. We all need to feel some skin after all. The fact of the matter was I really liked wild sex, and that wasn't something you shared with someone you were definitely going to see in the field or on scenes. I was very free with my sexuality, and I would have fucked him in that alley if I didn't think I'd see him at work or if I wasn't making plans with his best friend to do girly things later in the week. I was comfortable with what I liked, but I also didn't want it out in the open either.

As I hopped into my baby, I checked the glove box for my gun out of routine. It was right where I'd left it, and I started up the engine. I was still really hot, and my panties were soaked from that session in the alley. I couldn't help but wonder if he was the kind of guy who was able to give me what I needed to be satisfied. He was so fucking hot; thinking of the way he'd slammed me up against the building gave me goose bumps all over again. I was definitely going to have to get out my little toy when I got home to curb that desire.

The rumble from my car's engine only fueled my need for release. I couldn't get home fast enough. I slowly touched myself, massaging between my legs on the ride, thinking about the alley. Normally, when I got home, I poured myself a drink, but I couldn't wait to pleasure myself and immediately stripped down to my bra and panties and headed for my bedroom practically panting. I was completely soaked, and the cool between my legs when the air hit the wetness had me heading for the drawer next to my bed immediately.

Thinking of Matt and his huge cock pressed up against me, I grabbed the big one; the one you only pulled out once in awhile. I leaned back on my bed, turning the soft vibration on, and touched it to my most sensitive spot, rubbing it along my clit over my underwear. With my other hand, I pulled down my bra, exposing one of my breasts. I licked my finger and started to circle my nipple, making it even harder than it was before. I couldn't stand to wait any longer, so I used my vibrator to push my panties aside and slid it inside me slowly while increasing the vibration's intensity. It felt like it was jerking inside me with an intense vibrating pattern, and I felt my release coming faster. Pinching my own nipple, imagining Matt biting gently on it then flicking at it with his tongue, the wave came up on me, and I cried out, arching my back, with my vibrator deep inside me, coaxing me through.

After I finished, I lay there on my bed for a moment thinking about how it would feel to have Matt actually finish me off the way I wanted. He was a single guy, not appearing to want to be tied down. Maybe he would have been a good choice to take to my bed. I certainly wasn't going to go home with him. He had a roommate. I didn't want roommates in my business, and I felt safe at my place. I wondered when I'd see him again. *He certainly left an impression*, I mused to myself, staring at the ceiling fan above my bed.

The last thing I remembered was watching it whirl around, cooling me down, when my alarm went off. I woke startled and realized I must have passed out the night before. I went into the bathroom and inspected myself in the mirror, raising my fingers gently to my lips, thinking of the night before. Our moment in the alley was hot, and I was getting turned on just thinking of touching his tight abs and how he'd slammed me against the wall. And could he kiss, oh my God. I shuddered at the thought of his touch and got my ass ready for the gym. I worked out almost every day, definitely at least six days a week. I had always been pretty obsessed with it.

I belonged to a martial arts gym that mostly trained fighters and mixed martial artists. I didn't train to fight, and I never competed, but the workouts consisted of such intense agility and strength training that I really felt like it was the best mix for me to stay in absolute top condition. I hated running, but I'd do it once in awhile. My sister loved doing fun races like 5Ks for charity, so I did those with her as long as there were celebratory cocktails afterwards. She was the runner for sure; in fact, she had done a handful of marathons, which I couldn't even fathom. I mostly worked with a trainer and did crossfit type workouts, which were varied every day but always intense.

One of my favorite workouts was Muay Thai, which was essentially kickboxing that allowed you to throw elbows and knees at your opponent or the bag, which I simply loved to do. That's where I learned how to throw the elbow I gave Matt to those beautiful abs of his, and I knew I had hit him pretty hard. All really great self defense tactics, but also for someone as small as me, and in my line of work, having multiple ways to get a leg up on an unruly perp was critical. I had a tendency to drink fairly often, but other than that, I took my health and my fitness seriously.

I wanted to get my workout in early, so I could hit the gun range in the afternoon and stay there as long as I wanted. I had qualifications coming up again, which I wasn't worried about, but it was always wise to get out and practice a little. Plus, I really enjoyed shooting. My partner, Kevin, usually went with me, but he wasn't available today; he was helping his parents with some home improvement projects. He was very handy and always helped them keep their house up. He was a good guy, and I was lucky to have him for a partner. Since it was just going to be me, I planned to take some of my other personal guns to play around with. It was looking like a good day ahead.

MATT

I woke up the next day annoyed as fuck, and it was because of that goddamn detective. *Who the fuck acts that way?* Not only did she hit me, fucking hard, she left me hanging and hard as hell in the alley, which I still could not believe. I had no appreciation for a tease like that, and I went to bed feeling dumbfounded, turned on, and pissed off all at the same time. I got up and shook off the night before as I got myself ready for the gym. I usually worked out with my brother or Jax or both, but since we all had the day off from work, Brian was hanging out with Jo and going to the beach. They did that a lot on their days off, and I actually even went with them sometimes. Brian and I would fish, while Jo read books and lay in the sun with SPF 2 billion on so she wouldn't burn like a lobster.

I walked into the kitchen, where Jax was dressed already, but not for the gym. "Hey, are you gonna hit the gym with me today? I was planning to go shooting later too."

He was finishing his coffee and shook his head as he put his cup in the sink. "I have an appointment at the VA today. I'll probably be there all fucking day, so count me out for this afternoon."

"Maybe someday they'll get their shit together, man. Sorry. Everything ok?"

He grabbed his keys by the door. "Yea, of course. Just routine shit. No big deal. I just never know how long it's going to take, is all. I'll catch up with you later." He headed out the door quickly.

"Later, man." I waved in his general direction. Jax got out of the Marines two years prior, and he really didn't talk about it very much at all, other than that his platoon were his brothers and that the desert was awful. He had been deployed three times in the eight years he had been in, and said he'd never go back. We went to high school together, and besides being a firefighter, all he'd ever wanted to do was serve his country. We all thought he would make a career out of it and were shocked when he decided not to re-enlist after his last tour. He had become one of my best friends besides Jo, of course, before he'd left. He had already been to the fire academy with us when we were young and was a staple down at the station just like the rest of us through high school. Always happy and always a friend to everyone. He came back different; more quiet and thoughtful. But when we asked about it when he first came back, he said he was just happy to be home, in the U.S., and never really elaborated. I made a note to ask him again when he wasn't in a hurry sometime soon, and I headed to the gym.

Even though I enjoyed going out, and I certainly liked to have a few drinks, working out was really important to me. The job was fun, I couldn't imagine doing anything else in the world, but it was physically demanding and stressful sometimes. We've always been into working out; Brian and I both played sports since we were little, so it was just something we'd always done. I didn't go to a fancy gym. I worked out at the firehouse gym, which was actually pretty nice. It was early in the day, so there wouldn't be too many people there, and I could get my workout in and get cleaned up and out on the range around midday.

I ran into a few of the guys from the other shift at the firehouse, but I was still so rattled by Isabel that I didn't stop to shoot the shit like I normally would have. I absolutely hated running, but I did it every single day, even if it was only two miles. As much as I loathed the hamster wheel of a treadmill, I hopped on it, popped my ear buds in, and ran. I listened to System of a Down and a bunch of other hard rock. It always pumped me up and got me going, and with the mood I was in, I was able to take my aggression out on the run.

After about thirty minutes, the endorphins kicked in, and I wasn't feeling so deranged over a woman anymore while I got to the other part of my workout. I always started with a run, but I always finished with a crossfit type workout, because I really felt like it was the best kind for what we did for a living. You could lift heavy shit up and put it down, and you could curl your arms a thousand times, but that wouldn't necessarily train you to be agile in an emergency situation, which was always my goal. We hadn't had any particularly challenging fires in a while, and that always made me feel like we were about due for one. What we'd call the "big one."

A firefighter could go his whole career without the "big one," the fire that you see on the news in some warehouse or giant office building; the fire that caused guys to wonder if they could really do the job. I was made for that fire, and I was always training for it. I think that was why Jax and I got along so well. He was like the resident Boy Scout that was always training too, and always prepared for an emergency. Our house was the same way. We were prepared for the apocalypse, frankly. We had everything you could possibly need to survive in a disaster situation in our basement; rope, candles, MRE pre-packed military food, tools, you name it. We also had weapons. Lots of them. I had become a bit of a gun collector over the years, and essentially, between Jax and me, we had a small arsenal.

As I finished my last set of burpees, thinking about going shooting made me smile. The day might not have started out that great, but I knew it would be a great afternoon by myself, shooting and enjoying the sun.

Isabel

After my killer workout, I showered and gathered my two guns and supplies to go to the range. I just had my issued pistol, as well as a smaller pistol that was easier to conceal. I didn't really see a need for much more than that. The range was outdoors, so I grabbed my sunscreen, my safety glasses, my guns, ammo, and ear protection and headed out.

Normally, I wouldn't wear my badge out and about on my day off, but since I was going to the gun range, I clipped it at the waist of my jeans. I didn't especially care to explain myself as a woman when I went places like that, and with my badge, they'd just assign me a lane and send me on my way. While I knew the owner and most of the people who worked there, on occasion, some new guy wanted to show me how to shoot, or talk to me about shooting, and I couldn't possibly be less interested in a conversation when I was going to focus.

Thankfully, when I arrived, the owner was working, and I was able to go right outside to a lane by myself. As I set up my targets, I saw a familiar silhouette out of the corner of my eye. *Sonofabitch, it's Matt Cavanaugh. Walking my way.* My pulse quickened, and I felt immediately short of breath as I flashed back to the night before. I looked away quickly, but it was too late; I had caught his eye, I could tell even through his aviator sunglasses. *Was he this hot last night?* I looked back up as he got closer and noticed his jeans fitting him snugly in all the right places and his t-shirt clinging to his muscular arms, while he carried what looked like quite a few things for a day at the range.

He set his stuff down in the lane next to mine and turned to me, taking his sunglasses off. "Well, hello there, Detective. Fancy meeting you here today." He smirked and rolled his eyes at me. I suppose I deserved that a little bit. I certainly didn't think I'd see him this soon after last night.

I took my sunglasses off and set them on the table next to me. "Well, I *am* an officer, Cavanaugh, so it's not entirely unlikely I'd be out shooting." I couldn't tell if I was flirting or being a bitch, probably both. Sometimes I couldn't help myself. I thought I'd better apologize, or at least make it sound more like I was flirting, or definitely change the subject, but I couldn't speak.

"I suppose you're right, Detective." It was really bothering me how he emphasized *detective*, like he didn't want to say my name.

"You can call me Isabel, Matt." I huffed it at him.

"Oh, we're being friendly again, are we? Should I protect my ribs?" He dramatically took a step back and protected his body with his arms. I put my hands on my hips and cocked my head at him.

"In my defense, you came running up behind me in a dark alley." I paused and thought about what happened next. "And you seemed alright when I left last night." I smiled.

"Ohhhh, you call leaving someone like that alright, do you? Remind me never to get left *not alright* by you," he retorted sarcastically, but gave me a huge smile. God, he and his brother really were beautiful. I looked at his eyes as he watched me, trying to figure out my next move, but all I could think of was getting lost in the green, with maybe flecks of blue that I could see. I wanted to get a closer look. Then I was brought back to reality. "Isabel, is everything ok?"

"Oh, yea. Of course, it is." I shuffled back to my lane to finish setting up my targets. "I have qualifications coming up again soon, and I enjoy practicing anyway. What brings you here today? It looks like you have a lot of stuff with you."

"I'm actually here quite a bit. And yes, I do have a lot of stuff with me. I have several different firearms. I'm a bit of a collector." He started to settle into the lane next to me, which had my heart racing even more, and I was totally turned on by the fact he enjoyed shooting. I wasn't sure why, because I never dated cops, and they all went shooting of course. There was something about him that kept catching my eye, but I did actually want to practice a bit.

"That's interesting. You'll have to show me what you've got. Maybe after we practice a little bit." I felt my lips curl into a little smile like I couldn't stop them.

"I'd love to."

He turned to finish unloading his arsenal, and I adjusted my holster so I could practice drawing my gun from it. It wasn't particularly difficult once you were adept at using your firearm to be able to shoot a target consistently. What was more difficult and required practice, was safely drawing your gun, presenting it at the target, and assessing the situation quickly. There were a lot of different kinds of holsters, and we were allowed to use whichever we felt most comfortable with, which was nice.

My preference was the outside-the-waistband holster, which was essentially a holster that attached to your waistband on the outside of your pants. I found this option was the best way to get a completely locked-in grip on my gun right from the holster. When I wasn't on duty, I used an inside-the-waistband holster, depending on what I was wearing, which concealed the gun a bit better and slipped between you and your clothes. Most concealed weapons carriers used one of these two. I only concealed my weapon when I was off duty, and I didn't really go out that much, so I didn't have a need to conceal it often.

Trying to ignore the ridiculously hot firefighter in the lane next to me, I practiced drawing my weapon quickly down range a few times before I got my eye and ear protection on. I took a deep breath as I looked down range at my target and tried to put Matt out of my mind for a moment to focus, which was damn near impossible. I was certain I could smell him, that manly, freshly-showered scent, and it was intoxicating me. As I checked my weapon, loaded it, and holstered it, I saw him watching me, and I glanced in his direction.

"Do you mind if I watch?" he asked me softly.

"No, not at all." I smiled and refocused.

I had the all clear to shoot, so I went for it. It wasn't the first time I'd done that, of course, but for some reason it felt different having him watch me. It actually made me feel powerful, and with that realization, I drew my gun from the holster, set my sights on the target, and squeezed the trigger in rapid succession until the gun was empty, then dropped the magazine one handed, reloaded with the other hand, and did it again. A total of thirty shots fired in about two minutes. As an officer, I was allowed to carry a fifteen-round magazine, while most civilians carried a ten- to thirteen-round magazine, depending on the type of gun.

I could tell I shot well, and the draw from my holster felt smooth, which was good. I didn't draw my gun quickly often; in fact, I'd only ever had to do it twice on the job in the twelve years since I became a cop. I drew it from its holster on a regular basis, just not in this manner. I set my gun down on the counter in front of me and took off my ear protection.

"Nice shooting!" Matt exclaimed.

"Thanks," I grinned at him. I knew I could shoot, but for some reason, I was feeling like I wanted to show off to him, show him what I could do. Being around him made me feel like a woman, and I wasn't used to that. He made me feel feminine and strong at the same time. I was one of the guys at work, and of course, I had to be kind of tough, so I wasn't used to feeling so soft. It was outside of my comfort zone, and yet I was enjoying it at the same time.

"Let's see it. That was what, thirty rounds?" He came and stood close enough for me to smell him again, making my head swim with desire. I felt my hands want to touch him, and I stopped myself. *Maybe he'd let me see if I left a bruise on those delicious looking abs of his,* I thought to myself before shaking it off.

"Yea, thirty rounds. I can't ever imagine a scenario in which I'd need to shoot that many, but it's good practice and lets me see if my shots are consistent or not. Plus, it's kind of fun to rapid fire like that, don't you think?" I flipped the switch that brought my paper target back to me on a zip line, so we could take a closer look at it.

He laughed while we watched the paper approach us. "Well, we aren't all allowed to carry quite as many rounds as you, but yes, I agree. It's definitely fun. Holy shit, Isabel!" His eyes got huge as he looked at my target, which had a hole blown right through the middle of it. Even I was shocked. There were no stray shots at all, just a perfect little blown-out hole in the chest of the target caricature.

I laughed as I pulled it off the clip it hung from and examined it more closely. "Well, I guess my work here is done," I joked.

"I'd say so. Jesus Christ, girl. That's some goddamn good shooting." He kept staring at the paper.

"Thank you. So, why don't you show me some of your arsenal over there? I mean, if you don't mind." I realized I had just invited myself into what looked like some alone time he may have had planned. I knew a lot of people, like myself, often went shooting to work things out in their head, or to not think about things for awhile, which made me wonder why he was there and what might be going on in his head.

He looked down at me and smiled again. "I'd love to show you what I've got." His smile turned into a smirk, and I felt my face get hot and flushed from the innuendo.

"Relax, Isabel. I was talking about my guns. Get your mind out of the gutter, woman." He turned around to get his stuff sorted, while I forced a giggle out and tried to regain my composure, once again thinking about how hot he was and kicking myself for not going home with him the night before.

"Ok, so this is an AR-15. I'm sure you've seen plenty of them, but have you ever shot one of these?" He held it up for me to see.

"No, actually, I haven't." I admired it. That gun was powerful, and in the wrong hands, deadly, as politics in this day and age would attest to. Many of the criminals we went after had them, and on the streets, they were bad news.

"Okay, well, today you're going to. I think you'll like it. It's pretty fun to shoot, I'll be honest." Flashing me that million-dollar smile, he set it on the counter in front of his lane and got the magazines and ammo ready. "Here, load this magazine with these rounds." He handed me an empty magazine and pointed to a box of ammo, and I got to work loading.

"Ok, all done." I had loaded three magazines, while he had done the same.

"Do you want to watch me do it first, or do you want me to show you how to shoot it, and then you can go?"

"I want you to show me how. I'm excited to try it." I really was excited to shoot it and didn't want to watch him do it. Mostly, just because I was impatient. Normally, you'd need to wear your ear protection the whole time you were out there, because people were shooting nonstop, but we were the only people at the range that day, and we had taken it off after I shot my rounds. Now, we put it back on, and I looked over to him for my instructions. I was excited, but I was all about gun safety too, so I wanted to pay close attention.

"Ok, come over here. I'm going to stand behind you and show you how to hold it, and then we'll fire the first couple of rounds together. Then you can shoot on your own if you want, ok?" He motioned for me to step up to the counter in his lane, and then he pressed himself up against my back, reaching around me for the gun. I almost flinched at his touch, which he must have sensed. "Isabel, just relax."

"Ok," was all I could muster. I needed to shake off the anxiety a bit. It wasn't like I'd never shot a gun. I had just destroyed my own target a couple of minutes prior. His touch was distracting but comforting as well. I took a deep breath and sighed, settling myself into his arms comfortably, then relaxing into him. I was so turned on by him, and a little apprehensive but equally excited about shooting the rifle. I could feel my heart racing and wondered if he could feel it as well. He placed the gun in my hands, wrapping himself even closer around me, and helped me adjust my hand positioning by placing his over mine. He maneuvered my fingers into the right places and then showed me how to load the magazine into place, using his hand to guide mine to do the work.

He leaned in close to my ear and said, "Ok, now we'll take these first couple of shots together, then you can shoot away. Sound good?" It was hard to hear each other with earplugs, but I heard him and nodded my understanding. "Nod when you're comfortable and ready," he said loudly. I took another deep breath as he moved his right hand over mine on the trigger of the gun, then I nodded.

Together, we squeezed the trigger slowly, igniting the gas piston and firing the rifle. The recoil was unexpected, causing me to lose my footing a bit and pushing me backwards roughly into Matt's rock hard chest. It. Felt. Amazing. I could feel him chuckling behind me, while I readjusted my feet, and we shot again. After about ten rounds of shooting slowly, he relaxed his grip on me and stepped back a little bit, his fingers lingering over mine as he left the gun in my hands.

I could still sense his presence behind me, but I was in control now and fired off the remaining rounds in the rifle. I counted ten more after he surrendered it over to me, then it ran out, and I set it down and started giggling. Taking my earphones off and turning around, I caught Matt standing there with the biggest smile, making me flushed. He was not only hot, but he was handsome. He was Mr. All American with those pools of green and those perfect teeth as he stood before me, arms crossed with his biceps bulging, just smiling at me.

"Was that fun or what?" he asked.

"Oh my God, that was awesome. Thank you so much for letting me shoot it. That was amazing." I felt like a little kid at Christmas. It was exhilarating to shoot a powerful weapon like that. You could feel your entire body reverberate.

"If you want to hang around and shoot some other fun stuff, you're more than welcome to. I've got guns from most of the major American wars I have collected and was planning to shoot this afternoon. If you're not busy." He lifted his glasses to his head to look directly at me. I lifted my glasses and placed them on top of my head to meet his eyes.

"I would love that, if you're sure you don't mind." I really did enjoy shooting, and honestly, I enjoyed his company.

"As long as you promise not to hit me again, I don't mind at all. Jax doesn't let me yammer on about my guns anymore, so it'll be fun for me to show them to you," he smiled and put his glasses back down, while he started to get the other guns out of his bag.

MATT

Isabel was just too hot for words. She had me wound up all morning, and I wanted to be pissed off at her when I saw her, but one look at her ass in jeans, followed by watching her assume a combat stance and rapid fire shoot her pistol, and I completely forgot what I was mad about. All I wanted to do was bend her over the counter, slap her ass for the other night, and fuck her. Literally, it was the first thing I thought. Then when she got anxious about shooting the rifle, I wanted to wrap my arms around her and comfort her.

I had never taught anyone to shoot like that, but she was so tiny, I knew the recoil from the gun was going to knock her right on that sweet ass of hers if I wasn't standing there. Being that close to her again was such a fucking turn-on, and I tried like hell not to look like it, but I sure couldn't help but feel drawn to her after last night and the position we were in. I was certain she could feel my heart beating through my chest right into her back. As I inhaled behind her, I could smell coconut and flowers, taking me someplace else in my head. She smelled like the beach on a hot summer day. It was intoxicating. I wanted to taste her so badly I actually felt saliva pool in my mouth as if I were hungry and smelled something I had been craving.

Amy Briggs

We spent the rest of the afternoon shooting, while I showed her some of the guns I'd collected. I had been collecting guns from the major American wars, plus a few fun ones too. She wanted to hear all about them, so I went through a few of them for her. I was really surprised at how interested she seemed, but maybe as a cop, she had an affinity for firearms too. From WWI, I had a Springfield M1903. It was a five-shot, bolt-action rifle; it was the basic issued rifle for the Army and saw use up to Vietnam as a sniper rifle. It had a wooden stock and iron works and was heavy as hell. It had to suck lugging that thing around.

From WWII, I had found an M1 Garand. General Patton had called it the "greatest battle implement ever devised." It was a semi-automatic rifle fed with an eight-round clip, not a traditional magazine. What was interesting to me about this gun was that after the eight rounds were fired, the clip would eject from the top of the weapon with a very distinct sound, so the enemy could detect when our guys were out of ammo. As it turned out, they found a way around that by tossing empty magazines onto the ground where it would make the same pinging sound, and trick the enemy into thinking our guys didn't have fully loaded weapons waiting for them.

In the Korean War, they still used the Garand, but I had an M1911 .45 pistol that supposedly belonged to someone in our family who got it during the war. My mother had given it to me for Christmas a few years ago, and while I didn't know if I believed the story behind it, I certainly enjoyed shooting it.

The last of my "war guns" was the M16, ever popular and used in Vietnam, of course. The M4, which I also had, was built on the same platform, but the M16 was longer, and the Vietnam era rifles

330

weren't built for attachments like sights and flashlights and the other fun stuff I could put on my M4. I didn't bring the M4 or the M16 with me that day, but I did tell her about them, and she listened like I was telling her a bedtime story, asking me questions about when I got them and why I picked the ones I did. She was so easy to talk to. I had completely forgotten being annoyed with her that morning.

No surprise to me, her favorite gun was the .44 Magnum revolver, which was the same gun Dirty Harry used in the movie. Every time she shot it, she giggled from the kickback. After we had both shot all of my guns and she'd practiced with her pistol a few more times, I realized we had been shooting for hours. We hadn't really talked much except about the guns and how to use them; it was hard to talk and shoot, of course, but we were also just enjoying the time. I had known Isabel for a few months now, and this was the first time I felt like she had ever relaxed, except for in the alley the night before; but even then, she hadn't been relaxed. She was always looking around, observing, being a cop, basically, and I was thoroughly enjoying spending time with her. Most women liked to go out and shoot around here because it was a way to spend time with the guys, but with the exception of Jo, in my experience, they had no interest in learning about the guns or becoming more proficient. Isabel's desire to master each of them was appealing to me; I could tell she was a perfectionist like I was, and I was definitely attracted to that quality in her.

When we were shooting, there was less sexual tension, but I swore the moment we started putting everything away, it was like a heavy blanket covering us. I would have done anything to find a reason to touch her again.

"I really had a lot of fun today. Thank you so much for letting me shoot all of your guns. I feel like I had a history lesson today too." She smiled up at me while helping me wrap the guns back up and put the ammo away.

"It was totally my pleasure. I come out here fairly often with Jax or with Jo, or both, but they were both busy today. I like to practice, and it kind of clears my head too. There's something calming about being out here on the range, as strange as that may sound." I honestly did feel that way. I enjoyed the thrill of shooting, of course, but becoming one with the weapon and working on a goal, whether it be to hit a bullseye, do drills, or whatever the case may be, gave me a sense of accomplishment every time I came out.

"Are you back to work tomorrow?" she asked me in a way I was hoping meant she wanted to continue our time together.

"I am. I'm on for twenty-four tomorrow with the usual crowd. What about you?" I should have just asked her out to eat or something.

"I am back to work tomorrow as well. We are doing twelve-hour shifts right now, but it keeps changing. We have the same budget issues you guys do, I'm sure."

I smirked a bit. "Yea, every year it's something. Fortunately for me, that's more Brian's problem than mine; as long as I have a job."

"Ah yes, I don't have to deal with that stuff, but I have my own fair share of bullshit paperwork to do on a regular basis. That's the one thing about becoming a detective I never gave any thought to: paperwork." She rolled her eyes dramatically and grinned.

"Yea, I can only imagine." Every time she spoke, I was waiting for her to finish so I could ask her to eat or drink or make out, or something to keep this day going, and yet the words never came out of my mouth. Then she hit me with a surprise, which was her way, I was learning.

"So, would you like to come over to my place for some food? After letting me shoot your guns and use your ammo, it's the least I can do to say thank you. I'll cook us something, or we can just get takeout and have a drink or two if you'd like."

"You cook?" That was what I chose to say. I was a fucking moron. If I could have slapped myself for that one, I definitely would have. And my mom would have slapped me too.

"Uh, yea, I cook." She looked at me with a raised eyebrow and was definitely waiting for me to say something less stupid.

"I'm sorry, I didn't mean it how it sounded. I would absolutely love to come over for dinner, but you don't have to cook for me. I don't want to be any trouble."

"Maybe I like trouble, Cavanaugh." She was definitely flirting with me. "But in any event, I love cooking for other people. So let's get your shit, and you can follow me home. I live about ten minutes from here. You can park behind me in the driveway."

"Sounds great." I grabbed my stuff, which was all packed up, and followed her to the parking lot.

I watched her get in that goddamn hot rod, and the rumble from the engine as she started it actually sent a jolt right to my cock. I was starting to wonder what I was getting myself into with dinner at her place, because I definitely wanted to pick up where we left off the night before.

I secured everything in my truck, and as she pulled out, she waved to me and smiled. I quickly got in and hightailed it behind her, since I had no idea where she lived. I didn't want to get left behind. I decided at that moment I was going to let her control the situation. There was no way a woman like her was going to let me take control. I had no idea if this was just dinner or not, but either way, I wouldn't have said no for the world.

Isabel

I really just didn't want the day to end. I didn't want to go home and cook for myself. Besides, everyone had to eat, so dinner could have been a totally innocent and friendly meal, just two people who spent the day together, eating and socializing. That was all.

I wasn't kidding myself one single bit, really. I wanted to spend more time with him, and after I'd ditched him the night before, there was no way he was going to initiate dinner or continuing the day, so it was all I could think of. I was hoping I had something decent to cook for us. I was definitely going to need a drink. That man's smile had been melting my fucking panties all day long, and I needed to calm down. I got chills thinking about his arms around me, teaching me to shoot firearms I was unfamiliar with today. It was one of those moments where you needed to surrender and trust, which wasn't in my nature at all, and yet I felt perfectly comfortable with him.

I lived in a two-story condo I had bought a few years prior, and luckily for me in this city, there was plenty of parking. Once we pulled in, I watched him get out of his truck and tuck his hands in his pockets, a sign of nervousness, which brought a smile to my face. I loved all of the things about people's mannerisms I learned as a cop. I could almost always tell when someone was lying or hiding something, and being able to read people like that gave me a feeling of control in most situations.

We walked up to the front door, and I could smell him come up behind me. After we had been shooting all day, there was a hint of gunpowder, but I could also smell a bit of his cologne or soap; it had a musky scent that hit my senses in such a way I couldn't think of anything except how much I liked his closeness. I turned off the alarm as we got in the front door and led him into the kitchen and dining room area.

"Can I get you something to drink?" I asked as I took off my holster and badge and set them on the counter in their usual spot.

"I'd love a beer if you have one. And can you point me to your bathroom so I can go wash my hands?"

"Of course. It's down the hall there, first door on your left. And I'll grab you a beer while I get dinner started." I began rummaging through the fridge to see what I could come up with on the fly. I opened an import beer for him and put it on the kitchen island behind me.

I found frozen shrimp, rice, and some random veggies, and decided I could pull together Spanish rice with shrimp for us. I had started to make myself a martini when he popped back into the kitchen.

"Is shrimp ok? Are you allergic or anything?" I asked.

"I love seafood. Well, I love food actually, so yes, shrimp is great." I pointed to the beer on the counter, which he took and brought up to his lips, distracting me from what I was doing, causing me to spill vodka on the counter.

"Why don't you let me make your drink while you start

dinner," he offered with that million-dollar smile. Those Cavanaugh boys really should do toothpaste commercials or something; they had the most beautiful smiles I'd ever seen in my life.

"Ok, that sounds reasonable. It's just a vodka tonic, and there are limes right over there in the fruit bowl. They should still be good too," I laughed. It was fairly often I threw away every single thing in that fruit bowl without ever having eaten anything in it. I forgot about it all the time, and then the fruit would just go bad. "I was going to make shrimp with Spanish rice if that works? I eat pretty healthy for the most part, so I have lots of veggies and stuff."

"Sounds amazing. Is there anything I can do to help? I feel kind of bad just watching you cook for me." He handed me my drink, and I took a huge sip of it, letting the warmth from the vodka begin to dull my inhibitions about the evening before it even kicked in.

"Nope, just hang out there and tell me how you got into collecting guns, and I'll get this show on the road. I don't know about you, but I'm starving." I got the pans I needed out and started chopping veggies, while the shrimp thawed out.

He took a long sigh, which made me look up. He seemed lost in thought. "Well," he said staring off into the living room, "I think it really was just that I wanted to protect people. My mom mostly?" He said it like a question, then turned his eyes back toward me.

"What do you mean?" I felt almost concerned for him, for whatever story he was about to tell me.

"I think because my mom was a single mom, my brother and I were always sort of protecting her. When we got our first guns as young men, Jo's dad Jack used to take us out shooting and spent a lot of time going over safety; how to use them, when it was okay to use them. One time, he talked to us about what to do if anyone ever showed up at our house uninvited. It really stuck with me."

"So Jack taught you what to do if an intruder came into your house?" I was kind of surprised.

"Yea, he took Brian and me out to the range one time, without Jo, which was unusual. He said she was doing something else. I can't even remember what now; it was so long ago. He seemed concerned, and he wanted Brian and me to listen seriously to what he was saying. He never explained why, but I always felt like he was implying we needed to be on the lookout or something, and that we needed to be looking after our mom. As it turns out, Jack and my mother had a longstanding relationship none of us knew about, which might explain why he wanted to give special attention to us in that regard."

"Wow, no way. Jack and your mom? Does everyone know now?" I was shocked and felt my mouth gape open.

"Well, Brian and Jo are the ones who told me, and then I talked to my mom about it. I think it's cool. I feel bad he's gone, because apparently, they were quite close."

"That's really interesting." I honestly didn't know what else to say.

"Yea, so anyway, after that day with Jack at the range, I just kind of developed a fascination with guns. I took a few classes on combat shooting, gun safety, things like that, and started to become a collector. A historian of sorts." He grinned and went back to drinking his beer. "It smells amazing in here. Are you sure I can't do anything to help?"

Dinner was well underway at that point, and I was just

enjoying hearing about his family and learning something new.

"Nope. Just hang out. Relax. Dinner is actually almost done. I picked a pretty easy dish to make if I'm being totally honest. Are you ready for another beer?"

"Are you trying to get me drunk, Detective?" He raised an eyebrow at me with a smirk.

"I'm quite sure you can handle more than a couple of beers, Cavanaugh," I retorted while grabbing him one out of the fridge and then immediately finishing my drink.

"Well, I'll make you another drink and set the table or something. How's that sound?"

"That sounds wonderful, actually." He had already gotten up and walked up next to me. Our hands touched as I handed him my glass, sending a chill up the back of my neck and causing me to look up at him. He was almost a foot taller than I was, and at that moment, all I wanted was to feel him pressed up against me again.

Quickly moving, taking the glass from me and taking a step back toward the fridge to get ice, he asked, "You don't really want the tonic, do you? You strike me as a vodka on the rocks kind of woman to be honest."

I laughed, tossing my head back while stirring vegetables in the saucepan. "You're absolutely right, Cavanaugh. But I do like the lime in it. How did you guess?"

"Not a guess at all. Detectives aren't the only ones who observe. I can size up a scene too, I'll have you know." He glanced sideways at me and carried on making my drink and going through my cabinets looking for dishes. "How do you reach anything in here, Isabel? And while I'm at it, how do you find anything? Seriously, it's so disorganized. Everything most people use on a regular basis is like two feet further away than I believe you can reach without climbing the counters. My OCD is in overdrive over this." He was right. My dishes were not where anyone would ever put them if they ever planned to use them. My dad didn't ever pull dishes out for anything in his own home, so it was no surprise to me after I moved in to find things in terrifically non-useful places.

"I keep meaning to rearrange it all. When I moved in, my dad put all that stuff away, and every time I go to get something, I make a note to rearrange it all, but seriously, who wants to spend their free time rearranging their kitchen cabinets?" I shook my head at the thought of spending a day doing something so frighteningly boring.

"I'm going to have to fix this at some point. It's maddening." He rolled his eyes and handed me my cocktail. Taking the plates and other dishes and silverware he found, he set the table, almost formally. It was amusing to me, considering I was just whipping up shrimp and rice and nothing much else, due to my lack of grocery shopping, which was pretty common. When I was working on a case, I could get totally consumed by that and not shop for weeks sometimes.

Since we had been shooting all day and never had lunch, I could feel the vodka doing its job, warming my insides, loosening me up a bit. I was always a little high strung, I suppose; I think it came with the job. However, a couple of cocktails always helped me relax, and since I hadn't had a man in this condo in quite some time, I certainly needed it. I was thoroughly enjoying our banter, and truth be told, I loved cooking for someone other than myself, especially a man. I thought feeding someone was sexy, and at this point, everything about Matt felt sexy. The more I watched him move about my house looking at things and observing, the more I wanted to climb all over him. A carnal need was smoldering in my core, and I was working in overdrive to keep it at bay, which wasn't working at all.

"Ok, dinner's ready." I brought the pot I had mixed everything in over to the table and set it in the middle. "Can I get you another drink with dinner?" I asked before sitting down.

"I think you're trying to get me drunk, Isabel," he smirked at me, those green eyes twinkling. I returned his expression with a sly smile and a shrug. "I'll have what you're having this time, actually." His tone was almost challenging. We both had to work tomorrow, so while I wasn't sure where this was going, the teasing was getting me excited, and I began to consider my options.

As we ate, Matt told me more about Brian and Jo's relationship, and how Brian wanted to propose. He expressed his concern about it, which seemed legitimate to me, as I've never felt that way about anyone and couldn't imagine sleeping with the same person forever if I was being honest. But, to each their own, I supposed. I felt myself getting quieter as dinner started to conclude. I wasn't sure what to say to get him to my bedroom the way I wanted him, and the growing need to climb all over him was overwhelming my thoughts as I watched him get more comfortable in my space

"So, Isabel, let's talk about last night." He leaned forward across the table and addressed me questioningly and seriously with his eyes, looking directly into mine.

"Ah, I was wondering when this would come up, Cavanaugh. What part of the evening would you like to discuss exactly?" The need to make my move was looming in the air, washing over me like a heavy fog. I stood up to get our dishes and put them in the sink to break the tension I was feeling, and to create the illusion it didn't exist at all.

"I'd like to discuss why you left me hanging in the alley when you quite clearly wanted exactly what I was offering." He stated it so matter-of-factly I was taken a bit off guard, tilting my head like a puppy at him from the kitchen sink just a few feet away.

"What was it that you were offering, just so we're clear?" I shifted my weight, putting a hand on my hip, realizing my move was coming.

He got up and walked toward me, his voice getting low and his stature growing as he approached, taking over my personal space. "I like you, Isabel." He waited for my reply.

"Well, I want you to fuck me like you don't."

MATT

In all of my life, I'd never been speechless. Not once, not ever. Until that moment. I knew my jaw dropped, and the rest of that moment happened in a blur. I lunged at her, grabbing her face and crushing my lips against hers, shoving my tongue into her mouth, exploring hers roughly. As she pressed herself against me, I felt her grip my lower back, roughly pulling me into her, sending chills down my spine and igniting my need for her even more. I had restrained myself the entire day, and she was letting me have what I'd been craving since yesterday. I grabbed her tiny frame, lifting her up onto the kitchen island so she was eye level with me. Immediately, she wrapped her legs around my waist, pulling me in close. As my cock rubbed against her center, I roughly grabbed her head, moving it to the side so I could lick and bite that delicious, long neck of hers. Her soft moan sent me into overdrive as my hands groped every inch of her over her clothes.

I stopped for a moment to regain my composure and process what she had said. *I want you to fuck me like you don't.* We were both breathing heavily, and I watched her chest rise and fall as we both anticipated our next move. As fucking hot as what she'd said was, I wanted to be sure that's what she really wanted, and then I wouldn't be stopping my assault on her sexy body. Resting my forehead against hers, I placed my hands at the base of her neck beneath her long, brown hair.

"I will give you exactly what you want, Isabel. Are you sure that's what you really want? Once this starts, please don't make me stop." I sucked in my breath, hoping she'd drop something filthy from that beautiful mouth of hers.

Still connected to me, the corners of her mouth upturned into a grin, she leaned to the side and forward to whisper in my ear. "I want you to fuck me tonight, Matt. I want you to shove your rock hard cock inside me and fuck me like we were in the alley last night. I want you to own me like property tonight." Her lips grazed my neck as she finished her sentence, making my cock strain against my jeans. Fuck me sideways, I'd never had a woman say anything so fucking filthy and amazing to me in my entire life. I didn't think I could be gentle with her at that point even if I wanted to, which I most certainly did not.

"Where is your bedroom?" I demanded, barely able to speak I was so fucking turned on.

"Upstairs," she whispered. I grabbed her off the counter and bit her neck gently as she landed on her feet in front of me.

"Take me there. Now." I seriously couldn't form full sentences, and I definitely sounded like a fucking caveman commanding orders. She obviously didn't give a fuck. I followed behind her and slapped her ass as we made it halfway up the stairs, causing her to let out a little whimper, igniting the fire in me. When we got to her room, she turned to face me, waiting for me to make a move, and it was then that I decided to go full alpha caveman on her. If she wanted me to claim her, I was going to. I roughly pulled her to me by the waist of her jeans and began to undo them, staring into her eyes. I couldn't decide if she looked lost or excited, but I continued taking control of the situation and planned to continue doing so unless she stopped me, which she didn't.

"Take your clothes off." I took a small step backwards so I could watch her undress as I adjusted my aching cock. She slowly finished sliding her jeans down her beautiful, tanned legs, kicking them off. I started to salivate as she grabbed the hem of her t-shirt and pulled it over her head, revealing her black lace bra and matching panties. Her body was incredible; she was built like an elite athlete, and I wanted to devour her. She looked up at me in a demure and pouting way, waiting for approval, which she had from the moment she let the words *fuck me* escape those full, pink lips of hers.

I had always been a man who liked to take charge in the bedroom, but I'd never been with a woman who let me command her this way, and I was taken aback by her overt sexuality and desire to be dominated by me. It was a turn-on in ways I couldn't comprehend. She wasn't like women who were easy; she knew what to say to me to turn me into the beast I was about to become.

"Do you want me to tell you what to do, Isabel?" I hoarsely whispered with one hand in my front pocket, while the other one was tugging at the waistband of my own jeans. I was thirsty for a taste of her sweet pussy, but I was going to savor this moment as long as I could. She nodded, giving me innocent doe eyes that screamed she wasn't innocent in the least. I yanked my shirt over my head and tossed it aside, watching her eyes get round as she looked me over. I couldn't stop staring at her full breasts heaving over the top of her lacy bra. I didn't want to spend another minute not touching her.

"Get over here and put your lips on me, Isabel." I loved saying her name. She sprung toward me quickly, but then touched me so gently, it was almost burning my skin. She swept her lips across my chest, leaving small kisses in her wake as she gently stroked my abs, causing me to shudder. She looked up at me, and I commanded, "Don't stop. Don't you dare stop." It was then that she gave me the wicked smile that would engrain itself into my brain forever, setting me completely on fire. She started to undo my jeans while licking and nipping at my torso, causing my brain to fog and give in to the sensations she caused in me. I ran my hands through her soft hair, taking handfuls of it and guiding her lower. She undid my jeans, providing relief to my cock that desperately ached to be inside her, and when she touched it ever so gently, I almost stopped her and tossed her onto the bed.

"Isabel!" I demanded, and she stopped in her tracks, looking up at me again, confused. "I want your beautiful lips wrapped around my cock, but I need to know what you want..." I couldn't just demand things of her without checking in again. It wasn't my nature, and even though she was doing things to me that were making me see stars, I had to know it was what she wanted. I had to know I wasn't pushing the limits with her, even though I already knew she'd stop me.

She slinked her sexy body upright, barely touching mine, but just enough all the way up to drive me wild, and said, "Matt, I want to do what pleases you. I want you to dominate me tonight. You have my permission. No more questions. You have my permission to take me. Do you understand what I'm saying to you?" I finally understood what she needed, what she wanted. I grabbed her wrists that were still stroking my sides gently and pulled her toward the king size bed that was in the middle of a giant room I had barely managed to take in. As I sat on the edge of it, I pulled her on top of me until she was straddling me. I let her hands go, and she reached up to touch my face. Then she began kissing my neck, which was my fucking sweet spot, diminishing my control completely.

I tossed her off of me and yanked my jeans down, kicking them off and across the room. She watched me look at her like a hungry animal, and I crawled up on the bed. She knew what I wanted her to do. I didn't even have to command it. I sat back on my knees and watched as her hungry mouth approach me, and when she licked her lips, we both knew what was coming. Using both hands to pull down the waistband of my boxer briefs, she unleashed my cock, which sprang to life in front of her. She looked like she couldn't wait to devour it, and I couldn't wait to watch those pouty lips take it in before I fucked her, which I was definitely going to do.

Isabel

I unleashed his giant fucking cock, and my mouth watered, wanting to take it all. I licked my lips and then crawled closer, taking his beautiful dick immediately in my mouth. I could taste the salty pre-cum, and all it did was ignite my libido more. As Matt grabbed a handful of my hair and muttered the words, "Fuck, Isabel, that's so fucking good," my pride swelled because I loved turning him on. I hoped he would dominate me tonight the way I desired. He seemed like such a nice guy, but I believed he had an animal in him waiting to get unleashed by me.

On my knees in front of him, taking his monster cock down my throat, I massaged his balls with one hand and stroked him with the other. As his grip on my hair got tighter, I felt the wetness between my legs increase, and my sex pulsed, wanting him to fuck me so badly. The rougher he grabbed me, the more I wanted him, the more I wanted to please him. He moaned while I continued to suck on him, savoring every taste of him. I was turned on in ways I hadn't felt in as long as I could remember.

"Do you like the taste of my cock, Isabel?" he murmured. I looked up at him, not slowing down, and nodded my head, humming, "Mmhmmm," while he watched me take him in and out of my mouth. "Do you want me to put that cock inside that sweet pussy of yours?"

"Mmhmm," I affirmed again, continuing to devour him. I wanted to make him come. I loved making a man come. Being the cause of someone unleashing their inhibitions, letting it all go, was a thrill to me. I wanted to please him, and I hoped he would fuck me how I wanted to be fucked.

"Oh fuck, Isabel. I'm so close!" He started to pull away, but I pulled him closer, making sure he knew I was going to let him finish right where we were. Feeling my signal, he gripped my hair harder, causing me to let a little sound out, and as he began to clench, nearing his release, I stroked him harder and faster. "Fuck!" he cried out as I felt the hot, sticky warmth hit my throat. I slowed down and swallowed. As he leaned back on the bed to recover, I sat up on my knees, pleased with myself, smiling and relishing in his glow.

"You're a very bad girl, aren't you, Isabel?" Matt smiled at me with a heaving chest. I simply nodded in reply. "What am I going to do with you now? That was amazing." I smiled shyly again, noticing my panties were completely soaked. When he leaned forward, a growl began to escape from him as he made his way slowly toward me. My heart raced in anticipation of his touch; the room felt cold without it. Not saying a word, he grabbed a handful of my hair at the nape of my neck, yanked my head to the side, and began the most glorious assault on my body I had ever experienced.

Gently biting my neck while still holding my head in place for himself, he used his other hand to undo my bra, setting my breasts free. Immediately, he began to knead at them and then squeezed my pebbled nipple, sending a shockwave to my core. I was on fire inside and wanted my own release so badly I could hardly stand it. Letting my head go, he moved his mouth to my chest and began sucking on my nipples, first one, then the other, roughly. He gently bit one, causing me to suck in air, the sting coming, and then his tongue gently flicking at it, driving me wild.

"Enough of this. I need to taste your pussy now." He grabbed me by the waist, off my knees, and tossed me on my back in front of him. "I want you to grab that headboard, Isabel, and you are not to let go of it. Do you understand me?" I reached up behind me, grabbing the wrought iron headboard of my bed, smiling and nodding in anticipation. I wanted to be devoured, and I loved taking orders from him. He was gruff with me, but in a sexy way that made me want more.

"You're so fucking sexy, Isabel. So. Fucking. Sexy." He looked at my body like he wasn't sure where to begin, and then he leaned in to lick and play with my nipples again, causing my hips to rise and my back to arch. I started to let go and reach toward him. "Don't you let go. It's my turn to taste what I want. If you let go, I'll have to tie you up there. Be a good girl," he whispered. Oh my God, I couldn't believe my panties didn't explode off of me at that exact moment. They surely could have melted from the heat escaping between my legs. Once I put my hands back where he wanted them, he nodded at me and made his way down my body, taking my panties off and throwing them on the floor.

My knees were bent, and he grabbed my ankles, opening me up to him and smiling. As he moved his face between my legs, I closed my eyes and gripped the headboard tighter, knowing he would touch me in the most intimate way at any moment. "Open your eyes!" he commanded, startling me. "I want you to watch me devour you." He smiled at me as he lowered his head and ran his tongue flat against my pulsating sex. I immediately threw my head back with pleasure, then shifted my focus back to him and watched him intently. He gave long, slow licks along my slit, then used a finger to play with me while he continued licking and watching me watch him. My heart began to race even more, and as he slid a finger inside me, I let out a soft moan. As he continued to fuck me with his finger and suck and lick on my clit, I was nearing the need for release faster and faster. Before I even realized what he was doing, he removed his finger, grabbed my ankles, and spread my legs as wide as his arm span before he aggressively went back to my pussy, causing such a sensation that I couldn't take it any longer. As my climax began to build, I tried to arch my back, but his hold on my legs kept me at his mercy, and I had no choice but to let go. I grabbed the headboard as tightly as I possibly could and cried out in ecstasy as I came all over his face, feeling the wetness as he continued to lap it up.

"FUCK!" I yelled out as my entire body shook.

"Oh, that's what I'm going to do to you next," he said as he leaned back and let go of my legs. I panted, feeling as though I'd just finished an amazing workout, and lowered my arms.

"Did I say you could take your arms down?" he questioned me, looking me directly in the eyes, his giant, exposed cock standing at attention.

"No," I whispered, excited to find out what my punishment was for disobeying.

"Well, bad girls get punished, Isabel. And you've been a bad, bad girl. Haven't you?" He smiled his Captain America smile, looking devilish.

"Yes, they do," I whispered longingly.

"I think bad girls should get spanked, what do you think about that? Do you think bad girls should get spanked, Isabel?" He started to come toward me, crawling over me between my legs.

"Yes, I do."

"Yes, you do, what, Isabel?" He wanted me to say it. He was so fucking hot, and I couldn't possibly have been more turned on.

"Yes, I think bad girls like me should be spanked."

"That's right." He nodded and kissed my abdomen. "Bad girls should get spanked right before they get fucked. Don't you agree, Isabel?" Every time he said my full name like that, I almost came on the spot again. I knew what he wanted me to say, and I was all for getting spanked and fucked.

"Bad girls should definitely get spanked and fucked," I whispered and began to push myself up on my forearms.

Leaning back again, he waited for me to continue pushing myself up before he grabbed me, flipping me over roughly. "That's right," was all he said.

I felt coolness from the room between my legs where I was completely soaked, and as I settled myself onto all fours, he hovered over me, kissing my back softly. He was so much larger than me, that when he wrapped his arms around me, he covered me completely. He grabbed my wrists, lifting me upright, placing my hands on the headboard again. I could feel his cock graze the inside of my thigh and wanted him to shove it inside me desperately, when all of a sudden, smack! He slapped my ass, while I held on to the headboard, one of his hands holding mine in place, his dick dangling between my legs, and my tits bouncing from the smack. It stung, and he rubbed the spot he'd smacked to soothe it, making my climax start to stir inside me. He leaned back, grabbing my breast from behind, pinching my nipple, and slapping my ass again, causing me to audibly moan as I arched my back into him, relishing in his touch. Massaging my nipple, and again soothing the sting on my ass with his hand, he leaned in close to my ear and whispered, "That's what happens to bad girls, Isabel. Are you ready for me to fuck you now? Because I am ready for your pussy to be wrapped around my cock."

As he took his hands away, I could hear him opening a condom and whispered again, "Yes, please." I could still feel the sting on my ass, and the sensations he'd brought me had me feeling heady and weak. It was wonderful.

"Your skin is so soft," he said in a hushed tone. He had moved his hand to the small of my back, and I could feel him lining that beautiful cock up to my slit, while I grinned in anticipation of him entering me. As soon as he penetrated my folds, I cried out in pleasure, and he groaned with me. "Fuck! You're so fucking tight, you fucking bad girl." He was fully seated inside me and began to rock in and out slowly. I couldn't help but vocalize my pleasure.

"Fuck, Matt, you feel so fucking good! Fuck me harder!" I wanted him to take his frustrations out on my pussy and pound into me. He didn't pick up the pace at all, and I was starting to wiggle and writhe to get more friction between us. His cock was so big and so fucking hard I could barely stand it.

He grabbed my hips and stilled me, pulling me onto him from behind, bringing him deeper into me. I let go of the headboard, leaning back into him, while his hand ran up my abdomen, making its way gently to the base of my throat as I leaned back. I could feel his breath quickening as he whispered hoarsely, "Beg me, Isabel.

Beg me to fuck you like the bad girl you are."

I smiled at his filthy words; they did things to me I'd deny in any court of law. I would happily beg him to fuck me. "Cavanaugh," I whispered, his hand still gently at my throat, "I'm such a dirty girl. I deserve to be fucked. Please fuck me hard. Please fuck me like the bad girl I am." I hoped I had pleaded enough for him to unleash the beast I had created for myself tonight. To my overwhelming pleasure, he let go of my throat, pushed me down on my hands, and began to slam his cock into my pussy. With each thrust, I cried out, "Yes, yes!" and as he picked up his pace, nearing his climax, he began to groan louder, yelling my name.

Within a few minutes of pounding into me, he yelled out, "Fuck, Isabel, I'm going to come!!!" which was my cue to let myself fall over the edge as well, slamming myself back against him with each thrust. As my release came and sweat started to cover me, I screamed out loudly, "Fuck yes! Give it to me! Yes!" Just moments later, he came, and even through the condom, I could feel the heat of his cum. He yelled profanities as he gave me his final thrusts, slowly finishing.

MATT

Collapsing on top of her after the best sex of my entire life, by a landslide, I tried to steady my breathing and not crush her. "Jesus Christ, Isabel. That was fucking intense." I begrudgingly pulled out of her and rolled over, grabbing a tissue to put the condom in and grabbing another to clean up with.

She rolled over onto her back next to me with what appeared to be a satisfied smile. She was a fucking minx. I've never had a woman say such filthy, hot things to me, and just reliving it for a moment gave me a little twitch, even though there was no way I could go again at that moment. My whole body was spent as if I had just gone for a run or fought a raging fire; I was still catching my breath. I glanced at her. She was on her back with her eyes closed and a smile spread across her face that gave me a warm feeling of satisfaction.

As she took in a deep breath, she sighed, "That was exactly what I needed." I leaned up on my side to look at her. She was flushed and so fucking beautiful. She was model beautiful, and looking at her like that, I found it hard to believe she was a tough as nails cop. She opened her eyes, glancing over at me observing her, and looked confused. "What?" she said.

"You're beautiful." It was the first thing that came out of

mouth. It was also true.

She rolled her eyes at me and said, "Cavanaugh, stop. It's not like that. You don't need to flatter me. We now have some pretty serious carnal knowledge of each other." She lay back down and stared at the ceiling.

"You are beautiful, and you'll take my compliments." I leaned in closer to her, smelling the sex in the room. My body was still on fire, and I could feel the heat radiating from her as well as she looked back over at me, questioning me with her eyes. "Yea, that's right. I'm going to tell you how this is going to go." Her chocolate-brown eyes widened, almost challenging me with a raised eyebrow.

Pulling the sheets up over her delicious breasts, she leaned up on her elbows. "Oh really? Are you now?"

"Yes, I am. So listen up."

"You have my attention, Cavanaugh." Her lips spread into a sly smile, just barely showing her sparkling white teeth between those plump lips.

I leaned in and bit her neck gently, causing her to let her head fall back, giving me access, and I quietly growled, "When we are doing this," I paused, "I am in charge. We both know that's exactly what you want, and I've never been more turned on in my life." I sucked on her neck, licking the same spot, causing her to moan quietly. "Am I clear?"

I pulled away, scanning her face for her understanding. Glancing up at me through her thick black eyelashes, the corners of her mouth barely upturned, she replied, "What makes you think this is going to happen again?"

Laughing and leaning back over to what I was officially deeming my side of the bed, I replied, "Oh, it's happening again.

Often."

She quietly giggled, lying back as well. "We'll see about that, big guy."

I launched myself on top of her, caging her in with my arms, taking her by surprise. I looked at her intently and in a low and gruff voice said, "Baby, you're not going to deny me, or yourself, the pleasure of a repeat of that fucking heat. So let's not kid ourselves and just admit that was fucking amazing, and it's definitely happening again. You hear me?" I leaned in close, my lips grazing hers.

"Ok," she whispered. Getting the reply I wanted, I pressed my lips to hers and kissed her passionately. She reciprocated, touching my chest with her palms, searing her heat into me.

Pulling back from the kiss, immediately missing her lips on mine, but thoroughly exhausted, I said, "But for now, sleep. I have to be at work early as fuck. I need to sleep a little bit."

"You're staying here?" she asked me, shocked.

"Yes, I am. I'm exhausted. It's late, and your sexy ass wore me out. It's completely your fault." I pushed myself back over to my side and reached over to set an alarm on my phone. "Now, get over here. Detectives need sleep too." I wasn't trying to be romantic, but I was way too fucking tired to get dressed and drive my ass home at that point. I pulled her in tight and inhaled her scent, causing her tense body to relax. Planting a soft kiss on her shoulder, I whispered, "Night, Detective," and shut my eyes, starting to drift off immediately.

"Night, Cavanaugh," she whispered.

Isabel

I fell asleep in Matt's arms, completely consumed by his huge frame around mine. I was uncomfortable and anxious at first; I didn't really ever let men stay over, but I knew he had to be at work way earlier than me, and who doesn't like to sleep next to someone if only for a little while? As I was nodding off, I acknowledged to myself I was already breaking rules when it came to him and sighed as his arms closed around me.

When my alarm went off, my eyes sprung open and I looked over to the other side of the bed, which was empty. For a brief moment, I wondered if the night before had actually even happened, but as I began to wake and feel the after effects of a good fucking, I smiled and rolled over, feeling satisfied. I was definitely more satisfied than I could ever remember being. I'd slept like the dead last night. He had bossed me around and dominated me in a way that made me feel like the most sexual and desirable creature on earth. Knowing I had to get up for work as well, I sighed and sat up, noticing a note on the end table at the other side of the bed.

I rolled over to that side of the huge bed and grabbed it.

Until Next Time.

There WILL be a next time.

Be safe at work, Detective,

MC

I grinned a little, and setting the note back down, got up to start my day. I had to be at work in about two hours, which was just enough time to get some coffee going and spend some time in a hot shower, enjoying the stiffness in my body from the night before. When I walked into the kitchen, I found another note next to the coffee maker.

I couldn't take it.

You're welcome.

Be safe today

MC

Couldn't take it? Couldn't take what? Then it hit me. I started opening my cabinets, and saw everything was reorganized. Every single thing. I could reach the mugs and glasses, and the plates were in a useful spot. The entire contents of my dishes had been taken out and put where they should go. *Well played, Cavanaugh, well played.* I got myself a coffee cup from an extremely easy to reach location and grabbed my phone to send a text. While we didn't exchange numbers, I already had his number from when he'd called me during the investigation when Jo was in the hospital.

Thank you.

I set my phone down, but it dinged with an incoming text almost immediately.

For last night or because you can actually
reach a coffee cup now?

I smirked and even let out a little laugh, replying,

```
For both lol
```

I waited for another reply for a minute while making my coffee, but it never came. I was almost a little disappointed, but I had shit to do. And we weren't dating. We were fucking. Well, we had fucked. And according to him, we were going to be doing it again. The thought gave me butterflies that made their way to my core, and completely turned on and grinning, I headed for the shower.

I ended up making it to work early, which was a miracle considering where I lived. Traffic downtown was always a nightmare, but I insisted on driving myself and not taking public transportation. Besides the fact that I was simply not interested in commuting with other people, why on earth would you have a beautiful car like mine if you weren't going to drive it? I never understood why people would buy classic cars and not drive them, giving them what they need, the open road. Although with the traffic here, the open road was usually twelve miles per hour on the highway most of the time.

My partner, Kevin, lived closer to our precinct and was already at his desk. "Hey Izzy, how was your day off?"

As I thought about the events of the day prior, and especially the evening, I smiled. "It was uneventful, really. What about you?"

"You're smiling awfully big for your usual shitty disposition, Cruise. What did you actually do on your day off?" He smirked at me from across his desk as I sat down at mine right across from his.

I laughed, "I ran into one of the firefighters at the range

yesterday. Turns out he's a collector of guns from various wars. So I ended up spending the majority of the day shooting his guns. I got to shoot an AR, Kev. It was awesome." I felt myself grinning like a kid on their birthday, thinking about how fun it was.

"Ah, nice! My brother-in-law has one, and we've gone to shoot it. It's a good time."

"Yea, for sure. So what did you do? Spend your day off with Emily?" Kevin had a girlfriend, who was all right. I had met her a few times here and there, but she really didn't like Kevin being a cop, and I mean, that ship had sailed. He was a cop when she met him, and so the fact they seemed to argue about his choice of profession was obnoxious to me.

"Actually, we broke up yesterday." His tone fell low, and his head dropped.

"Oh no, what happened? I'm sorry." He looked sad, and that made me feel bad, even though I really didn't like her.

"Honestly, Izzy, the same old shit. I can't keep arguing with someone over my career. It's what I've wanted to do my whole life, and if that's a problem, it's just never going to work. She kept bringing up things like going to work for her father and shit, and I couldn't possibly want to do that any less. Being a cop is who I am, and at the end of the day, if that isn't good enough for her, then it's time to move on." He shook his head.

"I understand. I'm sorry. We'll grab a drink after work. Come on, let's get to the briefing." We didn't have an active investigation going on, so we were probably going to have to execute a warrant today until we were assigned a new case.

Every day, we had a briefing to go over the current investigations and any other activity from overnight. As a detective, it was altogether possible to get called in overnight, when the vast majority of crime happened, but oddly enough, with the exception of some fairly straightforward cases, we hadn't had any major crimes in a while. We were definitely due for something soon. In a big city like ours, there was almost always a drug deal gone bad, burglaries, homicides, you name it, but we had been in a dry spell for about a week, which was almost unheard of.

As the captain briefed us on the crimes that had happened overnight, he mentioned there was a huge fire downtown, which peaked my interest, knowing Matt was working that day as well. If it was deemed arson, police would get involved, but otherwise, it was just a fire that had little to do with us, and certainly not detectives. While it may sound like an elitist statement, the fact of the matter was detectives got involved or assigned to more complicated cases that required an in-depth investigation. There were probably plenty of beat cops watching the fire, and if Brian or Matt gave their opinion, getting in the way.

"Cruise, Connor! I need to you execute a warrant for a deadbeat dad today," the captain interrupted my thoughts.

"You got it, Captain," Kevin replied, and we stood up to get ourselves ready to go.

Normally, executing a warrant was pretty uneventful, so it looked like another uneventful day on the force for us today.

MATT

As I hauled the hose into the front door of the strip mall store with Jo behind me, I couldn't help but think this fire spread awfully fast. It had quickly turned into a three alarmer, requiring us to call in neighboring stations to assist in battling the flames.

Through my mask, I yelled to Jo, "You with me?" The thick, black smoke around us was all consuming, and we hadn't even gotten to where the fire was in the back of the store. The ladder company was on the roof, trying to saw a hole up there to force the flames to go where the air was coming, a pretty standard practice for this sort of fire.

She yelled her acknowledgement back, and we made our way around the front desk and through the door to the back of the store. I was assuming the fire was in the storage room, that's where most of this type of fire originated, but we had yet to happen upon the flames, which was odd considering the amount of smoke. We were hauling a deuce and a half, which is the nickname for the two-and-a-half-inch hose, which, frankly, was heavy as fuck. Jo never complained about it though; she knew big fire meant big hose, and she and I trained with it quite a bit, because it could really lift you right off the fucking ground if you weren't prepared for it. Being as small as she was, it was always something she worried about, being able to handle things like that, but we made a perfect team.

We got to the back room, and a couple of the other guys were in behind us, but there was no fire. Using the TIC, the thermal imaging camera, Jax realized the fire was in the eaves of the roof, which meant it didn't even start in the store we were in.

"Fuck! It's in the roof, guys," he yelled through his mask, sounding muffled. It was pretty likely the fire started in the store next door based on how fucking hot it was where we were at, but the other problem was that it was becoming pretty clear the entire strip mall had a shared attic, meaning every single store was going to be affected. I got on my radio to report to the chief what was going on.

"Chief, we have zero fire in this store, but the TIC indicates massive fire in the eaves of the roof. We are backing out." He was going to need to send a second crew in to the store next door, and we'd have to get out and regroup.

"Copy that. Already have another crew entering next door," he replied. Jax got behind Jo and helped us haul the massive hose back out of the front of the building so we could figure out what the next move was and check our air levels. We had been in there about fifteen minutes or so, just maneuvering around furniture and such, as it looked like a doctor's office of some kind. Once we got out, we took our masks off and looked around the scene, and my mouth dropped open.

"Holy fuck," Jo said before I could. The entire strip mall was almost completely engulfed in flames, except for the one store we had been in. The tones dropped for a full evacuation from the building, and I glanced in Brian's direction as he was yelling over the radio for all personnel to evacuate. This was now a massive fire, and it was completely unsafe for anyone to be inside fighting it.

There is a critical point in all large fires when Command needs to determine whether or not the structure can be saved without putting the team at further risk than they would normally be in a fire. This structure was not going to be saved at this point, and Brian determined the next best course of action was a surround and drown. Essentially, that just meant we shot massive amounts of water on the building from the outside and tried to drown the fire that way. It was basically a last ditch effort to try to save the structure, but basically, it was fucked. It was now putting water on the fire for show, so it looked like we were trying to save something, but once Command called for evacuation, it meant what the other crews were seeing was bad news.

We made our way over to the manpower pool, which was essentially where we hung out to wait for more orders, when Brian waved me over to him. I picked up the pace and jogged over in his direction with Jo in tow.

"What's up, Chief? What do you need?" I asked.

Sweating, and with a furrowed brow, he looked me dead in the eye, "Something is wrong here. I don't know what, but this fire spread way too fast for an ordinary strip mall fire. Once we get it contained, I want you and Jo to climb up in the attic and see what you can find. There's just no way it should have spread this fast, which makes me believe it was set intentionally." He looked extremely concerned and spoke quietly enough so only Jo and I could hear him. Something about that was unusual, even though I couldn't put my finger on it at the time.

My brother had an instinct for fire like no one I'd ever seen except Jo's dad, our old chief. He just had a way of knowing things you couldn't ever really know. It was hard to describe, but if Brian felt like something sketchy was going on with a fire, or if he felt like something unusual needed to be looked into, I just did it, and of course, so did Jo, because we trusted him; and frankly, he was Mr. Safety at all times. I mean, we all were, but I think Brian felt especially compelled, being my brother and Jo's boyfriend, as well as Jack's protégé, to really look after all of us. I could honestly say I never wanted to be chief. Ever. Too many decisions to make, and at the end of the day, I really wanted to be responsible for my partners and myself, but not the whole kit and caboodle.

Jo, Jax, and I all waited and watched for over an hour as crews continued to battle the flames, and even Jo asked Brian twice if we could go back in to try and put out the fire, but he got more stern with her than I'd seen him since before they were together. He definitely had a bad feeling about this one, which gave me a bit of a sinking feeling in my stomach. We hadn't had a big fire like this in a long time, and while it was contained to the strip mall, if it had been residential or deeper in the city into the downtown area, it could have escalated into something far more serious than it was so far.

Finally, after about two hours of drowning the fire, it had become safe to go back in. While we waited, we watched the windows blow out of the convenience store, the side wall of the trophy making store on the end crumble, and the doctor's office we had been in eventually catch fire in the back, burning out all of their inventory and half of their exam rooms. Several firefighters from other companies begged Brian to let their crews go back in, but he refused, saying it wasn't safe. Once it was overhaul time, when firefighters can go back in to make sure the hot spots won't catch fire again, Brian indicated with a nod to Jo and me he wanted us to go into the attic to take a look at things.

"Be careful." He grabbed the brim of Jo's helmet and gave it a yank, making eye contact with her.

"You know it, Chief," she winked at him and walked toward the building. I gave Brian a nod, indicating I had her back and knew what the job at hand entailed, and we went into the building. While we were dressed in our full PPE, our turnout gear with airpacks, etc., we didn't have our masks on; we just took some tools with us to go poke around. I had a Halligan bar and a water can, in case we happened upon any hot spots, and she had her axe with her.

"Ok, I'm going to go up," Jo indicated as we pulled the attic stairs down from the convenience store, where we assumed the fire had originated, just based upon the damage.

"I'm coming right behind you. Watch those fucking stairs though." I watched her pull the attic stairway down by a string that somehow didn't burn up in the fire, and followed right behind her on the stairway, a rickety one at that, with or without fire damage.

"Yea, yea, I hear you. Just shine your flashlight around me." She climbed her way up, and with my face more or less right in her ass, I climbed up behind her.

"MOTHERFUCKER!" she exclaimed before I made it up, and as I came up behind her, I saw what she was referring to. In the corner of the attic space was a pile of gas cans, five of them, melted but still recognizable.

"Holy shit, Jo," was all I could muster. What we saw was essentially the point where the fire began. All around the gas cans the area was a crisp, black, charred mess of wood. The truss roof around us looked as though it had been burned almost completely through as well, and I knew we needed to get out of there. When a building structure, particularly a roof, is burned to that degree, it's simply unsafe, and the entire structure could collapse around us. I started making mental notes about what to put in my report as we began to observe our surroundings. It was one of those situations where you didn't realize what was going on in front of you until you had seen it yourself. We didn't see anything like that next door in the building we had been in, and all signs pointed to this fire being set intentionally.

"Jo, we gotta get out of here. It's not safe." I tugged on the back of her coat.

She reached inside her coat and pulled her cellphone out. She saw me looking at her funny, and she knew I was wondering what she was doing. "I'm gonna take a couple of pics of this just in case we need them. This whole place could crumble to the ground."

"Ok, hurry up though. I don't like this. You see what I see, and it's bad news." We locked eyes. She nodded and began snapping pictures of the attic. After a few moments, Brian came over the radio, asking for an update.

"Interior, what's your status?" he asked.

"We're on our way out, Chief. There's too much damage to stay up here. No hot spots though." I replied while creeping back toward the stairs on my hands and knees, pulling on Jo's coat. "Let's go, Jo. Seriously, that's enough."

"Ok, ok. You don't have to pull on me. Sheesh." As we made our way back down the old attic stairway, the acidic scent of gasoline was all I could smell. It was overwhelming my senses, and I stopped my descent. "What's wrong?" Jo asked me, also stopping on the stairs.

"Do you smell that? I didn't smell it before." I clicked my flashlight back on and pointed it around the area below us. That's when I spotted it, another large gasoline can with rags shoved in the opening, that somehow had yet to ignite.

"Holy shit, let me get a picture of that real quick," she replied and grabbed her phone again.

"We need to get the fuck out of here and get the overhaul crew in here to handle the rest of this. We don't have the tools we need for this. Come on!" I snapped at her. Sometimes, Jo really pushed her luck for what she considered the greater good, but this whole place could catch on fire again with that gas can, and we didn't have anything except for a small water can. We needed to go.

We came out of the building and made our way over to Brian's truck, where he had Command set up. There were a bunch of people milling around, including owners of the various store fronts. Because this was most certainly a crime scene and could very well be insurance fraud, I didn't want to report what we had seen with a crowd around us.

"Well, what did you find?" he asked curtly.

I looked over at Jo, who was waiting for me to tell him. "Chief, I need a moment of your time privately to discuss the interior." I said it as professionally as I could, so he would know I had something important to say. We were all pretty casual with each other most of the time. In an effort to assist, Jo jumped in.

"Chief, I'll hang out here with the store owners. Matt can brief you." She smiled and nodded us away, tossing me her cellphone at the same time.

As we walked around to the front of his truck to talk privately, he seemed like he hadn't picked up the hint this needed to be discrete.

"What is this all about? I've got crews from all over town I have to deal with, Matt. I don't have time for pow wows." He lifted his sunglasses to the top of his head and looked down at me, folding his arms.

"Dude, this is an arson. We found a stack of gas cans upstairs. I mean, a stack of them. Jo got pictures, of course, but on our way back out, we found one of those larger industrial cans with rags stuffed into the top of it that hadn't ignited in the fire somehow. So there's evidence in there, and I didn't want to tell you all that while the business owners were loitering around up your ass, in case one of them is a fucking criminal." I handed him Jo's phone to look at the pictures while I was talking. "It could obviously be insurance fraud or whatever, so I wanted to be discreet."

"Thanks, man. Someone from downtown was supposed to come and deal with the public, but somehow they're not here, so I'm stuck trying to do my job while answering their questions nonstop, which is obviously making me crazy. I'm gonna hold on to her phone. I'll give it back to her at the station, but I want to get these pictures off of it. I'll send the overhaul crew in to make sure that other can is taken care of." He began to walk off, getting on his radio and indicating the overhaul team needed to address some fuel on the lower level.

As we regrouped back at the other side of Brian's truck, the interior crew replied, "Chief, there's no fuel in here. What are we looking for?"

"Interior, there is a gas can at the base of the attic stairs inside the convenience store. I need you to bring that out."

"Sir, there's no gas can here. I'm standing at the base of the stairs." When he met my eyes, I knew something was wrong. In the last ten minutes, someone on this scene had removed evidence. That was not a sign of good things to come.

Isabel

We rolled up to the address on the warrant. I noticed it was actually a nice-looking house. The yard was well manicured; nothing looked overgrown or out of place. There was a nice middle class sedan in the driveway, along with a few kids' toys. My guess was this guy was keeping all of his money for his new family and not paying his child support to his ex. It was a pretty familiar story.

As we casually walked up to the front door to do a simple arrest and take him in, I peeked into the side window and saw a young woman crying, while a man was standing over her. Waving to Kevin to stop, I unholstered my gun and pointed to the front door, mouthing the words, *He's inside, something's wrong.* Kevin nodded his acknowledgement, drew his gun, and we addressed the front door on either side. I tried the doorknob, which was of course locked, so shaking my head, I bowed out of the way for Kevin to give it a swift kick near the lock, which would almost always break a door in.

Kevin kicked the door wide open, and I rushed into the living room to the left of the foyer where I had seen the perp hovering over the young woman. Startled, the woman started screaming and stood up, while the man shouted, "What are you doing in my house?"

"Sir, are you David Chavez?" I asked, pointing my gun in his direction.

"Yes, I am. Who are you? Why are you in my fucking house, bitch?" He raised his hands about halfway. His slightly long, greasy, dark hair fell in his face as he yelled and his face became red with anger.

"We have a warrant for your arrest. Put your hands on your head and step away from the couch," I demanded loudly, pointing my gun at him.

"Ma'am, you need to get up and raise your hands as well," Kevin told the woman who was muttering something and looked like she was about to start hyperventilating.

As the petite woman raised herself off the couch, she lunged at Kevin, clawing at him. Chavez found the moment he was looking for to try and run past me out the front door. Knowing he was going to try and knock me over with his towering size, I prepared myself and leaned into it as he charged toward me. He had me in size, but I was fast, and since he was so much taller than me, I was able to take us both to the ground as he hit me. I could hear Kevin cuff the small woman after shoving her off of himself. I could also hear him calling for backup.

In a situation like this, where you've already got your firearm out and a perp is resisting arrest, you have to be careful to stay in control. As we had fallen to the ground, Chavez tried to kick me in the stomach to push me away. Fortunately, he just barely grazed me as I was scrambling back to my feet, feeling a sharp pain in my hip from the fall. Our positions had switched, so he was closer to the open door now, making me think he would try to run again. I had my gun on him again and was screaming at him to freeze. Gun in one hand while I steadied myself to the foyer wall, I yelled, "Stay down, Chavez. You are under arrest. Every—"

"Fuck you, bitch," he said as he turned and ran out the open door.

"Sonofabitch!" I muttered as I ran after him. He might have been about seven inches taller than me, but I was way faster. I could hear our backup's sirens coming, and as I caught up to him in the front yard, I tackled him to the ground, taking him down to his knees.

"You fucking bitch! Get the fuck off me!" I had maneuvered myself on top of his back, and while he was squirming, I was able to get cuffs on him as our backup screeched into the driveway and assisted in restraining him.

My tight ponytail had come loose from all the commotion, so I holstered my gun and pulled it out to fix it as Kevin walked out to the front yard, shoving the screaming blond lady in front of him. I started laughing, because she was quite loud and obnoxious and continued to fight him like an angry kitten all the way to the black and white patrol cars that had come to assist.

"Oh my God, lady, shut up already," he rolled his eyes and snapped at her. "She's all yours, guys," he laughed as he transferred her into the other officer's custody.

"Oh, thank you so much. I cannot wait to listen to her screech all the way back downtown," the patrolman replied sarcastically and grinned at us. "You alright, Detective?" he asked me.

"Yea, I'm fantastic. Thanks." I looked down to Chavez, who was still lying in his front yard, cuffed, now with six officers including Kevin and me around him. As he glared at me, I put my sunglasses back on and smiled. "Guess you'll pay that child support next time, eh, Chavez?"

"Fuck you, Detective. You should be home serving your man," he spewed at me. I couldn't help but laugh when my thoughts drifted to the night before with Matt. *I definitely served him last night,* I mused to myself.

"You guys got this from here?" Kevin asked the patrolmen.

"Yea, we'll take them in, no problem, Detectives." The young patrolman picked Chavez up off the ground and put him in the back of his vehicle.

"Ugh, let's get the fuck out of here," Kevin said to me. "It's just a warrant, they said. It'll be fun, they said," he was mocking the situation. I couldn't help but laugh.

"Well, look at it this way, we got most of our workout in already." I shoved him to the driver's side of our vehicle.

"Oh geeze, and now you want me to drive? Cruise, you're getting high maintenance," he teased me.

"I just need a moment to fix myself up, man. I'm still a girl, even when I gotta tackle the big guy and you take on the little girl."

"Um, she came after me. Zip it, woman," he laughed.

"Uh huh, yea, yea," I chuckled back. I loved our relationship. We had been partners for about two years and knew how the other worked on a scene. We played good cop/bad cop a lot, and I was always the bad cop, because he said I had resting bitch face. Basically, I looked like a bitch when I wasn't making any face at all. We had worked enough cases together that we really played on each other's strengths, and I trusted him one hundred percent, which was pretty crucial in a partner.

We got in and took off. It was about lunchtime anyway, and truthfully, I wanted to scroll through my phone and see if I had any messages from a certain tall, handsome firefighter. I couldn't help it. The previous night was creeping into my memory, and I was feeling like another round with him would definitely be in order soon, even though I'd been coy about it. I certainly wasn't going to tell Kevin that though.

MATT

After dinner at the firehouse, I went to my bunk room to sleep and have a moment to myself. I hadn't had time to do anything except work, clean equipment, and then work more, which was fairly unusual. We had back-to-back calls the majority of the day, and after the situation that morning with the arson, my mind was tired and my body was spent. When I finally lay down on my bed and relaxed my body, I immediately recalled the last moment I relaxed, with her.

I wanted to see her again. Being stuck at the firehouse for twenty-four hours could really cause a crimp in your style, but it did mean I had the next day off. I wondered how her day was, and I imagined her face when she realized I had rearranged all of her dishes and shit. I was pretty pleased with myself, since I had set my alarm an extra hour earlier to do it. Mostly because I thought it would be funny as hell, but I also couldn't stand disorganization like that; and if I didn't do it, she certainly never would have. I decided I'd reach out to her; we weren't dating, but we sure as hell were intimate now, and the memory of thrusting into her from behind while she called out my name had my dick hard in seconds.

How was your day?

She replied right away.

Action packed. How about yours?

Same, back-to-back calls all day. This is the first time I've sat down.

I heard about the strip mall fire. Sounded big.

Yea, and suspicious. We'll see what happens though.

Suspicious? You have me intrigued.

Definitely a cop response. I couldn't tell her anything; it was an active investigation, and even with her being a cop, that was just not something I could do.

You know I can't talk about it. lol. Let's talk about something else.

Fair. What would you like to talk about, Cavanaugh?

I'd like to talk about having a repeat of last night.

Oh, would you now?

Yes. Immediately. If not sooner.

Well, you're at work, and I'm out having drinks at the moment. So it'll have to wait… you know, if I were interested…

She was being a smartass, and I loved it. Her playful attitude and confidence was so fucking sexy. I couldn't wait to get my hands on her again.

Oh, you're interested. Do I need to spank you again for being a bad girl?

You might have to. I'm a bad, bad girl, Cavanaugh, and I don't usually learn my lesson very quickly.

You're killing me, woman.

My cock was seriously aching then, and all I wanted to do was drive over there and bend her over every piece of furniture in that house.

Sweet dreams, Cavanaugh. I'm sure we'll see each other soon. Somewhere.

Oh, you're blowing me off. I see how it is. Now I'll really have to punish you for that sass.

You enjoy my sass. Maybe I'll let you punish me tomorrow night.

```
Your  sass  is  gonna  get  that  ass  in
trouble.  Tomorrow,  I'll  have  to  remind  you
and  that  sweet  ass  of  yours  who's  in  charge.
```

```
Me  and  my  ass  will  await  our  punishment
until  then.
```

She was so fucking hot. I needed to end this conversation, so I could just look forward to fucking the hell out of her the next day.

```
Have  fun  tonight.  Be  safe,  was  all  I  said.
```

Always, she replied. Then she sent a second text.

```
You  too,  Cavanaugh.
```

I tossed my head back on my pillow and groaned. She was almost too hot for me. I'd never been with a woman who was so confident in general, let alone sexually, and I shuddered with excitement at the thought of fucking her again. The girls I usually dated absolutely wanted to get in my bed. Between the good genes in my family and being a firefighter, finding someone to warm the bed wasn't generally difficult, but there was something about her. She was so intense in the bedroom, so serious at her job, and then she'd become cute and sweet in a moment. I couldn't put my finger on what it was, but in the last forty-eight hours, I had developed a magnetic pull to her that felt carnal. I had to have her, and own her. But I also felt an unusual desire to just be around her. I'd never felt that way before, and while I didn't know what it meant, it couldn't be real feelings; that just wasn't my thing. I loved it and felt anxious about it at the same time.

Just as I was starting to doze off, fully clothed, with even my boots still on, there was a faint knock at my door. It had to be Jo, and I never turned her away, so I got up to answer it.

"Hey, were you sleeping already? I'm sorry. We can talk later," she whispered.

"No, no, come on in." I rubbed my eyes. "What's going on? Is everything ok?"

"Well, yea. I just wanted to talk to you about this morning. We were so fucking busy today we haven't had any time to talk. Let alone think."

I sat on my bed, well, on the bottom bunk where I normally slept, and motioned to the chair in the room for her to sit on. We were really lucky our budget supported having individual rooms for the firefighters on duty. It wasn't like a hotel or anything, but each room had a bunk bed, in case you needed to double up, a dresser, nightstand, and a chair. It was nice to be able to go back to your room if you wanted, or go to bed early, and not get disturbed unless you had a call.

"Yea, this morning was strange, and I'm really concerned someone on that scene moved that gas can."

"Well, someone on the scene *did* move the can. The question is whether or not they belong to a department. Do you think we should tell Isabel about it?" she asked me. *Isabel. Mmm.*

"No, I think we need to just do our jobs, and that does not include fiddling around in an investigation. That's Brian's job. If he wants to get the police into an investigation, which I'm sure he will, he'll handle it. And Isabel doesn't work this type of crime, I don't think, does she?" I wondered what kind of crime she did work on besides the one case that involved Jo's dad.

381

Suddenly, my thoughts went to her dealing with the underbelly of society, and her mentioning she had an action packed day. I wondered what she'd meant by that, and wished I had asked her, feeling what could definitely be likened to worry about it. *It's just sex,* I reminded myself. I honestly didn't want anything more than a good time, but I wasn't a douchebag either. *We have dangerous jobs, that's all. We always worry about our brothers and sisters in police, fire, and EMS. It's nothing more than that,* I thought to myself.

"I actually have no idea what type of crime she typically works on. Maybe I'll call her tomorrow. I said I would when we were out the other night. Maybe I can go have drinks with her. I haven't had a girlfriend in a long time," she said.

Rolling my eyes in her direction, I sarcastically replied, "Maybe if you didn't spend every waking moment with Brian, you would." It must have come out far nastier than I intended, because Jo's face dropped, and she reached over and punched me in the arm.

"What the fuck is with you lately? Do you have a problem with me and Brian still?" She was almost pouting, but she definitely expected an answer from me.

"No, no. Sorry, I didn't mean for it to sound that way. It's just still kind of weird for me, I guess. I don't have a problem with it at all, and in fact, I'd way rather you ended up with my brother than any of the other douchebags I've seen you date." I was hoping my lighthearted tone would keep her from being mad at me. I never wanted to upset Jo; she was literally my favorite person to be around, and she was my best friend.

"Go fuck yourself, buddy. Just because I fell in love and you're still banging hussies with no brain, you don't get to be shitty with me. You just wait. You'll meet someone one day, and when you look at each other, you'll say, oh my God, it's you. I've been waiting for you," she lectured me.

"I sincerely doubt that. And I enjoy my hussies for now, so don't get your hopes up you'll be best friending some chick in my life."

Rolling her eyes at me for what seemed like the tenth time in ten minutes, she said, "We'll see. I can't wait to say 'I told you so.'" She stood up to leave, then looked down at me. "Back to the other thing. You're right. I haven't talked to Brian about it. I really wanted to get your thoughts first, since we were the ones who saw everything. I sent him all my pictures, and I guess we'll just wait and see what happens. There was definitely something not good about that whole scene. I'm hoping it was just some kind of asshole insurance fraud or something. It just worries me when one of us could get hurt over some jerk setting his business on fire because he can't pay his bills."

"Yea, I agree with you there. Hopefully, that's the last of the day too. I'm fucking exhausted." I sighed and lay back on my bed when our pagers went off for another call.

"Ugh, here we go again." We both left my room and headed out to the engine bay to get our gear and find out what the umpteenth call of the day was.

Isabel

Having drinks after work with Kevin was always a nice wind down to our day. My hip was hurting from the altercation earlier that day, and the vodka was settling my nerves and taking the edge off the pain.

"How's your hip?" he asked me.

"I'll be honest, it fucking hurts. That guy was like a damned tank." I smiled. We were at the same dive bar we usually went to after a shift; it was a place where we didn't get treated differently for being cops, and we could just hang out and have a few drinks to unwind before going home. Kevin lived alone too, and while we'd talked many times about how great it was to live alone, there were certainly times when it was too solitary and we didn't want to be left alone with our thoughts.

"Well, you're a tough one. I'm sure he's hurting worse, being taken by surprise and all." He laughed, sipping at his beer. "I hope we get an actual investigation soon. While I never want to wish for more crime or anything, serving warrants totally blows."

I couldn't have agreed more. It was a total drag not having something to solve like a puzzle, which was why I wanted to become a detective in the first place. Obvious crimes were basically about paperwork, and I enjoyed solving the mystery of a real case.

"Yea, hopefully tomorrow we'll get something. So, what are you gonna do about the girl? Do you want to talk about it?" I thought Kevin was the sweetest guy I knew and really did wish for him to find someone. He seemed lonely to me.

He took a deep breath, looking away as if he was thinking of what to say exactly. "You know, Isabel, I just don't know anymore. I feel like women want to date a cop because it makes them feel safe, and I totally get that. It makes me feel like a man to be with a woman I can make feel secure. I do love that. But on the other hand, the women I've found seem to want that at first, but then flip a switch once things get more serious, and they want to keep me from doing what attracted them to me in the first place. I feel like I should tell women I'm a fucking chef or something, so I don't even have to go down this road with them. It's the same thing over and over and over."

He was right. Women did want to be with someone who made them feel safe, but the tables always turned, and they wanted to keep him from doing the job he was born to do. "Honestly, I think the right one is out there. She's someone who has her own life and her own career and shit. Someone who understands the system though. Maybe you'll meet a paramedic or a nurse or something like that. Someone who understands the whole emergency thing and appreciates it, and no, I'm not talking about my sister. In all honesty, even though sometimes it seems impossible, I hope that for myself someday as well," I confessed.

Kevin's mouth fell open, and he set his beer down in shock. Leaning into me from across the booth table, he said, "I'm sorry. Do my ears deceive me? Did you just say you hope you find someone who understands you? Like love? Did you bump your head today when you tackled that guy?"

I felt my lips curl to a little smile and took a sip of my drink before setting it down. "Oh, shut up, Kevin. I'm still human. At the end of the day, we all crave love. We all long for affection and attention, and just because I don't necessarily need someone to feel safe, doesn't mean I don't wish for that feeling too from time to time." I watched him tilt his head at me like a puppy dog listening.

"I feel like it must be a full moon or something. Did you meet someone?" he questioned me pointedly.

"No! I didn't meet anyone!" I was probably a little too defensive in my reply, but I couldn't help it. I hoped I would be able to cover my tracks a little bit. After all, I didn't just meet Matt, and there was no love, no relationship happening. It was just phenomenal sex. Sex I would be having again the next day, apparently, to my surprise and excitement. As I felt my body get warm and flushed, I realized I might have been blushing.

"Ahhh, me thinks you might be protesting too much. So, who is he?" Kevin grabbed his beer again and sat back taking a long tug on it.

"No, seriously, there is no 'someone.' I was being general, and fuck you. I was trying to open up and relate." I turned the tables on him.

"Uh huh. I don't believe you. You're little miss love 'em and leave 'em. Don't get too attached, keep them at arm's length. I think you brought someone to your home and you might even bring them back again. That's cool though. Don't tell me. I'll find out eventually. You know, I'm a detective too," he teased.

I laughed, relieved we were moving on. I could feel the flush in my face dissipating and went back to sipping my drink. "Yea,

yea. Listen, in the unlikely event some guy sweeps me off my feet, you'll be the first to know. My current standard is what it always has been. I like having a physical relationship, just like anyone else would, but anything more than that is not something I'm seeking out."

"Ah, yes. Not seeking out. But what if it finds you, Izzy? When you're not even looking..." he mused.

Rolling my eyes at him, I replied, "I'm sure he is lost on his way to find me. But in the event someone gives him directions or he finds his way, I'll be sure to fill you in on the details. But until then, it's business as usual in my neck of the woods."

Matt was really anything but business as usual, particularly for me. Most of the men I had been with couldn't get me going the same way he did the night before. Other men were weak, and while I made every attempt to bring my feminine to the bedroom, they allowed me to dominate them, which provided for lackluster fucking and limited satisfaction for me. At work, I had to be in charge all fucking day, dominating situations; in the bedroom, I wanted to be used for pleasure. It gave me pleasure to satisfy a deep, animalistic desire in a strong man.

As my thoughts drifted to the night before, I reminisced about how he'd handled me. His strong hands, his large stature towering over me had made me feel small but powerful sexually. His reserved but then enthusiastic reaction to what I said brought me pleasure. I could feel the warmth between my legs forming as I thought of his firm smack to my ass as my punishment, followed by his soft touch, soothing where he'd made contact. The look in his eyes when I gave him permission to dominate me was that of a hungry lion that wanted to devour me. When he'd said it would happen again, I hadn't thought I'd want to. I generally tended not to go back to the same man's bedroom a second time, but a desire to fuck him again was taking over.

"Earth to Isabel?" Kevin interrupted my thoughts, bringing me back to reality. "What's going on in that head of yours?"

"Oh! Nothing. I just got lost for a moment, relaxing and daydreaming, actually." I smiled. At that moment, both of our phones started pinging with a message. Another large fire was happening right that moment, just under a block away from us, and we were specifically requested at the scene.

"That's unusual, while a fire is still burning," Kevin said as he flagged the waitress down to pay our bill. "We're being requested specifically too, that's odd. Let's go check it out. It's not far from here anyway."

"From what I understand, it's been a busy day for the fire department. Maybe something is up." I finished the rest of my drink and stood up.

Kevin quickly paid our tab, while I called in we would be responding, as well as our location, and we walked out to our car. As we exited the building, we could see the lights from the emergency vehicles, and the air was thick with the pungent smell of smoke. It appeared to be a rather large fire, and while I couldn't see the flames from where we were, the smell was overwhelming and the haze in the air was visible from our location, which was close, but not that close; it had to be a big one.

Dispatch informed me we were requested on scene specifically because it was the third sizeable fire of the day and suspicious activity had been reported at one of the fires earlier that day. That must have been the one Matt mentioned in his text. That number of fires in one day, along with one suspicious report, was enough to open an investigation to see if there was a common thread among them. Looked like I'd be seeing Matt much sooner than I'd anticipated, and not under ideal circumstances, which would have been my bedroom, of course.

As we pulled up to the scene, we saw an apartment building fully engulfed in flames. I had actually never been to a fire scene that large, and as I got out of the car, I could feel the heat from the flames against my face.

"Jesus Christ, this is a big fire." Kevin looked over at me. "Fuck, it's hot."

"Yea, it really is. Let's go find the chief first." I stared at the flames rising out of the roof and through two windows of the apartment on the end. There appeared to be five apartments across, and two stories. Displaced residents were watching in awe as well.

As we made our way over to Brian Cavanaugh's command vehicle, I noted he looked very concerned. His brows were furrowed, and he was yelling orders into the radio as more firefighters showed up to assist from all directions. The chaos of a scene like that was fairly new to me. I didn't normally run investigations like this. It was late in the evening, and the flames were so big they lit up the block as if the sun were shining.

"Chief, I'm Detective Connor, and you know my partner Detective Cruise. We'd like to talk to you when you have a moment. I understand you requested us." I nodded at Brian, continuing to take note of his concern for what was going on around him.

"Give me a minute, Detectives." He turned away from us, putting his ear up to his radio. "Ok, I want everyone out of there.

This is a surround and drown. I repeat, all firefighters out. NOW."
And with that, the horns on the trucks sounded three times in quick
succession, several times. What I learned later was that when the
interior of the building was deemed unsafe to continue fighting the
fire inside of it, the chief would call for the firefighters to leave the
building immediately. Because of the chaos and noise at times,
they don't always hear the orders, and so the sound of the horns
blowing quickly in succession three times is the indication they
need to get out immediately.

"There is way too much going on for him to talk to us right
now. Let's walk around," I said. I motioned to Brian we were going
to walk around and would be back. When he nodded his
understanding in my direction, we started to observe our
surroundings more intently.

"So, if this is the third large fire of the day, it's either a really
busy town all of a sudden or something fishy is going on. What do
you think, Cruise?" Kevin wiped some of the sweat forming on his
forehead off with his shirtsleeve.

Fanning myself from the heat as well, I replied, "Well,
dispatch said something suspicious was reported at the fire this
morning, so I guess we'll need to ask the chief what that was.
Normally, they would just tell us when we call in, so I already find
everything about this odd. I don't follow the fire wire, but three
large fires in one district in one day certainly raises an eyebrow and
throws up a flag for me."

"Yea, me too." As we walked around, I took mental pictures of
my surroundings. The apartment building, the number of
firefighters on the scene and what they were doing. And I did look
for Matt, but with them all dressed the same, it was impossible to

tell them apart, really, except for their names on the backs of their coats, and I didn't see his. For a moment, I wondered how hot it must be to wear all of that heavy equipment in weather like ours here. It's so hot to begin with, and to wear a heavy coat and pants as well as all that gear must be arduous at best.

Kevin and I both knew that at major scenes of any kind, you wanted to get a good look at the crowd. The people watching the scene often left clues, and as much as I hated to admit it, often a criminal in a situation would watch the aftermath of a crime they committed if they had the chance. We learned early on at the academy that often people who committed crimes did it so they could participate in the spectacle. Sometimes, they would engage the media as an innocent bystander. Sometimes, they did it so they could be a hero and help save the day. Why they did it was always a mystery, or at least it was until we figured it out. Without saying a word, we began to observe the faces and the reactions of the onlookers. In my head, I asked myself, *Does anyone look happy? Does anyone look sad? Does anyone look nervous?* Thinking and watching, I didn't notice Brian had waved us over.

"Come on, the chief wants us now," Kevin nudged me. I simply nodded, turning my attention away from the growing crowd. I hadn't noticed anything worthy of additional attention and figured we'd probably have better luck talking to residents.

As we approached Brian's truck, he said something to a firefighter next to him before he walked toward us, away from his vehicle. As the other firefighter turned to watch Brian walk away, I immediately realized it was Matt, and I felt a flush as our eyes met. He didn't smile but gave a slight nod, and then turned back to the radios and other equipment at the back of the truck. I knew full well this was a real emergency scene, a big fire, and what they did for a living, but I couldn't help the slightest disappointment that crept in from his lack of acknowledgement. Shaking myself free of it so I could do *my* job, I spoke up first as Brian ushered us further away from any people so we could talk privately.

"So, you requested investigators here? What's going on? It sounds like a hell of a day. Is everyone accounted for?" I asked.

Taking a large sigh and looking around nervously, Brian began to explain the events of the day. "We had a pretty large fire this morning, and while two of my guys were inside investigating after the fire was out, they discovered a gas can that had not ignited in the fire. It had rags stuffed right into the top of it. Jo got a picture of it, actually. When I sent a backup crew in to get it, it was missing. Gone." He ran his hands through his sweaty hair, and I caught a glimpse of his green eyes, lit up from the fire and lights around us. I immediately noted they were the same eyes I'd stared into the night before, except these didn't belong to Matt.

"So someone definitely tampered with evidence at fire number one," Kevin scrawled in his little notebook, repeating what Brian said.

"Yes, but there's more. Look, we are a medium-sized department. We have some busy days, but never, and I mean never in the twenty years I've been riding fire trucks in this town have we had three major fires in one day. It's fucking suspicious. The fire we have going on right now spread to three apartments before we could even get here, and we aren't that far away. I suspect when we finally get the flames out, there will be traces of some kind of an accelerant, because there is no other way for this type of construction to go up that quickly. This is new construction, made of a multitude of fire resistant materials. That should at the very least slow the spread of fire."

"Ok, we'll definitely need to get the evidence guys down here. I'll make the call now, actually. Please keep telling Detective Cruise about the rest of the situation." Kevin walked off, taking his cell out of his pocket and calling in for a crime lab unit to be sent out to this scene.

"Is everyone alright, Brian?" I had to ask. I didn't see Jo anywhere. I mean, there were a ton of firefighters from multiple districts at that point there, helping out, but rarely had I ever seen Jo without either Brian or Matt by her side.

"Yea, all of my guys are ok. Jo is fine, if that's what you're asking. She was on the initial interior team, but they've all been pulled out now. She's over at rehab, cooling off and getting hydrated. It's so fucking hot out here tonight."

"Well, I'm glad she's ok, and I saw your brother. I assume everyone else is alright. So tell me about the second fire today."

"The second fire today was a mechanic's garage. You familiar with Mike's over on Minnesota Ave?"

"Yes, I am, actually. I took my car there once. Is it gone?" I was disappointed. I liked taking my car to smaller mechanics who have an appreciation for the classics like me. I also hadn't heard about that fire, since we had been busy serving that warrant.

"Oh, it's gone alright. When a garage like that goes up and we don't get a call right away, all the chemicals and shit light up pretty fast. He happened to be closed today, which is normal for a Monday, so it didn't get reported right away. The long and short of it is, we've now had three major fires in one day, all of which included accelerants of some kind, and I'm getting fucking concerned for the safety of my guys and whether or not any of these might be connected."

"What would make you think they're connected?" I examined Brian's face, looking for a sign that would speak to me.

"Honestly? It's a gut feeling."

"A gut feeling?" Kevin chimed in loudly and fairly sarcastically, turning our attention to him.

"Yes, a gut feeling. I've been doing this a long fucking time, Detective, and I know when something isn't right. And something about everything that has happened today isn't right."

"Ok, ok. Everyone calm down for a minute," I interjected. "Kevin, I believe that if the chief here thinks something is wrong, then something might actually be wrong. Brian, why didn't you directly report to the fire marshal for this? Why did you get us involved yourself?" I was puzzled. Traditionally, the state fire marshal's office would handle this sort of an investigation and involve the police after the fact.

"Well, to be honest, because I clearly had some sort of interference or tampering with evidence this morning. I believe this is a criminal matter. I looked into it this afternoon, and it is within my jurisdiction to recommend this be turned over to the police and not the fire marshal's office," he replied.

"That doesn't really answer my question. Why?" I stared into his eyes, looking for an answer.

Looking around again, he leaned in closer to Kevin and me before speaking. "I'm concerned it is one of the firefighters."

MATT

When I saw Isabel on the scene, part of me wanted to grab her, but after the day we'd had and the continued burning of the building in front of us, I barely had a moment to acknowledge her. Brian had asked me to take over the scene so he could go talk to the detectives. I was guessing the guy with her was her partner, and I couldn't help but wonder what their relationship was. He probably wanted to fuck her. Who wouldn't? Not that it was any of my business, really.

I took over the scene for the remainder of the incident, which kept me busy, and I ended up losing track of Brian as well as the detectives. We finally got the fire under control, and as it started to die out, I could feel my body doing the same. Even in good shape, it was exhausting to fight fire, let alone three fires in one day, and I could feel my muscles begin to ache. Jo and Jax had been assigned to operations earlier, and when the fire was under control, a new team took over, and they made their way to me.

"Hey, where's the chief?" Jo asked. She never called him Brian on a scene, which was funny to me. It was completely professional, just always amused me.

"He is talking to the cops over there somewhere," I waved in the direction I had last seen them.

Jax rose an eyebrow of suspicion. "Is there something particularly suspicious about this fire? Or is the fact we've been running our asses off today at what looks to be three arsons in a day?" He did always have a way of simply putting it all out there, calling attention to the elephant in the room.

"I'd say it's the latter, but I didn't ask." I figured Brian would tell me what he wanted me to know. Even though we were brothers and we were close, it wasn't my place to question things at work, unless I had what I thought may be an alternative way to operate on a scene or something. I respected authority. While every chief had their own style, and Brian was much different than Jack, he was extremely competent, was one of the best firefighters I'd ever met, my brother or not, and a fire department frankly runs more smoothly when the Chain of Command is kept intact.

Jax and I were both Lieutenants and had both been asked to apply for the Deputy Chief position, although neither of us had yet. I really didn't know if I wanted that additional responsibility. Well, I mostly didn't want the additional paperwork ruining my fun as a firefighter. I enjoyed the thrill of riding the truck, fighting fire, and going inside, that kind of thing. As a Lieutenant, I still got to ride the fire trucks, I got to actually fight fire, and I still got the perks of teaching new guys and contributing to budget requests and expenses based on what we as firefighters needed. I felt like I had the job of my dreams, so staying where I was appealed to me.

"Hmm," Jo hummed. "I think something fucked up is going on, and I can tell you one thing; I'm goddamn tired now. That was a lot of work today, and I cannot wait to get back to the station and take my fourth shower of the day at this point." She leaned against the side of the truck and took a bottle of water out of the pants' pocket of her bunker gear. Taking a long sip, she sighed, and Jax moved over and leaned next to her.

"I agree. I'm fucking spent. That was fun, but now I could sleep for a day," Jax agreed.

The scene was winding down, and I continued to direct crews to look for hot spots and begin overhaul. The overhaul process meant tearing down any loose debris, looking for smoldering fire and embers, putting them out, and also looking around for evidence if need be. While I didn't ask anyone specifically to look for evidence, I did instruct the interior crews to be observant and look for anything out of place. I hoped they picked up what I meant and expected they'd likely understand after the day we'd had.

Since I was running Command, people continued coming up to me, asking for directions and such, and it was seriously getting annoying. I kept looking around for Brian and the detectives, and my mind shifted to looking for Isabel as much as I was looking for Brian. It was then I saw them walking back toward us, Isabel's partner holding his notepad and writing things down Brian appeared to be telling him. As they got closer, I locked eyes with Isabel and immediately felt that animal attraction to her again. The corners of her mouth turned up into a half smile, and I felt my dick get instantly hard. She always had a smirk around me, and it was so fucking sexy, I couldn't shake it. Thankfully, through my bunker pants you'd never know, but the closer she got, the more my body reacted. My pulse quickened, and I felt overwhelmingly thirsty as my mouth dried up.

"Evening, Cavanaugh. Busy day, I hear," she said when they arrived in front of us.

"You could say that," was all I could muster. All of a sudden, I was completely stupid and couldn't think of what else to say. *What the fuck does she do to me? And those fucking jeans she has on would look so much better crumpled up with the rest of her clothes on my bedroom floor.*

Both Jo and Jax said their hellos, and as I commanded the crews to finish up so the chief could go inside and take a look, presumably with the detectives, I had to turn away so I could concentrate. She had her long, dark hair pulled back in that conservative detective ponytail, which was making me think about grabbing her by it while I fucked her from behind again. The thought made my cock so hard I had to adjust myself and shake it off so I could do my job; well, do Brian's job. As I gave a few more instructions and started shooing people away so we could wrap up the operations side of the job, I waved Brian over.

"Hey, you ok doing this?" He came over and asked.

"Yea, it's fine. I'm glad it's not my full time job though," I said. "I'd like to get this scene wrapped up, Chief. The fire is definitely out, and it looks like the hot spots have all been addressed. If you want to go in with the detectives, now is the time before too much gets destroyed in overhaul."

"Alright, can you hold down the fort for a little bit longer while I take Jax and the detectives inside to look around?"

"Yea, do your thing. You know I got this."

He patted me on the shoulder and nodded his thanks. As I watched him grab an axe and the camera from his truck and walk toward the building with Isabel and her partner, all I could do was sigh. I had a bad feeling about the entire day, and a twinge of concern for all of us crept in.

Isabel

I hadn't actually been to a lot of fire scenes, not even as a beat cop. Not for any reason other than it just didn't work out that way. The chaos around me was quite fascinating. The flashing lights everywhere were something I was used to, but I was stuck on the smell of the scene; the dirt and smoke permeated my senses, invading my lungs, and making my eyes blur. I had heard this type of debris in your system was a carcinogen, and my thoughts drifted to how well Matt took care of himself. I remembered reading an article about the firefighters who responded in NYC on 9/11 coming down with various forms of cancers, autoimmune diseases, and other serious issues after spending so much time in the debris on that scene. I couldn't image a mass casualty incident like that and what it could do to you emotionally and physically. I admired Matt's commitment to health and hoped he took precautions against things like that even on a regular basis at these types of fires.

I watched him point and direct people, noticing how tired he looked. After hearing Brian explain everything that had happened that day, I knew he had to be exhausted. A small nurturing piece of me poked a little hole in my darkish heart and pushed me into an unusual place where I wanted to take care of him, not just sexually.

He looked like he needed to be fed and rest, and a part of me wanted to provide that place for him.

An uneasy feeling came over me, knowing something nefarious was definitely happening. This many serious fires in one day, in one district, was something that definitely didn't happen often, and if Brian thought something bad was happening, then it had to have been. I trusted his judgment. Kevin and I had a standard way of operating on a new scene: he would take notes, while I would engage, so that one of us was continuously connected to whomever we were interviewing or talking with. We walked toward the apartment building, following Brian and stopping at the entrance before walking in.

"Ok, I want you to stay behind me until I'm able to fully assess what's in front of us. I'd like to make sure it's safe. Detective Cruise, you stay with me. Detective Connor, if you could stay with Jax, that would make it easiest for us to cover the most ground and look around." We nodded our heads in agreement and made our way into the building.

It was still quite warm, and there was water and what looked like suds dripping off of just about everything.

"Chief, what's all the soapy looking stuff?" Kevin asked.

"That's foam. It's a chemical that helps smother a fire a little bit better than water in some cases. We started the operation with water, and then, since the fire was spreading so rapidly, we decided to go in with foam before it got out of hand. Unfortunately, I don't think it helped much. We had to evacuate and drown the fire out anyway," Brian replied.

As we made our way into the unit Brian assumed the fire had started, we looked around for the point of origin of the fire. Again,

I wasn't a forensic fire expert, but I was most certainly a crime scene expert, so I treated the scene as I would any crime scene, leaving nothing disturbed. I made mental images of the burned-out couch in the living room and continued observing everything in the room, from the charred curtains that hadn't completely burned up, to the group of small houseplants that sat on a table that had also not totally burned up. It was striking to me how some of the building had been completely charred, and yet some parts were almost untouched. As if the fire didn't have it out for those things.

Not seeing anything of note in the living room, when he was done snapping pictures, Brian led us into the kitchen, and Jax took off upstairs with Kevin. "What are you looking for, Chief?" I asked. I wasn't entirely sure what to look for other than something suspicious, which could've been almost anything in there.

"I'm looking for an area that would have some sort of a smoke pattern on the walls or the floor, indicating an accelerant was lit or used to spread the fire. It will look like it burned differently, and likely it would leave a clue of some kind."

"Ok, that's helpful. Is that how you tell if it was arson?" I asked.

"Well, it's how we tell a fire was started. I believe it to be arson just because of the day we've had; however, there are no clues leading me to believe that really yet. Normally, my first assumption would never be arson, but today I feel differently." He sighed. I examined him and watched as he poked at debris from furniture that had burned up, as well as pieces of wall that had been ripped out. "We rip the walls out to try to find the fire as well. That's where you would find an electrical fire in some places. This is all new construction, so there is a lot of space in the walls for fire to grow. A fire needs three things, Detective: fuel, oxygen, and heat; along with a chemical reaction or ignition. The fuel in new construction is the wood that frames it out, as well as the drywall, which burns as well. The air pockets in the frame provide lots of oxygen, so it's a matter of figuring out where that third piece comes into play."

I hadn't realized how much chemistry and science was really involved in fires. I think I might have known deep down, but I was fascinated learning something new at the same time. "That actually makes a lot of sense. It didn't occur to me at first, the chemistry of it all," I admitted.

"Yea, it's not all hot guys climbing ladders and getting wet, you know," he tried to make a joke.

"No, no, I know. So, I've got to ask you, Chief, while it's just you and me, did you request me on this case? Because I'm not an arson investigator, and I'm not sure how well I'll be able to help solve these crimes with my little knowledge of fires and fire scenes." I wanted to help, but I didn't want Brian to get his hopes up I was some kind of specialist in this area at all.

Stopping to look at me directly, Brian looked around before meeting my eyes. "Isabel, you are a friend of the fire department and a friend of my family. Someone is putting my family in danger, and that makes me trust very few people right now. I trust you. This is not something I can handle and investigate on my own, and frankly, asking for help isn't my thing. But I knew you would help. I did call today and speak with your captain this afternoon and requested you be put on this case indefinitely, and discreetly. I hope that's okay with you." I stared into his green eyes. They shined brightly against his dirty, pale skin.

"You can trust me. You can also trust my partner. I'm sure we'll figure out what's going on here, and then we can all move on. This sort of thing doesn't usually drag on, and there has to be a reason of some kind for these events. Motive always presents themselves, and we'll find out who did this and put them away."

Going back to searching, he simply replied, "Thank you."

We continued to poke around and take pictures, looking underneath everything, locating the furnace and other appliances that could cause a fire, until we had searched everything downstairs and came up empty-handed.

Brian called up the stairs, "Jax, you find any point of origin up there? We're coming up with nothing down here!"

"No! There's actually very little damage up here overall." They met at the stairs to regroup and discuss the next steps.

"I'd like to look in the kitchen again, actually. Something isn't sitting right with me," I said.

"We already checked the kitchen, Isabel," Brian said, seeming confused by my request.

"Yea, I know. Something is nagging at me. I want to look again. It was totally burned out, but we didn't find any point of origin anywhere, and I feel like it has to be somewhere in that kitchen."

All four of us tromped back into the kitchen, and the three men watched me poke around. I put on a pair of latex gloves from my pocket to keep my hands clean, but also to preserve anything I touched, and began looking around more closely.

"What are you actually looking for, Isabel?" Kevin asked me.

"I'm not sure yet. The fire had to start in here, and it obviously didn't start with one of these appliances. The stove is burned, but it's not where the fire started, so it *has* to be something else. But it's not something with a motor or electrical. At least I don't think it is." I ran my hand along the counter, which was charred but not completely disintegrated, while I thought. *Where would the fire start if the stove, the fridge, or the dishwasher didn't cause it?* While they were all burned out, they were not so badly burned to be the cause.

As the boys watched me think and walk around slowly, I began to open cabinets until I found exactly what I was looking for. "Come here! I found it!"

They gathered around to see what I had found. A hole had been cut out of the drywall through the back of the cabinet, and what we found was the perfect pattern of fire damage, proving the origin of the fire was that very spot. The cabinet hadn't been burned to nothing, simply because whatever was used to set the fire was shoved into the space between the walls, and the fire had spread that way. Upon opening all of the other cabinets, we found similar holes in other walls. Whoever set this fire didn't expect for the structure to be salvageable. They had definitely expected the building to burn to the ground, destroying this evidence.

MATT

"So, what did you find in there?" I asked impatiently as Brian, Jax, Isabel, and her partner came out of the building and walked over to the truck I was still standing at. I was really over this day and wanted to go the fuck home to sleep. Knowing I still had to go back to the station was annoying me more than anything as exhaustion had truly set in.

"We definitely have an arsonist on our hands," Brian stated without any emotion. He appeared to be equally exhausted, and while I didn't know exactly what they found inside, it was apparent there was more to the story judging by the troubled look on his face. I looked over at Jax, who met my eyes and shook his head, signaling to me they had found something pretty bad inside.

The fact it was arson wasn't really surprising to me after the day we'd had; what was more troubling was the fact it was an apartment building and people could have been seriously hurt or killed in a fire like this. The last two fires had been set at businesses, which meant the motive could've been insurance related or something like that, much less human collateral. Once you're talking about arson related to a residential setting, you're talking about possible murder charges. Fortunately, in this fire, everyone appeared to have gotten out safely, but it certainly could have gone a different way.

"Jesus Christ," I shook my head. "Are we ready to get out of here?" I ran my hands through my hair, the sweat dripping down my neck. I caught Isabel's eyes, and she quickly looked away, avoiding my glance.

"Yea, we can wrap it up here. The investigation needs to be turned over to the detectives here, and we've already got the caution tape set up, so it looks like we're good to go. Thanks for manning things over here, bro." I simply nodded and gathered my helmet, coat, and other shit to take back to my truck.

"Do you need anything else from me? I'm going to go back with Matt and the rest of my crew," Jax asked Brian.

"Nope, thanks for your help. I'll see you back at the station," Brian replied.

"Detectives, sounds like we'll see you soon," I muttered in their direction.

"You can count on it," Isabel replied, finally meeting my stare with her big, brown doe eyes. I quickly scanned her face and noticed a slight smirk forming, causing me to smile back. She was totally into me, and I loved the secret we had between us. Her little remark put a spring back in my step. Something about her really just got me worked up all the way around; she was hot as fuck but super smart too. It was funny to me, thinking back at how I disliked her early on when we'd first met.

"Sounds fantastic," I grinned as Jax and I took off to meet Jo and the rest of our crew at our truck. I really did need a shower and at least a nap before going home to crash after this hellacious shift.

"Dude, is something going on between you and that detective?" Jax asked me as we walked.

Surprised and not wanting my secret out, I attempted to shut it down immediately. "Hell, no. I still think she's a bitch. Why?"

"No reason. Just seemed like you guys were sharing some kind of inside joke or something." He raised an eyebrow at me questioningly.

"Nope. She's not my type. You know I like them blond and not that smart or bossy," I laughed.

"Yea, you definitely do have a type." That was thankfully the end of that conversation.

Once we got back to the station, none of us wanted to talk. We were all far too exhausted. I knew I'd catch up with Brian later anyway, and Jo and I talked every day, so we all got our showers and crashed in our bunks for a few hours before the end of the longest shift in history. When I woke up at seven the next morning, I felt like I had been in a coma and couldn't wait to leave.

Quickly grabbing my shit, I got to my truck to go home but decided to make a stop first. I decided to go see Isabel and address the hard-on she gave me last night by just standing near me. Figuring she'd be up, I sent her a text and hauled my ass to her place. She lived relatively close to the firehouse, so I was there within about ten minutes, already feeling my dick get hard in anticipation.

I pulled into her driveway on a mission, having gotten myself worked up on the short drive. She knew I was on my way, so when I knocked on her door, it flung open almost instantly. There she was, in the smallest white shorts I'd ever seen and a black tank that hugged her tits and accentuated her tiny waist. She had that squat ass I could not get enough of, and for a brief moment, I was speechless.

"Cavanaugh…" she said like a question, holding the door open for me to enter.

"Detective… I'm not here to talk." I walked in past her, turning around to face her as she shut the door.

"I don't expect you to," she said.

And with that, I launched at her, immediately picking her up by that beautiful round ass, crushing my mouth to hers. She welcomed my tongue into her mouth passionately and squeezed her legs around my waist as I pushed us up against her front door. She tasted like coffee and toothpaste, and in that moment, she was what I wanted for breakfast. With her small frame, I was easily able to hold her against the door with one arm under her ass, while the other was free to rove over those perky tits.

I felt her heart racing against my chest, and all I wanted to do was be inside her. I pulled away, looking intently into those big, brown eyes, and whispered, "Bedroom. I need you. Now." She nodded and started licking and nipping at my neck, driving me absolutely wild.

As I carried her up the stairs, feeling her tongue gently taste me between my neck and my shoulders, my knees buckled from the sensations of pleasure tingling through me. Since she was holding on to me tightly with her legs, my aching cock was rubbing against her, begging to be freed. When we reached her bedroom, I gently set her on the edge of the bed and kneeled between her legs, salivating already, knowing I was about to taste her again. She watched me intently, waiting for me to control the situation, which just got me fucking hotter. I pulled my t-shirt off over my head and tossed it aside before I grabbed the bottom of her tank top and pulled it up just over her round tits. She wasn't wearing a bra, and her little brown nipples were stiff peaks, letting me know how turned on she was, making me even harder, if that were possible. I leaned in to take the left one into my mouth, sucking and licking the little pebble, and pulling her into me while I kneaded the other, just barely squeezing it between my thumb and forefinger. As she let out a little moan, she arched her back and spread her legs open even more for me to get closer. I moved to the right breast to get a taste, letting out a groan of my own. I fucking loved sucking on her tits, and it drove her wild, which made it even hotter for me.

I leaned back to look at her beautiful body, that tank top resting on top of those delicious breasts, leaving her torso and beautiful, flat stomach exposed. It was time to take charge a little more before I totally had my way with her. I put my hands just inside the waistband of those tiny little shorts near her ass, feeling her soft skin down the small of her back, and whispered, "Have you been a good girl, Isabel?"

Her breath hitched, and she met my eyes intently, shaking her head no. A smirk of anticipation crossed her face as I yanked her shorts down around her ass then down her legs to her ankles abruptly. I noticed a big bruise on her hip and gently ran my hand over it. I wanted to know what happened to her, but now wasn't the time. I needed to deal with my naughty girl, and the anticipation was creating a fully involved fire inside me.

"No?" I questioned as I removed the shorts from her ankles, exposing her naked sex to me. Again, she shook her head no to me. *God, she's so fucking hot,* was all I could think. *How the fuck did I get so lucky that this chick wants me to fuck her like this and play these games with me*? I'd never been so turned on by a woman in my life.

"You know what happens to bad girls, don't you, Isabel?" I asked her as I unbuttoned my jeans to give some relief to my aching cock. She nodded her head yes. I ran my hands up her thighs, grabbing her ass and pulling her toward me, her ass just barely at the edge of the bed now, causing her to lean back onto her elbows with her legs spread to me. I couldn't wait another minute to taste her and leaned in, gripping her thighs tightly, immediately going for her clit with my tongue. I couldn't resist torturing her as her 'punishment' for being a bad little girl, and even though I wanted to smack that beautiful round ass again, I had to eat that pussy first. She leaned her pelvis into me, giving me exactly what I wanted. Her breathing became heavy, letting me know how much she liked it.

As I flicked my tongue at her hard little nub, an idea came to me, and I sat up, stopping abruptly. Clearly taken by surprise, she leaned back up toward me with a pouty look on her face since I'd taken away what she wanted. "I know you have toys, Isabel. Where are they?" Her eyes got huge, and she pursed her lips, knowing I was about to torture her. She didn't reply, so I slipped a finger inside her dripping wet pussy and asked again, "Where are they, Isabel?"

Panting now, she whispered, "In the drawer next to your side of the bed." I removed my finger and stood up, taking note she used the phrase *your side of the bed*, getting me even more excited to torture her with pleasure.

"I'm going to let you pick which one I use on you today. Go get one," I demanded. She stood up, getting ready to remove the tank top that was still tight over the top of her tits. "No. Leave it. I like the way it wraps around the top of those delicious breasts." She stopped and smiled at me, walking over to the other side of the bed, while I stared at that ass and took my jeans off, leaving me in my boxer briefs, hard as a fucking rock. As she opened the drawer, she paused and looked back at me, wearing nothing but that tank top. "You better hurry up and pick one. Don't keep me waiting."

She grabbed something pink before she demurely walked back over to me. Standing in front of me, she slipped the small, pink vibrator into my hand while looking up at me with wanting eyes. Leaning down to her, I pulled her ponytail out, freeing her hair, and inhaled the coconut smell of her shampoo as I licked her neck. "You're so fucking hot, Isabel. I'm going to torture you now, and you're going to beg me to fuck you today. Do you want to beg me to fuck you?" I loved asking her filthy questions like that.

"Yes," she let out in a whisper.

"Get on the bed and lie down on your back," I demanded. As she got on the bed, I examined the little vibrator and clicked the on switch, getting a feel for it. I wanted her to enjoy my dick more than the toys, so I was only going to go so far with it. I made a mental note to go through that drawer and take anything I didn't want her using without me. I watched her get on the bed, leaning up on her elbows again, spreading her legs to me. I loved that she wanted to open to me, that she sat up ready for me.

Crawling up toward her sweet pussy, with the little vibrator humming in my hand, I gently rubbed it against her clit to see how sensitive she was. Isabel licked her lips and took in a deep breath as soon as I touched her, and I could feel drops of pre-cum forming at the tip of my dick. Watching her get turned on was the ultimate fucking turn-on for me. I was going to make her come hard for me today.

"Do you like that, Isabel?" I asked as I watched her squirm under my touch with the gently humming vibrator. She panted and tried to continue sitting up, but couldn't. She didn't answer me. "Answer me, Isabel," I demanded in a hoarse voice. I was so turned on I could barely speak myself, but making her answer me was so hot.

"Matt, you're torturing me. It feels too fucking good," she cried out quietly.

"That's right, I am. That's what happens to bad girls who turn me on and make my dick hard when I'm at work." Her lips pulled into a smile. I started to work the vibrator gently over her slit and slid it inside her while I used my thumb to rub her clit gently. Her back arched on the bed as she leaned back, and she started to run her hands up her own torso, under her breasts. "Touch yourself, Isabel. I want to watch you come for me before I fuck you." Following my instructions, she continued to slide her hands up, cupping her breasts and taking her nipples into her little fingers, pinching them. This whole scene was hotter than any porno I could have watched, and I reached into my boxer briefs with my free hand to stroke my cock because I couldn't stand it anymore. As I pumped her gently with the vibrator, stroking her clit, I could feel her getting closer to release, so I turned up the vibration, causing her to moan loudly.

"Fuck, Matt, I'm going to come!" she cried out.

"Yes! Come for me, baby, come now," I coaxed her. Her body began to quiver, and her hips rose off the bed as she fell over the edge into her release, crying my name out again. Hearing her call out my name while I watched her climax had me in overdrive.

I gently pulled the vibrator from her, turning it off and setting it on the nightstand. As she lay there in the aftershock of her orgasm, I grabbed a condom and put it on quickly before I crawled above her, caging her in below me. I took a moment to look at her face, slightly shiny from sweat. She didn't have any makeup on, and her thick, black lashes hung heavy over her eyes as she looked up at me. I leaned down to kiss her softly. I wanted to slow things down just a bit, only to make it last longer. But as her lips touched mine, I lost control, my head spinning. She deepened the kiss, exploring my mouth with her tongue, rising up to meet me. I placed an arm around her and spun her over on top of me, causing her to place her hands on my chest for balance.

As I roamed over her perfect body with my eyes, I ran my hands up her sides, avoiding that giant bruise that actually looked painful. I took her tank top off over her head as I reached its hem around the top of her chest. Gently sliding my hands back down, I grazed her hard little nipples with my thumbs, causing her to quiver as I lingered. As I got to her tiny little waist, I got a better grip and lifted her up just enough to let her know I wanted her to ride me and I wanted to be inside her now. She took the hint and reached between her legs where my cock was aching for her to position it at her entrance. Just before letting me inside that sweet pussy, she leaned over and kissed my neck, driving me absolutely wild, causing me to moan.

"Fuck, Isabel, let me inside you, baby," was all I could say. She slid down, letting me enter her, both of us groaning out loud. Her pussy was so tight, and as she started to move her hips up and down my shaft, I could feel myself almost ready to lose control. She tried to sit up, and while I wanted to watch her bob up and down on my dick, I held her close, kissing her more and running my hands down her back. Having her mouth on me felt better than watching her, and I loved the sensation of having her soft skin against mine. I felt her pick up the pace, sliding up and down my cock, bringing us both to our climax. As she cried out, I grabbed her hips roughly, pulling her into me as hard as I could and yelled out myself. It felt as though I'd launch her right off of me, I came so hard. As we finished together, she collapsed on top of me, panting into my neck. "Fuck, Cavanaugh, that's a hell of a way to say good morning," she exhaled with my dick still inside her, pulsating.

She started to attempt lifting herself off of me, but I held her in place. "Stay still. I want to enjoy being inside you for another couple of minutes." She looked at me with a raised eyebrow in surprise, and then laid her head back down and stayed perfectly still, while I stroked her lower back. After a moment, she let out a big sigh, and I just held her like that. Pushing her hair away, I pulled her face to mine for a kiss. A real kiss. While she seemed to hesitate at first, she gave in, finally kissing me sweetly in return.

I loved kissing her. Those lips were so soft, and she always tasted sweet, like caramel candy or something. I knew this wasn't a relationship, but after the last shift, all I wanted to do was come to her. I was drawn to her, and I was starting to think it wasn't just her voracious appetite for amazing sex that had me making a beeline for her place as soon as I left the firehouse this morning. I enjoyed the game of cat and mouse we played, but lying here with her intimately, just touching her, had me wanting to spend all day there.

Sadly, I knew she needed to go to work, and if I didn't go home and get some sleep at my own place, Jax would probably send out a search party. He never mentioned how I didn't come home the other night and just showed up at work, but he did give me the 'I know what you did last night' smirk, even if he didn't know whom I was with. I let her roll off of me, wincing as my cock left its favorite spot.

"I have to get ready for work, but you can rest or whatever. I know you had a long night," she said as she walked naked across the room to get some things out of a drawer.

"Thanks, beautiful, but I'm gonna get cleaned up and get home to sleep for a while. Are you investigating the fires now?" I got up and disposed of the condom in the bathroom trash.

"You know I can't really talk to you about that, Matt." She had put on a little robe when I popped back out of the bathroom.

"I didn't ask about the investigation, Detective. I asked if you were going to be working on it. You're allowed to tell me what's on the agenda for the day." She was getting defensive all of a sudden, and I was so tired I didn't want to accidently walk into an argument.

"Sorry," she looked confused. "Yes, I'm going to be investigating the fires. Look, if that makes things weird with what we've been doing, I totally understand, and we can just—"

I interrupted her. "Isabel. You have a job to do. I have a job to do. Do your job. It has nothing to do with what's going on between us. Loosen up a little, babe. Seriously, it was just a question." I was hoping that squashed any upset the topic of conversation caused.

"Okay, you're right. I just didn't want to... Well, I didn't..." She hesitated.

"You didn't what? Want to feel like you have to answer to me?" She just stared at me, mouth open. "You don't. I don't have any expectations for what's happening here, yet." I added the yet, because I was feeling like I did want to have some expectations, but we weren't there. Isabel had some serious walls, and I wasn't going to ruin the fun we were having by placing any labels or expectations on us, but I'd been considering how I might want to at some point. Of course, I had just realized that at that very moment, so I didn't know what else to say either. I also didn't want to think about it anymore.

"You certainly have a way with words, Cavanaugh," she smirked. She was always smirking at me, never really smiling though. Suddenly, I wanted to make her smile. Once I was dressed, I walked over to where she was standing in her cute little, purple robe and cupped her face in my hands.

"Isabel."

"Yes, Matt?" she replied with some sarcasm.

"Calm the fuck down. Go fight some crime. Take down some bad guys. I'll text you later." I kissed her softly with her face still in my hands, then turned to leave.

"Matt," she called out to me when I reached the doorway.

"Yes, Isabel?" I sang back to her.

"I'm glad you came over. Sleep well today." She almost gave me a real smile.

Grinning back at her, I said, "I am too. Be safe. I'll talk to you later, babe." I was starting to break down her walls and loving every minute of it. I hightailed it out of there before I made her get in the shower with me and she never made it to work.

Isabel

When Matt had texted me that morning he was coming over, I had gotten immediately excited. I wasn't even surprised for some reason; I was actually kind of happy. Obviously, I loved having sex with him. He gave me exactly what I needed, but having him near me felt so good too. He was so manly and gave me such pleasure sexually that I was starting to crave him when he wasn't around. But he was also so sweet and calming at the same time. When I had gotten defensive with him about the investigation, he immediately diffused the situation, calling me out, which no one ever did except Kevin. He wasn't afraid to give it to me straight, and it was extremely attractive.

I still didn't think this thing between Matt and me was going anywhere, but occasionally, I was starting to forget why I felt that way. I wanted to shake it off; there was no point in getting caught up in the idea of a relationship as far as I was concerned. I had always felt a relationship and commitment ruined the fun between two people, and the pipe dreams of true love were just that, pipe dreams. Perhaps that feeling is created by the examples you are brought up with.

While my parents were still together, they didn't exactly treat each other lovingly. They certainly cared about each other, but they weren't passionate, and I couldn't ever remember them being that way. As little girls, my sister and I would play dolls and daydream about weddings and things all little girls do, but somewhere along the way, I became jaded about relationships. I'd had boyfriends in high school and even in college, but I never felt swept off my feet. The fairy tale daydream faded away, and the men I dealt with professionally were just that, professional. I always thought my choice to be a police officer would negate any romance in my life. Deep down, I still desired that person who would make things different, and I still had that little bit of fairy tale in my heart like I'd mentioned to Kevin, but it just didn't seem realistic.

Thinking about all of that and having Matt show up at my house in the early morning before work had my head swimming a bit. I found our status to be a conundrum and knew it would have to change at some point; but for the moment, I decided to enjoy the unadulterated pleasure he brought me and cross the bridge of what was next when I absolutely had to. In the meantime, I needed to get to work and figure out what was going on with these fires. I was hoping there wouldn't be any more that day, and perhaps it was a one day fire bug on the loose, but a nagging feeling inside told me this was only just the beginning.

Kevin and I arrived at the station around the same time after I had my workout at my favorite place like I did most mornings. My legs were shot from the encounter with Matt that morning, but I still killed my workout and felt amazing by the time I got into work. It was Kevin's turn to bring coffee for both of us, and he handed me mine in the parking lot.

"Good morning, Detective. Manage to get any sleep?" he

asked.

"Eh, I'll be honest. I have been racking my brain about why someone would start fires the way they have. I'm trying to come up with some motives for three very different types of fires. I'm also hoping we don't have to spend the whole day at more fires and we can just go back to the scenes and look around," I said before taking a sip of the amazing coffee. Kevin happened to have a little Brazilian café near his house with ridiculously amazing coffee, so the days he got it were the best.

"Yea, I was thinking we could just check in for the morning briefing and get ourselves on the road. I want to see the scenes we didn't get to go to and see if there are any clues or any witnesses we can talk to."

"Agreed. Let's get to it."

Knowing we would be poking through fire scenes today and likely getting dirtier than normal, I had on jeans and a black t-shirt, my standard uniform, with some tactical boots I'd bought for these sorts of occasions. It was hot in Florida a good portion of the time, so we didn't really wear jackets much unless we absolutely needed to. Today, I had my badge on a chain around my neck as opposed to clipped on my belt. I did love not having to wear a uniform anymore. In my female opinion, not wearing that unflattering uniform was almost a good enough reason on its own to become a detective, although I'd never admit that to anyone.

After the daily morning briefing, we filled the captain in on what we'd encountered the night before at the apartment fire and headed out for the strip mall, the first scene. There was already evidence demonstrating this was an arson, so that wasn't really what we were looking for; we were more interested in talking to witnesses and the business owners to see if we could determine some motive that may link it to the other fires or that would help us determine why the fire was started. As we pulled up to the scene, I looked around to see what else was there. I was looking for apartments or other residential areas people may have watched from, porches folks may have been sitting on when it started, or other areas from where someone could have observed everything. Arsonists, and actually any calculating premeditating criminals, had a tendency to get off on watching a scene unfold, so I wanted to figure out from where they could have achieved that.

"What do you think, Izzy?" Kevin asked while pulling out his camera and taking pictures from a variety of angles. We always did that so when we went back to our desks, we could sit and stare at them, waiting for ideas to pop up.

"Well, it looks like someone could definitely have watched from that parking garage over there. Unless it was a resident, which I'm thinking is out because there were so many fires around town. It had to be someone else." I pointed across the street to a small parking garage that was previously reserved for a building of doctor's offices that was no longer there. "The only people who use that parking garage are folks who would be shopping in this area, and there just aren't that many stores. I think we should go check that out and see if it looks like anyone was hanging out watching from up above."

"Ugh, yea, you're probably right," Kevin groaned. "Let's get it over with." We both knew this was the shit part of investigations. The following of the cold trail, as it were. Essentially, we were going to go to each floor of that garage—thankfully, it was only about seven floors—and we were going to look around to see if anyone had left any evidence that seemed like they had been hanging out for a long time, camped out and monitoring the scene. It was a long shot but certainly worth a look, and so far, our only possible lead.

We reached the third floor and still hadn't found anything. Walking along the edge of the garage facing the scene, we were starting to get deflated. Investigations could be so boring, and this was like finding a needle in a haystack, but I still felt like this was the spot. Somewhere, there had to be evidence someone had been hanging out here, watching. I just knew it. By the time we reached the fifth floor, Kevin was agitated and sweating.

"This fucking blows," he muttered.

"Yes, yes, it does," I kind of laughed. That pretty much summed it up in a nutshell. Then I saw what I was hoping for: a pile of cigarette butts. I couldn't believe it. "I found it!" I exclaimed.

"Oh thank God. What is it?" He raced over to where I had kneeled down. Looking over my shoulder, he saw them too. "This is the spot. You did find it. And look at the view from here. You can see absolutely everything from this spot. And there's perfect cover as well." I stood up and looked out the garage, and sure enough, you could see at least two full city blocks, including our scene directly across the street. You'd have been able to see the entire fire clearly, and you'd have been able to see the emergency response as well. Whoever was here had watched everything unfold, and they had been here for a while. The cigarette butts were fresh; they still had a white color to their filters, as if they were new, indicating they hadn't been there very long.

Kevin snapped pictures of what we found, as well as of the view from the spot, while I put gloves on to gather the butts for evidence. We wouldn't be able to get fingerprints on anything here;

a public garage would be a waste to get the crime lab out for, but it was possible to get DNA off of cigarette butts. I collected them into an evidence bag and sealed them once Kevin got all the pictures we needed.

"Do we need to go through the building across the street, you think?" he asked.

"I don't think so. Brian emailed us the pictures that were taken immediately after the fire, so I don't think there would be anything more we need. I mean, you and I both know the biggest problem with a fire investigation is that so much of the evidence is destroyed. Plus, my understanding is the fire marshal was out here, and we can go talk to him and see what he has to say about it later. We won't find anything he didn't already see, in my opinion." I thought about who would start fires, and it was common knowledge, or rumor, that in a series of arsons, firefighters were often the prime suspects. That thought had nagged at me since the moment we became involved in the investigation. Kevin knew I was more or less friends with several of the folks in the fire department. We hadn't discussed what we both knew yet, but I knew it was coming eventually.

"Yea, I agree. Let's move on to the garage fire and see if we can find a link." He motioned for us to leave. The garage was only about a fifteen-minute drive, and when we pulled up, the owner, Mike, was out front taking pictures himself.

I got out of the car first and walked over to him. "Mike, I'm so sorry."

"Hey there, Detective. Thanks. It is a real sonofabitch. I mean, that's what insurance is for, but I'm real careful with the chemicals here, so I don't understand how this happened. I'm guessing that's what you're doing here today?"

"It sure is," Kevin chimed in as he came to my side.

"Mike, this is my partner, Detective Connor. We are investigating all the fires that happened yesterday as possible arsons. Do you know anyone who would do this to your business? Have any enemies or anything? Anyone who would hold a grudge against you?" He nodded to Kevin, then turned back to me.

"I don't. Honestly, my customers and my partners I work with are all on the up and up. You know what kind of a business I run here. Fair prices, quality service, and we treat your babies like we would treat our own. I don't have any gripes with anyone. All my customers are paid up too." He hung his head and sighed. He was a large man, well over six feet tall, a full, thick head of dark hair and light blue eyes I always noticed when I came into the shop. He wasn't particularly good looking, but he was kind and welcoming, and damn good at fixing cars. He had taken over the business from his father about five years prior, after his dad had been fixing up cars, specializing in classics for as long as I could remember. He looked tired; I was sure he'd been up all night trying to figure out what to do next.

"Well, we're going to look around a bit and take some pictures of our own. I see you're taking pictures too. Did you find anything unusual here?" I asked.

"No, ma'am, I sure didn't. At least not yet. I'm taking pictures for the insurance, because I'm going to need to file some claims for the vehicles that were stored here and destroyed, as well as for regular insurance, even though they're sending someone out too. I'm waiting to go inside to take the rest of them for my records. The police and firefighters yesterday asked me not to until the Fire

Marshal had come out, and he hasn't been here yet. I'm expecting him any moment though, actually. I guess he had himself a busy day as well, from what I hear."

"Yea, you can say that again." Kevin started to walk around the building, just observing and taking pictures of the building itself and the grounds as we had on the last scene. I immediately started to look around the area, hoping I'd find another location that appeared good for observing, which I'd hoped the smoker had been doing during this fire too. As I walked around, I didn't see anything as obvious as at the last scene that would be a good lookout spot, but I knew the guy had been watching. He'd had to be. Criminals have egos, and they like to see the damage they cause in most cases, so I kept searching around, while Kevin and Mike both took pictures of the structure, knowing I would find a clue eventually.

As I meandered around the premises, the Fire Marshal arrived. I decided to keep doing my thing. It was obvious I was a cop from the badge hanging around my neck. Kevin could deal with him for now. The Marshal was new to the county. I didn't know him, and I was on a mission. As I got further away from the scene, I continued to scan for what would be the best vantage point if I wanted to watch, since there were no obvious or large structures like the parking garage to hang around in. I decided the only place our perpetrator could have been was way across the intersection by the strip mall, which had a small convenience store, a coffee shop, and a dry cleaner. The area in general wasn't super populated, so there weren't a lot of other places to hang out, except at residential porches, which I just didn't think our guy would do.

In front of the stores, the sidewalk looked like it had been swept, but as I walked around to the side of the building to an open lot, I found it: another pile of cigarette butts. Same brand, still new-looking. This was our guy. My heart started to race from adrenaline as I pulled my cellphone out to take a picture. I looked at the screen and saw I had a text message from Matt, which made me smile. I really needed to stop that. I opened the message, which had been sent a couple of hours ago. He must have woken up this afternoon and sent it.

You're sexy as fuck. That is all. Be safe.

I actually laughed out loud and shook my head. I didn't have a good response to that at the moment, so I closed the message and pulled up my camera to get some shots of my sweet evidence find. Normally, I would have called Kevin over with the nice camera, but I could see him across the way talking to the Fire Marshal, so I figured I'd just handle it myself and bag up the evidence. I got the butts into the brown paper bag, sealing it with red evidence tape, and made my way back to the scene, stopping at our car first to put the bag in there. In light of knowing that firefighters were always suspects, I had no intention of sharing my find with the Fire Marshal. I decided we could run concurrent, separate investigations and see where we landed later on.

After I stopped at our car, I went back to the garage and walked inside, to where everyone had relocated. The chemical smell of the burned-out building on the inside actually took me by surprise it was so pungent. I walked over to where Mike, Kevin, and the Fire Marshal, whose name I couldn't remember, were all standing near a cabinet market HAZMAT.

"Hey, guys. Find anything of interest in here?" I asked, nearly choking on the fumes from the place.

They all turned around. The Fire Marshal thankfully reintroduced himself to me. "Hi, Detective, I'm Bill. Bill Wilson, the new Orange County Fire Marshal. I believe we met once before?"

Smiling, I replied, "Yes sir, we did one time a few months ago. I'm Isabel Cruise. So what do we have here? Is this HAZMAT cabinet where the fire started?" It didn't look like that cabinet had caught fire at all, so while it probably sounded like a stupid question, I still wanted to hear his response.

"Actually, it is not. Which is what we were all just questioning. It seems this was definitely some kind of malicious fire. I'll just call that right now in my professional opinion, but the HAZMAT cabinet is not where it started. I was just about to ask Mike here to step out while I conducted my investigation to determine the cause. You detectives are, of course, welcome to stay." Looking over at Mike, he said, "I'm sorry, Mike. I know this is hard for you, but I have to do my job, and you'll have to step out so I can do that. I'll turn your property and building back over to you as soon as I'm done."

"I understand, sir. I'm actually going to head back over to my house and make some phone calls. The insurance adjuster is going to need to come out, and I've got plenty of customers to call as well. Detectives, thanks for your help as well." Mike turned around to leave, and I turned my attention back to Fire Marshal Bill and Kevin.

"So, what do you think, Bill?" I asked, folding my arms and looking around the burned-up garage.

"Well, what I think is, someone wanted it to look like the cabinet full of chemicals here is the cause of the fire, but the problem is, the fire they set wasn't anywhere near this cabinet, never even made it over here. Follow me." He picked up a little box that resembled a fishing tackle box, and we followed him across the bay floor. The garage was quite large and had three full-size bays for cars, two of which were occupied. The car furthest from where we were standing was completely burned out, while the car next to it was not, though it was certainly destroyed. It was a beautiful classic Camaro similar to mine; I couldn't help but feel a tinge of upset over it, since I loved my car so much. The third bay, which was where we had been standing, was empty except for some tools and other random things.

Stopping at the passenger side of the car furthest away, Bill set his tackle box down and turned to us. "Someone actually started the fire on this side of the building, assuming these cars would catch each other on fire, and then catch that cabinet on fire." I rose an eyebrow, thinking that was a bit of a stretch in assumption, as I didn't see any evidence leading to that conclusion.

"Ok, so how do you prove that, Bill? Because what I see is one car caught fire, however that may be, and the owner is lucky the fire didn't spread to the other side, where the majority of the chemicals are. It's lucky the entire building didn't burn down, yes, but how do you figure they expected it to reach over there?" I was extremely skeptical of his assumptions without real proof.

He laughed at me. He laughed out loud at me. Scrunching my face up and crossing my arms again defensively, I glared at him. Kevin took a step closer to me, knowing I had a short fuse for being laughed at in these situations.

"This, my dear detective, is why we as investigators need to work together. Take a look at this," he pointed to the burned-out back seat of the vehicle. "This is the origin of the fire right here. You can tell by the deep hole that goes all the way to the floor from the fire. The rest of the car became fully involved fairly quickly, because it is a classic car filled with combustible materials. Now, look at the Camaro here next to it. Most of this damage is heat damage, but guess what?"

"What?" Kevin asked. He stepped in to keep me from getting bitchy, which was definitely going to happen.

"I bet if we open the trunk of this car, we'll find fuel of some kind." My skepticism was on overload at that point.

"Let's do it," I said sarcastically. Low and behold, upon opening the trunk, there was a very small gas can in the trunk. "So, what do you make of this, Bill? I'm still not understanding where this is going." I was running out of patience with him.

"Ok, I'll cut to the chase here, Detectives. There's no point in a tiny gas can like this. It was definitely planted here, so that once the fire caught, it would be destroyed with the car, likely what happened in the first car, where it was in the back seat. Now, I didn't point this out when Mike was in here, because I need to write up my report first; that's just how the bureaucracy of investigations works, as you know." We both nodded, knowing full well we'd have a mountain of our own paperwork to do too. "I noticed the floor was wet, but it had a kind of slick sheen to it. One would typically presume that's just water and oil from the fire department putting out a fire in a greasy garage."

"Yes, that's what I would assume," Kevin replied.

"Well, I happen to know that this particular garage had applied for a permit to use some nontraditional materials when they upgraded their facility a few years ago when Mike took over from his father."

"Ok, keep going," I said.

"The majority of this building is noncombustible. The paint on the floor is actually fire retardant paint. No one would know that, except someone who reviewed previous fire inspections. Mike received insurance breaks for upgrading his building to hold up in the event of a disaster like this. So what the perpetrator didn't know is that the building wouldn't have burned to the ground unless it had been on fire for days. But everything along the walls over here is completely saturated in some sort of accelerant, likely gasoline, as that seems to be this particular arsonist's accelerant of choice." Looking pleased with himself, he continued, "So, basically, it appears that it was made for the fire to start in car number one, carry over to car number two, and then catch the walls and such on fire on its way to the HAZMAT cabinet, which would have taken the rest of the building over if it were made with traditional materials. I'll have to run a few lab tests, of course, to document and confirm everything, but I've been investigating fires for over twenty years, and I'm quite certain that's how it went down."

"Well, I'll be damned, Fire Marshal Bill. You do know your stuff. I had no idea they even made paint that resisted fire. Looks like Mike got luckier than he could have, and it paid off for him in this case." I relaxed my stance, totally impressed by what the Fire Marshal concluded. "I'm going to have our crime lab come out and take some samples as well. If you'll excuse me, I'm going to go call them now." Feeling like we got some great evidence at this scene, I called the lab guys to come out and do their thing.

I couldn't get out of there fast enough. While the garage was a large space, in the interest of securing the crime scene, the bay doors were closed and the fumes were killing me. Even though we didn't have motive or suspects, we had some evidence and were collecting some clues that would hopefully lead us to some closure.

It was going to be a long day; we still had one more scene to visit, the apartment building from the night before. Now that we had something besides the cause of fire, which we already knew, we could look for another pile of butts and any other evidence, then get them all to the lab for processing. With any luck, this guy might be in the system.

MATT

"So where did you go this morning?" Jax asked me after we were both awake from our coma-like naps most of the day.

"This morning? Oh, I had a couple of errands to run before coming home to crash." I was definitely trying to cover my tracks and felt guilty as hell for lying.

"Errands? At seven in the morning after the worst shift ever?" He raised an eyebrow at me and smirked over his coffee cup. "So what's her name?"

"Name?" I laughed. I was absolutely dodging this line of questioning, and I wasn't going to be honest if I did answer.

"Oh my God, you're really not going to tell me, are you?" He looked surprised, like he expected me to confess what I'd been up to.

"Nope, not happening." I just smirked.

"She must be important then. Interesting, Cavanaugh, very interesting." He took his coffee cup with him into the den and flipped on the television. "Are you going to be around later or you having dinner with mom and the lovebirds?" he called from the other room, while I was still in the kitchen.

"Dinner with mom. You know you're invited to come. She asks about you all the time."

"Please tell her I appreciate it, and maybe next time, but I think I may go out for a bit tonight. Or I might just fall asleep with the remote in one hand and my dick in the other," he laughed at his own joke.

"I'll be sure to let her know what you're up to then," I teased back. He loved my mom, but he didn't love the sit-down dinners, really. Everyone loved my mom; she was that mom who was like the den mother for everyone. Her cooking was amazing too, and she insisted we try to come over for dinner as a group whenever we could. The only problem with these family dinners since Brian and Jo got together was everyone's insistence I find a nice girl to date I essentially could bring to these dinners. The girls I dated were not the kind of girls you brought to your conservative Irish mother's house for family dinner.

I'd take a girl like Isabel there though. I knew my mom would love her; she loved a strong woman, because she was one herself. Besides the fact she helped raise Jo sort of, it was one of the things about Jo she loved. She was another strong woman. Raising us on her own after our deadbeat dad left, she did it all. My thoughts drifted to Isabel and what she might be doing at work to find out who was setting those fires. I had texted her when I got up, but she hadn't responded. Then, of course, my thoughts drifted to that morning and those fucking tiny white shorts she'd had on. She really had the nicest ass and the tightest little body. I couldn't keep my hands off of her if I tried, and once again, she'd let me demand things of her. That was indeed a hell of a way to say good morning. I found my thoughts always went back to her the last few days, and if I was being entirely honest, it wasn't just about the amazing sex we had.

I liked her. *Oh shit, I really do like her.* This was not the realization I was hoping for about my life that afternoon. I never caught feelings, and I had definitely caught some here. I was thinking about her all the time. I wondered what she was doing. I was planning when I could see her again in my head. *Fucking feelings. Fuck. Fuck. Fuck.* That wasn't what we were about at all; and she was so closed off emotionally. Hell, we both were. I groaned quietly to myself and went upstairs to shower before heading to my mom's for dinner. I decided I was going to have to put this whole sentiment on the back burner or something while I got my head right.

I went off to shower like I was having a temper tantrum with myself, almost as bad as the night she bailed on me in the alley. I definitely needed to get my fucking mind off of that whole situation, but every thought led back to her. I started to wonder what, if anything, she found out today about the fires. Knowing she wouldn't tell me, I wasn't going to ask, but maybe Brian would know something. I made a note to ask him at dinner. In the shower, my stomach started to growl, and I realized I hadn't eaten since sometime the previous day. I got excited to get to my mom's.

When I pulled into the driveway at my mom's house, Brian's truck was already there, so I pulled in behind him and checked my phone real quick before getting out. Isabel still hadn't texted me back, and it was definitely the end of a typical workday, so I was feeling a little put off by it. As I reminded myself she wasn't technically mine and didn't owe me a text or a reply per se, I put my phone back in my pocket and headed into the old house I grew up in.

"There you are, Matthew!" My mom came over to squeeze me.

She seriously gave the best hugs on earth.

"Hi mama. Sorry I'm late. I'm sure Brian and Jo told you what a day we had yesterday. I've just been in slow motion today."

"Yes, they did. I worry about you three so much. Come in here and have a drink. It's a whiskey day," she winked at me. My mom was a straight up whiskey drinker. Sometimes in her tea, sometimes on the rocks, but she got her whiskey either way. She was Irish through and through.

"Well, that sounds perfect." I followed her into the kitchen, where Brian and Jo were having their drinks at the table. They raised their glasses to me.

"Hey bro, get any rest today?" Brian asked me.

"Yea, I was pretty much in a coma most of the day. I'm still exhausted though." I took the drink my mom just made me and sat down at the table with them.

"What a crazy day," Jo said. "I heard the detectives were going to all of the scenes today to really get into their investigation. Isabel is investigating with her partner, Kevin I think his name is."

"Yes, I heard that too. Has anyone heard any word on progress or anything?" I asked.

"No, not yet. I'm going to go down to the police station tomorrow to see Cruise and her partner and see where they're at. It's only been a day, but the Fire Marshal was out at the scenes today too, so hopefully we've at least got some idea of what the causes were, besides the obvious," Brian told us.

"Ok, who's ready for pot roast and veggies tonight? You all look like you could use a good, hot meal, and you know how much I love having us all together here," Mom said.

In unison, we all replied, "Yes please," and I got up to get dishes for all of us as my mom pulled out serving stuff. Once all the food was out, it got pretty quiet while we ate like we hadn't eaten in days, which was exactly what it felt like. My mom started to laugh at us about it too.

"You kids. I haven't seen you all eat like this since you were teenagers." She took a sip of her whiskey on the rocks and relaxed in her chair. "So, how is everyone doing otherwise? I know yesterday was hell on wheels, but what's going on in my children's lives, since none of you stop by enough for my liking?"

Jo spoke up first, while Brian and I continued to shovel food into our faces. "Well, I think my house is going to be done soon, and then I can move back in if I want to."

We all looked over at Brian to see his reaction, which was one of shock and disappointment. "Is that what you want to do? Move back there?" he asked her in front of all of us. It was getting awkward, especially since my mom and I both knew Brian was planning to propose soon.

"I don't know... Don't get mad about it, babe. I'm just saying my house will be all fixed up from the fire, and if I *want* to, I can move back in. I didn't say I was going to. We can talk about what we're gonna do later."

I started to snicker at the awkward moment, and my mom smacked my arm pretty hard. "Matthew, that's enough."

"Sorry, mama." I went back to eating and enjoying the show. As I would have predicted, my mom interjected her opinion on the situation.

"Brian, Josephine grew up in that house. It belonged to her father. I'm sure she would like to spend some time there, deciding what she would like to do with it next. Whether that be move back in or make some other use of it. Jack was special to all of us, and that was his home as well. Don't be pushy."

"I'm not being pushy. I was just asking what she wanted to do, mama," he pleaded with her.

"Ok, ok, hold on everyone," Jo finally spoke up. "I don't know what I want to do with the house. I know half my stuff is still there, and I need to sort through the rest of my dad's stuff, and then I'll figure it out." She turned to Brian. "You need to calm down. I have been living with you in your house, but it's your house, not mine, not ours. So give me a break. I didn't say I was going anywhere. It's only three miles from your house anyway." She rolled her eyes at him.

"Well, for the record, as far as I'm concerned, my house IS your house; it's our house." He actually looked hurt, which made me feel a little bad for laughing. I knew Jo loved him, but she did move in with him about five minutes after they declared their feelings for each other, and only because her house had been set on fire.

She reached over and took his hand. "Brian, nothing is changing. We can talk about whose house is whose and where everyone is going to live later, ok? Nothing is changing anytime soon, so don't be upset about this conversation. I love you, and you know that. We will figure it all out together, ok?" She seemed to soothe him. He reached over to touch her face and gave her a kiss.

"Ok, baby, we'll figure it out," he said softly. We went back to eating peacefully after that. My brother really was a hothead, and I was too at certain times, but his fuse was way shorter than mine.

I felt my phone vibrate in my pocket, and hoping it was Isabel, I hurried to finish my dinner. My mom had a strict no cellphone at the dinner table policy. She was pretty old school with family dinners and things like that, and we all respected it. As teenagers, it was pretty annoying, but as an adult, it was actually quite nice to have the break from technology and just talk as a family. Once we'd all finished eating and the dishes were cleaned up, we went out to the sitting room we used to not be allowed to sit in. I think everyone's family has one of those rooms the kids aren't allowed to sit and be comfortable in because everything is nice or white; and even though as adults we were allowed in there to socialize with my mom, it was still always a little awkward.

My mom refreshed everyone's drink, and we sat down to just relax as a family. "So, Matthew, when are you going to bring a nice girl over here for family dinner?" My mom always had to go there.

"There's no one special, mama. You'll be the first to know, I promise," I replied, rolling my eyes at this conversation.

"Oh, I don't know. I heard you didn't come home the other night and that you were missing this morning after the fire before you went home to sleep," Brian interjected.

"What the fuck, dude?" I snapped.

"Language!" my mom yelled. Jesus Christ, why he would even say that in front of our mother was beyond me, but what a dick move.

"Sorry, mama," I apologized. "Dude, that kind of thing isn't discussion for family dinners, man. Seriously." Meanwhile, Jo was giggling like a little girl, and Brian was snickering along with her. I looked over at my mom, and even she had a little grin on her face.

"Matthew, I know how you boys can be, but if there's someone special in your life, it would mean so much if you brought her around," she said sweetly.

"Oh my God, mama. There's nothing special going on right now. Brian is being a word you won't let me say in this house. There's nothing going on. Why is everyone trying to marry me off all of a sudden? These two are living in sin over at whosever house. Let's pick on them instead?" I pointed at Brian and Jo, giving them a *fuck you guys* look with a smirk like a five year old.

"Living in sin? Really?" Brian said.

"Alright, alright, that's enough, boys. Brian and Jo have a special relationship, and I'm not so foolish and old that I don't know what goes on." Now mom was rolling her eyes at all of us. I couldn't help but start laughing. I couldn't believe we were even having this conversation about unmarried sex, me not coming home, and all of us finding love. My family was both ridiculous and awesome at the same time.

Once I started laughing, we all did and enjoyed the rest of the evening just shooting the breeze and having cocktails until Brian got a phone call.

"Excuse me, I have to take this." He got up and went out to the porch to take his call in private.

"Hmm, that's odd. Normally, he doesn't take calls when we're visiting," Jo said with slight concern in her voice.

"Well, maybe it's about the fires from yesterday," I suggested. After all, Brian was the chief now, and even on his technical day off, the district was still under his purview, so he needed to stay in the loop. Not gone very long, he came back in from the porch with a different demeanor, looking frustrated.

"I have to go. There's been another fire."

"Do you need us to go in?" Jo asked. I didn't want to go in on my day off, but I would too if needed.

"No, the C shift has it, but I need to go meet the detectives there, and I'm going to need to talk to the press too." He sighed. Brian really loved his job, but he did not like talking to the press. They rubbed him the wrong way. I knew as well as he did they were going to start asking questions about the number of fires.

"No worries. I can take Jo home," I said.

"That would be awesome. Is that ok with you, baby?" he asked her.

"Of course, it is. I'll wait up for you at home, so keep me posted, ok?"

"I will. Hopefully, it won't be an all-nighter. Matt, can you move your truck so I can get out?"

"Yea, of course. I'll be right back, ladies. Then you can continue giving me a hard time about my love life if you want," I winked at the girls and walked outside. Brian went over to kiss Mom and Jo goodbye and met me outside.

"Thanks for taking her home, man."

"Of course. She's my friend. And soon-to-be sister-in-law," I joked.

"Yea, once we get through all this shit with the fires and investigation, I still want your help planning something fun and cool as a proposal, I think. What do you think all that about the house was?" he asked me.

"Honestly? I think she misses her dad, man. That was his house. All of his stuff is still there. It's not the thing to go all caveman over. Bring out your sensitive side for that conversation. She isn't going anywhere, I can promise you that. Don't turn it into something it's not."

"Yea, you're probably right. Sorry about bringing up your

shenanigans in front of mama."

"Yea, fuck you very much for that, by the way. I am entitled to keep some things personal, fucker. So when I'm ready to bring someone around, I'll bring someone around. I don't need my shit broadcasted, and Jax is gonna get his ass kicked at home for bringing it up to begin with," I sneered. That really did piss me off; Jax could be so strange sometimes. *Why would he even mention it*, was all I could think.

"I get it. Sorry again, bro. Alright, now move your truck. I've got to go. Ugh." He groaned and rolled his eyes. He seemed tired still too, and we were having a nice relaxing night with Mom and Jo, so it was definitely annoying he had to leave.

"Be careful. This whole thing really bothers me. There's something fucked up going on. I don't like it." I really did have a sinking feeling things were going to get worse before they got better, and it had me on edge.

"I'm always careful. And me too. I'll catch you later." I moved my truck out of his way and after he left, went back inside. After hanging out with my mom for a while longer and having her send us both home with leftovers for Brian and Jax, I took Jo home. I figured I'd find out what the house conversation was all about on the ride, because while I did think Brian was kind of a dick in how he responded to things like that, I knew where his heart was, and I certainly knew where hers was too.

"So, what are you going to do about the house, Jo? You know Brian doesn't want you to move out of his house. Is that what you want to do?" I asked.

"Well, no, not exactly," she replied.

"Ok, what do you want?"

"What I want is to have a conversation about what our game plan is."

"Game plan?" I questioned.

"Yes, game plan. He's it for me. He's the guy. And I'm pretty sure he feels the same way about me, so I want a conversation about where we want to live, not an assumption I'll just want to stay at his house. I like it there, and he makes me feel like it's mine, but it's *not* mine. It's his. All of my stuff is at my dad's house. My pictures, my decorations, my stuff; its all there. I want to be someplace that is *ours*. So maybe neither house, to be honest. Maybe a new house we pick out together. But I don't like being put on the spot like that, so we'll be having words at some point about it, honestly," she admitted.

"I think that's fair. And if you want my honest opinion, first of all, you're his person. You soothe him, and you definitely complete him." She blushed and smiled. She was so smitten with him; it was awfully cute to see, truthfully. "Also, I know Brian well enough to know if you wanted to move to the moon, he'd be calling NASA to find a real estate agent for you. So whatever it is you really want in your heart, he's going to give you." *Wow, that was mushy as fuck. Who have I become?* I waited for her commentary on that one.

"Wow, Matty, you believe in love all of a sudden? Be honest, are you seeing someone?" she pleaded.

"I'm not seeing anyone seriously, Jo. You really would be the first person I would tell. I've been hanging around with one girl in particular more than I typically do, yes. But that's all you're getting. I'm not anywhere near ready to talk about my feelings, or lack thereof, or where anything is going, so don't even ask." I stated the latter firmly as if to end the conversation, forgetting I was talking

441

to a woman.

"Come on, Matt," she pleaded more. "Who is she??"

"Jo. I'm serious. I really need you to just mind your own business right now." I thanked the Lord silently we had pulled into Brian's driveway and I was dropping her nosy butt off. I loved her, she was my best friend, but I was so uncomfortable with how I had been feeling about Isabel in the last twenty-four hours, there was no way I could verbalize it even if I wanted to. And I most certainly did not want to.

Huffing and hopping out of the car, she said, "Fine. But when you are ready, I better be the first to know, or I'll kick your ass."

"I do believe you would." I laughed at her. She was like five foot four and always threatening to kick my ass; I believed she might too.

"Alright, I'll see ya later. Thanks for the ride."

"Anytime. Text you later," I said. I waited for her to get inside the house before I pulled out of the driveway and pulled my phone out for the first time in hours, forgetting it had gone off in my pocket earlier.

Seeing it was, in fact, a text from Isabel brought a ridiculously big smile to my face and gave me a half hard-on, just thinking of her. When I opened it, I was even happier.

If you're off tomorrow, meet me for lunch at my house. I won't be serving food. ;)

I slammed my head back on the seat of my truck. Sonofabitch. Full hard-on commenced.

Isabel

No real surprise, we found a pile of butts at the apartment fire scene, which looked much different than the night before, of course. After we had explored the scene with the sun still up, we were able to walk around where bystanders had been the night before, and it looked like in this case, the smoking watcher had just been standing with the rest of the crowd behind the caution tape, watching things unfold.

Kevin and I were on our way back to the station so we could drop off all the cigarette butts at the crime lab in the hopes there would be some DNA on them, when I finally pulled my phone back out to reply to Matt's text. I invited him over for lunch tomorrow if he was off, and I'd be serving *me* for lunch. While it was technically my day off, the investigation was well underway, so I knew I'd probably have to go back in at some point. However, with the late night last night and the likely long night ahead of us, I definitely hadn't planned on going in until the afternoon at the very earliest.

"Ok, so let's discuss where we stand," Kevin said, tearing me away from my thoughts.

"Alright, we have three piles of matching cigarette butts, essentially indicating we have a chain smoker who likes to watch fires. The Fire Marshal is going to solidify each of these were arson, but we definitely already knew that from the evidence at each of the scenes. Gasoline seems to be the accelerant of choice. We have no witnesses though, and there doesn't seem to be anything related to any of the fires other than the fact they all happened on the same day. So far, no new fires today, so no new leads yet. That about covers it, unfortunately," I replied, going through my recollection of everything we'd done and seen to that point. "I think once we can at the very least confirm with the lab all the butts were from the same smoker, we can start looking for witnesses who might lead us to who the guy is, whether we find a match in the system or not."

"I think you're right. Even if the guy isn't in the system, if we can find a local or resident who can identify a man clearly chain-smoking and standing in one place, we can at least get a description, and maybe a composite or sketch, and start looking for this guy."

"Ok, so we drop this stuff off at the station and then go through the fire report to see if anyone gave any descriptions of how the fire started when they called so we can start finding people to interview. I think that's our best bet, to use the names on the chief's report before we start knocking on all the doors in the neighborhood or get a sweep going. Agreed?" I really didn't want to knock on doors all damn day, and if we had a handful of people who were already witnesses for Brian, we could call on them to be witnesses for us as a start.

"Agreed. Guess it's gonna be a late night," he said.

"And this is why we are both single," I laughed.

"Seriously. I'm not coming in tomorrow until at least after lunchtime. I'm exhausted," he laughed as he informed me. *How convenient for me*, I thought.

"Works for me," was all I said.

As I settled in for the twenty-minute ride back to the station, our police radio informed us we would be heading somewhere else. Another fire. Fires do happen from time to time that are not worthy of a full investigation, obviously, so I was hoping there was a reason we were being called back out of our way.

"Ok, well, off we go to the other side of town then, I guess." Kevin flipped on our low profile emergency lights so we could get there faster.

"Here's the game plan. I'll talk to the chief, while you look for our perp in the crowd if there is one, which I assume there will be. Deal?"

"Yea, works for me. Do we have any idea what kind of fire it is?"

"Nope. I heard the same thing you did on the radio," I gave him a sideways look for assuming I had some kind of psychic ability to know more than what we were both just told.

"Oh, yea. Duh," he chuckled.

We arrived on the scene, and what we found was actually what appeared to be an abandoned building engulfed in flames. As we got out of the car, we could once again feel the heat, and I wondered why anyone would want to be a firefighter in Florida. Seriously, it was so hot, and the fire just added insult to it. I made my way over to Brian, who was in civilian clothes with his coat and fire helmet on. He was standing with Fire Marshal Bill and another firefighter, who appeared to be running command of this scene, but I didn't know him.

"Chief, what have you got here?" I interrupted the trio.

"Detective Cruise. I'm sorry to have to see you under these circumstances so soon, but it appears we have another large fire. And while nothing suspicious has been uncovered yet, we felt that calling you in sooner rather than later would be wise," he informed me.

"You did the right thing," I replied. I turned to the man I didn't know. "I'm Detective Isabel Cruise. Are you in charge of this scene today?"

"Uh, yes. I guess I am. I'm Lieutenant David Dorner. I work the C shift at Station 23." He turned to Brian. "Sir, if you'd like to take command?"

"No, Dorner, I would not like to take command. This one is yours. There appears to be no possible victims, and I'd like to get home to my woman at some point before the sun comes up. It'll be your treat tonight." Turning to me again, he said, "Detective, let's take a walk with Bill here." He motioned for the fire marshal to join us, and we walked away from the area set up for command of the incident.

"So what do you think, Fire Marshal?" I asked.

"You can call me Bill." I nodded. "I think it's too many real fires in two days. Other than that, motive and shit is your game, not mine. I collect evidence and tell you what caused the fire. Until the fire is out in this case, not much I can surmise by looking at it. So far, I don't see any common threads between the fires other than that I believe the accelerant in all of them is gasoline, but I have to have the lab confirm that, of course."

"Ok. Did you find anything else of note at the other scenes?" I asked.

"No, I did not. The only one that had any salvageable evidence

THE BROTHERHOOD OF DISTRICT 23

was the garage, because of the fire resistant paint, and then the holes in the cabinets you found over at the apartment complex."

"Alright. Well, our plan is to start interviewing people who may have seen something, and we intend to start with your list of witnesses from your report, so I'll be by tomorrow for a copy of that." I motioned to Brian.

He was looking at something on his phone, and his face dropped.

"Brian, what is it?"

"There's a call at my mother's house. There's some kind of fire. I gotta go!" And with that, he ran to his truck and took off down the road with his emergency lights on.

I searched the crowd for Kevin, and when I saw him, I screamed out to him, "Connor! We gotta go! RIGHT NOW!" When he stopped in his tracks and ran to meet me at the car, I hopped in the driver's seat and took off in the direction Brian had.

"What's going on?" he panted, catching his breath from running.

"There's a fire at the chief's mother's house. I'm starting to think this is personal. Look up her address. I have no idea where it is. This is just the direction he went."

He read me the directions, and we hauled ass to get there. When we arrived just a short ten minutes later, we pulled up to a beautiful older home with a wraparound porch. In the driveway in front of the house was a vehicle completely engulfed in flames. Brian's truck was parked in the front yard, neighbors were coming out of their homes, and I could hear sirens from the fire trucks making their way off in the distance. It was pure chaos.

"I'm going to go find Brian! See if our guy is here anywhere!"

I ran toward the house, calling out for Brian. Several cars showed up and parked on the street, but what caught my eye was Matt rolling up at top speed, screeching to a halt in the grass next to Brian's truck. I stopped, not sure where to run suddenly. I watched as he jumped out of his truck and ran toward the front door right by me, so I ran in after him.

"Mama!" he yelled, running inside.

"We're in here!" Brian yelled from the front room off to the side of the entrance of the house. Thus far, I hadn't said anything at all, but I scurried after Matt to the front room.

"What the hell happened?" Matt yelled, out of breath. A need to calm him washed over me, and I had to remind myself I was there for work.

"Did you see anything?" I finally spoke to the older woman. She was beautiful and looked up at me from the couch she was sitting on with the same green eyes her boys had.

"You must be detective Cruise?" she asked me, visibly shaken by what was happening.

"Yes, ma'am, I am. Can you tell me what happened?" I asked.

"Hold on one minute!" Matt snapped at me. "Mama, are you ok?"

"Matthew, calm down. I am fine. My car, however, is most certainly not ok at all, it seems." She smirked and looked up at Brian, who had his arm around his mother in a comforting way. Matt was not amused at all, but Brian and I did share a little grin over her comment.

Taken aback by Matt's tone with me, I shifted my weight uncomfortably. "I'm sorry, ma'am. I'm glad you're ok. If you don't mind, can you tell me exactly what happened as best as you can remember?"

Matt paced angrily back and forth across the room but didn't acknowledge me in any way. I had a job to do, and he was just going to have to let me do it, whether he liked it or not.

"Of course, dear. And you can call me Catherine. My name is Catherine Cavanaugh. As you can see, my boys are a little wound up this evening. My apologies, dear." I smiled at her and sat down in the chair next to her before I nodded for her to keep going. "I was just reading here in the front room and having a nightcap when I heard glass breaking outside. I went over to the window and saw a shadow of a man throw something onto the back seat of my car. Then, before it even registered with me, the entire car was completely engulfed in flames. I dialed 911 and then called the boys, since I knew they would hear about it. Unfortunately, I didn't get a good look at the man, other than to say he was tall and rather thin. Other than that, I'm afraid I don't have much to add. I'm sorry, dear." She sounded disappointed.

"No need to apologize. You did exactly the right things. Which direction did the man run away in?"

"He ran east, toward the woods," she pointed.

"Ok, great. Mrs. Cavanaugh," she looked at me to correct me. "Catherine, does anyone here smoke?" She smiled at my recognition of her request.

"No, dear, no one here has smoked since my ex-husband, and that was over twenty years ago. Why do you ask?" She was confused, and with good reason.

"I'm just checking all angles, ma'am. I don't have any more questions, so I'm going to leave you with your boys for now, but another officer will be in shortly to get your official statement, if that's alright?"

"Of course, dear. Whatever you need."

Brian looked up at me from the couch and asked the million-dollar question. "Isabel, do you have any leads on this? Now it feels personal. First it's three fires on my shift, then a pointless abandoned building fire, which feels like a distraction while my mom's car gets lit up? Something fucked up is happening here."

"Brian Patrick! Language!" His mother smacked his chest.

"Sorry, mama." He rolled his eyes in my direction.

I grinned at the exchange and took in a deep breath. "Brian, I'll be honest with you. I have some evidence that links the fires together, but it's not conclusive yet, and I don't have any suspects. If you think it's personal, and I'm leaning toward agreeing with you after tonight, we need to sit down and go over who would hold a grudge against you or the fire department. None of the loose ends we've been chasing led to any personal connection until this fire." I was just as disappointed as they all looked. "Also, if you're concerned about the safety of your family, I can have a patrol assigned for the next couple of days to watch the house, if that helps."

"I don't need anyone hanging around watching my house all day. That's annoying," Catherine chimed in.

Finally, Matt stopped pacing and looked at his mother. "Mama, what is annoying is having your mother's car torched in her driveway, and her not taking it seriously. It's very serious. That could have caught the house on fire with you in it. You realize that, don't you?"

"Listen here, young man. I know how fires start. I've listened to the two of you, and Jack and Jo for that matter, for over fifteen years, so pipe down. I'm still your mother, and I'll still be making the decisions about my life, thank you very much." She took a sip of amber liquid in front of her. Whiskey, I guessed. "I'll cut you a deal, Matthew. Why don't you get your truck off of my front yard, and then you can sleep in your old room and protect your mother. How about that?"

"What about me?" Brian asked, suddenly sounding like a child.

"What about you? You need to go home and protect your woman. If someone is out for you, or me, or one of us personally, you need to be taking care of Josephine, and you cannot be two places at once. Matthew can stay with me until we have this sorted out a little better." I observed how the matriarch of the family kept those boys in line, and I was truly in awe of her power over them. She was a smart cookie. "Brian, you can also get that monster truck of yours off my lawn, and when all this calms down, you can both fix the grass I'm sure you ruined." She took another sip of her drink, ending the discussion. It was all I could do to keep from laughing out loud. She was my hero.

"Isabel, will you stay here with mama while we move our monster trucks off the lawn and check on the crew outside who put the fire out?" Brian asked me.

"Of course, I will," I smiled and sat back down. Still not making eye contact with me, Matt walked out first, Brian following him, leaving Catherine and me alone.

"You're such a tiny thing to be a detective. Do you enjoy it?" she asked me.

Thinking for a moment, I replied, "Honestly, it's my calling. I was absolutely meant to do this job, and I thank God every day for

451

the opportunity to help other people and to put the bad guys away." I meant that. I loved my job.

"I'm so sorry for the way Matthew was acting. He's had a rough day, apparently, and those boys worry about me more than they need to."

"No reason at all to apologize. I know Matt from work a bit, and he's had a rough couple of days. They all have. It's sweet how he protects you and wants to take care of you," I said softly. Catherine took my hand and gave it a squeeze just as Matt walked back in. He seemed to have relaxed a little bit.

"The fire is out. Obviously, the car is totaled. It was fully involved when we got here before the fire department ever had a chance to put it out. I'll help you get it handled or whatever you need, mama." He glanced in my direction and shuffled his feet before speaking to me directly. "Isabel, I'm sorry I snapped at you. I'm a little emotional at the moment and worried about my family."

"Cavanaugh, you have nothing to apologize for." I stood up, Catherine rising with me. Leaning forward to give her a hug, I said, "We're going to catch this guy. I promise." She gave me a hug that was so warm and inviting it could prevent wars. I didn't want to let go. Finishing it with a big squeeze, she let me go, and I made my way for the door.

"I'll walk you out, Isabel," Matt said as he held the screen door open for me. I walked past him out to the porch, pausing to look up at him. His eyes were full of worry, and in that moment, I felt myself soften. I wanted to hug him. He needed someone to take care of him too, and I wanted to be that person.

"I'm going to catch this guy, Matt," was all I said.

Running his hands through his light hair and taking a huge

sigh, he looked across the yard to the driveway, where the burned-out car was still smoking. "I know you will, but I'm worried, Izzy."

"What are you worried about exactly? Talk to me." I folded my arms over my chest and looked into those magnificent green eyes, getting lost for a moment.

"I'm worried someone is going to get hurt. These fires are clearly not random, but they're getting scarier. We train for this, and we know what to do, but setting an apartment building on fire? People could have been home. That garage fire could have been a HAZMAT incident. This car could've caught my mom's whole house on fire. I'm fucking concerned for the people I love," he confessed to me.

I pursed my lips, contemplating what to say. "So far, no one has gotten hurt. I've got some evidence to take to the lab tonight, and you're going to stay here with your mom. Brian will look after Jo. I'm going to catch this guy. It's what I do, Matt."

He tilted his head to the side in thought. "Who's going to protect you, Isabel? Who's going to make sure *you're* safe?"

I was taken aback by his question. "I don't need anyone to protect me, Matt. I'll be fine. My job is to make sure you're all safe." Not knowing how to answer a question like that, it was all I could think to say. I looked over to see my partner waiting for me at our car, so I tried to think of something else to say but was at a loss.

"I think someone should be looking after you too," he said quietly.

"Listen." I leaned in a little closer so I could speak more quietly. "I'm going to be fine. Take care of your mom, and let's take a rain check on lunch tomorrow while we get this thing under control, ok?"

Scrunching his face at me, he replied, "Only because I'm going to stay here with my mom. How about you make yourself free tomorrow night for some one-on-one time with yours truly? It's been a rough couple of days. I have an idea I think you'll enjoy." He was grinning then, pleased with whatever idea he'd come up with on the fly.

"Are you asking me on a date, Cavanaugh?" I definitely didn't want to do that. I wasn't ready for that.

"Not a date. Time set aside just for me and you, is all. No different than *lunch*, but I'm picking a slightly different activity. An appointment, if you will."

"You have me intrigued. Since I like you bossy, I'm going to let you get away with it." I was flirting at that point and needed to stop it, because he was turning me on with his charm and those fucking eyes.

"I know you like me bossy, babe. I'll see you tomorrow night. I'll text you the details later, Detective," he whispered. "Don't even think about trying to bail either; I know where you keep your toys." That he whispered so barely audible I could hardly hear it, especially over the sound of my own heart beating out of my chest. Goddamn, he was so fucking hot, and in the middle of this chaos and shit storm going on, I had soaked panties and an aching desire for him.

Shaking myself of his spell, I straightened myself back up and pretended to be professional again. "Ok, Cavanaugh, we'll be in touch."

As I walked away to the car, I could hear him say, "Yes, yes, we will."

"Let's get all this shit back to the lab. What a night," Kevin said

THE BROTHERHOOD OF DISTRICT 23

as we got in the car.

"Yea, for real. Fingers fucking crossed that's it for today. I need some sleep. Let's keep our day off tomorrow unless we get something from the lab? I have some shit I'd like to do, and I'd love to actually get some sleep too."

"You got a deal. I'm fucking over this investigation already. I talked to the chief outside, and he thinks it might be personal. I'm starting to think he might be right."

Sighing, I replied. "I think so too. We just have to figure out the motive, and we'll find this guy. I know we're close though, and he's got to fuck up soon. They always do."

"Yea, they always do."

We dropped the evidence bags from earlier in the day off at the lab, got them logged into evidence, and did all the paperwork associated with the lab, then called it a night. I went home to crash, and I'm sure Kevin did the same.

I was fucking drained.

MATT

After Isabel left, I went back inside to hang out with my mom. I couldn't believe she wasn't more scared or worried about this. Someone came to her home, where she lived by herself, and intentionally torched her car. I was losing my mind over it.

"Mama, are you sure you're ok?" I sat down on the couch next to her and put my head in my hands. I was so frustrated.

"Matthew, I'm fine. It's just a car. If someone wanted to do something worse, they most certainly could have. I'm sure that detective will figure out who it was, and we'll be able to move on and forget all about this. I'm far more concerned with the stress on your face, my love." She reached over and rubbed my back like she used to when I was little and didn't feel well.

"I'm fine. I'm just frustrated. And I'm tired. You know, Brian and I are well aware what we do for a living can be dangerous, but I have such a bad feeling this has something to do with us, and I can't stomach people getting hurt because someone might have it out for us or something.," I essentially exhaled all of that out to her. She turned her body to face mine and put her hands in her lap before replying thoughtfully.

"There are people in this world who do bad things for what they think are good reasons, and some who just do bad things because they are cold inside. We have to just take care of the people we can and look after our loved ones. It is the best we can do. You boys take the weight of the world upon you sometimes, and you need to remember you cannot fix everything. I know it seems hard to do, but I promise you this will all work out in the end the way it is intended."

I knew she was right, but it didn't make the situation suck any less. I was actually glad I was staying with her; she had a way of making me feel much calmer. Isabel did the same thing to me; she brought me peace, and we fit together in a way I couldn't explain, like she was part of a puzzle I'd been looking to solve without even knowing it. While she may have hesitated and she may have reservations about dating or relationships—and hell I did too; I hated that label that tended to ruin things—my desire to break down her walls and bring her into mine was overwhelming my thoughts.

"I know you're right, mama. I just worry." I leaned back on the sofa, relaxing a little bit and getting lost in my thoughts of the investigation, the fires, and Isabel.

"I saw you outside taking to that beautiful detective. She seemed to know you quite well." My mom was trying to get information out of me now.

I turned my head to her, seeing her smirk and raising eyebrow, causing me to laugh. "She's just a friend, mama. Don't start. Between you and Jo, I swear I don't know what I'm going to do with you."

"She might be a friend right now, but I saw something. You know I know things, Matthew."

"Not this time." I looked away, knowing she would be able to tell I was a big fat liar.

"Mmmhmm. I've said it before and I'll say it again. Have your secrets. I still know things. Would you like a drink, sweetheart?"

"Mama, I would absolutely love a drink. We're drinking the good stuff tonight though. I'd say we earned it." As I got up to fix us both a whiskey, she stopped me.

"You sit. I'll get it for us. And yes, let's have the good stuff. I'll make one for your brother too. I see him walking back up this way now."

"Hey, the crews are cleaning up and heading out now. You guys ok in here?"

"Yea, mom is fixing the three of us a drink. Then you should go home to Jo. You've been gone since dinner time, and she's called me three times. I texted her and let her know what was going on."

"Fuck, I completely forgot my phone in my truck. She's gonna kill me." He smacked his own head after checking his pockets and not finding his phone.

"She isn't going to kill you, because I told her you were outside handling things, Isabel was here, and I was staying with mom. I also let Jax know too, because you know he would've been over here in two seconds as soon as he saw the dispatch here."

"Oh, he wasn't home with you?" Brian asked.

"No, I actually don't know where he was. I assumed he was out having drinks someplace or something. We are roommates. We don't do everything together, you know," I replied sarcastically.

"Yes, I know. So, you gonna tell me where you were the other night when you didn't come home? Or where you were this morning?"

"Nope, I'm not."

My mama was saving the day with some drinks, thank the Lord. The three of us talked and sipped our whiskey on the rocks, agreeing the next afternoon Jo and Brian would come and relieve me so I could go do some things I needed to while someone would still be with mom. They didn't know those things I needed to attend to were Isabel, and no matter how many times Brian, Jo, or my mother questioned me, I was protecting what I had going on. Frankly, Jo and Brian had no room to bitch about it either, since they'd kept their little relationship secret for who knows how long before they both confessed to me. Once it was out in the open, it was up for scrutiny and judgment, and I wasn't game for that; and I knew Isabel sure as hell wouldn't be either.

The next morning, Mom made me an absolutely insane breakfast that consisted of bacon, eggs, toast, sausage, and she even tried to push pancakes on me too. Her cooking was amazing, but I wasn't trying to be a slug all day. I actually wanted to go to the gym at some point before setting my plan of breaking Isabel's walls down into motion. I still couldn't call what I felt about her feelings, because *ugh, feelings*; however, she was on my mind constantly, and just having a plan for the next time I'd see her made me happy.

Much of the day dragged while I checked my watch what seemed like a thousand times waiting for Brian and Jo to tag me out. After a good night's sleep and an amazing home-cooked breakfast, I was feeling much less anxious about the fires and how they might relate to us, and I was far more excited to go work out and see Isabel than anything else.

Once Brian and Jo arrived, we exchanged some quick pleasantries before I ran home to get changed so I could work out and then get the rest of my plan together. There hadn't been any fires that day, which was a welcome break for all of us, but that left a nagging feeling something was still looming. Knowing it was a waiting game, really, I went on about my business for the day, simply hoping for the best.

Isabel

After sleeping like the dead, I met Kevin back at the station to regroup and get our list of potential witnesses together while we waited for lab results to return. Fortunately, the overnight had been uneventful, and there were no new fires to investigate yet, so we were able to sleep and get back to the business of solving this crime. We briefed the captain on our progress and made our way back out to the scene of the first fire. Brian's report gave us a list of about five witnesses we would reach out to who had given statements, and I hoped one of them would be able to give us a description we could go on.

"So, do you think this arsonist is trying to make a statement or something?" Kevin asked me on the ride.

"You know, I've been thinking about that. I feel like he is, but it's only a gut feeling. I obviously have nothing to go on there," I replied thoughtfully, thinking through what we knew.

"I'm having the same feeling. It's obvious none of these fires are truly related, but the abandoned building fire last night truly did seem like a diversion from the car fire at Cavanaugh's mother's house."

"I think you're absolutely right. Today, we'll talk to the fire marshal about the building fire, because maybe some other clue was left behind. Those fires were so close together, I'm hard pressed to believe the same person started them both, but I still think they were connected." I definitely believed the building fire was a diversion, but that could mean two arsonists and not just one. "I think we should send the forensics team over to the abandoned building fire now, to get a jump on any evidence that might be there."

"Yea, you're right. Give them a call now, and we'll meet up with them after we talk to some witnesses."

I made the call. I explained our suspicions to the forensics team leader and requested a team be sent over right away to look for evidence outside of just the normal fire investigation. I also reminded him we had been finding piles of the same brand of cigarettes at each of the other fires in locations that appeared to be prime for viewing the scene, making sure he had his team looking for that as well. In the chaos of the evening and leaving that fire to get to Cavanaugh's mom's so quickly, we really hadn't spent any time on that scene, and I was concerned we had left something unfound in the heat of the moment.

We arrived at the first house and knocked on the door, where a small older woman with grey hair met us with a concerned look.

"Good morning. Are you Mrs. Lorraine Hill?" I asked.

"Yes, I am. Who are you?" She seemed scared.

"I'm Detective Isabel Cruise, and this is my partner, Detective Kevin Connor. We are investigating the fire that happened a couple days ago. We understand you gave a statement to the fire department, so we wanted to talk to you about what you saw. Do you have a moment?" We showed our badges, and she opened the

THE BROTHERHOOD OF DISTRICT 23

door fully, inviting us in.

"Please come in and have a seat. I'll tell you anything I can. Although, like I told the fire department, I didn't see much." She showed us to a small sitting room off of the front of the house. As I looked around, I saw several pictures of family on the walls, and a lot of books. This woman read a lot.

"No worries, ma'am. This is really just a follow-up. We have to do our own set of paperwork on things like this, so we want you to tell us what you told the fire department, and we'll go from there so we can get out of your hair." Kevin smiled at the woman. He could be very charming, and the lady was falling right into it, smiling back and even blushing a little bit.

"Well, I sit out here and read every night. That night, I heard the alarm for the store across the street go off, so I went to the window but didn't see anything. Sometimes alarms go off around here; most of the time, people just ignore them anyway. I went back to my book but couldn't get into it because of the sound. When I saw smoke coming from the back of the strip mall, I dialed 911. I went out to my porch to watch what was going on. A small crowd of people had started to form, mostly my neighbors," she said.

"When you say mostly your neighbors, were there other people standing around too?" I asked.

"Well, there was one guy I didn't recognize. This is a small little neighborhood; I know just about everyone. There was one guy standing in front of my house, smoking cigarettes, and I asked him to move down the block, because I just can't stand cigarettes." *Hot Damn!* That was our guy. It had to be.

Trying to not sound too excited, I exchanged a knowing glance with Kevin as I asked, "Mrs. Hill, can you describe that man for me?"

She looked at me thoughtfully for a moment, and then began. "Well, he was tall and fairly thin. He was white, and when he turned around to look at me, I noticed he had piercing blue eyes. They were cold. He didn't answer me; he just tossed his cigarette butt into the street out front and walked away. He didn't seem like a kind man at all."

"Mrs. Hill, do you think you could come down to the station and work with a sketch artist? Describe this man so we could get a better idea of what he looked like? We think you may have told the arsonist to get off your lawn, and having a description would be a tremendous help to us." Kevin went right in for it. He knew as well as I did this was the guy we were looking for and we had just struck gold with Mrs. Hill here.

"Of course, I can. If you could just give me a few moments, I can go right now. Anything I can do to help." She stood up and went into the kitchen, where I heard water running. She must have needed to clean something, I guess.

"Ok, I'm going to go outside and call this in so we have a sketch artist waiting for her. This is the lead we've been waiting for." I stood up.

"Yea, agreed. I'll figure out what she's doing, and we'll see if she wants us to take her or what. I'll meet you out front in a minute."

My adrenaline was pumping knowing we finally had a solid lead and soon we'd have our lab results and a sketch. We were closing in on this guy. That's what I loved about my job. He wouldn't be on the loose much longer. After I called in and arranged for the sketch artist to be waiting for Mrs. Hill, I wandered around the front porch area and the adjacent street just to see if there was anything of note. Sure enough, there was a small pile of butts right in front of the house. This guy smoked a ton and left us breadcrumbs everywhere he went. It was like finding Easter eggs.

Mrs. Hill and Kevin came outside, while I was putting the latest set of cigarette butts in an evidence bag. Kevin and I grinned at each other; he knew what I had found.

"Mrs. Hill is going to have us give her a ride over to the station. Her son is going to come meet her there so she can get home later," he informed me.

"That sounds lovely. Mrs. Hill, would you mind if we stopped for some coffee along the way? I could use a refill. It's our treat." I smiled at the little woman clutching her purse on her front porch.

"I'd like that very much. If your station is anything like the ones on TV, the coffee is probably terrible, so let's stop before we go," she said very seriously, making me laugh out loud.

Kevin chuckled as well and led Mrs. Hill to the car, letting her into the back seat and then meeting me in front of the car for a quick chat.

"So, it looks like our guy was going to watch from right here until Mrs. Hill told him to scram. That must be when he went over to the parking garage. I think by this time tomorrow, we might be able to make an arrest." I was almost giddy. "And he keeps leaving these butts everywhere. It's crazy he doesn't know we can pull DNA off of them. I could do a happy dance right now. I love catching bad guys."

"You're hysterical. Come on, let's get the fuck out of here and check in with the lab. I know they were backed up, so we might not have anything until morning, but between the sketch and the DNA, we should be able to identify him no later than tomorrow."

We hopped into the car and took Mrs. Hill and ourselves to get some decent coffee before we made our way back to the station. All of these fires and scenes were scattered around town, so it took longer than I would have liked to get everywhere we were trying to be, but Kevin and I agreed that after dropping her off with the sketch artist, we would take the rest of the day off unless we got a call from the lab.

Once we had our witness situated with the sketch artist, we dropped our latest batch of cigarettes off at the lab and checked in on how long it would take to process our evidence. Unfortunately, they informed us it was going to be at least late night, early tomorrow before they'd have anything for us. While that news wasn't the best news we could have received, we weren't really surprised. It's not like it is on TV; you don't get lab results in a few hours in any situations. Most labs are backed up by weeks, and in our case, because there could be felony charges associated with arson, we were getting moved up the list, but we weren't first.

I decided to go to the gym before going home and finding out what my appointment with Matt was about. I was kind of tired, but the thought of seeing him gave me a flutter, knowing how he made me feel every time I was with him. I knew anticipation coupled with a good workout would wake me right back up, and I was intrigued by what he had in mind. That devilish smile of his created a warm sensation right to my core.

When I got to the gym, I found Murphy, the owner, going over paperwork feverishly behind the desk. "What's wrong, Murph? You look troubled." I stopped to lean over the desk.

"Hey, Cruise. Just going over finances for the gym. The fighters aren't bringing in enough scratch, and we don't have a lot of members like yourself who come here to just work out and use the equipment, so I'm trying to figure out where I stand financially and whether or not I can keep the place. I'm getting too old for this shit, frankly." He ran his hand over his aging, bald head. A former professional MMA fighter, Murph started this gym as a way to bring a different style of training to everyone, but also as a way to train professional fighters. I believed he didn't know enough about business and was probably cutting too many people who were down on their luck a break.

"You thinking you might sell it?" I was genuinely intrigued. I also didn't want the gym to close. It was no frills; with all the equipment you would need to get a solid workout and plenty of space.

"I've been wanting to retire for years. The wife has about had it with this place and me as it is. I'm not sure what I'm going to do. I'd hate to foreclose, but I don't want to sell it to any douchebag who wants to turn it into one of those $10 per month gyms that gives away pizza to keep people fat and coming back for more," he groaned.

"Yea, I hear you there. I hate places like that. It's like workout fast food. Maybe someone will come along and make you an offer or something. Let me know how I can help. I've gotta get a quick workout in today, but I know a lot of people. Maybe I can figure something out with you."

"Thanks, doll. Have a good workout. What am I saying? You always do. You put half the guys in here to shame!" He winked at me.

"Thanks, Murph. I'll catch up with you later when I have some ideas." I walked off to the locker room to change and get my workout done.

As I punched the heavy bag and worked on some of my strength and conditioning, I observed the gym and the people using it. I loved going to that gym, and I'd hate for it to close. I wondered how bad off Murph was financially and if it weren't something I could invest in. I had plenty of money in the bank, no debt, and generally speaking, I had the time to take on a project like a gym. I mulled it over for a while, continuing to beat up the bag and myself, and made a mental note to call my accountant to see if it would be a worthwhile investment. Maybe if I owned the gym, I could get more cops and firefighters working out here. The more I thought of it, the more I liked the idea. Maybe Matt would come work out here. It's near his place, and oh how fun would it be to watch him work out?

Getting turned on thinking about his muscular arms around me, holding me where he wanted me while he had his way with me, all while bringing me such deep satisfaction, I became completely flushed in anticipation of seeing him. My workout almost done, I looked over at my phone to see I had a message from him. Hoping it was details about our appointment this evening, I opened it.

8pm. I'll pick you up. I promise you'll like it. Wear cowboy boots. Remember, it's not a date, it's an appointment…

Wear cowboy boots? I was not a cowboy boots girl. Okay, I had a pair somewhere in my closet my sister had convinced me I had to have. I had worn them that day and never again since. Where in the hell would he be taking me that I needed to wear cowboy boots?

I was significantly less excited about this appointment now, knowing there was a costume for it.

I wrapped up my workout; feeling perplexed about the night ahead, and decided to put my reservations aside. At the very least, I could humor him, and then we could have some mind-blowing sex, which was all I wanted at that point anyway. I was so worked up thinking about fucking him later, I almost pulled open the toy drawer, but then decided to just wait. It would be far more pleasurable to see what he had in store for me in the bedroom later, which is where we always ended up anyway.

MATT

I sent Isabel a text on my way to the gym, letting her know what to wear and reminding her it wasn't a date. Jax was meeting me at the gym so we could work out together. I hadn't seen him much in the last few days, which was weird, but we also didn't necessarily keep tabs on each other either. When I got to the station gym, he was already there, and I was praying I could get a workout in without a fire call happening. The fires had been so huge and often lately that if a call was tapped out and I was at the station, even if it wasn't my shift, I'd be expected to go, and I had plans I didn't want to change.

"Long time, no see," I said as I walked into the gym.

"Yea, we keep missing each other. How's your mom? She ok? I would have come over last night, you know."

"Oh, yea, she's alright. I probably should have had you come over this morning to help me eat the massive pile of food she made. You'd think she was cooking for an army," I laughed.

"Your mom's cooking is amazing. I'll definitely come over for one of these family dinners soon. I've just been so fucking wiped from the fires and shit. It's ridiculous. I hope the cops catch this guy soon so we can go back to our usual routine."

"Tell me about it. I hate being off schedule so bad. We basically lost a whole fucking day sleeping, and that drives me crazy."

"Yea, me too. Ok, so what are we doing today? Crossfit workout? We haven't really done a lot of lifting lately, but I'd like to get some plyometrics in and work on agility a little." He and I both lifted, but we really preferred doing more full body type workouts that were really using your own body weight more than barbells and such.

"Yea, let's do the box jump/burpee workout we both love so much, but we'll incorporate some balance shit with the bosu?" Basically, what I meant was, let's do burpees, which no one likes to begin with, but use a half stability ball to balance our pushup portion on. It was a move that totally sucked, but legitimately worked your entire body.

"Sounds like a suck. Let's do it." He walked over to the stereo and turned up the tunes loud enough so we couldn't talk. That worked for me. I didn't want to make up any lies about what I was doing later, so avoiding the conversation altogether was even better.

After about an hour and a half, we wrapped up our workout. "What are you up to tonight?" I asked Jax, knowing we were going to discuss our plans at some point.

"I'm actually going to take a ride with Scotty out to that outdoor supply store a couple of hours away. He asked for some help getting some shit for a camping trip he is going on with his family in a couple of weeks. You wanna come with us?"

A wave of relief washing over me, I replied, "No, I'm gonna pass. I might go get a couple of beers at Moonshiners. I haven't been in a while, and I've got a hankering for some country music."

He laughed out loud. "A hankering, eh? Well, you have fun

with that. And pick up a little cowgirl for yourself since you'll have the house all to yourself."

"I just might do that," I joked, knowing full well I was planning on staying at Isabel's house that night.

"Alright. Well, I'll see you at home. I'm gonna run a few errands, so if I miss you, have fun with the country honeys and I'll see you at work tomorrow." We got into our trucks and took off.

Jax seemed kind of off lately, not his usual joking self. I thought maybe when things calmed down, I'd be able to talk to him about it a little and see what was up. I always kind of worried he might have PTSD or something, but I wasn't going to harass him about his feelings. We were men; we didn't really do that unless it was critical. Our jobs could be so stressful sometimes too, and dealing with the bullshit of working for the government, even at the county level, could wear on you sometimes as well.

Brushing off the Jax thing for the moment, I turned my focus to Isabel. I intended to make her laugh and relax. That was my main goal for the night. She was wound up so tight most of the time, I wanted to show her how much fun she could have with me outside the bedroom. Not that I didn't want to end up back in her bed. I just wanted her to see another side to what we could be if she was open to it. The more I thought about it, the more I longed to be with her in a more traditional way.

I wanted to take her to my mom's for dinner. I wanted to go run errands with her. I wanted to just hang out with her at home on our day off and do couple shit. Oh my God, I wanted to do couple shit. As the realization hit me I wanted Isabel to be a bigger part of my life, it also dawned on me I had no clue what I was doing. I hadn't had a real relationship since high school. I was the fun guy.

I was the guy you called to go out with but wouldn't settle down with. I struggled with the notion I was both exexcited to win her over and freaked out by my own desire for more with her. No woman had ever brought that out in me before, and a sense of certainty she needed to be mine became the overarching theme of the evening for me.

Isabel

After I tossed clothing out of my closet all over my bedroom, I finally found a pair of short denim shorts and a flowy purple tank top I wanted to wear with these goddamn cowboy boots he'd asked me to put on. I wondered if maybe this was a fetish thing. As the thought of role-playing with Matt even more than we had dabbled in crossed my mind, I heard my doorbell ring. Throwing the shorts on quickly and grabbing the boots, I ran to the door, knowing it was him.

"Hey, there," I said as I flung it open, wondering if he could hear my heart racing. Every time he was in proximity, I felt like I had just run a race.

"Well, don't you look cute," he said as he walked by me to enter. I looked him up and down, noticing his green t-shirt that hugged those arms I dreamt about, stopping at that delicious ass of his in jeans, noticing that he too, had on cowboy boots. I didn't have a thing for cowboys until that exact moment. I wanted to climb him like a tree.

"Thank you very much, cowboy. Now, what are we doing?" I continued to eye fuck him while he leaned up against the island in the kitchen, crossing his huge arms across his chest.

"Well, little miss, that's still a surprise. So get those boots on and let's go before I have to take you to the bedroom first," he nodded in the direction of the boots.

"We could just do that you know," I offered.

"I'm in charge here, remember, Detective? You have an *appointment* with me for one-on-one time. Believe me, we'll make it back to the bedroom. I have plans for you later," he stated firmly.

Feeling both pouty and turned on, I put my boots on and went to a drawer in the hallway to grab my gun that would fit inside my boot when he stopped me.

"No guns tonight. No crime. No fires. Just me and you." He had lowered his voice, mesmerizing me. At first I had wanted to argue I didn't do that, but I was going to let him have his say tonight.

"Ok, but we have to compromise and put one in the glove box. Deal?" I gave him the poutiest lower lip I could muster, which caused him to laugh out loud.

"Yes, we can do that, you little badass. Now, chop chop. We gotta go." He smacked my ass as I walked by.

I hopped up into his truck, glancing over at him while he drove us to our unnamed destination, taking in his profile. His jaw was exactly what you'd think of when you referenced chiseled, and he always wore t-shirts that were snug at his biceps, accentuating them even further. He was sexy as hell in his uniform, and even sexier in jeans and a simple green t-shirt that matched those eyes I got hypnotized by.

We pulled up into a busy parking lot about twenty minutes outside of town that was already pretty full. I realized we were at a bar called Moonshiners, a country bar I'd heard of but had never been to. Country was not my thing at all.

"We're here," he said as he backed into a parking spot.

"What are we doing here, Cavanaugh? This is a country bar. I don't really do country." I turned toward him in the cab of the truck and raised an eyebrow at him. I didn't want to listen to hillbillies all night long. I wanted to go home and get fucked.

"Tonight, you do what I say. That's how this works. So tonight, you do country. We're here to dance." He smirked at me. He was fucking with me, and I didn't like it one bit.

"We're what? Dancing? I don't know how to dance to that kind of music," I huffed.

He hopped out of the truck, coming over to my side, and opened the door. "Tonight, I'm going to teach you how. Come on, m'lady." He held his hand out to help me hop out of the truck, and of course I took it. We walked to the front door, still hand in hand, when the bouncer recognized him.

"Cavanaugh! How are you, brother? Good to see you!" Matt dropped my hand and gave the bouncer a handshake and a bro hug.

"Cole! Good to see you too." Letting go of the man, he took my hand again. "Cole, this is Isabel. I'll be teaching her to two-step tonight. She's never been here before."

"Well, Isabel, it's a pleasure to meet you. You're in good hands with Matt here. He's a hell of a dancer. Have a great time tonight." The large, bearded man gave me a huge smile.

"Thank you so much," was all I could say. I was literally stunned.

Matt led me into the building and squared us directly up to the bar. "So, little lady, what will it be?"

"I think I need a shot. I'm out of my element right now," I said.

"Well, then shots it is." He waved over the bartender. We took shots of some kind of whiskey that burned immensely as it made its way down to my stomach, where it warmed my entire body. The music was pumping. It was country music but remixed into dance music, which was really entertaining, I had to admit.

"Come over here, babe." He pulled me into his chest and looked down at me, smiling. "Trust me. You're going to have fun, I promise. You gotta loosen up every once in a while." I got lost looking up into those green eyes when he took my face in his hand and pulled me closer with the other.

Our bodies were completely touching, and all I wanted to do then was get lost in my desire. I felt my body relax, and when he leaned down to kiss me, I forgot I didn't want to be there, I forgot the cowboy boots seemed silly, and I forgot where I was. This kiss was different. This kiss changed things, and as he swept his soft lips across mine, I realized he was what I wanted, and I didn't care what that meant. He took my breath away in a new and different way. Of course, I wanted him in my bed, but in an instant, I felt more. He kissed me in a way that felt like desire for me, that was more than just sex, and I completely gave into it. He caressed my face, slipping his tongue in my mouth, and I drank in that whiskey taste, completely consumed. As our lips parted, he whispered to me, "That's the kiss, Isabel. That's the one that changes things."

He was completely right. And I was completely speechless. We separated our bodies and both turned back to the bar to flag the bartender down for another shot, breaking the tension and making us both laugh.

"You're beautiful when you laugh, Isabel," he said matter-of-factly.

His comment was so direct it made me blush. I didn't know what to say, again, so I smiled and leaned into his side. He felt good. Everything about the moment felt good. Not wanting to be too intense or presumptuous, I decided to turn the topic back to the music and this dancing he'd mentioned. "So, dancing. What kind of dancing are we doing tonight?"

"Ah, yes, dancing. I almost forgot why we're here," he teased. "Tonight, I'm going to teach you to two-step. It's a basic country dance. You'll have it down in no time at all. And you can do the two-step to over half the songs out there, more or less."

"Hmm, the two-step. Ok, so is it only two steps?" I asked.

Laughing, he took my hand. "Come on, let's do it." He led me to the dance floor. I hesitated at the makeshift wooden fence around it. "Come on, Cruise. The fence is so people can watch and look for a partner. You're with me, it'll be fine." He tugged at me, and I finally gave in.

A fun song I was familiar with came on; my partner listened to country, so I had heard some. Matt positioned me how he wanted me. "Now, all you have to do is follow my lead. It's quick-quick, slow-slow. That's it. We can get fancy later." He winked at me. "Ready?"

"Ok, sure." I looked down at my feet.

He let go of my hand and lifted my chin up to meet his eyes. "Just look at me. Don't watch your feet. Feel it." And with that, we were dancing. He started right away, moving to the music, and I counted in my head, staring at his eyes. After a few loops around the dance floor, I was able to stop counting, and my body knew where it was supposed to go, led by him. I started to smile. Not a little smile; I was having fun. Real fun. I was enjoying the music, and we were dancing. I couldn't even believe it. Matt must have noticed, because he started to grin too and then said, "Ok, you're ready to get fancy now."

"No, no, I'm not!" I tried to stop him when he grabbed a hold of my waist and spun me around, bringing me right back into step within an instant, and we were back to our quick-slow routine.

"See? Now you're fancy." He laughed so hard I couldn't help but laugh too. It felt so good to be away from everything, just laughing and dancing and enjoying his company. It had always confounded me until that moment that this was what people must be talking about when they said they found someone they could be themselves with. I was completely relaxed and having an absolutely wonderful time, enjoying the moment.

As the night continued, we stopped dancing a few times to grab a drink or take a short break, but we spent most of the evening on the dance floor. As I got more comfortable, he taught me how to switch up our movements or add extra steps for different songs. It was so different from what I'd expected, but I was ready to go home. I wanted to put my hands on him in a different way. Clearly picking up my vibe, he leaned into me and said, "Are you ready to go home now, Isabel? You look like you need to get in bed."

Unable to control my enthusiasm for that, a huge smile crossed my face, and I nodded my agreement. "Yes, please."

"Let's go, babe." He took my hand, and we headed out the door. When we reached the passenger side door, he stopped, pressing his body to mine against the truck, and kissed me passionately, igniting everything sexual in me. He wrapped his arms around me, pulling my hips to his and crushing his mouth to mine hungrily. "Let's get the fuck out of here," he growled into my neck.

"Yes, let's," was all I said.

He pulled away from me and opened the door for me to climb in. As I did, he smacked my ass playfully, causing me to let out a little yelp.

"That's not the only noise you'll be making tonight," he said as he shut the door. The anticipation of getting home was like an outbreak. My skin was buzzing all over. We couldn't get to my house fast enough.

MATT

My plan was fucking working. Date, appointment, whatever you wanted to call it, she was into me for more than sex, and I was the happiest man in that bar if not all of Florida in that moment. That fucking kiss, holy shit. That's the kind of kiss that stops traffic. The one you tell your kids you fell in love with their mother over. Yea, those were the kinds of thoughts she put in my head. I wasn't even the same person because of her. I couldn't wait to get her home.

I was fairly certain I broke at least three different traffic laws, hightailing it back to her place with a hard-on from being in her presence and touching her all night. And those shorts she had on that showed off the shape of that beautiful ass of hers paired with those boots had every guy in that bar staring at her, something she hadn't even noticed. I couldn't keep my hands off of her, and even as she was fiddling with her keys to let us into her place, I was biting her neck and running my hands up and down her body.

As soon as we made it inside, she dropped the keys on the floor and spun around to meet me, hopping into my arms. The moment her hips grazed mine, I could barely see straight from the overwhelming desire to bury myself in her. I carried her up the stairs to the bedroom, kissing her the whole time. We hadn't stopped kissing except for when I was driving, and I was certain I'd die a happy man if that were all I ever did.

As I set her on the bed, I kneeled down to take her boots off, tossing them behind me. "Isabel, you've been a very good girl tonight," I said.

Giving me a confused look, she waited for me to continue.

"Good girls don't need to be punished, Isabel. Tonight, I want to worship you instead." I wanted to be close to her tonight. I'd had her in other ways, but in that moment, I wanted to devour her, consume her, and pleasure her. The corners of her lips turned up into a smile, and she scooted herself toward me, taking my face in her hands.

"Matt, right now, I'm yours, any way you want." Pressing her lips to mine, she kissed me softly and passionately like she had at the bar, sending me spinning. I pulled her to me by the waist of her shorts, then worked to undo them, yanking them off and revealing the sexiest fucking black underwear I'd ever seen in my life. She grabbed the hem of her shirt, pulling it off over her head, showing me the matching bra. She was literally the hottest woman I'd ever been with, and she had no idea what she did to me. I had gotten caught up in the moment, becoming motionless when she leaned forward to grab my shirt, pulling it up over my head. As her hands came down, she let them linger slowly down my chest, giving me chills. Before I lost all sense, I grabbed a condom out of my pocket and tossed it on the side table as she made her way to my waistband. My cock was aching for her at that point. I wanted to be deep inside her so desperately it was all-consuming. I had to kiss her again, and while she went to work undoing my pants, I brought her lips to mine.

As she reached in to free my cock, I let out a little groan, her touch causing me to lose my breath. She continued to stroke it, while I kissed her, until she pulled away just a bit and whispered, "Take your pants off, Matt, and get in this bed with me. Please?" She certainly didn't need to ask me twice. I sprung up, stripped off my pants and got rid of my constricting boxer briefs as well. I watched her crawl to the head of the bed, where I followed her immediately, climbing over her.

"How do you want this, Isabel? Tell me." I knew what I wanted, and I had told her, but I needed her to tell me what she desired, what she needed.

Placing her hands on my chest as I had her caged in, she looked up at me longingly. "I want to be close to you, Matt. I want you to..." she trailed off, looking away, afraid to say it.

"Do you want me to make love to you, Isabel? Because that's what I want," I said the words. I always wanted to fuck her. She was hot, a goddamn vixen. But tonight, I wanted to relish in her, get lost in her.

"Yes, please, Matt," she whispered to me, meeting my eyes once again. With that, I had all the confirmation I needed to do things my way. I was going to consume her right there, making her mine. She had lit something inside of me, creating a fully involved fire of desire that burned for her constantly. Her reply caused me to smile, and as I leaned in to kiss her neck where it meets her shoulder, I inhaled that tropical scent only she had. Her hands found their way to my back, and as I hit the spot she loved so much, her breathing got heavier.

I rolled to my side just a bit so I wouldn't crush her under my weight and began to kiss her shoulder, while she gently touched my throbbing cock. Sliding her bra strap down her shoulder, I tugged the lace gently away, unveiling her beautiful tit to me, and immediately latched on to it, sucking and licking at her pebbled nipple. I had figured out how much she loved that as her hips rocked, and I freed her other breast, gently rubbing my thumb across that nipple.

Her hand was now gripping my cock, pumping and stroking it, while I continued nibbling on her nipples. I took her hand gently off my cock, positioning myself over her again for a kiss before I went down for my favorite treat. As she ran her hands through my hair, I had to remember to take it slow this time, even though she was making me insane with her touch.

"It's time for me to taste your sweet pussy, Isabel. I've been dreaming about having this all day." I started to lick and nip at her all the way down until I reached my destination. I could smell her desire, and as I settled in, she relaxed her legs open to me. Flattening my tongue, I swept it across her clit, evoking a moan that made my cock twitch. As I sucked and licked at her sweet pussy, she began to pant, and her hips started to rock. I grabbed her by her ass, bringing her into my mouth, holding her there, while I coaxed her orgasm from her with my tongue. As she cried out, shaking, I licked up everything she had.

"Matt, oh my God. What are you doing to me?" she let out breathlessly. She perched herself up on her elbows and leaned over to the nightstand to grab the condom I'd thrown there. "Jesus Christ, Matt, put this on and get that beautiful cock inside me before I lose my mind."

Always a man who did what a woman told me, I put the condom on and crawled over her, the tip of my cock at her entrance. "Is this what you want, Isabel? You want me inside you?"

"Yes, please!" she cried out, reaching for my hips in an attempt to pull me closer. Unable to wait any longer myself, I thrust my cock inside her, causing us both to groan.

"Fuck, Isabel, you're so tight. Oh my God." I was trying not to lose it. I needed to go slow or I was going to explode. She was rocking her hips into mine, making it impossible for me to control myself, and she didn't want me to.

"Don't stop, Matt, please," she begged me. I finally let go and pumped into her with long deep strokes. With each time, I felt like I was going deeper, and she cried out with pleasure, driving me to go faster. As her hips met mine, I lost control and moved faster, causing her to yell out even more. The sounds she made as we connected drove me over the edge, and I couldn't stop.

"Fuck, Isabel! I'm going to come!" I groaned. She moved her hips into mine faster, and we fell over the edge together, yelling and panting. I was holding myself up with shaking arms, trying not to crush her as I looked down at her beautiful face smiling up at me.

"You're going to kill me, woman," I joked, giving her a quick kiss and then rolling over to my side of the bed to regain my composure.

Propping herself up on her arm and looking at me, she said, "Me? I didn't do anything. It was your charm and that Captain America smile, Cavanaugh. It does things to me." She grinned. I loved her smile. She didn't smile often enough. I was going to make it my mission to make her smile every fucking day.

"Come here and snuggle with me, Detective." I pulled her to me, and she settled right in beside me. The same position we both woke up in the next morning.

Isabel

The night before was different. It was passion and fire, not just lust. We fell asleep tangled up in each other in a romantic way, and several times before I drifted off to sleep, I felt him kiss my head and stroke my hair in a soothing and calm way. It was wonderful. Something was different between us, but I didn't want it to ruin the dirty-talking, dominant man I was more into than ever before, so when I woke up first, I decided to wake him up by stroking his beautiful cock so he'd use it on me one more time before work.

His sleepy eyes opened as his cock began to get hard in my hand, and he instantly smiled. "Good morning, baby. Are you ready for round two?"

"I am. Let's shower together though. Come on." I let go of his now rock hard cock and pranced to the bathroom in nothing but my thong, which I'd never taken off the night before. As I leaned in to turn the shower water on, he came up behind me, grabbing me around the waist and turning me toward the mirror in the bathroom, which had started fogging up already.

Standing behind me with his huge cock grazing my ass, he leaned over my back, kissing my shoulder, and whispered, "I think you want to be a bad girl this morning, don't you?"

"I do. I really, really do." I quivered in anticipation as I felt the moisture pool between my legs.

"Well then, I guess I'm going to have to torture you right here then, aren't I? You can watch me do it in the mirror." He reached up, taking my breasts in his hands, causing my nipples to harden in his fingers instantly. As he pinched my pebbled nipples, sending sensations straight to my core, I watched him in the mirror as he looked at me. "Do you like seeing what I do to you, Isabel?" he whispered in my ear.

"Fuck," I hissed. This was so fucking hot I was about to explode all over the bathroom.

"Answer me, Isabel." He pinched my nipples a little bit harder, making my breath hitch.

"Yes! I love watching you torture me, Matt," I breathed out heavily. My head dropped for a moment, and I spotted another little toy from my drawer, as well as another condom on the counter. He came prepared. My beautiful Boy Scout was ready for anything.

"I think maybe you need to be spanked?" he asked.

"Oh? Do I?" I whispered excitedly. I loved the sting of him slapping my ass, followed by his smooth, soothing touch. It was such a turn-on to hear the sound of his hand meet my ass swiftly when he was taking me from behind.

Grabbing a handful of my hair and pulling me to him, he reached down to touch my clit beneath my panties, rubbing it gently with his finger, setting me completely on fire. He let my hair go, gently pushing me back down with my hands on the counter and my ass facing him. When he smacked my ass once, I let out a little cry. The sting was warm, and he rubbed it gently before sliding a finger under the string of my thong and ripping it off. He then rubbed his cock up and down the crease of my ass toward my opening, teasing me. I was pulsing, waiting for him to enter me.

"Not yet. I'm not done torturing you. Look what I found..." He held up a tiny anal plug I'd actually never used before. "Have you used one of these before, Isabel? I took it out of the package this morning." He showed me. Watching me shake my head no, he smiled and slapped my ass again, then soothed it once again. Reaching down between my legs, he began to rub my clit, then slid two fingers deep inside me, pumping me for only a moment.

As he pulled his wet fingers out of me, making me miss them immediately, he slid them near my ass, putting the tiniest bit of pressure at the hole. "You're going to enjoy this, Isabel," he whispered as he coated my opening with my own juices. I'd never felt anything like this before, and while I was scared at first—no one had ever crossed that boundary—I was also dripping with anticipation. I watched him in the mirror as he put the condom on himself before he started to slide the plug near my hole. As he entered me with it, I gasped and then quickly adjusted to the sensation, which was heightening my pleasure already.

"Feels fucking good, doesn't it?" he growled. I turned my hips up more, which was creating a new pleasure. Then he entered me from behind, thrusting into me over and over so hard I couldn't hold myself up. The intense pleasure I was experiencing was something I'd never had before. It was overwhelming all of my senses.

"Oh my God, Matt, I can't... I can't take it," I cried out.

"Yes, baby, come for me. Look at me," he demanded. As I met his eyes in the mirror, I couldn't control my body any longer and fell into the most intense orgasm I had ever experienced. "Yes! Oh my God, baby, yes!" he yelled out as he found his release as well.

Hunched over the counter and completely spent, I realized the water had been running and the bathroom had completely filled with steam. My entire body was quivering. Matt gently removed the plug, causing me to gasp again slightly, and then slid himself out of me and disposed of the condom.

"Jesus Christ," I said.

"Yea, that was amazing, Isabel. Fuck. You do things to me I can't control." He leaned on the counter, pulling me to him. "Let's shower. I know we both have to go to work today." He kissed me and pulled me into the walk-in shower already running.

We took an amazing shower together, washing each other, kissing and even laughing. I couldn't remember a time when I had smiled as much as I did when he was in my presence. I had considered myself a happy person, but I didn't think I had known what that meant.

As be both got dressed for work and met back in the kitchen, I wasn't sure where this left us. It felt like something had changed between us in the previous twenty-four hours. However, I was fearful to draw attention to it. Matt was never afraid to speak his mind, and as he got ready to leave, he pulled me into his arms.

"I want this to be more," he said with a sigh.

"More than what?" I glanced up at him.

"More than what it started out to be."

Not sure how to respond, I said, "How much more?"

He pulled away and held me at arm's length, meeting my eyes with his. "I want this to be an *us*, Isabel. We don't have to put a label on it if you don't want to, but I want it to be you and me. Not sneaking around. Just *us*. Being together. *Us*."

Hesitating for a moment and realizing we wanted the same thing, I said the words out loud, "Me too, Cavanaugh. *Us*."

MATT

I could have danced the Irish jig right on out of her house. We were an *us,* and my heart was happy. I was starting my day off with my woman. *Yep, my woman.* I loved the sound of that.

"Well, that was easier than I thought it would be," I chuckled.

"I have feelings for you, Matt. I just don't want to rush into anything. This is all very new, uncharted territory for me."

"Babe, you and me both." I kissed the top of her head and pulled her in for a squeeze. "I really don't want to, but I have to leave. And your phone has been blowing the fuck up, so you should check it. It better not be another boyfriend," I teased.

"No labels! And shut up. It's probably work." She looked at her phone, and her face fell.

"Fuck, I gotta go. We have a positive ID on our arsonist. Move it, move it," she hustled us both out the door. She was so fucking sexy with her hair all pulled back again, wearing her gun and her badge. She had on jeans and boots again and a conservative t-shirt that still didn't leave much to the imagination in terms of her curves, but she looked like she could beat someone's ass. Topping off her attire, she put on some aviator sunglasses when we got outside, seriously sealing the deal. My woman was a fucking badass.

"Alright, alright. I'll call you later. I'm working a twenty-four, so if you catch this guy, stop down and see us at the station." I wanted to say, stop down and give me a celebratory romp in the hose room, but I wasn't a total douche.

"I will. Be careful today. If I can't find him right away, he'll still be out there," she warned.

"Don't worry about me, baby. Be safe." I kissed her one last time before getting in my truck to leave.

"I will. Thank you, Matt." She got in that hot rod of hers and looked over to blow me a kiss.

Hearts and flowers and unicorns. That's what I was feeling. Fucking Jo had been right. Someone showed up and caught me off guard. I'd do anything to make that woman smile. *Another lost pussy to love*, I mused to myself.

I had what I needed to go straight to work, so I met the guys and Jo on shift and started the coffee maker as part of my daily routine. I was generally an early riser, so it was no chore to me. I must have been humming out loud when Jax walked in and said, "Someone definitely got laid last night."

"Ha! And this morning. I'm a happy man, Seth Jackson. A. Happy. Man."

"So, who is this chick? It's the same one you've been out MIA with before, isn't it?" he asked.

"Yes, it is. I'm gonna tell you, because we talked about it not being a big secret today. It's Isabel." My man's mouth dropped wide open.

"Shut the fuck up. Isabel Cruise? The detective?" he questioned.

"Yea, man. Not sure how it happened, but we've been talking

and seeing each other for a little bit now, and something just changed. She's hot as fuck, smart as fuck, and seriously, she's fucking sweet too. I'm a lucky motherfucker." I was beaming.

"You sure are. Well, I'll be damned. Does Jo know yet? Because she's going to be off her rocker when she finds out you have a woman," he laughed.

"Nah, I came straight in from Isabel's house. I figured I'd just see Jo here anyway and tell her." And right on time, she walked in.

"Tell me what?"

"Your boy has a girlfriend," Jax sang to her.

"WHAT? SHUT UP! A girlfriend? Who is she? Why don't I already know about this?" She spewed her questions at me.

"Calm down, woman. I'll tell you all about it. It's Isabel. The detective."

"Get the fuck out." She was shocked.

"What?"

"I'm just stunned. Well, sonofabitch, Matt. Nice job. She's amazing. I'm gonna need all the details, because you've clearly been keeping shit from me."

"Yea, yea, I know. Sorry. I wasn't ready to talk about it. You of all people should understand that," I reminded her.

"Hmph. Touché, sir," she conceded.

"Alright, enough about my romantic life. Let's go do our truck checks and pray the arsonist gets caught today."

We spent the remainder of the morning in blissful firehouse peace, doing our truck checks, training a little bit, we even washed a fire truck. I knew Jo wanted to dish with me, but that was something we usually did late at night when it was quiet, so I'd just tell her all about it later. We had no calls, and it was a treat and a half to be left alone for the morning, but that wouldn't last long.

Just as we were walking in for lunch, Brian met all of us in the hallway, looking extremely concerned.

"What's wrong?" Jo asked.

"There was a 911 call dialed from Mom's house and then hung up. Could be nothing, but we're going over there. It's absolutely not standard protocol, but I think you should bring the crew and we should go over there and see what the hell is going on."

Isabel

I completely neglected to check my phone all night and all morning, distracted by Matt, and missed a call we had identified the arsonist. I called Kevin as I raced to the station.

"Sorry, man, I was caught up. What do we have?"

"Cruise, get to the station. We need to find this guy right now. It's definitely personal."

"Who is it?" I asked.

"The guy's name is Patrick Cavanaugh," he replied as if I should know who that was.

"Who is Patrick Cavanaugh?" And then I realized. "Oh my God, it's Matt and Brian's father?"

"Yea. I don't know what the motive is, but the fires definitely got more personal. We haven't had a fire in over twenty-four hours, so he's got to be up to something bad right now. We need to find him. Swing by and pick me up, and we'll go straight to the mother's house again," he said. "There was a 911 call and hang-up about five minutes ago."

I didn't have lights or sirens in my personal vehicle, so while I could speed and get away with it, it was still going to take me about five more minutes to get there and another five to get to her house.

I came to a screeching halt in front of the station, and Kevin jumped in. "Let's go to the mother's house first, check on her and see if she's heard from this guy. Apparently, he's been missing in action for years, and the mother filed for an uncontested divorce about fifteen years ago."

With my car being as loud as it was, I parked it a few houses down so we had the element of surprise if we needed it. We had no idea where to find this guy, but he had already torched Catherine Cavanaugh's car, so it was escalating, and it was likely he wanted something from her or from the boys.

"Let's do a quick perimeter search," I said as I strapped my bulletproof vest on. I wasn't taking any chances today. Kevin already had his on, so we unholstered and did a quick walk around the house. Underneath the kitchen window was another small pile of cigarette butts. Our guy had been here watching. I pointed to them so Kevin would see them too.

It was definitely time to go in. I radioed dispatch quietly we were going to enter the home. We had reasonable suspicion the arson suspect was inside, and that he was hostile. They identified that backup was on the way, and we got in place at the front porch.

I peered through the window but couldn't see anything. I suspected he had her in there, but I really didn't know for sure. We agreed to knock and pretend we were just following up on the 911 call hang-up as standard protocol.

"Is anyone home?" I yelled as I knocked.

I heard a chair move, and then Catherine answered, "Hello? Who is it?"

"It's the police, ma'am. Detective Cruise. We had a report of a 911 call that was dialed and then the caller hung up. We have to come out and check those things. Can you please come to the door?

We have to see you're ok," I called.

"Uh... just a moment," she called out. I heard a hushed whisper and was certain our guy was in there holding her hostage.

The door opened just a few inches, and there she was, standing before me. "Mrs. Cavanaugh? I'm Isabelle Cruise. We haven't met before. We were in the area when someone dialed 911 and hung up. We have to check on those calls. Is everything ok?" I repeated as I met her eyes. I lied so she would know I knew something was up.

"Yes, yes, everything is fine." Then she mouthed the word NO. I nodded my understanding of the situation. "It was a mistake. I thought if I hung up fast enough, it wouldn't go through."

"Not a problem, Mrs. Cavanaugh. I'm going to head back to my patrol now. Let me know if anything suspicious happens, and we'll come right out, ok?"

"Of course. Sorry for the trouble, officer. Just a mistake. I wasn't paying attention. Do you need anything else?"

Kevin never spoke or moved until just then when he quickly whispered to her, "Hit the floor when we come in," and held up his hand counting down from five, four, three, two, one...

I pushed the door open, shoving Catherine to the ground and yelling, "Police! Freeze!" while Kevin ran in toward the back of the house. "Catherine, get outside NOW!" I hustled her outside, making sure she was safe, and then returned my attention to where in the house this guy was. "Connor!" I yelled for my partner.

Suddenly, I heard a gunshot, and the doorframe near me splintered. That was fucking close, and I went for cover in the front room. Going for the radio on my shoulder, I yelled into it, "Badge number 2345! Shots fired! Shots fired! Need immediate assistance on scene!"

I had only heard one gunshot, and it had whizzed past me, so I knew Kevin hadn't been shot. I couldn't figure out where he was when I heard him yell.

"Cavanaugh, you need to put your weapon down right now and surrender! This isn't a joke," he screamed.

"I'm not going anywhere! This is my house, and I'm taking it back, or burning it to the ground. Take your pick." He came out of the kitchen holding a gas can and a lighter, with a revolver shoved into the front of his pants.

"You gotta be kidding me," I said. "Drop the fucking gas can, Cavanaugh!" I yelled at him.

"Not happening, sweetheart. Hey, wait a minute. Aren't you the one who's been running around with my son, Matthew?" He'd been following all of them, I thought, and that was how he'd recognized me.

"Am I adding stalker to the charges today, Cavanaugh?" Kevin had rejoined me, and we both had our weapons drawn, pointed at him, when the front door swung open and Matt and Brian rushed in, giving Patrick Cavanaugh a chance to drop the gas can and grab his weapon again.

"Well, look here, it's my boys! Hey, sons!"

"What the fuck is going on here?" Matt exclaimed.

"I'll tell you what the fuck is going on here. Your girlfriend with the gun is trying to keep me from getting my family back. This house was mine, and your mother made me leave. And then that fire chief took care of all of you, leaving me with no family. I'm here to get it back." He sounded almost drunk, certainly deranged.

"Matt, Brian, please step aside," I commanded. "Patrick, you are going to jail today, or are we carrying you out of here? You're guilty of arson, kidnapping, and apparently stalking, so you need to put the fucking gun down right now. We're not having a standoff here all day!" Never taking my eyes off the perp, I could hear the gas spilling out of the can. Hopefully, he didn't realize that was happening, as now he had a lighter in one hand and his gun in the other.

"I'll tell you what's going to happen, pretty cop lady. I'm gonna burn this house to the ground, and you're not gonna fucking stop me. If I can't have it, my ex wife can't have it either. She can go live at her dead boyfriend's house."

"Are you seriously our dad?" Brian chimed in. "What the fuck, man? We needed you. Our whole fucking lives, we wished you were there. Jack stepped in when you walked out!"

"I didn't walk out. Your mother made me leave."

"Because you're a drunk and a cheat! This house doesn't belong to you. We aren't your family. You decided you didn't fucking want a family twenty years ago, old man. You've put countless people in danger. You can go fuck yourself." Brian was getting angry, and I didn't want it to egg Patrick on.

"Alright, that's enough. You either put the weapon down, or I'm going to shoot you, Cavanaugh," I said.

"You're what?" Matt finally spoke. "You can't shoot him!"

"Matt! You need to stay out of this!" I yelled.

"Isabel, you can't shoot my dad!"

"Listen to him, honey. You can't shoot me. He'll never forgive you." I could feel the sweat dripping down my back. Something had to happen soon. This standoff was going on too long. Our backup had to be coming soon, and I hoped they would come in the back door through the kitchen.

"You need to drop the gun, Cavanaugh. I'm not going to ask you again," I repeated.

"Drop the fucking gun!" Kevin yelled.

"Wait! Wait!" Matt yelled.

Just as it appeared from the corner of my eye that Matt was taking steps toward his father, Patrick took his chance and lit up his zippo lighter, dropping it to the floor next to the gas can, which immediately erupted into flames. Everyone scattered, creating chaos. In the same moment, our backup crashed through the back door, catching Patrick off guard and tackling him to the ground without any further shots fired.

The living room was starting to burn, and as Kevin, Matt, the other officers, and I scurried outside, Brian, Jax, and two other firefighters I wasn't familiar with came in with the fire hose and began putting the fire out. Mrs. Cavanaugh was out on the front lawn with Jo and some of our other officers, and Patrick Cavanaugh was cuffed and hauled away to a squad car. I peered in Matt's direction as he walked over to his mother, scooping her into a hug. I truly didn't think he would forgive me for threatening to shoot his father. A father who'd left him and held his mother hostage, but his father nonetheless.

I put my gun away and walked over to one of the squad cars to catch my bearings and to internally and ceremoniously kiss goodbye the only relationship I'd ever really had.

MATT

I was so confused. My mom looked so upset, I had to go straight to her to make sure she was ok. I had checked on her quickly before running into the house with Brian, but I had known Isabel was in there too, and I had to protect her if I could.

Apparently, my dad was a criminal, and in the last several days, he had effectively set five fires, displacing countless people from their homes, ruined no fewer than five small businesses, torched his ex wife's car, and held her hostage. Turned out my dad was a real piece of shit, and a little bit crazy.

My mom promised to tell us why she threw him out twenty years ago, and Connor said they would tell us the laundry list on his rap sheet when we came down to the station the next day to give our statements. Apparently, he was some kind of chain smoker, and they had matched a bunch of cigarette butts from crime scenes to his DNA. He was in the system because of a bunch of petty thefts and other small crimes he'd performed over the years.

Connor was the one who told me this much, because I couldn't find Isabel. She had threatened to shoot my dad in front of me, yet she couldn't even tell me all of his crimes herself and had disappeared. I looked all over for her. I was angry and disappointed, but I knew I needed to find her. Something was definitely wrong. She had a job to do and was protecting all of us, so I couldn't understand why she would just leave, especially after our talk this morning.

"Where is Isabel?" I asked Connor.

"She left," he replied.

"No shit, she left. I can't find her. Where is she?" I was getting angrier.

"She went back to the station, dude. We still have work to do. Just leave her alone, Romeo. She'll be at work tomorrow when you come in to fill out your statement, and you can talk to her then," he snapped at me.

Tomorrow? This guy was crazy if he thought I was going to wait until the next day to talk to her. I decided I'd go to her house later. I didn't want to confront her at work, but I certainly wasn't going to let this sit until the next day.

I went back over to talk to my mom, knowing I'd have to wait to see Isabel anyway. She was still standing over by the trees in the front yard with Brian and Jo.

"Mama, what the hell happened here?" I asked, running my hands through my hair, exasperated.

"Oh Matthew. I don't even know where to begin," she sighed as she stared at the house. People were going in and out of the house; it was a crime scene now and a huge mess.

"How about you tell us what exactly he wanted from you today? Then you can tell us what happened all those years ago, ok?" Brian asked.

Turning her attention back to us, she took in another deep breath before beginning. "Well, boys, I always told you growing up that your father left us. That is mostly true. I talked to Brian about this one time many, many years ago."

I felt my face getting hot from anger knowing there was more to the story and it had somehow escalated to today's events. Finding out Brian also knew some of this was just adding fuel to the fire I was feeling, but my mom continued telling us before I could set some of that anger free.

"Patrick was a good man when we got married. He wanted a family, he worked hard, and he took care of us. Once we moved into this house though, he started to drink. Not like we do, a bit of whiskey now and again. I was finding bottles everywhere, and he had stopped going to work. He told stories of the job not needing him those days and went out to run errands and such, but he was out at the bar, spending money we didn't have.

He was never mean to you boys, but you were rowdy, which was often too much for him. He complained to me constantly about wanting quiet, and for what? For nothing. He stopped doing anything. Finally, I told him he needed to straighten himself out or leave. It wasn't as dramatic as today would make it seem at all. One day, we had a big argument, like we'd had so many times before. I said the same thing I had kept saying, and he left. Only that time, he never came back."

"Did you look for him? Weren't you worried?" I asked.

"Of course, I was worried. I had the police involved, but they couldn't find him for a while. I stopped looking for someone who did not want to be found. Eventually, a few years later, I received notification he was in New York City. He had an apartment, a girlfriend, apparently, and had moved on from us and obviously wasn't coming back. I filed for divorce, had him served, and he signed the papers. I moved on with my life and even had a beautiful relationship with Jack, as you are all aware. I've never heard from Patrick once over all these years." I looked over at Jo, who was also listening intently.

"He knew what we were doing, Mama, who we were with. He had been following us all," Brian said. "He knew about Jack."

"Yes, it seems he did. It seems Patrick has been watching all of us throughout the years. All he said to me was I'd moved on and didn't leave a place for him in his own home. It's very sad, but I think he has some emotional issues he will need to deal with, in addition to his drinking, which appears to still be a problem." She hung her head. I moved over to hug her; she looked like she needed one. While most of the time, we went to her for those hugs, it was definitely her turn to receive some comfort now.

Holding on to her, I too hung my head. What a fucking day. "Mama, I don't think you'll be able to stay here tonight. Do you want to come to my place?" I asked.

Brian interjected, "I already asked her to come stay with us for a few days. The damage isn't that bad; it will only take a couple of days to get it cleaned up. I am pretty sure she doesn't want to hang out at your bachelor pad with you and Jax."

"Thank you, sweetheart. I'm going to stay with Brian and Jo until this little mess is dealt with. Besides, don't you have something you need to do?" She had pulled away from my embrace and poked me gently in the ribs.

"What do you mean?" I asked, knowing full well she meant Isabel. How that woman knew everything escaped me.

Rolling her eyes at me, she said, "Go. Go to her. She is confused, but you can fix that, sweetheart."

"Are you sure you don't need me?" I was kind of relieved Brian had already handled taking Mama in, even though Jax and I would absolutely take her too.

"I'm taken care of now, sweetheart," she said.

"Uh, Chief? I need to take the rest of the shift off." I looked over at Brian with pleading eyes. This was a moment where having your brother as your boss wasn't so bad.

"Do what you gotta do, man. I'm going to see if we can find someone to take Jo's shift too, so we can take Mama home. But where are you going?" It occurred to me Brian was the only one who didn't know anything about Isabel and me.

"Matt has a girlfriend!" Jo blurted out.

"What? Get the fuck out of here. Is that why you've been so shady?" he asked me. Meanwhile, Jo and my mother were now giggling. I needed to leave and find her; I didn't have time for these shenanigans.

"Dude, I'll explain it all later. Isabel and I are a thing. That's the bottom line." I started to walk off, realizing I didn't have a vehicle.

"Well, I'll be damned. Nice work, bro," he said.

"Matthew, take the old Ford out back," Mama waved. We had an old Ford truck we kept here mostly because it ran. Every once in a while, my mom would need a truck for something. For instance, when her ex husband lights her Buick on fire. But also, this was a perfect time for an extra car.

"Thanks, Mama," I kissed her on the forehead. "I'll catch you guys later. Yes, Jo, I will text you." Jo smiled at me. She always appreciated when I knew what she was going to ask before she actually said it.

I took off to get the keys and make my way to Isabel's. As I drove to her house, trying to figure out what to say, I was at a loss. After hearing everything my mom had told us, plus the events of this day, I just needed to understand why she'd left in the middle of all of that; it couldn't just be work. Especially when we'd agreed that very morning we were an *us*. I needed *us* now. I parked in her driveway next to her usual spot and sat myself down on the front step to wait.

About an hour and a million thoughts later, I could hear her car coming from up the street and thought how her neighbors must hate that beautiful Camaro of hers. My heart immediately began to race, and for some reason, I felt nervous.

"What are you doing here, Matt?" She said as she got out of her car, still wearing her sunglasses.

"What do you mean, what am I doing here? You left the scene without even saying two words to me," I replied.

She walked past me to open the door. "What do you want, Matt? You don't really want to be here right now."

"What do you mean, I don't want to be here? Did you bother to stick around and ask me? You're my fucking woman, and we need to have a fucking chat about what happened today." She put her sunglasses up on top of her head. I noticed her eyes were red as if she'd been crying, and she was sniffing her nose.

She motioned for me to enter, so I stormed in past her and turned around to face her head-on. "Why did you fucking leave the scene before I could even talk to you?"

"Because it was the right thing to do, Matt. I threatened to shoot your dad. In front of you, and in front of your brother. That's not something that calls for a discussion right then and there with

507

all of those emotions running high. And I would do it again to protect myself and everyone else there if I had to. I really didn't know how to tell you all that this afternoon. I know that's not something you could ever understand or forgive, so I left." A tear crept out of her eye and rolled down her beautiful face.

Lunging forward, I took her into my arms. "Baby, I know you had to do that. Did you think I wouldn't understand? I was just shocked in that moment." She started to cry a little bit harder, letting it all out, and I held her tighter. "Don't cry, baby, shhhh." As her crying lessened, she pulled away to look up at me.

"You're not mad at me? I just assumed you would be. I don't regret what I did. It had to be done," she said, staring up at me with those big, brown eyes.

Taking her sweet face in my hands, I wiped away a tear with my thumb. "Baby, I'm pretty sure you saved my mom and who knows how many of the rest of us. We are all lucky you showed up before we did, if I'm being completely honest. Of course, I'm not mad. I mean, I'm mad about you, maybe, but that's all." I was trying to get a little smile out of her.

She sniffled and let out a little giggle. "I told you I'm not good at this relationship stuff, Matt. I don't know what the hell I'm doing. I jump to conclusions like this, and I don't want it to ruin what we talked about this morning."

I pulled her in again, stroking her hair and inhaling that sweet scent that now felt like home. "It's just *us,* Isabel. No labels. Just *us.* I'm not going anywhere."

"Just us," she whispered back as she finally relaxed into me and sighed.

The End

508

ACKNOWLEDGEMENTS

Every book you write has a team of people who helped put it together, and every author has a support system they rely on for guidance, encouragement, and sometimes just for a drink or two.

I've said it once and I'll say it again; my brother Jesse is the man. He and my sister-in-law, Maye, support all of my crazy ideas, and I'm so lucky to have them in my life. A big huge thanks goes to my oldest and dearest friend, Janelle, who I've now been friends with for over twenty years. She takes care of me, and she takes care of my feline entourage when I travel for signings; I'd be lost without her friendship and help.

Writing and working from your cave full time can be isolating, and if it weren't for the friends around me, I might go stir crazy. Brandy Haas, Jaisha Burr, Gina Crocker, Donna Caruso, Stephanie Snock, all my crossfit friends, Pam Delaney and Justina Hopkins from ProBody Sports, thank you for checking on me and making sure I get off my chair every now and again.

The writing community has been inspirational to me, and I continue to find my tribe of people, the ones who understand what it feels like to have ideas buzzing in your head like bees. Carina Adams, you are amazing and always there for me when I need you.

Stevie Cole, you're my Panda #2, and I'll always float in a bamboo canoe with you, no matter what. Jess Epps, you're the sister I never had. I don't know how I survived not talking to you for an hour or more a day my whole life. You're Panda #3, and I love our little panda bowl. Jillian, working out story ideas with you is one of my favorite past times now. Thank you for being such an amazing friend. Judi, you're still my yoda; I love you tons and am so grateful for your friendship and your amazing eye for design. M. Robinson, thank you for your generosity and kindness to a newbie; you have no idea how much it means. Cassy Roop, LP Lovell, BT Urella, Heather Roberts & Mikey Lee, Cara Gadero, Patti Correa, Jillian Toth, and all the rest of my inner circle, thank you for the laughs, the advice, and the outlet in this crazy book world.

Thank you to my PA Tiffany Holcomb, for being a fast reader and making sure I'm writing when I should be. My betas, Jillian, Tiffany, Jess, Mary, Ninfa, Patti, and Murph, thank you for your honest feedback; it means a lot to have you help me along the way.

This cover was especially awesome, because my friend, David Hernandez, took that picture at a fire back in New Jersey and allowed me to use it. We took Fire Officer together a million years ago, and I can't thank you enough for the beautiful shot that captures the essence of this book perfectly.

Readers and bloggers, what can I say? You're amazing. You make me laugh, you make me cry, and you make me cry laughing. I love the enthusiasm, and I cannot wait to keep creating awesome book boyfriends for us to share and swoon over.

Lastly, thank you to everyone who protects and serves his or her community. It's a difficult job to protect others, and I honor you.

CONTROLLED burn

BESTSELLING AUTHOR
AMY BRIGGS

DEDICATION

For anyone who thinks you are alone; you are not.

JAX

I am safe. I feel this way because of my past experiences. I have survived before. I will survive this now. I recited this again and again trying to calm my racing heart. Every morning I had been telling myself these phrases, for the last few months at least. *Coping statements* is what my therapist from Veteran's Assistance, the VA called them. Yes, my therapist. In all my thirty-four years on earth, I never thought I'd say those words. I had a therapist. Because I was broken. I couldn't cope anymore on my own, and I didn't even know it until a routine visit, where I was instructed to see him after I had casually mentioned my sleeping problems and recurring nightmares during my physical. And the next thing I knew, I had a therapist.

I didn't want anyone to know; it was weird and embarrassing. But I honestly looked forward to most of our discussions once I had gotten used to the idea. The nightmares I'd been having were considered part of my Post Traumatic Stress Disorder, or PTSD diagnosis, which came from my time in the Marines and even potentially with the fire department, or so Dr. Rosen said. As I lay in my bed, staring at the ceiling fan spin around, trying to do some deep breathing he taught me to slow my heart rate down before I got up to start my day, I thought over my time in the Corps.

As I had explained to the good doctor, there hadn't been anything in particular that made me feel upset, sad, or anxious when I was in, or even when I got out for that matter. That's what made the new anxiety and nightmares particularly frustrating. I was becoming distracted and introverted, and I had no idea why it was happening so suddenly. It seemed like the whole thing started overnight.

I could hear some laughing coming from downstairs, which meant my roommate, Matt, and his girlfriend, Isabel, must be up and making breakfast. Matt had been renting from me for a couple of years. When I got out of the Marines, I bought my own house, which was entirely too much house for one person, but I got a spectacular deal on it, and with Matt paying me rent, it was an even better deal. Sometimes they stayed at Isabel's house, and sometimes they stayed here in my house, but they were planning to move in together any day now. She had a nice condo across town, but they weren't committed to moving there; and they were going into business together and buying some decrepit old gym and turning it into a professional MMA gym. Everyone needs a hobby, I guess. They seemed to think they could turn it into something big. I've always been all for supporting my friends in their adventures, so I was supposed to go with them to talk to a realtor later and visit this gym as an impartial third party.

As I rolled my eyes at the thought of going into business with someone I was banging, I swung my legs over the edge of the bed to sit up. The pounding in my head I felt almost every morning had started to subside as my heart rate slowed, and after an internal rally, I was ready to get up and face the happy couple to see what we had in store for the day. We had all been spending a lot of time together, and in all honesty, I thoroughly enjoyed their company. Matt was more or less my best friend; we were friends in high school and went through the fire academy together. When I came back from the Marines, he helped me get the job at the fire department in District 23, where we grew up. I had lived in Florida my whole life, and this area of the state is where I spent most of my time when I wasn't traveling for the Marines, of course.

I ran my hands through my hair and got up to join the world. Walking into the kitchen, I watched the two of them laughing and smiling while Isabel made coffee and Matt was cooking.

"Morning, kids, what's for breakfast?" I inquired.

"Hey, sunshine, welcome to the land of the living. Late night?" Matt joked with me.

"Nah, I stayed in last night. I wasn't feeling the party thing. Called it an early night in fact."

"No way, I didn't even realize you were home," Matt said. He wouldn't have, I was in my room, just trying to clear my head and trying to find some quiet.

"Would you like some coffee?" Isabel asked me.

"Why, yes, darlin', I would love some." I smiled in her direction. When we had first met Isabel, I wanted her for myself. I had called 'dibs' in fact, and then ended up distracted with some random chick and missed my opportunity. In retrospect, it was really neither here nor there, because I wasn't a settle down kind of guy, and if I was being totally honest, I liked them together. They weren't a couple that made you sick like a lot of others did. They were just cool people who ended up finding each other, and when we all hung out, they didn't have to be up each other's ass at all.

Isabel was a detective in the same district we worked, and she was great at her job. The three of us went shooting quite a bit; she always shot better that Matt and me, no matter whose weapon she was using. Our friendly competitions were something I always looked forward to, even if I was getting my ass handed to me by a girl. If it was going to be any girl, it may as well have been a badass detective. Nobody even knew that Matt and Isabel had a thing going on until after she almost had to shoot Matt's dad during a really rough case and, they kind of came out to everyone. It was pretty dramatic. Matt's dad had been an arsonist in town, and Isabel was assigned to the case, not knowing he was the guy doing it. Somehow they came out of that a couple that just didn't give a fuck about tradition. They were their own team, and I did admire and respect them for that.

Now for me, I never minded being single; in fact, it really was my preference to not be tied down. However, nobody likes to be the odd guy out with a bunch of couples, either. But Matt and Isabel never made anyone feel that way; they were like hanging out with two friends that just so happened to be in a relationship.

Isabel handed me a fresh cup of coffee, and as the aroma hit my nose, I smiled. This was my one vice really, coffee. I drank it all day, every day. I was pretty sure the caffeine didn't affect me at all anymore, but it was my little cup of sunshine all day long.

"Thanks, Detective," I winked at her.

"You want some bacon and eggs? I'm feeding all of us before we go meet with the realtor... What's her name again, babe?" Matt looked over to Isabel, forgetting the realtor's name.

"Vivian. Vivian Deveraux. She's the one with signs and billboards all over town, remember?"

"Why docs that sound familiar?" I asked.

Isabel turned to me again, leaning up against the counter by the coffee maker. "I don't know, but she's popular, and you've probably seen her face. She's a killer negotiator around here. She's super young, though, for someone with such a high-profile reputation. So I looked into her, and she seems on the up and up."

Laughing, I said, "Of course you looked into her. Always the investigator, eh?"

"Hey, it's a lot of fucking money, Jax. And it's one of my job's perks, being able to check people out. If she can get us the right price on this gym that's beneficial for everyone, then it's worth the investment. But I want to meet her in person and get a feel for her. Since she seems pretty young for all this, I want to be sure she's the right person to be handling our finances on this deal." Isabel crossed her arms and glanced over at Matt again. "It's a pretty big investment all the way around, ya know?"

"Oh yeah, I totally get it. You keep saying she's young. How old is she?" I asked.

"She's only twenty-five. But again, like I said, she's got a great reputation. And she's adorable, right up your alley," she joked and went back to making another cup of coffee for herself on the Keurig. She had the same love for coffee that I did, and when they stayed here, she always got up early and made some for both of us. Isabel was thoughtful, and I was glad she was with Matt. As I watched them interact in the kitchen, sipping on my coffee, I smiled. *This is my family. These are my people. My life is good.*

The nightmares and headaches will go away. They have to.

Vivian

As I listened to the sadness in my mother's voice, I reminded her that I had to work. "Mom, I know you worry. I'm fine, but I'm really busy today. I am meeting with some new clients on a really big deal. I'll call you in a few days, and I'll plan a trip as soon as I can, ok?"

My parents were living in New Jersey now, taking care of my grandmother, who was not doing well. They still had a house in Florida where I lived, but until there was improvement in my grandmother's health, or...well, they weren't coming back down anytime soon and wanted me to come up and visit them. My mother consistently forgot that I was an adult with a job.

"Your father and I miss you, Vivian. You could take time off. You're the boss of you now anyway, so can't you just come up here and spend some time with us? Your grandmother would like to see you too."

"Mom, I promise that I will work it out. Soon. But I really have to go. I don't want to be late for my appointment. It's a commercial sale, and it's a big deal. I love you. Please don't worry so much about me." I sighed. I knew that everyone's parents were pretty much the same, wanted us to spend more time with them and all that jazz, but ever since my older brother died last year, my mom had tried to tighten her hold on me, and I was kind of happy they were in New Jersey and I had finally some space.

"Ok, ok. Please call me in a couple days, dear. I know you think I worry too much, but you know why. Don't make your old mother fret too much." I could hear the concern in her voice. I didn't want to upset her, I tried not to hustle her off the phone, but I really did need to go.

"I promise, Mom. I really have to go now, though. I love you." I waited for her reply before hanging up.

"I love you too. Talk to you soon." She hung up. I always waited for her to hang up first for some reason; it made me feel like she'd decided to be okay for the moment. I didn't like to leave her feeling bad, but my brother died almost a year ago, and me not working to appease her wasn't going to bring him back.

I loved my parents so much, and I missed having them nearby. But they had decided to go back to New Jersey for who knows how long, and they had encouraged me to stay and run my business at the time. I'm one of the top realtors in central Florida, and at my age, only twenty-five, I had been ranked in the top ten under forty the last two years. My business was thriving, even in a market that was a little flighty. There was something about helping people find the right home to raise their family in, or the right place to run their new business out of that had always appealed to me, and I had a natural ability to make it work for them. And, of course, it worked for me.

Real estate was a lucrative business if you played your cards right and invested your money into your business and into more real estate. I got my license when I was twenty-one years old, and while most of my friends were juniors in college, drinking their way through their bachelor's degrees, I had already made my first $20,000 on a home sale for a nice couple that was friends with my parents. Everyone in that deal made out. I wasn't shady. I was just smart about people. It was in their eyes. The eyes tell you everything you need to know about a person. Whether they're desperate, they don't care at all, they're longing—you can tell when you talk to clients what they're really looking to gain out of a real estate transaction. Some people are looking for money, while others are hoping for a way out or a fresh start. My job was to give them the experience they were expecting and represent them to the best of my abilities. I was born for the job.

I once sold the house for a young girl who was looking to relocate. She had inherited the house when her mom had died. She had been living there most of her life and had taken care of her mom through multiple illnesses, racking up debt along the way, while her mom still held the title to the house and only owed a small amount on it. When her mother died, she really didn't know what to do. She was a successful professional, but after years of taking care of an old home and helping her ailing mother, she was ready to leave it behind and get a fresh start.

I could see the desperation in her face, knowing that this house was all she had left and it was hard for her to move on, but I could tell it was what she needed to do. After we made some minor renovations she taught herself how to do, I assured her I could sell that house to the right people.

As we began to organize some showings, I could see the stress leave her face. Her shoulders rose with confidence, and she began to gain her independence as she made progress and people started showing an interest. I knew how hard that had to be for her, but she made it work. One could still see the spot in the hall closet where her parents had marked her height as she grew up. It was endearing, and when she asked if she should paint over it, I told her no. I felt that if a potential buyer saw that, a young couple for instance, that it would help them envision doing the same with their young children. She ended up leaving the state and moving a thousand miles away to start over before we ever even sold the house.

In any event, the house sold to a sweet, young couple about two months later, after she had already started over, creating a new chapter for herself. It was so wonderful to be a part of that, to help facilitate that closure as well as being a part of her starting something new. It was beautiful, and that was the kind of thing that made this job awesome for me. That's the stuff right there that hits you in the feels, making it more than just a job to me.

My new clients were a detective and her firefighter boyfriend. Isabel Cruise, the detective, had contacted me after seeing my advertising around town. She was looking to purchase a building that was currently a fairly run-down gym. It was a private sale, meaning the building wasn't on the market or listed. The buyers had contacted me with the seller's permission to facilitate the sale of the property on behalf of both parties. It turned out the owner of the gym wasn't necessarily looking to sell actively until Isabel had talked to him about it. While the gym itself wasn't doing well, the location was prime real estate downtown and worth quite a bit of money. They wanted me to establish a fair sale price for everyone based on the value of the property and any renovations that needed to be done.

I was meeting the buyers at a local coffee shop to go over the transaction and expectations, and then we were going to go to the gym so that we could look over the property together and meet with the current owner. It still needed a new appraisal, which I could oversee with one of my contacts, and they would all need to agree to terms. Since the buyers and sellers had agreed to the private sale and they had both decided to work with me, the full commission was mine, which was pretty sizeable. It was the first time that's ever happened for me, and I was excited.

I checked myself out in the mirror. I was wearing my beige shift dress, beige heels, and a matching beige blazer. I always dressed conservatively; it was just my nature. It seemed kind of bland to some, but keeping my look toned down like that was more appealing to a wider audience. Marketing yourself was part of the job too. And in my profession, you just always wore some kind of a suit most of the time anyway. Being only five foot three inches, I almost always wore heels so I could at least be closer to looking people in the eye. I glanced at my watch and realized it was definitely time to go, I grabbed my keys and my huge Louis Vuitton purse then ran out the door thinking about how many purses I could afford after this sale went through.

JAX

As I looked around the coffee shop waiting for this real estate chick with Isabel and Matt, I thought about what I wanted for my future. As long as I could remember, I wanted to be a fireman, and then when the opportunity arose to serve my country, I was all about it. I loved being in the military; it gave me a sense of real purpose for a long time, and I love my country. After two long deployments, one to Afghanistan, and one to Iraq, I had enough of being overseas, had seen a lot of tragedy and wanted to come home and go back to the fire department. I thought that setting some roots down might make me happy.

It wasn't that the tragedy was more than I thought I could handle seeing when I was in the military, but I couldn't do anything about it. Fixing things isn't really what we did, even though we tried. I spent most of my time getting shot at or waiting around in the desert to get shot at. At least at the fire department, I was truly helping people. I was also a paramedic and occasionally rode the ambulance or helped people medically when needed in addition to fighting fires, performing rescues or whatever came our way. That job truly made me feel like I made a difference, like I had a purpose. Even if I had forgotten it sometimes lately, it was still there.

"Hey, you alright?" Isabel shook me from my thoughts.

"Me? Oh yeah. Just daydreaming."

"Anything good? It's certainly not the coffee here; it's not as good as ours." She laughed.

Smiling back in agreement, I noticed her as soon as she walked in. As she approached our table, I took note of her long, blond hair, which was almost sparkling in the sun through the coffee shop window, her perfect sunkissed skin, and as my eyes made their way down her petite frame, I also noticed the insanely high heels she was wearing. As she stopped at our table, I felt my cheeks get warm. She was stunning, just like her pictures that I immediately recalled seeing.

"Hi there, are you Matt?" she said to me. I was still taking in her beauty and didn't respond while she stared at me with her beautiful blue eyes; I was completely lost in them immediately.

Pulling me out of my second trance of the day, Matt stood up and introduced himself and Isabel. "Hi, I'm Matt Cavanaugh, and this is my girlfriend, Isabel Cruise." Then pointing over at me, he said, "This is our good friend, Jax, who does know how to speak. He works with me at the fire department," he looked at me like I was crazy, and with good reason. I had totally frozen up.

"Seth. My name is Seth Jackson. My friends call me Jax." I took her hand.

"Well, it's an absolute pleasure to meet you all." She had a nice, firm handshake like she meant business, but her tiny hand was so soft, I wanted to hold on to it for a moment longer. "Mind if I sit down?" she asked as she pulled up a chair.

"Of course not, please do," Isabel motioned. "We're very pleased to meet you. We've heard great things about the work you do, and you're certainly well represented in your advertising across town."

Letting out a slight laugh, she replied. "Yeah, I've always thought it was a strange practice for realtors to put their picture on everything, but hey, whatever works. If it ain't broke, don't fix it, I guess." She began pulling papers out of her giant purse. It looked expensive. This girl was fancy; way too fancy for someone like me. She sure was nice to look at, though, and spunky.

"Well, it helped us find you, so it definitely works," Matt said. "So, what do we have here?"

"First things first. Since both you and the seller have verbally agreed to a private sale, we will need to get all of that in writing. I've drawn up a standard contract that states that I will serve as both the buyer and seller's agent. If you all agree to that, then we move forward with getting a fresh appraisal of the property. Before we do that, I'd like to go over to the property with you and take a look, which will give us a chance to document any issues with the building we'd like addressed before the sale, or that you would be willing to take cash back or a lower sale price for. I have looked into the property of course, but it's always much better to look around ourselves and take notes on things. So, can you tell me a little more about your plans for the gym? I know we talked briefly over the phone about it, but I'd like to hear more about your thoughts and plans."

"Okay, well we are looking at this as a long term investment property," Isabel began. "Our goal is to refurbish some of the gym, but keep it's current vibe, which is kind of no frills; it's a place to work out, not a place to get your wheatgrass and chill all afternoon."

Vivian laughed, the cutest laugh I've ever heard. "I totally understand. When we go over there, I'll make notes of some things for us to discuss with the seller and all that jazz. Understanding your short and long term goals with the property just helps me get a better overall picture of what your needs are," she said.

I watched her talk, staring at her perfectly pink-glossed lips, when my thoughts turned to where I'd like her to put those lips on my body; I simply couldn't help myself. I was mesmerized not only by her obvious beauty, but also by how smart she was. I listened to her talk about property value and taxes and some other things I don't care about, and all I could do was watch her. That conservative little dress she had on left so much to the imagination that it had me thinking about what was under there. Did she wear matching panties and bra? I bet she did. She was perfectly matched from head to toe like a little Barbie doll, which was giving me all kinds of dirty thoughts.

As I quietly listened and observed, Matt and Isabel quizzed her on a multitude of things related to the gym, and then the young realtor stood up and started shoving the papers back in her purse.

"Okay, so let's go over to the gym to talk to Murphy and let me get an in-depth tour of the place. Sound good?" Matt and Isabel stood up as well, so I followed suit. I hadn't even noticed it was time to go; I had been too busy staring and daydreaming.

"That's great. See you in a few minutes," Isabel said.

As Vivian walked away, Matt smacked me in the arm. "What is with you, dude?" he hissed at me.

"What? What did I do? I didn't say a word."

"No, you didn't, but you eye fucked her the entire time. Don't be a creepy douchebag, man. She's our realtor, for Christ's sake."

He rolled his eyes at me.

Isabel on the other hand started to laugh. "I actually don't think she even noticed. She is ridiculously pretty in person though. Can you blame him?" she asked Matt.

"Oh, I'm not walking into that trap, Detective. Nice try. She's a realtor and that's all I noticed, so there," he said firmly, causing Isabel to laugh even more.

"All right, all right, let's get out of here. I'm totally interested in seeing this gym for myself now too," I said.

"Our realtor is a no-fly zone, Jax." Matt looked at me sternly.

"What? That's ridiculous." I hadn't given any legitimate thought to trying to get with her until he said that; now it was stirring up some more desire. The forbidden fruit will get you every time.

"No, I'm serious. Until this deal is done, you keep your hands to yourself. She needs to focus on the deal before you distract her and break her heart."

"Dude, I'm no heartbreaker. Come on now. I'll heed your wishes, though, because I love you so much, Matty," I started to sing to him like a song and tried to hug on him.

"Ugh, you're ridiculous. Get away from me." He started to laugh, shoving me away.

"Good lord, boys, let's go. I'd like to move this paperwork along, because once we get this situated, we need to decide what our long term living situation is; we live like hobos right now," Isabel settled us down. Her comment made me wonder what she meant by 'long term living situation', though. I had just assumed they would move into her condo together at some point, although they still spent quite a lot of time at my house with me.

The thoughts of being completely alone began to creep over me, almost like a chill in the air. I had known deep down they would end up having their own place, but the reality hadn't hit me until that moment for some reason.

It looked like soon, I'd be all alone more often than not. Alone with my thoughts. I was unsettled by the notion, but tucked it away as we piled into Isabel's classic Camaro to head to the gym.

Vivian

As I headed to my car to get over to the gym before the buyers did, I could feel their friend Seth's stare burning into my back. From the moment I had walked in, he'd stared at me with those hazel eyes, and while it didn't make me uncomfortable necessarily, it did catch me off-guard. He was so handsome and also so quiet. Normally, guys like that talk and talk to get your attention, yet he just sat and observed, listening the entire time. When he shook my hand, his giant hand engulfed mine, and something about his touch made me linger for a moment.

While I was sure he was a perfectly nice guy, I was on business. The trip to the gym was short, and when I pulled up, I grabbed my notebook out of my purse to make some notes on the exterior of the property. The first thing I noticed was that the roof needed to be inspected; I could see some loose shingles, which here in Florida was definitely a problem.

It was getting hot out, so I took my jacket off and tossed it back in the car. That was the only thing about working in Florida; trying to look conservative and professional could be difficult without sweating like a dog. By mid-day, there was no way you could keep wearing a suit jacket and not be on the verge of passing out; and I was always warm anyway. I stood there fanning myself for a moment with my notebook while I waited for them to arrive.

As a rumbling hot rod rounding the corner caught my attention, I realized that it was them as they pulled into the parking lot next to me. I found it amusing that Isabel was driving the two guys around in her car. Something about it made me smile, perhaps because she was such a tiny little thing herself, while her boyfriend and his friend were so tall and muscular. As I watched them get out of the car, I caught a glimpse of Seth Jackson's beautiful stature. He had been covered up in a long sleeve shirt when we'd met at the coffee shop, but now his body was on display and perfectly framed by a dark gray t-shirt. I could see that both of his muscular arms were completely covered in tattoos down to his wrists. It was incredibly sexy and instantaneously caused me to suck in a breath in surprise when I saw them.

As they approached, I held the door open for Isabel to walk in ahead of me, when Jax jogged over behind me to take hold of the door. "Ladies first, Miss Deveraux." He smiled, waving me to go ahead of him.

"Thank you very much." I blushed and returned his smile. I could sense his eyes on me as I walked in, even through his sunglasses. I felt an intense attraction to him. He looked like a bodyguard or a rock star, which was a complete turn-on. Something about the way he looked at me made me want to get him to talk more. So far, he had only spoken two sentences to me, and I was intrigued, mostly by his appearance; but whatever, I'm only human.

The pungent smell of sweat and mold in the gym hit me immediately, and as I took a step back in surprise, I bumped right against his rock hard frame. Of course I didn't realize how close behind me he was, and he grabbed me to keep me from falling backwards saying, "You alright there, darlin'?"

Looking up at him over my shoulder, I replied, "Yes, yes, of course. I'm so sorry about that, Seth." I could smell his fresh, masculine cologne, and realized that I hadn't righted myself yet. His hand fell lower, resting on my hip, turning me to Jell-O on the spot.

He flashed that million-dollar smile at me again, still resting his hand on my hip. "You can call me Jax, darlin'." I'd have called him anything he wanted if he was going to keep calling me darlin'. I've never been such a clumsy nerd before in all my life, but this man was a specimen, causing me to lose my poise entirely.

Finally righting myself and surrendering the moment, I said, "Ok, Seth, thank you." Then turning to everyone, "Let's find Murphy and have him show us around, and we'll make a list of potential improvements, etcetera, and go from there?"

"Sounds great. Obviously, we've been here a few times, and Isabel works out here almost every day." Matt put his arm around Isabel, who looked a bit apprehensive about the whole situation.

"Isabel, why don't you show me around, and Matt, why don't you and...Seth find Murphy for us, so we can all walk and talk?"

"Will do," Matt replied, and Seth followed in tow.

"So, Isabel, why don't you tell me more about your plans for this building and this location, so I can get a better understanding of your needs, your budget, and your strategy for this project?" I felt that having a chat with Isabel alone for a moment would give me more perspective than in the larger group, as it seemed this was more her dream than anyone else's.

"Well, I've been working out here for as long as I can

remember, really. I like the no-frills approach, but obviously it could use some work. I'm looking for an investment that I can give a shit about, that brings me some satisfaction in between working cases, of course. Retirement as a detective will probably not pay that great with the way things are going, and I'm looking for a business proposition with long term potential that I can stand behind and be involved in." She looked off in thought for a moment before she continued, "I want to turn this into a legitimate training center for fighters."

"Wow, really?" I certainly loved an ambitious woman and wanted her to have her dream, but this gym was in kind of crappy shape.

"Ok, so let's talk budget, realistically. Are you looking to renovate and pay someone for those renovations? I can see some things that are out of code that Murphy will have to pay for in order to transfer the title to you, so you don't have to worry about those as long as he can foot that bill, but there are other things here, obviously." I looked around at the shabby equipment, the boxing ring that looked like it needed to be replaced among fresh paint and some other things, then looked back to her.

"Here's what I want. I want Murphy to pay for the things it needs to get up to code, and then Matt and I are going to take care of the rest. We're planning on doing much of the renovations ourselves. The way his shift works he often has several days in a row off, and I'm home most nights and weekends lately, so we are going to work on it. It's our baby. We're planning to put professional fighters through here at some point, and between us we have enough money to cover a reasonable down payment, and our salaries will afford the rest. It's important to us. I know it doesn't look like much now, but I have a vision." She gave me a sweet smile, and I understood. This was going to be her project and their legacy.

"Ok, well, I see the boys coming this way, so why don't we find a place we can sit down and I can get the information I need to draw up the paperwork. Sound good?" I asked.

"Sounds great. I'm really excited about this, and I'm glad we found you, Viv—can I call you Viv? You look like a Viv to me." She winked.

"You sure can."

Murphy came over and introduced himself, "You must be Miss Deveraux?" He reached out his hand to me.

"Yes, sir, I sure am. It's a pleasure to meet you in person." I returned his handshake and smiled. He was older and looked like he spent most of his time in that gym, trying to keep it going.

"Is there a place we can all sit down and talk about the property, the codes, and things like that so I can draw up the paperwork?" I asked.

"There sure is. Follow me. I have a small conference room in the back set up. We can all sit and talk there without any interruptions. Does anyone want coffee?" he asked.

"Yes!" Both Jax and Isabel said in unison, while Matt shook his head no.

"Isabel, you know where it is. Why don't you get some java for you and Captain America over here, and meet the rest of us back in the conference room?" He pointed at Jax when he said Captain America, which caused me to giggle out loud.

"Captain America? Well, I've been called worse," he said with a slight southern drawl and a chuckle.

We made our way back to the conference room, where we settled around the long rectangular table. Jax sat across from me, watching the conversation take place after he'd gotten his cup of coffee, which seemed to make him extremely happy. As I started talking to the actual parties involved in the sale, I couldn't help but glance at him out of the corner of my eye, which he caught me doing at least twice, to my total embarrassment.

After about two hours of talking about the must-do repairs, who was responsible for what, and a timeframe for closing the deal, which would be about a month in my estimation, everyone seemed pleased, and I packed up my things to go. I wanted to go back to my office and start getting the paperwork together, as well as call the appraiser to see if we could get an appointment. I was disappointed that Seth Jackson didn't speak much, but he did smile at me every time I caught his glance.

We all left the gym at the same time, and as we said our good-byes in the parking lot and I secretly longed to hear Seth talk again, he extended his hand to me. "It was a pleasure meeting you, Vivian Deveraux. Until next time." Then that sexy thing winked at me. He *winked* at me. *Why is that so hot?* Swoonworthy. One hundred percent.

Feeling my mouth drop open, I replied, "Nice to meet you too... Seth." I collected myself and finished my good-byes to Matt and Isabel before I got in my car to crank the air conditioning on myself.

Whether it was him or the gym with its terrible ventilation system, I was overheating and needed to regain my composure. The rumors were true. Firefighters are hot, and that one was gonna be on my mind. I hoped I'd see him again, although I couldn't imagine why or how that would happen.

JAX

That woman was too adorable for words. When she about got knocked over from the musty smell of that old gym and backed into me, I caught a whiff of her scent, and goddamn if she didn't smell like a fresh fucking field of flowers blooming. I might have held on to her to "steady her" longer than I had to, but whatever, I'm still a guy who loves a beautiful woman. She was like a little bouncing sunshine.

I actually loved that she called me by my name, not my nickname. Hearing her say Seth made me wonder what it would be like to have her whisper it to me. Buttoned up all tight and conservative; she was sexy as hell. She's not the kind of girl who hung out with guys like me, so I'd probably never see her again, except for her billboards, of course. Thinking of her billboards all over town, I let out a little chuckle in the back seat of Isabel's car.

"What's so funny, lover boy?" Isabel turned around from the passenger seat of her own car to give me a look over her sunglasses. She wore aviators, just like every cop, which I always found pretty funny too.

"Lover boy? Who? Me? Nothing's funny at all, Detective." I grinned at her. "Except maybe your typical cop glasses."

"Ahhhh, go fuck yourself, Jax." She started laughing. "You were laughing before that. So what's funny, smartass? You liked my underage realtor, didn't you?"

"She was very cute and is a very professional little thing. And she's not underage. She's twenty-five, you said so yourself." I started thinking about her sexy little body and those pouty pink lips of hers causing a little twitch in my dick.

"Oh God. Seriously, Jax? You're almost thirty-four. That makes her a little young for you, don't you think?" Matt chimed in.

"Oh, you got a girlfriend now, and suddenly you're the dating and sex police? I didn't say more than two words to her, so everybody calm the fuck down." I was getting defensive at that point. I was a perfect gentleman, so everyone needed to settle themselves. I didn't date anyway. I occasionally brought a girl home for some fun, but that was about it, and it was my preference not to bring them home. In fact, I hadn't been bringing anyone to my home in quite a while. If I did hook up with a girl, it was either super classy and somewhere sly in public, or I went to her house.

"Sorry, man, sorry. You're right. And you can bang anyone you want," Matt replied.

Suddenly, I was feeling a little put off and territorial about the bang comment about that beautiful woman; she was worth more than a bang for sure. "I'm not banging anyone at the moment, so let's all just move on. Are you feeding me now after making me come with you? Why *did* you make me come with you?" I asked with some serious attitude. I don't think they ever told me why they wanted me to accompany them; they simply insisted.

"Yes, we are feeding you. Since we all have the day off, is anyone opposed to lunch cocktails too?" Isabel asked. "I could certainly use one myself."

"I'm in," both Matt and I replied in unison.

"Thank God," Matt added.

Shortly thereafter, my question about why they asked me to join them still unanswered, we pulled into one of our favorite local watering holes that had a nice patio, decent food, and of course, alcohol.

To no one's surprise, I flirted shamelessly with the waitress, all the while thinking of Vivian. Even her name was stuffy. But I liked it. She was classy. I wondered what she did to loosen up. I wondered what her bedroom looked like. I envisioned pink everything and stuffed animals on the bed. Probably won at local fairs from her high school boyfriend. She wasn't wearing any rings at all, so she wasn't married. She probably had some conservative douche boyfriend who wore polo shirts and khakis with flip-flops.

As we sipped our drinks on the patio, we talked about this business venture they were getting into. I was curious what would make them want to invest all that money in a gym, but also why they were going into business together. Yea, they were a couple and all, but it wasn't like they had been together for years and years; so I was intrigued at their thought process on this, and I figured I'd ask.

"So, let me ask you guys. Why a gym? And why together?"

"What do you mean?" Isabel asked.

"Well, I get that you're looking for an investment or something, but that gym needs some serious work. And I've heard you mention that you want to turn out professional fighters. What's that about?" I asked.

"Why not?" Isabel replied. "I love mixed martial arts, and I think that running a real bonafide training facility would be not only a great investment, but also a fantastic was to stay involved in the community through our eventual retirements."

"Ok, I can see that. Why together? Don't get me wrong, I love you two, I do. But I'm curious what would make you go into business together and tie all that money up together." I didn't want to offend them. I was honestly curious at the thought process behind it and they hadn't been together for years or anything, so it seemed risky.

A thoughtful smile immediately spread across Matt's face before he replied. "I'll be honest with you, bro. I figured, why the hell not? At the end of the day it's just money, but it seems like a really fun proposition to get into with my girl. Sharing a business, which is really more of a passion, is something we talked about doing. Neither of us wants kids, so they gym is going to be our baby."

Shocked that he didn't want kids and had decided at thirty-four that he wasn't going to, I had to probe more. "Why no kids? I pegged you for a white picket fence at some point kinda guy." I glanced in Isabel's direction to gauge her take on this conversation.

Noticing my line of questioning was directed at her as well, she chimed in. "I can't have kids, Jax. So it's not on the table for us. And with our dangerous lifestyles, and our passion for it, this was the next step for *us*.. We were looking for something that would be fun to do together, that would grow with us."

I certainly wasn't expecting that answer, and I watched as Matt reached under the table to take her hand in comfort. "Shit, Isabel, I'm sorry. I didn't mean anything by it, I swear."

"I'm not upset, Jax. Nothing happened to me. I found out

when I was a teenager I couldn't have kids. It's a weird genetic thing, and my body just wouldn't carry a baby. I never got attached to the idea of having kids. Besides, we're hoping that Brian and Jo have a shitload of them we can spoil and play with then send back."

Brian was the fire department chief and also Matt's brother, and his fiancée, Jo, worked with us as well. They were definitely the couple that would be having a basketball team worth of kids, and they were another couple we all loved being around. They'd both had a crush on each other since we were kids, but neither one of them did anything about it until we were all into our thirties; and even then, they struggled making it work together for quite a while.

Now, if I were to describe what I thought true love was, it would be them. Most people didn't see it, but I'm an observer. We all work together, and I've seen them steal glances and little smiles at each other. I've watched his hand linger on hers when they were passing something to each other, like a tool or a paper. They went out of their way to be professional at work and not act like a couple, and I don't think most people would notice the things I'd seen. It was the stuff that turned cold hearts like mine a little bit softer every now and again.

Isabel and Matt laughed, causing me to smile and relax about my comment. I was afraid I'd hurt her feelings or struck a nerve in some way. The truth of the matter was that they had really become my best friends, and if it weren't for them, there were a lot of days lately I might not have gotten out of my bed at all. They didn't know what I was going through, but their friendship kept me going some days.

"Well, I'm still sorry. That was a dick thing for me to say. Honestly, I was just talking out of my ass. I'm excited for your little gym project, and I'll be there helping you do whatever you need. And as for Brian and Jo, you think they'll start having the rugrats soon?"

"I think they'll start right away after the wedding. Brian could barely wait to get engaged, so I think he's all about procreating the next generation of firefighters." Matt chuckled. "After everything they've been through, I think that Brian wants Jo to stop working at the department too. That should be fun to watch." We all knew that Jo would never quit working, especially not at the firehouse, it was all she ever knew. Her dad had been the chief before Brian, and when he died, Brian took over. She'd definitely haul her pregnant self around the station until it was go-time when that day came.

"How are the wedding plans coming? Does anyone know?" Isabel asked.

"All I know is that her and my mom are constantly on the phone talking about it, and all the liquor in Florida is probably not going to be enough of a supply for this shindig. Should probably call in a mutual aid cover for the station, because we'll all be hammered and out of service." Matt took a swig of his beer and sat back, looking relaxed.

Turning his attention back to me, he raised an eyebrow. "So, Jax, the Chief's test is coming up. Are you going to take it?"

I felt the look of surprise wash over my face, causing me to hesitate. "Well, I hadn't given it much thought. I was going to take the test, but I just assumed you were taking that job. Why do you ask?"

Matt took a deep breath, leaned forward and smiled again. "Nope."

"Nope? What do you mean, nope?"

"I mean I don't want it. I don't want to be Deputy Chief. I don't want to be Chief."

I looked over at Isabel, who had a huge smirk on her face, like the Cheshire Cat. Turning back to Matt, I asked, "I thought that was your dream, dude. You know, your legacy or whatever."

"It's not. It's Brian's. I'm my own man, and I'm making my own path. My legacy is this gym, with Isabel. So, you know what that means, right?"

"No, what?" I was afraid he was going to say exactly what he said. The fear of failure and weakness, of not being good enough, started to simmer in my stomach.

"You're going to be the next Deputy Chief."

I can't handle it. I can't do it. I am not good enough for that job. I cannot be responsible for others in that capacity. Every negative thought I had about myself rose to the surface like a diver coming up for air.

Vivian

After I finished all of the preliminary paperwork for the sale and set up the new appraisal and some inspections, I decided to reward myself with some retail therapy, so I called my best friend to meet me out. Jessica used to be my roommate, however when I got successful, I got my own place, because I could afford it; but we still hung out all the time. She had agreed to meet me at the mall before we were going to have dinner and drinks together.

"So, tell me about the sale today. I hear that the firefighters in this town are smoking hot. My neighbor had to call them, because her oven had caught fire like six months ago, and she said she would have burned the place to the ground if she had known they were so good-looking," Jess took a sip of her wine.

Reminiscing of the afternoon I spent with them, well, of Seth really, I gave her a nod and a smile. "Jess, I can't even begin to describe the hotness. And, by the way, two of the clients are a firefighter and his badass detective girlfriend. Seriously, they were like Superman and Superwoman or something. And they brought an even hotter friend along with them. His name was Seth... Jax." I felt warmth spread over me, radiating in my core thinking about how hot he was.

"What the hell kind of a name is Seth... Jax?" she asked,

raising an eyebrow.

"Oh, his name is Seth. Seth Jackson. But his friends call him Jax. He told me I could call him Jax, but I like Seth. I'm not even kidding you; I practically drooled. It was all I could do to maintain my professionalism when I wanted to climb him like a tree. The owner of the gym called him Captain America, and seriously, he was. Million-dollar-toothpaste-commercial smile and everything."

Choking on her wine in surprise and laughing hysterically, she stared at me. "You? You wanted to climb a man like a tree? He must be one hell of a specimen for that not so conservative little statement. Oh. My. God. Viv! Did you talk to him? Did you flirt? Give me details? Where can we find him?" she demanded in rapid fire.

Feeling myself blush at my own candor, I told her what little I knew about him and how I had nearly fallen back into him at the gym. "He's like six foot four, has dark blond hair and hazel eyes. He looks like Thor from the movie, not even kidding you. He literally barely spoke to me. I think he may have said exactly ten words to me. He was beautiful, though," I sighed.

"Oh my God, Viv, you're smitten. I've never seen such a thing. I love it. Over a rugged working man in a uniform too. So, so hot. So, are you going to see him again?" She was almost too enthusiastic.

"I don't think so. I mean, I can't imagine why I would unless he comes with them to inspections or to closing. I don't really have any other reason to see him." Disappointment settled in, replacing the little fire that had ignited for him.

"Well, I think we should try to find a way for your paths to cross again," Jess stated matter-of-factly.

"What on earth for? He wasn't even into me."

"I sincerely doubt that. Everyone is into you. You're adorable. You're tiny and blond and spunky, and you ooze an undercover sex appeal. You just haven't let it loose since—" She cut herself off and looked down at my fidgeting hands. I knew why. "I'm sorry Viv, I—"

"No, no, it's ok. You're right." I glanced back up at her, letting out the breath I hadn't realized I'd been holding. She was referring to my brother's suicide.

After my brother killed himself, I closed myself off from a lot of things; everything except my job and my parents, and of course my friendship with Jess. I needed her. She gave me time to grieve and was unconditionally supportive on good days and bad.

The worst part for me was that I still couldn't believe that Michael had been suffering in silence for so long, and that none of us knew. I was devastated. He never asked for help. He was in so much pain that taking his own life was the choice he made to stop his suffering. I can't even begin to imagine how horrible that must have felt, and my heart ached every day for him. I can say with certainty that the guilt of not being able to have helped, not being able to intervene, not showing that I was there for him, will haunt me until the end of days. A black cloud would always surround me.

As I tried to shake off that horrible darkness I learned to tuck away in the last year, I changed the subject to get us back to having fun, talking about men and fun.

"So what are your plans for the weekend?" I asked her.

"I have a date; a second date in fact." She was beaming. She must have really liked this one. Jess was more of a love-them-and-leave-them kind of girl. She wasn't going to settle for less than the perfect guy, and she felt like there was no point in a second date unless they had something to offer that might lead to more.

"Holy crap, seriously? I cannot believe it! Who is this unicorn?" I teased her.

"His name is Jeremy, and he is a veterinarian. I took Hector to the vet for a checkup last week, and I swear to God, I almost hoped he was sick so I could come back again. My vet retired, which I didn't know, and Dr. Jeremy Shaw took over his practice."

"That's awesome. I presume Hector is okay?" Hector was the friendliest cat on earth. It didn't matter who you were, if you went to Jess' apartment, this guy would snuggle with you. He knew when you were sad too, and would spend extra snuggle time with you, which I certainly took advantage of on more than one occasion myself.

"Oh yeah, he's great. Still a snuggle monster." She giggled.

"So, anyway, I know you don't ask guys out. So did he ask you out while he was giving Hector a checkup?" I thought that would be pretty ballsy for the new vet to do, but what do I know?

"Oh, no. I ran into him at the grocery store that night. We got to chatting in the parking lot, and before I knew it, my ice cream had melted because, ya know, it's Florida, and anyway, he asked me out to dinner and to ice cream to make up for mine that melted." She was blushing full on now. It was adorable. I loved this chick like my own sister. I couldn't believe she met him at the grocery store too; they always say it's a great place to meet men. In my experience that hasn't been true, but I hadn't been looking in a long time, either.

"Jessica May! That is so awesome. I'm so excited for you!" I held up my wine glass to toast her.

As she raised hers to toast me back, she of course had to throw in, "Now we need to find you someone, Viv. Seriously, it's time to get back on the horse. You've been single for like two years. Let's at least get you back in the game?"

"I'm not opposed to being in the game. Sheesh. When someone interesting and worthwhile crosses my path, we'll see. In the meantime, let's just celebrate you." As my thoughts turned back to Seth, I wondered what he was doing. He seemed a little too charming to be spending much time alone, that's for sure. I knew I needed to shake off that encounter and maybe start thinking about dating again, and moving on with my life or at least getting more of a social life of some kind.

JAX

"Seth, let's talk about your personal life today." Dr. Rosen started right out of the gate with the big dog, clicking his pen and leaning forward to gauge my reaction.

"What would you like to know, Doc?" I smirked, looking directly into his steely eyes.

"Well, Seth, I'd like to talk about your romantic life. I think it's important that we spend some time talking about your relationship with women, and where you're taking your life as you move forward. " Leaning back and crossing a leg over, Dr. Rosen patiently waited for me to speak. As I examined the lines that had formed around his eyes over time, I wondered what he wanted to hear me say. I didn't do relationships, so I wasn't really sure how to even address his question.

"Doc, I'm not sure I know what you mean. Are you asking me if I'm dating anyone? Because if that's your question, the answer is no. I don't date, really. Why does that matter anyway?" I could feel my heart rate pick up and shifted in my chair; something about this line of questioning was making me uncomfortable.

"Ok, I'll just cut to the chase then. Our goals here, in talking with one another over time, are to help you establish a degree of normalcy in your life where you are comfortable moving forward. And what normalcy means is doing average, normal things, like dating." As I scowled at him, his head tilted slightly, watching my reaction. "Yes, Seth. I'm suggesting that you date."

"I get plenty of action with the ladies." I grinned, trying to turn the subject.

"You're avoiding the topic, and now I'd like to know why. What about dating scares you, Seth? We have already talked about the relationship you have with your mother, and you seem to have a very healthy relationship outside of the geographic distance, and your parents have a loving relationship from what you've said. So, tell me what you're scared of." The doctor's tone turned sterner, which it only did when he knew I was avoiding his line of questioning.

"I'm not afraid to date necessarily, but I don't know if I'm..." I hesitated. "I don't know if I could..." I trailed off, not wanting to say the rest out loud.

"You're not sure if you're good enough? Is that what you're trying to say, Seth? Say what's on your mind. That's what you're here for." I sucked in air, knowing he would make me admit it. I didn't believe I had anything to offer a woman outside of a short-term good time. "Seth, I want you to talk to me now."

Hanging my head, I rubbed my hands through my hair. "You're going to make me say it, aren't you?"

"Yes."

"Fine. I can't exactly imagine a normal life for myself, not in the way you're describing. I don't even know what normal is. But I can tell you this, Doc; I know that if I can't shake the darkness, how on earth could I be with a woman for more than one night or for anything other than a good time? How would that be fair? No one deserves to deal with that baggage. No one. I am a lot of things, Doc, but I'm not a shitty guy, and the women I'm with now, they don't expect anything from me. I'm honest with them. They get what they see, which is a good time, and that's it. I couldn't put anything more on anyone; they don't deserve it. I just can't bring that darkness into someone else's life." I felt like a deflated balloon, letting all of that out into the room. The reality of what I admitted floated around, sinking in, even to me.

Dr. Rosen leaned forward again, resting his elbows on his knees and taking in a deep sigh. "Normal is relative. What I'm saying is that I think it's time for you to start branching out and not being so closed off. Particularly in your romantic relationships. I think that you'll see in time that there is much to be gained from romantic love. Seth, the darkness you think you have inside you is temporary. I know it doesn't feel like it now, but taking steps toward a normal life, with your career, your friendships, your love life, all makes a difference. Bringing you closer to peace; real peace and real joy. You deserve to feel joy, Seth, and once you realize that, it's going to alleviate the anxiety you're feeling."

As the words he spoke sunk in, I shifted in my chair again. I have always avoided commitment and real dating. I think the last real date I went on was to the prom, and I wasn't even sure that even counted since it was a group thing and we all went together.

"What are you thinking, Seth. You look thoughtful right now," Dr. Rosen interrupted my thoughts. I debated what to tell him.

"Doc, I'm not opposed to giving it a try, but I don't know what I'm doing. I've never dated, really. I kind of just... well I kind of just bring girls home and then don't usually call them back." I hung my head. Admitting that out loud made me feel like a douchebag, and I honestly didn't want to be that guy. Saying it out loud made it pretty real.

"Look, I get it. You're a playboy. But, I would bet you that one of these girls is probably a nice girl whom you'd enjoy getting to know if you gave getting to know her some effort." He smiled at me, giving me a reassuring look.

"Ok, so let's say there was a girl. What would I do?" I felt like a teenager again, having no clue what I was doing.

"You talk, Seth. You get to know each other. You spend time doing things not work related. You go to dinner or something, whatever seems natural," He paused. "Let's make a deal, though, to keep you on track."

"What kind of a deal?" Apprehension set in, and from the look on the doc's face, he thought it was funny.

Letting out a slight laugh, he said, "No sex."

"What?" My mouth dropped open.

"No sex. Not right away. The purpose of this exercise is for you to eventually find a special woman, but right now, it's about opening yourself up to the possibility. Sex clouds judgment, and I'd like you to spend some time emotionally invested."

"For how long?" I knew I sounded a bit like a dick, but no sex? That sounded virtually impossible.

"Until it means something." Seeing my shock hadn't dissipated, he continued, "I'm not a gambling man, but if I were, I'd bet this won't be as hard as you think it will be once you get used to the idea that a real connection is possible and you find a woman worthwhile of the exercise. A connection besides the one you have with your Marine buddies and your colleagues at the fire

553

department."

"Well, I'll have to take your word for it for now, Doc," was all I said.

"Our time is up, Seth. Let's talk again next week."

I stood up to leave when the doc stopped me. "Seth, trust me."

"I do. I promise I'll do what you say. I'm not sure how." I let out a sigh and then chuckled. "But I will."

"Atta boy. See you next week." He patted me on the shoulder on my way out.

When I got to my truck and stuck the key in the ignition, I racked my brain about whom I could really see myself going on a real date with, the way that Dr. Rosen described. The women I typically found myself with intimately involved weren't exactly great conversationalists. Or maybe they were; I truly had no idea, but I didn't want to go backwards. It needed to be someone new; a fresh start. As I was driving home, it came to me. Vivian. Vivian Deveraux, the stunning little conservative real estate agent. She was the girl I'd date.

Vivian

Almost every morning I went for a run, I felt like it cleared my head and gave me quiet to think at the same time. On my runs I'd think about Michael a lot. We had been quite close, or so I had thought. The way he died burned inside me, making me question almost every conversation we'd ever had; and it made me question relationships in general. If I had thought we were so close, when he didn't think he could come to me for help, had we really been that close? I questioned how close we were if I wasn't able to see what was going on with him. I didn't know what to think about it anymore.

I was starting to miss my parents more, though, and I made a mental note to call my mom and to look at some flights up to NJ. I wanted to visit before it got too cold up there and I'd be miserable the entire time. Once you've spent some serious time in the south, going north, particularly when it's fall or winter, the cold can be unbearable for some people. I was definitely one of those people. I hated being cold more than anything.

I started to head back to my house when the burn in my legs began to slow my pace. I was completely soaked in sweat, even though it was still very early in the morning, it was already warm, and I'd had a hard run. I typically did about five or so miles on these runs. I wasn't a fitness nut by any stretch; in fact, I was already salivating at the thought of the glazed donut I was going to eat for breakfast. I had a serious sugar addiction and not a care in the world about it. It was worth every mile to eat that sugar.

After taking a shower and picking out another conventional suit from my extensive collection, I grabbed my things and headed to check out some new properties that had come on the market. I had a growing list of clients, and the market was picking up. There were lots of homes for all types of people popping up in town, and it was an exciting adventure for me both financially and personally.

At the time, I was looking for a starter home for a young couple that didn't want to live in an apartment or condo anymore. They wanted a house with a yard, but their budget was small, so I was on the hunt for them. I drove around and checked on a few of the properties I saw in my database, then headed back to my home office to email them some times that we could go look. I did a bit of other work, and checked my messages.

When I looked at my email, one caught my eye, and jaw dropped. The subject line "Looking for Some Real Estate Help & Dinner" initially caught my attention, but what floored me was who it was from. Seth Jackson, the tall drink of water from the other day. I stared at the email for way longer than necessary before I opened it, and I couldn't help but feel a little flushed and excited.

I clicked on it and read,

Dear Miss Deveraux,

It was a pleasure to meet you the other day when you helped my friends begin the process of purchasing their new gym. I got your contact information from a passing bus yesterday; I see your face daily, it seems… I am currently considering relocating and potentially selling my house, and wondered if you would be inclined to have dinner with me and discuss the process and what my options might be.

Sincerely,

Seth Jackson (Jax)

I probably read that email ten times before calling Jess immediately after I believed it was real.

"Uh, have you called him yet? Because this is exactly what we were discussing!" she exclaimed.

"No! I called you, Jess. This isn't an invitation to date. This is an invitation to a business dinner. Right? I mean, come on." I couldn't decide which it was, but I was excited to see him either way, and I hadn't even responded yet.

"Viv, this is totally a ploy to get you out. One hundred percent. That guy digs you, and this was his way of reaching out to see you again. Oooooh, I'm so excited! Email him back with your phone number and make some damn plans and let me know. I have to get back to work, but text me immediately when you hear from him." She paused for a moment while I was still silent. "Viv, this is awesome. It's time to enjoy yourself a little. See if he wants to sell his house or whatever, but have yourself some fun. You deserve it."

"Thanks, Jess. I'll text you later." I hung up the phone and put my face in my hand. I was giggling out loud by myself. I was excited to talk to him; he was so intriguing when we met, and I was so nervous that I had butterflies.

I didn't want to seem too eager, but if it was truly business, I didn't want him to wait, either, so I replied.

Dear Mr. Jackson,

Thank you so much for getting in touch. I'd absolutely love to sit and chat about the market and your plans for your home.

If you'd like to discuss over dinner, that would also be lovely. I am free tomorrow evening if that works for you, just let me know. You can also contact me on my cell at 407-555-5555.

I look forward to hearing from you.

Best,

Vivian

It took me a solid twenty minutes to hit send. I figured giving him my phone number that wasn't on my ads would be nice, so he wouldn't get routed to my answering service if I was busy. I also wanted to be able to hear back from him myself. I was suddenly feeling like a high school girl, smitten or something, and it wasn't anything—yet. I mean, anything is possible, but if he was looking at relocating and selling his house, that certainly didn't make him anything except a good time.

Maybe just a good time was what the doctor ordered. It had been a long time since I'd had any real pleasure, and that man was walking hotness. As the warmth of arousal began to stir, I thought about what it might be like pressed up against him. Falling backwards into him was amazing, I could only imagine falling forward into him, I giggled to myself again. Interrupting my sensual thoughts of him, my phone dinged with an email.

It was *him*, already!

Vivian,

I'd love to take you to dinner tomorrow night. I'll pick you up at 7:00.

I'll text you.

Looking forward to it,

Jax

I pulled out my phone and texted Jess, letting her know that we had a date. Well, it was kind of a date. It wasn't really a date. Jess said it was definitely a date and she wanted to come over and go through my closet tonight to make sure I wasn't going to pick out something terrible to wear. He'd already met me before, so I didn't really see what the point of that was, but another side of me was extremely nervous about it too.

I went about the rest of my day, trying to get work done, setting up appointments with potential clients, and filing a variety of paperwork that came with working in realty. I'd be lying if I said that I was completely focused, because frankly, that man was on my mind. I hadn't been touched in so long that it was practically all I could think about. I knew that I shouldn't get my hopes up and that it was probably a legitimate business meeting, but something told me that it might not be, and that was the part I was holding on to.

After I finally finished working, I texted Jess that I was all done and headed downtown to run a few errands before she came over. I needed to pick up some food. My fridge was totally empty and I was low on wine, which was never a good thing, especially with Jess coming over.

I absolutely loathed grocery shopping, and I hated cooking even more, but I was frugal and refused to eat out or order delivery more than once a week unless it was business related, because it was such a waste of money. So, begrudgingly, I got myself to the grocery store and pulled out my list of things I didn't want to cook and was only half sure I wanted to eat. When I pulled into the grocery store parking lot, it was a madhouse. I guess I wasn't the only one who needed food, right at dinnertime.

I meandered around the grocery store in my own little world, being petulant with myself about being there at all. Being an adult was awesome, but there sure were some things I missed about my parents being here, like my mom feeding me. Before I realized how little attention I had been paying as I was shoving my cart along, it stopped abruptly, taking me off-guard wondering what I ran into. As I looked up to apologize to whomever the unsuspecting citizen was, hazel eyes locked with mine and I was searching for words.

"Oh my God, I'm...so...uh, sorry. Oh God." I felt my face get red hot with embarrassment as I looked up at Seth, and then over at Matt. As I looked at them standing there in their uniforms, looking like honest to God heroes, I wanted to wither and die. I had just crashed my cart right into Seth. *Dear God, please just strike me dead, this is so embarrassing.*

"Well, darlin', couldn't wait to run me down? We haven't even gone out yet," he joked.

"No!" I squealed. *Oh my God, what is wrong with me?* I smacked my face with my hand. "I am so sorry, Seth...uh..."

"It's fine, darlin'. Where you off to in such a rush? You hungry? Should I be feeding you today and not tomorrow?" He leaned over my cart and winked at me.

That made me laugh, and I peeked at him through my hand and grinned. "I am so clumsy, Seth, I'm so sorry. Did I hurt you?" I felt like the world's biggest dumbass.

"I'm fine, darlin'. Is this your grocery store?" he asked me. It was one of the smaller of the chains in the area, and I liked it because it was so small and generally easy to get in and out—unless you went at prime time like me, of course.

"Oh yeah, it is. I live a few blocks away. What are you all doing here?" I waved my hand in the direction of the other handsome guys he was with, all in uniform, standing at the deli counter.

"Our station is the one up the road. We come here for dinner sometimes. I'm on duty until tomorrow morning." He looked over at Matt, who motioned they were heading out.

"Looks like you gotta go?" I asked. I was talking like a five-year-old with nothing intelligible to say. I needed to work on that before dinner the next day, that's for sure.

"Uh, yeah. But I'll text you later, alright? We good for tomorrow?" he asked me.

"Yes, and I promise I won't run you down tomorrow." I smiled shyly.

"Ok, awesome, I'm gonna hold you to that." He started to back away. "I'll text you in a little bit after we take care of some things at the station." He gave me a little wave and another wink. Seriously, I usually think winking is so stupid, but he was so hot, it was adorable.

"Sounds good. Be careful out there." I waved.

"Always, darlin'!" he called out and disappeared.

I let out a huge sigh that I guess I'd been holding in, when a small older lady next to me gave me a little elbow and said, "Well, that was a handsome bunch, wasn't it, dear? Makes me want to start a fire."

I laughed and agreed, "It sure was, ma'am. It sure was."

I smiled during the rest of my little grocery trip before I got home to meet up with Jess and tell her about my encounter. *She's gonna love this story.*

JAX

That Vivian is fucking gorgeous. She looked so mortified, which made her that much more adorable.

"Who was that little beauty queen, Jax? Another one of your conquests?" Brian teased me on our way out of the grocery store.

Before I could even answer, Matt jumped in. "That was my realtor. It seems Jax has been talking to her on the sly?" He looked at me out of the corner of his eye with a sneer.

"Ok, hold up. Number one, not a conquest; I'm not a total dirt bag, fellas. Number two, I contacted her to get an appraisal on my house, that's all. We're going to discuss it over dinner tomorrow. You know, like civilized human beings? You've all heard of going out to dinner." I was being sarcastic, overly so, and trying to cover up the fact that yes, it was a shady-ass way to ask a girl on a date, but I did it anyway. I had no idea what the hell I was doing. It was the best I could come up with, and she agreed to it, so they could all fuck off.

"Why would you want an appraisal on your house? Are you selling it? Going somewhere?" Brian asked, looking a little concerned.

"No, but I wanted to find out what the property value was."

There was really no good explanation for my bullshit, and I'm pretty sure we all knew it was bullshit.

"Uh huh. I see," was Matt's reply. "Well, don't be messing around with my realtor before my deal is closed, for Christ's sake. Isabel will fucking kill me. And you for that matter, she knows how. She literally knows like a hundred different ways to kill us," he said rubbing his chin thoughtfully.

"Jesus, gentlemen, it's dinner...and a discussion about real estate. Settle yourselves, you hound dogs," I teased them all.

Scotty, our driver, just chuckled, never chiming in. He was a bit younger than us, kind of quiet, but seriously great at his job and becoming one of us. He hadn't grown up in the same town as us, so he was relatively new to the fold in terms of longevity, but he'd proven himself time and time again on a scene, so it didn't matter. The truth was that we could be a little bit of a clique sometimes, and new guys—or girls for that matter—sometimes had trouble fitting in, simply because we'd all known each other for so long.

We piled into the truck, and I pulled my phone out. I decided to text her now. And probably later too. She was on my mind, and thinking about her the past couple of days had kept a lot of the darkness away somehow. Maybe I was getting better, maybe it was her, but the coincidence was certainly there. I sent her a quick text before I put my phone back in my pocket and looked across the truck at Matt, who was giving me the stink eye.

"Oh, settle down, I'm not gonna do anything. It's just dinner." I flipped him off and rested my head back against the seat. I was already seriously attracted to Vivian; even the sound of her name was sexy. I couldn't wait to say it out loud again. It rolled off the tongue. It sounded fancy, like a special treat or something. There it was, my dick started to twitch again, thinking about her, what it would feel like to touch her again for more than a lingering moment. I was going to need to get that shit in check. Dr. Rosen said no sex. I mean, not forever, I hoped, but certainly not right away. I'm supposed to get to know her. My cock certainly wanted to get to know her all right.

When we got back to the station, we piled into the kitchen area to eat our dinner, and I checked my phone. She hadn't replied yet, and I immediately wondered why. Usually, I wouldn't care, so I didn't really know what the difference was, but for some reason I was feeling antsy about it.

I must have made a face, because Scotty nudged me and asked quietly, "Waiting to hear from your girl?"

"Sort of," I mumbled to him. "I don't want to discuss it."

"You're allowed to dig a chick. Fuck them." He gave me a smirk and we continued eating. I didn't say anything back, but I gave him an appreciative nod.

The thing about the firehouse is that yeah, we're all brothers, and we're all family, but with that came the ribbing and giving each other a hard time that was usually fun, but not always if you were on the receiving end. I really wasn't up for getting a hard time about Vivian. I didn't even know her, and all I wanted to do was try like I was supposed to. Scotty never cared about that kind of thing; he just said and did what he wanted when he wasn't being quiet. He was a bit younger than the rest of us, and an awesome addition to our team.

We ate and gave each other some shit like usual, however the darkness started to creep into my thoughts. I was doubting Dr. Rosen's advice, and with that, I also realized I had become the kind of guy I wouldn't want my sister to date. Letting those feelings in brought me lower, and realizing that I've been a douche was frustrating. My "date" with Vivian was supposed to help this, but fuck if I wanted to wait. I knew that this dating shit wasn't supposed to fix me per se, but since my discussion with the doc, I had been feeling better, more optimistic. I had been becoming a moody dickhead; I needed to get that shit squared away, or at least not let Vivian see it.

We went out after dinner to do some truck checks; testing all the equipment on the trucks to make sure they had fuel and were working properly. Plus, it was fun to play with the stuff we had. Once we had gotten through all of that, a few of us settled on the benches outside. It wasn't that hot out, and there was a nice breeze.

Matt came over and sat with me, which was completely normal, but of course I was defensive out of the gate and gave him a don't-give-me-a-hard-time look. Recognizing it immediately, he put his hands in the air. "I'm not gonna give you shit, I promise."

"Uh huh, sure." My reply was laced in sarcasm.

"I swear. I did want to ask you about the test, though. Have you talked to Brian yet? I didn't tell him yet I wasn't taking it; I was kind of thinking we could talk to him together, you know; we could spring it on him, because he loves surprises so much." Matt chuckled.

Laughing as well, I said, "Honestly, I hadn't given it one bit of thought. I'm going to take the test like I said before; I just haven't done anything about it since we talked last. It's the next logical career move for me, and the position is vacant since Brian finally got the official promotion to chief. You're absolutely sure you don't want it?" Just then, I felt a buzzing in my pocket from my phone, so I pulled it out to check while we talked. *It was her.*

"Yeah, I'm sure. I'm not a keep-rising kind of guy. I'm a branch-out kind of guy. I am super pumped about this next adventure with Isabel, and it's not like I'm leaving the department or anything. Hey, are you listening?" he asked.

"Oh shit, yeah, sorry. I just wanted to reply to this text." I shoved my phone back in my pocket.

"You know, you've been really secretive lately. Everything ok?" he asked me.

"Yeah, of course everything's ok. I'm not being secretive. I just don't really have much to share most of the time. I'm not that interesting, man, you know this," I said. In all honesty, that was truly how I felt at the time. I obviously wasn't telling anyone about my arrangement with the doc, and they all knew I went to Veteran's Affairs regularly for a variety of things. It was part of my benefits after all, and even if I got the runaround at almost every turn when I was there, the one place I did actually get help was from Dr. Rosen.

"Ok, well, what's up with you and little Miss Real Estate? She's pretty, but she's not your usual type; and since when do you 'do dinner'? Be honest, is this a date?"

he asked just as Jo walked up.

"Who's got a date?" She smiled as she chimed in, plopping herself down right next to me.

"Now you have to tell. Nobody can lie to Josephine Meadows, soon-to-be Cavanaugh," Matt said, causing a huge smile to spread across Jo's face. Her smile was infectious, and I felt myself smiling again right away too.

"Who says I'm changing my name?" she said jokingly.

Everyone knew she'd change her last name. Brian was really traditional when it came to that kind of thing, and it was important to him. I heard them arguing about it one night in his office with the door shut. We all generally worked the same shift, and for the most part, Brian and Jo were completely professional; you wouldn't know they were engaged at all if you didn't know them. Sure, there was an exchanged glance here and there, but professionalism was important to both of them, and they went out of their way to not make their relationship a thing, unless it was just amongst us friends, or outside of work.

"Oh, please, Jo, everyone knows you're changing your last name. That way there can be little Cavanaughs running around the firehouse," I said. I could totally picture a whole brood of little dark-haired babes with light eyes playing on the fire trucks and running around the station. It made me happy to think about that future for them. To see them finally planning this wedding was really cool.

"Oh, lord. We're a ways off from that, bitches. Now…who's got a date?" she said in a sing-song manner. "It couldn't be Matty here, because he's busy getting put in cuffs every night by Izzy, *so* it must be you." She pointed at me.

"Good God, woman, put that finger away. I'll have you know it's not a date. Your bestie over here is giving me shit because I asked his realtor, who, yes, is a total fucking fox, to dinner with me so we could talk about real estate. Nothing more, nothing less. He's just giving me a truckload of bullshit about it, because it seems he thinks that I do not eat with women. So, tell him, we eat together all the time," I winked at her.

Raising her eyebrow at me skeptically, she replied, "Well, that is true. We do eat together all the time. Sounds to me like Matty is just being a pain in the ass." She laughed. She totally covered for me. She's a cool fucking chick. She knew. She's not an idiot and I was appealing to her sweet spot. Jo was all about love. Once she fell in love, she wanted everyone to be in love; it was both annoying and sweet at the same time. I completely took advantage of that in this conversation to shift the focus from myself.

Rolling his eyes dramatically, Matt said, "Oh, whatever, you two. I call bullshit. But in the meantime, let's go watch a movie. It's getting late."

"Sounds good," Jo and I both agreed.

I tried to restrain my grin as I felt my phone in my pocket vibrate again.

Vivian

We had been texting back and forth throughout the evening, of course with me showing Jess just about everything. Immediately after the incident when I ran him down at the grocery store with my cart, he texted me.

You look beautiful today, even when you're trying to kill me.

I'm so, so, so sorry about that. I really am.

I'm just teasing you, darlin', except you really are beautiful.

Thank you. That's very sweet of you to say.

Well it's the truth ;) What are you doing?

I have a girlfriend over, drinking wine mostly. What about you? Are you working now?

I am. I work until 7am tomorrow. We do 24-hour shifts here.

Oh, wow. That's a long day. Were you busy?

Not even a little bit. It's been very slow, but that'll probably jinx it. lol.

`Well, if you do have to save lives`
`tonight, be careful.`

I really didn't know what to say; he was so flattering, and I was terrible at taking a compliment. I also didn't know that much about firefighters, except for their unbelievable hotness that I'd just come to learn about, and you know, the obvious, that they fight fire.

`Oh, I'll be careful. I have important`
`dinner plans tomorrow.`

`Haha, ahh yes. I'll bring my laptop so I`
`can show you some comparable listings to`
`yours to give you an idea of the property`
`value.`

`You can leave the laptop at home.`

`Are you sure?`

`You don't need the laptop. I promise.`

I was starting to think that this was not about real estate at all, and I was one hundred percent ok with it.

"Jess, he told me not to bring the laptop!" I squealed at my friend, who had been sitting two feet away from me on the couch almost the entire time.

"Well, no shit, Viv. Because it's a date. DUH. Nobody brings laptops on dates; ok, maybe nerds do, but whatever. He's a hunky fireman. By the way, did you know that his picture is on their department website?" she asked me.

"Uh, what? Is it? Get the hell out of here," I said.

"Uh, you heard me. That is a goddamn good-looking bunch, Viv. Like a superior race of hotness. I'm about to touch myself, not even kidding." She laughed.

"Oh my God, shut up. He's really good-looking, right?" She showed me her phone, where every firefighter belonging to District 23 was listed with a picture and their rank. *Ooh, he is a Lieutenant. That sounds important.*

"Yeah, he is. Your babies would be little super blond, blue-eyed smarty-pants heroes. It would be amazing." She loved teasing me. I couldn't stop laughing. She was such a nut.

"Stop it! There're no babies. There's just talking and dinner." I was hoping for more than that, like making out would be nice. Just the idea of his touch had my libido going into overdrive.

"Yeah, yeah, whatever. So, what are you going to wear? Besides ridiculously high heels? A dress?"

"I don't know. To tell you the truth, I'm not sure exactly. Let's go to my room and go through some stuff. I don't have any idea where we're going, but yes, I'm definitely going to wear heels. If you saw how tall he is in person, you'd wear heels too."

"Alright, let's find you something that says, 'I'm conservative and a smart, independent woman, but you can grope me on the first date, because it's been a while. But I'm not going home with you tonight. You'll have to take me out a couple more times'," she said.

My eyes got huge, and I started laughing so hard that I had tears streaming down my face. "Jess! You are so messed up! But also, so right. That's exactly what I want my outfit to say." I was squealing with laughter getting the words out.

We ended up doing a fashion show that entailed me trying on almost everything in my closet and modeling it for Jess; we should have had a soundtrack for it. We were like teenagers. I had a moment where I found myself happy, just happy. I couldn't remember the last time I had felt excited and optimistic like that without the darkness of my brother's death being just around the bend.

We settled on black skinny jeans and a sparkly tank top. I made a mental note to remember a sweater or something in case it got chilly at night, which it was starting to. We agreed the shoes of choice would be my Louboutins. I mean, every girl deserves a pair the moment she can afford them, and they should be worn often, especially on first dates.

We spent the rest of the evening laughing and drinking wine, and talking about men. It had been such a long time since we had a good old-fashioned slumber party. It was a Thursday night, but neither of us had particularly busy days that Friday, so we stayed up doing our nails and plotting life without any darkness encroaching at all.

The next morning, I woke up with butterflies. I felt like I was on a countdown to the date, and I was super fussy. Jax and I had been texting, but then he'd stopped abruptly. I assumed he had fallen asleep or something, but really had no idea. Jess walked into the kitchen rubbing her eyes.

"You hear back from lover boy?" she asked.

"Nah, but for all I know he was out saving lives all night, ya know, being a hero," I joked.

"Probably. Or he fell asleep in a chair with his phone in his pocket. That seems pretty likely if you ask me. You'll hear from him, though," she replied.

Just then my phone vibrated on the counter with an incoming message, immediately bringing a smile to my face. I needed to tone that down; I was getting nervous I was a little too excited. It was a "sort of" first date, but nobody ever said it was a date. Whatever, I checked the message and it said,

Good morning, beautiful, sorry I crashed with my phone literally still in my hand last night.

Well, how cute was that?

Jess made herself some coffee and started getting her things together to go home before work. It was early, around 6:30am.

No worries, my girlfriend was here hanging out and we ended up crashing too. Hope you slept well.

Better than I have in a while. I'm looking forward to seeing you tonight.

Me too. 7 still good? I asked.

Sure is. I'd like to pick you up, is that cool?

That would be great. I sent him a little smiley face, because I'm a total dork.

I'm about to get off work and have some stuff to do, but I'll text you when I'm on my way, ok?

Sounds good. I'm off to work soon myself.

Have a really good day. See you soon ;)

I felt little butterflies. I decided to not ruin it by overthinking it any more. Everyone loves a flirtation, and especially a flirtation with an insanely hot firefighter.

"By the doe-eyed look on your face, I'm guessing that was him?" Jess asked with a raised eyebrow and a smirk.

"Yeah, he's going to pick me up at 7. I'm like super nervous, Jess. Is this normal? I feel like I'm gonna puke," I joked with her, only half joking.

"Yep, totally normal. All right, text me a picture of your sexy ass later, then I hope not to hear from you until tomorrow, if you know what I'm saying," she said giving me a smirk while making her way out.

"Sounds good. I'll keep you posted. Thanks for your help!"

"Anytime." She waved and made her exit, taking my coffee mug with her.

I decided to go for a quick run before getting my workday started and shake off some of those nerves. I had a few appointments that afternoon with clients, but other than that, I pretty much had the day to myself. Realtors are generally quite busy on weekends, but I didn't have a whole lot scheduled, which was fine with me, I had been so busy lately.

I preferred to try to get all of my appointments into clusters back to back, particularly when I had open houses or showings of a particular property. One, it was safer for me as a female to have back-to-back appointments, because as one was ending another was beginning, and so someone was always on their way to see me. It also gave the buyers an implied sense of urgency, because other people were interested in the same property. It happened to help sell properties faster when potential buyers thought there was competition.

I popped my earbuds in and set out for a quick few miles. I couldn't run without music; for some reason music, had become extremely important to me over the years. It could instantly enhance or change your mood. I had been on a country music kick the last year, and was listening to Garth Brooks' Greatest Hits album on repeat when I was running. I ran down the street singing Thunder Rolls to myself, when I started to get emotional. It was another unseasonably warm morning for October, and I had a later start than normal because Jess had been there, and as my sweat mixed with my tears, I started to get short of breath. I stopped for a moment to regain my composure.

Leaning against a telephone pole, I ran my hands over my face, rubbing away the sweat and tears that had pooled around my eyes. I had such a good morning that it was frustrating for me to suddenly start feeling all of these emotions again. I hadn't cried in quite a while, yet in that moment it was all I wanted to do. I finally just gave in to it, and let a sob out, which compelled more, practically choking me.

After a few minutes of my uncontrollable mini breakdown, I got myself together. Stretching my legs and taking a few deep breaths, I regained my composure and decided to just walk home. I was only about a mile from home, so I put my earbuds back in and headed back.

Wondering what came over me, I tried to turn my thoughts back to happier things like my date-non-date, whatever it was. I shook my head at myself thinking I better get my mind right before he picked me up, or he'd think I was some kind of basket case. Which maybe I was, but I didn't want him to know that, certainly not on the first time we were spending time together, or it would be the last.

JAX

I knew I had been laying it on a little thick with my text messages to her, but everything I said was true. I wanted her to get the impression that it was a date; I was just too weird about the whole dating thing to flat out ask her on one, and I was kind of afraid she'd say no if she thought it was a date out of the gate.

I had some errands to run and wanted to clean my truck before I picked her up, so Matt and I took off after work to run around together on our day off. He had some shit to do too, and this was a pretty standard morning of our day-off routine for us to do all of our adulting crap together.

"So, what are you up to tonight?" he asked me as we walked out to my truck.

"I'm taking Vivian out to dinner tonight." I hesitated telling him, but I'm not a liar, so I figured I'd just be honest about it and he knew it was coming.

"That's tonight, eh?" He gave me a skeptical glance.

"Yeah, I want to wash my truck before I pick her up. It's a fucking mess in here." I pointed around it.

"Yeah, it sure is." He laughed. "So, where are you going to take the youngster?"

"Fuck off. She's not that young," I said. "I'm not sure. I haven't figured out where to take her where we could have an actual conversation," I admitted.

Rubbing his chin in thought, he offered some actual helpful suggestions. "Why don't you take her that new place over on Virginia? They have a nice patio, and the music isn't that loud. I heard the food was really good. Isabel has wanted to go there too, and you know how picky she can be about where to eat. So you can check it out with your lady friend, and then report back on the food," We both laughed. Isabel was laid back about many things, but not about what or where she ate.

"That's a good idea, and it should be fairly nice out." I paused for a moment, contemplating telling him why I was interested in a normal date all of a sudden. Part of me thought he'd understand, but the self-consciousness caused my jaw to clench, so I simply explained that I found her interesting, and that it wasn't a big deal. "You know, I realize everyone thinks it's weird that I'm going on an actual date or whatever, but honestly, I am curious about the market and she also seems like a cool chick."

"Dude, we're just busting your balls. I know you wouldn't do anything to make my business with her weird, and honestly, I have no beef with you dating someone. Look what happened to me. I have absolutely no room whatsoever to talk."

He was right. He didn't have any room to talk at all. He was my wingman until he fell for his girl, and while we still went out, it wasn't like it used to be. We were all growing up, and at the end of the day, it was probably time for me to grow up too. Even if it didn't go anywhere with Vivian, it felt like a positive step in getting over whatever it was that was keeping me in the darkness. Getting to a place where I wasn't constantly reverting to the solitude in my head was important, and if Dr. Rosen thought this was a good idea, I was going in headfirst. I trusted his judgment, he hadn't been wrong about anything so far. I also considered the fact that finding someone might be quite nice.

We ran around doing our usual bullshit errands of going to the bank, getting the truck washed, stopping at the hardware store. There was always something one of us needed at the hardware store, and we always managed to spend way more time than we needed to; same thing would always happen if we went to the auto parts store. Some things about us guys are as typical as anyone would guess.

After we were done, I dropped Matt off at the firehouse, where we had left his truck, and I headed home. It was mid-afternoon, so I still had plenty of time to fuck around at home and get out of my own head before picking up Vivian. I still needed to get her address, so I sent her a text.

```
Hey beautiful, hope you're having a good
day. Need your address so I can pick you up
promptly.
```

She replied right away.

```
Hey there, busy day, but not bad. It's 224
South Orange Ave. You'll see my car in the
driveway. 7pm still good?
```

```
Sure is, looking forward to it.
```

```
Me too. See you then! ☺
```

```
;)
```

Girls love emojis. Every girl I've ever texted used them constantly. I used to find it stupid and annoying, however, I thought it was cute she sent me a smiley face. So I sent a wink back. I didn't know why, but I liked sending the last text too.

As it got closer to the time to pick her up, I stared at myself in the bathroom mirror, thinking about what I was doing. I was completely out of my element, causing the anxiety to creep in. I ran my hands through my hair one last time and muttered "It's just dinner" under my breath before heading out.

Vivian only lived about ten minutes away from me as it turned out, so I was in her driveway before I had too much time to psych myself out. I noticed she had lots of flowers planted around her front door in little pots, and what looked like a bunch of herbs and stuff too. Feeling my heart rate pick up, I took a few deep breaths before I rang her doorbell.

Vivian

When the doorbell rang, I jumped. I practically ran to answer it, stopping by the hall mirror really quickly to check myself out, fluff my hair one last time, and check for lipstick on my teeth, of course. I opened the door, and I couldn't stop my mouth from falling open. Standing before me, leaning up against my doorway, he looked like a model. He had on a greenish plaid button-up shirt, tight at his biceps and rolled up to his elbows showing his tattoos, with a white t-shirt, jeans, and brown boots. I knew how good-looking he was, but every time I saw him, I was floored anyway.

Quickly getting my bearings, I invited him in for a moment. "Hi, there, please come in. I'm almost ready. I just have to grab my shoes and purse."

"You're looking absolutely stunning today, darlin'." He smiled at me, causing my temperature to rise.

"Thank you, Seth. You, uh, too." I tried to recover from the moment, stumbling over my words.

He walked in past me, and as I caught a whiff of his manly scent, a mix of cologne and that same fresh soap I remembered smelling before; I was definitely swooning.

"Your place is really nice." He looked around, seemingly

admiring my condo.

"Oh, thank you. I just bought it last year. It needs a little bit of work, but it was a steal," I said as I rummaged through the closet looking for the gold heels I wanted to wear. Putting them on, I walked over to him now standing in my kitchen leaning up against the island. "Um, I'm ready now if you are?" I asked hesitantly.

"Ok, great, do you want to bring a jacket or anything? I thought it might be nice to sit outside?" he asked.

"Oh, that's a good idea. I have one hanging by the door. I'll grab on our way out." I started to lead the way as he followed, hands in his pockets.

"Those shoes are really sexy, Vivian," he said quietly from behind me. I turned around and flashed him a little smile.

"Thank you very much." I grabbed my purse and ushered him out in front of me, so I could lock the door. When we got out to his truck, I went over to the passenger side and realized it was a lifted truck that was way too high off the ground for me to get in without some help.

"Oh, shit," he said quietly behind me. I looked over my shoulder at him, confused about what to do. "Let me help you." He opened the door, gently grabbed me by the waist, and lifted me up into the cab, causing me to giggle. "What's so funny?" he asked.

Now looking down at him from the inside of the truck, I said, "You just lifted me up here like I weighed nothing."

Giving me that handsome yet devilish smirk of his, he replied, "Darlin', you are a tiny thing." He shut the door and walked around to his side and hopped in the truck.

"Are you sure you don't want me to bring my laptop so we can go over comps and things like that for your property?" I was fidgeting with my hands, unsure of what this was still.

"Yeah, about that." He turned to me, placing one hand on the steering wheel and the other between us. Leaning closer to me, he said, "I'm really more interested in talking about you than about my property tonight."

Surprised and flattered at his honesty, I went ahead and asked the question of the day, "This isn't really about business, is it?" I'm certain I was whispering, slightly afraid of his reply.

Turning back to the steering wheel and revving up the engine, he said without looking back at me, "No, it's really not about a business at all." Grinning, he backed out of my driveway, and to my excitement, we headed out on our confirmed, actual date.

I'm usually good at small talk, but in this case I really didn't know what to say, so I just asked how his day was.

"It was a good day. I was looking forward to picking you up most of the day. Other than that, I ran errands like I usually do on my day off. Tell me about your day, darlin'. I'm sure it was much more interesting."

Seriously, something about the southern twang in his voice when he called me darlin' was panty-melting. If I weren't a responsible adult, I would have jumped over to his side of the truck and insisted he had his way with me. I didn't even care that I barely knew him. If he kept calling me darlin' and giving me that million-dollar smile, I knew I'd never be able to behave myself.

"Well, I had a few showings this afternoon. They were all pretty standard. Two couples, and then this single guy. He was a little creepy, but whatever. Uneventful for the most part." That guy today was really creepy.

"What do you mean, the guy was creepy? What did he do?" Jax

583

snapped a little, surprising me.

"Umm, well, he didn't seem that interested in the property, really. He had me give him a tour, during which he was very quiet and just kind of stared at me a lot. When my next appointment showed up, he took off. It was weird, but whatever."

"Do you always do all of your appointments by yourself like that? It doesn't seem safe at all to just be meeting strangers alone in empty houses." He seemed more concerned than I would have expected. We pulled into the new restaurant I had heard opened but hadn't had a chance to go to yet, making my stomach growl from the thought of some food.

"Well, sometimes I do. Um, most of the time I do." I looked over at him as he parked. "That's just kind of the nature of the business, really. I line all of my appointments up back-to-back whenever I can, so that I always have another one coming up except for my last one of the day, of course. But I'm always in touch with someone, so I'm expected someplace or people expect to hear from me. It's my job." I explained it the best I could, really; he was right, it's not super safe, but you have to trust that people are inherently good. And I had a system, sort of.

"I can see I'm going to have to worry about you, Viv," he said before hopping out of the truck and walking over to help me get out. It never really occurred to me that someone would worry about that kind of thing besides me; it was endearing. He was protective, which was attractive, like everything about him.

He reached in to help me out of the truck, which was obscenely big, and as he let me down slowly, my body glided along his, giving me goose bumps. The fact that I hadn't really touched a man other than a business handshake was messing with my senses, and I'd become super sensitive to touch it seemed. He placed his hand on my lower back as we walked toward the restaurant and got seated on the patio outside. There was a guy singing inside, and while we could hear him lightly through the speakers on the patio, it wasn't so loud that you had to yell to each other, thankfully.

Being ever the gentleman this evening, Seth pulled a chair out for me, then sat across from me at the table looking at me with a sly smile.

"What?" I asked. I was sure I had a booger or something and he was staring at it.

"I'm honestly just enjoying the view, darlin'." He leaned forward, placing his palms together on the table in front of him. I didn't have any clue how to take his compliments. He was quite flattering, but it just wasn't something I was used to.

"Uh, well, thank you." I let out a small laugh.

The waitress came over and took our drink orders, then quickly came back for our food orders; and all the while, we'd been quiet. I was extremely nervous and wanted him to take the lead on conversation, but being nervous made me chatty. So I quickly began the barrage of questions as soon as we were done dealing with the server.

"So, what's your story, Seth? Are you from here? Does your family live here? Did you always want to be a firefighter?" I almost asked him about the distinct Marine tattoo that reminded me of my brother, but decided not to go there yet for both our sakes.

"Ha ha, that's a lot of questions, darlin'. Uh, my story—well, it's long. I am from here. I grew up in this area and have lived here most of my life, except for when I was in the Marines and was deployed elsewhere. My parents live in South Florida, Boca Raton, to be exact. They retired there about ten years ago, and I don't see them as often as I should. I have an older sister, who also lives nearby with her husband and kids. Did I always want to be a firefighter? Yes. Definitely yes. From the time I was a little kid having a fire truck birthday party, I knew it was for me. I joined the Marines after high school, though, and had a break for a few years while I was away. But I came back, because they are my family too. Now it's your turn for the inquisition." He smiled again. He smiled a lot, but there seemed to be something behind his eyes. He seemed to be having fun, but it looked like something else was on his mind.

"Ok, well, what would you like to know?"

Leaning in closer across the table, he lowered his voice and looked into my eyes. "Vivian, I want to know everything about you."

JAX

I felt like I was staring at her, inspecting her. Waiting for her to see through me. Her piercing blue eyes looked at me so directly, so intently, that I felt like I was wearing all of my flaws and insecurities like a mask across the table. I wanted to turn the topic of discussion to her as quickly as possible. This exercise was about connecting with someone, and I couldn't do that if all I was thinking about was how fucking sexy she was, coupled with how uncomfortable I was talking about myself.

I sipped my beer, awaiting her response, pretending to be cool and collected. "Well?" I asked and smirked.

"Everything? Well, ok, let's see. You already know what I do for a living—" I interrupted her.

"Yes, and at some point I'd like to discuss a better way for you to be safer, because I don't like the idea of some creepy douchebag making you uncomfortable for even one second." I really didn't. I wanted to find that guy and teach him a fucking lesson about how to behave. She looked at me, clearly surprised by my interruption, before she continued on talking with a bit of a smile on her face.

"My parents are in New Jersey, where we used to live, taking care of my grandmother. We all live down here, but I'm 'from' there. I'm not sure when they're coming back. I know they will eventually, but they keep trying to get me to go there to visit, and I don't want to because it's cold."

"I'm not a fan of the cold, either. I can't really imagine living anywhere but here."

I watched her shoulders relax as she got more comfortable and she continued. "For real. They've been super overprotective since— "She stopped herself and looked around, trying to find words.

"Since what, Viv?" I prodded.

"Since my brother died. But I don't want to talk about that. I'm sorry I brought it up. My parents are just super protective and want me to be with them all the time, is all I meant." She took a sip of her wine and leaned back into her seat.

"I'm sorry about your brother. And I'm sure your parents just worry about you, is all. Having family that gives a shit about you is special. Not everyone has that, you know?" I needed to change the subject. She looked uncomfortable. I was so horrible at this dating business. So far, I'd had to lift her into my douchebag truck not designed for sweet girls like her to climb into, and now I had brought up something that made her sad. *Ugh.*

"It's ok. It's been about a year now. Anyway, right now it's just me here doing my real estate thing." She let the corners of her mouth turn up into a slight smile.

"Ok, let's change the subject. Tell me something you've always wanted to do but just haven't for whatever reason."

"Hmm, good question." She smiled big that time, thank God. "Sleep on the beach."

"Sleep on the beach? Really?"

"Yeah, I've always wanted to camp out on the beach. Have a

fire, snuggle up, and fall asleep listening to the waves crash. It seems like the absolutely most perfect moment. What about you?" she asked.

"I want to steal yours," I said. That sounded so peaceful and glorious. Like I might be able to fall asleep that way.

"You can't steal mine!" She laughed.

"Oh, but I can, darlin'. That sounds magnificent. The only thing I'd have to add is doing all of that with someone special, because if you're going to camp on the beach and watch the sunset, you need someone to cuddle up with." I was back to flirting. I was really shameless.

Blushing, she replied, "Well, hopefully you'll find someone to share that moment with."

"Oh, I think I already have, Viv. She just doesn't know it yet." As her mouth fell open in shock from my blatant statement that was obviously about her, I felt victorious. I wasn't trying to make her uncomfortable; I wanted her to feel wanted. Hell, she *was* wanted. From the minute she opened the door barefoot in her tight little jeans and tank top, I had to keep reminding myself to be a respectable guy and treat her like a respectable woman. The thoughts of getting my hands on her were overwhelming, and I caught myself dreaming about what she'd taste like.

"You're shameless," was her reply. She just called me out on my shit.

Laughing out loud, I had to agree. "You're right, I am. But honestly, Viv, I feel like it's totally your fault. You're beautiful and smart. I'd be a fool not to lay it on thick." I winked at her while she gave me a playful eye roll.

"Oh, please. I can see you're the kind of guy who likes to tell a girl what he thinks she wants to hear."

Almost hurt but knowing I deserved that, I leaned forward again to grab her attention. I lowered my voice, wanting her to pay close attention. "Vivian, I used to be that guy. I won't lie to you. I wasn't always the gentleman. But I'm working on that. I am genuinely interested in getting to know you, even though every time you speak I'm staring at those perfect lips of yours." That was as honest as I could get, and I stared right at her pouty little mouth waiting for her reply.

"That was quite possibly the most honest response anyone has ever given me, Mr. Jackson. Thank you." She picked up her wine glass and held it up to clink against my beer bottle. I loved observing her. She was so confident at work, but had a silly side that I got to see at the grocery store, and I was witnessing her thoughtful side now as I watched her try to figure me out. *Good luck with that one* I thought. .

"So, tell me about being a firefighter. I don't know anything about it, but it's very intriguing. It's obviously dangerous; are you an adrenaline junkie?" She leaned back in her chair, crossing her legs and getting comfortable.

"Well, no, I'm not an adrenaline junkie." I grinned. "I will tell you that it is fun riding the fire truck, though. I think it's every little boy's dream to go cruising to a fire with the lights and sirens blaring. But that's not why I do it. My dad was a firefighter before me. He was a volunteer; it wasn't his career. I always had such a respect for him going to work all day as an electrician, and then answering calls and helping people in his spare time. I know my mom thought he spent way too much time at the firehouse, but it was something that made him feel important. We always related to each other in that way." I thought about my dad and how he had taught me early on how important contribution was. I felt the darkness creep in as I realized how I'd lost sight of that in recent years.

"I think that's wonderful. It's so important to feel like you are doing something important for people. So did you start out as a volunteer too?" She brought me back to the moment.

"Yeah, I did. The section of town we lived in had a department that was a combination department, half paid staff, mostly during the day, and volunteer staff in the evenings and on weekends. So that's how I got started. When we moved closer to the downtown area, I joined District 23 for a couple of years when I met Matt and Brian at school."

"Who's Brian?" I totally forgot she didn't know everyone. I was talking away, getting more comfortable just telling her my story, I didn't even realize.

"Oh, sorry. Brian is our Chief. He is Matt's older brother. We went through high school together with Jo, who is now engaged to Brian and is Matt's best friend." As I thought about how complicated that sounded, I laughed. "That probably sounds way more Melrose Place than it really is. We all went to school together, and Jo is a firefighter too. Her dad was the Chief before he died, and Brian moved into the job."

"Were Brian and Jo high school sweethearts?" she asked.

"Oh God, no. They didn't get along at all. Which leads me to believe they probably loved each other since they were little kids." I chuckled thinking about it. If I had a dollar for every time Jo rolled her eyes at Brian in high school, I'd be retired on a beach in the Mediterranean.

"That's funny. So you all work together now full time?" It was weird for me having this conversation; none of the women I usually spent time with were such good listeners or asked so many questions. It was nice.

"Yeah, we're like a family. It's pretty cool. So what about you? How did you get into real estate at such a young age? I mean you must do pretty well. I see your face everywhere." I wanted to get her to talk to me more about herself; I really wanted to get to know her better.

"Well, I always worked for as long as I can remember. I've kind of always been an entrepreneur, I guess. I used to make friendship bracelets and sell them when I was a kid, then I would tutor or babysit. I was always working some kind of little job. When I was in college, I had saved up a pretty decent amount of money, when a little run-down house went up for sale and I decided to buy it and try to flip it. I wanted the challenge. I paid so much in commission on the sale of a run-down house, I decided to get my real estate license and broker my own deals. So I've been a realtor for almost five years now." She had a proud smile on her face.

"That's fucking incredible. I don't know anyone who would work like that; it's admirable." She was a little hustler. It was sexy.

Our food had come, and we ate and continued exchanging stories, getting more comfortable as the evening continued. I realized that I was really enjoying myself, and she seemed like she was too. When the server brought our check, I paid—even though she tried to split it with me, which would never happen. Ever.

I didn't want the night to end, and it wasn't that late, so I suggested a local bar nearby we could walk to for a couple of drinks.

"I'd love to. Let's go." She picked up her giant purse, which looked expensive and like you could carry a small child in it. Literally, it was like a suitcase or something.

"What the hell do you carry in a bag that big?" I had to ask her.

"Well, I like to be prepared. Shut up." She nudged me as we walked side by side. Inclined to put my arm around her, I refrained and kept my hands to myself.

"Prepared for what? In case you have to sleep in it? Seriously, it's huge. Is it heavy? Should I be carrying it for you?" I teased.

She started to giggle and leaned into me again, setting my heart racing. "Be quiet. I have girl stuff in here. And sometimes I put my laptop in here. So it's gotta be big enough for that stuff."

"Let me look in it. Come on." I grabbed the edge of it with my finger and pulled it open slightly to peek inside.

Gently swatting at me, she exclaimed, "You get out of there, Seth Jackson! You don't go through a woman's purse!"

"The more you fight, the more intrigued I am. You realize this, right?"

"I just realized that. But I'm still not giving away all of my secrets, so stay out." She smiled up at me and pulled her arms around herself.

"Are you cold? You look cold." I saw her let out a little shiver.

"No, no, I'm ok."

"You're cold. Come here." I pulled her into me and put my arm around her, causing her to put her hand on my ribs, which sent chills through me that landed right in my cock. I was hoping she didn't notice, but having her that close was such a fucking turn-on, and pulling her in to keep her warm felt good.

"I forgot my jacket in the truck. I'm sorry," she said quietly.

"Don't apologize. I wanted you to forget it, so I could get my arms around you. All part of my plan, you see." I gave her a little squeeze and felt her relax. "We're almost there, and we'll warm you up with a cocktail. Sound good, darlin'?"

"Yeah, that sounds great."

Vivian

When he pulled me close and put his arm around me, I almost fainted. As my hand rested on his ribs to steady myself, I felt what good shape he was in. I couldn't resist the urge to slide my hand along his side to feel that rock hard body; all I could think about was what it would be like to touch him without being so sneaky. He was so sexy, and I was having such a good time. I was happy he'd suggested getting drinks after dinner, because I really didn't want the night to end, but didn't know how to extend it myself.

"Here we are, milady." We stopped in front of an Irish pub, where he took his arm back and pulled the door open for me to enter. I immediately missed his closeness.

"Great. This place looks fun," I said.

"It's got a nice, chill vibe. I thought it would be cool to continue our getting to know you chat over drinks on the patio out back here. There're some patio heaters here, too, so you shouldn't be cold, but if you are, we can stay inside." Looking at him as he awaited my reply, I noticed his eyes sparkle from the neon lights around the bar.

"No, I like the fresh air. Let's go outside. If I get cold, I'll just have to steal your arm again," I flirted. I actually flirted a little bit.

I was making myself blush.

"I like your style, Viv." He put his arm around me and led us out to the patio. There were no tables left, so we went up to the bar, where he found two seats and helped me climb up onto one.

"Thank you, Seth. You're always lifting me up, I guess," I joked around. I really didn't think I was that short or small, but around him, I felt tiny.

"I'm at your service, darlin'. Now, what can I get you to drink?"

"Why don't you let me get the drinks since you got dinner?" I didn't want him to have to pay for everything. I had plenty of money.

"Let's get one thing straight right now, Vivian." He got serious, and I felt my eyes get big. "When you're with me, your wallet stays in that giant purse of yours. This is not a negotiation, either, you understand me?" Lightening up, he winked at me, melting me again.

"Ok, ok. I understand." I pretended to pout, sticking my lower lip out dramatically.

"You better put that lip away, Viv," he leaned in and said quietly, his closeness making my heart race.

"Or else, what?" I whispered back.

Reaching his hand up near the back of my neck, he pulled my face even closer to his. The corners of his full lips turned up into a smile before he leaned in and pressed his lips to mine gently, sending a burn through my entire body, taking my breath away.

As he pulled away gently, he replied, "Or I'll have to kiss you, darlin'." I couldn't even remember what I wasn't supposed to do or I'd get kissed, but I wanted to do it all the time.

I caught my breath as he leancd back on his stool and flagged the bartender for us. "Did you want the same wine you had before, Viv?"

Shaking myself back to reality, I shook my head. "I'll have a Guinness this time."

"Excellent choice. I'll have the same." He motioned to the bartender then turned back to me. I think I hadn't moved since he kissed me. "So where were we, darlin'?"

"Uh, I was going to leave my wallet in my purse, I think?" I grinned, remembering that my pouty lip started it all.

"Yes, yes, you are. And if you pout, I'll have to stop you, but you don't seem too upset about that part."

"No, the stopping part I'm a fan of." I was still trying to flirt and felt my face get hot and flushed. "Makes me want to pout more." I was laying it on thick.

He laughed and rested his hand on my leg as our beers arrived. He rubbed my thigh gently and didn't move his hand away for the rest of the night until we decided it was time to go. We had continued to chat about our jobs for most of the night, and the more we talked, the more comfortable I felt. I had forgotten how wonderful it felt to have a man's company, let alone a good-looking, life-saving, interesting man.

When we got back to the truck, he had to help me get in again, which was kind of awkward, even though he picked me up with such ease. If we went out again, I thought that perhaps I'd mention taking my car, but I didn't want to get ahead of myself. I suspected that he wouldn't love that idea.

When we got in the truck, we were quiet for a moment before he turned to me and sighed.

"Is everything ok?" I asked a bit nervously.

"Viv, darlin', everything is great. I had a really great time with you tonight, and I hope you did too."

"I really did, Jax." I gave him a shy smile. He smiled back and reached across the seat to take my hand in his. He held my hand, rubbing along my palm with his thumb the entire ride back to my house.

He of course helped me out of the truck again and walked me to my front door. "Would you like to come in?" I asked. I knew it was too soon for that, but he was so hot, and in that moment I'd have done just about anything with him.

He leaned in close to me, pressing his body into mine gently against the front door. "Vivian, I would love nothing more than to come in, but I'm working on being a gentleman, so I'm going to take a rain check. Would you do me the honor of letting me take you out again?" His hand found its way to the base of my neck again, making my body tingle at his touch.

"Yes, of course. I'd like that a lot, Seth," I whispered.

He lowered his face to my level, bringing his lips to mine again. This time, the kiss was more consuming, causing those butterflies in my core that make you forget who you are. As his lips parted, I let his tongue explore my mouth, while he pulled me in tight against him, giving me the opportunity to feel his heart. I could taste the faintest bit of Guinness and a mint he'd eaten on the ride home. That sweet flavor filled my mouth as my muscles relaxed, and I gave into the moment. I dropped my purse beside me and wrapped my arms around his torso, running my hands up his back as he deepened the kiss.

Too soon for me, he pulled away, causing me to gasp slightly.

"Viv." He met my eyes with a soft glance.

"Yes?" I breathed out.

"You're addicting." He gave me a soft smile and rested his forehead against mine. I could feel his heart beating, and as he sighed, I relaxed into him and softened my grip on his back.

"I hope that's true," I said quietly.

As he pulled away, taking my face with both of his hands, he said, "You have no idea, Viv. Now, get inside and warm up. Can't have you getting sick before we have another date, which I'd like to be sooner than later, darlin'."

"Thank you for tonight." I felt wonderful, like I'd finally let myself enjoy an evening in a way I couldn't even recall. Those first date, wonderful moment butterflies fluttered in my stomach, making me smile.

"Oh no, thank you, darlin'. Thank *you*." He planted his lips on mine one last time before pulling completely away, leaving me wanting so much more as he walked back to his truck.

I let myself into the house and turned around to see him in his truck waiting for me to get inside. I gave a little wave, and after he waved back, I went inside, shut the door, and squealed while doing a happy dance as if I just scored the winning touchdown at the Superbowl.

JAX

I waited for her to close the door before I left; I wanted to make sure she was safely inside. It also gave me a moment to get one last look at her. When she waved to me before closing the door, a pounding in my chest made me smile more than I can remember doing in a while. She was captivating, and if I weren't following the doctor's orders, I might have taken her up on the invitation inside, although this being a gentleman thing was kind of a fun challenge after tonight.

Surprising her with that first kiss was electric; I hadn't planned it out or anything, but I'd been staring at those pouty little lips all night, watching her talk. I couldn't resist anymore. It was going to be difficult to keep this gentleman thing up if I was touching her, but every chance I had tonight, I had my hands on her. As I drove home, I listened to the classic rock station and Poison's *Every Rose Has it's Thorn* came on, which had a nice slow sexy beat, but made me think about how there was no way Viv had any thorns.

I wondered what had happened to her brother. When he came up, she was firm she didn't want to discuss it. She was young, so unless her parents were extremely old, he had to be relatively close in age to her, which would have made him quite young when he died. It occurred to me in that moment that I wanted to be the kind of man who she would want to talk to about something like that. Something about this exercise of becoming a gentleman, connecting with people—with her—was both uplifting and depressing at the same time. I felt like I had this wonderful opportunity to experience the kind of joy Dr. Rosen described as possible for anyone who wanted it. On the other hand, it also pointed out many of my past selfish, poor choices. Indiscretions that I thought were who I was as a person and that I felt defined me as a fun guy, made me feel unworthy of someone as kind and genuine as Vivian Deveraux.

As I lay down to sleep that night, reflecting on my evening, contemplating who she was, I resolved that this time would really be different. While I had already committed to the exercise Dr. Rosen had me following, I wasn't sure my heart was really in it until then. I had an appointment with him the following day, and I was looking forward to talking with him about what I was experiencing. I drifted off to sleep that night, thinking about how sweet she tasted and how good she felt in my arms.

The next morning, I woke up to the smell of coffee and immediately realized I didn't have a headache, and I had slept more soundly than I had in weeks. Immediately, a smile crossed my face, and I hopped up out of bed to go see Matt and Isabel, who were obviously in the kitchen doing the breakfast thing.

"Good morning, friends!" I exclaimed more loudly than I intended, because both Matt and Isabel flinched from surprise.

"Well, hey, there, sunshine, you must have had a fantastic evening. You're practically glowing," Matt teased.

"Well, fuck you very much. Yes, I did have a lovely evening with Miss Deveraux. And how are you two heroes this morning?"

Isabel started laughing immediately. "We are fantastic. In fact, even though all of the paperwork isn't done yet, we are heading over to the gym to measure some things, so we can start setting up to paint and do some stuff like that. Would you like to join us?"

"I have an appointment around lunchtime at the VA, but I can meet you over there afterwards. Sounds like it's all coming together?" I replied.

"Yeah, it's getting pretty exciting. We want to remodel and get ready to put new signage up so we can start promoting a grand reopening in about a month. Murphy is helping us reach out to some fighters, and we are going to host an open house with some mixed martial arts demonstrations and stuff to draw in some new blood." Isabel appeared enthusiastic about the whole thing.

"That sounds really cool," I replied.

"Yeah, we want to have a kids program too, so we are going to incorporate more classes and offer incentives to the fighters to participate as guest instructors and shit, so that the kids who come in stay and become adults who work out and represent the gym eventually as they start to compete. It's one of our longevity strategies for the business," Matt explained.

"Dude, that's awesome. I love that idea. Let me know how I can help in any way," I said. I was totally on board for the whole project. Besides shooting, I didn't really have a lot of hobbies, and this sounded like something I'd love to be a part of more regularly.

Without even asking, Isabel handed me a full coffee cup with a smile and went back to the table to finish her breakfast. "Thank you, darlin'." I winked at her.

"Easy with the flirting shit, pal," Matt ribbed me.

"Oh, leave him alone," Isabel defended me. "Besides, look at that face. He's in puppy love, can't you see it?" She thought she was hilarious obviously, so I gave her the one-fingered salute from across the kitchen while taking my first glorious sip of coffee.

"As much as I'd like to tell you both to go fuck off, I'd have to listen to it through the walls, so I'll just say *piss off* in traditional Irish fashion. Isabel, what kind of coffee is this? It's different than the norm, and it's fucking delicious," I proclaimed cheerfully, changing the subject.

Laughing, she replied, "I wondered if you'd notice. I found it at that coffee shop downtown on Third Avenue. Matthew here didn't notice a difference. No accounting for taste, I guess." She poked him from across the table.

"It's amazing. My new favorite. Thanks, Detective. You're aces with me." I winked at her. I winked a lot I was realizing. *I should keep that shit on reserve for Viv* I thought to myself. "Alright, well, as much as I'd like to shoot the shit with you two lovebirds all morning, I need to go to the auto parts place and take care of something for the truck before my appointment, and then I'll meet you at the gym around 2:30. Does that work?"

"Yep, sounds great. See you then," Matt replied.

I took that glorious cup of coffee with me to the shower and got myself ready for the day, feeling optimistic even though I definitely had some stuff I wanted to run through with Dr. Rosen.

I hit up the auto parts place that was near the VA, so I could maximize my time. I hadn't heard from or talked to Viv yet, and while I wanted to text her when I woke up, I decided to wait until after my session, so I'd know better how to play my cards. While that may sound divisive, it was really because I didn't want to fuck it up.

"Well, Seth, how are you today? You're looking quite positive, I must say." Dr. Rosen shook my hand when I came in.

"Well, Doc, I had a fantastic evening yesterday." I took a seat on the oversized chair in his office and got comfortable.

"I trust that you're following the rules?" He raised an eyebrow at me; clearly, he thought I wouldn't have.

"I sure am. To the letter, in fact." I grinned, feeling accomplished.

"Well, do tell, Seth. Let's chat."

Vivian

Even though it was late when I got home that night, I immediately texted Jess a bunch of hearts, so she'd know I was home and had had a fabulous evening. As soon as she was awake and functioning the next morning, she called me.

"Soooooooo?" she squealed.

"Well, good morning to you too, sunshine," I teased her.

"Oh, cut the shit, Viv. I saw the hearts! Did you get some last night? Oh God, I hope you did," she rambled.

"No!" I exclaimed.

"Well, that's disappointing. Did you at least get to second base?" She really could be too much sometimes, but she made me laugh anyway.

"Oh my God, Jess, shut up. He was a perfect gentleman the entire evening." I felt a little excited churn rise up from my belly. "We did kiss, though. And Oh. My. God. Jess... I can't even tell you how sexy he is. Well, I can."

"I'm gonna need ALL of the details," she said.

"Well, duh." I laughed at her. I loved that we had a best friend relationship that felt almost like high school. I mean we could be serious when we needed to, but me going on a first date, and a fabulous first date at that, was something we could have a lot of fun talking about.

I proceeded to tell her about how he made it known from the moment he picked me up that the business talk was just a ruse, and how he had to lift me into the truck.

"He had to lift you physically into the truck? How big is this truck? It's not a small penis compensation truck, is it? He doesn't have rubber testicles hanging from the tailgate, does he?"

I laughed so hard that I let out a mini snort. "No! I mean I don't know what his penis size is. Yet. But there are definitely no dangling ball sacks hanging from the tailgate. Only you would think of that, oh my God, Jess." I couldn't stop laughing.

"Well, these are valid questions, Vivian. I mean, seriously, they are."

"Yes, you're totally right." I was still laughing but continued telling her about the evening.

"So, when you stuck that pouty-ass lip of yours out because you wanted to pay for drinks, he shut you up with a kiss?" she asked.

"Yep. That's exactly what happened. It was incredible."

"Oh, boy, someone is a smitten kitten, aren't they?" she teased me.

"I sure am. Not gonna lie. I invited him in last night, and he said that he was trying really hard to be a gentleman, that he wanted to come in, but he thought he should go. But we totally made out on my doorstep before he left. And he asked if we could go out again," I gushed.

"Well, Miss Viv, it looks like Stella Got her Groove Back. I'm proud as hell."

"As silly as it sounds, I feel like I did! After we kissed, he somehow had a hand on me at all times. Doing little things like gently rubbing my thigh, stuff like that. He was even trying to keep me warm with his arm around me when I forgot my jacket in the truck."

"You forgot your jacket in the truck? You saucy little minx. You never forget your jacket. You did that shit on purpose, didn't you?" She totally knew me.

Laughing, I admitted it. "Yea, I did. I wanted to see what he'd do if he thought I was cold, or if he'd notice. He totally put his arm around me to keep me warm. Let me tell you about his rock hard body, Jess. Seriously, I couldn't help but give a little feel on those washboard abs of his when he had me pulled in tight. Oh. My. Gawwwwd." I definitely squealed a little bit on that one, reminiscing about touching his hotness.

"Viv, I'm so goddamn happy for you. This is excellent. Have you talked to him since?" she asked.

Making a bit of a pout, I said, "No, not yet. I don't want to text first. I don't know what his schedule is or anything, so I don't want to bother him, and I definitely don't want to come off like a stage-five clinger or anything like that."

"I wouldn't worry about it. Men like that have busy lives and lose track of time and space and shit. If he already asked you if he could take you out again, and he didn't try to bang you on the first date but was kissing on you and stuff, you'll hear from him. Just be 'busy' until you do," she advised. As much as I hated playing the game, and I really wanted to send a text thanking him for the evening, I knew she was right. And being the normally mature, busy professional that I was, I needed to be dignified and adult

607

about the whole thing.

"Oh, you're right. It's Saturday, so I have a short open house in a bit, and then me and you, we're doing drinks at that martini bar downtown?"

"You know it. Ok, go sell a house so you can buy me liquor," she teased.

"Yeah, yeah. I'll text you later. Have a good afternoon nap," I teased her back. She always took a Saturday afternoon nap. She insisted on getting up early every day, so it was part of her routine, but she couldn't handle it and always took naps on Saturdays and Sundays. She was so funny.

I didn't feel like working out, so I showered and put on one of my usual shift dresses that doubled as a suit. Realtors had become more casual over the last ten years, but I found that dressing up more professional and conservative than trendy gave me credibility I lacked due to my age. After the conversation I had with Seth last night about being alone in houses, coupled with the weird guy from yesterday, I decided to ask one of my colleagues from town to join me at the open house just so I wouldn't be alone.

Sometimes open houses went really well, and sometimes they were a total flop. They were kind of old school, but people out on a drive did like to stop by and check out houses that were for sale on a whim, so we always did them anyway. It was almost tradition to do a few of them for properties that had great curb appeal. The house I was showing today was no exception. It was a small, Florida traditional bungalow, and it was priced to move. It has a sweet little backyard, which was a commodity this close to the city, and while it needed some upgrades, it was a perfect starter home, which was my favorite to show.

This particular home was still occupied, so it was furnished and lived in, which helped sell houses better. Staging could be tricky when a house was unoccupied, because it's so empty. While that makes the house seem bigger overall, it made it harder for potential buyers to envision it being lived in. Normally, I ask homeowners to ensure their pets are out of the house, but it was a single woman selling and she had a cat, and had no one to take care of it while she was out of the house letting people walk through it. I told her that she could keep the cat there, and that I'd make sure he didn't get out.

Normally, I'd be worried about potential buyers being allergic and things of that nature, but I just didn't care. I liked this woman, and truth be told, I loved her cat. I wanted to get one myself. I loved them. They're so sweet and loving and funny. I played with Jess' cat, Hector, all the time, and anytime she went away, I took care of him. I made a mental note to go to the shelter soon to get myself a little companion soon.

My colleague, Mike, who was supposed to join me, ended up having a family emergency and called to let me know he couldn't come at the last minute. I wasn't really nervous, to be totally honest; it was Seth's expression of concern that made me more disappointed that I'd be alone than anything else. I headed out to the house, which was only about fifteen minutes away, even in city traffic, figuring I'd be bored out of my skull, and having no idea how wrong I'd be.

JAX

"So, it sounds to me you like this Vivian, yes?" Dr. Rosen asked me. I felt my face get warm; I think I was blushing.

"Yeah, I do. She's cool as hell, Doc. She's beautiful, smart, funny. She's been through something. Her brother died. She didn't want to talk about it, but I found myself wanting to be the person she'd talk about that kind of thing with. Honestly, most of the women I've spent time with in the past were about passing time, I think. This feels different," I admitted.

"So tell me, Seth, you said that you were following my rules. Was it easy, or was it difficult not to spend the night with her?" He crossed his legs and looked at me thoughtfully.

"Both," I blurted out.

"Interesting." He smiled at me. "Explain."

"Well, obviously, I've told you she's a fox. I mean, have you seen her billboards?" I asked him. He chuckled at me.

"Is this that blond girl who sells real estate? Her picture is everywhere?"

"Yes!" I exclaimed. "Listen, I know you're a married guy and all, but you've seen her billboards. She's hot. Of course my first instinct is to get intimate with her. But, and thanks for that, you were on my mind the whole time. I was thinking about how my actions would make her feel, and I wanted to make sure that I was listening to her. That I was attentive to her needs, even on a first date."

"Well, that's good. Tell me, how did it make you feel?" he asked.

"It made me feel good and shitty at the same time, Doc. That's one of the things I wanted to talk to you about today. I'm doing everything you said, and even though she invited me in last night at the end of the date and I said no, against my instinct, I still felt like a douchebag."

"Ok, tell me why."

"Well, it has occurred to me what a stone cold dick I've been to other women. For example, I never even realized that women could barely get themselves into my lifted truck until I helped her and picked her up last night, because she was way too short to get herself in. I felt like a jackass."

The doctor chuckled. "Well, self-reflection is a part of the process, Seth. While this isn't about making you feel bad, it is about coming to a place where you recognize where you are versus where you want to be, and closing that gap. So it sounds like you learned something about the kind of man, or potential mate for someone, you want to be versus who you've been in the past. Is that fair to say?"

"Yeah, I'd say that's pretty accurate. Today, I went and installed steps on the truck so that she wouldn't have so much trouble getting in. I mean, I still want to help her, I like helping her, but I don't want her to feel totally helpless. Nobody wants to feel that way," I said. Realizing what I'd said, I felt a grin spread across my face as I met the doctor's eyes.

"You just had yourself a little breakthrough, didn't you?" he asked.

"Doc, I sure did. I understand what you mean by making a connection. Not focusing on how hot she is, which wasn't easy, but listening to her and observing her, actually made me feel better than it used to when I'd ignore those things and focus on physical connection. It's kind of crazy to realize it like this."

"It's not crazy. It's human nature, Seth. Humans were born to love," he said. Noticing my skepticism, he continued. "Let me explain. If you go back to the times of the cavemen, they mated for life. They found someone to build their home with while they hunted and gathered for the family. It's almost a basic instinct. But let's take that to today's day and age. Humans cannot thrive without six basic human needs."

"What are those?" I was genuinely curious.

"The four needs of personality are certainty, uncertainty, significance, and love. The last two, which are needs of the spirit, are growth and connection. The theory behind living a fulfilling life is to prioritize them in ways that are resourceful and meaningful. For example, if you were to rank these in order of importance to you, how would you rank them?"

I pondered them for a moment. I thoroughly believed that significance used to be important to me, but in the last few weeks, love and connection had become front-runners for me. "Well, I think that now, after spending time with you and reflecting more, love and connection are the most important to me. Is that right?" I asked hesitantly.

"There is no right or wrong answer, Seth. It is about

determining your destiny and becoming fulfilled."

"Yeah, ok, Doc, but let's be real. A few months ago, I think I would have ranked significance as number one, and that doesn't seem right. It feels selfish, and I don't want to be selfish. After spending time as recently as last night listening, like really listening, I would rank connection at the top of my list. It's hard to separate that want for connection versus my physical desires, though."

"Well, the good news is that you're human, Seth." He grinned at me. "This isn't a test where you have to get a perfect score; it's about developing a balance in your lifestyle where your motivation shifts from being about taking in for yourself and instant gratification, to achieving a level of confidence and self worth where you receive joy from making other people happy, and connecting with them. The love actually develops automatically from those behaviors and actions."

"I don't know how I feel about love, Dr. Rosen. That seems like a pretty huge leap from just developing a connection. Having someone rely on me day to day, that makes me anxious." I was being honest. I liked Vivian, but it had been one date, and now the doc and me were talking about love? How did we make that leap? I wanted to see her again, though, and I definitely didn't want some other dude swooping in on her, that's for sure. The thought of that made my blood boil.

"You look like you just had a multitude of realizations, Seth. What's on your mind, really?" Dr. Rosen was really starting to pick up on my facial expressions or something.

"Ok, here's the deal. I had a great time with Vivian. She's beautiful. She's smart. She's funny as hell. But the thought of getting so involved that she might rely on me scares the ever-loving shit out of me. I mean, I get by taking care of myself, but I have to come see you every week to keep my head on straight. I'm sleeping a couple nights a week without the nightmares, but I still wake up regularly in a panic, sweaty and confused. The headaches have lessened, but they aren't gone. I can't imagine bringing that into someone's life, and I'm not even sure that I'd want to."

"Tell me why you wouldn't want to share all of yourself with someone," he asked me point blank, giving me pause. I hesitated, unsure of my answer, and he spoke again. "Be honest with me, and be honest with yourself. What are you afraid of, really?"

I surveyed his eyes looking for an answer that was truly only within me. I sighed. "I'm afraid." I hung my head as if I was defeated.

"What are you afraid of?"

"I'm afraid of disappointing people. I'm afraid of not being enough. I feel all of this responsibility to make people happy, and it weighs on me like a Mac Truck. I'm afraid I'm not strong enough to take it on. If I continue going like this, I'm going to end up having feelings for this girl, and what if I can't keep it together?" I felt like such a failure just admitting that.

"Seth, it is not your job to take on the anxiety and troubles of the world. If this Vivian is the girl, if she's the one for you, time will tell. If you're truly giving of yourself, giving of your time, your energy, and your real, raw emotion, she will stay. If she doesn't, then it was not meant to be anything but a stepping stone, a lesson on your path." He paused and leaned toward me over his knees, getting my attention. "Is she the girl? The one? I don't know. You've been on one real date in your life at this point. But do you owe yourself the opportunity to find out? To explore the possibility? You're goddamn right you do." And with that, he sat back, letting me absorb his words.

"I want to see her again. I slept like a rock last night, Doc. And I woke up without a headache. She was the first thing I thought of this morning, and I was happy about it. I'm just afraid to fuck it up."

"Seth, this is totally normal. Believe me. Even with my wife, I'm afraid to fuck it up sometimes. Relax, enjoy the moment, and remember that true connection with someone comes from giving of yourself. What that means is that in order to really receive love, you have to be open to it. You have to give from a place that is meaningful, and that is going to mean sharing. Sharing your story. Sharing your truths. Maybe not like we do here, but you will need to be authentic with her if you want something real."

"I think that I do. I know it's only been one date, but she's special. So I need to keep doing what you said?" I had to ask. I was hoping he knew what I meant.

"Do you mean no sex?" He smirked at me.

"Yeah," I replied cautiously.

"I think it would be wise for you to refrain for a bit. I'd hate for you to get lust or passion mixed up with connection. I know that it probably seems frustrating, but first dates are about getting to know what someone does for a living, what their hobbies are, things like that. If you are serious about establishing a relationship with this woman, then you are going to need to dig a little deeper, and it is my opinion that for you, sex would cloud that judgment. I'm not saying you can never be intimate again, or intimate with her for that matter. I'm just saying, don't make that a priority, and see where it takes you."

"Ok, Doc. I trust you. And I do know what you mean. Don't get lost in the magnetism. Get to know her. I want to know her," I admitted.

"That's absolutely wonderful, Seth. Now, you said you slept well, is that becoming more regular?"

"Not especially. I mean, I slept well last night and didn't have any issues this morning. I went to bed extremely relaxed, and I've been working on the meditation stuff we went over, which helps. I'm trying not to take the pills; they make it hard for me to wake up in the morning, and I feel like I'm in a fog on the days after I take them to sleep." Dr. Rosen had prescribed me sleeping pills to take when I needed them, and we agreed that we would not make them a regular thing. I didn't like the idea of getting addicted to something like sleeping pills, and I didn't want to fix my problems with drugs. We agreed that I'd let him know weekly how many times I needed to take them to get a full night's rest, and then we'd continue to evaluate the situation.

"Alright, so if you're taking them three days a week or less, I think we're fine. Keep me posted on that, and we'll talk about it again next week. Sound good?" He stood up, signifying that our time was up.

Standing up to shake his hand, I said, "Thank you, Doc. I'm starting to see the light at the end of the tunnel more, and I know it's from being able to talk to you about this shit."

He smiled and nodded. "Seth, there will always be shit. How you deal with it is what makes you the man you are, and you're doing everything you should be to get your mind right and become the person you want to be. Keep up the good work."

"Thank you." I turned to walk out, feeling like the world was on my side. The first thing I did was grab my phone from my pocket to text her.

Vivian

Nobody had showed up to the open house that day. Frustrated and cranky about it, I gathered my things and made my way outside when the time had finally passed and I could go. That was a house that I'd have to sell and show to one of my clients; an open house just wasn't going to cut it. As I was packing up my car to leave the property, I saw a truck that reminded me of Seth's pulling into the driveway next to my car. It didn't take long for me to realize it was him; when I did, I felt a smile form, changing my day around in an instant.

He hopped out of his truck in the driveway and sauntered over to where I was standing at my car. "Hey there, darlin'," he said with that slight southern drawl. I loved the sound of his voice; it was smooth, and when he spoke I would hang on every word.

"Um, hi there, Jax. What are you doing here? Uh, not that I'm not happy to see you." I was putting my foot in my mouth within moments.

"Well, you didn't return my text, so I figured you were busy showing this house, and I wanted to see you, so I figured I'd come to the open house then."

Quickly grabbing my phone from my bag, I saw the text

message and visibly rolled my eyes at myself. "I'm so sorry. I must have had it on silent. I didn't hear it. I've been sitting here doing not much of anything by myself here all day too."

"By yourself?" he asked, giving me a scowl.

"For the record,"—I placed my hand on my hip and pointed at him—"I'll have you know that I did have someone scheduled to be here with me. However, they had a family emergency at the last minute and had to bail. So I didn't have a choice. Not. My. Fault."

"Alright, sassy pants, not your fault, but I don't have to like it, either, you know." He took his sunglasses off to look at me, and of course flash me that smile that was simply irresistible.

"Oh? Sassy pants? You have no idea." I started to giggle. "So really, what are you doing here?" I took my jacket off, now that I was technically off the clock. It was still pretty warm out during the day, and my dress was kind of thick, so I was hot. I grabbed a pair of flip-flops from my back seat and dropped them in front of me awaiting his answer.

"I really just wanted to see you, darlin'." He leaned against his truck. "I was hoping I could take you to lunch or something?"

Immediately, I was disappointed. I already had plans with Jess, and we just don't cancel on each other. "I have plans in a little bit, I'm sorry. But if you're not doing anything later, my best friend and I will be downtown getting drinks if you'd like to meet up?" I didn't want to miss the opportunity to spend some more time with him.

"Downtown, eh? What kind of trouble are you little ladies getting into downtown?"

"No trouble, just drinks. Just a normal Saturday night." I laughed.

"Well, Miss Sassy Pants, I think I just might take you up on it. I want to see more of you. Your friend going to be okay you invited me along?"

I slipped my feet out of my heels, making me four inches shorter, and put my flip-flops on. I didn't like to drive in heels; it ruins them. I always had a spare pair of shoes in my car. "She won't mind at all. Her new boyfriend is going to be meeting us out too. You can quietly judge him with me." I smiled up at him, then leaned up against my car across from him

"Oh, is that what we're going to do? Make some poor dude uncomfortable?"

"Well, they'll be silently judging you too, so it'll be totally fair, really." He laughed and slid his hands in the front pocket of his jeans.

"Well, I would love to join you in this judging event." He grinned. "I am going over to the gym shortly to help Matt and Isabel with some stuff the rest of the afternoon if you're really not going to join me?" He stuck his lower lip out and pouted like I did the night before, making me laugh.

"You know what happens when you pout?" I attempted to flirt and playfully looked up at him through my lashes.

"I know what happens when *you* pout, but what exactly happens when *I* pout, sassy pants?" He stepped toward me, closing the distance between us.

Curling my lips into an excited smile, I leaned into him and rose on my tippy toes, balancing myself against his chest with my hands. "I think turnabout is fair play, don't you?" I said quietly.

"I'd say that's totally fair." He brought his smile down to mine for a kiss. When his lips touched me, the burning sensation all through me was almost impossible to control. It felt as though we were wrapped in a blanket, and the rest of the world disappeared, just leaving us standing there, connected. His lips were so soft and warm. I honestly could have died happy at that moment, just wrapped up in him.

I lowered myself back down and ran my hands down his chest. "This pouting thing totally works for me." I let out a small giggle.

Laughing back and pulling me in for a squeeze, he agreed. "I'm going to have to agree with you, sassy." He kissed the top of my head, which was one of my new favorite things, then released me and stepped away. "Ok, it looks like we both have shit to do, so I'll see you tonight then?"

"Yes, definitely. I'll let you know where we are, and we can definitely meet up."

"All right, then I'll see you later, darlin'." He came in to give me a quick peck on the lips before walking around to the driver's side of his truck to leave. I gave him a little wave and got in my car as well, where I sat for a moment to relish in the moment.

My heart raced when he was around, and I was almost short of breath. He was so damn hot. Whenever he was in my presence, I wanted to be touching him. I absolutely loved when he wrapped me up in my arms; he felt so warm and comforting. He was also so sweet, and his demeanor toward me was playful, but also very loving. Twice he'd brought me close and kissed the top of my head, resting his above mine for a moment, and something in that gesture made my heart skip a beat.

I called Jess on my way home to let her know that he was planning to meet us out. I thought I'd lose my hearing from her squeaky excitement on the phone.

"Get out! Really? So, we are going on a double date!" she yelled.

Laughing, I replied, "Yeah, I guess we are. That's pretty funny. I mean, he's just meeting us out wherever we are, he said."

"This is totally amazing and I cannot wait. What are you wearing tonight? Something slutty? Pretty please?" she teased me.

"Oh my God, Jess, you're too much. I hadn't even given it any thought yet."

"You need to wear something tight and short to show off that rocking body of yours. You went casual before, now it's time to bring out the big guns. I'm serious. You could very well be getting laid tonight, and I'm as excited as if it were my own pussy!" she exclaimed.

Shaking my head and laughing like a teenager, I was thankful that my windows were up and no bystanders could hear my Bluetooth speaker from the car at the red light I was sitting at. "Good lord, Jess, you are too much."

"Yeah, too much, whatever. You love me, and you are just as excited, even though you're pretending to be cool. You forget I know you. I happen to know that your vagina is sad, and it wants attention from a sexy-ass firefighter."

"That might be true." I started to laugh uncontrollably.

"Alright, I gotta go. I need to call my parents, and I have a few things to do before I come over. I'm just gonna get an Uber so I don't have to deal with parking downtown. I hate driving," I said.

"Ok, sounds good. Then your sexy hero can just take you home." I rolled my eyes. She really was too much. While I totally wanted to have sex with him already, that was largely based on how long it had been since I'd had sex last. It had been a while. A long while. He made it clear he was trying to be a gentleman, which I appreciated, so I didn't think tonight was the night. That certainly didn't stop me from thinking about what I could wear that would make him wish it was.

JAX

I really fucking hated going downtown. I absolutely avoided it at all costs normally. There are too many people, too many rookies out and about on a Saturday night doing shots, screaming and yelling and not pacing themselves. I always preferred the bars and restaurants on the outskirts of downtown that had a more relaxed vibe compared to the overwhelming noise of the downtown bars and nightclubs.

That all being said, if little Miss Sexy Sassy Pants Vivian was going downtown on a Saturday night, I was going too. Besides the fact that I frankly didn't want some other douchebag hitting on her, which he absolutely would, I wanted to see her. Something in her sweet face calmed me every time I was in her presence. I had brought her into my arms twice now, just to hold her, and it was quickly becoming my favorite thing. I towered over her, and bringing her to my chest and resting my head on top of hers felt comforting. I could smell the scent of her shampoo and her perfume mixed together lingering in my nose.

I'd be lying if I didn't admit I had a raging hard-on every time she was in the vicinity as well. I anxiously ran my hands through my hair knowing that she'd be wearing something sexy for a night downtown, and I was going to have to control myself. In an effort to give myself a pep talk, I reminded myself the sexual hiatus wasn't forever, and eventually I'd bring her to my bed and claim her over and over. Those thoughts ended up making it worse, so when I pulled up to the gym, I had to try to think of something else before I could go in. The only way to calm that shit down was to think of sad puppies or some shit, but fuck all if it wasn't near impossible to get the thought of my hands on her out of my mind.

When I went inside, there were a handful of people working out, but it was dead for the most part. I found Matt and Isabel across the gym floor pointing at something on the wall.

"What's happening over here, kids?" I asked, announcing my presence.

"Hey, dude, we were just discussing taking all of these mirrors down and re-sheetrocking the walls," Matt replied.

"Well, that sounds like a pain in the balls, but these mirrors are old and shitty and unnecessary for the type of gym you're trying to build," I said knowing full well, I'd be helping sheetrock that wall.

"That's what I said," Isabel replied. "What if we took all that shit down and put up some whiteboards or chalkboards people could use to put their work out on, or something like that?"

"Well, why don't you just paint that entire wall in chalkboard paint? Then you'd have nice smooth walls all the time. They'd be black, which is cool looking, but also you could put your own messages and stuff up, and it would be easy to clean up with water or erasers or whatever." I had seen some home show on TV do chalkboard paint on a door in a kitchen so the family could write their weekly chores and shit on it, and sometimes the mom used it to write messages for the family. Seemed like a pretty cool idea that would work for the gym too.

"I love that idea!" Isabel exclaimed. "I want to do that behind the counter at the front too. That way when there's news or something, we can just put it up there and change it super easily. Write that down, Matt." She motioned to him. He was holding a notebook and was clearly her scribe for the day.

"Your wish is my command," Matt teased her.

"Sorry, babe, I don't mean to be bossy." She lowered her voice and gave him a flirty look. She was totally playing him, and it was hilarious.

He laughed, knowing the scam she was running on him, and I knew full well he didn't care. "Sure you do, babe, but that's ok. I'll be bossy later." He smacked her ass, causing her to jump and give him a smirk as she walked off to look at more walls in the gym.

Turning to me, he asked, "How was the VA? I keep meaning to ask if everything is cool?"

"Yea, everything is cool. I've been seeing a couple of doctors there for routine shit mostly, and they also have some great resources for information and stuff that I like to use."

"Oh, that's cool. I just wanted to make sure you're ok. You are ok, right?" He gave me a concerned look, furrowing his brow in my direction.

"Yeah, of course I am. Why would you even ask?" I was defensive and concerned that maybe I hadn't been playing it as cool as I thought I had been lately.

"I don't know. You just seem tired lately. I'm your friend. I'm just doing a buddy check, is all." He seemed to be trying to play off his concern.

"Yeah, I've had some trouble sleeping lately, but I'm alright. I have a doc there who gave me something I can take on nights I'm not at the station so I can get a good night's rest, but I don't love taking it. You know me. I'm not much for taking drugs of any kind, really." That was honest, without giving any information. There're millions of people who have trouble sleeping, and it doesn't mean a thing.

"Alright. Cool, man. Well, if you ever need anything, you know you can count on me, and even on Isabel for that matter, right?" The thought of telling Matt how my anxiety had been lately gave me even more anxiety, so I tried to blow the whole thing off.

"Yeah, of course. But no need. Everything is cool, man." I changed the subject. "What are you two up to this evening?"

"We are just gonna hang at her place tonight, watch movies or something. Why? What are you up to?" he asked.

"I am meeting Vivian and her friend and some dude downtown tonight," I replied.

"Well, well. You had your first date last night, and you're already going to see her again? And downtown nonetheless? You hate downtown." He laughed.

"I do indeed hate downtown. I do not, however, hate her. She's a cool chick, and that's what she wants to do, so I aim to please." That was mostly true. If it were up to me, I'd run off to the beach with her and climb in the bed of my truck for a sleepover like her perfect day. I made a mental note of what a fantastic idea that would be for another night when it was just the two of us.

"So, you really like her, eh?" he asked me.

"I do. I mean it's new. I'm trying not to be *that guy*, though."

"What guy is that?"

"The usual douchebag who doesn't call the next day and doesn't really care to chit chat. I like talking to her; she is interesting, and she makes me laugh," I said.

"Dude, if you find a chick who makes you laugh and makes your dick hard all the time, you fucking keep her. Believe me. I never thought I'd settle down, but I can't get enough of Isabel. She makes me laugh, she looks after me even though I don't think I need it, and she rocks my fucking world," he gushed over her.

"Yeah, you two are pretty awesome together, I have to admit it. I'm not sure what I'm doing, but I know that since I met her, she's on my mind all the fucking time; and since last night, all I want to do is spend more time with her. There's something about her, man. I can't explain it."

"Eh, you don't have to. I give you a lot of shit, because that's what we do, but I want you to be happy. In fact, I think that finding a sweet girl would make you less of a dick." He started laughing.

"Ah, yes, fuck you very much, sir," I replied, laughing myself. This was how we were. Brothers act this way; even if not by blood, we were absolutely brothers.

Isabel walked back over to us, taking the notebook from Matt. "What are you two laughing about?"

"I was just telling Jax here how much I care about his happiness." Matt could barely even say it; he was still laughing.

"Oh, I see, you two clowns have your little secrets then." She rolled her eyes at us. "Don't tell me, that's fine."

"No really, we were having a *broment*." I started laughing again, making up the word.

"See? I'm not a dick, baby," Matt pleaded to Isabel.

"Oh, I didn't say that. You're a dick, but you're a dick who cares

628

about my happiness," I said. At that point, I was practically crying I was laughing so hard.

"Oh God, collect yourselves, children." Isabel started to giggle. "I can't take you two anywhere, I swear."

"You love us," Matt said and grabbed her up in his arms, making her laugh out loud finally.

"Yes, yes, ok! I do. I love you! Now put me down. Jesus!" she exclaimed.

"Ok, ok. What can we do now for you, my love?" Matt said, bowing in her direction mockingly.

"I need you two to figure out how much Sheetrock we need to redo that wall, and how much paint it will take to do the back counter and that other wall in the chalkboard stuff. And then I need to know how much paint it will take to cover up the rest of the place in one color so it's uniform-looking and not peeling and shit. Then can you go get some paint samples in the colors we discussed so we can mull them over? I have to go into the precinct and finish up some paperwork from a case I'm working on. I was helping that Detective Seth Lane I told you about on one of his cases he just closed and need to sign off on the reports." She handed the notebook back to him after taking a look at the notes.

"Yes, ma'am," he said to her. "Jax, can you take me to Home Depot and then home? It appears my girlfriend has shit to do and we came together in her car, she is abandoning me" He looked over to me making a sad helpless face.

"Of course, I'm here to help." I smiled. "Let's go before she gives us more chores, though."

"See ya, babe. Let me know when you'll be home so I can be the bossy one," he teased her before giving her a quick kiss and grabbing her ass.

Smacking his hand away, then smiling at both of us, she replied, "Shouldn't be long. I'll call you on my way home."

I waved, and we made our way to Home Depot, where we had literally just been a day ago. Typical.

Like a married couple, we fished through the paint samples, attempting to find a shade of blue that the detective would approve of, then ended up taking one of all of them. There was really no use in picking one we liked, because we honestly didn't care that much which shade as long as it made Isabel a shade of happy. The best way to do that was to let her pick it herself. If I'd learned anything about women in my lifetime, it was that if they sent you to run an errand that involved guessing what they wanted, you were totally fucked and your best bet was to bring all of the options back with you, or as many as you could.

"Dude, did you install steps on the truck this morning?" Matt asked.

"I did. That was the auto parts run I had this morning. Installed them in the parking lot there; wasn't as big of a pain as I expected it to be." I was pleased with myself.

"Well, well. I see you want the little lady to be able to get in here more easily. Well played sir, well played indeed." He teased.

"Yes, well when I had to physically lift her into the truck, which as fun as it was to have my hands all over her, I felt like a fucking dick that I didn't have a vehicle she could get into more easily."

"You had to actually lift her in?" He was laughing.

"Dude, no joke. She's tiny, like a little fairy. Even with a running start, I don't think she could have leaped in on her own,"

I started to laugh too. "It's about time I turned this into somewhat of a grown up truck I suppose anyway, right?"

"You'll hear no arguments from me. I think it's cool man. That's actually really nice of you," he said.

When we got back to my place, Matt got his truck and headed over to Isabel's, leaving me back at my house alone. I really did like my house, but when no one was there at all, it left me with my anxiety and my thoughts; not the good ones. I had a few hours before I needed to go, and I didn't really have anything particularly important to do, so I decided to lie down for a bit and try to erase the dark anxiety that was creeping in. Dr. Rosen did say that sometimes it was going to happen, and not because of a trigger necessarily. He told me that in those cases where I could chill out and practice meditating to settle my mind, I should do that.

He gave me some music that I would never *ever* show anyone I had on my iPod that was for meditating. It was mid-Eastern chimes, more or less, and shit that was supposed to help me visualize energy and focus on relaxing my muscles, and therefore my mind. I didn't particularly like it at first, but after about two weeks of making myself listen to it quietly alone, I found that it did change my state; it completely relaxed me, helping me clear my head of the junk that fogged it up. The mellow sounds, and the singing or chanting I couldn't understand, vibrated in my ears, taking my mind away from everything else.

I laid my head on my pillow with my ear buds in, focusing on the music and shutting my eyes. I had felt a headache developing shortly after Matt left, so as I laid flat on my back, listening, I imagined a soft light relaxing me from head to toe, making me sleepy. These were all techniques Dr. Rosen had gone through with me in the office. He had done what he called 'a guided meditation' when I first went to see him, to calm me down, and then walked me through doing something similar when I was alone. As I relaxed, my headache dissipated, and I dozed off.

Vivian

I was so excited that Seth was going to come out, the butterflies in my stomach felt so bad that I got nauseous. Jess was completely spot-on; I was smitten. I was also really scared to get involved with someone. It's a strange thing when you've been single for a while and you've gotten used to doing your own thing. You have bouts of loneliness that you have to fight off; they lead you down a dark path to depression if you're not careful. Then, when you're having an up day and you get excited about something, disappointment can feel like getting punched in the stomach. I was scared of getting my hopes up or investing in something that would turn out to be nothing. I had to remind myself a hundred times that we'd had one date, that's all, and that it was too soon to tell.

Everyone who's already in a relationship loves to tell you that you should do this, or do that, and they're definitely always telling you how great dating is and how you should enjoy it. I get it, but seriously, dating gave me anxiety. The not knowing, the acting like a flipping idiot, which I do all the time; none of that was fun for me. That was the stuff that would make me just want to stay home.

I was drawn to Seth, though. He seemed troubled in some way

that I couldn't put my finger on. I wanted to get to know him, the real him. Of course he was charming and insanely good-looking, but I felt like I had barely scratched the surface in just one date. I knew tonight probably wasn't going to be a getting to know you evening, but being near him anyway was a step in the right direction, even if I was scared and nervous. In the grand scheme of things, that's what alcohol is for anyway; to take the edge off. So I planned to wear something sexy and enjoy the evening with my best friend, her new man, and what could very well be my new man.

Jess and I were going out by ourselves, and the boys were meeting us later when we'd be going to some nightclubs and bars. We wanted girl time of our own, so I met her at one of the martini bars downtown in the early evening instead of her house, which was the original plan. Downtown was between our houses, and it was really just easier to meet in the middle for our girl talk before the boys came.

"It's about time. I've been here for like twenty minutes," I said when she rolled in.

"Parking was a bitch! You know how it is down here," she explained.

"Yeah, I do. Which is why I don't drive in the city. Total waste of time. And at the end of the night, the last thing I want to do is walk six blocks to my car," I said.

"Yeah, yeah. Well, let's get a look at you, sexy." She motioned for me to stand up.

Laughing, I accommodated her request and did a little spin at the bar for her. I had chosen an off-the-shoulder dress with long sleeves. It was sort of 50s style, very fitted, showing off all of my curves, not leaving a lot to the imagination. I chose blue, simply because I loved wearing blue, and I picked out black for my heels of choice that night. People always asked me how I walked in them, but I had been wearing them for so long, it was easy. I guess practice makes perfect, and if you found the right ones—by which I mean pay top dollar—sexy shoes can be very comfortable.

"You look absolutely fuckable, Viv," she exclaimed.

Mortified, my eyes got huge. "Shut up, Jess! Now, sit down and have a drink with me!"

Following my orders, Jess, who was also dressed to kill, took the seat at the bar next to me. Her black mini skirt was very mini, and she had on boots that came up over her knee, skimming her thighs. She had on a fire engine-red top that was truly eye-catching.

"Ok, ok! Well, you do. And so do I, for that matter." She laughed, flagging the bartender over. I was already sipping on a dirty martini with blue cheese olives. There was something about a little snack with your drink that made me happy, and they worked their magic quickly. After she placed her order, she turned to me. "So, let's talk about Mr. Hotty Hot Firefighter, shall we? How did it come to be that he will be joining us downtown? Which pleases me to no end, I might add."

"Well, he came to my open house today," I said.

"Yes, you mentioned that earlier. What was that about? What did he say exactly?"

"He said that he wanted to see me." I felt my face get flushed with embarrassment.

"Well, that's fucking adorable, Viv. For real. Tell me more," she demanded.

"Well, as I was leaving from a total waste of an open house, he showed up and asked to take me to lunch. I told him that I had plans but that if he wanted to meet us out, he was totally welcome to come, and he seemed fairly pleased about the invite?" I kind of questioned my recapping of the exchange.

"You had your first date last night, and he showed up at your open house today to take you out again. This is fantastic. I like him already." She raised her martini glass so we could toast. "Here's to a fun evening of judging each other's man and having ourselves what could definitely be described as a double date." We clinked glasses before we sipped our drinks.

The vodka was warming me through, and I was already less anxious about seeing him, and far more excited. I had texted him where we would be so he could come whenever he wanted, and I let him know that if we went someplace else, I'd let him know. I didn't hear back, but he did say that he would be busy at the gym with Matt and Isabel, so I assumed that's what he was up to. I was on my second martini and knew I'd need to take it easy or I'd be smashed by the time either of the boys showed up.

Since Jeremy was coming soon, I had Jess fill me in on what was going on with them. She seemed happy, and it looked like Hector the cat was a big fan too. That was a huge deal breaker for Jess; if you didn't like cats, she didn't like you. I thought that was a pretty good policy; after all, animals have instincts that the rest of us do not. Immediately, I wondered if Hector would like Seth, but since he's a firefighter, he had to, right? The thought made me giggle a bit.

Not long after we got our gossip out of the way, Jeremy arrived. He was very handsome, and Jess lit up like a Christmas tree as soon as she spotted him.

"Hey, babe, you look amazing," he said, giving her a kiss.

"Thank you so much. Jeremy, I'd like you to meet my best friend, Vivian Deveraux," Jess introduced me, and I extended my hand.

"Vivian, it's a pleasure to meet you. Jess has told me so much about you. And of course, I've seen your signs," he said, shaking my hand.

"Oh, yes, they are indeed all over the place. As silly as it is, it brings me quite a bit of business." That billboard always came up when I met people, but in reality, it was the best marketing ever. My parents took pictures of it when it was put up, which was embarrassing and hilarious. My mom had mused about how proud my brother would have been, and then the day took a turn downhill. But she's on her own grief schedule, and there's not much you can do in a situation like that. As my thoughts drifted for the moment, I watched Jeremy interact with Jess. I wondered where Seth was, and then realized that I hadn't checked my phone in a while.

"Well, shit," I said, looking at my phone.

"What's wrong?" Jess asked.

"Oh, I missed another message from Seth. I keep doing that. Not looking at my phone. Looks like he'll be here any minute now too. I'm going to run to the ladies' room real quick and freshen up." I grabbed my purse off the little hook under the bar and went to the ladies' room.

I checked myself in the mirror, wanting to look perfect, fixed my lipstick, fluffed my hair, and inspected my dress to make sure nothing was out of place. I was antsy and excited to see him, but nervous about all of us hanging out together. As I walked back to the bar, I spotted him standing there with Jess right away. Much taller than the average guy, he was at least a head taller than most of the men in the bar. As I approached, he saw me and smiled, giving me goose bumps all over again.

"Well, hey there, darlin'. Forget to check your phone again?" Not waiting for an answer, he gave me a quick kiss on the lips right in front of Jess.

"Um, yes, I did. I really must get better about that, I'm sorry," I said, forgetting anyone else was there until Jess cleared her throat, waking me from my little daze.

"Oh, I'm so sorry. Seth, this is Jess, my best friend, but it looks like you've met?" I said.

"I spotted him walk in and flagged him down. We were just making introductions," Jess answered. She turned to Jeremy, who had taken a spot behind her and introduced him, "This is Jeremy. Jeremy, this is Seth."

As they shook hands, Jeremy said, "I'm Jess' boyfriend. It's nice to meet you, Seth." I made eyes at Jess, who shrugged her shoulders and smiled. She clearly didn't know he was her boyfriend until that moment, which was downright adorable. Seth settled in at the bar, standing next to me, and as I caught a whiff of his cologne, I became weak in the knees. It wasn't the martinis. He smelled downright amazing.

After he ordered a drink and we were all chatting, he leaned down to whisper in my ear, "What are you trying to do to me in that dress, sassy?" I leaned into him, feeling his muscular chest against my back, and giggled.

"I don't have any idea what you mean." I glanced over my shoulder to tease him when he brought his hand gently to my throat to hold me for a kiss. I had never been one for public displays of affection, but I wasn't going to argue with this man's lips on me. After he let go, his fingers gently slid across my neck to my shoulder and he leaned in to whisper again.

"You make it very hard to be a gentleman, Miss Deveraux."

"Nobody said you had to be," I whispered back. I was being a little lippy; I guess the liquor was getting to me a little bit. But I was having fun.

"So, are we ready to move on to another spot?" Jess stood up.

"Whatever the ladies would like," Jeremy replied.

I grabbed my purse to pay my tab when I realized Jax had already taken care of it. "What are you doing? You don't need to do that," I said.

"Want to. Hush about it, darlin'. You alright to walk around in those shoes?" He pointed to my fabulous heels.

Scrunching my nose at him, I said, "Yes, of course I am. I wear heels all the time, Seth."

"Oh, I've noticed your sexy little feet," he replied with a smirk. "So, where are we off to?" he asked.

"We were thinking of that rooftop bar over on Church Street? Is that ok with you?" I forgot to even ask him what he wanted to do.

"I'm happy with whatever or wherever you'd like to go, milady. Lead the way." He motioned toward the door so he could follow. Jess and I met at the door, and the boys followed us. We were whispering to each other while the guys got to know each other walking behind us. The bar was only about two blocks away, so it wasn't a far walk.

"Secrets don't make friends, ladies," Jeremy called from behind us.

Laughing hysterically, we stopped to let the boys catch up with us, and we coupled back up. Jess and Jeremy led the way the last block, and I watched as he put his arm around her, pulling her close and kissing her on the cheek. It was sweet, and I was so happy for her.

"What's on your mind, sassy?" Seth asked me as we fell in line behind them.

"I'm just happy for Jess. She's dated some real jackasses—I mean, I guess we all have—but he seems like a nice guy, and that makes me happy for her."

"Have you been dating jackasses before me?" He winked.

"Well, yeah. I mean I'm single, so I sure didn't meet any good ones," I said with a little bit of a snark, thinking about the cheating troll that was the last one.

"I don't think you'll be single much longer, sassy." He reached down for my hand, giving it a squeeze.

Teasing him, even though I wanted to jump his bones for such a romantic comment, I said, "You trying to make an honest woman out of me, Seth Jackson?"

"Quite the contrary, Miss Deveraux. It is you who is making an honest man of me." It was in that moment that I started to catch the feelings. Like a plague that takes your rational mind away. I was in. I leaned into him as we finished the walk to our next stop, and we held hands the entire way.

JAX

The world was against me. When I saw Vivian walk toward me in that skintight dress, my dick took over my brain. She looked like a fucking pin-up model, while she was still so cute and conservative at the same time. She didn't have everything on display; her dress was at her knees, but it hugged every curve and yet still covered them up like a present I wanted to unwrap. I could barely keep my hands off of her from the moment I saw her.

We were heading over to this rooftop bar on Church Street and I was holding her hand the entire way. Something about holding on to her continued making me feel alive and connected, not in a fog. The usual fuzzy, indifferent feeling I had most nights when I went out was completely gone in her presence.

When we arrived, we all went up to the top, taking the stairs. She was a little tipsy already, and that tight dress of hers was making her hips sway even more as she took the steps. It was almost comical that her ass was right in my face as we walked up three flights of stairs; it was all I could do to keep from putting my hands all over it. When we reached the top finally, and my torture was over temporarily, she pulled me to the side to talk.

"Hey, I'm buying you a drink and I don't want any lip about it, ok?" She pointed her tiny little finger at my chest.

"Alright, sassy pants, settle down. I'll let you buy me *one* drink if it will make you happy." I laughed.

"It would make me very happy, so you should let me do it." She batted her eyelashes at me dramatically.

"As you wish," I said. "But can I have a little kiss right now?" I negotiated.

She turned her head sidewise slightly like when you talk to a puppy. "Well, of course you can. You can have as many of those as you would like." She started to smile, but my lips were on hers immediately. She was uninhibited, probably from the martinis she had. Most of our kisses had been sweet, but this kiss was more. She reached around my waist and grabbed near my lower back, making my cock completely hard again. I pulled her to me, exploring her mouth, tasting her. I wanted to leave with her, immediately.

I knew she wanted to be out with her friend, though, so I pulled away, but not before leaning into her ear to whisper, "If you kiss me like that again, we have to leave. I can't keep my hands off of you, Viv."

"I'll keep that in mind," she whispered. "Now, let a girl buy you a drink?" Her charming smile took over, lighting her up.

"If you insist." I winked at her and ushered her over to the bar where her friend was waiting with her boyfriend.

We kept up the small talk for a while; I believe we were doing the "judging" that Vivian mentioned earlier. The dude, Jeremy, seemed cool, and her friend Jess was a trip. She was hilarious, and by the way the two girls interacted, you could tell they'd been friends forever. The original plan had been to go to one of the clubs, which I had been dreading, when Vivian asked me if I minded not going.

"Do you mind if we skip the club and just hang out here for a while before going home? Jess and Jeremy are going to head out shortly, and I don't really feel like dancing or anything. I like it up here; the breeze is nice, and it's not too crowded tonight," she asked me.

"We can do whatever you want, darlin'. I told you that."

"Thank you. I want you to have a good time too, though. What would you like to do?"

"Honestly, Viv, Doing whatever you'd like to do makes me happy. Well, and that dress; that dress makes me happy, except I don't like all these other guys checking you out. Maybe you should come sit on my lap so they know you're with me." I pulled her to me.

"Oh, please, nobody is looking at me. You're silly." She was blushing. I loved that. As sexy as she was, she was sweet too, and it felt so good to be around someone who didn't have any clue how captivating she was.

"Come here and kiss me again. I can't get enough," I demanded.

"You got it." She smiled and sat on my lap. She had one arm around my neck and the other over my heart, which was beating out of my chest. As her lips touched mine again softly, she melted into me. I stopped hearing the music, and the sound of the other patrons disappeared. It was just her and me in that moment. After the kiss ended, she put her forehead to mine and smiled.

"I'm happy I met you, Viv," I said.

"I'm happy I met you too, Seth," she whispered. "You want to get out of here? We could go back to my place and just watch a movie or something. I'm kind of tired of being out tonight. What about you?" She stood up in front of me, my hands still on her hips.

"I thought you'd never ask." I got up and we walked over to Jess and Jeremy to say good-bye.

The girls shared some secrets, and I shook Jeremy's hand before we took off.

"How did you get here? Is your car here, Viv?" I asked as we left.

"I took an Uber. I hate driving in the city. It's annoying, and finding parking makes me crazy," she said matter-of-factly. "Did you bring your monster truck?" she teased.

"Yes, I did. I parked a couple blocks away from here. Can you make it?"

"If you're asking about my shoes again, yes, I can make it a couple blocks. My whole shoe collection is like these. But, if you're asking if I'd like to get home faster, the answer is also yes." She gave me a little hip check with that sexy ass of hers.

I knew I was going to have to watch myself here. I felt like she was inviting me for more than a movie, and it was definitely too soon. At least that's what Dr. Rosen would have said. I got to see her, kiss her, and spend some time with her, but if anything more happened, then I wasn't following the rules. I wanted to know her. Really know her. The rules were no sex without the connection, and if I slept with her tonight, that would change everything, and not in the way I wanted to emotionally. Not yet at least. I'd just be doing the same thing, hiding behind physical attraction to keep my feelings at bay.

We walked along in silence, holding hands while I racked my brain on how to get out of having sex with her that night. The irony of the situation was also not lost on me; I'd never in my life tried to avoid sex, especially not with a sassy little fox like her. The internal dilemma was creating an anxiety I wasn't sure how to handle. This was definitely not something some meditation and coping statements were going to work on, and I was getting nervous.

When we got to my truck, I walked her over to the passenger side and opened the door. The new automatic step I'd installed slid out from under the truck on a hydraulic piston, giving off a little hissing sound.

"Oh my God, Jax, did you install a step on the truck? So I can get in easier?" She covered her open mouth with a hand to hide her shock. She was pleased, which was what I'd been going for.

"I did, darlin'. I can't have you feeling like you can't get in and out on your own. I'm still gonna help you, though, because I want to," I replied, beaming with pride.

"Come here." She pulled my hand around her back and stretched up to kiss me. "That was really thoughtful, Seth. You didn't have to do that." I accepted my reward kiss happily.

"Sure, I did, darlin'. Now hop in, so we can get you home." I took her hand and held her steady while she climbed in using the new step.

There was a little traffic from all the Saturday night revelers, and I could see there was also a fire truck off to the side of the road, one of ours. The other shift must have had a call. It didn't look like anything serious, and I wasn't going to stop. I was busy, but I was of course always curious.

"Do you know those guys?" she asked as we passed them.

"Yeah, that's my station, darlin'. I know most of those guys," I told her.

"Is it a fire?" she asked.

"Doesn't look like it. If I had to guess, it is probably an alarm system of some kind that went off. We get a lot of those. If they get too dusty, they can go off on their own; or sometimes there's some smoke from something, but since they're all hanging out around the truck, it looks like they're just waiting for the business owner to show up with a key."

"You guys wait for people with keys?" She seemed shocked.

I laughed. "Yes, we will wait for a key if it's not serious. If there were fire coming out of the windows, we'd smash our way in, though. Is that what you're asking?"

"Yes, that is exactly what I'm asking. It sounds fun to smash your way into a building," she said thoughtfully.

"You know what, sassy? It definitely is fun to smash your way into a building from time to time." I laughed again. She was so cute, and she really knew nothing about fires, or firefighters, or the fire department. It was endearing, and a refreshing change from the girls who went after guys in uniform explicitly. We called them badge bunnies; they were always chasing cops and firefighters mostly, and they often got passed around a station if they didn't latch on to someone. My Viv was not that kind of girl.

"I haven't been sassy at all tonight, you know." She looked at me from across her seat, resting her head on the headrest.

"Eh, I think you're always a little sassy. But that's a good thing. Your sass is cute."

"My sass is cute? So I'm cute, like a little kid?" She didn't look pleased.

"Your sass is cute, you are cute, but you're also many other things, Viv," I stalled, waiting to see if she was mad or if she was fucking with me. Either was completely possible.

"I'm just messing with you. You looked nervous, though. Did you think I was mad?" She started giggling.

"You know, darlin', I wasn't sure. You had me going for a minute." A wave of relief washed over me, and I squeezed her hand, causing her to smile over at me. Her eyes were little blue oceans that I could totally get lost swimming in.

We pulled into her driveway, and I ran over to help her out. The ride must have made her sleepy. She looked like she was ready to curl up and go to bed. *Bed, bed, beds are for sleeping, not having my way with her.* I kept saying to myself over and over in my head. I followed her to the front door and hesitated before entering.

"Don't you want to come in?" she asked me as she opened the door.

"I really do, Viv, but I don't want to rush things here," I said honestly.

She inhaled deeply and ushered me into the front room. "How about this," she proposed. "How about I put on something more comfortable and we just hang out and watch a movie or something? And we just promise each other that tonight's not the night? I'll be honest with you, Seth, I'd love to have you slam me up against the wall right now and take me, but I also think I would be much happier in the long run if we just spent a little bit of quiet time together." She raised her eyebrows and tilted her head at me with that questioning look again.

I sighed and pulled her to me for an embrace. "I would like that very much, Viv. Very much." I kissed the top of her head and released her to go change into something meant for being cozy on the couch.

"You go get yourself something to drink and get comfy. I'll be back in just a few minutes." She kissed me softly before she floated away.

Vivian

As I scurried off to my room to find something adorable but sexy to hang out in, I assessed my feelings about the whole situation. Part of me was relieved that he was still trying to be a gentleman, yet the other part of me really wanted to jump him. I couldn't believe he installed a step on his truck that very day for me to get in and out of it more easily. He really thought of everything, and I'd never experienced anything like that kind of consideration.

I threw on a tank top and some yoga pants, and returned to the living room to find him on the couch, with his shoes off and a movie on the TV. "What did you pick to watch?" I asked.

"There's a Christmas movie on. I thought that might be fun? It's only October, but it's still my favorite season, so why not get in the spirit early? Does that work for you?"

"Christmas is my favorite too." I moved myself over to the couch and snuggled into him.

"You comfy, sassy?" he asked.

"I am. Are you?"

"I don't remember the last time I was this comfortable," he replied.

His arm was around me, and I'd snuggled into the nook of his torso, with my hand on his amazingly toned abs. I couldn't help but stroke the washboard gently with my fingertips. He started to play with my hair, petting my head gently, which was causing my heart rate to rise. As I leaned my face into his neck, all I wanted him to do was kiss me and give me some relief from the burning for him that I was trying to control. Completely unable to control my desire for him, I sat up a little and softly kissed his exposed neck, sliding my hand up his chest.

He let out a soft moan and wrapped his arm around me more tightly. I maneuvered myself to face him more and continued to lick and kiss him as softly as I could control myself to do along his neck, and below his ear. I could feel his heart beating under my hand, and as I inhaled him, his manly scent made my head swim. I stopped to look at him, sitting back just a bit so I could see his eyes. As I'd hoped, he was filled with desire as well, and he moved his hands to my hips.

In one quick movement, he lifted me onto his lap, allowing me to straddle him as he moved his hands up the back of my shirt. Everywhere he touched me left a burning sensation, making me completely wet for him.

"Viv, you are so fucking sexy," he growled before he crushed his mouth to mine, claiming it. I could feel his hardness between my legs, causing the want in me to grow. As he pulled me into him, his arms wrapped around me, he began to roughly kiss my neck, making his way to my chest, which sent tingles to my nipples before he'd even touched them. His hands were making their way up my sides, and as he began to caress my breasts, I threw my head back and let out a soft moan of my own. He started to pull the top of my tank down lower, exposing more of breasts to his mouth as his thumb started to rub over my pebbled nipple. The thrill of his touch caused me to rock my hips gently into his hardness through our clothes, and I was sure I was going to lose it fully clothed like this.

As he moved his mouth over mine again, he whispered, "You make it very hard to be a gentleman, Viv."

"Maybe I like it hard," I breathed out, pressing my body against his even more.

Before I knew what was happening, he shifted us effortlessly and was hovering above me on the couch within seconds. His control over me was hot, and even though we still had all of our clothes on, I could barely control myself. He started kissing my neck again, then sat up slightly, raising my hands above my head, pinning them there.

"I want to kiss you all over, Viv, but I don't want this to go too far tonight. You're making this impossible," he said almost inaudibly.

"We can do whatever you want tonight, Seth. Anything." I meant anything. I wanted to feel him inside me. I wanted to feel his skin against mine.

He sighed deeply, then kissed me deeper than he had before. It wasn't rough; it was purely passion. As his lips pulled away from mine, he began to plant soft kisses down my neck and across my chest. He pulled my tank top down again, more this time, exposing my sensitive, pebbled nipples. Taking one into his mouth, he gently grazed it with his teeth, causing me to rock my hips upward into his. As he swirled his tongue around one, his hand moved to the other, gently stimulating me to the point of madness. His licking and suckling my nipples began to set me over the edge as I started to lose myself and my release built up.

"You taste so good, darlin'," he whispered between licks.

"I can't take it, Jax. You're making me lose it here," I panted, short of breath from the intensity of my desire.

"Good," he rumbled as he took the other nipple into his mouth, leaving the first cold and wet from his attention, making it painfully hard, and yet still feeling so intensely pleasurable. He moved a hand between my legs and began rubbing me gently as he devoured the other nipple, now tripled in sensitivity. My legs began to shake, and the pleasure I felt was uncontainable as I started to pant and roll my hips into his roving hand. As he rubbed my clit gently, with my tit firmly in his mouth, I cried out in ecstasy. I couldn't control it any longer, was completely unable to control the massive orgasm for another second.

"Seth! Oh my God," I moaned out breathlessly. I still had one hand above my head, the other around the back of his head as his tongue feverishly flicked at my nipple, intensifying every nerve in my body. The waves of my release washed over me with such magnitude, my eyes rolled back and I moaned loudly.

"Yes, that's it, baby." He increased his movements to align with mine, coaxing my orgasm out, making it last longer. As I came out of my euphoria and my hips fell to the couch, he unlatched his mouth and gently covered my breasts up with my shirt again. I was soaked. I had never had an orgasm fully clothed like that; it took my breath away, and as my chest heaved, he moved his lips to mine. "You're amazing, Vivian," he whispered to me.

Barely able to speak, I said, "Seth, that's never happened like that. I can't believe how much you turn me on." I was still practically panting at him as he began to get up, bringing me up to straddle him again.

"Baby, there's so much more where that came from." His eyes roamed my body as I sat face-to-face with him on his lap.

"We don't have to stop," I whispered, leaning in to kiss him when he held me in place.

"We do. We have to stop, Viv." His firm grasp on my hips prevented me from moving closer into him.

"Why?" I pouted. "What about you? I want you to feel as good as I do."

"Put that pouty lip away, sassy. Believe me, I feel amazing. You have no idea," he said, softening his features. He brought our foreheads together and closed his eyes, sighing. "I don't need anything else tonight but you in my arms, ok?"

"Ok." I leaned to the side so I could sink into a full embrace with him. He rested his head on my shoulder, slumping into me a bit, and held me tightly. "Are you ok, Seth?" I slid off of his lap to sit next to him and look at him.

"I am, Viv. I've been troubled in the past, but right now, I'm really great," he replied, stroking my face.

"We've all been in the darkness, Jax, it's what you do to stay out of it that matters most," I whispered, wondering what troubled him.

"And that is what I'm working on, darlin'. I promise you." His gaze retreated from me to somewhere else for a moment; I wasn't sure where. Then he asked me, "Where does your darkness come from, Vivian?"

Pursing my lips, unsure I was ready to talk about it, I stiffened my posture. I figured that if I was going to catch the disease of feelings after two days, I might as well just say what was on my mind and see how he reacted. "I told you that my brother died and

653

that it was obviously very hard on my parents."

"Yes, you did. What happened to him, Vivian?" He looked directly into my eyes, searching for something.

Without any movement, a tear fell from my eye before I even spoke. "He killed himself shortly after he came back from Afghanistan. He never told anyone anything was wrong. He just left a note saying that he was sorry and that he just couldn't take the pain anymore. We don't know what pain. But it had to be horrible for him to suffer alone like that, and it troubles me daily, Seth. There is not a single day that goes by that I don't wish I had been a better sister, a better friend to him. Every day I fight the urge to scream at him for not coming to any of us, for taking on the burden of his demons alone; some days I feel like I'm lost in black fog, searching for the answers to why he did it."

I had looked down to try to prevent any more tears, and when I looked up, the color in Seth's face had completely drained; he was pale as a ghost, taking me by surprise.

"Seth, are you ok?" I gasped.

"I... Umm... Your brother was military?" he asked me quietly.

"Yes, he was a Marine. When he came back from deployment, he was quiet and didn't want to talk about it much, but we thought that was normal because we wouldn't understand or something. We didn't come from a military family. He was the first in ours to join the service."

"Well, you know I was in the Marines as well obviously," he said, still looking shocked.

"Yes, I remember you telling me." I ran my fingers softly over his tattoo. He placed his hand gently over mine resting on his forearm. "Do you think something happened over there that he couldn't recover from emotionally?" I asked quietly.

"I don't know, Vivian. Deployment can change you no matter what you see or you do there. It's hard to explain. Sometimes you don't have to see or experience any specific incident or any kind of loss to be troubled or to be suffering in a way you don't know how to recover from," he replied softly, reaching up to wipe my tears away. I felt so vulnerable in that moment, sharing my sadness about Michael's death. The pit in my stomach grew, making me cold.

Seth shifted uncomfortably in his seat, his gaze turning away from me. I presumed that he must have been thinking of his own deployments that surely brought him his own demons. I wanted to comfort him. "Seth, I'm sorry I brought it up." I looked down at my hands, fidgeting with my nails nervously. I knew how to ruin a moment, that's for sure.

He looked back at me, shaken from whatever had stolen his thoughts for a moment. "Vivian, never apologize for sharing your feelings; especially about this. I just don't think I'm ready to talk about how I feel right now though. I'm sorry." He took my hands in his and brought them to his lips, resting them there. It was a moment I'd never forget as I watched him struggle internally with whatever darkness was occupying his mind.

"Viv, it's getting late. I'm going to go home." He stood up abruptly.

"Seth, I'm so sorry, you don't have to go." I stood up with him, almost pleading.

"Darlin',"—he caressed my face—"don't be sorry. It is really late. You didn't do anything wrong. Please don't think that, ok? Promise me." He looked intently into my eyes.

"Ok," I whispered, feeling like I had ruined the night.

I followed him to the door after he put his shoes on and gathered his keys, wrapping myself in a blanket on the way. Before opening the door, he turned to me and said, "Vivian Deveraux, you're special in ways I cannot describe, and in such a short period of time, you bring me light. Don't ever let me dim that light in you." My eyes welled up with tears that were going to fall at any moment as I simply nodded, afraid to speak.

He cradled my face, brought his lips softly to mine, and whispered, "I promise this isn't good-bye or anything; it's just good night, beautiful. I've got to go, but I'll be back. I promise." And with that, he kissed me softly and disappeared out the front door. As soon as the door closed, a waterfall of tears fell from my eyes, completely silently.

The striking similarities between Jax and Michael brought me to my knees, and I sat on the kitchen floor, silently weeping. The overwhelming guilt of losing Michael continued to consume me. Like a heavy, wet blanket wrapped around my heart, my chest tightened and my despair turned to the thought of losing Seth before I even had him, and how I'd brought up something painful for him as well. He seemed to be such a good man. He was thoughtful and attentive; and I was so foolish and naïve to not think of his feelings when I brought up Michael's suicide. Clearly, I had struck a nerve with him, and surely he had his own darkness, his own troubles he wasn't ready to share, and I quite possibly ruined the chance to truly get to know him. Loss loomed over me, choking me like smoke as I cried on the floor, feeling like a fool.

JAX

Fuck. Fuck. Fuck.

Feeling like I had been stabbed in the gut and survived to tell the tale, I pulled out of her driveway short of breath and practically hyperventilating. Her brother, a fellow Marine, fucking killed himself after he got home. Fuck. I couldn't handle the overwhelming similarities between him and myself in that moment, and I wasn't sure how I even felt about them. I probably should have stayed and consoled her, maybe even confessed my demons, but the walls felt like they were closing in on me, so I fled. Like a fucking coward, I ran.

I slammed my hands on the steering wheel, cursing myself for how I handled that conversation. The very conversation that Dr. Rosen wanted me to have I completely cut and run out on. I could tell that she was upset, and I was so torn on how to handle that. I was a leader at work, and I was a leader in the Marines; however, I had no idea how to take care of her, or myself for that matter, when it came to this. I knew that leaving at that moment hurt her. I definitely fucked this up; and if I wanted her to be in my life, which I was pretty sure I did, I was going to need to figure out how to fix this. But first, I was going to drown in the pain and darkness.

When I got home, I immediately went to the fridge and grabbed a beer, sucking most of it down immediately. Another no-no on Dr. Rosen's rules; however, since I was breaking them anyway, I might as well break them with a buzz to dull the fucking pain a little bit. I paced around my kitchen, running my hands through my hair, not even really trying to regain composure yet. Mostly, I was just processing the last couple of days. Not only had I started to fall for a chick in a matter of days, I'd made her come, then I made her cry. Fucking stellar job. I was kidding myself that I could do this; be normal. I grabbed another beer immediately, thankful that I was alone and Matt and Isabel weren't there.

Unable to organize my thoughts at all, I drank away the pain. I drank away the pain of my reality, of my whole fucking existence. I was an asshole for leaving her like that, and I was fucking weak for not being the kind of man that would stay. As I pictured the tears well up in her sweet face, I cursed myself more for hurting her. She opened up to me about her darkness; she was so strong, and so beautiful. She deserved so much more than me. As I sank lower in my self-wallowing, finishing several beers on top of what I'd already had that evening, I got myself stinking drunk. I ended up passing out on my couch for who knows how long, but when I woke, it looked like the sun was starting to come up.

I was supposed to go to work that morning. I only had one day off that week, but I called Brian to tell him I was taking a sick day. He wasn't pleased with the last-minute notice, and I knew that it was especially frowned upon to call out on a Sunday, since Saturday was a party night. Whatever, I never called out, ever, and I needed to be alone. I wanted to be alone. I wanted to feel shitty, which I did. Punishing myself by spending the day with my darkness was what I deserved. I moved myself from the couch to my bed, a headache already forming, and tried to sleep away my guilt.

Sometime around noon, I woke up from what had been a horrible sleep. The alcohol, the emotions, the nightmares, all of it left me feeling like shit. I peeked out the window to see what it was like outside. The sun was shining, barely a cloud in the sky. What I would have done for a dark, gloomy thunderstorm to fall from the sky. I went to the kitchen and grabbed another beer for what I was calling breakfast, presuming it would help the headache go away. Drinking it on my way to the bathroom, I set it on the counter and looked at my reflection. The man looking back at me was broken. Not the man I thought I could become. Not the man a precious soul like Vivian deserved in her life. As the thought of losing the opportunity to know her came into focus, I felt warm tears fall down my face.

I began to lose the faith I had that I could ever be well. That I could become the man someone like her deserved. She deserved light in her life. She was like sunshine, burning brightly with that beautiful smile and sparkling eyes, and I was the dark storm cloud ruining a perfect day. Even with her sadness and grief, she was brilliance like the stars on a summer night. She literally sparkled when she spoke, and I would ruin her. Knowing that I had made her cry brought more of my own tears, and I stepped in the shower in an attempt to wash them away. I'd never cried. Even through loss or terrible trauma at work, even through the things I witnessed in my lifetime, I'd never shed a tear in my life. I held in my feelings for so long, I didn't even know what they felt like, and as they rose to the surface, I choked on my tears. As the warm water hit me, I sunk to the floor and let them all out. Every emotion I'd ever kept inside. Every hurt. Every loss I'd suffered. Every soldier that didn't make it home. Every life we didn't save on the job. I cried for all of them. I wept for every single one of them.

Vivian

I gently cried myself to sleep knowing that I had upset him, wishing I'd thought better of the story I told. I know he was the one who asked me about Michael, but maybe I should have thought how that might affect him as a fellow Marine. It was terribly insensitive of me to let my emotions get the better of me, especially after what had been such a wonderful evening together. I didn't blame him for leaving when he did; it just stung, and I felt the little pit in my stomach grow as the day had gone on without hearing from him.

He said it wasn't good-bye, it was just good night, but it felt more final than that. He looked as though he'd had the wind knocked out of him when he left, and I was worried for him. I refused to make the same mistakes I did with Michael, and I decided that I'd take matters into my own hands. While he did walk away last night, I couldn't in good conscience fault him. I had no idea what he'd seen, what he'd been through in his life. He'd been deployed just like Michael. Who knew what happened over there? Nobody ever tells you the whole story. Adding to that, his actual job was to save people. I'm not so naïve as to believe that he's been able to save everyone. My heart broke for him, the pain he must be in.

I rescheduled all of my appointments for the day and got in the shower. I needed to talk to Jess, and I definitely needed to talk to my parents, and then if I still hadn't heard from him, I planned to just go see him. Even if he didn't want to talk, his parting words left me feeling like he was lost in the darkness and feared that would affect me, and he needed to know that my grief was different. That he wasn't alone if he didn't want to be. I would be there for him if he'd have me; there was something that drew me to him, to his heart, like he needed me and I needed him as well.

I called Jess first after I got out of the shower and told her everything that happened.

"So you're telling me that he got you off, with all of your clothes on, and then somehow your brother's death came up, and he bailed out?" she exclaimed.

While that was kind of the short version of what happened, I replied, "Yes, more or less. I mean we talked. He asked me what happened to Michael, and I told him the truth. They were both Marines, you know, and I think that something I said triggered him, and he immediately stiffened up and said it was getting late and he needed to go home."

"Well, did he say anything else, or did he just leave it like that?" She had a skeptical tone in her voice, indicating to me that she didn't like that he'd run out. I knew how she thought.

"Yes, he said that I was light, and that I should not let his darkness dim my light," I repeated quietly.

"Well, fuck, Viv. That's some deep shit. You know, he might be too brooding and troubled for you. Are you sure you want that in your life? It took you so long to come out of the fog after Michael. I don't want to see you dragged back down into your own darkness again." She sounded concerned.

"I can honestly say that while I shed a few tears talking about Michael to him, the grief didn't consume me like it used to. I didn't fall backwards into that pit. I am more upset that I'd said something that upset him. I'll always miss and love my brother, but I've learned to just kind of let it go. I can't change what happened. But I can cope. I can move on. Michael would have wanted all of us to move on, I know that. We all know that, right?" I rationalized.

"That we do, Viv. Your brother's death affected all of us, but he always wanted you to be happy. I've never in my life seen siblings who didn't ever give each other shit, who just genuinely supported each other wholeheartedly, and I think he'd be so proud of you for seeing that."

"Thanks Jess. I think so too."

"So, what's your next move then? What are you going to do about the brooding hero?"

"I haven't heard from him. Part of me thinks I should leave him be, but I have an overwhelming urge to go to him. I want to find him and see if he's ok. Is that totally stupid?" I asked.

Letting out a hefty sigh, she replied, "I don't think it's stupid, but I think you should prepare yourself if he pushes you away. You can't make something work if everyone involved isn't on the same page. On the other hand, if he sees you as his light, and you want to be that light, then you should be. I would give him a day, though. You have no idea what he's doing, and he might need a little bit of space."

"Yea, maybe you're right. I was looking at flights, and there's a deal if I go see my parents today but come home tomorrow night.

It's only a two-hour flight. I thought maybe I'd go surprise them, and then when I get back, hopefully Jax and I will have talked. What do you think?"

"I think that's a fucking fantastic idea. Book it, I'll come over and take you to the airport, you can surprise your parents. It would make their day, and then maybe your mom will get off your case a little bit since she gets to have you tonight and tomorrow."

"Ok, I'm going to do that now. The flight was at three, so if you could come in an hour and get me, that's plenty of time, because I don't have a bunch of luggage or anything for a one-night trip."

"Sounds good. I'll see you then."

After we hung up, I texted my mom to make sure that she and my dad would be around later. I asked under the pretense of calling her later and making sure she was available to chat. My mom had become quite the texter and told me way more information than I needed to make my plans. I was able to find out that they were going to be home all evening, and my mother was very excited about not cooking and ordering takeout. I kind of laughed at that one. My mom used to love cooking for the family, but over the years she said she was exhausted from feeding the boys. I think she just really enjoyed getting all dressed up and going out to eat. I got my love of fashion and shoes from that woman, and anytime we had a chance to dress up, we did.

I quickly grabbed a few things and threw them into a duffle. I was only going for one night, so I didn't need much, but knowing my mom, she'd want to go out for a nice breakfast or something, so I planned accordingly.

Before I knew it, I was at the airport, sitting on a plane and heading to see my parents. I still hadn't heard from Seth, but I was optimistic that I would. I did decide that I wouldn't text him first, at least not until I got home the next night. I was hopeful that giving him space for a day would give him the time he needed and we could talk, or better yet see each other when I got home.

JAX

In the late afternoon, I finally managed to pull myself together, get composed, and call my sister. We were close. We didn't see each other as often as we wanted, but she had kids, my niece and nephew, a job, and a husband. Her life was busy, and I worked odd hours.

"Hey, Savannah, how goes the mom life?" I tried to sound upbeat.

"It goes the same as usual. Everyone here makes a mess and I'm horrible for making them clean it up. And then I'm the favorite. And then they're crying. Every day is a new and exciting challenge." She laughed. "How are you, little brother? Haven't heard from you in a while." Her southern accent was much more prominent than mine, and especially when she got riled up, it really came out. Hearing her voice made me smile a bit.

"Yeah, I'm sorry about that. I know I'm due for a visit to your place to see the kids and all, but I was wondering if maybe you could meet up with me for a drink tonight?"

"It's kind of hard, but let me see what Randy has planned. A night with the kids on his own would do wonders for his appreciation of me. Are you ok, Seth?" She sounded concerned.

"I've been better, Savannah. I could really use family right now, and I want to fill you in on everything face-to-face."

"Ok, how about seven o'clock at Shea's? I know it's on my side of town, but it's quiet and you can get away from your side for an evening," she suggested.

"That sounds good. Thanks, sis. I appreciate it. I know it's a pain in the ass to get away, but I just need to talk some shit out, and you're the only one who gives me good advice," I confessed. Dr. Rosen gave good advice too, if I'd fucking followed it. At least I didn't sleep with Viv before I bugged out. I'd never be able to fix that kind of colossal fuck up.

"That's what big sisters are for. I'll meet you there. We'll have some quality time. See you at seven," she replied before hanging up.

A bit of the weight of my emotions lifted knowing that I could be honest with my sister. The only reason I hadn't told her I was seeing Dr. Rosen in the first place was because we were both so busy, I didn't want her to worry. After my fucking breakdown today, I felt like a little kid who needed his parents, and my sister was the next best thing. I decided that I needed to send Vivian a text too. I felt like such a fucking jerk; I hoped she wouldn't be mad at me and I'd be able to explain what I was going through.

I spent the next couple of hours hoping to hear back from Vivian, which I did not, making me completely sick to my stomach. I'd received texts from Matt, so my phone was definitely working; she just wasn't responding. As the thought that I'd ruined my chances with her became more real, I began to rack my brain on why I cared so much after only going out with her a couple of times. The answer was simple. I was falling for this chick. I dropped my head into my hands and audibly groaned in frustration. *How did any of this even happen?* One minute I was just a cool dude, doing my own thing, working on battling my demons; and the next minute I was a hot fucking mess, fretting over a beautiful, young, sassy real estate agent. *Fuck.* My life was already better with her in it, and she wasn't speaking to me. *Fuck.*

I pulled into the parking lot of Shea's just before seven. My sister was prompt unless the kids were into some shit, but since I told her I needed to talk, I was pretty sure she'd be on time, if not early. Sure enough, she was already there in the parking lot waiting for me.

"Hey, sister." I gave her a huge hug immediately.

"Hey, brother," she replied as we made our way in.

Once seated, we quickly ordered drinks and she began questioning me. "You look like shit, Seth. What is going on with you? Are you sleeping at all?" She looked at me intently, scrunching her brows as she examined me.

"Well, thanks, Savannah. You look lovely too," I tried to tease her, but she wasn't having it.

"Seth, let's cut the bullshit." She leaned forward, taking one of my hands in hers. "What's going on with you? Something is clearly not right for you to call me and want to talk in person." She softened her tone, causing me to relax my nervousness and open up.

"I've been seeing a shrink," I blurted out.

"Ok. That's not the worst idea I've ever heard. Through the VA?" she asked.

"Yes. He thinks I have PTSD, even though there isn't anything in particular that happened that triggered it when I was deployed or anything. He thinks that the deployment itself, along with my day job and the things I see day in and day out, has gotten to me, and that I've closed myself off from meaningful relationships as a result of it." That seemed like a fairly appropriate summary of Dr. Rosen's initial diagnosis.

"Keep going," she coaxed.

"I've been having a lot of nightmares and trouble sleeping, so he's been trying to help me... uh...well, he's been trying to help me become the man I want to be."

"And who is that, Seth?" she asked softly.

I sighed, and leaned back in my seat. Looking for the words to say, I glanced around the room. I immediately spotted Jess, Vivian's best friend. She met my eyes and glared at me, shaking her head. I couldn't figure out what that was about, but it dragged me from my thoughts when my sister snapped in my face to bring me back. "Who is the man you want to be, Seth?"

I once again put my face in my hands and sighed. Looking up at her from across the table, I said, "I want to be a man who knows how to deal with demons and keeps them at bay. I want to be a man who deserves to be loved, a man who's capable of loving. I want to be someone's light, Savannah. And most of the time, I have an overwhelming darkness inside me that keeps me disconnected. I go through the motions. I hang out with my buddies, I spend time with the wrong kind of girls I'd never introduce to mom and dad, and I drink too much. I don't want to be that guy anymore. I want more, but I haven't been able to figure out how to do that on my own."

"Seth, you're a good man. You've served your country. You continue to serve the community. Why would you think you don't deserve love? What happened to you?" She had tears in her eyes as she looked at me with pity.

"Please don't cry, Savannah. Please?" I reached back out and took her hand. "I don't know what happened. Somewhere along the way I just got lost. But I'd been getting much better. I even met a girl. A woman. She's amazing, actually. I think I may have seriously fucked it up, though," I admitted.

"What happened?" Savannah asked, brushing away the tear that had fallen.

"Last night, we were at her house, watching a movie, sort of. We were talking, and exchanging stories, and I asked how her brother died. She had mentioned him before and didn't want to talk about him, but then she kind of brought it up, so I asked."

"Oh no, what happened to him?" Savannah put her hand to her mouth waiting for the bomb to drop.

"He was a Marine. He must have seen some shit, some awful shit, Savannah." I searched for the words and then just came out with it. "When he came home from his deployment, he killed himself."

"Oh my God, that's awful," she gasped.

"It *is* fucking awful, and I didn't mean to make her cry. I had no idea. I made this sweet, beautiful girl cry, Savannah. I'm such a dick."

"I'm sure that you specifically didn't make her cry. It's a sad and horrible thing to lose someone, especially like that. Memories can evoke emotions, that's how it works," she reassured me.

"Oh, it gets worse." I held my hand up to stop her from consoling me more.

"Oh, shit. What did you do?" She made a face that looked like she was waiting to get hit with something. She was.

"I fucking left. I completely bailed. I told her it was late and I had to go. She knew something wasn't right. She was apologizing and holding back tears, and I fucking left her like that because I was too big of a fucking pussy to just open up to her. I froze when she told me about him, and I just fucking left." Groaning into my hands, I ran them through my hair, exasperated with myself as I leaned back in my booth seat.

"Well, shit, Seth. I need another drink, goddamn." She ran her hands through her short hair as well. Shaking her head at me, she didn't need to say anything else.

"Yeah, fucking tell me about it." She flagged down our server and pointed at our drinks, indicating our need for more.

"Well, tell me about this girl. You fucked up, yes, and you look like fucking dog shit, so tell me what you're going to do about all of this. All of it." She made a motion with her arms opening them wide.

"Well, I've been seeing this shrink like I told you. This all started with him. He wanted me to connect with people on a deeper level. It seems that my coping mechanism for dealing with shit was to disconnect and have meaningless relationships and just go through the motions. So he's been working with me on some things like meditation that helps me calm my mind and sleep. I've been drinking a lot less, except for today and last night, of course." I held my beer up. "So, anyway, I've been doing all of these things to quiet my mind when I'm losing composure or can't rest, etcetera."

"Is it working?" she asked.

"It is. I'm not becoming a yoga-teaching hippie or anything, but the meditation really calms me, and I've been sleeping a lot better. The next step was for me to start trying to connect more, particularly with women."

"Ok..." she sounded confused.

"Look, I go out with the wrong kind of girls, that's no secret. But the reason is so that I don't have to open up. I don't have to have a meaningful relationship. I don't have to let my guard down, and I don't have to be myself. Well, as it turns out, that's not appropriate or healthy." I rolled my eyes. "Dr. Rosen wanted me to try going on actual dates with girls who I would consider to fall in the category of someone I'd see more than once. He wanted me to limit myself to no sex, just talking and connecting." I muttered quietly.

Letting out a big laugh, she said, "No sex? You? How did that go for you?" She was giggling at my expense. Fucking helpful.

"Shut up. I'm trying to open up to you," I snapped at her. "Do you have any idea how hard it is for me to talk about all of this, Savannah? Any clue?"

She immediately stopped. "I'm so sorry, Seth. Please, keep going." She took a sip of her drink and went back to listening.

"So, I met this girl. She was Matt and Isabel's realtor. You know they're buying that run-down gym downtown." She nodded. "Well, she's fucking beautiful, Savannah. Like goddess beautiful. And fucking smart. She started her own business, and she's one of the top realtors in the county. Her picture is everywhere. Buses, billboards, you name it, and her fucking beautiful face is on it."

"Vivian Deveraux?!" she exclaimed.

"Yeah, do you know her?" Just what I needed.

"I don't know her, but she sold my neighbors' their house. They raved about her. What a small world," she said.

"Yeah, she's amazing. We've been out a couple times, and I'm fucking hooked on her. She's like a little ray of sunshine. I think about her all the time. I think about ways to make her smile at me. I'm a ridiculous mess. We have so much fun together; we laugh and tease each other, and she is fucking smoking hot. She is the whole package."

"So, how does she feel about you?"

"I have no idea. I texted her today, but she hasn't replied. I think she's not speaking to me after last night. Maybe she needs to cool off?" I said hopefully.

"Maybe you should man up and do more than send a text. You *are* a pussy," she said matter-of-factly, causing my jaw to drop in shock.

"Whoa! Did you seriously just call me a pussy? My sister, Savannah Jackson Walsh, you kiss your kids with that filthy mouth?" I teased her, using both her maiden and married last names.

"Oh, piss off, Seth. You know I'm right. Your fucking generation with your texting and shit; it's ridiculous. You do remember that little computer in your pocket makes phone calls, right? When you hurt someone's feelings, you call them. Or better yet, you show up to make it right."

"You're not that much older than me, Savannah."

"You're missing the point as usual, Seth. Listen with your ears." She talked to me like she talks to my nephew.

"Ok, ok. You're right. What do I do? I want her back. I want to tell her everything. I want to be honest, but I'm so fucking scared," I pleaded for answers.

"If you love her, which you do—don't even bother denying it, or we wouldn't be having this conversation—you need to take that risk. You need to do what the doctor told you to do, which is open your fucking self-up to it. You want to feel real love, Seth? The kind of love where even after a long fucking day working in construction you send your wife out with her brother because you love her and he needs her? The kind of love where on a Sunday when you try to sleep in but your kids decide that they want to have brunch with their parents, you get up and cook for everyone and steal kisses from your husband in the pantry? Yeah, that's right. We do whatever it takes to stay connected, and it's not always easy. It's work. But it's worth it. You have to have faith that when you open your heart to someone and they receive your love that they're giving you theirs as well. That girl opened up to you. She showed you her weakness, the chink in her armor, and you didn't do the right thing. So you need to remember that when you talk to her. She. Opened. Up. To. You. Now, it is your turn to come clean. Show her the man you are, and the man you aspire to be. We're all works in progress, Seth. All of us. Man the fuck up."

She sat back and watched me absorb everything she said. She was so fucking right. She was right about everything; Viv did open up to me, and when she did, I shut down.

"I don't deserve her," I said.

"Yes, you do. That's a cop out. You do deserve her. You just haven't realized how special you are too, Seth. Mom and Dad would be lost without you, I'd be devastated, hell, my kids would be devastated. You are loved so much more than you even realize. You deserve the love we're talking about; real, deep, true love."

I felt a smile form as I thought about love. I used to think it was all bullshit, but it was just me hiding from it. My sister was right. "Thank you," I said quietly.

"So, what are you going to do about it?" she asked me.

"Well, she hasn't returned my message, so I'm going to try calling her when we're done, I guess. And if I don't hear from her, then I guess I'll have to track her down. She isn't that hard to find. Her face is everywhere," I joked.

"It sure is," she laughed. "She is a pretty one. You have some high-end taste, little brother." She was teasing me, and it was like old times. Savannah was only two years older than me; in fact, she graduated from high school with Brian. We were always pretty close, but we definitely gave each other a lot of razzing and shit.

I laughed at that comment. "You would love her, Savannah. She's feisty as hell."

"I have no doubt that anyone who spends anything more than five minutes with you would need to be feisty. You need someone who'll put you in your place, you know, for when I'm not around to do it." She grinned at me from across the table.

"Thank you for meeting me tonight. I know it's a pain in the ass. I mean it. I promise to come see the kids soon, or you should bring them down to the station. They haven't come to see the trucks in forever. The guys love it when they come down to see us."

"It's not a big deal. I was just making a point, is all. I'm always here for you. Next time call me sooner, though. Not when everything's fucking falling apart, for Christ's sake." She reached across the table and squeezed my hand. I was really lucky.

I needed to remind myself more often of how lucky I was. I wasn't grateful enough for the good things in my life. That was going to change.

Vivian

When I got on the plane, I saw I had a text from Jax, but before I could reply, the mean flight attendant came over to make me turn it off or put it in airplane mode, whatever that is.

His text said:

> Viv, I'm so sorry about last night. Let me make it up to you, please?

It was sweet, and I'd planned to reply later, but now I was going to surprise my parents. All of the emotional crap of the last day made me so tired, and I was glad to be taking a couple of days off, even if it was a one-nighter trip to hang with my parents. It was a break, and it was much needed.

I drifted off to sleep immediately, completely missing takeoff, and I didn't wake up until we touched down in New Jersey. I looked out the window, recognizing the city lights. Since it was a surprise, there was no one to greet me at the airport, but I was easily able to grab a taxi to my grandma's, where my parents were. The cool October air of the Northeast hit me as I walked to the taxi stand and caused me to pull my jacket closed tightly as I walked. I definitely didn't miss the damn cold, that's for sure, and I was glad I packed a sweater.

It was about a twenty-minute ride, and while my excitement to see my parents built up, I forgot about my phone completely. When we pulled in front of the house, all the lights were on, literally all the lights in the entire house. I shook my head and smiled. I knocked on the door and heard footsteps approaching making me even more excited; I just loved surprises and my mom was going to be over the moon.

She opened the door, her mouth falling open immediately upon taking me in. "Hi, Mom! Surprise!" I yelled.

She gasped and pulled me into a big bear hug. "Baby! I'm so happy! This is the greatest surprise ever! Come in, come in! You must be freezing," she exclaimed. She was right.

"Hi, Daddy!" I yelled across the house.

"Is that my Vivian?" He poked his head into the front room. "Oh my God! What the hell are you doing here?" he asked.

"I wanted to surprise you guys. I missed you." I hugged them both again, then set my bag in a corner. "Now, I have to go back home tomorrow night, but we have all night tonight to hang out, and I thought we could have brunch tomorrow before I head back. I know it's just a quick trip, but I have to work and stuff."

"I wish it was longer, but I understand, baby girl. I'm so excited you're here. Are you hungry? We have leftovers."

"No, I'm fine, Mom. Let's just hang out and catch up. Is grandma up?"

"She's resting right now, but you can go see her in a little bit. She needs to rest after she eats."

"I understand. Well, let's have some tea, and you guys can fill me in on all your shenanigans here in the north. I can't believe how flipping cold it is up here! I'm sorry, but I do not miss this one single bit."

They both laughed, and my dad replied, "Yeah, I don't miss it, either. We'll be back to Florida soon. Is it still warm and wonderful?"

"It sure is. It's been a little cool in the evenings, but that's because the humidity is gone. It's that perfect time of year where it's like eighty degrees but you're not dying in the humidity. It hasn't rained in weeks. It's been super sunny." I already missed it. I felt like I couldn't warm up; that cup of tea was going to hit the spot.

"I'm going to go get the tea going. You want the usual, Miss Viv?" my mom asked me.

"Yes, please, earl gray." We've been big tea drinkers my whole life. I'm not even sure where that came from. I still drank coffee in the mornings, but my mom always made tea for guests, and she made us tea when we didn't feel well.

My dad and I sat down across from each other in the front room of my grandma's house. He took a spot on the couch, while I nestled into an overstuffed lounge chair like a little kid, folding my knees under me.

"It's so good to see you, kiddo, but why the surprise? We've wanted you to come for weeks," he asked.

"Dad, Mom wants me to move here and hang out with you guys until who knows when. Come on, now. I missed you guys, and I saw a really cheap ticket, so I snatched it up. I haven't taken any time off in forever, so I figured, what the heck?" That was mostly true. I wanted to get away for a day to escape everything too, but they didn't need to know that.

"Your mother just worries about you, honey. But I do

understand. You look tired, honey. Was it a rough flight?"

Thinking back to all the crying I did last night and the soul searching I did earlier, I just shook my head no. "No, I'm just tired from working a lot, I guess. I took a nap on the plane ride here."

"Well, I know how important your business is to you, but you need to make sure you're taking care of yourself too, baby."

"I know, Daddy." I smiled at him. I was so happy to see them. I wished they were all back in Florida, including my grandmother.

Mom came back in with her tea set on a little tray with some shortbread cookies too. "Oooh, shortbread cookies?" I said.

"I know they're your favorite. I figured you might like a little snack with your tea, sweetheart."

"Thank you so much. Now sit, sit, tell me what you crazy kids have been up to with grandma." I took a bite of one of the shortbread cookies, and as it hit my tongue, it practically melted. It was heaven with the hot tea, warming me up and hitting me with my love for sugar. All the angst had drifted away.

"Oh, please, dear. We are old. We are all just hanging around, trying to keep grandma comfortable. Your father here has been to two Jets games, though, so he's in hog heaven. I've been reading nonstop, and I have some books for you to take back if they'll fit in your bag. Other than that, I read to grandma and I am trying to quilt. It's quite a bit harder than I expected." She laughed.

"I think it sounds really hard, and tedious so good for you, Mom." I giggled.

"So tell us what you're up to, kiddo? Taking over the real estate world of central Florida, I'm sure," my dad said.

"Yeah, remember that commercial sale I told you about? Well, that's moving along, and should be closing in the next two weeks I think. The buyers and sellers know each other, so it's been super easy, and my commission is nothing to sneeze at. The people I'm working with are awesome too. It's a couple, one is a firefighter, and the other is a detective. They are buying an old gym and converting it to a gym/training facility for MMA fighters, you know, mixed martial arts."

"Well, you seem very excited about it, dear," Mom said.

"I am. They brought a friend with them to the meeting, another firefighter. We ended up hitting it off and have spent a little time together." I dipped my toe in the water of telling my parents about my dating life.

"Well, well, a firefighter, eh? What an admirable and difficult job. What's this boy's name?" My dad asked it like we were in high school.

"His name is Seth. Seth Jackson." I smiled. "He was a Marine too." I dropped the little bomb on them.

My mom froze for a moment, then shook herself of it when it was apparent that my dad and I had noticed. "Well, isn't that lovely. I wonder if he knew Michael."

"I don't think he did. Seth is a bit older than Michael and was probably getting out when..." I trailed off, not wanting to upset them.

"How much older is this Seth character?" my dad asked.

"He's not old, relax. He's in his early thirties," I said defensively.

"Well, is he a nice guy? I'm guessing you really like him if you're telling us about him," my mom offered.

"He is. He's one of the kindest, most gentlemanly men I've ever been out with. He might be a keeper," I blushed a little thinking about him. I hoped that he was all right, and I made a note to reply to his text when I went to bed that night.

"Well, that's good enough for us then, dear," my dad replied. "Hopefully, we'll get to meet this gentleman when we make our way back to Florida soon."

Lowering my shoulders and remembering that they were only here to take care of my ailing grandmother, I asked the question, "How is she doing, really?"

My mother sighed. "She's not doing that great. We are really just making her comfortable at this point. There's not much more the doctors can do, and we have a nurse who comes every day. She'll be very glad to see you, though." My grandma was a stubborn lady who we'd begged to move to Florida, yet she wouldn't budge on staying in the Northeast.

"I'm so sorry, Mom." I went over to her and gave her a big hug. We held that embrace for quite a while.

"It's so good to see you, sweetheart. It's starting to get late, so why don't we get you a bed set up, and then we'll get some rest, so we can have a nice brunch or something tomorrow? Does that sound good?"

"That sounds perfect, Mom. I love you." I forgot how great it was to get a hug from your mom. "I know things have been hard, but it'll get better," I whispered.

"I know, dear. I know." She squeezed me a little tighter then came with me to get me settled in the spare bedroom.

"Night, Daddy." I ran over and gave him a big hug too.

"Good night, sweetheart, thank you so much for surprising us." He gave me a great big bear hug.

My mom helped me put some fresh sheets on the bed, then

she sat down on the edge. "So, this Marine firefighter, you really like him?" she asked.

I sat down on the bed too and leaned into her. "I do, Mom. I told him about Michael last night, and he got very upset. I haven't really talked to him since then, though, so I'm not really sure it's going to work out, but I hope it does," I confessed to her sadly.

"Well, sweetheart, we learned the hard way that the military and deployments can do awful things to a man's psyche. Tread carefully with him, for you do not know what he has been through. But don't make the same mistakes we did with Michael. If you care for him, talk. Even when you don't want to, make sure you're both ok." She leaned into me, resting her head on mine. "We didn't know how badly he was hurting, Viv, and we didn't know what to do. Not a day goes by that I don't think about him. Losing a child is the worst thing that can happen to you in the world. You have children thinking they will be there, you will watch them grow up, and you will pass away before they do. There's something unexplainable that happens to you when your child leaves this earth before you." She turned to me. "You know that's why I hover over you, right? I worry. I know that you're not him, but you're our baby, and it would kill us to lose you too." Her eyes began to fill with tears.

"Oh, Mom, I know. I'm sorry that I get snippy with you. I love you so much." I hugged her again.

"Ok, sweetheart, get some rest. Your flight is tomorrow evening?"

"Yep, it's at seven tomorrow night, so we have the whole day to sleep in, visit with grandma, and best of all, eat!" I giggled.

Smiling back at me, she said, "Sleep well, baby girl. Thank you for the present of surprising us. You have no idea how happy you've made me."

"Night, Mom."

After she closed the door and left me by myself, I grabbed my phone from my purse and turned it on. Several messages from Jess popped up, and when I read them, I tossed the phone to the side and lay down. I wouldn't be responding to anyone's messages, instead, tears fell from my eyes and my heart sank.

JAX

She hadn't returned my messages, and I had to go to work in the morning, so I couldn't camp out on her porch. I did drive by and saw her car was in her driveway, but all the lights were off. If she had gone out downtown, she wouldn't have driven, so she could have been anywhere.

I took myself home, checking my phone every five seconds until I decided I really did need to try to get some sleep. I had tried calling her on my way home from meeting with Savannah, but it went straight to voicemail. While everyone else on my shift was doing a forty-eight-hour shift, I was doing a twenty-four because I'd called out today. They'd get me back for it the next day, and I'd be doing all the bitch work, so getting some rest was pretty crucial. I decided that it was a sleeping pill night; there was no way that the anxiety wouldn't keep me up all night.

When I lay down on my bed, I thought about everything that had happened that day. Unsure of my ability to fix things with Vivian, I again resolved to try. My sister said I was in love with her. Was I in love with her? I wasn't sure, but I was certain that I needed to set things right. I owed her an explanation. I definitely didn't want the last time I saw her to be the last time I saw her for good.

I turned on my meditation music. Unable to shift my thoughts completely away from her, I fell asleep with my phone on my chest, hoping that her call or text would wake me.

Early the next morning, I woke with a headache after not having slept well at all despite the sleeping pill. I wasn't really surprised, considering how I felt when I went to bed. She had never returned my text, and so with my head hanging low, I took a shower and got myself to the station to start my shift. When I arrived a bit early, Brian was in his office reading and yelled to me as I walked by.

"Jax! You feeling better?" He gave me a sarcastic look over his coffee cup.

"Yeah, I am. Sorry about yesterday," I said.

"It's fine. If it were anyone else, I'd be pissed, but honestly, you never take a day off. Maybe just try and schedule it instead next time?"

"You got it, Chief. I have quite a bit of time saved up, might even take a real vacation at some point," I replied.

"I'm going to insist that you do. There's going to be a new policy in effect soon that you can't carry it all over for years, so start planning. And hey, while I've got you here, let's talk about the Deputy Chief's position, shall we?" He waved me to come in and take a seat, which I did.

"What would you like to talk about?"

"Well, you and Matt are the only two qualified for the position, and as I understand, Matt has no intention of taking the test." I didn't realize Brian knew Matt didn't want the job. He continued, "I'd be thrilled to have you move up into the position, Lieutenant," he said. "Honestly, I think the job was meant for you, Jax. You've worked your ass off, the department respects you, you're ahead of everyone when it comes to technology. It would be an honor to have you. Can we talk about it?"

I bit my lower lip debating how to handle this situation. I hadn't even had any coffee yet. "Well, Chief, I think it would be an honor to move up into the position as well. In the beginning, I honestly hadn't given it any thought, because I assumed Matt wanted it, so that's why he said that."

"Even if he did want it, I'd still have picked you."

My eyes widened in surprise. "What?"

He chuckled. "I don't know why you're so surprised. Just because Matt is my brother doesn't mean I'd have hired him into the position. The fact of the matter, Jax, is that you're a leader, whether you see it or not. Your experience here, coupled with your military experience, is exactly the kind of long-term leadership I'm looking for. I kind of always suspected that Matt would not want to move up the ranks. You and me, though, it's in our blood. I can't imagine doing anything else and I see that in you." He leaned back in his chair and looked at the shock on my face.

"Wow, thank you, Chief. I don't know what to say." I really was speechless. This had quite possibly been the strangest week for me in terms of my feelings about everything. The things Brian had just said filled me with pride. I did the things I did, the research, the extra time at the station, learning things I didn't necessarily need to know to do my job because I loved it, and it seemed like the right thing to do. If you're going to do something, do it right, more or less. But it had never occurred to me that it was noticed by anyone else.

"You can say that you'll hurry up and get the paperwork done."

He handed me a large manila envelope. "I've printed all the paperwork for you so that you don't even have to hunt it down."

"Thanks, Brian. I really appreciate that." I called him by name, because we were friends, and he definitely didn't have to do that. He was making this process easy for me, because he genuinely wanted me to do it.

"Bro, I'd do anything to help you. Literally. We are family, always have been, always will be."

"Thanks, man."

"Are you ok? I thought you were full of shit and had a late night Saturday, but you honestly look like shit, man." He casually pointed up and down at me, assessing just how shitty I looked.

"I had a rough day, but I'm alright. I have had a little trouble sleeping off and on the past few weeks, but I'm getting squared away." I didn't want him to send me home, and I didn't want him to think that my problems were bigger than they were or that they were a problem on the job. After talking to my sister, things had become clearer to me, and it was time for me to man up.

"Alright, well, get this paperwork done today if possible. Fingers crossed we don't have a crazy day, and maybe you can get a little rest later. Isabel sent Matt in with some new gloriously delicious coffee yesterday. I just made a fresh pot, so go get yourself some." He pointed to the door.

Letting out a little chuckle, I replied, "Yeah, that coffee is the shit, right? She has fantastic taste."

"In coffee, yes, in men, ehhh maybe." We laughed. "Alright, get out of here. I have shit to do, and my fiancée will be in here any minute to quietly give me a hard time about planning this wedding."

I laughed and stood to leave. "Good luck with that, man." I saluted him casually on my way out, heading immediately to the kitchen for some of that coffee.

Matt was already in the kitchen as well and gave me a what's up nod. "Hey, man, feeling better?" He used air quotes.

"Yea, I am." I poured myself a cup of coffee and sat at the large table.

"Must have been a hell of a night out for you to call out sick on a Sunday of all days," he said.

"You could say that," I muttered.

"You all right?" he asked.

"Yeah, yeah, I'm fine. Just not completely awake, I guess."

"So, tell me about Vivian. You've seen her a few times, and you weren't here yesterday, so something must be going on there?" You'd think that men didn't gossip like women stereotypically did, but you'd be wrong. We are just as bad, if not worse sometimes.

"She's pretty awesome," was all I said. I was still worried she wasn't going to talk to me or want to deal with my shit since she still hadn't returned my text or call yet.

"Come on, tell me more!" he teased.

"I don't know. She's a great girl. Too good for the likes of me," I confessed. "I haven't talked to her since Saturday night though so we'll see."

"Why not? Did something happen?" Matt sat down and gave me a genuinely concerned look. "Look, I know I gave you a lot of shit about it, but if she's the girl, then I'm all for it."

I took a long sip of my coffee, letting it awaken my senses before continuing. In that moment, I decided that the new me, the me who connects with people, the me who was honest was going to be honest about everything. "It wasn't an argument or anything, but I left her place under kind of shitty circumstances Saturday and we haven't talked since. I've tried to text and call, but she isn't getting back to me."

"Did you say something stupid? We've all been there," he joked.

"Well, more like I didn't say anything at all." I paused. Matt was looking at me intently, genuinely concerned and interested, so I went ahead and told him what happened. "The long and short of it is that we were talking about some things, getting to know each other and all, and the subject of her brother came up. Turns out he was also a Marine. Here's the thing, when he came back from his deployment in the Middle East, he killed himself."

"Jesus Christ, that's awful."

"Yeah, it is. And it's more common than you would think and I didn't handle it well at all. Did you know that twenty-two veterans a day commit suicide? Twenty-two a day," I informed him, shaking my head at the staggering statistic.

"What the fuck? No, I didn't know that," he said, shocked.

"Yeah, it's an epidemic. In any event, this kid came back and did what he did. When she told me, I froze. I didn't know what to say; it hit me hard and I didn't even know the guy. She was telling me something important, something that she didn't go around telling people, sharing with me, and I handled it like a complete and total fucking ass." I thought back to that moment and how I would do everything differently if I could have a do-over.

"Well, she has to know that you've seen some shit in your lifetime. I'm sure she'll understand. What did you do?" he asked.

"I left. I told her I had to go. She was on the verge of tears, and

I took off like a pussy. There's really no excuse for it. I was shocked by his story, and it's close to me. I didn't know him personally, but I know others, plural, who have done the same thing. It's a hard thing to have on your mind every day, and I should have told her that, but I didn't." I rolled my eyes at myself and took another sip of my coffee.

Matt was silent for a moment, obviously processing what I'd said. Taking in a deep breath, he replied. "You need to fight for her."

"What?" I said, surprised, looking over my cup at him.

"You heard me. You need to fight for her. For her to share something like that with you, knowing that you were also a Marine, that's a big deal. People don't go around telling that story unless they're comfortable with you; that's something that was hard for her, I'm sure of it. You're one of the very few people she'll meet in her lifetime who can understand what she's been through. You need to fight for her. She's special."

Still stunned, I replied, "I think you're right. She's not returning my calls at the moment, so I'll have to take more drastic measures, it seems."

"Did you swing by her place yesterday?"

"I sure did." I laughed. We were obviously on the same page with that. I recalled a time that Matt himself had to camp out on Isabel's front porch until she would talk to him. "Her car was there, but it looked like no one was home, so I guess she was out or something."

"Well, try to call her again today. And if she still doesn't answer, show up at her place in the morning. You know I've done it, it usually goes in your favor after some sweet talking and begging if you have to. No shame in the love game man." He grinned.

"Thanks, man. I appreciate it." I sighed, appreciating this chat. In our younger years we would have never been so honest about our feelings, and the truth was that it felt good to be authentic about things like this. I genuinely appreciated having the ability to have this conversation with Matt.

"Bro, all kidding aside, we're not kids anymore. Finding a chick who has her shit together, who also appreciates who we are now, who we used to be, and who we want to be is clutch. Seriously, having a chick like that in your life is what it's all about; there's nothing better. I'm truly a better man with Isabel in my life. No bullshit," he said.

"I think you're right, Matt. Hopefully, I'll be able to fix all this bullshit. I feel like a fucking jackass."

"It won't be the last time, believe me." He laughed, teasing me. I cracked a grin myself.

"Ain't that the truth, bro." I held up my coffee cup as if we were toasting.

Vivian

Through brunch with my parents, I had to pretend like I wasn't upset. I had flown all the way to New Jersey to spend some quality time with them, and I wasn't going to let Seth ruin it. I didn't know when I was going to see them again, so I pushed the thought of him aside. I'd deal with it later.

"Is everything ok, dear?" my mom asked.

"Oh, yes, of course it is. I wish I was able to stay a little longer," I lied. Well, it wasn't totally a lie. In reality, I wished they'd come back to Florida so I could see them whenever I wanted. But I was still freezing and looking forward to getting back to my palm trees even though I was happy to be with them.

"Why don't you change your ticket?" She gave me a sly smile.

"Mom, you know I need to get back to work." I gave her a knowing smile.

"I know, I know. It was worth a try, baby girl."

"Grandma seemed really good this morning," I changed the topic. "She just seems tired. It's hard to believe she's so sick."

"She has her good days and her bad days. I think getting to see you made it a good day for her."

"Well, that makes it a good day for me too." I smiled.

"So, what's on the agenda for you this week?" My dad asked in between bites of French toast drowning in syrup.

"I'm going to try to expedite the paperwork for that gym sale so that's done, and I have a few clients I'm showing properties to over the next few days. I think I'm going to stop doing open houses, though. They're such a waste of time."

"Oh, really, how so?" he asked.

"The last one I had, not a soul showed up." *Except Seth*, I thought. "And the one before that, there was a weirdo who I don't think was even in the market for a house. They just don't sell houses anymore the way that they used to. Taking my clients to visit properties that are on the market is really where I've had the most success, so I think I'm just going to focus on that. Having that one on one experience seems to serve me way better, but I also think that moving into more commercial real estate would be a good move."

"Hmm. Well, make sure you're safe at these showings. I don't like weirdos showing up with my daughter around." He looked at me with a raised brow.

"I know, I know. Anyway, I think that commercial real estate in the city is really taking off. There're a lot of properties that are kind of run down, and there seems to be an influx of thirty-somethings who want to remodel and turn the properties into new businesses. I'd love to be a part of that. This gym concept is great and has a lot of potential if they get it off the ground. I had a lot of fun working with them." My thoughts drifted to Seth again, and then to the message I received from Jess last night, changing my mood.

"Well, meeting that firefighter probably didn't hurt, now, did it?" my mom teased me.

"I'm not sure that's going anywhere, Mom. We've only been out a couple times. We'll see how it goes. I just told you so you wouldn't think I was turning into a spinster."

"Alright, dear, as long as you're happy. I'll mind my own business for now." She smiled at me. "Now, eat. You're too small, Miss Viv. You need to eat more."

I picked up my fork and moved eggs around on my plate. My stomach was revolting against brunch, which was normally my very favorite thing. The night before when I turned my phone on, I had a voicemail from Seth and a couple messages from Jess. I listened to the voicemail first, in which he said that he was sorry, he wanted to explain himself, and asked me to please call him, or come see him at the station to talk, which was definitely not happening.

There was one message from Jess that changed everything about how I felt.

The firefighter is out having drinks with a blonde lady, and they're cozy AF. Fucking asshole. I'm sorry, Viv.

In all honesty, he didn't owe me monogamy; he didn't owe me anything at all. He was free to date as many people as he wanted, or sleep with, or whatever. That didn't take the sting away, though. I thought we had a connection. After the last night we saw each other, I guess I should have known that was just how he was. It got way too serious for him, and he cut and run. It was probably a good thing I hadn't slept with him, because then I would have been that much more hurt than I already was. And it wasn't for lack of trying; I certainly would have after that first date.

Thanking my lucky stars he didn't want to sleep with me, I forced some of my food down so my mother didn't have an intervention on me. I pretended not to be totally crushed by the whole mess. I'd just cry to Jess later when she picked me up. My mom was going to head back to the house to take care of my grandma, and my dad and I were going to do a little shopping before he took me to the airport.

When we said good-bye, my mom started to cry. "Thank you so much for coming to see us, baby girl. You made my day. I love you to the moon and back." She's said that to me since I was little, and it caused me to tear up too.

"Mom, I'll see you again soon, I promise." I hugged her tight.

"Let me know when you make it home safely."

"I will, I promise."

My mom's birthday was coming up, so my dad and I went to the little shopping district in town to walk around, have coffee, and just enjoy some father-daughter time. While in one of the little shops, looking at some scarves I thought my mom would like, my dad said something out of the blue that I never expected to hear.

"You know, Viv, it's not our fault. The guilt that you carry over Michael isn't your burden to bear." He touched my arm gently, pausing to look at me.

"What?" I stopped in my tracks, almost dropping the scarf I was looking at for my mother.

"Michael was a troubled man, Viv. He was always a little bit troubled, and I tried to talk to him. In fact, when he came home from overseas, I tried to take him to see someone. I don't think anyone, including him, knew what the struggles of the war had done to him. None of us realized how hard it could be to come back and pretend you never saw the things you did. But it's not your fault for not knowing. I know how close you two were. But you need to stop carrying the weight of his death on your shoulders. You're allowed to move on, and I can see how it's held you back."

"Oh, Daddy." Tears started to stream down my face. He pulled me into his arms. "I just don't know how to move on sometimes. I feel like I should have known how bad it was for him."

"None of us knew. Viv, you're all we have left. You deserve to be happy, and that's what he would have wanted for you too. Your mother and I, we will always have sadness, and you don't ever have to forget, but you have to move forward and live a happy life. Don't get yourself stuck, Vivian. You have to promise me that you'll try to be happy. Don't go through the motions like he did." He squeezed me tightly.

"I will, Daddy, I promise. It's hard sometimes, though. It weighs on me that we couldn't help him. I feel like we should have known how much pain he was in, yet we didn't," I said, wiping the tears away.

"He didn't want us to know. That's the problem with society right now, is that these veterans so often feel like they have nowhere to turn, and they think that they're less of a man for talking about it, that it makes them weak. It's infuriating. They defend our country and then feel like they cannot get the help they need to integrate back into civilian life. It's shameful."

"If we had known, we could have helped him."

"Maybe, maybe not. Listen to me, Viv. Michael isn't the first veteran to go through this. Did you know that on average, twenty-two veterans a day commit suicide?" he asked me.

I was appalled. "Jesus Christ, no, I didn't know that!" I

exclaimed, utterly shocked by that statistic.

"Yes. Twenty-two. A day. We did the best we could with the information we had available to us, Viv. Your brother is at peace now, and it's our job to cherish his memory. Not wallow in our own guilt and self-pity over it. What we can do now to honor his memory, is tell other people what happened to him. Be there for those who need us. Contribute. That's the best thing we can do. And live our lives. I want you to be happy, Vivian. You deserve to be happy." He pulled me in again.

I let a few soft sobs find their way out as I laid my head on my dad's chest. I felt like a child again, being consoled. My heart hurt for Michael. It also hurt for Seth, even if he was not the man I thought he was. It hurt for everyone who was facing this kind of pain and sadness in their life.

"I love you, Dad. I'm glad we got to spend a little time together today." I wiped my tears away on my sleeve like a small child would.

He ruffled my hair like he did when I was little. "I am too. Now, let's get your mother this scarf, and we should get you one too. You look cold, baby girl."

I giggled. "Ok, Dad. Thank you."

We purchased the scarves, and I put mine on right away, snuggling into it simply because it would forever remind me of this moment with my dad. When we got to the airport, my dad got out of the car to hug me good-bye.

"Viv, remember what I said, ok?"

"I will, Daddy, thank you." I was sad to be leaving, but so grateful for the conversations I'd had with both of my parents.

"And Viv... Take care of that Marine of yours. He will need

you." I simply nodded in response and hugged my dad before making my way into the airport. My bag was much heavier than when I left, now that my mom had filled it up with books for me to bring back home.

As I checked in and then got myself a pre-flight glass of wine at the bar, I thought about what my dad said. Take care of that Marine... Well, he wasn't mine to take care of, but I didn't want to tell my dad that. Now that I had some alone time and room to think, I found myself getting angry with him. He laid it on so thick with me, but then didn't even want to sleep with me. He was probably sleeping with that blonde girl he was out with, though. I deserved better than that bullshit.

The glass of wine was settling in and warming me up. I couldn't wait to just get home and get back to normal. When I boarded the plane, I snuggled into my scarf and drifted off to sleep, trying not to think of him.

JAX

Busiest. Day. Ever.

Shortly after the talk over our morning coffee with Matt, we got tapped out for a car accident on the highway. That was a real treat in rush hour traffic. People in this town drove like maniacs; it would never make sense to me. On the up side, no one was hurt; it was really more of a mess and a roadblock than anything.

We'd been back at the station for about an hour when we got called to save some baby ducks that had gotten trapped in a storm drain. While not technically our job, we'd never say no to helping. We had to attach a hook to the storm drain to pull it up using the truck, then Scotty jumped in to grab them and hand them up to safety. I was hoping that Scotty would become the next Lieutenant when I moved up to Deputy Chief; he had what it took to be a leader, and he was smart. He had gone to college and had a degree in fire science. He was destined for big things. Well, bigger than rescuing baby ducks from a storm drain at least. But it was good public relations for the department.

No sooner had we cleaned up from that run, when we were called to a fire just outside of town. That took up most of the rest of the day and into the evening. A farmhouse had caught fire and somehow had spread to farm equipment, as well as a barn. There were about four stations involved and we were second on scene, mostly because we had barely pulled into the station when we turned around and pulled right back out.

The house was about a mile outside of town, where the properties were bigger, and there were a handful of farms. For whatever reason, maybe just simple convenience, the owners parked all of their tractors and other farm equipment in a row between their house and their barn. When the fire started in the kitchen, because it was old wood frame construction, it spread quickly before anyone even knew what had happened.

It appeared that the flames had spread to the exterior window of the home, extremely close to a tractor, which was of course filled with fuel. When we arrived, the equipment was catching on fire in a domino effect, spreading from one machine to the next very quickly.

"Well, shit," I said as we pulled down the long driveway.

"It's a hot one. Holy hell," Matt said.

"All right, boys, I'm going to take Jason into the kitchen to try to stop the interior fire. I can hear the other units coming, so try to protect that barn from catching and work with the guys already there to put out the machine fires," I said. I radioed Brian to let him know our plan and get his okay on it. When he confirmed, we were just parking and jumping out.

The property was just far enough outside of town that there were no hydrants, so we were going to need water tankers to keep this one under control; there was no endless supply like we usually had. I motioned for Jason to grab the hose, and I was going to back him up. He was a newer member of the department, quite a bit younger, and it was a perfect opportunity for him to have the nozzle and get some action.

"Let's go, kid," I yelled.

As we entered the porch that connected to the kitchen, the heat from the fire hit me right away. It had been a while since we had a real fire, and yes, it was terrible for the homeowner, but for a firefighter, this is what we trained for. It was exciting, and the team inside before us had already performed a search, ensuring there were no victims to rescue. It was our job to simply put the fire out at that point. We dragged the hose to the entrance of the kitchen, where the stove was completely charred, and the fire had spread to the walls and cabinets; the room was almost completely engulfed in flames.

I demanded water over the radio and steadied myself against Jason, preparing for the force of the water as it filled the hose. The pressure could knock you on your ass if you weren't ready for it. Once the line was charged with water, I elbowed him in the back to indicate it was time to let her rip. He nodded and opened up the nozzle, spraying a smooth stream of water in a circular pattern above the fire.

Cooling the ceiling first like that would help make the fire smaller right away, and as the flames began to go down, they'd stop spreading. I was extremely proud of him; he did exactly what he was taught. As the flames started to lessen, he started to hit the stove directly, as well as the cabinets, now really putting the fire out. Once we had tamed it, drowning it out was the mission. Several other firefighters from other stations entered the kitchen as it had cooled off tremendously, and they began pulling the cabinets off the wall to make sure there weren't hot spots, and opened the oven, so we could shoot water inside of it as well.

Once the fire appeared to be mostly out, Jason shut down the nozzle and looked back for my approval. Nodding at him, I slapped him on the back in acknowledgement and grabbed another nearby guy to take my place so I could go outside and report back our status.

I pulled my helmet off and ripped my mask off over my head as I walked to the chief's truck. "Fire's out in the kitchen. They're doing overhaul now and putting out hot spots. How's it going out here?"

"Well, they lost three, maybe four tractors, but the barn was saved, so that's a win," Brian said.

"Man, that one spread fast. Why the hell would you park all that shit right next to your house?" I shook my head.

"Who knows, man? How bad is the kitchen?"

"They won't be serving us dinner tonight, that's for sure. It's completely burned out on one side. The window sucked a lot of the fire out to the side where the tractors are, so some of it might be salvageable, but the smoke damage is pretty bad. It looks like it didn't spread anywhere else, though, so they could consider themselves lucky."

"Yeah, they sure can. None of the family was home; they were on a supply run. Someone must have left something on the stove, you think?" he asked.

"Almost definitely. The stove was the source for sure. They're gonna need a new one." I grinned.

"Well, that's probably the least of their problems now," he replied.

"Yea, you ain't kidding. I'll go back in and see how it's going inside. Radio me if you need anything." He nodded at me and I went back in to check on things.

Overhaul takes forever. Literally forever. Unless it's a good old-fashioned conflagration, or you have problems, a fire is usually put out fairly quickly. It's all the other bullshit that takes forever. I tromped back into the house, where the crew was still pulling things apart.

"Take that stove out to the front yard," I directed a couple of guys from station four.

"You got it, sir," they replied. The least we could do was unhook it and get it out of the house for them. Some company would have charged them an arm and a leg to do it. Everything else seemed more or less in order for a burned-out kitchen, so I instructed Jason and the other guy to get the hose out and start cleaning that up.

About two hours later, and into the dark of night, we were finally able to go back to the station. I was starving and exhausted. Between the events of the last few days taking their toll, it had been an absurdly long and busy day, and we still had to do a bunch of work back at the station to get ourselves back in service.

As we piled out of the truck, someone mentioned dinner and what we were going to do. I wanted to suggest going to the grocery store, just because it meant I had a small chance of bumping into Vivian there. Pizza ended up being the winning vote, which was fine, really. If I was going to talk to her, I needed more than a run-in at the store. I needed time to come clean about my feelings with her, and that wasn't going to happen at the deli counter in the grocery store.

Matt, Jo, and I went to the day room to sack out in lounge

chairs while we waited for our food to arrive. I had my phone in my hand. I'd been checking it incessantly since we got back, trying not to send eight billion more texts to her.

Matt looked over at me, feet up in the lounge chair, "You talk to her yet?"

"Nope. Haven't heard back. Trying not to send yet another message to her at this point. I guess I'll have to go tomorrow and bang on the door until she talks to me." I laid my head back, exhausted and frustrated.

"What did you do, Jax?" Jo asked. She was also lying back in a lounge chair, but she had her feet curled up under her. Women loved sitting like that, curled up like a cat.

"You don't even want to know, Jo," I groaned.

"Romeo over here caught himself a case of the feelings," Matt joked.

"For real, dude, it's like a disease around here. You people have infected me," I replied sarcastically.

"Oh, shut up, you both know it's nice to have someone, so cut the shit. What did you do to fuck it up, Jax? You didn't run around with another girl, did you?" she said sternly.

"No! Why does everyone think I'm some kind of douchebag? Fuck. Once I started seeing her, she was the only person I wanted to see anyway." I closed my eyes, picturing her smile. "I realize that in the past I wasn't exactly a one-woman guy, but that was before. And I was never a cheater. So let's just get off that right now."

"I'm sorry, you're right. So why haven't you heard from this girl?" she asked. I really didn't want to tell the whole fucking story again; it was draining.

"It's a long story, Jo," I sighed.

Matt jumped in. "He didn't tell her how he felt when he definitely should have. Major case of poor timing. He bolted on her, and now she isn't taking his calls so he can fix it." That was a fair recap of the situation, more or less.

"Well, you're going to fix it, right?" she asked.

Still squeezing my eyes closed, I replied, "I'm certainly going to try in the morning when we get off. Until then, there's not much else I can do short of calling her all night long which I think would make it worse at this point."

"Going to see her in person should help. It always does. Things always get fucked up and lost in translation over text and shit." She was right. There wasn't any way that I could explain myself to her via electronics; it had to be in person, so we were going to have to be face-to-face in the morning. Hopefully, she'd be there; and hopefully, she'd listen.

"I hope you're right, Jo. She's special," was all I said. We sat in silence after that, just waiting for our food, which I had lost my appetite for.

Vivian

My flight was uneventful. In fact, I slept through it just like on the way there. Something about the hum of the engine, I guess. I always fell asleep on flights or long road trips. I found them relaxing. The events of the last couple of days along with the chats about Michael with both my mom and my dad had left me emotionally drained.

Jess was waiting outside to pick me up with her usual upbeat and supportive attitude. "Welcome home, Viv! I missed you!" she exclaimed.

Giggling, I replied, "I was only gone since yesterday, you dork."

"A whole day without you, though. It's more than I can handle." She hugged me. "You doing ok? How are mom and dad? How's grandma?"

I let out a little sigh as I got settled into the passenger seat. "Grandma is doing all right. They don't think she'll make it to Christmas, but she was in good spirits when I got to see her. Mom and Dad were totally surprised to see me, so that was awesome. I had very interesting conversations with each of them privately about Michael. It feels like they've done some healing."

"Interesting," she said. "What did they have to say?"

"Well, they both said that it was time to let go of the guilt. I guess they've been feeling similar to the way that I have about not being there for him. You know, we never really talked about it as a family or anything, so it was eye opening to know that they were feeling the same way that I have been."

"Of course they have, Viv. They lost their only son. Nobody expects that to happen. Did they seem better?" she asked.

"They did. They seemed more at peace about everything. I guess having time to think and spending time with grandma has given them some perspective." I continued, "In other news, I told them about Seth before I'd seen your message, of course. So, how did you happen upon this bit of information?" I huffed out. I wanted to know the whole story, of course, but I also wanted to pretend it wasn't real and that he was the gentleman he said he was trying to become.

"Jeremy and I went to Shea's across town for a late dinner last night," she began. "While we were there, I saw him having drinks with a blonde woman."

"Did he see you?"

"He definitely did, and I gave him a nasty glare and shook my head at him. I didn't confront him, though. Jeremy didn't think it was appropriate. If he hadn't been there with me, I would have chewed that man out in front of that hussy. Have you heard from him?"

"I have. Several times, " I told her.

"And? Have you talked to him?" She seemed surprised.

"And nothing. I haven't replied. He called me and left a voicemail. And he's sent a handful of text messages about wanting to explain his actions from the other night. He didn't mention the other girl. I don't even know if he knows I know." The thought of him out with another girl after I thought we'd connected made me nauseous. I felt my face get hot from embarrassment and anger. "I guess he's just not the guy he claimed to be. There's not much else to say about that. It's disappointing, but it is what it is."

"He didn't mention the other girl at all? That's weird. He definitely saw me. He gave me a look when he saw me."

"What kind of look?" I asked.

"I don't know, a 'what the fuck did I do' look," she said. This conversation was going nowhere, and it was honestly just making me more upset.

"Yeah, I don't know, Jess. It's just done, I guess. I thought when I came home I'd be able to talk to him, you know, apologize for making him uncomfortable. I've learned a lot in the past weekend about veterans and what they go through after deployments, and I think that it would have been helpful to know more about his past and his history before I dropped the Michael bomb on him. I think there are a lot of similarities between Seth and Michael, and that didn't occur to me until after I talked to my dad today." My voice fell soft and trailed off. I was sad.

"Well, that may be true, but he didn't stick around to talk about it, and then he went out the next day with some other chick, which is one hundred percent not cool. Not cool at all."

"You're right. He's tried calling a few times, so I guess at some point I'll just have to shut him down if he doesn't stop, but until then, I'm going to ignore it. Maybe he'll just go away," I said softly. The truth was, I didn't want him to go away. Even if he was out with another girl last night, he still tried calling me several times and something about that didn't settle well with me.

"Well, tonight, just go home and shut your phone off. You've already talked to everyone you need to, like me of course. Just take a night to yourself, put some music on, have some wine, and call it a fucking night. It's been a weird week to say the least, ya know?" She looked over at me to gauge my reaction, I'm sure.

"Yeah, you're right. Thanks again for chauffeuring me around, Jess. I appreciate it," I told her. "And while I'm at it, your boyfriend seems like a nice guy." I smiled over at her.

"You know what, Viv? He really is. That whole boyfriend thing was a surprise, but we are on the same page; he makes me happy. And Hector likes him, so you know, there's that." She laughed.

"Hector's approval is super important, I totally understand." I laughed back.

After she dropped me off, I didn't even bother unpacking. I just put my bag in the living room and went straight to the wine rack to choose my poison. I settled on a smooth and inexpensive Pinot Noir I picked up at the grocery store. You'd be surprised how little you have to spend on some really great wine. The expensive stuff isn't always that great, and I didn't have to make a special stop for this, which made it a winner out of the gate in my book.

I poured myself a big glass and went to my room to change into something comfy so I could just drink wine and watch the Hallmark Channel or something equally sappy. Since it was late October, they were starting to show some holiday movies to get people in the mood. I didn't even care if it was all a ploy to get me to start holiday shopping early. I loved those movies. They always had a happy ending. They also always made me cry, but that's ok. I didn't even mind.

I cozied up on the couch under a blanket, leaving my phone off on the coffee table. I reached out to grab it a couple times, but stopped myself. Jess was right. I should just leave it for the night. Even though something about him trying to reach me today wasn't sitting right with me, I decided to just shove it aside. Instead, I watched movies for a couple of hours, crying with the characters over their lost love, their Christmas love, a stray cat they took in. I cried about everything.

The next morning, I woke up on the couch, an empty wineglass on the coffee table next to my phone. Rubbing the sleep from my eyes, I got up to stretch and took the glass to the kitchen sink. All the Hallmark emotion coupled with real life must have knocked me out. Well, and the wine too. I decided to take one more day off to just get my head right. I needed to do some things around the house anyway, and I didn't really want to get all dressed up and deal with people. I needed a *me* day.

I went to the bathroom to brush my teeth and have a good look at myself. My reflection was as I expected; I looked like crap. I brushed my teeth, washed my face, and piled my long hair into a messy bun on top of my head, deciding that was going to be the look for the day. It wasn't like I was leaving anyway. I had on my favorite Johnny Cash tee shirt, and I changed into a pair of cutoffs suitable for hanging around my own house all day.

As I made my way back to the kitchen, a loud knock at my door startled me; it was more like banging on my door. I scurried over to the door and looked out the peephole.

"It's me, Viv, can we talk, please?" It was Seth; he showed up at my house. At seven in the morning. *What the hell?* My heart fell into my gut, and then started pounding violently against my chest.

JAX

When I pulled down her street, I wasn't sure what I was going to say other than that I wanted to explain. I was trying to think of the right thing to say without admitting my faults. Nobody wants to do that, and I was no different. As weak as it may be, I was falling in love with this girl and I needed her to know that.

Tail between my legs, I knocked on her door. I could hear the television on, then the sound of her tiny feet coming to the door. As the shadow formed over the peephole she was looking at me through, I said, "It's me, Viv, can we talk, please?"

She opened the door just enough for me to take her in, looking her up and down. She had her long, blond hair up on top of her head in a messy bun and she was wearing little jean cut offs with a black tee shirt. She had never looked so amazing to me since the day I met her, and she wasn't even trying. I was speechless. "What do you want Seth?"

"Can I come in? I just want to talk." I pushed lightly on the door to see if she'd give.

Thankfully, she did let me in, but she sure gave me a hefty sigh for such a tiny little thing. "Seth, what do you want?" she repeated.

"I want to explain what happened the other night. I told you that I was trying to become a better man, and it's been hard. I need you to know where I'm coming from. Please let me explain myself, Viv," I begged her.

"Seth, the other night doesn't even matter now. I know you went out with someone else." *What the fuck was she talking about?*

"Someone else? What? There's no one else." I had no idea what she meant.

"Now you want to talk? You knew how I felt the other night. I shared things with you, I thought we were connecting, that's what you said you wanted. And when I did, you ran away. And adding insult to injury, you went out with another girl the next day? What could you possibly have to add to this?" She waved her angry little hands in between us dramatically. It was so fucking adorable I could hardly stand it. I knew she was mad, and I was there to fix it, but goddam if she wasn't like a little angry dragon huffing at me, though.

"Whoa, hold on one second, Viv." I put my hands up in surrender. "I didn't go out with anyone else. What are you talking about?" I was honestly getting upset she thought I was out with another woman. The thought made me sick.

"Jess saw you at Shea's with some blonde chick. She was there with Jeremy. So don't even deny it. She said she saw you, and she said you definitely saw her too." She rested her hands on her hips, satisfied she'd put me in my place when I started laughing.

"That explains the nasty fucking look she gave me," I said, still laughing.

"What's so funny about that?" She scrunched her little nose up at me.

"That was my *sister* I was out with. Savannah lives across town, and I asked her to meet me so we could talk. I've been dealing with a lot of shit, Viv, and I took my *sister* out for drinks to talk."

"Well, shit." She dropped her hands from her hips and gave me a confused look.

I felt like a fucking asshole. Here I was, in love, not falling, it happened, and she thought I was skipping out to be with another woman. All I could think was that I had to say something to fix it, and my dumb ass decided to ask about her fucking shirt. "What's with the Johnny Cash shirt?" Yeah, that's what I said, and she just shook her head at me and walked to her living room. Of course I followed her, running my hands through my hair as panic that I might not be able to fix this started to set in.

"Do you even know anything about Johnny Cash, Seth?" she asked me curtly, putting her hand on her hip again in perfect sassy fashion.

"Honestly, I do not. You're a big fan, I take it?" *Still, nothing smart to say, obviously.*

"Johnny Cash and June Carter Cash shared a love that fairy tales and stories are written about. After *years* of him begging her to be with him, she finally fell in love with him, and they spent like thirty-five years together until they retired. They had been through a ton of shit together. They were best friends. Then, they were madly in love. When she died before him, he died just a few months later. He died of a broken heart over losing her. He was so heartbroken that he covered the Nine Inch Nails song *Hurt*, which will rip your fucking heart out, by the way. It's the kind of love that anyone would want. It's inspiring. It's what romantics dream about finding. So, *that's* what's with the Johnny Cash shirt."

I couldn't stop myself. I lunged forward to her, taking her face in my hands and crushing my lips to hers. She resisted for a moment, then gave in, letting my tongue seek out her mouth. I was out of breath trying to consume her as she reached around and slid her hands up my back. I started to run one hand down her side, pulling her closer to me as I reached her waist, when she put a hand to my chest, pushing me away slightly.

"Seth, what are you doing here, really? The other night you ran out—"

I interrupted her. "The other night, I got lost in my own thoughts, Viv." I pulled her back in just to hold her, resting my chin on top of her head. "I need to tell you some things so you understand what goes on inside my head. It's not all unicorns and kittens for me, darlin'." I paused. "My darkness comes in waves, and sometimes I can't control it, and that night, talking about your brother, well, it reminded me of myself." I sighed, holding her tightly, hoping that she would relax into my hold on her.

Her arms reached back up around me, welcoming my embrace, relieving some of my anxiety about my confessions. "I'm sorry," she whispered. Hearing her apologize for something she didn't do brought tears to my eyes.

I pulled away and took her face in my hands, "Don't you dare apologize, Vivian. You did nothing wrong. Do you understand me? You're perfect. I should have stayed, and I should have opened up to you." I rested my forehead against hers. "Let me explain?"

She nodded. I took her hand and walked us over to the couch so we could sit and talk, and I could finally come clean about everything.

Not letting go of her hand, I started, "So, you know I did two tours in the Marines. I was deployed in Afghanistan, and then again in Iraq. I didn't experience anything that I thought was particularly horrible. It's not a great place, I'm not saying that. But I didn't lose anyone on my team while I was there. I just did my job. Now, maybe stuff happened that would have affected other guys, I don't know. I was a take-orders kind of guy, so the whole thing to me was my job, and you just do your job."

She nodded again, looking up at me with those beautiful, blue eyes, listening intently. "When I came home the second time, I decided that I wanted to go back to the fire department and work there. Matt helped me get my job there, while I finished out my time. No big deal. Over the last couple of years, we've seen a lot. We don't save everyone, Viv. We can't. We do the best that we can, but it's one of the reasons I avoid riding the ambulance and I try to stick to the fire truck. When your job is to rescue someone and you can't get to them in time, or they simply don't make it, those things can wear on you after a while."

She raised her hand up to my face, caressing my jaw. I brought my hand to hers, closing my eyes for a moment, collecting my thoughts before I brought her hand back to my lap and continued. "The last few months I've had trouble sleeping. I started having nightmares and anxiety. Walls feeling like they're closing in on me, the whole nine yards. You remember I told you that I was trying to be a better man?"

"Yes," she said quietly.

"Well, that is true. I wasn't always that great of a guy, Viv. I used people. I was never dishonest about it, but I never went on real dates. I didn't spend a lot of time outside of the bar talking to a woman. After one night, it was pretty unlikely they'd see me again. And I drank a lot. On my days off, of course, but certainly more than I should have. I was trying to drown out the noise in my head. I was heading down a path of self-destruction, and I really didn't know what to do.

"I was at the VA getting a physical, and I mentioned to the doctor that I was having trouble sleeping, so he made me go see a therapist. Big shocker, I didn't want to, but you have to do what they tell you to, or you can't keep going there for other things. So, I went. Viv, Dr. Rosen is the one who helped me see the light. He told me that I was never going to get out of that darkness if I didn't work on making meaningful connections with people. And then I met you."

The corners of her mouth turned upward into a small smile. "Then you met me," she repeated.

"Yes, you were the light, darlin'." I couldn't contain the grin her little smile caused me to have. "I met you, and after our first date, I had the absolute best sleep I can remember in months. I was hooked on you from the moment we met. Even if you are sassy and you weren't sure about me." I tried to lighten the mood a little bit.

"I thought you liked my sass." She scrunched her nose at me again. Definitely one of my favorite looks on her.

"I love your sass. I love everything about you. I lo—" I hesitated and then I just blurted it out. "Fuck it, I love you, Vivian. I'm in love with you. I know it hasn't been long, but you know when you know, and I know that what you've been through makes it hard for you, and if you don't love me yet, maybe you will someday, but you need to know how I feel about you. I. Love. You." That was some word vomit that I'd not soon live down. I was almost out of breath from trying to get it all out quickly while I had the courage.

She raised her tiny hands, placing them gently on either side of my face. Looking up into my panicked eyes, she whispered softly and with a slight smile forming, "I love you too, Seth Jackson." A ten-ton weight was immediately lifted from my shoulders.

"You do?" I asked cautiously.

"Of course I do, you sweet, sweet man." She grinned, showing her beautiful full smile. "Everything that happens to us happens *for* us, really. Even when it doesn't feel like it, everything that's happening around us brings us to each new special moment, Seth. Everything that happened with Michael brought me to you. I was meant to be light for you, and you for me. Don't you see it?"

"I do, darlin'," I replied, pulling her into me. "I can't believe how happy having you in my life makes me, Viv."

She squeezed me back, holding on to me tightly. "I told my parents about you yesterday when I saw them," she said.

"You saw them? Are they back in Florida?" I asked, relaxing my hold on her. I hoped I could meet her parents soon; I suddenly wanted to meet the people who raised the woman I love.

"No, I flew there for a night so I could spend time with them. After you left, I just wanted to hug my parents, and I felt like they needed me too," she explained softly.

"You flew there? For a day? Is everything ok, darlin'?" I asked. She looked slightly sad at first, then her eyes brightened and she smiled at me again.

"Everything is great, .I spent some time with them separately, and we talked about Michael, and for the first time, we talked about what happened. It's time for me to let go of the guilt; that's what they both wanted me to know."

"They're right, you know. He would have wanted you to be

happy. He loved you, even if he couldn't help himself." My heart ached for her. I knew how hard it was to lose someone, and the burden can be so hard to let go of.

"I know that. I think I always sort of knew that. But I felt like if I moved on, it was betraying him in some way, if that makes any sense. My dad told me how he'd tried to help Michael, how he'd try to get him help, to talk to someone, and how he just didn't want it. He reminded me that sometimes all you can do is give your love and hope it's enough. What happened isn't my fault, but I don't want history to repeat itself, Seth. You opened up to me, and I want you to know how much that means to me. I do love you, and I will love you on good days, and on bad days, and every day in between."

"Well, you're stuck with me now." I laughed.

"Come on." She got up yawning, pulling me along with her.

"Where are we going?"

"We are going back to bed." She smiled.

I gladly followed her to her room, practically floating from letting go of the angst and fear. A sense of relief had taken over; I was exhausted, and all I wanted to do was hold her.

Vivian

I led him back to my bedroom by his hand, then turned to face him, placing my hands on his chest softly. He still had his uniform from work on, and I started to undo the buttons on his thick shirt while he stood in front of me motionless, watching me. His eyes were heavy, and while it was a sensual moment, undressing him, I wanted him to rest. I slid his shirt off his shoulders, leaving him in his undershirt and pants.

As I made my way to undoing his belt buckle, his body stiffened, and his hands stopped mine. "Viv, we don't have to do this right now," he uttered breathlessly.

I stopped and pushed him gently to sit on the edge of the bed. "I know, Seth. We're just going to rest together; you need to sleep. I can see it in your eyes."

I helped him take off his boots and then went back to his pants. As they dropped to the floor, I took note that he was noticeably hard, his size and arousal causing me to become wet with desire immediately. Trying to focus on taking care of him, I motioned for him to lie down and get under the covers in his boxers and tee shirt. He never took his eyes off me, watching me intently. I walked to the other side of the bed and undid my shorts, letting them fall to the floor before I slid under the covers next to him.

He raised his arm for me to snuggle in close, the feeling of our skin against each other igniting that controlled burn I had for him. As I rubbed my leg against his, I slowly moved my hand up his chest, under his shirt, outlining his abs with my fingertips. As I made my way back down, tucking my finger gently into the waistband of his boxers, he sucked in air and quickly rolled on top of me.

"Is this what you want, Vivian?" he whispered into my neck as he gently licked down to my shoulder.

"Yes," I breathed out. He quickly sat up and yanked his shirt off, exposing all of his tattoos and muscles for me to enjoy. Those beautifully tattooed arms reached back down to the hem of my shirt, where he gently pulled it over my head, causing my hair to fall from its bun into waves around my shoulders.

"You're so fucking beautiful, Vivian. I'm so fucking lucky." He looked at my almost naked body like I was dessert. I pulled him back down to me, letting the heat of our skin converge, causing the burn for him to bubble to the surface. As he began kissing me, making his way down my body, I shuddered with desire. I wanted him to ravage me, but he wanted to take his time with me, and I was going to enjoy every minute of it. "I want to taste every inch of you," he whispered.

He made his way to my breasts, sucking and nuzzling my nipples. I started to rock my hips up against him, feeling his hardness against me, which was driving me crazy with desire. He kissed his way to my stomach and softly kissed my abdomen, as his hands started to pull my panties down gently. As he pulled them down my legs, taking them off, I lay there watching him. Watching him worship my body. He stood up and took his boxers off, completely exposing his beautiful form to me. He had moved to the end of the bed and kneeled down, gently grabbing my ankle, kissing it softly. As he continued moving up my thigh, I tried to control the urge to leap up; the sensations of his gentle, soft lips along my thigh were turning me into a quivering pool.

As he reached the top of my thigh, he paused and looked up at me. "I'm having you for breakfast, because you're mine," he said in a raspy voice. Not waiting for an answer, he gently spread my legs wider, licking me in my most sensitive spot. I let out a stifled moan, causing him to go in deeper, suckling my clit, then sliding a finger inside of me. Ecstasy started to build inside me; I'd never felt so consumed, or experienced so much pleasure at once. The emotions of the day coupled with my overwhelming desire for him came to climax as I cried out, letting the pleasure take me away.

"Seth!" I cried out as my hips rocked and shook. He held me in place with his muscular arms, continuing to eat me out until my hips fell to the bed, spent. I was panting, unable to speak from the intensity of the orgasm. He moved to the side of the bed, getting something from his pants, and came back to the bed.

Still trying to catch my breath, I looked over to see him smiling that stunning grin at me. "I could do that all day long, baby. Are you ready for more?"

I just nodded as my chest continued to rise and fall dramatically. I watched as he ripped the foil and rolled the condom on before sliding in next to me again. Pushing myself up, ready for round two, I encouraged him to lie next to me so I could climb on top of him. "Oh yeah?" he said, helping me straddle over him.

"Oh yeah," I replied as I slid myself on top of his length,

causing us both to moan. "Oh my God, Seth," I cried out as he filled me up slowly.

"Fuck," he growled, as he grabbed my hips roughly. "Oh my God, Viv, you feel so fucking good." He held me in place as my body adjusted to his size, and then allowed me to rock myself gently on his cock. I leaned forward, placing my hands on his chest, sliding up and down gently, watching him enjoy the sensations with me. As my own climax started to build, I started to go a little faster, which caused him to stop me. "Viv, you're killing me," he sighed out as he rolled us over so he could be on top of me.

Hovering over me, he took control, kissing me while we made love, watching my face. I was about to implode again, and as he picked up his pace, we both began to moan loudly, shouting out our release together. He collapsed over me, trying not to crush me and rolled on his side before going into the bathroom. When he came back, still completely naked, I drank him in with my eyes.

"Are you ok, darlin'," he asked me as he crawled back into the bed, pulling me close.

"I am great. Are you ok?" I asked.

"I've never been better. I'm in love." He kissed me gently. "Can we rest together today, or do you have to work?"

"We can rest together." I laid my head on his chest, listening to his heart as we both fell fast asleep.

JAX

I slept like the dead that morning, well into the afternoon. The weight of my guilt, my demons, it all lifted when I told her how I felt about her; how I felt about everything.

When I woke up, she was missing from the bed, so I sat up looking around for her. I couldn't figure out what time it was, but from the light in the window, it looked like the sun was going down already. I must have slept the entire day. I grabbed my boxers and my pants, and went to look for her. I could hear a faint noise, music of some kind coming from the kitchen.

As I approached, I was overwhelmed with the scent of something delicious, making my stomach rumble. I realized I hadn't eaten since the day before, and I was starving. When I made my way to the end of the hallway, I spotted her in the kitchen, her hair tied back up, radio playing softly, while she was dancing around and singing while cooking something. I could wake up to this vision every day for the rest of my life. A smile spread across my face as I realized that was possible. I loved her, and she loved me back. She was mine.

I stood there watching her dance around until she noticed me and jumped. "Oh my God, Seth! You scared me!" She did that scrunching thing with her nose, making me smile even more.

"Hey, darlin', whatcha doing in here? Smells amazing." I took a deep breath in.

"I didn't want to wake you, but I figured you'd be hungry when you woke up. I did some cooking." She was beaming.

"I thought you didn't cook." I smirked at her.

"Well, as it turns out, I cook for you."

I made my way over to her, taking her in my arms and planting a kiss on her sweet lips. "Well, aren't I the luckiest guy in the world?"

"Well... you haven't tasted it yet, so if it doesn't kill you, then yes, you definitely are." She laughed.

"If I die from the food the most beautiful woman in the world cooked for me because she loves me, I'd die a happy, happy man right here and now." I kissed her again.

She stopped and embraced me. "I really do love you, Seth. No matter what, don't ever forget that."

"I'm going to spend the rest of my life showing you how lucky I am to have you in my life, darlin'. I promise you that. I have a little surprise for you today."

"A surprise? For me?" She blushed.

"Yes, for you. You're my girl, and I'm going to be full of surprises to make you smile for a very long time, darlin'."

"I like that idea very much." She set a plate of food in front of me and kissed the top of my head, like I always did with her. She was so affectionate with me, which filled my heart up so much it felt like it would explode. She sat across from me at the table and watched me. "So, what's the surprise?"

"I don't know if I should tell you yet," I teased her.

"What?" She scrunched that little nose up, making me laugh.

"Okay, okay. But first, is there any way that you can take one more day off tomorrow?" I asked. That was a crucial part of my plan.

"Yeah, I can do that. Now, what's the surprise?" She squealed and clapped her hands together in anticipation.

"Well, I packed up the truck with camping stuff before I came over this morning." She gave me a sideways look, confused. "I thought we could pack up some stuff and go to the beach, sleep in the back of the truck down by the water. Listen to the waves tonight and wake up to the sunrise together."

A huge grin crossed her face just before she leapt up and ran over to me, throwing her arms around me. "Oh my God, Seth! That is my perfect day! I would love to do that!" She squeezed me tight, then kissed me passionately. Her kiss warmed me all over, and I wrapped my arms around her with her on my lap now, thanking God for having her in my life.

"I want to spend the rest of my life making perfect days for you, darlin'. Every day with you is perfect for me," I said.

"I love you so much, Jax," she whispered in my ear as she held me tight.

That night, we bundled up and parked the truck on the beach to catch the sunset before we made love to nothing but the sound of the waves crashing. It was the first of many perfect days we shared together. The darkness came and went from time to time, less often over time, and she never left my side. We were a package deal from then on out in good times and in bad, almost always good, though.

The End

ACKNOWLEDGEMENTS

Every time you write a book, you give a little piece of yourself to your readers. This book was no different. A departure from my other books, this was emotional for me. I too, have lost colleagues and friends to suicide. Before I thank everyone, I cannot say enough how much I care about you. Yes, you. If you ever feel that you're alone, you are not. If you need help, call, write, text. Send smoke signals. Never ever give up. If you don't need help, do a buddy check. Make sure your friends are ok.

My family always deserves a thank you for their completely unconditional support. The calls between my brother and me to talk about what we're up to are my favorite conversations in the world, and every time we talk, I'm more motivated than ever to do more and be better than I was the day before. I'm truly blessed.

Jessica Epps, you are the Thelma to my Louise; you're my partner in crime, and I'm grateful for your support and our hysterical chats every single day. I can't imagine not talking to you throughout the day no matter when or where. I'm so lucky to have you for a best friend.

Mikey Lee, what can I say? From the time we locked eyes from across the room at a signing, we've literally been buddies ever since. So excited for all of the awesome projects we've got going on, and so grateful to have you and Heather in my corner. Your support means so much, and I hope to be moving in with you guys soon, but only when it's warm outside.

I can't possibly name everyone who has helped me with my books, my business, and my life, but some of my friends in the writing community have been insanely supportive and deserve huge shout outs from the rooftops. Stephanie Hoffman McManus, Heidi McLaughlin, Jennifer Armentrout, BT Urruela, Cassy Roop, Judi Perkins, Patti Correa, Sharon Abreau, Jillian Toth, and Tiffany Holcomb, just to name a few whom I talk to regularly to complain, cry, ask for advice from, you name it. I'll be forever grateful for your input and guidance, as well as your never-ending encouragement.

The biggest thanks of all goes to the readers and bloggers. You are literally why we keep putting stories out there. It is an absolute honor to have found my way to your kindle, your tablet, or even as a good old-fashioned paperback. I'm genuinely honored to have you read my words.

WHERE YOU CAN GET HELP
&
HOW YOU CAN GET HELP

If you are in crisis, please reach out for help.

National Suicide Prevention Lifeline:
1-800-273-8255

For more information on how you can help raise awareness of Veteran's suicide, below is a list of nonprofit organizations where you can learn more:

Honor Courage & Commitment
http://www.honorcouragecommitment.org/

Honor the Sacrifice
http://www.honor-the-sacrifice.org/

The Wounded Warrior Project
https://www.woundedwarriorproject.org/

Founded under the nonprofit, Honor Courage & Commitment, 22KILL works to not only raise awareness toward veteran suicide, but also to the issues that can lead them to suicide. To learn more about the 22KILL project that raises awareness of veteran suicide please visit: https://www.22kill.com/

VETSports is a nationwide non-profit helping veterans achieve better physical, mental, and emotional health through sports, physical activity, and community involvement. For more information, please visit: http://www.vetsports.org/

BONUS CHAPTERS

BRIAN CAVANAUGH

I grabbed two beers out of the fridge, handing one to Matt before plopping down on the couch and putting my feet on the table. I glanced around the room taking in all of the wedding gifts and clutter that had become commonplace the last few weeks at my house.

"She's gonna kill you for putting your feet on there," Matt teased, raising an eyebrow at me.

"Nah, she doesn't care, she's not mom you know," I replied. Taking a long sip of my beer, I grinned and relaxed into my seat comfortably. "I can't believe it's finally here," I said, relishing in the thought that tomorrow was my wedding day. I never thought I'd get married; it just didn't seem like something that I'd ever do.

"You excited?" Matt asked.

"Honestly, I am. Truthfully, I'm relieved," I replied.

"What do you mean, relieved? That's a strange answer."

"I'm relieved it is going to be over tomorrow. Man, none of this hoopla is what we really wanted, but I also insisted she have her day, ya know? She deserves to be the star of the show for everyone to see. She fought me on it, but I saw the look in her eye after mama took her wedding dress shopping, and I wouldn't want to rob her of that moment." I thought about how her blue eyes sparkled when she came home from shopping with my mother; I could feel her enthusiasm as if it were my own as she told me about her day. Not to say I wasn't enthusiastic, I was. From the moment I discovered how I felt for Jo, all I wanted was to make her mine forever.

Jo's parents were both gone, and that added a bit of sadness to the day for her, but that moment, where she twirled in front of me, I knew the day had to be more than us simply making our relationship official. She was demonstrating what she'd done in the store, and watching her dance around, laughing and smiling about that moment reminded me of how special she was to me.

"Yea, you know growing up, sometimes it was easy to forget she wasn't one of the guys. You're right; it's the woman's day any way you look at it. I think her dad would be really happy; really proud right now," Matt said thoughtfully.

"I hope so man. He was a hell of a guy to look up to all those years. I'm glad she has our mom to be there for her right now. It feels like our family just keeps getting bigger, and I love it."

"Yea, me too man. Who would have thought we'd be where we are now even a year ago?" Matt laughed and sipped on his beer. "Tomorrow, we'll both be married dude. It's fucking crazy."

"I still can't believe you and Isabel ran off and got married without telling anyone. You know mom's never going to get over it," I replied giving him the same stern look we all gave him when he made his announcement at work. Matt took a long weekend recently and came back married. No notice to anyone that it was even going to happen; they showed back up to work that Monday with wedding rings and a story. At first my mom was devastated that she wasn't included, but that's just how Matt and Isabel operated. They definitely weren't traditional, and they marched to the beat of their own drummer.

"Oh my God dude, you all need to get over it. Izzy and I just don't want all the shenanigans that come with a big wedding and everything, and we just decided on a whim that we'd do it. Our intention was never to make anyone feel shitty man, I don't know how many times you want me to say it. And, while I'm at it, I didn't want to steal your thunder," he tried to explain.

"Oh, steal my thunder, eh?" I let out a laugh.

"Fuck off. You know what I mean. You and Jo, you're different."

"Different how?" I asked. I didn't really know what he meant, but since we were having this conversation, the night before I tied the knot and we had nowhere else to be, I wanted to know.

"You and Jo were meant to be together dude," he stated, matter of factly.

"You say that, but what do you mean, really?"

"Jo is your lobster."

"What the fuck does that mean?" I asked.

Rolling his eyes at me like I should have known what the fuck he was talking about, he replied. "Lobsters mate for life. They find their other lobster, and that's it. Jo was always it for you. You think it took you years to figure out, but we all fucking knew she was for you from the time we were kids. You always had your eyes on her, you always looked out for her even when she had no idea. It just took both of you for fucking ever to figure it out yourselves. The rest of us all knew. Ask mama. She'll tell you," he got up. "You ready for another one, or can we switch to whiskey now that we're having a heart to heart the night before your wedding?"

I flipped him the bird before replying, "Yea, let's have the good stuff. We're celebrating." I pointed to the liquor cabinet where we had some pretty good whiskey that had shown up as wedding gifts, and Jo didn't really care for it, so she wouldn't mind if we tapped into the stash. Besides, she was staying at my mom's house, because we were being traditional and not spending tonight together. I hated not having her here, but there was something about tradition that I loved, and sharing traditions with Jo made them that much more enjoyable.

Jo loved our traditions; I wasn't assuming that, I knew. Every time I shared something with her that our mom shared with us growing up about Ireland, and how our ancestors did things, she listened intently. We shared everything, and part of our wedding was about combining our traditions together. She was my heart; it beat for her.

I didn't say anything while I watched Matt pour us both a generous glass, watching the amber liquid splash into the glass; I was thinking about his lobster analogy. Reflecting my past with Jo, and our history, he was right. I've known her since she was born. Our mom's were friends, and when her mom passed, my mom sort of stepped in. It was as if she was born to be with me. I felt my heart swell like I was a teenager swooning again. A grin had formed across my entire face that Matt must have noticed, when he handed me my drink.

"Oh Lord, look at you glowing," he teased as he handed me the tumbler.

"Fuck off, you're glowing too asshole," I rose my glass to toast his.

"You're God damn right I am," he clinked his glass to mine. "Did you ever think – I mean really think – this is how we'd end up?"

"Honestly? I didn't even know these feelings existed. It's hard to explain," he cut me off.

"Oh, I get it. Butterflies? Excitement? Checking your phone non-stop? I get it... believe me," he rolled his eyes.

Leaning forward, shocked he knew how I felt I said, "Dude! Exactly. Like I know I'm coming home to her at night, and still, all this random shit that happens during the day, she's the first person I want to tell about. And forget about seeing her at work. I can't even help myself, as professional as I try to be, when she does something on scene, I'm puffing my chest out, like *she's mine* fellas," I started laughing uncontrollably, the liquor hitting my system now.

"I thought it was just me man," Matt started to laugh as well. As we began our giggling fit like teenage girls, he continued. "All fucking day, I'm about seeing what she's doing and shit. I mean I also worry about her crazy ass. She's come home with some nasty bruises where I'm asking who do I need to fuck up, and she puts me in my place, and I don't even care!" He kept laughing hysterically.

"You know mom thinks all of this is hysterical too right?" I said, wiping tears from my eyes, still chuckling.

"Dude, I'm not stupid. Any man as close to his mother as we are, is totally gonna end up like us. I just didn't see it coming; it was like getting hit with a fucking truck. I don't even care. I feel like I was the biggest fucking dummy for not seeing it sooner, but then again, I guess that's what Isabel was for me. So, really... You're the dummy. You've known Jo since we were in diapers and it took you thirty-five years to figure it out."

"Damn, that's fucked up dickhead," I replied, barely able to get the words out I was laughing so hard. Thinking about what he said, I began to realize how right he was, and in a way, felt bad I wasn't with her longer. My demeanor changed from laughing hysterically with my brother, to ashamed it took me so long to make her mine. I should have manned up and figured out how I felt sooner, and I felt my shoulders slump a bit thinking about it.

"Brian. I can see you thinking. It's creating a smoke condition in the room," he looked over at me from the couch. "I was just teasing you. Man, everything in this life happens for you, not to you, and that goes for her too man. You got together when the time was right. You saved her life, and she saved yours. It's all good things man, don't let yourself get lost in the 'I should have' moments. Focus on tomorrow, and making her yours officially, and giving mama some grandbabies, so I don't have to," he chuckled, trying to lighten the mood.

"No, I get it, you're right. There's a part of me that feels like she should have had all of this already, and that she deserves better than me," I could tell I was delving into one of those semi-drunk 'she's too good for me' moments. And regardless of how much I drank, I knew I was lucky to have her, and she would always be too good for me.

"Bro," Matt leaned forward, holding his almost empty glass in his hand while he rested his elbows on his knees, trying to get my full attention. I looked him in the eye, acknowledging his serious tone. "Of course she's too good for you. Relish in that shit," he smiled. "She's been my best friend since the sandbox. She asked *me*, to give her to *you* tomorrow. That shit almost made me cry motherfucker! I can't even begin tell you how much it meant to me.

We were destined to be family, all of us. Show her every fucking day how lucky you know you are to have her to come home to. That's it. It's that simple man. She loves you. I mean seriously, she loves you unconditionally. She's your fucking lobster." He pounded the rest of his drink; satisfied he'd made his case with me, which he had.

My heart swelled. I was getting married the next day. Forever. There were no what if's, there were no maybe's, it was forever for us. I knew her; I'd known her since the she was born, and she was born to be mine. I loved her with everything I had, and I'd spend the rest of my life showing her how much I loved her and how lucky I felt to be in her life. Tomorrow, I was marrying my best friend, with my brother by my side; I honestly couldn't imagine a more perfect day.

MATT CAVANAUGH

The cool breeze came over the ocean, blowing Isabel's hair behind her just slightly, exposing her long neck in her profile. As I gazed at her beauty, I couldn't help but think how crazy our little ride had become, and yet how completely at peace I was with everything we were doing.

She caught me looking, and opened her lips into a wide smile, "What are you looking at?" She swept her long dark hair to the side and turned to face me.

"I'm just looking at my beautiful bride to be is all," I smirked at her.

She laughed and placed her face in her hand, "Are you sure this is a good idea?" She looked up at me wistfully.

We were sitting on the balcony of our hotel room in Puerto Rico, overlooking the crystal blue water that I couldn't help but look back to before responding. "Isabel, I've never been more sure of anything in my life. Me and you baby, we're easy. We don't need all the pomp and circumstance of the whole district coming to a wedding. Let Brian and Jo have that. That's for them, it's not us. I always promised you it was just us, no labels and we do what we want." Technically getting married in secret was definitely giving us a label, but I knew that she knew what I meant.

"You know our families are going to kill us right?" She laughed, making her way over to my lap, her sheer, white sundress flowing around her. Isabel didn't wear dresses very often, but when she did, she blew my mind with her sexiness and femininity. She looked like an angel floating over to me.

As I wrapped my arms around her tiny waist, pulling her in for a little kiss, I whispered, "Baby, who cares?" She smiled into my kiss, softening herself into me and wrapping her fingers into the back of my hair. The way she touched me had my cock coming to attention in seconds.

I started to move my lips to her delicious neck, causing her to let out a little moan. This of course, drove me wild. Every sound that came out of her turned me on, I couldn't ever get enough. It was my idea to come on vacation and elope, and when I'd presented the idea, I didn't even have a ring. In retrospect, that was a douche move, which I planned to rectify in a moment.

She pulled away, inspecting my face. "You're up to something Cavanaugh, I can feel it."

Huffing at her cop intuition, I replied, "Don't always ruin a surprise with your smarts and cop shit woman." I reached into my pocket and pulled out the box. Isabel would never wear a diamond solitaire; it just wasn't her. And with her job, I'd be lucky to get her to wear a band, but that's what I bought. I picked out a thin white gold band, surrounded with small diamonds all the way around it. It wasn't too flashy, but it said she was spoken for, which she was and I wanted people to know. I'm a cool guy, but I want my woman to be mine just like anyone else would.

"What is this?" She exclaimed more playfully than her usual

demeanor.

I carefully removed her from my lap, setting her down in the chair I was in on the balcony. Adjusting myself down to one knee, I watched her face form a surprised expression just before she covered her mouth with her tiny hands.

"Isabel Cruise. You are the love of my life. You rock my world. I know you didn't want some fancy ring or all of the spoils of a big wedding, but you deserve a proper proposal before we get hitched today," I knew I was surprising her, and scanning her face to take in her shock, had my heart racing. "Would you officially do me the honor of marrying me, and making me the happiest man on earth?"

A tear fell from her eye, which I didn't expect at all. As I reached up to wipe it away, she grabbed my hand and rested her face against my palm. I started to get worried something was wrong, until she leaned forward, softly planting her lips to mine. "Of course I will Matt," she started to sniffle and then fan her face to get rid of the tears.

"Baby, don't cry, this is our day!" I exclaimed.

"I know, I don't know what my problem is. I guess it's just all becoming so real," she said, gaining her composure.

"Are you having second thoughts Cruise?" I teased her, getting up off my knee, and pulling her into an embrace.

"Of course not," she replied, resting her head on my shoulder, squeezing me back around my waist. *Mission accomplished*, I thought to myself. I wanted to take her by surprise, and I felt like I won; not that it was a competition. But if it were, I totally won.

"Okay now baby, let's finish these drinks and get down to the beach. It's about that time for you to become a Cavanaugh," I said excitedly.

She giggled. "You know that the only reason I'm changing my name is so we can call the gym Cavanaugh's and it's still fifty-fifty me and you, right?" Again, that was her idea, not mine. I would have named the gym whatever the fuck she wanted to, but she thought Cavanaugh's sounded like a place fighters would want to train. She also explained to me that she felt it was a true family operated business if we named it that, and while we weren't exactly the most traditional couple, there were some traditions that were meaningful to us. It was in that moment that I blurted out, *'then we need to get married, so it's our family business'*. She never really said yes or no, it was just happening after that. It's how we rolled.

"Baby, I don't care what your name is. I feel like you already know this," I grabbed her hand and started to pull her into our hotel room.

"I do, I just like to give you a hard time and keep you on your toes." She smiled as she came with me into our giant room.

We weren't rich by any means, especially since we'd bought the gym that would probably always need fixing up, but we splurged on our vacation slash secret wedding and had a huge suite. We had already started consummating our soon to be marriage around the place, and I couldn't wait to make her call me her husband while I was fucking her later. In fact, more than anything, I couldn't wait to call her my wife. But we needed to get moving. Since we didn't bring our own witnesses, the hotel had arranged for people to be there at our small private ceremony, but that also meant we needed to be on time.

"Well, in a few minutes, you'll be able to say that it's officially your job as my wife. Let's go make this official babe," I was God damn excited to marry her. I felt like I'd won a title fight or something; Isabel was a prize and I was the winner. It never crossed my mind once that it was too soon or that it was a bad idea to run off and get hitched without telling the important people in our lives, our family.

I knew our families would be upset that we didn't include them in the nuptials, but Isabel and I always did our own thing. I told Jax before we left what we were doing, but I swore him to secrecy and I knew I could trust him. Besides Jo, Jax was my best friend, and as a guy, I felt he understood what I needed to do, and how I needed to do it. I wanted desperately to tell Jo, but she would have told Brian, who would have told my mom, and then chaos would've ensued. Jo would be super pissed at me, but she loved love, and knowing that I was in love and had married my person, the *one* so to speak, would make up for it.

Isabel told her sister June, who wasn't thrilled, but completely understood why we were running off. Isabel's family was fairly traditional and not small by any means, and would have wanted a big huge wedding with all the family from all over the country, and all Isabel and I could think of was how it would have spiraled out of control into the circus we didn't want. Between her well to do parents, the police department and the fire department, we felt like all that pressure took away from what we were really about. Isabel and I, from day one, were about us. Our connection to each other was what defined our relationship from the moment our lips touched in the alley for the first time.

We really did need to get going, so I evaluated what we looked like. I had on tan linen pants and a white shirt, customary 'island wear' for a formal occasion, and she had on that sexy as fuck white flowing dress with little spaghetti straps I wanted to snap right off the dress. Her olive skin against the white dress was so striking, that everywhere we walked, people stared at the woman that was about to be my wife. We made our way out to the beach, leaving our shoes on the sidewalk, simply not giving a fuck if they were there when we got back or not.

As we walked to the makeshift arch out near the water covered in flowers, and some flowing white material, a woman we'd met with earlier handed Isabel a bouquet of white flowers. In the presence of strangers, on the beaches of Puerto Rico, we recited our vows hand in hand, never taking our eyes off of each other. Nothing extraordinary, we didn't write some flowery version of our love for each other, but we recited what the officiant said, grinning at each other almost as if we were about to laugh, like we had a secret no one knew about.

Once he announced, "I now pronounce you man and wife," I kissed her like I was thirsty for her taste. Picking her up and carrying her off, we didn't wait around for any other formalities. What no one tells you about destination weddings is that usually you're technically married by the time the ceremony takes place; you sign all the licenses and paperwork beforehand, so you're married on paper by the time the ceremony happens. The ceremony is for show, and that was the case for us. I was ready to consummate the marriage, and enjoy the rest of my vacation with my wife.

I carried her all the way back to our room that night, where we explored each other in ways most men only dream about. My wife was my ultimate fantasy, and now she'd be mine forever. Business partners, best friends, and lovers.

SETH "JAX" JACKSON

I watched as Viv tried to reach a plastic green cup that was four solid inches out of her grasp. I told her that she didn't want to put her favorite cups up there, but she was stubborn like me, and so I leaned against the doorway waiting for her to ask me to get it for her. The fact that she had these weird plastic tumblers she insisted on drinking out of was funny enough, they looked like they were meant for a child, but watching her struggle was priceless.

Sensing my presence and not even looking in my direction, she said, "I'm not asking you to get this God damn cup Seth. I'll climb this counter like Spider Man." She huffed it out in her usual angry little dragon way that made me laugh out loud.

"How about while you're up there, you grab all of them and move them somewhere you can reach them? I mean it's just a suggestion, I'd never move them from where *you* put them of course," I teased her. She knew that if she didn't move them, I was going to as soon as she wasn't looking.

"You know that I hate it when you're right," she gave up on the cup, turning around to look at me, she leaned up against the counter.

I walked over to her, pressing my body against hers and

reached up behind her to grab the silly cup. "I know you do, but in any event, here is your cup my love," I handed it to her, but not before I stole a kiss from her sweet lips. She set it on the counter behind her, then stretched up on her toes to kiss me again. She always tasted like caramel, or something sugary to me, and I could never get enough.

"I love you," she whispered against my lips.

"Not more than I love you darlin'," I replied, pulling her into an embrace. I never considered how much one woman could mean to me until I met Vivian Deveraux. When I fell in love with her, I fell hard. I crashed into her like a steam engine, and she caught me completely, taking in every part of me, the good and the bad. We'd been dating for almost a year, and I had finally convinced her to move in with me. I'd been asking for at least six months. Hell, probably even longer than that.

She rested her head against my chest, and as her sweet smell found its way to my senses, I kissed the top of her head. It was one of my favorite things to do. She was so much shorter than me, and especially when she was barefoot like she was then. I felt the ring burning a whole in my pocket, but it still wasn't quite the right moment. I had wanted to plan something special, something that she'd never forget, but I hadn't devised the perfect plan even though I had the perfect ring for the perfect girl.

My sister Savannah went with me to pick out the ring; she couldn't have been more excited. All of a sudden, we were all getting married or talking about getting married. They say when you know you know, and while I don't know who this *they* is, they're right.

We were still in the process of moving in together; there were boxes everywhere; she had a lot of stuff. On the upside, I did not really have a lot of stuff. She leaned back and looked up at me as I was looking around at the chaos in our house. "Are the boxes and stuff bothering you?"

"Nope. Not at all darlin'. I love having you, and all of your stuff including your sass here. I would have loved having it here months ago," I released her to get myself a drink from the fridge chuckling to myself. She took the cup and poured herself some water.

"Well, I'll be all done by tomorrow, I can't stand all the clutter," she rolled her eyes.

"Whatever works for you Viv," I honestly didn't care how long it took her to unpack and move shit in, around, wherever. Having her in my bed every night, and waking up to her sweet face every morning that I wasn't sleeping at work was all I cared about. "So listen, I was thinking."

"What's up?" She looked at me sweetly with those crystal blue eyes I would forever get lost in.

"I happen to have this weekend off, as you know."

"Yes, I am aware," she giggled.

"Mmhmm. So anyway, smarty pants, I was thinking we could go to the beach and stay down there Friday night. Camping style in the back of the truck. We could stay Saturday too, but I know that's a long time away from modern amenities for you," I teased her. "I know weekends are when you're the most busy, but any chance you can squeeze in a weekend away?"

Scrunching her nose at me, and giving me a sideways glance, she replied, "Are you up to something Seth? I feel like you're up to something." *How did she know?* Seriously, she was a mind reader.

Nervous she was onto me, I tried to act as cool as possible,

"Who me? *No*," I said dramatically. "No I'm not up to anything, why would you say that?" I was definitely talking too much. She was going to figure it out.

"You're being weird. But, yea sure, we can go camp out, but let's just do the one night? I think it's supposed to get chilly," she replied, giving me the fish eye. She definitely suspected something was up, I needed to get out of there.

"Ok cool, well I've got some shit I need to do. I am gonna run to the station and catch Brian while he's there, we have a report to go over," I said, totally lying through my teeth.

"Uh huh, sure ya do," she said sarcastically.

"Babe, why would I lie about that?" I grinned. Oh, my God, I was losing it, I needed to go immediately.

"You're up to something. Have your secrets Jackson. It's fine," she said with an acerbic tone, definitely not believing me at all.

Not wanting her to be upset with me, I walked over and scooped her into my arms. "Darlin', I just want to spend a weekend away from work, away from packing, unpacking, moving... with you. That is all, I promise."

"Are you sure you're okay with all of this Seth? It's a lot of change. For both of us," she met my eyes with a concerned glance.

"I've never been more sure of anything in my life. You are the best thing that's ever happened to me. You could never unpack a box, and just wake up with me each and every day, and I'd be the happiest man alive, I promise you darlin'," I cupped her face in my hands and brought her lips to mine.

Returning my kiss, and gently touching my abs, which drove me wild, she whispered to me, "I love you Seth." My heart soared when she said my name since everyone always called me Jax. I couldn't imagine my life without her. As we kissed passionately, I started to forget I had things to do, and unfortunately, she pulled away reminding us both. "I have to get out of here baby, but if you want to go camp tomorrow, we can do that. I'll rearrange a few things today, ok?"

"Yes please," I pulled her in for one more kiss, before swatting her on her ass as she walked out of the kitchen.

I went down to the station, not because I had any real work to do, but because if I spent one more second with Viv, I was going to ruin my own plans and spoil the surprise. Since I'd become Deputy Chief, I didn't have to work quite as many twenty-four hour shifts as I used to, just based on the way my new contract worked I was home a lot of nights and worked way fewer twenty-four shifts. While I had a lot more flexibility in my schedule, I had a hell of a lot more paperwork, so if I had the opportunity to get out of the house to escape fucking my own plans up, going to the station to do paperwork was a perfect excuse.

When I got there, I ran into Scotty, who I'd started calling Scott when I could remember, because he wasn't nineteen anymore. "Hey man, how goes? You ready?"

He looked around to make sure no one heard me, "Yea. I think tomorrow is the day. I have the official offer from the county. I can't believe it's really happening."

"I'm gonna miss you around here, you sure it's what you want? You're a hell of a firefighter man," I offered. I knew he was making moves in his career, but I was going to miss our crew.

"I appreciate it man. I'm sorry I won't be around to take orders from you officially," he teased me. He and I had really bonded over the last year or so, he seemed to be the only one that knew something was going on with me, and encouraged me to go for Viv for real, not just as a conquest. We all sowed our oats, but when the right girl came along, you had to take a leap of faith, and even though Scott was still single, he somehow understood that.

"Ah, funny guy. You'll be working for the man, staying clean all day, pushing papers around... You'll miss us, no?" I asked.

"You have no idea man. It's actually been a way harder decision that I expected it to be. I worked all this time for it, but now I'm just like 'shit, is this for real'?"

"Haha, you'll be okay. Best news about the whole thing is you get to stay here, so we'll be working together regardless," I offered.

"Yea, that is probably the best thing about it. So anyway, you pop the question yet or what? Getting married fever seems to abound District 23 these days. First Brian and Jo, then Matt and Isabel eloping. Now you? You ready for that?" He asked in a joking way, but I knew he had my back. He was the only one I'd told I was planning to propose this weekend, and I felt like he knew things about my feelings I'd never told him somehow.

"I am. Bro, this ring is seriously burning a hole in my fucking pocket. Since I bought it, it's all I can think of, and I've actually been avoiding her," I confessed.

"That's fucking hysterical. She must think you're off your rocker man," he chuckled at me.

"She has asked me four thousand times what's wrong and keeps scrunching her face at me, so yea," I laughed as well. Man, I loved it when she scrunched her tiny little nose at me. She was fucking adorable.

"Well, tomorrow then, right? You get her to agree to the weekend away?" He asked me, knowing what my plan was.

"Yea, she said she could rearrange some stuff. It sucks that so much of her big work is on the weekends, but she kills it out there," I said.

"Oh I'm sure she does. Do you even have to work?" He teased me.

"Probably not, but let's be real. I'd lose my fucking mind if I didn't have this place. It's who I am," I replied thoughtfully. After everything in my life that I'd gone through in my head, my therapist at the VA, this place, and Vivian were without doubt what saved my life. I was a miserable fuck with no motivation to be better.

"I think we all would," Scott replied with a sly smile, getting back to work.

I went to my office, but all I could think about was how to not spill the beans early. Vivian deserved a moment, something that she'd remember forever. I wanted to give her that perfect engagement story. I wasn't worried about her saying yes or anything; she and I had talked about it a couple times, and just acted like it was what was going to happen. I had absolutely no cool about this at all.

I shuffled some papers around for awhile, just avoiding home, when she texted me to ask if I'd be home for dinner.

Hey babe, you gonna be home for dinner? I was gonna make steaks if you are?

What would you eat if I wasn't coming home?

Cereal

Well we can't have that darlin', I'll be home in fifteen. I'll man the grill, it's my job.

I was hoping you would say that, see you soon

I love that coming home means to you

(I couldn't help it, she had me hooked)

Me too. Love you. Xoxox

(I loved the extra "x" she always put in there)

As I headed home, I got caught in the daydream of our lives. When I met Viv, I was not the same guy I am now. I was trying to be, but it was her that brought out the man I had become. Since we had met, I'd studied for and taken the Deputy Chief's test, and was promoted to the position Brian left vacant when he became Chief. I had become a leader. I was sleeping through the night, not waking up with headaches. It was her that changed it all.

When I got home, she was in these little black insanely short shorts and a tank top that said "COFFEE" across the chest. It was from a Veteran owned coffee company, and she'd taken to wearing their sexy little tanks around the house; they had a machine gun as part of their logo, frankly, it was sexy as fuck. When she turned around and spotted me staring at her, she pointed some kitchen tongs at me.

"Whatcha staring at babe?" She flashed me that million-dollar smile, and I knew I couldn't wait. I pulled out the ring and dropped on one knee.

"Darlin', I have a question for you."

SCOTT WALKER

All the studying, juggling twenty-four hour shifts and forgoing a social life for the last four years had all come down to that moment. It was go time. I'd been with the fire department for almost eight years, going to school online and on weekends where I could to finish my degree. It was finally time to graduate. It took me more than the average guy to finish my fire science degree, which wasn't at all necessary to be a firefighter, but for my next career move it certainly was, along with several additional certifications.

I had the night off, and since I had forgone anything that resembled a social life for my studies and for work, I didn't have much to do, so I decided to head to the gym down at the station to work out. While I worked out every day, it was mostly to clear my head; I didn't really have a hard time staying in shape. The station was kind of my home, I spent most of my time there for as long as I could remember, and my friends were there. I figured I might find Jax there, he was supposed to propose to his girlfriend over the weekend, and I hadn't heard yet how it went.

Jax had finally become the Deputy Chief, a role we all knew he should be in. It just took him a long time to figure it out for himself.

Over the last year or so, Jax had become one of my best friends, we had late night chats at the station over all kinds of things. He was quiet a lot of the time, often only talked when he felt there was something important to say. We had an unspoken friendship previously over the years until he met his girl Viv. Something about that relationship softened him in a way, and he opened up more. That was also when he realized he wanted to move up at the fire department. I've always been an observer, and maybe that's why it was so great to watch that change in him.

He was the only person who knew that I was planning to resign. I'd always wanted to be a firefighter but I also always knew it wasn't my final stop in the service. My degree was in Fire Science, but my area of concentration was arson investigation. Part of me always wanted to be a detective too, and so for me, this was the best of both worlds. Those jobs don't really pop up often though, and the stars aligned in my favor when the position opened up in our district.

I asked the commissioners not to announce that I'd accepted their offer until I was able to resign appropriately myself, which wasn't exactly customary. Our chief, Brian Cavanaugh, was a friend though, and I wanted to tell him myself. I didn't want him to hear it at a meeting or something. Since I was a firefighter in the same municipality, the commissioners obliged my request, and tomorrow was the day I would hand in my resignation.

"Hey man, how goes?" he asked as I walked into the gym.

"I was just wondering where you were. I saw your truck outside. I'm good. What about you? Are you betrothed now?" I teased.

"Why yes, yes I am," he grinned. You could tell how happy he was.

"So, did it all work out? The big weekend away? Romance and all?" He had planned to take her away for the weekend and propose on the beach.

"Yea, uh, no." He hung his head but still laughed.

"What? All that planning? What happened?"

"Bro, I couldn't wait. I told you that ring was burning a hole in my pocket. When I got home that night after talking to you, I just dropped to my knee in the kitchen. I had to," he explained. "But she said yesss!" He sang.

Laughing, I replied, "I don't think that was ever a concern man. You two were meant for each other."

"Thanks man. Now, you need to get yourself out there for real. You've had your nose in a book for four years. It's time to spend some time with the ladies," he said.

"Yeah, yeah, I know. You sound like my mother, thank you very much." He was right though. I hadn't dated in forever. There wasn't even anyone I considered dating when I was working on my degree. I probably wouldn't have noticed them anyway.

"Well your mother is right. Plus, if we find you a girl, then our girls can go do girl things, and we can go do man things. It works out fantastic. I love Viv. Can't imagine my life without her, but seriously, I'm not going shopping with her ever again after that one time I went to the shoe store with her."

"Was it that bad?"

"Was it that bad? Yes! Besides the fact that she paraded eighteen thousand pairs of fuck me heels in front of me for two hours and I could do nothing about it, I spent two hours in a fucking shoe store. Nope. Never again. No way. I told her I would buy all of her shoes for the rest of my life if she never asked me to go again," he said seriously.

"Did she take you up on it?"

"She's not stupid. Of course she did," he laughed.

"You two crack me the fuck up," I replied.

We worked out, and continued to shoot the breeze for awhile, thankfully changing the subject from my nonexistent dating life. Once I was settled into my new job I'd consider getting back out there. I was ready. I wanted someone special in my life, but it needed to be on my terms, my timing, and the timing hadn't been right when I couldn't give anything the attention it deserved besides work and school.

After I went home that night, I finished writing my resignation letter, which I'd worked on every night that week. I'd rewritten it so many times I practically ran out of printer ink. When I was finally satisfied that I'd expressed my gratitude for my time as a firefighter, and stated that I was moving on to another position in the district, I carefully signed it, then slid it into a large envelope to give to Brian. It was what I wanted, what I'd been working for, but it was still hard to make the move. Not seeing the guys every day would be the hardest.

The next morning, up and out of the house early to catch Brian at his desk before the hustle of the day got underway, I pulled into the station. My heart raced realizing that everything had come down to this moment. As I approached Brian's office, a newfound confidence washed over me.

"Hey Chief, you got a second?" I asked, knocking on the open door.

"Of course Scotty, come on in!" He said cheerfully, before

noticing my expression. "You look like this is important."

"Yea, it is important Chief," I handed him the envelope, and as he opened it, reading the letter, a smile spread across his face.

"Congratulations man, we're going to miss you here," he came around his desk, and gave me a solid hug, surprising me completely. "This is the next chapter for you. I'm sad to see you go, but it's time for you move ahead. I'm so fucking proud of you."

As I let out a sigh of relief, I realized he was right. The next chapter was starting.

Read Scott Walker's story in Hot & Cold: an Ignited Romance by Amy Briggs and Mikey Lee, releasing January 2017.

CHARACTER INTERVIEWS

Interviews with

Brian Cavanaugh, Matt Cavanaugh and Seth Jackson on life and how it's going with the women in their lives

BRIAN CAVANAUGH

Did you always know you wanted to be a firefighter?

Oh hell yea, for as long as I can remember I wanted to be a firefighter. Growing up with Jo and her dad as the fire chief, he was always my role model. I can honestly not think of anything I'd rather be doing with my life.

Who hogs the sheets?

Haha! That would definitely be Jo. No question. She also manages to steal most of the bed, and comes over to my side in the middle of the night, every single night.

What's your favorite thing about your partner?

My favorite thing about Jo? There's so many, but I'd have to say it's how much she loves me. I know that sounds totally lame, but she is the most giving, kind and caring woman I've ever known besides my own mother. She looks after me even when I don't need it, and she keeps an eye on everyone. She's without a doubt the best thing that's ever happened to me.

What's your biggest pet peeve about your partner?

That's a hard one. I think in general, my biggest pet peeve about Jo would be that she is so stubborn. But I have to admit, I kind of like it too. I love everything about her, can't help it.

Your favorite place to go out to eat?

We eat out so much with the fire department, I really prefer eating at home when we can, but if I had to pick a place it would be this little place across town called Shea's. They have the absolute best burgers in the world there.

If you could live anywhere, where would you go?

I'm a Florida guy, I love it here. I guess California would be nice too, but I love it here. I think Jo and I will eventually move closer to the beach someday though.

Who does the dishes?

We definitely take turns or do them together. We both work 24-hour shifts, and often the same shift, so we just do all of our housework together in between.

How do you keep your relationship...hot?

Oh, now we're getting personal... Well, I'm always hot for Jo. As far as keeping our relationship hot, I try to make sure she is happy by remembering things that are important to her, shit like that. When I pay attention to her needs, mine are automatically met. She drives me wild with just a smile, and I can't see us ever needing to try to keep things hot.

Coffee? Tea? Liquor?

Coffee and Liquor. Those are definitely my jam. I'll admit, I like having tea with my Irish mother, but I like it better when she puts some whiskey in it.

What's the best advice you can give someone looking for love?

Oh God, I'm no expert on love, but what I can tell you is that when you find someone, the person that makes your heart race, the person you know you need to see every single day, chase them. Catch them, and never let them go. Do whatever you have to do to keep them in your life. You won't be sorry; I know I'm not.

MATT CAVANAUGH

Did you always know you wanted to be a firefighter?

I think I did. My brother was a firefighter before me, and it was just something that we did together growing up. Jo's dad was the chief, and he was sort of our dad for a long time, and it was our rite of passage so to speak. I don't think I'll be a firefighter forever though; I have other things I want to try. I will always love the brotherhood, but eventually I'll do something different.

Who hogs the sheets?

Definitely Isabel. I don't understand how it happens either. I wake up every morning with no covers, and she's basically wrapped up in a cocoon.

What's your favorite thing about your partner?

That she can totally kick my ass.

What's your biggest pet peeve about your partner?

That she can totally kick my ass.

Your favorite place to go out to eat?

We love going to Houston's, a local steak joint. They have an awesome happy hour, and Isabel and I really like to eat. We work out a lot, so we have to!

If you could live anywhere, where would you go?

Ah, I'm a Florida guy; I have no use for seasons. Being outdoors all year round makes me happy, so Florida works for me, but I could see us living on some island that has perfect weather all year round too.

Who does the dishes?

Ugh, usually me. Isabel cooks most of the time, so that's her rule. If she cooks, I clean. I briefly considered trying to cook so that I could make her do the dishes, but her food is so good, it's just not worth it.

How do you keep your relationship...hot?

Well, Isabel and I don't have much trouble in that area, it's always pretty hot. That being said, we're no strangers to bringing some toys into the mix now and again, and we like to try new things together.

Coffee? Tea? Liquor?

My mom is a big tea drinker, and it's really not my thing unless she's tipping the whiskey into it. I have coffee every morning; my girlfriend is a coffee nut, so we always have some fancy brew around. As for liquor, who doesn't like that?

What's the best advice you can give someone looking for love?

Don't look for it. Do your thing. Your person will show up when you least expect it, and they will click right into your life like a puzzle piece. I never looked for it and now I'd never look back.

SETH (JAX) JACKSON

Did you always know you wanted to be a firefighter?

My dad was a firefighter, so yea, I think I did always want to be a firefighter. When I left to join the Marines, I missed it. When I got out of the military, going back to the fire department was at the top of my list of things to do. They're my brothers, and I can't really imagine doing anything else.

Who hogs the sheets?

Definitely Vivian. I don't understand how such a tiny little thing needs so much blanket.

What's your favorite thing about your partner?

Oh, it's definitely her sass. She gives me these looks, and scrunches up her little nose at me and gets lippy about the funniest things, and I find it completely irresistible.

What's your biggest pet peeve about your partner?

That she works so much. I wish that she'd cut back a little bit and relax more. I'm working on that though.

Your favorite place to go out to eat?

We don't go out to eat a lot, but we order takeout a lot these days, and my favorite place for that is Anthony's pizza. It's the closest thing to northeast boardwalk pizza that you can get down here in Florida, and Viv and I love it.

If you could live anywhere, where would you go?

I think we'd like to live closer to the beach, but we wouldn't leave our little section of heaven here in central Florida. Viv used to live in New Jersey, but she says she doesn't miss the seasons, so I think we're lifers here in the south.

Who does the dishes?

Definitely me. That girl hates cooking and cleaning. I don't mind it. It makes me feel like I'm taking care of her a little bit.

How do you keep your relationship...hot?

Hmmm, wow, what a question. Well, honestly, I can't keep my hands off of her since the moment I met her, I've got to be touching her. Keeping it hot hasn't been an issue because I quite simply can't get enough of her.

Coffee? Tea? Liquor?

Coffee. Coffee. More Coffee. And Liquor on occasion. I cannot survive my day without copious amounts of coffee in my day, and I've gotten really picky about it since Matt's girlfriend Isabel introduced me to fancy brews.

What's the best advice you can give someone looking for love?

Oh, I don't know. I'll tell you what it was for me. Once I learned how to open up and give of myself – like truly give without expecting something in return, I found real love. So, be real, and be honest, and give. It all comes back to you in love, in friendship, whatever. It's all about giving.

OTHER *Books*...

Fired Up – Book 1 in the Brotherhood of District 23

Fully Involved – Book 2 in the Brotherhood of District 23

Controlled Burn – Book 3 in the Brotherhood of District 23

A Brotherhood of District 23 Coloring Book

ABOUT *the Author*

Amy Briggs is an Orlando-based writer, consultant, and entrepreneur. Amy runs several small businesses from the comfort of her home while spinning realistic, thrilling, and romantic stories. Formerly a firefighter and EMT in New Jersey while living next to a military base, Amy was drawn to creating stories around emergency services and the military, and draws on her experiences to show the depth and emotional side of those lifestyles.

Amy loves to hear from readers and is extremely active on social media.

You find her here:
Facebook: www.facebook.com/amybriggsauthor
Twitter: @amybriggs23
Instagram: @amybriggs23
Email: amybriggs.author@gmail.com
www.amybriggsauthor.com

Made in the USA
Columbia, SC
06 May 2018